SERAPHIM ACADEMY

THE COMPLETE SERIES

ELIZABETH BRIGGS

Cover Designed by Covers by Christian

Interior artwork by Jessica Allain

www.elizabethbriggs.net

WICKED WINGS

SERAPHIM ACADEMY BOOK ONE

1

OLIVIA

S eduction is a dangerous game, but one I have no choice but to
play. And, as I've learned from my mother, seduction and
deception often go hand in hand.

They do tonight, anyway.

I move through the party and try to ignore the growing hunger
inside me. It's hard at times like this, when music is pulsing, drinks
are flowing, and bodies are dancing a little too close. Inhibitions are
down, temptation is in the air, and boy does it smell sweet. To me, at
least.

I find a corner where I can survey the crowd, trying not to get
too close to anyone. College kids at various levels of drunkenness
dance, play beer pong, and try to talk over the loud beat of the
music. A guy standing off to the side catches my eye and gives me a
warm smile. He's got the face and shoulders of a small-town college
football hero, and for a second I'm tempted. I picture digging my
nails into those broad shoulders as I ride him hard, but I quickly
glance away. He looks like a nice guy. The kind who brings you
flowers on your first date and wants to take it slow. The kind I avoid.

Trust me, I'm doing him a favor.

A guy with sleeve tats and a dark goatee walks into the room with a "don't-fuck-with-me" vibe. I bet these rich snobs invite him to parties for one reason alone: he sells drugs. He's exactly the kind of man I need tonight.

Chester's hand clasps my elbow possessively. "There you are."

"I was waiting for you." I flash him a fake smile. He's one of those kids who only got into USC because his parents bribed someone. Sandy blond hair with a perfect curl over his eye, dark green polo shirt, expensive smile—you know the type. His confidence makes him more attractive than he really is, as does his money. This is his house—bought by his parents so he wouldn't have to live in a dorm with the common folk—and his party. It's St Patrick's Day, he's wearing an "I'm Not Irish, Kiss Me Anyway" pin that lights up, and his breath smells like whiskey. It takes a good bit of acting not to cringe away from his touch, but Mother taught me well.

We met in the bar where I work, where he flirted with every girl he could before I took him home. Now he only has eyes for me. What can I say? I have that effect on people.

Chester pulls me up against him. "I missed you. Let's go back to my bedroom."

I play with the buttons on his shirt. "Only if I get a drink first. I'm dying for one of those green beers everyone's got."

He nuzzles the side of my neck like a ravenous bear. "Can't it wait? I need you now."

I might have gone a little too far with him last night. I swat his chest playfully and put on a cute pout. "Everyone's had a drink but me. Please?"

He has no idea I'm doing him a favor. If we sleep together again, he won't survive it. Humans can only handle one night with a succubus—or even a half succubus, like me.

"Fine," he says, but he tightens his fingers around my arm. "One drink and then you're mine for the rest of the night."

His mouth crushes against mine, and I can't help but take a little of what he's offering. His lust for me is delicious, but every second our lips touch puts him in more danger. The guy is a possessive, snobbish jerk, but I don't want him dead.

I push him away before I can do any real damage. "Go find me that green beer, and then we'll continue this."

His eyes are glazed and unfocused, his face a little paler than it was before, and at first I think he won't let go. Did I take too much? But after a second the daze passes, and he stumbles off to go get me a drink.

I blow out a long breath and search the room for that tattooed guy I spotted earlier. He's easy to find, with a group of entitled students passing him money in the corner in exchange for something in a little baggie. I use a tiny bit of my powers to catch his attention, and his gaze locks on me. Others in the room turn too—both men and women—and I know I can have any one of them if I want. Desire is powerful, and succubi are hard for humans to resist when we put on the charm. The only people immune are those in true love, and they're few and far between, especially in places like this.

He pushes through the crowd and makes his way over to me. "You alone, baby?"

"Not anymore." I rest my hand on his arm and tug a little with my magic, making his emotions flare.

He suddenly grabs me around the waist and plants his lips on mine, kissing me hard. Oops, I tugged a little too hard. Mother would chide me, but I'm still getting used to these powers and the thirst that comes with them. I hear it now, the little voice in my head that tells me to yank open his jeans and climb him like a tree. That voice is getting harder to ignore with every passing day.

I end the kiss slowly. "I could use some fresh air. Let's go onto the balcony so we can continue this."

He grunts and leads me outside, his hand on my ass. Subtle, he is not. I lean against the balcony and he leans against me. From below, the sound of people laughing and splashing in the pool filters up. It's a perfectly clear blue Los Angeles day and the sun hits my bare shoulders, filling me with warmth. I'm wearing a little red dress that shows off all my curves, and my new friend is definitely enjoying the view.

His hands circle my waist. "I'm Trey. What's your name?"

"Olivia." I toss my hair back. "But everyone calls me Liv."

Chester comes barreling outside at that moment and yanks the guy off me. "What the fuck, man? You think you can come into my house and touch my girl?"

"We were just talking," I say.

"Looked like a lot more than that," Chester snaps. He shoves a green beer at my chest, and a little of it foams over. "Here, take your damn drink while I kick this guy's ass."

I grab the beer from Chester. As I do, I brush against his hand and unleash a little more of my power, heightening his emotions.

"I'd like to see you try," Trey scoffs as I take a sip of the green beer. It's disgusting, but I gulp a bit down anyway.

Chester gets right up in Trey's business and he's so angry now his face is bright red. "Stay away from my girl."

Trey takes a step closer and actually lets out a growl. "What are you going to do if I don't?"

Chester throws the first punch at Trey's face, unable to contain himself between his overwhelming lust and anger. Fighting breaks out between them, and I rush in a little late to try to break it up. As I do, I'm shoved backward, hard. My beer falls to the ground with a loud crack and my back hits the side of the balcony—and then I'm over it.

Falling.

Falling.

Falling.

Wings unfurl from my back with a loud snap, breaking up my screams. For a second I hover over the pool, black feathers flashing through the air, while everyone down below and on the balcony stares at me. Then I plummet toward the water again. The second I hit it, everything goes black.

Exactly as I planned.

2

OLIVIA

I wake in a hospital room with no idea how I got there and jerk upright when I realize I'm not alone. It's an honest reaction. No one likes to wake up and find a stranger has been watching them sleep, even if I expected a scene like this.

"Who are you?" I ask as I sit up straighter. "What's going on? Where am I?"

"You can call me Jo." The woman appears to be in her mid-30s with pale skin, shoulder-length honey blond hair, a sensible white blouse, and a black pencil skirt. Everything about her is professional, from her shiny nails to her closed-toe pumps to her black briefcase, but there's something about her that makes her stand apart from an average businesswoman. The symmetrical perfection of her face. The lustrous shine of her hair. The way the sunlight streaming through the window seems to gather around her. "Do you remember how you got here?"

"Not really." I place my hand on my forehead, trying to ease the ache there. I'm wearing a hospital gown, there's an IV in my arm, and my head is pounding. I stare at the IV and my jaw falls open. "Why am I in a hospital? What happened to me?"

"That's what I'd like to find out." She crosses her legs, her skirt swishing as she moves. "I'm here to ask you a few questions about what happened at the party tonight. Don't even bother trying to lie to me—it won't work. As long as you speak the truth, we'll both get along just fine."

I reach up to touch the necklace around my neck, relieved it's still there even though my clothes are missing. It's gold and heavy, with ornate curls and a big aquamarine gem that changes color depending on the light. As soon as I realize what I'm doing, I drop my hand, but she's already seen it. I swallow and begin talking. "I was at a party and a fight broke out. We were on the balcony and I got knocked over, I think. I fell?" My eyes widen. "There were... wings. Feathers?" I shake my head. "No, that can't be real. Was my drink spiked or something?"

"Your drink wasn't spiked, and I can assure you that what you remember was real."

Fun fact: my drink *was* spiked. How do I know? Because I spiked it myself when Chester handed it to me. I needed to pass out, and I knew the drug would be out of my system by the time anyone tested me thanks to my angel-demon metabolism. But Jo doesn't need to know that.

"No, it's not possible," I say, getting increasingly upset for her benefit. "I fell from the balcony, but I'm not injured. And the wings. Oh shit, the wings..." I press my palms against my eyes. "I must be dreaming. Either that or I've totally lost my mind."

Her perfect ankles cross as she leans forward. "You're not dreaming, and I believe your mind is perfectly intact, though you may be in shock."

"Who are you?" I sit up a little straighter in bed so that I'm fully upright. "What are you doing here?"

"You were brought to the hospital after you passed out. I was sent to find you after a video was uploaded to YouTube of a girl falling off the balcony and suddenly sprouting wings." She scowls a little. "This video was seen by no less than three thousand people online, not to mention all the people who witnessed it happen in person. We were able to get the video taken down without much trouble, but the partygoers are more of a problem. My team is still trying to track down everyone who was there so I can wipe their memories. You've caused quite a bit of work for us all."

Wipe their memories? Shit, this isn't just any angel, this is Archangel Jophiel, the only one with that power. I'm going to have to be extra careful with what I say to her.

"Not that it's your fault of course," she continues, "and we've certainly dealt with worse incidents before, though not many. Most people grow up knowing what they are." She pauses to study me. "Do you really not know? Remember, it's impossible to lie to me."

I stare back at her and reply without hesitation. "What do you mean? Know what?"

She considers me for a moment and buys my lies. "Olivia, you're an angel."

"A what?" I blink at her. "Like in the Bible?"

"Not exactly." She waves a hand. "They got some things right, and other religions are correct about different things. But you get the basic idea, anyway."

I let out a slightly insane laugh. "This is a joke, right? Angels don't exist. And if they did, I'm definitely not one of them."

She sighs. "Who are your parents? Are they...different?"

"Different how? My mom died when I was a kid, and no one knows who my father is." The lies roll smoothly off my tongue, and Jophiel never even reacts. I nearly touch my necklace again, but this time I restrain myself. *Thank you, Mother.* "I grew up in foster care."

Jophiel gives a terse nod. "As I thought. Your father must be one of us, but it's unlikely he will come forward. It's forbidden for our kind to breed with humans."

"Our kind?" I ask.

A rush of air sweeps through the hospital room as her copper-colored wings suddenly flare out from her shoulders. I let out a small scream and recoil against the bed, giving it my all as the wings spread wide, taking up the entire wall. There's no denying what she is now. With her wings out she glows with an inner light, and everything about her is a little too perfect. You might even call it *divine*.

"Angel," I whisper while clutching at the bedsheets as if they'll protect me. "It's true."

"Indeed." Her wings disappear back into her shoulders as if they never existed. "Now, let's talk about your future."

I blink at her with big eyes like I've just seen a ghost. I'm really playing up the naïve half-human part, and Jophiel seems to be drinking it all in. "My future?"

"Now that you've Emerged, your other powers will be manifesting soon."

My jaw falls open. "Other powers?"

"Of course." A touch of pity crosses her face. "We all get our wings and angelic gifts at twenty-one years of age, but most grow up among other angels and are well prepared for their Emergence. Since you had no idea what you are, it's no wonder you were a bit shocked."

"That's an understatement," I mutter as I drag a hand over my face, trying to pull myself together. "Sorry, this is a lot to take in."

"I'm sure it is, but now that we've found you, we'll take care of everything. Starting with your education. Every angel is sent to Seraphim Academy for Angelic Studies at around twenty-one or so, usually after they finish their human university studies. I've already informed the headmaster you'll be attending."

I hold up a hand. "Wait. I'm confused. I'm going to a school...for angels?"

"Yes. It's imperative that you attend Seraphim Academy and learn to control your powers and how to hide what you are from humans. It's a three-year program, and once you're done, we can help you find a suitable career for your skills."

"Three years," I say slowly. "That's a long time."

"It will fly by, I promise. No pun intended." She smooths her skirt as she stands. "It's fortunate for you that Seraphim Academy's next term starts in a few days, although that gives you less than a week before you need to arrive there. We will handle all travel accommodations and email you everything you need to know about the school."

Time to play reluctant. "Wait. A week? I need some time to think over this first, and—"

Jo shakes her head. "I'm afraid that isn't an option. If you don't learn to control your powers you will be a danger to yourself and others. Attendance is mandatory for all angels."

"But what about my plans for the future? And how will I afford this? I'm not exactly making a ton of money at the bar I work at."

She waves a dismissive hand. "Your plans for the future are irrelevant now that you know what you are, and you don't need to worry about the financial details. My company, Aerie Industries, covers tuition for all students, along with a small allowance for supplies." She offers me a clipped smile. "As you'll see, angels take care of our own. Even the ones who are half human."

I stare out the window with a frown. "I guess I don't have a choice, do I?"

"That's correct." She moves to the door, but then turns back. "One last thing. Where did you get that necklace?"

"Oh, this?" I touch it again. "It was my mother's." This is one of the first things I've told her that isn't a lie.

"I see." She looks skeptical, but lets it go. "As I said, everything will be emailed to you. All you have to do is show up at the school next week. If all goes well, I'll see you in three years when you come work for Aerie Industries."

She walks out of the room, and I finally drop the clueless act. I lean back on my pillows as a satisfied smile spreads across my lips. I did it. I got into Seraphim Academy, and they have no clue what I really am or who my parents are. My fists tighten around the sheets in my lap as I'm filled with resolve. *I'll find you, Jonah. I promise.*

W hen I get back to my apartment, Father is waiting for me. Of course.

I close the door. "I should have known you'd be here."

"This is a real mess you've gotten yourself into," Father says as he stands in the middle of my miniscule studio apartment between my bed and my TV, looking completely out of place. He's wearing a perfectly tailored gray suit with a crisp white shirt that stretches across his muscled chest and broad shoulders. "One I'm not sure I can get you out of."

"I don't want out of it." I drop my bag beside the bed. It didn't take much convincing to let me leave the hospital since I was physically fine, but traffic was so bad it took me forever to get home and now all I want to do is collapse.

Father pinches the bridge of his nose. If anyone saw us together, they would never think we were related. His hair is soft brown, his eyes are bright blue, and his face is smooth and impossibly handsome in a way that makes you want to trust him immediately. He looks thirty, thirty-five max. He's much, much older. "Why exactly are you doing this?"

I head into the small area that barely qualifies as a kitchen and pour myself some coffee, then heat it in the microwave. It's a day old, but coffee is coffee, and this addict needs her fix. "I'm going to find Jonah, and I need to attend Seraphim Academy to do that."

He follows me across the room. "I want to find your brother as much as you do, but this isn't the way. I've already got my best angels looking for him. Let me handle it."

I turn back and meet his eyes. "And where has that gotten you so far? It's been three months, Jonah is still missing, and we're no closer to finding him."

He crosses his arms and sets his jaw. "What makes you think you can succeed where I have failed?" His tone challenges me, but I do things my own way. What can I say? Stubbornness runs in the family.

"I have a different set of skills. The ones Mother taught me." A sinful little smile crosses my lips. "You know how persuasive she can be."

"Don't remind me." He sighs, and for a second the weight of an immortal life rests on his shoulders before it's gone again. "Going to Seraphim Academy is a bad idea. It's too dangerous for you. Your mother and I have worked hard to keep you hidden from our world for all these years. I know it's been tough sometimes, but you were safe. Now you're throwing all of that away."

I suck down the rest of my coffee and refill my mug before

popping it back in the microwave. It's hot pink and reads, *I'm a fucking angel*. Jonah got it for me for my twenty-first birthday, and it makes Father's eye twitch every time he sees it. "I'll be fine."

His eyes narrow. "I'm not sure you understand the implications. There's no turning back from this. Now that the angels know you exist, you have no choice but to attend Seraphim Academy for all three years. Unless they find out the truth about you, they'll make sure you attend each term. And if anyone finds out what you really are..." He trails off wearily. "I don't want you hurt."

"Don't worry. I plan to keep it hidden. As far as they know, I'm half human." When he still looks concerned and unwavering, I add, "I won't tell them who my father is either, if that's what you're worried about."

"No, of course not," he says, although there's a slight hesitation that I can't help but catch. I'm his biggest shame, and though he cares for me in his own detached way, I'll never be the child he wanted. Jonah is, and now he's gone. He clears his throat and straightens his tie, obviously uncomfortable. "Although it's probably best if you did keep that information to yourself."

"You got it." I give him a mock salute with my mug. "Anything else I should keep in mind?"

"Just be careful." He rests a hand on my shoulder, and I'm filled with a comforting warmth at his touch. Sunlight streams through the window nearby, hitting his slightly curling hair and framing his silhouette, and in that instant, I can almost see the outline of his silver wings. I'm awash with a wave of his power that feels like basking in the glow of the sun. I can't help but crave more of it, along with his approval, but then he takes his hand away. "Promise me."

"I'll be careful. I promise."

After giving me a long look, he disappears in a flash of light. One second there, the next gone, leaving me feeling like the conversation was only half finished. Teleportation seems like overkill when you can fly too, but that's one of the perks of being an Archangel—they have powers the rest of us don't.

I glance around my apartment. I still have a lot to do, but everything is going exactly as planned. I've dreamed of attending

Seraphim Academy ever since Jonah told me about it, and soon I'll be there. I just wish he could be there with me too.

Jonah is my half-brother and a year older than me. He should have been starting his second year at Seraphim Academy next week, but he disappeared at the end of last year's term and no one knows why. Father's been searching, but he hasn't found any leads. If there's something going down at that university, only another student will be able to uncover the truth. That's why I have to infiltrate the school and find out what happened to Jonah. Luckily, I can be very persuasive. And if I have to, I'll tear the place down with my bare hands to find my brother.

I just have to make sure no one finds out what I really am. Angels and demons have lived in an uneasy truce ever since the Earth Accords, but my very existence breaks all the rules. If anyone learns my true identity, I won't just get kicked out of Seraphim Academy—I'll be killed.

3

OLIVIA

"What's it like at Seraphim Academy?" I asked, trying not to let my jealousy show. Jonah started at the school a month earlier and wasn't visiting me as much ever since. I missed him already. I hadn't seen Mother in two years and Father wasn't exactly a common visitor those days either. I was pretty sure they both wished I didn't exist. Jonah was my last connection to the non-human world...and my only real family.

He lounged on my bed beside me while he threw a baseball in the air and caught it. He had our father's light brown hair, and at that moment it was a little long and curling up around his ears. He was handsome in that guy-next-door way, with the kind of face that made random strangers spill their entire life story. "It's like a normal college but everyone has wings."

"Smart ass." I rolled my eyes. "I wish I could go."

"It wouldn't be safe for you."

I sighed. "I know. It's just frustrating that everyone else can attend, while I have to pretend I'm human and hide what I am. I want to learn to use my powers too. I'd even settle for going to Hellspawn Academy."

He snorted. *"You'd be in even more danger there with the demons."*

"Maybe. At least I could feed openly there."

Jonah gave me a warm grin. *"Yes, but at Seraphim Academy you'd have a big brother to look after you."*

"Ugh, I don't need looking after."

"Sure you don't." He chuckled softly. *"But it really is a shame you can't go to the academy too. I could introduce you to all my friends. I think you'd like them. Especially my roommate."*

I sat up a little and arched an eyebrow. *"Why's that?"*

"He's something of a lady's man. A new girl every week. You two have a lot in common."

"Sure, except he does it for fun, and I do it for survival. And if he knew what I was, he would probably try to kill me."

Jonah wrapped an arm around my shoulders. *"I'd never let anyone hurt you, sis. Never."*

I punched him in the arm. *"Don't get all corny on me."*

He laughed and sat back. *"Sorry, I know you hate that shit."*

I didn't though, not really. I wish I'd let him know how much it meant to me that he was the one person I could be completely myself with—who knew what I was and loved me anyway. Especially since I only saw him two more times before he disappeared, and then it was too late.

———

I t's four days later, and I'm on my way. I've given up my job, my apartment, and most of my meager possessions, but it feels good to start fresh, without the weight of my past holding me down. Just about everything I need should be provided by the school anyway, or so I've been told.

It's a long drive from Los Angeles to the northern-most part of California, but I follow the directions that were emailed to me and head into the mountains, then take an unmarked road that leads higher and higher. The trees grow taller and older as I climb toward the sun, and the road becomes narrower and more treacherous. I nearly turn back—I'll admit I'm not the best driver—but the thought of my brother keeps me going, and I finally make it to my destination.

Seraphim Academy sits at the top of a tall mountain, isolated from the rest of the world by its location and a large stone wall covered in ivy. I stop in front of a black wrought iron gate with a winged logo and the letters S and A. The gate opens, and I take a deep breath. All my planning has led me to this moment. After months of waiting for Jonah to appear or be found, I'm taking matters into my own hands.

I park next to a pretentious-as-hell red convertible and nearly ding it—oops—then look for the print-out of the map I was sent...and can't find it. Of course. I try to load it on my phone and get no signal. Seriously? No cell service up here in the mountains? How do people survive? I'll have to ask someone for directions to the dorms so I can find my room and get settled in. I don't have much, just a few boxes in the trunk and backseat of my car with my clothes and a few other things I couldn't leave behind, like my mug from Jonah.

I climb out of my car and take in the school grounds. Seraphim Academy is beautiful, with a lush green lawn, tall redwood trees, and white stone buildings beside a lake that sparkles under an endless blue sky. We're surrounded by thick forest on every side and so high up that the sun feels a little closer and the air is crisp and warm. Angels get their powers from light, and the introductory email explained that this area in Northern California is one of the sunniest places in the world.

A few other students walk toward the stone buildings or the lake, and it all looks so perfectly normal you'd forget this is a school for angels—until someone flies overhead, blocking the sun for a second with their large, outspread wings.

After taking a deep breath, I head toward an imposing building that looks like a gothic church made of pure white stone. It's got the arches, the buttresses, the towers, the works. All it's missing are the crosses or other religious symbolism, although a huge stained-glass window depicts an angel with shining wings and light emitting from his palms. Above it, the roof forms a point over a steepled bell tower

—where three large, muscular men stand on the edge and stare down at me, as if unaware of the dangers of falling such a great distance.

Angels love to be up high, looking down at everyone else like the arrogant creatures they are. And I'm pretty sure those three men up there are the worst of them all, because they're the sons of the Archangels.

They're also my brother's best friends.

And my main targets.

4

CALLAN

I cross my arms and gaze across the campus grounds like a king overlooking his domain. I can see everything clearly from up here in the bell tower, from the lake to the headmaster's house to the parking lot. A few angels dart across the sky, but most of the students hurry across the lawn while carrying books, boxes, and other assorted things to the dorms. You can always tell the newbies because they're scared to pull out their wings.

Our second year at Seraphim Academy is about to start, but this time it's all wrong—because one of us isn't here.

I turn back to Bastien and Marcus with a scowl. "It's been months. Jonah should be back by now."

Marcus raises a shoulder in a shrug, his body lazily draped over the black leather couch. "Maybe he doesn't want to come back."

I shake my head. "Don't be ridiculous. He wouldn't miss the start of the new school year. Something's gone wrong. Have you foreseen anything, Bastien?"

"As I said the last three times you asked, no, I haven't," he replies dryly from the armchair he's sitting in, without looking up from the old book he's reading on fae magic. "None of my contacts have heard anything either."

I let out a growl as I start pacing on the stone floor. "Demons must have found out what he was doing and taken him. It's the only explanation."

"Let's not jump to conclusions," Bastien says. "There is no evidence of that."

"There's no evidence of anything! Jonah is one of *us*. The fourth member of our group. Practically a brother. Why am I the only one upset by this?"

Marcus runs a hand through his dark hair. "We're all upset. You think I want to go back to my dorm and see his empty bedroom? No, I really don't. But I have faith he'll be back soon, or we'll find a clue as to why he's been gone so long."

"Statistically speaking, the chance of finding anything at this point is low," Bastien says. "It's been three months. The case has gone cold."

Marcus reaches over to punch Bastien in the arm. "You're not helping."

I turn away from them and pinch my forehead. As much as I hate to admit it, Bastien is right. We've spent the last few months waiting for Jonah to return, or at least send us a message letting us know he's okay, but it's like he completely vanished. The Archangels have been looking for him too, without any success. Something must have gone wrong and stopped him from completing his mission and returning. I fear we might have lost him forever.

Through the open window, I spot a car I don't recognize as it enters the parking lot. It's a silver Honda Civic so ancient I'm impressed it's still running, with no less than three dents that I can see from this distance. The driver is a woman, though I can't make out too many details from this angle, and she drives slowly as she searches for a spot. She finds one—next to my car. Where no one else dares to park. I cringe as she barely misses my bumper, and she pulls into the space so crookedly I'm sure she'll fix it, but she doesn't. Whoever that woman is, she definitely needs to be kept far, far away from my car. Or off the road entirely.

She gets out of the car and shakes out dark brown hair that cascades down her shoulders in thick waves. I can't see her face, but she's wearing tight black jeans with an ass so fine I almost forgive her for her terrible parking job.

She grabs a messenger bag and shuts the door, then glances around the campus like she isn't sure where to go next. Another first year, no doubt. After a few seconds she begins walking toward the lawn with a confident step, but as she gets closer and her features come into focus, every muscle in my body tenses up. She's easily the most beautiful woman I've ever seen, but that's not the problem.

The problem is that I recognize her.

"It's her."

"Who?" Marcus gets up and moves to my side. His gaze follows mine out the window and he lets out a low whistle at the sight of the woman. She's nearly below us now, on her way to the building we're on top of, and we've got a clear view of her cleavage from the low V of her tight red shirt. She definitely knows how to wear clothes to accentuate those curves, and it's hard to look away.

"The woman in the photo." I take out my wallet and pluck the photo out. Bastien is on the other side of me now too, and he glances between the photo and the woman. She's younger in the photo, but there's no doubt it's her. Same wavy dark brown hair. Same intriguing green eyes full of secrets. Same red lips begging for a kiss.

"Are you sure?" Marcus asks.

"I'm sure." I shove the photo back in my wallet. "She's the one Jonah warned us about."

Bastien peers down at her. "That's the new half-human. She just Emerged last week. How is she connected to Jonah?"

"I don't know," Marcus says. "What are we going to do about her?"

I clench my jaw. "We're going to do what Jonah told us to do."

Marcus frowns. "Do we have to? It seems extreme."

I give him a stern look. "She can't be here at Seraphim Academy."

Bastien strokes his chin as he looks down at her. "We'll have to make her leave."

"How will we do that?" Marcus asks.

The woman catches sight of us, three large men standing at the edge of a bell tower looking down at her. She stops in her tracks to stare up at us and something in her eyes feels like a challenge. Now I'm even more intrigued.

"We'll do whatever it takes," I say.

Bastien nods. "Even if it means making her miserable."

"I don't like it," Marcus says. "It's a shame to make someone that hot leave so soon."

I give him a sharp look. "Quit thinking with your dick for once and remember our promise to Jonah."

Marcus lets out a dramatic sigh. "Fine."

"We have to do this." I step onto the ledge and let my wings unfurl with a harsh smile. "Now let's welcome her to Seraphim Academy."

I hear the snap of the other men's wings flaring wide, and then we descend upon the unsuspecting woman.

The poor thing. She has no idea what's coming for her.

5

OLIVIA

The angels stretch their shining wings out and catch the sunlight, practically blinding me—and then they descend. They hit the ground in a rush, landing in a triangle around me, so close that the rush of air makes my hair fly back. I'm suddenly surrounded by three of the most gorgeous men to ever walk the Earth, and you'd think that would make it my lucky day, except none of them are smiling.

The one in front of me is the biggest, with muscles Thor would be jealous of and the strong jaw and golden hair of Captain America. His wings are pure white and edged in gold, and everything about him is large and imposing and all male. He gives me a look that tells me he's the boss here, and he's used to getting his way. His alpha male attitude is a major turn on, I'll admit.

Until he opens his mouth, that is.

"You don't belong here."

Does he know who I am? Has Jonah told him about me? Time to find out. I prop my hands on my hips and face him down. "Is that so?"

"Leave now, and it won't be a problem," his voice commands. I'm not sure he has any other way of speaking. He's obviously used to telling people what to do. Unfortunately for him I've never been one for following orders.

"Hmm," I pretend to think about it with my head cocked. "How about no."

I start to brush past him, but one of the other muscular men stretches out a bronze and white wing to block my path. This guy's got olive skin, dark brown hair with a hint of a curl, and a sensual mouth I'd love to kiss. He stands with a deceptively casual pose and has a cocky tilt to his chin, like he knows how good-looking he is and knows that you know it too. He could be Latino, Middle Eastern, or something else—he's got one of those faces that could pass for just about anything. A lot of angels do, actually. Probably because they're not from Earth originally.

"We're not done speaking with you," he says.

"Listen to us," the third angel adds in a sharp voice. He's beautiful, as all angels are, but in an unconventional way. More interesting-looking than handsome, with strong cheekbones, a sharp jaw, and cold eyes radiating intelligence and arrogance in equal measure. He's tall and lanky, and with his shiny black hair he reminds me of a raven, even though his wings are dark gray with silver streaks. If he were in a superhero movie, he'd be the sexy villain you love to hate. "If we say you don't belong here, then you don't."

I let out a huff. "Is this because I'm half human?"

Their leader nods. "Exactly. We don't want your kind here."

"It's for your own good," the bronze-winged angel says. "You shouldn't be at this school."

"I think I know what's best for me, thanks." The sarcasm drips off me like sweat. This is not how I planned this first interaction with my brother's friends. Nope, my plan involved a lot more flirting and seduction and convincing them to reveal their secrets after a round or two of hot sex. That's definitely not in the cards now that I've seen what overbearing assholes they are. I'm going to have to come up with a Plan B to get information from them. "I'm not leaving, so you might as well put those flashy wings away and let me pass. Or better yet, tell me where I can find the dorms to put my stuff."

"I can help you with that," a female voice says behind me. She moves to my side while frowning at the men. "Really, you three. I expected better of you."

She takes my arm and leads me away while they scowl at us. She has strawberry blond hair, pale skin, and big, warm eyes with a hint of sadness that I nearly miss. I recognize her immediately from a photo I saw on my brother's phone.

"Thanks, but I was handling it." My blood is still burning after interacting with those jerks, even as it sings with desire too. I wanted those men, all three of them. One at a time or all-together, I'm not picky. Being a succubus is such a pain sometimes.

Except I'm not the only one experiencing the lust. A steady trickle of it gives me a little boost of energy, and I realize all three men are not only looking at me with disgust, but with desire too. *Thanks for the snack, boys.*

"I'm sure you were, but women should stick up for each other, especially when men are involved." She gives me a kind smile. "Besides, you seem a little lost. I can show you around. I'm Grace, by the way."

I can't believe my luck. First, I run into my brother's friends, and even though they turned out to be grade-A jerks, the encounter saved me from having to track them down. Now Jonah's girlfriend is befriending me. I can definitely work with this.

I give her a friendly smile, turning on the innocent, naïve act I gave Jophiel. "You're right, I could use some help, thanks. I'm Olivia, but call me Liv." I glance back at the men. They've returned to the bell tower and are glaring down at me through a large window, although they've put away their wings. "Is everyone here so rude?"

"Not everyone. Those are the Princes, as they're called here, and they think they can boss everyone around." She shakes her head. "I suggest you avoid them, if you can."

Following the path, we curl around the bell tower but not out of their sight, unfortunately. "Why are they called the Princes?"

"They're basically angel royalty. All of them have at least one Archangel for a parent." When I look confused, she explains, "Archangels are the oldest and most powerful of all angels, and the seven of them form the council that rules over us—which means those three men basically rule the school. They can do anything they want and get away with it."

I'm tempted to look back at the men again, but I restrain myself, even though I can feel the weight of their gazes upon me still. "Are they really so bad?"

"They didn't used to be. I was once close with them." Her eyes drop and her smile falls. "But something happened at the end of last term and everything changed." She takes a breath. "As I said, it's best you avoid them."

"I'll try." Except avoiding them isn't in the cards. They must know something about my brother's disappearance, and I'm going to find out what it is. "Do they always perch up there like crows?"

"Most of the time. They've claimed the bell tower as their own. That building they're in is the main hall, where most of your classes will be. Anything that requires sitting at a desk will be in there. I can show you around the rest of the campus too if you'd like."

I give her a warm smile. "That would be great."

She leads me down a path next to the large green lawn, toward the lake and other buildings in the distance. Students sit together on the grass or stretch out under the sun with their eyes closed, wings out and fluttering in the breeze as they enjoy a peaceful moment before classes begin. For a moment, I envy them. They don't have to lie about who they are or hide their true nature from everyone around them. They don't have to worry about what will happen if they get caught.

"That's the gym over there," Grace says, breaking me out of my thoughts. She's pointing at a large building beside a big field near the lake. "Combat Training classes are all held in there or on the field. You'll also be taking Flight classes there or at the lake."

I let out a nervous laugh. "Combat? Flight? Shit. I am totally unprepared for these classes. I've never fought anyone before, and I'm scared of heights."

"Don't worry, many people arrive here not knowing how to fly or fight. You'll get the hang of it all soon enough. What other classes do you have?"

I pull out my class schedule. "Angelic History and Demon Studies."

She nods as we continue down the path. "Every year you'll take Angelic History and Combat Training, and each year you'll have to take a Supernatural Studies course, but the order you take them in doesn't matter. Most of us take Demon Studies first so we know what we're up against."

I hold up a hand to stop her. "Hang on. Demons are real?"

She blinks at me. "Of course they are."

"Wow. Okay." I suck in a breath. "Sorry, this is all new to me. A week ago, I thought the world was full of humans and that was it, and now I learn there are not only angels, but demons too."

"And fae," Grace added. "Although they prefer to stay in their own realm, so you probably won't ever encounter one. Don't worry about them for now."

"Good idea. My head is spinning enough as it is." The lie is easy, always so easy, especially with Mother's necklace on. I can hear her voice in my head now. *One of the best ways to seduce someone—or deceive them—is to pretend you're not very smart or capable. People are always quick to believe someone is dumber than they are, especially when you're a woman. You can use that to your advantage.*

Grace gives me a smile that is almost pitying. "I'm sure this must be very overwhelming for you. Oh, you should also have a class based on your Choir." She glances over at my schedule. "That's odd. It says, 'to be determined.' Do you have any idea what type of angel you are?"

"Um, I didn't even know there *were* types of angels."

"There are four Choirs, and all angels belong to one of them depending on how they control light," she explains with the patience of a saint. "Erelim create a burning light that can injure others, sort of like a laser. Malakim use light to heal the body and mind and can make plants grow too. Ishim, like me, manipulate light to make themselves and other objects invisible. And Ofanim use the light of truth to sense lies, see through illusions and glamour, and some of them can even see the future on rare occasions."

"How would I know which one I am?" I ask as we continue down the path.

"It's genetic, so people take after one of their parents."

"No luck there. I grew up in foster care. They told me my father was an angel, but I never met him, and my mother was human."

"That could make this more challenging. Have you noticed any magic since getting your wings? Anything unusual?"

"Nope. Nothing." Lies, lies, lies. They're just rolling off my tongue now.

She shrugs. "Sometimes it takes longer. You don't need to worry. The professors here will help you figure it out."

I sigh. "Or maybe since I'm half-human I won't have any of these powers."

"I doubt that, but I don't know much about it, sorry. Headmaster Uriel might be able to tell you more." She stops outside another building, this one with an outdoor patio. "This is the cafeteria. It's a buffet, so you can turn up whenever you're hungry and get as much food as you want. You can also get food to go if you want to eat in your room or by the lake."

"Is it expensive?"

She laughs softly. "No, it's free for students. Pretty much everything here is."

My eyes widen. "Wow. That's really generous of the school."

"Aerie Industries funds the academy, and they take good care of us. As they should, since most of us work for them when we're done here."

My tour with Grace continues, and over the next few minutes she shows me the headmaster's house, the library, the student store, and then she leads me down a short path toward a four-story stone building. "That's the dorm. You should have been assigned a suite already, which you'll share with another First Year student."

"Dorms, huh? I've never stayed in one of those."

"Did you go to college?"

"Just a local community college for two years." I shrug. "What about you? Do angels go to college?"

"Some of us do. We grow up in angel communities around the

world, but since we don't get our wings until we're twenty-one, it gives us time to get a degree first if we want. I went to Stanford, for example. Seraphim Academy is sort of like a graduate school in that sense. Of course, sometimes it still feels like high school."

Her dark eyes catch on a group of women walking past us as she says this. They're beautiful, even for angels, and they hold their heads high and walk confidently, like they're used to people leaping out of their way. Every single one of them has an athletic figure and identical straw-colored hair. The one in front has her hair tied back in a perky little ponytail and she meets my eyes and sneers, before they turn as a group and head toward the dorms. The one in the back bumps me hard with her bag before she walks inside.

It's difficult not to call her out as she passes. "I see what you mean. Who are they?"

"Seraphim Academy's resident mean girls. They're all descended from Valkyries and think they're better than everyone else because of it. That one in the front was Tanwen, their new leader, even though she's also a First Year."

"Wait, Valkyries? I thought that was Norse mythology. You're saying *they're* real too?"

"They are. As you'll see in Angelic History, any sort of winged being in mythology or religion can probably be traced back to us." She waves a hand dismissively. "Anyway, I suggest staying out of their way as best you can. It's better if you don't get their attention."

"So, avoid the angel royalty and avoid the mean girls. Is there anyone I *don't* have to avoid?"

"Everyone else should be fine, I hope. Although we don't get many half-humans here, so some people might be rude to you about it."

"Just what I need," I mumble.

"I don't *think* anyone will bother you," she says with a smile. "If you ever need anything or have any questions, just let me know."

I give her a genuine smile in return. She's nice when she didn't have to be. I appreciate it. "I will. Thanks."

Grace seems like a kind and caring person, which makes me almost feel bad for deceiving and using her. *Almost.*

6

OLIVIA

Grace and I split up outside the dorms, and I head inside to check out my new home and meet my new roommate. This building is done in the same white stone and gothic design as the rest of the buildings on campus. There's a small lobby with an elevator and some vending machines, and a guy sitting behind a temporary desk with a clipboard. His nametag reads *Blake*, and he's got ashy blond hair and way too tan skin. Someone has been spending a lot of time in the sun.

"Checking in?" he asks. "Name?"

"Olivia Monroe."

His lip curls. "Oh, you're the half-human. Sign in here."

I sign the line, and he pulls a key from a drawer in the desk. I knew pretending to be part human would make me an outsider, but I had no idea it'd be this bad. It stings a little, even if I'm not actually half-human.

"You're in room 302 with Araceli." He snorts. "That's fitting."

I grab the key. "What do you mean?"

His lip curl turns into a full-on sneer. "No one wants that pointy-eared freak here either."

I roll my eyes. That's enough of that. "I can't speak for her, but

I'm not going anywhere, so you might as well climb off your high horse already."

He leans back and shrugs, and I pocket my key and stomp off. Looking for Jonah here might be harder than I thought if everyone is a total prick to me. Then again, they'd treat me a lot worse if they knew I was actually part demon. Breeding with a human is forbidden, but breeding with a *demon*? It's so taboo, it's unthinkable.

I peek inside the common room, which has leather couches, heavy wood tables, and chairs with thick arms. There's a large-screen TV on one end, but it's turned off. Floor to ceiling windows let in tons of light, and sliding doors lead to an outdoor patio with tables and chairs. A few students are lounging around reading books, using their laptops, or chatting with each other while eating snacks. One of them spots me and nudges her friend, and then the room goes quiet as the entire place stops to stare at me.

I give an awkward wave before stepping back from the door. So much for getting through this year without much notice. It's clear that everyone knows who I am, and they have a lot of feelings about it already. I don't really care what these people think, especially since everything they know about me is a lie, but I need to find information on Jonah, and it would be a lot easier if people would talk to me like a normal person.

I hop in the elevator and head up to the third floor. As the door opens, I step out and nearly bump into someone getting on. It's the sneering Valkyrie from before, who Grace said was named Tanwen. Her blue eyes narrow when she sees my face. "Get out of my way, human trash."

My eyebrows dart up. "What did you call me?"

"You heard me." She crosses her arms and looks at me like she's daring me to fight her.

The elevator door shuts before I can come up with a smart reply. What a bitch. I'm more angry than offended, especially since if Valkyrie girl knew I was actually a succubus, she'd probably piss herself.

I shake it off. I don't have time for petty shit, I have a mission to accomplish, and to do that, I need to get my base of operations set up.

There's another small lounge area here in front of the elevator, and on the other side is room 302. My key unlocks it, and I step inside a small living room with a mini-kitchen and a bathroom. Two doors on either side lead to the bedrooms, and I'm relieved to see I won't be sharing a bedroom with someone else. I'll still have a room-mate, but we each have a little privacy—a really good thing when you need to feed on sex to survive. Not that I expect to be doing much feeding here. That would be far too dangerous. But hey, you never know.

There are two women chatting in one of the bedrooms, so I head for the empty one before they see me. I dump my bag on the double bed and look around the small space. It's got a desk, a closet, and a window overlooking the lake. It's not much, but it's not bad either. Everything looks clean and well-maintained, although it's sparse enough for us to add our own touches. Reminds me a lot of some of the places where I lived while in foster care, and it feels just as lonely. Yes, I really did grow up in foster care, since neither one of my parents could raise me safely, and loneliness was my best friend —until Jonah.

There's also access to a balcony, which extends the length of the dorm suite, with two chairs and a table. It's big enough an angel could extend their wings and take off. That could come in handy.

I head back out to get the rest of my stuff, but I'm stopped by the two women. They look like they could be sisters, with the same soulful brown eyes, except one has a purple streak in her brown hair. The other stands with the confidence and grace of someone who has lived for hundreds of years, even though she looks no older than thirty.

"Oh honey, this must be your roommate," the older angel says.

"Hey, I'm Araceli," the purple-streak girl says, offering me her hand. "Nice to meet you."

"Liv," I say, as I shake it. "Short for Olivia."

"I'm her mother, Muriel." She gives me a big smile, then looks back at her daughter. "Do you need anything else? Should I stay and make you some dinner? Do you need help organizing your closet?"

"No, Mom," Araceli says with a groan. "I'm fine. Really. You can go now."

"Are you sure? Liv, do you need any help getting settled?" Muriel asks.

"I'm good, thanks."

Araceli's tone grows exasperated. "Mom. Please."

"All right, I'm going. Although I think your bathroom could be organized a little better..."

"Mom!" Araceli practically stomps her foot.

"Sorry, sorry." Muriel leans over and gives Araceli a kiss on her forehead. "I just can't believe my baby is already grown up and attending Seraphim Academy. I'm so proud."

Araceli rolls her eyes, but she hugs her mother. "Thanks for your help, Mom."

"Of course, honey. You call me if you need anything at all and I'll be right over. Liv, it was a pleasure to meet you." She gives me a warm smile before moving to the door. She hesitates again like she doesn't want to leave, but finally she gives a little wave and shuts the door behind her.

Araceli lets out a huge sigh and collapses on the couch as soon as her mother is gone. "Finally. I thought she would never leave!"

I glance at the door wistfully. "I thought it was cute. She obviously loves you a lot. You're lucky."

The words slip out, and I regret them immediately, but it's hard not to be jealous when Father is currently pretending I don't exist, and I haven't heard from Mother in three years.

She takes a closer look at me. "You're the half-human girl. I guess they stuck both the outcasts together in one suite. Strength in numbers or something."

"You're an outcast too?" Maybe I'll have one friend. Not that it'll help me since she's brand new, too.

"Yep." She pushes her purple streak aside and shows me one of her ears, which are slightly pointed at the top. "I have fae blood from my father's side, so I'm seen as a pariah among angels, even though I grew up among them and don't know my fae side at all. I'm sure you've noticed they're not the most welcoming group to anyone who is different."

"No kidding. I've already been told to go home by multiple people today."

She props her lime green combat boots up on the arm of the couch. "Just ignore them. Some people think angels should remain pure, or whatever." She rolls her eyes. "Did you really not know you were part angel until your Emergence?"

Perching beside her on the sofa, I decide to take any friend I can get at this point. "I didn't. This has all been a total shock. What's an Emergence?"

"That's what we call it when angels get their wings. For most of us, it's a joyous occasion."

I snort. "Mine was anything but."

"So I've heard."

My eyebrows dart up. "You know about it?"

She lets out a short laugh. "The angel community is small and tight-knit. *Everyone* knows about it. We've all seen the video of you falling into that pool. Even an outcast like me."

I swallow. "Great. No wonder everyone has been staring at me."

"Don't worry. We'll stick together and give the middle finger to anyone who gives us shit. Hey, what classes do you have?"

I like this girl already. I pull my schedule from my back pocket, and she looks it over quickly.

"Awesome, we have Combat Training and Flight together." She frowns as she stares at something on the page. "So you don't know what your Choir is?"

"Nope. I'm clueless about everything. What about you?"

"I'm a Malakim, or a healer, like my mother."

"Have you done much healing yet?"

"Not really. I tried practicing on some plants and a sick dog, but I don't really know what I'm doing yet. Before this I went to nursing school, so I have some idea how to help sick or injured people, but using magic is totally different from practicing medicine." She gives me a thoughtful look. "I don't get a Malakim vibe from you. You feel more like an Ofanim or something."

Crossing my legs, I settle in. Araceli is easy to talk to. "Maybe. I really have no idea. About anything. I've been pretty lost ever since I got the invitation to this school." I feel bad for lying to Araceli since she seems so genuine and open, and as a First Year student she isn't on my list of people to investigate, but I have to keep my ruse up as long as I'm here.

She gives me a wide grin. "Well, it's a good thing you got stuck with me as your roommate. I can help you figure this all out, and I know a bit what it's like to be an outcast in the angel community."

"That would be great, thanks."

She helps me bring up the rest of my things, and then we each head into our own bedrooms to finish unpacking and get settled in before orientation tomorrow morning. Except when I close my bedroom door, I notice something on the bed that wasn't there before. A square box wrapped in brown paper and gold ribbon.

I open it up carefully, in case this is some kind of trick, but I'm even more confused when I pull out a white, hooded robe and a plain white mask that completely covers the entire face except for the eyes. Underneath it is a card printed on thick paper with letters embossed in gold script. There's an image of a golden throne taking up most of the page, and below it is a date, a time, and coordinates. Along the bottom are the words: "Attend at your own risk. Secrecy is mandatory. Loyalty is paramount."

I nearly run out and ask Araceli if she got one also, but then I run my finger along those bottom words again. What if she didn't get an invitation? I could already be breaking the rules by even telling her about the invite. But what exactly have I been invited to attend?

7

OLIVIA

Once we're settled in, Araceli and I head over to the cafeteria for dinner. Like the dorms, the cafeteria has floor-to-ceiling windows that let in a lot of light during the day. White tables and chairs are set up across the wide space, and along the sides are buffet stations with all sorts of different foods, ranging from tacos to lasagna to roast beef.

At first, all I can do is gaze around the room and take it all in. It's hard to believe all of this food is free. My birth parents made sure none of my foster homes were too terrible, so I was never worried about food—but money was another story. Neither of my parents could have any ties to me, because according to them it was too dangerous to have anything connecting the three of us. That meant no support from them either. Everything I had—my car, my apartment, my education—I had to work for myself. Meanwhile, Jonah got everything he could ever want, grew up in a damn mansion, and was adored by everyone around him for being the son of two Archangels. Not that I'm jealous or anything. I love Jonah. But still.

The angels here take it all for granted as they walk around the buffet and get whatever they want, just like they do everything else at this school. None of them know what it's like to grow up with practically nothing.

I grab some fish tacos plus a salad, and then make my way to the table where Araceli is already sitting. Someone bumps into me hard and my tray hits the ground, spilling my food everywhere and making a loud enough noise that everyone in the cafeteria turns to look.

"Oops," Tanwen says with a smile that is anything but sorry. "Might want to watch where you're going next time, clumsy human."

"*You* bumped into me!" I reply, but she's already moved on, and her Valkyrie friends just snicker as they follow behind her. As I stare at their backs I wonder if they dyed their hair to match, or if they're all basically clones of each other.

I let out a huff and begin cleaning up the mess. One of the cafeteria workers comes to take over, and I apologize profusely for making their job harder before going to get another tray of food. I know what it's like to have to clean up after someone else.

By the time I get back, Araceli has almost finished her food. "I see you've already met the Valkyries," she says, as I sit down.

I throw a dirty look at the group of women, who have taken over a large corner table. "Lucky me."

Grace walks up to our table holding a tray and gives us a smile. Beside her is a curly-haired guy wearing a purple polo shirt and those hipster jeans that are just a tiny bit too short. "Can we sit with you?"

"Sure." I scoot over a little so they can both join us at the table. I'm happy to see them. Grace knows my brother, so hopefully the guy does too.

Araceli looks surprised by our new guests, but smiles. "The more the merrier."

"This is Cyrus," Grace says, gesturing to her friend. "He's a Second Year like me, and an Ofanim."

"Nice to meet you," I say.

"Good to see you again," Araceli says.

"How do you all know each other?" I asked.

Araceli leans back and pushes her empty plate away. "We all grew up in the same community in Arizona, near Yuma. Lots of sun there. How do you know Grace?"

"She was kind enough to save me from the Princes this afternoon, and she showed me around campus."

Araceli's dark eyebrows shoot up. "What do you mean, she saved you?"

"Shh, there they are now," Cyrus says, and we each turn to look.

All three men walk into the cafeteria like they own the place, and people practically leap out of their way as they move toward the buffet. The big, muscular blond guy is at the front, charging forward like he's on a life or death mission to get food. I don't think he does anything by half. The tall, black-haired one is just behind him, shooting daggers with his cold eyes at anyone who dares look at them. The third guy, with the olive skin and sexy mouth, walks more casually and flashes a smile to the crowd, like he's trying to reassure everyone they're not really so bad.

As I watch, the leader spots me and his eyes narrow. He stares at me with open hostility, and the two other men follow his gaze. Great, now everyone in the cafeteria is staring at me too, probably wondering why I've caught the interest of the Princes. At first I'm annoyed, until the lust and desire gives me a little boost. Even angels can't resist the allure of a succubus—including the Princes.

It's an eternity before the three men turn away to get their food, but the damage is done. I can already hear the hushed whispers going around the room, no doubt talking about me. If anyone in the school didn't know about me before, they most certainly do now.

"What was that about?" Cyrus asks.

"The three of them surrounded me when I arrived and told me I don't belong here," I say.

"Wow, I had no idea they hated half-humans so much," Araceli says. "They're even worse than I heard."

"I never thought they did either," Grace says with a sigh. "But people change."

Cyrus leans forward and says in a loud whisper, "She should know, she used to date one of them."

"Really?" I ask. "Which one?"

Cyrus waves a hand. "Not one of those three. There was a fourth Prince last year."

Grace's head drops and the sadness in her eyes returns. "His name is Jonah. He disappeared at the end of last term."

I'm thrilled the conversation has already come around to my brother. "Really? What happened to him?" I ask, as though this is the first time I'm hearing about Jonah, like it doesn't rip my heart out every time I think of him missing.

"No one knows," Cyrus says. "He vanished without a trace, and no one has been able to find him. Some people think he ran off, and others think demons took him."

"Do you think the Princes had anything to do with his disappearance?" I ask.

"No, they were like brothers," Grace says, as she picks at her food without really eating it. "But they changed after Jonah disappeared. They're harder now. Meaner."

We quiet down as the Princes finish getting their food, cast me one last hostile look, and then walk out of the cafeteria with it. The room seems to collectively relax as soon as they're gone.

"Well, one thing hasn't changed—they still never eat with us commoners," Cyrus says.

"What else can you tell me about them?" I ask.

Cyrus grins, and I can tell he loves to gossip. "The blond one is Callan, and he's the son of Archangel Jophiel and Archangel Michael. He's an Erelim and basically the leader of the Princes, just like Michael was the leader of the Archangels, and he doesn't let anyone forget it."

My eyebrows shoot up. "*Was* the leader?"

"Michael was killed two years ago by Lucifer. It nearly ended the truce between angels and demons, but no one could prove it was actually Lucifer who did it. He had an alibi, but we all know it was him."

"Of course." It sounds like something I should agree with. I have no idea if Lucifer killed Michael or not, but it's not really relevant to my search for Jonah, so I move on. "What about the others?"

Cyrus leans forward, clearly enjoying this. "The one with black hair is Bastian, and he's an Ofanim and a cold, unfeeling jerk. He's Headmaster Uriel's son, which is why the Princes get so many perks."

"What kind of perks?"

"For one thing, they get the entire bell tower to themselves, which they use as some kind of private lounge. They're always up there, and no one else is allowed inside unless invited by them. But you've been there, right Grace?"

"I have." She's focused on her food, obviously having a hard time with this conversation. She's either a very good actor or she really is upset over my brother's disappearance.

"I've seen them up there," I say. "They watch over the school like they own it or something."

"They pretty much do," Cyrus continues. "The third one is Marcus, and he's one of Archangel Raphael's many sons. He's a Malakim and he was Jonah's roommate last year. I heard he doesn't have a roommate this year, because Headmaster Uriel is hoping Jonah will come back to school any day now. They even left all of his stuff in there."

Grace shakes her head. "He won't come back, because he didn't run away. He would never do something like that, not without telling anyone where he was going, or taking anything with him." Her voice chokes up a little and she grabs a napkin and dabs at her eyes. "I'm sorry, I just really miss him, and I'm so worried about him."

Me too. I shove a bite of taco in my mouth to keep from talking.

"Someone will find him," Araceli says. "All the Archangels are looking for him. He'll be back soon."

Grace sniffs. "I hope so."

He will be, at least if I have anything to say about it. And now I know exactly where to start looking: Marcus's dorm.

8

MARCUS

C allan is pacing again. He's been doing it a lot ever since Jonah vanished. Back and forth along the edge of the bell tower, his footsteps so predictable on the stone I could write a song to the beat.

"We need a plan," he says.

I stretch my legs out on the couch and fold my arms behind my head. "A plan for what?"

"To get rid of that woman in Jonah's photo."

"Her name is Olivia Monroe," Bastien says in his matter-of-fact voice. "I did a little research on her after our encounter. Unfortunately there's not much in her files."

Callan finally stops pacing. "What did you learn?"

"She grew up around Southern California in various foster homes. Her mother died when she was six due to a drug overdose, and her father is unknown, although no doubt an angel. Until recently, she was working in a hotel bar near LAX."

"Choir?" Callan asks.

"Unknown."

"What's her connection with Jonah?"

"Also unknown."

"He never mentioned her to me," I say, with a trace of bitterness.

I'm still annoyed Jonah gave Callan the photo instead of me. I was his roommate and his best friend, but apparently he trusted Callan more.

Callan pulls out the photo again and smooths his thumb over it. "He gave me this only hours before he left. It was obviously important to him, and we made a promise to him."

"We need to learn everything we can about her," Bastien says. "Find out how she's connected to Jonah. Maybe she'll know why he hasn't returned."

"We *need* to get her as far away from this school as possible," Callan growls.

"How?" I ask. "She didn't seem very intimidated by us."

"Not yet, perhaps. We'll have to take more drastic measures."

"Like what?"

"We'll start by making her life miserable. If that doesn't convince her to leave, we'll take it up another notch."

The whole thing feels off. I shake my head. "I'm not comfortable with this. And I'm not sure Jonah would approve either."

I think back on that moment at the end of last term.

"Are you sure you want to do this?" Bastien asked.

"Yes, and we all know it has to be me," Jonah said. He wore his baseball uniform, and would be playing against the fae in the championship game in only an hour. And after that...I couldn't even think about that. "Don't worry. I'll be fine, seriously. But I need to ask you guys for a favor before I go."

"Anything," I said.

Jonah pulled out the photo and handed it to Callan. "If this girl ever shows up at Seraphim Academy, you need to make her leave, however you can. It isn't safe for her here."

"What are you talking about?" I learned over to look at the photo. I was immediately struck by the girl's beauty and intrigued by her.

"Who is she?" Bastien asked.

"I can't tell you that," Jonah said.

I raised an eyebrow. "New girlfriend maybe? Should Grace be worried?"

Jonah shook his head. "Just promise me you'll do whatever it takes to get her away from this place—for her own good."

I realized then how serious Jonah was, and how worried he looked. He must care about this girl. I thumped him on the back, trying to make him feel better and bring some levity to the situation. "Hey man, we promise."

"Thanks. I knew I could count on you guys."

"We made a promise to him," Callan says, bringing me back to the present. "We said we'd do whatever it takes, and we will."

I stand up and let my wings unfurl. "Yes, we did, but that doesn't mean I agree with your methods. But fine, bully her into leaving if you think that will work. Bastien can try to uncover all her dark secrets. I'll handle her my own way."

"Yeah, we all know how you handle women," Callan snarls.

I give him a wry grin. "Then you know I'm damn good at it."

I leap off the edge of the bell tower and spread my wings, letting the cool night air filter through them and lift me up. It's a short flight to the dorms, and though I could fly directly into my room through the balcony door, I decide to land on the ground and walk into the common area first. Maybe the woman in question—Olivia—will be there, and I can figure out what to do about her.

I pass by the common room and flash a dazzling smile at a few ladies I pass by, but none of them is the one I'm looking for tonight. A few of them give me seductive glances, and I could probably take one of them up to my room if I wanted, but I'm not feeling it. Truth is, I haven't been all that interested in women since that incident with Grace after Jonah disappeared. Until now. One glance at Olivia changed all of that.

On the other hand, it'll be rough heading back to that empty suite tonight. I hadn't realized how hard it would be until we returned for this term and I saw Jonah's door wide open, with all his things still inside. Bringing someone back to my room suddenly sounds like a good plan after all. But then the guilt comes back and the desire fades. I step into the elevator and resign myself to a long night alone.

Olivia appears in the doorway and slips inside just as the

elevator shuts. Her eyes slide over me for a moment and then she turns away, like she's pretending I don't exist. Fine, I probably deserve that. I wasn't exactly friendly to her earlier. Quite the opposite.

The elevator is old and slow, and my eyes can't help but roam over her. She meets my gaze and a spark of desire passes between us. We're alone in a small elevator and suddenly it feels very intimate. I can't look away, and I have the strongest desire to touch her, though I keep my hands to myself.

"About earlier." I clear my throat. "I really don't have anything against half-humans, you know."

She slowly turns those green eyes on me, which are not giving me any leeway. "Sure. That's why you and your friends told me to leave the school."

"It's for your own good, that's all. We're trying to help you."

She snorts. "Thanks, but I don't need your kind of help."

The elevator doors open to the fourth floor, and I get out and head to my room. She gets off the elevator too, but heads in the opposite direction, down the hall. I fumble for my key as she walks away, and she glances back just as I get the door open. Our eyes connect, and that same desire sparks between us. She quickly tucks back a piece of her dark hair and looks away.

I enter my room and close the door. She must have felt it too, this attraction between us. I've never been very good at denying myself anything once I want it—and she is definitely very tempting.

The guys have their own methods, and I have mine. They may not like it, but I'm going to use them. I'll get close to her, make her trust me, and then find out how she's connected to Jonah—and then I'll use that to fulfill my promise to him and get her far away from this school.

9

OLIVIA

My new plan is in motion.

My original plan was to befriend Grace and seduce the Princes, but only one part of that plan is working out so far. The four of them are at the top of my suspect list—okay, at the moment they're the *only* ones on my suspect list—but I need to look beyond the obvious too. If it were that easy, my father would've found Jonah by now.

Hence, the new plan. Last night I waited for Marcus to return to the dorms, and then I followed him back to his room. Now I know which one is his, and I'll break inside sometime when he isn't there so I can search my brother's room. I'm going to find out everything I can about Jonah's time here at Seraphim Academy so I can figure out what happened to him, and then I'll find him. I refuse to believe he's dead or gone forever. And if he is? Then I'm going to find the bastards who took his life and make them pay.

In the morning, Araceli and I head to orientation in the auditorium, which Grace showed me briefly during our tour yesterday. We find a spot in the middle of the rows of plush gray seats, and a few other angels look at us and whisper, or nudge their friends. Araceli gives them an overly large wave, making it obvious we know they're staring at us, and the students quickly turn back around. She turns to me and rolls her eyes. "Think they'll ever get tired of gawking at us?"

"One can only hope." I glance around while the other seats quickly fill up. I spot Tanwen and the rest of the Valkyries in the front with their identical straw-colored hair, and catch a glimpse of the Princes in the corner, glancing at the crowd like kings surveying their minions.

After everyone has sat down, a very tall, thin man with black hair steps onto the stage and moves to the podium. The entire room quiets immediately, and I sit up with interest because he looks a lot like Bastien, except this man radiates the power and magnetism of an Archangel. This must be the Headmaster.

As Uriel's eyes move across the auditorium he seems to focus on each one of us in turn, and many students squirm under his gaze. Uriel is an Ofanim, which gives him the power to detect truth, and probably other powers too since he's an Archangel. I shiver a little as that intense gaze falls on me and lingers there. The hair on my arm stands up, and in his eyes I'm faced with a vast, unknowable intelligence from centuries of living. I have the sense that Uriel can see into my very soul, and I'm terrified of what he might find. My necklace should protect me, but I can't help but clutch it and silently pray it's working, until Uriel finally moves his gaze to the next student. Only then can I breathe again, but I'm still rattled by the brief encounter.

"Welcome to Seraphim Academy," Uriel says, his voice reaching across the room even without a microphone. It's not loud or commanding, yet somehow we can all hear it perfectly as though we're in an intimate conversation with him. Archangels and their tricks. "I am Headmaster Uriel and it's my privilege to oversee Seraphim Academy as another term begins. I welcome both our new students and our returning students, and I'd like to go over a few things before you begin classes tomorrow.

"First, let me tell you a little about the school, for those of you who are new. Seraphim Academy was originally established in 1921, when many angels fled Heaven for Earth. This was the first mass exodus of angels, and there were very few angels who attended the school then—fourteen to be exact. Yet the school continued to grow as more and more angels fled the devastating war in Heaven, which of course culminated in the Earth Accords thirty-two years ago. At that point the school expanded dramatically, and every year it grows as more angels are born on Earth. This year we've set a new record with four hundred twelve students from all around the world, and we've added a few new professors to our roster as a result. I'd like to ask them to join us on stage so I can introduce them to you now."

He turns to the side as four people walk onto the stage. My gaze skims across the line of professors until my eyes stumble and trip over a man near the end. He's devastatingly handsome, with almost-black hair, dark stubble trailing down his jaw, and piercing green eyes. He's far too good-looking for any teacher to reasonably be, with a mouth made for kissing and a strong body that begs to be touched. I should know.

My breath catches in my throat as he gazes across the audience, and I sink down a little in my seat so he won't see me. At first I tell myself it can't be him. There's no way my luck is this bad, but there's no denying it. It's *him*.

I start to get up without realizing what I'm doing, and only Araceli's hand on my arm stops me. "What are you doing?" she whispers.

I shake my head, not really sure *what* I'm doing, only that my heart is pounding out of my chest, and I need to get out of here as fast as I possibly can, except doing so will only draw more attention to myself, and that's the absolute last thing I want at this moment. Shit.

I slump back down. It's fine. Maybe I can avoid him, and nothing bad will happen. There are lots of professors here, and I only have four classes, or maybe five if they figure out what type of angel I am. What's the chance that he'll be my professor?

Uriel gestures at the man I can't take my eyes off of. "I'd like to introduce Professor Kassiel, who will be teaching Angelic History at Seraphim Academy for all First Years."

Shit, shit, shit. There's no way I can get out of him being my teacher. This is bad, really bad.

Because I know him.

Intimately.

And worst of all, he knows me too.

He knows my secret.

He knows what I really am.

I'm screwed.

10

OLIVIA

F *our months ago*

T he bar is dead tonight, and I'm starting to think I might go to bed alone and hungry, until a man walks in who makes me suck in my breath. I would have taken anyone at this point, man or woman, no matter what they looked like, but an attractive person definitely makes what I have to do easier. And this guy? *Damn.* I lick my lips in anticipation as he approaches the bar.

He's wearing a black three-piece suit that I bet cost more than my monthly rent—which isn't cheap, since this is Los Angeles and all—and it fits him like it was tailored for his body. And wow, what a body it is. Broad shoulders. Tall but not too tall. A tapered waist that makes me think he's got a six pack under there. I'm planning to find out soon enough.

He removes his jacket and folds it neatly over the back of the bar chair. Now in only his white shirt and charcoal tie, he rolls up his sleeves to his elbows slowly, revealing masculine wrists and strong, sexy forearms. Why is it guys are so much sexier when they roll up their sleeves like that? I nearly leap over the bar and jump him right there. He's one of the most gorgeous men I've ever seen, and trust me, I've known plenty of gorgeous men...intimately. This guy puts them all to shame, and I can't even put my finger on why. There's something about him that draws me in like no one else has done before.

His hair is short, thick, and a brown so dark it looks black until the light hits it. He has matching stubble across his face, but it's his eyes that really get me. They're green, a lot like mine actually, and there's something about him that feels familiar and makes him irresistible.

He's exactly what I need.

Our eyes hold for a little longer than normal, and I wonder if he feels this strange connection too. Sexual tension simmers between us without even a word spoken. For a second I wonder if he's like me, but then I dismiss that thought. I wouldn't be able to feed on another Lilim, and I can already feel a trickle of his delicious lust giving me a touch of strength.

He breaks my gaze and clears his throat. As he folds his hands on the marble counter, I realize I've been polishing a glass this entire time so hard it'll probably have permanent streaks. This isn't like me to fall apart all over a guy. I pull myself together and give him a lazy, seductive smile. "What can I get you?"

"A scotch, neat."

Well that's just unfair. He has a British accent, as If he wasn't hot enough already. I bet women fall all over themselves to be around him wherever he works. I've known him one second and I'm drooling all over the bar already.

I pour his drink, taking my time. I've got this routine down, and all I need to do is stick to it. First, you slowly fill their order, letting them get a good look at you from every angle. Some drinks are sexier than others to make. This one is too boring and simple to do many of my tricks, like shaking the drink in a way to draw attention to my breasts, but his eyes linger on me anyway. It helps there's not much else to look at in here, unless he turns around to stare out the floor-to-ceiling windows at the view of Los Angeles at night or the airplanes flying in to LAX. This rooftop hotel bar is dark, with low inoffensive music playing in the background, and everything is glass, metal, and marble. High quality furnishings and expensive alcohol for a more refined traveler—my favorite target.

Hotel bars near large airports are prime hunting ground, second only to strip clubs. Mother taught me that, and she should know—she's been doing this for centuries. Of course, she prefers staying at the hotels during her endless travels across the world, whereas I work at one. I need a way to make money, and Jonah would never approve of me working at a strip club. Not that I see him much anymore these days. Besides, at strip clubs you get regulars, and that only leads to trouble. Feeding on travelers is much safer.

Unfortunately for me, it's Tuesday night, which is always the slowest travel night. LAX is dead, which means this hotel bar is dead too. Before this guy walked in I was gazing wistfully across the empty tables while my hunger grew. The strip club life was starting to look better every day—I'd never go hungry there, and I'd probably make more money too.

It's a good thing this guy arrived in time.

I set his drink on the counter. "What brings you to L.A.?"

"I'm here to see my father." His voice makes it clear he's not excited about the prospect. He takes the scotch and downs it quickly.

I chuckle as his empty glass hits the counter, and I grab the bottle for a refill. "That bad, eh?"

His mouth twists. "He's not bad, not exactly, but he's definitely challenging. Our relationship is...complicated."

"Trust me, I know all about that." My smile is genuine because I can actually relate this time. "I'm not sure who is harder to deal with —my mother or my father."

He glances down at his drink with a frown and I sense I've hit a nerve. This isn't going well. Normally by now I'd have the target begging me to go back to his or her room already.

I try again. "Where are you visiting from?"

"I just moved to Northern California."

"And what do you do there?"

"I'm a history professor."

"Really?" I raise my eyebrows.

"Why is that so surprising?"

"The way you're dressed. I pegged you for a rich corporate type. A finance guy. CEO, maybe."

"You can blame my father for that. He has impeccable style." He picks at the shining button on his shirt sleeve. "The devil's in the details, after all."

"So they say." The saying is a little too close to home. I need to regain control of this situation. I lean forward on the counter, showing off my ample cleavage. "There's nothing better than a good-looking man in a well-fitting suit."

"My father would agree with you." His eyes dance down my body. "Although I'd argue a beautiful woman in a little black dress is even better."

And just like that, I'm back in the game.

I reach out and caress his wrist lightly, using a tiny bit of my powers to ignite the desire in him. "I have a break in twenty minutes."

At my touch, a flicker of confusion passes over his face for the briefest moment, so fast I nearly miss it. Then he gives me an alluring smile. "Is that so?"

Thirty minutes later, I'm knocking on his door. He throws it open and at first we can only stare as the sexual tension rises—then we reach for each other without a word. Our lips meet, and the kiss is carnal and intense. I've never tasted anything like him before, and I need more, more, more.

My back hits the wall, and his hands are on my bare thighs, pushing my black dress higher. I grab the front of his shirt and yank it open, and yep, there's the six pack I was hoping for. His chest is lean and strong, and I run my hands down his hard skin, enjoying the feel of him under my fingertips. Then I reach for the front of his trousers.

"What's the rush?" he asks, as I pull the zipper down.

"I have to go back to work soon."

He lets out a sexy growl as he yanks me against him and hefts my thigh up. "Fine, but when your shift is over you're coming back for round two, and I'm going to take my time with you."

I wish that could happen, but for his own safety I can only sleep with him once. It's a shame, because I actually feel a connection with this guy, even though we've just met and have only shared a handful of words. If it were up to me, I'd spend all night in his bed. We'd wake up beside each other and have room service for breakfast. Maybe it would even turn into something more after that. Something I've never had—a relationship.

It's impossible. Succubi and incubi—known collectively as the Lilim—are doomed to live a life with many lovers but no real love. We can't get close to humans without killing them, and angels, demons, and fae are not much better off. We can sleep with supernaturals more than once without killing them at least, but over time we still drain them dry. It would require a group of very strong supernaturals to withstand the insatiable hunger of a succubus, and finding that is damn near impossible. If my mother, who has lived for thousands of years, hasn't found lasting love, I have no hope of it either.

But then he's shoving my panties aside, and I forget all of that. The only thing that matters is this moment with him right now, with his mouth on my neck and his cock sliding inside me. He thrusts hard, filling me up, caging me between him and the wall. Every time his hips rock into mine, I feel his delicious lust giving me power and strength, temporarily sating my hunger. I lean my head back and close my eyes, partly because it feels too good, and partly so he won't notice my eyes have turned black—a side effect of a succubus feeding.

He lifts me up and wraps my legs around him, and his mouth finds mine again, claiming it with every touch of his lips and stroke of his tongue. I normally feel nothing when I have sex with random strangers, but right now I can't *stop* feeling. Sex with this stranger in a suit is unlike anything I've experienced before, and it's intoxicating.

As he pounds harder, he hits me in just the right spot, and I'm close, so close. He takes my chin in his hand and captures my mouth again, sending me over the edge. I cling to his body as the climax hits me, and I feel him join me in release only moments later. I'm hit with a wave of power so strong it would knock me off my feet if I wasn't already wrapped around this man. His energy is so much stronger than anything I've encountered before, and I feel like I've fed on ten men instead of just one.

I don't know what he is—but I can tell he's not human.

He breaks the kiss and looks at me in surprise. "You're a succubus."

He knows.

I push him away from me, my heart pounding, my eyes wide. They're still black from feeding, confirming what he just said.

There are only three people in the world who know what I am. Until now.

I've made a huge mistake.

I throw open the door and run out of his hotel room as fast as I can. He shouts, "Wait!" but I'm already around the corner and banging on the elevator call button like my life depends on it, while simultaneously yanking down my dress. The elevator opens imme-diately and I rush inside, then press the Door Close button. He makes it to the elevator just as the door shuts.

I collapse against the mirrored wall, trying to catch my breath. How did he know? I made sure to keep my eyes shut, which means he must have sensed it when I fed on him. Shit, shit, shit. I should have known a guy that hot wasn't human, but I was hungry and reckless, and ignored everything my parents taught me. They will lock me up forever if they hear about what just happened.

I'll have to put in my resignation at the bar immediately. I might even need to leave the city. But he doesn't know my name or anything about me other than that I work at this hotel, and he doesn't live in Los Angeles. I won't ever see him again. I hope.

"And as a reminder," Uriel says, "flying is allowed over the campus, the surrounding forest, and to the nearby town of Angel Peak, but nowhere else. Thank you, and have a wonderful year at Seraphim Academy."

Other students stand up, and I blink rapidly as the world comes back into focus. Orientation is over, and I have no idea what happened after Professor Kassiel was introduced and my mind went back to that night we met. He told me he just moved to Northern California. He said he was a history professor. He obviously wasn't human. Dammit, I should have made the connection. Except Jonah went missing only a few weeks later, and I completely forgot about the encounter. Until now.

How am I going to get through this year when one of my professors knows what I really am?

Everyone starts to file out, and I hope I can slip out in the crowd without Kassiel seeing me. As I follow Araceli into the aisle, a tall, imposing man moves in front of me. Bastien's eyes narrow as he blocks my path. "Headmaster Uriel would like to speak with you in his office now."

I'm completely taken off-guard and dumbly ask, "He does?"

"That's what I said, isn't it? Follow me."

I cast one last look at Araceli, but there's no way she can save me. Why would Headmaster Uriel want to see me? What does he know?

People move out of the way like Bastien is a snake who might bite them, and we're outside the auditorium quickly, putting me out of sight of Kassiel at least. Bastien walks down the path and I walk beside him, my movements stiff. He doesn't say a thing, even though I keep glancing over at him. I can't help it. There's something about him I find so intriguing. I want to peel off his hard shell and arrogant layers and see what's lurking underneath.

He takes me to a two-story Victorian house that seems out of place on campus, and leads me inside the front door. "This is the Headmaster's house," Bastien explains in a clipped voice. There's an ornate staircase made of dark wood, and a blue and gold Persian rug under us, but the home feels cold and unwelcoming.

"Do you live here also?" I ask.

"Of course not. I live in the dorms now, like all other students."

"But you did before?"

His tone grows sharper with every question. "Yes, I grew up here."

I'm so curious about what it was like to grow up as Headmaster Uriel's son, living here on campus as a child. And what about his mother? Is she in the picture? But Bastien's glare makes me keep my mouth shut.

He stops outside a dark wooden door. "This is the Headmaster's office. Please wait inside, my father will be with you shortly."

"Will do." I hesitate at the door. Okay, just one more question. "Are you his assistant or something?"

He scowls at me. "I am, yes."

He turns on his heel and leaves me there. I'm so tempted to sneak around the house and poke through Uriel's things, or even better, find Bastien's childhood room, but I've heard rumors about Uriel, and I worry he'd know what I was doing, even with my necklace on. Probably a bad idea—I don't want to get kicked out on my first day of school. Or killed.

I step into the office and sit in one of the black leather wingback chairs in front of his thick mahogany desk. He has a bookcase with ancient-looking books on it bound in leather, some of the titles so faded I can barely read them. Old relics are scattered around the room—an antique globe on the corner of his desk, a silver sword with a sapphire in the hilt hanging on the wall, and a glass case with a single feather inside that seems to be made of darkness itself.

The door opens and Uriel steps inside. I stand up quickly, my heart skipping a beat. He's even more unnerving up close. He has the same subtle radiance as Father, except he's like the sun on a cold, winter day—it may be bright, but it's not exactly warm.

"Thank you for meeting with me." He moves behind his desk and takes a seat. "You may be seated."

I sit down again. "Bastien said you wanted to speak with me?"

"Indeed. I've been informed that you didn't know you were half-angel, and that you don't know who your father was. You also haven't had any indication as to what Choir you belong to. Is that correct?"

"Yes. This is all new to me, and I'm still not entirely sure I belong here." Keeping my face neutral under his scrutiny isn't easy.

His cold smile makes me shiver a little. "You do. Of that, I have no doubt. However, it might take some time for your powers to emerge like your wings did, especially if you have unconsciously been suppressing them. I'd like you to spend some time with Bastien privately so he can better assess you."

I nearly groan, but manage to keep it silent. "Assess me? How?"

"He'll use his powers as an Ofanim to detect truth, plus he'll run some tests and ask you some questions." Uriel holds up a hand in a gesture of placation. "Nothing too extreme or invasive, I promise."

I try not to squirm in my seat, but the thought of being alone with Bastien while he studies me like a lab rat makes my skin crawl. On the other hand, this might be the perfect chance for me to do a little assessing of my own to find out what he knows about Jonah's disappearance. "If you think it will help, I'm okay with it."

"Excellent." Uriel hands me a piece of paper with my new schedule on it. Where it read *to be determined* before, it now has instructions for meeting with Bastien at the library at the end of each school day. "With Bastien's help, I believe we'll be able to learn more about you, starting with your Choir."

"Great," I manage to squeak out. Except I already know which Choir I belong to, I don't need any help awakening my powers, and I definitely don't want anyone knowing more about me. Especially Uriel.

Except every time he stares at me I feel he like already knows every one of my secrets. A chill runs down my spine as his gaze falls to my chest. "That's an interesting necklace."

I drop my hand quickly as I realize I've been playing with the necklace for the last few minutes. It's a nervous habit of mine, and one I need to quickly squash if I'm going to stay here at Seraphim Academy. "Thank you."

"Such a unique design. Gold with an alexandrite gem, is it not? It reminds me of something I saw long ago. A fae relic." He arches an eyebrow. "I don't suppose you know anything about that, now do you?"

"I don't even know what a fae is, really." I shrug, and it takes all of my acting skills to remain calm. "I think it's just costume jewelry, but it was my Mom's so it has sentimental value."

"Of course," he says, although I'm not sure he's convinced. He closes the file he had open—my file?—and rests his hands on the table. "I hope you enjoy your time here at Seraphim Academy and find everything you're searching for. Should you ever need any assistance or have any questions, please visit my office any time."

Everything I'm searching for... Does he know why I'm really here? I can't tell if he's just being polite or if there's a hidden meaning behind his words, but the way he's looking at me is creeping me out, and I quickly jump up. "Thanks," I croak out, before I rush through the door.

I nearly crash into Bastien on my way out of the house, and he gives me a withering look. "Running away, are we?"

I turn around, gather my inner strength, and straighten up. I won't let these jerks intimidate or bully me. I'm not leaving the school, not until I figure out what happened to my brother, and they'll just have to deal with it. "Hardly. In fact, I'll see you tomorrow at the library."

A flicker of confusion crosses his face, and then he scowls and rushes back into the house. Uriel didn't tell him. A slow smile spreads across my face.

Day. Made.

12

BASTIEN

I storm out of the house, my hands balled into fists at my side. It's just like my father to do this without asking me first, or even telling me his plans. It's probably another one of his experiments, which you'd think I would be used to after twenty-two years of them, but he always manages to surprise me. The most ridiculous part is that he can probably discern the half-human's Choir much easier and quicker than I can, but he claims this is a training exercise for me. Another test to see if I am worthy of taking his place someday.

Uriel only had me in the first place because of necessity. When the Archangels saw how quickly other angels were breeding now that we lived on Earth, they worried they would lose power without any children of their own to potentially take their place someday, thus they all made a pact to have at least one child. Archangel Raphael had already had plenty at that point, but he sired Marcus anyway as part of the deal, and two more children since. My father agreed to the plan reluctantly, and chose another Ofanim to ensure that his child would have be of the same Choir. My mother, Dina, was a very well-respected prophet, but she had no love for my father and no desire to raise a child. She did it out of duty, and as part of the deal she gave me up when I was a small child to be raised by Uriel. I've only seen her a few times since she left.

Thus the Princes came about—five male children sired from the Archangels. Azrael's son Ekariel was the first, but he was killed when he was a child, presumably by demons, but no one can confirm that. Marcus and I were born next, followed by Callan and Jonah, who were sired by not one but two Archangels each, which means they face high expectations from the entire angel community. That's one reason it was even more of a shock when Jonah went missing. Of course, he didn't actually disappear—a few of us know where he went. But he should have returned by now, and it's troubling that we haven't heard from him at all.

I'm thinking about Jonah and our promise to him when I walk into the student store, which is a misnomer since nothing in here costs money. I still need to pick up my books for my second year at Seraphim Academy, and when I step inside it looks like many other students are in the same situation. The student store is filled with books, gym uniforms, and anything else we might need for our classes. It also has some snacks and things for our dorms, such as sheets, towels, and so forth. There are also a few items of clothing, ranging from important things like emergency underwear to sweatshirts with the Seraphim Academy logo on it. Everything in here is provided by the school at no charge, although students are expected to only take what they need. If someone is caught being excessive or greedy, they may have their privileges revoked at the student store and the cafeteria. It works as a good deterrent because no one wants to be that person who isn't allowed a meal, or who has to use their own money to buy something. The angel community is small and tightknit, and the potential shame keeps people in line.

I head for the textbook section and pick up the one for Human Studies, and when I turn I spot the half-human walking down the aisle while checking a piece of paper. There is no avoiding her.

Olivia stops beside me and grabs the Demon Studies textbook off the shelf. She cocks her head. "Are you following me?"

"Hardly. I have to get books too, just like every other student."

"Except you're not just like every other student, are you?"

"What does that mean?"

She gives a little shrug, drawing my eyes to her bare shoulders and her smooth skin. "I'm told you get certain perks like your own private lounge in the bell tower. I'm sure there are other things I don't even know about too."

"You don't know what you're talking about." My voice is even colder than usual, but she doesn't react at all. Any other student in the school would be running for the hills with the look I'm giving her, but she seems immune to intimidation.

"Why don't you instruct me then? Or is that what you'll be doing in our sessions?" Her dark eyebrows lift up and her words sound dirty, although that might just be her voice. Everything she says sounds sensual. The woman is dripping sex appeal, and even though she's very much not my type, it's impossible not to notice it.

I scowl at her. "In our sessions I will be studying you to determine what your Choir is. Nothing more. With luck, we will uncover your powers quickly so I can stop wasting my time on you."

She shrugs. "Suit yourself."

She turns and moves on to the next shelf to find another book. As she grabs it, I stare at her and try to sense something, anything, about her Choir. Most people's Choirs are obvious. Her roommate, for example, has an aura that screams in your face that she is a healer, a Malakim. The Valkyries are also obviously warriors, Erelim, and were practically born shooting burning light from their fingertips. But this half-human is a mystery. I can't read her aura at all, which worries me. I've never met anyone like that before. Is it because of her human side? Perhaps she doesn't have any powers. I'll need to do some research on other half-humans to better know what to expect.

I'm not looking forward to the sessions with Olivia, but it will give me a chance to study her better. Callan wants the girl gone as quickly as possible, and doesn't care what he has to do to achieve that goal. He's always been the type to set his eyes on something and make it happen, no matter who he has to shove out of the way to get it done. Marcus, on the other hand, thinks we should get to know her in order to learn about her connection with Jonah. But Marcus always thinks with his dick, and it's clear he wants to fuck the half-human too. He's not exactly picky, after all.

And me? My eyes narrow as Olivia saunters away, her hips swaying enticingly as she grabs some gym clothes in her size. I want to study her until I uncover her secrets. I'll tear down every wall she's hiding behind, until her past is laid bare and all of her truths are naked and on display. Then I'll know what to do with her.

13

OLIVIA

The next morning, I wake with a hard pit in my stomach. Classes start today, and my gut churns at the thought of attending Angelic History. There's nothing I can do about it other than leave the school, which I'm definitely not going to do. I'll just have to hope that Professor Kassiel doesn't recognize me. It's been four months. Maybe he's forgotten me entirely. I doubt it, but I don't know what else to do. If he does bring up that night, I'll deny everything—although I can't imagine he'd want the Headmaster to know he slept with a student either, especially not when he's just started working here.

It takes me a while to get ready because I have to work around Araceli. I haven't lived with another person since I turned eighteen and got out of foster care, and I forgot what a pain it is to share a bathroom. Demons get their powers at eighteen, and when you have a new guy or girl in your bed all the time it's a lot easier to deal with when you live alone. On the other hand, it's also a lot less lonely with Araceli around, and trust me, it's hard to forget she's there. She's constantly singing to herself, dancing around the place, and generally filling the suite with her presence. I can see this getting annoying fast, especially because angels are all morning people and I am definitely *not*, but at the moment I find it somewhat charming.

I chug a ton of coffee, we grab a quick bite to eat in the cafeteria, and then we head to our first class, Combat Training. Araceli and I are both wearing our gym clothes, which have the Seraphim Academy logo on a white t-shirt above dove gray shorts. Araceli is practically bouncing as we head to the gym, while the morning sunlight shines down on her skin, making it glow a little. She's got her brown and purple hair tied back, and I can see the slightly pointed tips of her ears from her fae heritage. She must not feel the need to hide that side of herself, which I admire.

"I can't wait for Combat Training," she says. "Mom taught me a little, but she's a healer and not a fighter, so her skills are a bit rusty."

As we walk, I tie my hair back in a quick, messy bun. The morning sun warms the back of my neck, and my angelic side drinks it in. "You'll do better than me. My skills are nonexistent."

"The humans didn't teach you any form of combat?"

"Not really. I took a self-defense course once, but somehow I don't think that's the kind of fighting we're going to do now."

"Probably not. Professor Hilda is a Valkyrie and a former member of the Angelic Army. I heard she's tough as nails."

"What are the Valkyrie exactly?" I ask. "Everyone talks about them like they're a big deal, but all I know about them is from mythology. I never imagined they'd be real."

"Valkyries are a division of the Angelic Army with all female warriors, known for their fighting skills and for being damn near impossible to kill. They once served directly under Archangel Michael, before his death anyway. Now I suppose they serve under Michael's replacement, Zadkiel. And speaking of Zadkiel, I see Tanwen is in our class also."

I groan at the sight of the blond girl walking into the gym ahead of us. "Just what I need. I'm sure she'll remind me many times that I don't belong here thanks to my human half."

Araceli holds the door open for me. "Tanwen is a total bitch, but to be fair, she does have more reason than most to hate humans. Her mother was the leader of the Valkyries, but she was killed by human hunters when Tanwen was a kid. Those are people who search for any sort of supernatural and wipe them out."

"I didn't realize there were humans who did that sort of thing. But that doesn't mean she should hate anyone with their blood."

"No, it doesn't. I think she just gets off on being the meanest girl around, and she'll use whatever makes you different or lesser to bully you. I've known her my whole life, and have gotten pretty good at avoiding her or ignoring her. Unfortunately her father is Zadkiel, and now that he's taken the empty spot on the Archangel Council, she's going to be insufferable. She's the only daughter of Archangel, even if he wasn't one when she was born."

Except, she isn't the only one, and my father's been an Archangel from the beginning. But I'll keep that little secret to myself.

We head into the gym, which looks like every other gym in every school I've been to, except there are old-fashioned weapons hanging on one wall and armor on another. Professor Hilda stands in the center of the room with her arms crossed as she watches the students file in. She's a large woman, built like a Viking with broad shoulders and wide hips, and has white-blond hair cropped close around her head.

The students stand around and chat, and Araceli and I make our way to the back wall to wait for class to start. That's when an angel I don't expect to see walks into the room. Callan doesn't look like he belongs in a combat training class for beginners. No, he looks like he should be out there on a battlefield swinging a broadsword and cutting down his enemy. Maybe that's why he walks to Hilda and begins talking to her quietly.

I nudge Araceli and nod at Callan. "What's he doing here?"

"I'm not sure. He should be in the Second Year class, not this one."

A handsome guy in front of us with dark skin and friendly eyes turns around and grins. "I heard he's so advanced in combat that he tested out of even the Third Year class. All that training from Michael, I guess. But they need him to do something, so he's working as Hilda's assistant during the combat classes."

Well, that's just great. There'll be no escaping him now. I thought since the Princes were all Second Years we might not have any of the same classes, but no matter where I go or what I do, one of them always seems to be in my face. But hey, at least I have a chance to beat Callan up in this class. Okay, who am I kidding? Look at the muscles on his arms, and the six-pack straining against his gym shirt. Even his thighs are impressive, from what I can see under those shorts. There's no way I can beat him up. If I do manage to land a punch, he'll probably laugh it off.

Hilda claps her hands, and when she speaks she has a strong accent that sounds German. "Welcome to Combat Training, First Years. I am Professor Hilda, and this is my assistant, Callan. We'll skip the part where I explain my history and why I'm qualified to teach this class and get right to the point. You're here to learn to fight, because even if the Great War is over, it's never going to be safe for us. There are still demon attacks we must defend against, and the humans grow bolder every day as they try to hunt us down. And who knows, maybe the fae will decide they want Earth next. We must be vigilant at all times." She slams a fist into her hand, and some of the students jump. Yep, this is definitely a lot more intense than my self-defense class.

"First, I need to see what I'm working with here," Professor Hilda says. "Some of you have had combat training before, and some of your parents have sorely neglected this vital part of your education, but no worries, I'll get you all up to speed in the next three years. When you graduate, you'll be ready to enter the Angelic Army, should you so choose. That is my guarantee."

Callan crosses his arms and surveys the students with an impassive, hard look on his face. When his blue eyes land on me, his jaw clenches. I wait for him to look away, but he doesn't. He just keeps staring, and I refuse to look away either and instead narrow my eyes in an open challenge. Heat spreads through my body to my core as we face off across the gym, and everything else around me fades away. It's just me and him, and the arousal growing between us. The staring turns from hostile to something else, something that makes my inner succubus hungry. Does he feel it too?

I can't help it, I lick my lips. Only then does he frown and look away. One point for me.

"When I call out your name, step forward and you'll be assigned a partner," Hilda says. She begins going through her list, and Araceli is paired off with the friendly guy in front of us, whose name is Darel. He gives her a big smile and seems like a nice enough guy, which has been rare so far at the school.

As Araceli walks to the front, someone mutters, "Glad I'm not paired with pointy-ears there."

Araceli's smile falters and she touches the hair by her ears self-consciously, but then she keeps going like we didn't all hear that line. I find myself angry on her behalf, even though I barely know her. Maybe because I can relate to what she's going through. I shoot a glare at the Valkyrie who said it, but she ignores me.

Hilda calls Tanwen's name, and the blond saunters to the front of the class with an arrogant smirk on her face. As the daughter of a Valkyrie, she's obviously had plenty of combat training and is ready to show it off.

"Your partner is Olivia," Hilda calls out.

My stomach stinks. Seriously, me and Tanwen as partners. Did Hilda do this on purpose? She must know Tanwen, and she must know about my situation. Why would she pair us up if not to humiliate me?

Once the entire class is paired up, Hilda moves to the side and crosses her arms. "Try to take down your opponent however you can so I can see what I'm dealing with here. Once they hit the floor, it's over. And remember, you may not use any of your angelic powers. That means you, Erelim. Don't make me send anyone to the healing room."

We spread out around the room and I face off against Tanwen, whose blue eyes take me in with disdain. My parents gave me a tiny bit of combat training, but not much. Just enough to get me out of a tight situation so I can escape and hide. I have a feeling that won't be good enough here.

A whistle sounds, and my back hits the floor of the gym, while

Tanwen's pretty face sneers down at me. It happens so fast I don't even have time to react.

This does not bode well for me.

As pain courses through my back, Tanwen shakes her head. "That wasn't even a challenge. Surely you can do better than that."

I pick myself up off the ground, already sore in numerous places. It's a good thing angels and demons heal quickly, although it still hurts like hell when we get our asses handed to us.

Which happens to me, over and over. Tanwen is intense, and taking me down isn't even a challenge for her. Meanwhile Araceli and Darel are giggling as they roll around on the mat, and I don't even need to be a succubus to feel the lust between them. I try not to pout, but why can't I be paired up with a hot guy, instead of being a Valkyrie punching bag?

Callan walks over as I hit the floor again, this time with a kick that sweeps out my feet from under me. I hit my side this time and Tanwen just shakes her head.

"I see you're putting the half-human through the ringer," Callan says, as he towers over me. From this angle I have a nice view of his very firm legs, at least.

"Of course I am," Tanwen says, flipping back her ponytail. "How else is she going to learn?"

"True, although I'm not sure she can get a blow in," Callan says.

Tanwen shrugs. "I'm not trying to teach her combat skills. I'm trying to show her she doesn't belong here."

I drag myself back to my feet. "That's what everyone keeps telling me, but I'm still here."

"This is only the first day," Callan says. "It'll be a miracle if you survive the week."

If I thought I might get any help from Callan in his role as assistant, I was wrong. He turns back to Tanwen and nods. "Impressive form. I can see you've been practicing."

"Always," she practically purrs. She's giving him a flirtatious smile and some fuck-me eyes. "How are you doing, anyway? It's been way too long since we hung out. We should get dinner sometime. Now that I'm a student here we can catch up."

"Catching up would be good," he says, but then he looks at me, and I know he doesn't want her, not like she wants him. Nope, as hard as he might deny it, his lust is directed at me and not her. It's enough to heal my aches and take the pain away, and I stretch my arms and neck with relief.

He walks away, and Tanwen looks like a cat who just caught a mouse as she grins at me. "Ready for another go? Since I'm in such a good mood, I might even let you get a blow in."

Spoiler alert: she doesn't.

14

OLIVIA

There's a short break to rest and lick our wounds, and then it's time for my next class, which is Flight. We stay in the same gym uniforms but head outside by the lake, and I'm so exhausted from Tanwen beating me up that I don't have to pretend very hard that I don't know how to fly. This first day is mostly an introduction to the idea of flight, where the professor makes sure we all know how to extend and retract our wings without a problem. Most of the class doesn't have a problem with this, although I put up a good show that I'm having trouble, and Tanwen rolls her eyes and whispers to her friends about me. I ignore their catty looks. I want everyone to underestimate me, even if it's frustrating sometimes. At least there are no Princes in this class.

After Flight ends, we have a longer break to catch lunch, and I change into some fresh clothes after taking a shower. I eat a sandwich, chug some coffee from my *I'm a fucking angel* mug, and then I head off to Demon Studies.

This class is held on the second floor of the main hall, and as I enter the large gothic church-like building I can't forget my first day here when the Princes swooped down on me from the bell tower.

None of them do that this time, presumably because they're all in class, which is a relief.

I notice the looks and the whispers as I head up the stairs, and wonder how long they will last. I keep my head high as I walk along the white stone floors, but when I enter the room I stop in my tracks —because Marcus is inside, sitting at one of the desks. And worst of all, the only open seat is directly behind him. So much for avoiding the Princes.

I refuse to let them intimidate me, so I walk toward the desk with outward confidence, even if I'm faltering a little inside. I remind myself that I need to get information from them, so maybe it won't be too bad having them in my classes after all, and Marcus seems like the most tolerable one. He gives me a little nod as I pass him, which I ignore. His dark hair is especially wild today, and as I sit behind him I can't help but notice how rich and luscious it looks. He's got hair a girl could envy. Or daydream about running her fingers through. Not that I'm doing that. Nope.

The professor walks in, and he's wearing a bowtie covered with tiny lightning bolts, making me think of Harry Potter. He's got on a dapper little suit to match it in off-white, and I wouldn't be surprised if his wings were the same color. He has a kind smile and bright blue eyes, with salt and pepper hair.

"Welcome to Demon Studies," he says. "I assume you're all here for Demon Studies anyway. If you're not, then you should hurry and find your actual class before it's too late. You definitely don't want to be late on your first day of class, after all!" He claps his hands together. "Now, as long as we're all in the right place I'd like to go over a little of what you can expect here. This is one of the only classes that has students from all three years in it, just like the other Supernatural Studies courses. Some of you I recognize from last year's Fae Studies course, and it's good to see you again." He does a little wave. "To the rest of you, I am Professor Raziel, and it is my pleasure to meet you all. I can't wait to help you learn about demons, our ancient enemy." He makes it sound like he's talking about teaching us to make a pie, and not about the denizens from Hell that angels have been fighting for thousands of years.

Marcus casually whispers over his shoulder, "Overly cheerful, isn't he?" He gives me a quick grin and then turns around again. If Raziel notices or hears him, he doesn't react. I bet the Princes get away with all sorts of things in class.

"This year we're going to learn all about the various kinds of demons, because just like angels there are many types. In fact there are seven types, which align with the infamous Seven Deadly Sins. I'm sure you've all heard about those before, and you may have heard things about demons from your parents or from other angels you know, but in this class we're going to try to stick to facts and not stereotypes or opinions. Some of what you've learned so far might be wrong, so I'd like you to keep an open mind. Demons are not our enemy anymore, not like they once were. Ever since the Earth Accords, we've been in an uneasy truce with them, and it's important to learn about them so we can understand them better."

"And so if they break the truce we can defeat them," Blake, that douchebag who gave me my dorm key, says.

Raziel looks flustered, but he nods quickly. "Yes, yes, of course, we must be prepared to fight them should it come to that. As I was saying, we're going to go over all the different types of demons, from imps to Fallen, and everything in between."

"And succubi, right?" a guy sitting next to Blake asks.

My hair stands on the back of my neck and I worry maybe someone here knows something, but the guy who asked is just grinning and nudging Blake like he said something funny, and I realize it's because he's a horndog who just wants to talk about sex demons.

"Yes, we will talk about the two different types of Lilim later this year." Raziel lets out an exasperated sigh like he's heard that question a dozen times before. "But first, let's discuss how angels and demons are similar and different. Like angels, demons have limited immortality, meaning they don't age after a certain point, but they can still be killed. They also have superior strength and speed, and heal faster than humans, just like we do. Another similarity? Due to their immortality, they found it difficult to have children in Hell, as we did in Heaven, but on Earth it is much easier for all of us to procreate. No one is entirely sure why, but it means ever since the

Earth Accords there's been a boom in both angel and demon popu-
lations."

He continues on, but I tune him out, and find myself staring at
the back of Marcus instead. The man is far too hot for his own good,
and he knows it. You can tell from the way he smiles, like everything
has come easily for him his entire life, and he just expects to be
worshipped. He turns and gives me that lazy smile now and I scowl
at him, even as my heart beats a little faster. Damn succubus blood.

I try to focus on what Raziel is saying, but it's difficult. As
Marcus runs a hand through his hair, I get a sexy whiff of sandalwood, and my hunger stirs. I bite my pen and concentrate harder on
the class.

"Now, let's discuss differences," Raziel says. "Whereas angels
get their powers at twenty-one, demons get their powers earlier, at
eighteen."

So far everything he's said has been true. I can only hope his
class will be fair and grounded and contain some actual knowledge.
And hey, at least I should ace this course, right?

Assuming I don't get too distracted by Marcus, anyway.

15

OLIVIA

Next on the schedule I have the class I've been dreading, Angelic History. It's also in the main hall, but on the third floor, and it feels like I'm marching to my doom as I walk down the long hallway. I try to think of a way to get out of taking this course, but if I reveal that I've been well-versed in both angelic and demonic history, I'll ruin my cover and expose what I am. I have to keep up my clueless half-human act, and that means I need this class.

Professor Kassiel is already inside, sitting at his corner desk with a book in his hand, but he doesn't look up when I enter. I let out a relieved breath and stick to the far wall as I hurry to the back of the class, keeping my head down and trying to draw as little attention to myself as possible. I find a seat in the back behind a tall angel and slouch down in my chair. So far so good. Now I just need to make it through the next few months without him noticing me.

Fat chance.

More First Year students file into the class, and I see a few familiar faces from my other classes, but no one I know by name. I'm sad Araceli is in a different Angelic History period, but not sad that Tanwen isn't here.

When the clock strikes the hour, Kassiel rises from his desk and moves to the center of the room. He's wearing another impeccable, perfectly tailored suit that obviously cost a fortune, and I can't take my eyes off him.

"My name is Professor Kassiel and I'll be teaching you Angelic History 101 this year. We're going to be covering the basics, and while some of you might think you know this stuff, you might be surprised by what you learn once we get into the details."

His voice is exactly as sensual as I remember with the lilting British accent, and it's impossible not to stare at his striking green eyes. I'm not the only one who notices. The desire in the air is palpable, and I shift in my seat uncomfortably, suddenly starving—and not for food. I knew being a succubus at an angel school might be a problem, but I didn't realize just how much until now. I bet the Lilim at Hellspawn Academy don't have this issue.

Kassiel clasps his hands behind his back as he begins pacing in front of the classroom, cutting a sharp profile. "History is important both to know where we came from and to learn from the past so that we don't repeat it. Unless you know what we've done, you won't know how to do better in the future. It also gives insight into the present and why the world is the way it is at the moment."

I can barely concentrate on what he's saying. All I can think about is how he tasted and felt under my hands. I cross my legs and shift in my seat, trying to ignore the growing ache between my legs.

"Let's begin with a quick overview, as I'm told at least one person in this class grew up in the human world."

Oh crap. That would be me. I sink a little lower in my seat, even as people glance at me and make it obvious I'm the one he means.

Luckily Kassiel keeps talking and doesn't notice. "There are four known worlds—Earth, Heaven, Hell, and Faerie. The one we're in is obviously Earth and is the world of humans. Angels all originally came from Heaven, while demons came from Hell, and fae from Faerie. Thousands of years ago, the fae learned how to open gateways between the worlds, and they shared this magic with angels and demons. This one action had many long-lasting consequences, including many wars, and the fae came to regret sharing that magic —but that's something for your Fae Studies course, perhaps. All we need to know right now is that it allowed angels and demons to visit Earth.

"Angels kept their gateways heavily regulated so only a few people came to Earth at any one time, and at first they sent people like Sandalphon and Metatron, who we will discuss in detail in a few weeks. Others later visited different parts of the world, bringing knowledge from the more civilized and advanced society in Heaven. Meanwhile, demons and fae also began to influence Earth, and humans started to worship our three races as gods. Many scholars have wondered why there are so many winged gods and goddesses in mythology, both good and bad—Valkyries, Harpies, Cupid, Isis, and so forth. Those are all angels, while some of the other gods, like the half-animal ones such as Horus and Pan, are demons. Many of the elemental and nature gods are based on the fae. As you can see, angels, demons, and fae have been impacting the human world for as long as we have recorded history, and we're going to learn more about that this year."

I know all of this already, but it's fascinating to hear it from his mouth. There's something about the way he talks that makes me want to prop my hand under my chin and watch him talk about history—never one of my favorite subjects—for hours.

"For most of history, angels, demons, and fae all lived in their own worlds, with a few exceptions. Angels were always very strict about who they let travel to Earth, and the gateways were controlled by the Archangel Council. Demons, on the other hand, allowed anyone to go through as they please, and many demons decided to live on Earth instead of in Hell, creating bloodlines that go back centuries. The fae rarely go to Earth and prefer to stay in their own world—and don't like people going to it either, especially after the Faerie Wars, which we'll cover next year. This year we'll be going in depth about the long war between angels and demons, which I'm sure you all know came to an end thirty-two years ago, when Michael and Lucifer signed the Earth Accords. Does anyone know why they did this?"

A girl in front raises her hand and seems a little flustered when he nods at her. "We'd lost so many angels that the council was worried we might be wiped out."

"That is a part of it, yes. Demons had the same problem. After thousands of years of war, with very few new angels and demons being born every year, both races were at risk of extinction. What else?"

"Heaven and Hell were both destroyed," a guy on the right calls out.

"Correct. Due to the war, both worlds were in ruins. They'd become desolate battlefields, with empty cities and burned fields. Both the Archangel Council and the Archdemons realized that in order to keep both our kinds alive, our future was on Earth. They called for a truce, and after many weeks of negotiations, they ended the war with the signing of the Earth Accords. Working together, Michael and Lucifer used a magical item created by the fae known as the Staff of Eternity to send every last angel and demon to Earth and seal off Heaven and Hell for all time. As part of the truce, there is to be no fighting or breeding between angels and demons, and we must keep our existence a secret from humankind."

"But what about demon attacks?" another girl asks. "They keep happening, even with the truce."

"Yeah, and what about Michael?" the tall angel in front of me chimes in.

"Demon attacks do still occur, but they're pretty rare, just as angel attacks on demons are also rare. When they do happen, the perpetrators are punished swiftly and decisively, so they are not seen as the beginning of a new war or a threat to the truce. Both angel and demon leadership take these attacks very seriously. As for Michael's death..."

He turns toward the student who asked the question, but then his eyes land on me. Shit. I was so intrigued by his words I forgot to slouch, and now it's too late. He does a double-take, his words forgotten, and his jaw falls open as his eyes rake over me. Everything that happened four months ago is laid bare before us, and I know he remembers it all, just as I did. Any hope that he's forgotten me or that I could stay under the radar is out the window.

I can see it in his eyes—he knows what I am.

He tries to recover from his shock and turns back to the board, but stares at it like he's completely forgotten where he is and what he's doing. Great, I broke our professor.

He glances at me one more time, while the other students send each other quizzical looks, and then he runs a hand over his face and takes a moment to recover.

"As I was saying," he begins. "Michael's death is a mystery, and since Lucifer had an alibi, at this time no one can prove it was demons who did it."

"Bullshit," someone mutters under their breath.

Kassiel clears his throat. "The investigation is ongoing. What we do know is that in the last thirty-two years both sides have tried to make peace, but it hasn't always been easy, and many people on both sides wish to start the war again. Old hatreds die hard, especially among immortals who were at war for thousands of years. But others hope that this younger generation, all born on Earth, will be different and can learn to live among both humans and demons peacefully."

His eyes meet mine again and my heart skips a beat as our gazes lock. Is he saying he won't turn me in, or that he accepts me even though I'm half-demon? That he doesn't hate demons as much as some others might? Or am I reading too much into his words?

What I'm not reading too much into is the sexual tension between us. Even across a classroom with a dozen other students around us, the heat is there. I know he can feel it too, and my inner succubus wants to leap over the desks, push him against that chalkboard, and wrap my legs around him until we're both gasping with pleasure. I tear my eyes away before I start drooling, and squeeze my thighs together. *Not now*, I tell the hunger. I'm definitely going to have to feed soon, or I'll never make it through the week.

He keeps talking, and I somehow manage to get through class without ripping off my clothes or Kassiel's, despite his many heated looks. It's a huge relief when class is over. I grab my bag and start to hurry out with the other students, but then his voice stops me.

"Olivia, may I speak to you for a moment?"

Shit. This can't be good.

I stay to the side until everyone has left the room and then I approach Kassiel slowly, where he perches against the side of his desk. He watches me come closer with a heavy, unreadable gaze.

I draw in a breath. "If this is about that night, neither of us knew who the other was, and—"

"That's what I need to speak to you about." He furrows his brow and I know he's going to bring up the succubus thing.

I interject quickly to stop him. "Don't worry, I won't tell anyone about what happened. In fact, the less we speak about that night the better, I think."

He frowns as he studies me, and I desperately want to know what he's thinking. "Of course."

"Is it a problem for me to be in class? Because we could ask Uriel to move me to another professor."

He stands up straighter. "No, it's not a problem. Our relationship will remain completely professional. Student-professor relationships are strictly forbidden, and I don't think either of us wants to jeopardize our position here."

I nod. "Agreed."

Except knowing it's forbidden? That only makes me want it more.

16

KASSIEL

I can only stare at Olivia as she leaves the room. How can it be?
I never forgot her after that night in Los Angeles. She ran
away once I realized she was a succubus, and after that I did a little
digging, but no one knew who she was, and eventually I let it go.
There are many demons who don't wish to be found, and it was
obvious she was one of those by her reaction. But what is she doing
here now? How can a succubus attend Seraphim Academy? Is it
some kind of mistake?

And the biggest question of all, does she know my secret too?

I pack up my things and leave the classroom, since I'm done
teaching for the day. I walk across campus to the professors' building, which has all of our offices and a lounge area. It also acts as a
dorm for those professors who live on campus, like me.

I head into the professors' lounge and grab one of the sand-
wiches there, then lean against the counter. Hilda and Raziel are in
here, each doing their own thing at separate tables. Hilda is wolfing
down a sandwich like she hasn't eaten in days, while Raziel is
reading a newspaper. I haven't talked to either of them much since
arriving at the school, but they've both been friendly so far.

"What do you know about that student, Olivia Monroe?" I ask, trying to keep my voice casual. I've heard the other professors gossip about their students before, so hopefully my question won't seem too odd.

"The half-human?" Hilda snorts. "She's going to need a lot of help if I'm going to get her into fighting shape."

Half...human? That can't be right. "Are they sure she's part human? How do they know?"

Raziel folds up his newspaper. "Her mother was a human."

"And her father?" I ask.

"No one knows who is he is," Raziel says.

"Coward," Hilda says. "He should step forward and own up to his mistake, for his daughter's sake. It's the right thing to do."

"Yes, it is," I say. "But how do they know she's an angel and not Fallen?"

Raziel's head tilts. "Well, she has wings, although they are black, which is a bit unusual I'll admit. But she can create light, so she's definitely not Fallen."

"There's a video of her Emergence, and it's pretty clear she's an angel from that," Hilda adds. "It should be in her files, although it was taken down from the internet by Aerie Industries."

My eyebrows dart up. "A video?"

Hilda nods. "Yeah, she got her wings at a party when she fell off the balcony. You should watch the video, it's pretty shocking."

"It must've given those angels at Aerie a lot of cleanup work," Raziel adds.

"Thanks," I say. "I'll check it out."

I grab another sandwich and head to my office. Once I'm inside, I pull up the school file on Olivia, which is only accessible to Headmaster Uriel and professors. I read through what little they know of her, including information on her mother's death, and feel even more confused. When I met her in the bar, Olivia mentioned she had a complicated relationship with her mother and father. She was either lying then or she's lying now. I have a suspicion I know which it is.

I hit play on the video. Someone caught the incident on their camera phone, and at first they're filming someone doing shots by the pool at a St. Patrick's Day party. There's a scream and the camera pans up to catch a girl flying above the pool, with black wings spread and light glowing from her entire body. She hovers there for a moment and then she falls into the water, where her wings vanish along with the light. Things turn into total chaos next as a bunch of people dive into the water to rescue her, and when they pull her out, she's unconscious. That's where the video ends.

I lean back with a frown. She's definitely an angel. Was I wrong about her being a succubus? No, I know what they feel like, and I recognized that black glow in her eyes after she fed on me. But she clearly has wings too, and I might have believed she was a Fallen except for the glowing light. Unless that was all fake, but Aerie Industries would have investigated her thoroughly after this incident.

Which means she's something that should be impossible. Something so forbidden it's never spoken about. Something that could change everything if people knew.

She's half angel and half demon.

No wonder she looked so nervous when our eyes met. And now that I know the truth about her, I'm not sure what to do with it.

I know her secret, but does she know mine? Did I say anything that night about my past? I wrack my memory trying to remember our conversation. We spoke of my father, and I mentioned I was a history professor, but little else. I don't think she knows anything about me, just as I know nothing about her.

Does Uriel know what she truly is? He must. He knows everything that happens at this school. If so, there's no reason for me to bring it up. She's obviously keeping that side of herself a secret, but what is she doing here? She must know it isn't safe, although I doubt the demon school would be any safer for her.

I stare at her photo on my screen, gazing into those mysterious green eyes. I'll keep her secret as long as she doesn't interfere with my own plans. I'll be her professor and nothing more, no matter how much my blood sings when she's near. It will be torture having her in my class, but I've survived worse before. If anyone can resist a succubus, it's me.

But damn, it's going to be a long year.

17

OLIVIA

Just when I think my first day of class can't get any worse, I remember I have to meet with Bastien.

I head to the library, which is on the other side of the lake and set back against the forest. The front of the building is covered in mosaics depicting angels fighting demons, and a grand door leads me inside.

Bastien is waiting by the front desk, and he gives me a sharp look as I enter. "You're three minutes late."

"Sorry, Professor Kassiel needed to speak with me after class."

Bastien's eyes narrow a little, but then he turns on his heel. "Follow me. I've reserved a private room for us to begin our testing."

He leads me through the library, which has tall shelves completely filled with books both new and old. I catch glimpses of ancient texts on demons combined with new texts on biology. Father told me that when angels had to leave Heaven they only had a week to gather the most important things to take with them. Most libraries had been destroyed in the war already, but the few texts that were saved were sent to this library. It's a strange feeling, knowing that most of angelic literature and knowledge is contained within these walls, going back thousands of years. Maybe that's not so impressive to immortals with such a long memory, but it is to me.

On the far side of the library are private rooms for studying, and Bastien leads me to one of those. He flips the lights on and takes a seat on one side of the table, his back straight and his posture perfect. I take a seat across from him much more slowly.

"By now you should know about the four Choirs," he starts. "I am one of the Ofanim, who can detect lies and see the truth, among other things."

"Have you detected any lies from me?" I ask.

His eyes narrow. "Not so far, but we'll see what happens during this session."

"I have no reason to lie," I lie. I nearly touch my necklace, but I have it tucked away inside the collar of my shirt today. I don't need anyone else noticing it and becoming suspicious, and I have to trust that it will keep me safe. Mother wouldn't have given it to me unless she thought it could handle even the strongest Ofanim.

"We'll see about that. I'm going to use the light of truth upon you now, which should reveal more about you to me."

He holds his hands close together and a glowing white light appears between his palms. He lets it get bigger and bigger until it's almost the size of his torso, and then he releases it toward me. I cringe as the light surrounds me and feel a little tingle, but nothing else happens. His scowl deepens and I know the necklace is working.

"Do you see anything?" I ask, trying to look and sound innocent.

"No. Very unusual. I should be able to detect something, but with you I get absolutely nothing. It's almost like there is some type of magic blocking it. You wouldn't know anything about that, would you?"

"No. I don't know a thing about magic."

He leans forward with determination in his gray eyes. "I'll try again."

He continues casting different truth spells on me, but still doesn't get any of the information he so desperately desires. A sense of satisfaction forms in my chest when I see how much trouble he's having, and it gives me confidence that I might actually be able to pull this deception off long enough to find Jonah.

"Has anyone tested your blood?" he asks.

I stiffen a little at the thought. Would they be able to detect demon blood in me? Probably. I shoot him a look of confusion to show I'm just a simple-minded human. "No, and I don't think I'm okay with that."

"Very well," he grumbles. He'd obviously love to stick me with all sorts of sharp objects, and maybe even that one in his pants from the way he looks at me sometimes and the little buzz of lust I detect from him. I can't decide if he wants me, hates me, or just sees me as one big puzzle. Maybe all of the above. I think that's how I'm going to get to him. If he sees me as some mystery he can solve, then he might be more inclined to open up to me about Jonah. If any of the Princes will know about his disappearance, it's Bastien.

He steeples his fingers on the table. "There are other ways to tell what Choir you belong to. We'll go through a list of questions. First of all, have you felt anything when someone has lied to you recently? Like a strong sense of wrongness?"

"No, I haven't felt anything like that. But maybe no one has lied to me."

"I doubt that, but let's try it now. The sky is orange. Anything?"

"Nope. Nothing."

"Hm. I do find it unlikely you are an Ofanim. Perhaps a Malakim? Have you ever touched an injured person or animal, or even a plant that was dying, and had it heal or come back to life?"

The questions continue on for the next hour and I answer in the negative for every single one. When our time is up, he's more frustrated than ever and no closer to getting any answers. He instructs me to meet him again at the same time and place tomorrow so he can run more tests, ask me more questions, and generally get even more frustrated.

The game is afoot, and I find myself quite liking it. I've always enjoyed a good game of deception, and if he can help me find my brother, I'll do whatever it takes, and I'll be whoever I need to be...as long as I win.

———

That night, after finishing dinner in the cafeteria, I tell Araceli I'm turning in early when we head back to our dorm. I wait until I'm sure she's in her own room, and then I quietly slip out onto the balcony wearing all black, with my hair tied back. I let my black wings unfurl, and carefully float down to the ground without making a sound. I haven't mastered flight yet, but I can at least land carefully.

My wings disappear, and I pad across the grass quietly, sticking to the darkest parts of the campus. At night, the grounds are pretty empty. Angels prefer daytime, while the night is for demons. My time.

At first, I don't see anyone outside. This is almost too easy. Then I hear some giggling and some hushed whispers and spot a small beam of light behind a tree. A man and a woman together, doing something that only increases my hunger. The succubus inside me is tempted to go over and feed off of them, but the angel in me sneaks past without them noticing.

When I reach the main hall, I hide in the shadows, watching the light from the bell tower. The Princes are up there, as I hoped they'd be. Every now and then I spot a glimpse of Callan pacing through the tall windows, but I can't get a better look at what they're doing without flying up there, and they might see or hear me if I do that. I wait, and wait, and just when I think I might need to return tomorrow night, Marcus walks past the window. That's all the confirmation I need.

I sneak back to the dorms and go up to the fourth floor. Thanks to Father, I have the gift of invisibility, like every other Ishim. I use it now by bending light around myself to hide from view as I pick the lock on Marcus's door—something Mother taught me. It takes me a few minutes, and I keep glancing around, worried someone will spot me even with my necklace and my powers, but the hallway is quiet and empty, and finally the lock picks do their job and the door clicks open.

I don't bother turning on a light as I quietly slip inside. I don't need it, thanks to my demon vision. The living room area is a lot like the one I share with Araceli, although this one has more personal touches in it, like some pictures on the walls. There's also a much bigger TV. I don't spend much time snooping around in here, and instead head for one of the bedrooms.

This one has the covers thrown back, along with clothes hanging over the back of the desk chair, and a red guitar tucked in the corner. This must be Marcus's room. I catch a glimpse of a photo on his desk with Marcus, Archangel Raphael, and a ton of other guys who look similar to them, but I leave the room. I have no idea when Marcus will be back and I need to hurry. As much as I'd like to go through all of his things—in the name of finding my brother, of course—I don't have time.

The other bedroom is completely the opposite. The bed is made, and everything is tidy, like it hasn't been touched in months. The sheets are a dark hunter green, Jonah's favorite color, and on the nightstand there's a picture of him and Grace by the lake. I touch his pillow, where I can almost see him lying in bed while reading one of the horror novels he loved so much. I run my hand along the desk, disturbing a light coating of dust, and imagine Jonah sitting here doing his work. I palm the worn baseball sitting in the corner and picture him throwing it in the air. My heart squeezes, my chest tightens, and I close my eyes as worry for my brother takes over.

I shake it off and go through his desk, but all I find are flyers for a pizza place in Angel Peak, some pens and pencils, and a few dusty paper clips. Nothing exciting. I was hoping to find a laptop or his smartphone, but I'm sure someone else got to them first.

Next I open his closet door. His clothes are hanging inside, and I rifle through them. I spot his baseball uniform and another pang of longing hits my chest. I check the rest of the closet, and I'm about to give up when I find a garbage bag on the floor in the back. Inside is a long gold robe and a matching mask, exactly like the one I got, except for the color.

I don't know what it means, but it's the only lead I have. Now I definitely have to attend that meeting—or whatever it is—this weekend.

I hear the front door open and shove the robe back in the bag and in the closet. Going invisible again, I stay still as I hear Marcus's footsteps move through the dorm. He pauses at the doorway to Jonah's room, and I realize I left the door open. He frowns, turns on the light, and then stares at the bed. I hold my breath as the seconds tick by, and I think for sure my cover is blown. I can't help but stare at the grief on Marcus's face, but I see something else in his eyes too —guilt maybe? Or am I imagining that because I just want to see it there?

He closes the door, and as soon as he's gone I can breathe again. I wait until he moves into his own room, and then I quietly sneak out onto the balcony and escape. That was close.

And now I'm one step closer to finding out what happened to Jonah.

OLIVIA

My second day of classes go about as well as the first. This time in Combat Training we're not paired up at least, so Tanwen doesn't get to beat me up today. Instead, we go through some basic stretching and martial arts poses to help us build our balance and practice getting in different positions. It's a nice break after yesterday's beat down, and since I've been doing yoga for years, I'm actually not too bad at this. Araceli and Darel make googly eyes at each other during the entire class, while Callan stands in the corner with his arms crossed, shooting daggers at me with his eyes as I stretch, emphasizing my assets to drive him a bit mad.

In Flight, we practice taking off by jumping from a ledge on to a soft padded area in the gym. I make a show like I'm still learning and fall a few times, and the mean girl posse nudges each other and laughs every time. You'd think grown-ass women would be above this stuff, but I guess some things never change.

In Demon Studies, I'm forced to sit behind Marcus again, and he gives me another of his charming smiles that no doubt makes most girls melt. If he keeps it up, it might work on me too, but for now I'm holding strong. That might change depending on how hungry I get.

Professor Raziel walks in wearing a white suit with a bowtie with green polka dots. "Hello class! Today we're going to discuss one type of demon, the Fallen. This is probably the demon you've heard the most about, so it seems fitting to start here since there are many misconceptions about them, and about their leader, Lucifer. What can you tell me about the King of Hell?"

"He was once an angel," Marcus pipes up. "All the Fallen were."

Raziel nods. "Yes, and what you might not know is that Lucifer was actually an Archangel. What else?"

"He left and went to Hell," Blake says.

"That's right, he did, although many people debate the exact reason why. Some say it was because he wanted more power. Some say it was because he disagreed with the way the Archangels were running things. Some say he saw an opportunity and took it. Maybe all of these things are true. Who knows? What we do know is that he left Heaven, the land of light, for Hell, the realm of darkness. There were already many different types of demons living there, but they were all separate tribes who sometimes fought against each other. When Lucifer became the King of Hell, he united these different groups and turned them into one organized Legion under his rule. Many angels followed him, mainly those who were also disillusioned with the Archangels, and others who were simply loyal to him. These angels all changed as they adjusted to Hell, and they started to feed on darkness and control it, much like we do with light. They became the Fallen, and their Deadly Sin is pride."

As he goes on about the Fallen, I wonder how this class would be taught by the other side. The Seven Deadly Sins are an angel creation—demons don't talk about themselves like that. And I notice Raziel doesn't mention that the Fallen represent the sin of pride because angels are so damn prideful already.

Also, demons tell a different story as to why Lucifer fell. According to them, he left for freedom. Not just for himself and for those who followed him, but freedom for humankind. Lucifer disagreed with the angels' belief that humans need to be guided, or as demons call it, "controlled." Demons believe freedom is the most important value, sometimes even to the point of anarchy and chaos. As such, Lucifer left the angels and banded together the demons to enact his own plans on Earth. That's not to say he didn't also do it so he could gain power and have his own people to rule. There are multiple sides to every story, and a little bit of truth in all of them.

Before we leave the class, Raziel says, "Oh, I almost forgot to mention. I'm going to pair you up with another student, and together you'll do an in-depth report on one type of demon, which I'll assign to you. I'd like you to focus on finding historical, religious, and mythological figures from Earth who are known to be that type of demon, and write an essay on them. This will be due at the end of the year and will count as your final exam. Now, let's see here..."

He begins to pair people up, and I already know I'll be paired with Marcus because that's just my luck. All I can hope for is that we won't be assigned the Lilim to study—that would be way too close to home.

"Marcus and Olivia," Raziel says, as I expected. I think even the professors have something against me. "You'll be studying imps."

Well, at least there's that.

———

After another awkward Angelic History class with Kassiel, and an unproductive session with Bastien, it's a relief to head back to my room to relax. Although there won't be much relaxing, because my succubus hunger is strong, and I need to do something about it before it gets so bad I'm giving fuck-me eyes at every angel I see. That'll lead to doing something that can blow my cover. Nope, I need to nip this problem in the bud fast, but first I need a cup of coffee and a few minutes to chill after a long day.

I exit the elevator and pull out my key, but then I freeze. Spray-painted on my door are the words YOU DON'T BELONG HERE in long black letters. It's a shock to see something like that, and for a long moment I can only stare at it. Then I glance around, but there's no one else around. Even if there was, I doubt anyone would be sympathetic, or tell me who did it. Not that I can't guess. I'm sure it was Tanwen, and I grit my teeth as I unlock the door and step inside. She can bully me all she wants, but it's not going to work. I'm here to stay.

19

OLIVIA

After spending so much time around so many tempting men, I need to feed sooner than I expected. Most succubi need to feed on a human once a week, and before I got my angelic powers I was the same. After I turned twenty-one, I learned I can feed on light the same way angels do, although it doesn't completely sustain me. I still need to feed my succubus side once every few weeks. Sex with Kassiel lasted me longer though, and Mother said that would be the case if I fed off of supernatural beings, especially powerful ones.

Only problem is I can't feed at the school, because it's way too risky. I've never fed on an angel before except for that time with Kassiel, and we all know how that went. I have to assume some of the other angels might be able to recognize me as a succubus too, which means I'm going to have to go somewhere off campus, and not to Angel Peak either. There's a small town on the main road at the bottom of the mountain, and I should be able to find what I'm looking for there.

I wait until Araceli is asleep, which is easy because she snores, and then I sneak out and head for the parking lot. I hop in my car and drive off, narrowly missing what Araceli told me is Callan's convertible. I'm tempted to nick it, since it wouldn't be more than he deserves, but I leave it be this time.

No one stops me on my way out, but I feel a keen sense that someone is watching me as I drive out of the gate. No doubt there are cameras recording me, but why should I care? This isn't a prison, and I can come and go as I please.

It feels like an even longer drive down the mountain, especially in the dark. I take it extra slow around some of the sharp turns near steep cliffs. By the time I reach the bottom of the mountain, I'm seriously regretting not flying. I'll have to make this quick if I want to get back in time to actually get some sleep before class tomorrow.

I stop at a dive bar with several trucks and cars outside, and figure this is probably my best bet for tonight. I check my makeup and smooth my hair in my rearview mirror, and then I get out of the car. I'm wearing a tight little red dress and some fuck-me heels that always get attention, especially with my curvy legs and hips. I'm not vain, but I am a succubus after all, and we're pretty damn good-looking. It's part of my nature to use my looks to my advantage to feed.

The bar is dark inside, with tacky neon beer signs, clichéd sayings framed on the wall, and sawdust on the floor. The pickings tonight are slim, but I survey the bar, taking everyone in. My eyes immediately hone in on a hot guy sitting against the wall with dark hair, a short beard, and no wedding ring. Perfect.

His head turns my way, and when our eyes lock, I give him a come-hither smile and put a little of my power into it. Not that I really need to, but I'd like to make this quick so I can head to bed. I have more classes in the morning, and I need to be alert in case I'm paired with Tanwen again for Combat Training.

A slow grin spreads across my mark's lips, and I think, *wow this is too easy,* as I start walking toward him. He stands and heads in my direction, and I worry maybe I used a little too much power on him already, but then he says, "Excuse me," and brushes right past me. My mouth falls open as he leaves the bar.

Damn, are my skills rusty, or what?

I smooth down my dress, brush off my ego, and charge forward. There are four other guys in the bar, and two of them have wedding rings, which knocks them out of the running. I might be able to seduce them, but I won't. I don't mess with married people. I may be a sex demon, but I have some principles. Maybe that's from my angelic side.

That leaves two guys, and one is at least sixty with a huge bald patch, while the other looks like he hasn't showered in a week. The only other people without wedding rings are in groups or pairs, and those would take a lot more time to work on. There's also the bartender, but I don't want to do anything with her in case I need to come back again. That leaves these two men. When I get close, the stench from no-shower guy makes this an easy decision. I sit next to the older man, trying not to get weirded out by the fact that he could be my dad, if my dad was human. The irony is that Father looks about half this guy's age, but is thousands of years older. That's immortality for you.

I could ease into this slowly, but the hunger is intense, and I just want to get this over with. I place my hand on the guy's arm and lean in close. "Need some company?"

I put some magic into my touch, and he responds immediately to me, looking at me with unveiled desire. His eyes go straight to my boobs, and I nearly roll my eyes, but I keep the smile plastered on. Sometimes it really bothers me that I have to do this, even though it's necessary for me to live. But seriously, feeding on only light or darkness would be a whole lot easier.

"Hell, yeah," he says, tipping the lip of his trucker's hat.

Yes, Hell indeed.

It doesn't take much work before we're in the front of his truck and I'm riding him with my eyes squeezed shut while his meaty hands cup my ass. The succubus in me is going *yes yes yes* while the rest of me is trying not to gag. I have no other choice, I remind myself. I have to do this to survive. But I still hate it.

The only way to make it better is to picture Kassiel's hands on my body instead. I remember his lips on my neck and the way he filled me up. I moan softly and my nameless partner moves faster, but it's the memory of Kassiel that is turning me on, not this trucker.

But then it's not Kassiel I'm riding, but Bastien. He stares at me with those intense, intelligent eyes and presses that sensual mouth to mine. I turn my head and now it's Marcus kissing me instead, and I weave my fingers in his thick brown hair as he lightly nips my neck. Then it's Callan, wrapping those big muscular arms around me and holding me close as he pounds into me.

With the four of them on my mind, I make it through the encounter quickly, and my eyes turn black as I feed off the man. Succubi—and the male version, incubi—can feed off of sex, or even lust and desire, in many ways. Having lust or desire directed at us is like a little snack, while sex is a meal—and orgasms are the perfect dessert. And sex with Kassiel? That was like an all-you-can-eat buffet that kept me full for a month. I can only assume that's because he wasn't human, but I haven't been able to test that theory on any other angels or demons since.

When we're done I say, "Thanks," and practically leap off him. I clean myself up with some tissues from my purse, and then head back to my car. The trucker calls after me in a haze. Humans get hit hard when we feed off them and get addicted to us fast, even though we can only sleep with them once without killing them. The feeling will pass soon, and he'll be fine after he sleeps it off, leaving him with a story he can tell his friends about how some hot woman screwed him in the front of his truck.

And me? I'm full enough for a little while. The all-consuming hunger for sex is at bay, for the time being. I just wish encounters like this didn't leave me feeling so damn empty.

20

BASTIEN

"I'm telling you, there's something suspicious about her," I say, while idly tapping on the keyboard and staring at the computer screen. I've already scoured Olivia's files, hoping they might have something that will help us unravel her secrets, but they proved to be worthless.

Father must know the truth of who and what she is, but he's keeping quiet on the subject so far. I'm on duty this afternoon while he's at some Archangel meeting. All I have to do is sit in his office and answer the phone. Easy enough...and extremely boring. Which is the only reason my mind wandered back to Olivia and what I saw last night, and why I called Callan and Marcus in here. The *only* reason.

Marcus twirls in an office chair with his head back, his hair wild. "You think there's something suspicious about everyone."

"He may be right this time." Callan looks out over the grounds through the large window, his arms crossed and his shoulders squared. "She's important to Jonah in some way. We need to find out how they know each other."

I shake my head. "It's not only that. Last night when we went back to the dorm, I noticed her car was gone."

Callan turns away from the window. "Where do you think she went?"

"I don't know, but we should find out." *As soon as possible.*

Marcus shrugs. "Lots of people leave campus at odd hours. There's no rule preventing them from doing so."

I shake my head. "But by car instead of flying? And at such a late hour? No, we owe it to Jonah to figure this out. If it's nothing, then we won't worry about it and move on. But if it is something, we should uncover it sooner than later." With her being connected to Jonah, we can't afford to leave any stone unturned. "I'm going to check the security cameras."

"Isn't that unethical?" Marcus asks.

My fingers are already flying across the keyboard. "Father has given me access to them so I can monitor the school for any threats. I think this qualifies."

"She's hardly a threat," Callan mutters, but he also stands over my shoulder so he can watch. Marcus scoots closer too.

It only takes a few minutes to find the footage of the parking lot from last night. I fast forward until it catches Olivia walking to her car wearing tall heels and a dress that accentuates every curve. She isn't carrying anything other than her purse.

Marcus whistles softly. "Where's she going in that outfit? On a date?"

I raise my hand to silence him as the footage continues. Callan winces as we watch Olivia nearly take out his car again, and then I switch to the gates as she drives away. We follow her on a few other cameras set up outside the grounds, but lose her down the hill.

A little over an hour later, she returns. She parks, and we use the cameras to follow her as she walks straight to the dorms, carrying only her purse again. Her hair looks a little mussed, but that's nothing that couldn't be explained by the wind. She walks a little slower, like there's something weighing her down, but it could simply be tiredness. She returns to her dorm room and disappears.

"Nothing," I mutter. Dammit.

Callan rubs his jaw. "Definitely suspicious though. We'll keep an eye on her, and when she next goes on one of those late-night excursions, we'll follow her. Meanwhile, keep putting pressure on her to leave the school. Remember, it's for her own good."

I nod. "Yes, and we might be able to use what we find to get her expelled."

"If she's doing anything wrong," Marcus points out, as he begins his spin in my chair again. "Have you learned anything from your one-on-one sessions?"

We've only had a couple, but they were frustrating, to say the least. "Not yet. But I'll uncover something soon. There is some sort of magic blocking me from discovering anything about her powers. Could she have fae magic and us not be able to sense it?"

Marcus pauses his spin. "How would she get that kind of magic? Do you think she's part fae?"

"Could she have a fae-made object?" Callan asks. "Like the Staff of Eternity, the one my dear old dad used to close Heaven with." The bitterness in his voice creeps in, like it sometimes does when we're alone and he talks about Michael. Only when we're alone though.

The office phone rings, and I hold up a finger and answer it. It's the mom of a Third Year student named Blake who hasn't been able to get ahold of her precious baby in days. I assure her I saw her son earlier, and I'll have him call her as soon as possible. After hanging up, I pull out my phone and text him. He's an idiot, someone I'd never associate with normally, but I keep everyone's numbers in my phone for just such reasons. **Your mother contacted the school worried about you. Call her. Now.**

He replies in seconds. **I'll call her immediately. Sorry about the trouble.** I didn't expect him to do anything less than call her that moment. When one of us tells someone to do something, they always do it. Except Olivia.

As I put my phone away, I answer Callan and Marcus's questions. "I haven't seen anything indicating she's part fae or possesses one of their objects, but it's too early to know for sure."

"I've been trying to put pressure on her to leave the school, but nothing seems to be working so far," Callan says. "She's very stubborn. I'm going to have to try harder."

"What you have in mind?" I ask.

"I'm not sure yet, but I might ask Tanwen. She's good at this sort of thing."

"Are you going to get back together with her?" Marcus asks.

Callan snorts. "Definitely not."

Marcus chuckles. "That's not what she's been saying. Careful, or she might get the wrong idea."

"I'll make it clear."

I fade out their conversation as my mind goes back to Olivia. I pull up the live security cameras and switch through them until I find her walking out of the dorm. She tucks a piece of dark hair behind her ear as the wind picks up, as it often does at this altitude. My eyes narrow as I watch her move out of view. *I'm going to uncover your secrets, whatever it takes. You can't hide the truth from me.*

21

OLIVIA

The rest of the week passes quickly in a blur of classes while avoiding the Princes and Valkyries as much as possible, and I'm just glad I make it to the weekend without any problems. Saturday night I'm supposed to attend that secret society meeting, or whatever it is, and I'll hopefully be one step closer to finding my brother then.

As Saturday morning arrives, Araceli busts into my room at the crack of dawn. She throws open the curtains and declares, "We're going shopping!"

Freaking angels. They're all such morning people. Me, I was looking forward to staying in bed until noon. I'm still used to a bartender schedule. Or a demon one.

I eye the window, through which I can see a gray sky and trees blowing hard in the wind. It's the kind of day you can just tell is going to be chilly and miserable.

"Today? It's way too cold." I pull the covers up to my nose and hide.

Angels absolutely hate the cold, so I have to pretend I do also. It's why Seraphim Academy's school year runs spring to fall, with winter off. Demons, meanwhile, dislike heat. The whole thing about

Hell being fire and brimstone? Yeah, that's angel propaganda. It's more like a perpetual realm of night, according to my Mother, anyway.

Araceli peers outside. "Can we take your car? It's got a heater, right?"

"Yeah, sure." I don't love the idea since my car is such a piece of crap, but I have to keep up the ruse, and I'm not the greatest at flying yet. "But I'm warning you in advance, I'm not the best driver."

"Aw, we'll be fine." She waves her hand. "Flying would be torture this morning, and I want to go."

"All right, but give me a few minutes to get dressed and down some coffee. You know I can't function without it."

She rolls her eyes but says, "Fine, fine."

I take a quick shower, chug my coffee, and we're out the door in an hour. When the cold air smacks us in the face as we exit the dorms, I reconsider flying. With both demon and angel blood, I don't have a strong hatred or preference for cold or heat, but it's actually pretty damn cold out today, especially for the end of March.

We walk toward the parking lot, but then I spot the Princes prowling around. I yank Araceli back to hide behind the brick building of the main hall.

"Hang on." I have not had nearly enough coffee to deal with their shit this morning.

"What?" She looks around in alarm. "What is it?"

"The Princes." I peer around the wall, watching as they saunter toward Callan's car. Araceli ducks down to look under my arm, and another student walks by and gives us an odd look. I picture what fools we must look like, hiding behind the building, and I straighten up. "Come on."

"Why?" Araceli follows me toward the parking lot, but she's more hesitant than I am. "I don't want to deal with them, either."

"If we hide from them, they win." Even though I believe what I'm saying, I can't help but let out a little sigh of relief when Callan's car drives away without them seeing us.

After they're gone, we hurry to my car. The sooner we get it started, the sooner it warms up. I waste no time pulling out of the parking lot, and it's only a short drive to Angel Peak, with Araceli giving me directions since my phone's GPS doesn't work well up here. Nope, that would be too easy.

We make our way into the tiny town, which has only enough shops to keep us from needing to go to a bigger town. It's the quaintest thing I've ever seen. Each storefront looks like it's been teleported straight out of the 1950's, all done in pastel colors with decorative trim. I find a parking spot and as we get out I look around while trying not to let my chin drag the ground. A cobbler, seamstress, office supplies. There's even an ice cream shop.

I turn in a slow circle. "Wow."

"It's a trip, isn't it?" Araceli grins at me. "My aunt lives here, so I spent a lot of my childhood visiting."

I can't help the envy that trickles through me at hearing that. Even the half-fae outcast had a happier childhood than I did. Pushing those thoughts away, I try to suppress the negative emotions toward the person that has been nicest to me since coming to Seraphim Academy. She doesn't deserve them.

"We should be able to get some fun stuff for our dorm here," Araceli says.

"Okay, but I don't have a lot of money," I say.

Araceli looks up from her purse. "Didn't they give you your allowance? I know it's not a lot, but it should be enough."

"No, although I remember being told that I'd receive some sort of stipend. I wasn't sure how to get access to it." And wasn't sure I wanted to either. Nothing in life is free. I learned that lesson early on.

"Come on." She grabs my elbow and pulls me down the street. "We'll go to the bank first. I bet it's there."

"There's an angel bank?" That's something I didn't know.

"Yep. In the human world it passes as a credit union for employees of Aerie Industries, and it only has branches in angel communities. Lots of angels have accounts at other banks as well, but this one is just for us, and run by angels. The town is enchanted to ward off humans anyway, so it'd be nearly impossible for one to open an account even if they did find the branch."

The bank is at the end of the street in a building that looks like an old Victorian house, painted pastel blue. We step onto the front porch and the planks under our feet creak with age. I arch an eyebrow at them, wondering if they'll hold.

Araceli grins. "Quaint."

Quaint isn't a strong enough word. We step inside, and Araceli walks straight to one of the tellers waiting for customers in a little booth.

"Hello," the lady says in a bright voice. "How may we help you?"

"I need to make a withdrawal from my account, and so does my friend, Liv."

"I'm not sure if I have an account at all." I give a little finger wave and an apologetic look. "If you could check, I'd really appreciate it. Olivia Monroe, please."

"Of course." The redhead taps away at her computer. "Do you have any ID?"

I hand her my driver's license and watch her check it. This experience has been such an odd mix of human and angel procedures.

"Everything seems to be in order, Ms. Monroe." She hands me my license and looks at me with her perfectly manicured eyebrows raised. "How much would you like to withdraw?"

"How much is there?" I ask.

"A thousand." The redhead's bland smile is unsettling. To her, a thousand dollars is no big deal. To me, it's a lot.

I stumble over my words. I have an account that I didn't open or ask for, with a bunch of money inside. Aerie Industries is paying me a thousand dollars just to attend school. For a second I almost feel bad for deceiving everyone, but then I get over it. I'm here on a mission. The angels can't find my brother, so they can damn well pay me for doing their job for them.

"Is that for the school year?" I ask. I do some quick math in my head. I have a couple hundred dollars saved up from my job at the bar. I should be able to make it work for the next year even without a job, considering I can get a lot of things free, and since I'm not paying for an apartment anymore. I'll need gas in the car, which is paid off at least, plus money for insurance and my phone, even though it doesn't get service up here.

"No, just the month," Araceli says as she looks at some paper in her purse. "It's pro-rated since we're only here some of March. You'll get two thousand next month."

My jaw drops. What in the world am I expected to spend two grand a month on?

Nothing, that's what. That shit is going in my dorm in case I need to make a quick escape. I might hide some off campus too. If anyone finds out I'm part demon, I'll need to be ready for anything.

"I'll take it all, please." I try to sound confident, like a cool thousand for half a month doesn't make me want to crap my pants.

The clerk, who I'm suddenly very fond of, hands me ten one-hundred-dollar bills, counting them out into my hand. I fold nine of them three times and tuck them into a tiny pocket in my black jeans. The other one I put in my wallet to spend today. I've never carried this much money in my life before, and it makes my head spin.

Araceli withdraws some money too, and then we head out again. "I've had this account since I was little. There's a branch of this bank in Arizona as well." As we walk out into the cold, her face brightens. "There's Grace and Cyrus. They flew."

They land on the sidewalk and Grace gives us one of her warm smiles. "Going shopping? Can we join you?"

"Of course," I say, as I eye them in their short-sleeve shirts. Araceli and I are bundled up like we're going out into the snow. "How do you stand the cold?"

"It's something we learned this week in Light Control, which you'll take next year," Cyrus says with a grin.

"Just gather a bit of sunlight around you, like this," Grace says. She focuses, and a glow wraps around her and then vanishes again. "It keeps you toasty warm."

Grace and Cyrus head into the bank, and while we wait Araceli works on pulling light around herself like a warm winter coat. I want to try it also, but doing so would reveal that I can use my angelic magic, and I can't have that. So instead, I just shiver, while she makes herself toasty warm.

"You'll figure it out," Araceli says while rubbing my shoulder, and I feel another pang of guilt for deceiving her. "Soon all this angel stuff will make sense, I promise."

"Thanks," I say.

"Araceli!" Darel practically skips along the street toward us. "What are you doing here on this lovely morning?"

"We're going shopping," she says with a laugh. "Care to join us?"

"I'd love to escort such beautiful ladies." He gives her a wink and then takes her arm like a gentleman. The two of them stroll off down the road, forgetting about me completely. It's tough to ignore a succubus, but love will do that, even the first stirrings of it. I'm not mad, though. I hope it works out for them. Plus, I enjoy the taste of their lust growing too.

Grace and Cyrus walk out, and they chuckle when they see Araceli has ditched us. "I guess that's going to be a thing," Cyrus says, delighted by this new gossip.

"Seems that way," I say.

"They're cute together," Grace says.

"We can hear you," Araceli calls back.

We all burst into giggles, and for a second I feel something rare: happiness. It's easy to pretend with these people. They're friendly and open with me, accepting me into their fold even though they've only known me for a week. I wish it all wasn't a lie.

As we walk down the street and admire the cute little shops, I chat and laugh with the others, but I also remind myself I'm here for a reason. When Cyrus and Darel slip inside a clothing shop for men, I use the opportunity to grill Grace and Araceli some more. I need to get all the information I can.

After we get a coffee at a little stand on the corner, I ask them, "Hey, have you heard any rumors about a secret society on campus?"

"A secret society?" Araceli asks with a little laugh. It sounds forced, and her eyes dart side to side. "At Seraphim? No way."

Grace waves her hand dismissively. "Those are just rumors. They go around every year, and everyone speculates on who got invited to join and who didn't, but then they die down again because there's nothing to them." She shrugs. "Sorry. It'd be pretty cool if the school did have one though."

I take a little sip of my coffee. "I figured it was just a crazy conspiracy theory."

It's hard to tell if they know anything or not, although Araceli definitely reacted oddly. Was she invited to the meeting tonight? Or Darel, I wonder, as he walks out of the men's shop empty-handed and heads straight for my roommate?

Cyrus appears at my side carrying a shopping bag. "Where to next?"

We wander through town for the rest of the day, and even though I tell myself I'll only spend a tiny bit, the prices are higher here than in Los Angeles. After buying a pretty day planner to keep track of my assignments, some pictures to hang in our dorm room, plus a pair of jeans I spied through a window, my wallet is a lot lighter. I guess angels can afford a premium price so they can have a place where they don't have to hide their wings or their magic. It's common here to see someone flying overhead, or glowing softly as they pass by, and everyone seems to know everyone else. Except me, of course. I still get the weird looks and the hurried whispers, although with friends at my side, they don't bother me quite as much.

22

OLIVIA

That night, I silently move through the forest toward the location on the invitation, wearing the white mask and robes. It's pitch black out here, with no moon to light my way, but it doesn't bother me. Here on top of the mountain it's so clear it's like I can see every single constellation in the sky—very different from where I grew up in Southern California.

Soon I come upon a small clearing where two people in white robes and masks are already waiting. I can't tell who they are, but they must be first years like me. One of them is probably Tanwen, knowing my luck. Both robed figures give me a nervous glance as I take a spot in the clearing a little distance away from them. We all stand around awkwardly as a few more people walk in, until there are fourteen of us total. I'm not surprised—seven is a sacred number for angels, just like six is for demons.

People in gold robes and masks suddenly emerge from all sides of the forest, surrounding us in the clearing, and it's hard to tell how many of them there are. One of them has a gold crown over his or her mask, and when they speak, the voice is unidentifiable. "Congratulations. You have been chosen from all of the angels at this school to possibly join the Order of the Golden Throne, the most ancient secret society in this world. Created three thousand years ago, the Order has been working from the shadows to guide humanity and angels on Earth for all of history. We recruit directly from the academy from both students and professors, and when you leave this school you will go on to become leaders of angel society." The leader pauses and glances among the people in white robes. "However, just because you received an invitation to tonight's gathering does not mean you have been accepted into the Order. No, at the moment you are initiates only, and to join the Order you must pass three tests. Only then will you become a full-fledged member at the end of the school year."

If this secret society went back that far, then my parents gave me a seriously lacking education. I've been starting to figure that out over the last week, but it's a lot worse than I realized, and there's so much I don't know. This secret society stuff sounds like more of the "angels are holier than thou" philosophy I can't stand, but I'm pretty sure my brother was a member, and this is the only clue I have so far. Which means I have to pass whatever tests they're going to throw at me.

"Before we give you the first test, we want to talk about our core values," the leader continues. "We believe angels are superior beings, and our purpose is to control Earth from the shadows to guide humanity to a brighter future. We believe demons are evil and must be eradicated from Earth to protect humanity. And finally, we believe that loyalty to the Order is paramount, along with discretion. You must not talk about the Order or this meeting with anyone, even if you do not become a member. We will find out if you break this rule, and there will be consequences."

Oops, guess I already broke that rule. I wonder what these dire consequences will be?

The person to my right snorts, and he must be thinking something along the same lines. All of the golden masks turn toward him at once, and he visibly stiffens. There is nothing more unnerving than a dozen or more people in masks all staring at you.

"Do you find this amusing?" the leader asks, in their unnatural voice. "Initiate?"

The person—who I assume is a man based on their body type, though I could be wrong—adjusts their mask. "No, it's just that everybody already knows about the Order. People talk." Like the leader, this person's voice is masked somehow, just like their face.

"See that you are not one of them," the leader orders. "Now, you may wonder why we have chosen you to become initiates. We have been watching you for some time, and at least one of our members has nominated you because we believe you have the traits we are looking for. Some of you come from a well-respected angelic family, while others have shown a strong hatred for demons or a willingness to help guide humans toward the light. Do not question yourselves. If you received an invitation, then you deserve to be here—but keep in mind that only a few of you will make it to the final trial.

"For the first test, we ask you to demonstrate your utmost loyalty to the Order. To do so, you must steal an item from a professor, or even the headmaster, if you so dare. Make sure you don't get caught, as you will likely be suspended or fired for such an act. You have a month to procure this item, after which you'll receive another invitation to the next meeting, where you will present it to us. Make sure it's something good, or we might reject your offering. Should we accept it, you'll be given the second test. Good luck."

With those last words, the golden-robed people step back into the darkness of the forest and disappear, leaving those of us in the white robes standing around awkwardly. We glance at each other, but since we can't recognize anyone, we can't really size up our competition.

I can't help but wonder who nominated me. I don't meet any of their criteria, and I find it hard to believe they would invite the half-human with unknown parentage. Either someone knows who my father is, or I've been invited for some other reason. For all I know, it's a prank. Or maybe the invitation was meant for someone else, and it got put in my room by accident.

Whatever the reason, I'm taking advantage of it. I have no interest in actually becoming a member of the Order, or in any of the things they believe in, but I feel like I'm on the right path. My gut tells me this secret society is the key to finding Jonah, which means I'm going to pass whatever tests they throw at me. Bring it on.

———

After I return to my room, I find myself unable to sleep, and my mind drifts back to the night I met Jonah.

A noise outside my window got me out of my bed in a hurry. Father had just left, and Mother rarely came to see me, except in dreams sometimes. Whoever was out there couldn't mean anything good for me.

My current round of foster parents didn't pay much attention to me, so they hadn't noticed when I hid a baseball bat under my bed. I grabbed it and flattened myself against the wall, then peeked out the window with the braveness of a ten-year-old who was used to taking care of herself, but also knew there were definitely monsters out there that might get you.

To my surprise and relief, a gangly boy about my age pressed his face against the glass. I was on the second story, but his wings kept him hovering at my level. I gaped at him for a minute, and then I cracked open the window, raising my bat, just in case. "Who are you?"

"Jonah," he said, a little too loud. "Who are you?"

"Shhh! I'll ask the questions." My foster parents watched a few too many police shows on TV and they were rubbing off on me. "Why are you flying around outside my window?"

"I came to see why my dad was visiting you," the boy said. "I followed him here."

"Your dad?" I blinked at him and lowered my bat, then spoke without thinking. "He's my dad too."

"Really?" Jonah's face lit up.

Uh oh. I wasn't supposed to tell anyone about my real parents. Father was teaching me about my people, and he warned me many times that if they found me, they'd want to hurt me, but I was too excited at the prospect of meeting someone else like me. I opened the window all the way and waved Jonah inside.

"You have to be quiet." I sat on my bed and set the bat beside me. "I'm Olivia, but you can call me Liv."

Jonah didn't sit, and instead vibrated with excitement, his wings still out. They were sparkling white with silver streaks, and I really wanted to touch them, but I knew that wasn't okay. "You're my sister?"

I nodded while biting my lip. His hair was dark blond and his bright smile looked nothing like my own, so it was hard to believe we could be related. His blue eyes were almost gray, while mine were a strange green that people usually commented on when first meeting me. "How can you fly? I thought angels don't get their wings until they're twenty-one."

"I got mine when I was seven," he said, as he looked around the room, checking everything out. There wasn't much there, since I'd only moved in a few weeks ago. "Mom says it's rare, but it happens sometimes."

"Who is your mom?" Could it be possible? Was there someone else like me?

"Archangel Ariel."

"Oh," I said, disappointed. He was a full angel, and I was...not.

All of a sudden, Father appeared in the room in a flash of light, and Jonah and I both let out a cry of surprise. He took us in, looking stern and scary. "Jonah, what are you doing here?"

Jonah looked up at his dad with defiance. "I wanted to know where you sneak off to sometimes. Why didn't you tell me I have a sister?"

"It was for Olivia's protection. No one is supposed to know about her. Not even you."

"You should have told us." I got a little warm glow in my chest for siding with Jonah. I had a brother. I wasn't totally alone anymore.

Father pinched the brow of his forehead with a sigh. "Perhaps you're right. But Olivia is safer if no one knows about her. Jonah, I'm going to have to get Jophiel to wipe your memories. I'm sorry."

"No!" we both cried out.

I grabbed onto Father's sleeve and looked up at him with eyes on *the brink of tears. "Please, Father. I don't have anyone. Don't take Jonah away too."*

He stared at me, and for once, his hard demeanor melted. He touched my head gently in a rare act of tenderness. "All right. But you both need to promise me you will never tell anyone about each other. That goes especially for you, Jonah. None of your friends can ever know about Olivia."

"And if I promise, I can come back and visit Liv?" Jonah asked.

"Yes, whenever you want," Father said.

"Then I promise!"

"Me too!" I chimed in.

Father grabbed us both in a hug, and as he held us there, I felt something rare...belonging. I had a family. I wasn't alone.

From that night on, Jonah came to visit me regularly, and we kept our promise. He didn't care that I was half-demon, because I was his sister. He told me all about the angel world, and his visits were the highlight of my life. And then he disappeared, and I remembered what it felt like to be completely alone in the world again—and I swore I'd do anything to find him.

23

OLIVIA

On Monday, Bastien, Callan, and Marcus walk into the cafeteria as Araceli and I head out after breakfast. Stiffening, I try to sidestep them, but they plant their big selves in my way.

Of course.

Marcus gives me a suave smile, but it has a bit of a predatory gleam. "In a hurry?"

"I hope so," Callan growls. He's my least favorite of the Princes, by far.

This time I'm not going to hide from them like a coward. I refuse to budge, and just cross my arms and glare at them until they huff and pass around me. *Another point for Liv.* For anyone else I would've politely sidestepped, but not these jerks. They can get out of my way.

With a small grin, I stroll out of the cafeteria, with Araceli gawking at my side. "That was great," she says as she glances behind us, like she's worried they might come after us. "As soon as I saw them, I ducked out of the way without thinking, but you stood up to them."

I shrug a little. "It's no big deal. I just don't think they have the right to waltz around like they run the school."

"You and me both, but I'm not crazy enough to challenge them. You're brave, girl."

My good mood lasts me precisely until it's time for Combat Training to start, and I'm faced with Tanwen kicking my ass again. Surprisingly, she doesn't. Not surprisingly, she's so busy kissing up to Callan that she forgets to bother me. I spend the time sparring with Araceli and Darel, while getting little snacks from their lustful energy, along with Callan. Because even though Tanwen wants him, he wants me.

I keep my guard up for the rest of the day, but it passes without any major complications. Marcus and I ignore each other in Demon Studies, where Professor Raziel is still teaching us about the Fallen. In Angelic History, Professor Kassiel tries to pretend I don't exist and fails, and I squirm the entire time listening to his sexy voice. While he lectures, I stare at the stubble on his neck and daydream of running my tongue along it. If I want to pass that class, I need to get control of myself. Afterwards, Bastien spends our time together grilling me about my childhood. It sounds more like he's looking for loopholes in my story than a way to figure out what my Choir is. The session only makes him grumpier.

At dinner, I grab some pizza and sit at our normal table with Araceli, Grace, and Cyrus. Darel, who Araceli is already half in love with and fully in lust with, joins us too. It's nice to have a group of friends, even if I know our friendships can't last. They'll never stay friends with me if they find out what I really am, or that I've been deceiving them, but for now it's nice.

"What are these flyers I'm seeing around campus for a football game against demons?" I ask.

"It happens every year," Cyrus says. "We have games against the demon school, Hellspawn Academy, and with the fae school, Ethereal Academy, as part of a way to build connections with them in a friendly environment, or some shit like that."

Darel smirks. "I heard it's so we can go up against them without having any real consequences. Burn off some steam and let out that aggression, since it's illegal to actually fight them."

"So, there's a demon academy too?" I ask. "Is it seriously called Hellspawn Academy?"

"It really is," Cyrus says. "They don't consider it an insult, believe it or not."

"The games are pretty fun, even though no one is allowed to use their powers," Darel says. "No flying, no burning light, none of that. But we can still use our superior speed and strength since supernaturals all have those. It makes for a pretty fast-paced and intense game." He grins. "I made it onto the team this year, so you all need to come to the games."

Araceli flips her hair and smiles. "We wouldn't miss it."

Cyrus swallows a big bite of pizza. "The first game is here on campus against the demons. Then the fae and demons have a game at Hellspawn Academy, and we have a game with the fae. At the end of the year, two winning teams face off for the championship."

"Does the school have other sports teams too?" I ask.

"No, the sport rotates every year since we don't have enough students for different teams. Last year it was baseball, and this year is football."

Baseball. Jonah's favorite. I'm sure he played on the team. I'll have to look up who else was on the team with him and see if they'd have any reason to do him harm.

I poke at my pizza and try to sound innocent. "Is it safe having demons and fae here on campus?"

Grace gives me a slightly pitying smile. "Pretty safe. There are plenty of professors and official people around to make sure nothing bad happens. Sometimes a fight breaks out, but nothing serious. You don't need to worry."

Cyrus glances at her quickly. "Well, I mean, Jonah did go missing after the last championship game against the fae, but that was probably a coincidence."

I glance up quickly, then shove a piece of pizza in my mouth to hide my surprise. This is news to me.

Grace's face grows pinched at the mention of my brother. "We don't know if it's connected or not. The Archangels cleared the fae of any involvement."

I don't know much about the fae, but it sounds like I need to learn more...and figure out what happened at that game.

Araceli and I finish up our dinner, say goodnight to our friends, and head out the door. When we step out into the cool night air, I spot Marcus leaning against the wall outside, looking deliciously sexy in a black leather jacket while the breeze teases his wavy hair. His dark eyes catch mine and lust flares between us, so strong I nearly tremble when it hits me.

"There you are," he says, straightening up. "I'd like to talk to you. Alone."

Araceli gives me a nervous glance, but I nod at her. "It's fine," I say. "I'll meet you back at the dorm."

"Okay." She hesitates, but then rubs her arms and darts away.

When we're alone, I ask, "Were you waiting for me?"

"I was," he says. "We need to set up a time to work on our project for Demon Studies."

"Is that all?" I let out a soft laugh. "You had me worried there when you said you wanted to speak alone."

He gives me the sexiest little grin. "I just wanted you all to myself."

I roll my eyes at the cheesy line. "I'm free at 4pm on Wednesday. Does that work?"

"Sounds good. Meet in the library?"

I nod. "See you then."

As I walk away, he calls out in a teasing voice, "We both know you wanted to be alone with me, too."

I pretend I don't hear him, but I hate how right he is. I do want him alone. In my bed. On a table. On the floor. Doesn't matter, as long as we're both naked. But that's not going to happen, so I swallow my desire and head back to my dorm...alone.

24

KASSIEL

At midnight, the campus is deathly quiet, especially out here by the lake. The moonlight glistens off the black water as it moves softly in the wind, and I take a deep breath and take it all in. After a long day of teaching, it helps me clear my head to have a moment alone to myself out here.

"I never imagined I'd see you out of your suit."

The sultry, familiar voice makes me jerk upright, and I turn to spot the owner of it walking toward me. "Olivia."

She's wearing a black hoodie, and she pushes it back as she approaches, then shakes out that beautiful mane of dark hair. "What are you doing out here?"

"I could ask the same of you."

"I couldn't sleep, so I thought I'd take a walk around the lake. I didn't expect to see anyone else out here."

"Sometimes I unwind out here after a long day of teaching." I should get up and say goodnight to her to avoid her as much as possible, but I find myself rooted to the bench I've been sitting on. Something in her eyes looks so vulnerable and lost I can't send her away. I pat the spot next to me on the stone bench. "Care to sit with me for a few minutes?"

She glances at her watch and nods her head. If she was half-human like everyone thought, she wouldn't have been able to see it in the meager moonlight. But she's not, and she just confirmed it for me without even realizing it. *Careful, my dear, or someone else will catch on soon too.*

"I guess I can spare a few more minutes." She perches on the edge of the bench and stares at the water, like she's purposefully trying not to look at me. Then it hits me...she's hungry. Lilim are always hungry, especially young ones like her. Since she's only half succubus, I'm not sure how often she needs to feed, but she can probably feel my own desire for her every time I look at her, and it probably makes it even worse.

I jerk my gaze away from her and try not to think about how much I want her. "How are you doing? With your...special diet?"

Her body visibly stiffens. "I don't know what you mean."

"Sure you don't." I lean over and pick up a rock, tossing it into the lake. With my superior strength, it skips all the way to the other side and out of view.

"Nice throw."

"I've had a lot of practice."

She arches an eyebrow. "How old are you? Or is that weird to ask an angel?"

I chuckle softly. "It's considered rude to ask, because the older you are, the more powerful, but it's fine. I'm only one hundred seventy-two years old."

"*Only?*" she asks, with a little laugh.

"In the supernatural world, that's practically a baby."

She shakes her head with an amused smile. "And in the human world, it's old enough to be my great-great-grandfather or something like that."

"Time is different for those of us with immortal lifespans. Years will start to fly by, and you'll wonder where they went. Then you'll look up, and suddenly all the technology is obsolete, and you need to learn everything all over again."

"So what you're saying is, you're old," she says with a teasing grin.

I grin back at her. "Pretty much, yeah. Now get off my lawn, youngster."

"Not a chance." She tilts her head as she studies me, and I'm struck again with how lovely she is. "You definitely don't look old. Especially in jeans and a t-shirt. I thought you lived in those suits."

"Only when I'm in public. Like I told you before, my father ingrained in me that a man is only as good as his suit, and it's hard to get over that even after all these years. But then, you understand how complicated relationships with parents can be, don't you?"

It's a leading question, going back to what she said that night, and with it she instantly tenses again. "I don't know who my father is."

"Is that so?" I ask. "A pity. Maybe now that you're here, he'll claim you. What about your mother?"

"Dead."

"That's not what you told me back at the bar that night."

"You must have heard me wrong." She looks at the water and stands. "It's late. I should get back to my room."

She's falling back upon her lies then. I hoped she would be honest with me, but I understand her need for secrecy better than anyone. As she starts to walk away, I call out, "Olivia."

She turns and looks at me in the dark, easily meeting my eyes thanks to her demon blood. "Yes?"

"I won't expose you." I can't explain why, but I won't give her up. Not unless I'm forced to. "Your secret is safe with me, I swear it. And not just because I'm worried about an inquiry for sleeping with a student. So if you ever need to talk...I'll be here."

Her eyes lower to the ground for a few seconds. Then she meets my gaze again and gives a curt nod. "Good night."

As she walks away, I let out a long breath. Getting close to Olivia is dangerous for so many reasons. For one, it's forbidden for a teacher and a student to have a relationship. For another, she could find out what I am and expose me too. I can't afford to have my cover blown, especially not when I'm closer than ever.

And the most dangerous reason? When she's around, I feel more than I have in a century.

25

OLIVIA

L EAVE NOW BEFORE YOU GET HURT
Wadding up the paper, I stuff it deep into my bag before anyone else sees it. "Assholes."

The threatening note is the latest of a long line of them left in my bag, slipped under my dorm room door, or under the windshield wipers of my car. I even found one shoved in my bag after I shopped in the school store. Tanwen was nearby that day, so I'm sure she's behind the notes.

I just finished up my last session with Bastien, and after a long day of classes all I want to do is go to my room and take off my bra, but that's not in the cards today. I stop by the cafeteria to grab a coffee, and then head back to the library. I'm a few minutes early, but Marcus beats me there anyway, already waiting in one of the private rooms.

"Hey, gorgeous." He stands when he sees me and holds out my chair for me. "You ready for this?"

He's got several books on imps out already, which I don't need. Mother told me all about the other demon races, and I'm not sure I trust these books to be unbiased anyway. On the other hand, I thought I knew everything about angels too before coming to

Seraphim Academy, and I've learned a lot in the last week. Maybe there will be something helpful in the books after all.

Marcus flips one of them open. "From what I've read so far, imps represent the Deadly Sin of envy and can create illusions. They feed on attention and awe, so they tend to have jobs like actors, musicians, and magicians. That should make this project easier."

"Do we have to do a presentation or just the paper?" I ask, as I grab one of the books.

"We have to do a 3D model of an imp using its powers." Marcus stares at me like I should've known this.

"You're joking." A 3D model? Out of what? Paper mâché? I don't think so. "That's a bit much, don't you think? And imps look just like humans, they just have the power of illusion."

Marcus bursts out laughing. "We don't have to make a 3D model. Just write a paper."

"Oh, I see how it is." I can't help the smile that spreads across my face as he laughs. His features, sharp and handsome, soften as he chuckles.

He opens his notebook and checks his messy handwriting. "We're supposed to find historical, religious, and mythological people who are imps and write a ten-page paper on them by the end of the year. We did a similar thing last year in Fae Studies."

"That shouldn't be too hard. There's Loki, Houdini..."

Marcus's eyebrows shoot up. "How do you know they're imps?"

Shit. Mother told me. I'm not supposed to know this stuff. For a second I forgot. I give a little shrug and try to play it cool. "Grace told me. She took Demon Studies last year."

"Cool. We can definitely research those two. I think we need another person. Maybe a woman. Let's see what these books say."

We spend the next hour combing through the books Marcus brought while taking notes, and making an outline for what we need to research more. Though I originally pictured Marcus as more of a cute jock type, he's smarter than I expected.

"Hmm, there's a book we don't have." Marcus shuffles through the books on the table. "It's about the darkness of imps, and how they're seen as the more innocent of demons, but it outlines the atrocities some of them committed. I know I've seen it before."

"That could be useful."

He snaps his fingers. "I know! It's in Uriel's private library. I'll get it next time I'm there with Bastien, and I'll bring it next week when we meet again to finish up the research."

"Uriel has his own private library?" I ask as I help gather up the books on the table, keeping my voice casual. I still need to steal something for my first trial, and I have less than a month to do it. I remember seeing a bookshelf when I met with Uriel before, but I was pretty distracted and overwhelmed at the time.

"Yeah, in his office. Mostly stuff that's considered dangerous or not fit for students to read at their leisure. Dark magic kind of stuff. Old demonic tomes."

We put the books back on the shelf, and I peruse some of the other nearby books on demons. One of them looks interesting, and I pluck it off the shelf and flip through it.

"Same time again next week?" Marcus asks.

"Sounds good," I say, closing the book. I'm going to check it out and take it back to my room, because it has a section about Lilim that looks interesting. Surely I know all there is about my kind, but given what I've discovered I don't know about angels and demons, there might be something in the book I could learn too.

He leans against the bookshelf next to me and I catch a whiff of his scent. Sandalwood. "This was fun. We should hang out more."

My succubus side wakes up and purrs, and I'm tempted to bury my face in his chest and breathe him in. I clutch the book to my chest to stop myself. "I don't think your friends would approve."

"That's their problem. I want to get to know you better. Maybe over dinner sometime. What do you think?"

"I think that's a really bad idea." By now, my hunger has grown considerably and all the sexual tension with Marcus doesn't help in the least. "I'll see you in class."

I spin on my heel and start to head out. Why is Marcus suddenly being so nice to me? Is this some new angle to trick me into trusting him, then deceiving me? I've seen plenty of high school dramas on the CW, I know how this stuff works. Or am I being too suspicious? Maybe he actually...likes me? But that's a problem too. I can't have a boyfriend. Long term relationships are not possible for a succubus. I'm destined to be alone for the rest of my immortal days. Letting Marcus get close is only going to cause problems for both of us.

"Liv," he calls out. I turn to see him walking toward me with my planner in his hand. "You forgot this."

"Thanks." I hold out my hand, and Marcus places the planner in it, his fingers brushing mine. Desire shoots through me, strong and potent. I haven't felt anything like this since the night with Kassiel. This is different, though. I'm not sure in what way, yet.

Sucking in a calming breath, I pull my hand away and put the planner in my bag. Walking away with my desire stoked and hunger gnawing at me is one of the most difficult things I've done in life.

———

I find Kassiel by the lake again that night. I'm not sure why I come back, except perhaps because I believed him when he said he wouldn't expose me. He must have figured out by now that I'm half demon and half angel, a creature forbidden to even exist, but it doesn't seem to bother him. It's a relief to be around someone who knows what I truly am. For the short time with him, I don't have to pretend.

I sit beside him in silence, unsure what exactly to say. By coming here, I'm acknowledging that I do want to talk with him and that he's right about me, but I won't admit it out loud either. There's also the unspoken tension between us as two people who once had mind-blowing sex together, but can't do it again...no matter how much we want to.

"What's your favorite class?" he asks. "And don't say mine, I've seen your eyes glaze over when I talk about things that happened thousands of years ago."

I laugh and relax a little on the bench. "Flight, obviously. Isn't that everyone's favorite?"

"Okay, other than that one."

"Probably Demon Studies."

He chuckles. "Because you're so well-versed in the subject already?"

Well, yes, but... "No, because Professor Raziel is funny. He wears the silliest bow ties."

"That he does. And I've never seen him wear the same one twice. He must have dozens of them."

"One for every day of the year, maybe?"

I find myself grinning as we talk about classes and professors until the moon is high, and we only stop when the air changes and the sky starts drizzling on us. We both laugh and stand up, holding our hands out to the tiny drops. While we've been sitting here a spring storm has gathered above us, and could unleash at any moment.

"I'm going to fly back before it starts pouring," Kassiel says, as he rises. "I suggest you do the same."

I nod. "Good idea."

"See you soon, Olivia."

His wings appear, as black as the night itself, and almost identical to mine. Except when he turns his back to me, I notice his feathers have shining silver tips, and when he extends his wings wide it's like looking at the night sky sparkling with stars. They're so beautiful they take my breath away as he launches into the air.

My own wings are shining black, so dark they look like ink, and I fly up beside Kassiel for a moment, enjoying the cool, damp air brushing against my face. We circle each other, a dance only for angels, and my chest tightens at how romantic it is to be flying with him. Then we move apart, me going to the dorms and him to the professor housing, and I remember that the two of us can never be.

26

OLIVIA

Weeks have passed since school began, and I'm finally starting to find my groove at Seraphim Academy. People still steer clear of me for the most part, but otherwise the bullying has mostly stopped, except for the annoying notes from Tanwen. The Princes are a problem, but I've gotten used to dealing with their haughty attitudes. Marcus and I meet every Wednesday to work on our paper, and he flirts with me shamelessly while I try not to let him wear down my armor entirely. Callan continues to toy with me during combat training, and Bastien still can't figure out what I am. Kassiel and I have met a few more times by the lake at night, and he tries to get me to confess what I am with pointed questions, all of which I dodge. On Sundays, I go to yoga class on the lawn, and even though Tanwen is there too, it helps keep my head clear and my body flexible. Two important things when you're part succubus.

Sometimes I almost forget why I'm really here. It's easy when the classes are interesting, and I have actual friends to hang out with for a change. But last night I found another invitation from the Order of The Golden Throne, and I realized it's been a month since the last meeting. I need to bring something to the trial tomorrow night, or I won't pass this first test. This secret society is the only lead I have, and I can't blow it.

I've done everything else I can think of to find Jonah. I watched a video of the championship game against the fae last year, but it was so boring I nearly fell asleep. Nothing happened that seemed suspicious, and no one I questioned saw anything odd that night. Another dead end. I checked out the other members of the baseball team, but none of them have any reason for hurting Jonah. And so far, neither Grace nor the Princes have given me any other leads, even though I've been getting closer to all of them and trying to subtly ask them questions about Jonah.

The Order of the Golden Throne is my only hope of finding him. Ever since Marcus told me about Uriel's private library, I've been observing the headmaster using my Ishim invisibility and Mother's necklace. He keeps a strict schedule, which isn't good for his security, but it's great for my need to steal something from his office. There must be something in there I can steal, and I purposefully waited until right before the next meeting to steal it. I don't want my stolen item anywhere near me if he notices it's missing and goes on a hunt for it.

Even with a plan in mind, I'm a bucket of nerves. I've skipped out on Angelic History, complaining to Kassiel that I have a headache, and he gave me a pointed look but nodded. He probably thinks I need to feed, which is true, but I've been surviving off of light and the lust I receive from him and the Princes and I'm okay for now. I'll need to feed pretty soon though.

With my lock picks in my pocket and the light bent around me to make me invisible, I walk out of my dorm and make my way toward the Headmaster's house. Since the bell has rung and everyone is in fourth period, it's easy to move undetected across campus. At this time of day, I know the house will be empty because the Princes have class and Uriel uses the time to walk around the campus and meet with some of the workers.

I tiptoe onto the front porch of Uriel's home, but footsteps behind me make me freeze. Bastien walks up the path toward the house. Are you kidding me? They've followed the same pattern for a month, then on the day I'm breaking in, Bastien has to bring his sneaky ass here. Why isn't he in class?

I freeze, afraid if I move the wood under my feet might creak and he'll hear me. I stand to the right of the door, and there is just enough room for Bastien to use his key to unlock and open the door. If he moves a few inches to the right, he'll bump into me. I hold my breath.

As I wait and try not to move, silently urging him to go inside, he stiffens and breathes deep. He looks all around, and a white glow fills his eyes. He must suspect there is an Ishim hiding near him, but even his Ofanim magic can't get past my necklace. He sees nothing.

"Weird." He opens the door and strides in the house without bothering to make sure it closes behind him. I slip in on his heels and breathe a quiet sigh of relief when I make it without the door bumping into me.

I start to head for Uriel's office, where I visited on my second day here, but I want to scream in frustration when Bastien goes straight for the room I need. But then, luck! He unlocks it with his own key, and doesn't close the door behind him. I sneak in and watch him sit at Uriel's large desk and turn on the computer. I creep behind his shoulder silently to watch what he's doing. The monitor lights up, showing views of all the cameras on campus. Bastien fiddles with the controls and brings up the parking lot, then rewinds through the entire freaking night. But he doesn't go at full speed, oh no. He goes slow enough that he can keep a close eye on any movement in the lot. Pausing a few times when he thinks he sees something, he continues backing up until yesterday evening comes on and the sun reappears.

This is taking forever. Bastien needs to leave so I can get a book off the shelves and get the fuck out of this house. If Bastien is still here when his father gets home, I might be busted. I still don't trust that my necklace is really working with Uriel, and I don't want to test it again.

Bastien hits a few buttons and looks at the live feed, scanning through the cameras like he's searching for something. "I'll catch you leaving again, Olivia. It's only a matter of time."

The sneaky asshole is looking for me. He knows I've been leaving campus at night. Damn it. That means I'll have to fly from now on. I'm getting better, and I can probably make it to the town, but I don't want to. The thought of soaring over all those trees makes me nervous. What if I get too tired to fly back? I've never gone long distances before.

Just when I think we'll be in here forever, Bastien stands and leaves the office, locking the door behind him. Good thing I brought my lock picks.

First thing's first. Find a book that's dark and scary enough to impress the Order of the Golden Throne. After searching Uriel's bookshelf, I find what I need on the top shelf: *Daemon Death*, imprinted on a cover that looks suspiciously like skin. I shudder and put the book in a pouch slung cross-body just for this purpose.

The sound of footsteps have me flinging myself toward the window, praying it opens without a sound. Uriel must be back from his meetings. No time for lock picks, I need to get out *now*.

I dive out the window and tuck myself into a roll, landing on my feet and running toward the front of the house and around the corner. We learned that in Combat Training last week, and I silently thank Hilda for teaching it to us.

Once in front of the house, I dart down the path, praying Uriel isn't looking out a window and Bastien isn't about to jump out from behind a bush. I'm much more comfortable creeping around at night, even though my Ishim magic should protect me, but I feel a lot better when I near the cafeteria. I hide behind a tree, until I'm sure it's clear, and then I release the light bent around me, coming into view again.

Leaving the protection of the tree, I walk into the cafeteria like I would any other day of the week. Nothing strange to see here. Just a girl getting some food with a dark and dangerous book resting on her hip.

27

OLIVIA

The meeting is in the same spot as last time, so I make it there with no problem, even in the dark. This time, my white mask and robes only match ten other people's. We stand for some time in a line, waiting for the meeting to begin. Without warning, the golden-robed figures emerge from the trees and surround us.

"Your numbers are considerably lowered," the leader says, standing in front with the crown on his or her head. "But it's as we expected."

Another robed figure steps forward, with a smaller build. Female, I think, though it's hard to tell in the robes and with the voice-altering masks. She holds out her hand at the person on the far left. "One at a time, bring your stolen objects forward."

The person walks forward and pulls a bracelet from under their white robes. "Professor Hilda's bracelet."

The leader nods and the mysterious voice speaks. "We accept your offering."

The white-robed person moves to their spot again with a sigh of relief. The next person steps forward. "One of Professor Raziel's bow ties."

The smaller person in gold takes the bow tie. Another golden-robed figure steps up and shakes his or her head. "This does not belong to Raziel. There is none of his essence on this." The masked figure tilts his or her head. "You bought this in a store and hoped to deceive us, didn't you?"

"Um, no, never..." sputters the person in white.

"Your offering is unacceptable," the leader says. "Leave this clearing and never speak of anything you've seen here."

"What?" the initiate asks. "You're wrong! I got it from his bedroom, I promise!"

"You think we can't see through your lies?" asks the second robed figure. Something about the way he speaks and moves reminds me of Bastien. Could it be him? "Fool."

People in golden robes suddenly surround the initiate, grabbing the person's arms, and dragging him or her out of the clearing. There's a lot of yelling, and then it goes eerily silent. After a few minutes, the masked figures return to their places among the trees. Everyone in white shifts nervously, now that we've seen what happens when we don't have a good enough offering.

After he leaves, the next person steps forward with a pair of tight black briefs. "Professor Kassiel's underwear."

Oh, damn. The thought of Kassiel in those briefs sends a zing of lust through me, along with jealousy too. How did this person get his underwear? Is Kassiel getting involved with another student? I quickly dismiss the thought, since it doesn't seem like something he would do, especially if he can resist me. This person must have snuck into his bedroom to get these.

"Are they clean?" the female in gold asks, sounding almost amused. I hear several snorts and coughs.

"Yes, they are. And it was fucking hard to get into the professor dorms without anyone noticing."

There's a long stretch of silence, and I worry we'll have another person escorted out, but then the leader says, "We accept your offering."

They continue moving through the group, until it's my turn. I swallow hard, step forward, and try to dislodge the book from the bag under my robe. Damn it.

"Hang on," I grunt, but my voice sounds weird. I pause, then realize it's the voice change. Get it together, girl! I manage to get out the book, ready for the strange voice this time. "This is a restricted book from Headmaster Uriel's private library."

The golden-robed figure hesitates before taking the book. "*Daemon Deaths.*" The dark eyes behind the mask are familiar to me, but I can't place them. I need to find out more about these people, and a plan hatches. "Do you know this book is cursed?"

I yank my hand back. Good thing I got it earlier today. Who knows what it would have done if I'd kept it in my dorm for weeks. "I did not."

Silence stretches over the clearing, and I hold my breath, worried the object being cursed will be a problem and they'll drag me out of the clearing too. But then the leader nods. "Your offering is accepted."

I breathe a huge sigh of relief as I move back to the line. I've passed the first test. I'm one step closer to finding Jonah.

They continue down the line, sending one more person home, until the last initiate has made their offering.

"Congratulations on passing the first trial. Your next task, if you are up to it, is to guide a human to confession. You must prove that you're willing to help lead humanity down the path we have chosen for them, and take action against humans who commit evil. Many humans have dark secrets and have done things they're not proud of. Find one, convince him or her to reveal his secrets, and then expose them."

"Sorry, but I'm out," the initiate to my left suddenly says. "Stealing an object, fine. Ruining a human's life? Nope. I am not on board with this."

"You must do this if you want to join the Order."

"Yeah, no. This is not my jam. Thanks, but no thanks."

The person walks out of the clearing, while the rest of us stand there, stunned. The golden-robed figures whisper among themselves, shifting around uncomfortably at the disturbance, but the leader holds up a hand to silence them. "It's fine. That person will change their mind and come back to us. If not, they do not deserve to be in the Order anyway."

I'm disgusted by this task too, but I have to do it and it shouldn't be too hard with my succubus powers. Still, I'm seriously impressed by that person for walking away when this didn't feel right to them. That's hard to do, especially in a group like this.

The leader begins to speak again. "A camera will be left for you to record the confession. The camera is a fae relic, just like the masks you wear. You cannot fool it, and there is no way to cheat out of this test. You either do it, or you do not. Once you've completed the mission, leave it here, and if we accept your offering you'll receive an invitation to the next meeting."

With that, we're dismissed, and the others in white robes head back into the forest. I move a little way away from the other seven people, and then bend light around myself to disappear. Then I head back to the clearing. Time to find out who these fuckers are.

With my hand wrapped around my necklace, I double back just in time to see a glimpse of gold through the branches. Hurrying forward, I catch up to the group of masked figures. They walk on silent feet toward the lake, and when I think they're going to walk out of the woods and into the open air, they stop beside a boulder. The first person in the line grabs a branch on a nearby tree and yanks. The boulder rolls to the side as if several large men manipulate it, but nobody is close enough to touch it.

Not creepy at all.

A cave has opened up, and the members file into it one by one. I dart forward, on the heels of the last person to go through, and barely make it inside. The boulder must not be able to sense me with my necklace on, because it tries to roll back as soon as the person in front of me enters. I almost crash into them as I narrowly avoid it, and the boulder slams shut behind me, trapping me inside.

The tunnel behind the boulder leads downward in a sharp slope. I'm not expecting it and nearly trip and fall on my ass. I catch myself on the rough stone wall, and continue into the darkness. The ground levels out as the walls and floor dampen. Based on where we entered and how far we've walked, I guess we're under the lake by now.

The golden-robed figures enter a large cavern with ornate stone benches arranged in a circle. There's a small gap, leading to a large throne made of what looks like gold, carved with intricate designs of angels and demons in battle. It looks ancient.

The members of the Order take their seats on the stone benches, and the person with the crown stands in front. Oddly, he or she doesn't sit on the throne. Is it not for the leader? Who else would sit there?

"We begin another meeting of the Order of the Golden Throne. Has anyone made any progress in our mission?"

Silence. I clasp my necklace harder and stare at the robed figures. Who could they be? Why won't they remove their masks? Does that mean even the other people in the Order don't know who the other members are? Studying height and builds, I can't tell anything. I don't know these people well enough, even after all the time I've been on campus, but I'll figure it out. I've snuck in here once, I can do it again.

"Disappointing," the leader says. "Our master will be most displeased."

Master? Who could that be? I'm dying to know who these people are, but there's nothing I can do but watch and listen. I can't even move, for fear someone might hear my footsteps on the cold stone ground.

One of the masked figures speaks up. "The initiate that refused the second trial and left. She's the one we need, isn't she?"

"Yes, that was her," the leader says.

"How are we supposed to do this without her?" another person asks.

"We'll have to convince her to join after all," the leader says. "Perhaps we'll remind her of the evil of demons, and show her that the Order is the only way to stop them."

"What do you have in mind?" another person asks.

"I have an idea. We'll take action at the football game against the demons."

"Even if we can use her, what makes you think we'll be able to succeed this time? Jonah is still missing. If he failed, what hope do the rest of us have?"

My ears perk up at the mention of my brother. I knew this was the key to finding him. They must know where he is!

"We need to focus on finding Jonah," a different masked figure says. "He's been gone way too long now."

"Has anyone heard from him?" another asks. "Anything at all?"

"No, there has been no contact with Jonah, despite our best efforts," the leader says. "But once we have the girl, we can send a team to find him. Which is why we must convince her to join, no matter what dark deed it requires."

I don't like the way the leader is speaking, and I can't help but wonder who the girl is and why she's so important. How is she going to help them find Jonah? I need to figure out who she is.

"I'll send your orders when I have a plan in motion. Be ready for them. You're dismissed."

The masked figures stand, and some of them begin to file out, while others clump up into groups and whisper to each other. One of them moves to the leader and speaks in a hushed conversation. I really want to listen to what they're saying, but I'm also worried about getting trapped down here. Plus I have an idea.

I follow one of the people up the tunnel and out of the cave, watching when they press a stone to open the boulder. I continue moving silently behind them as they head through the forest for a distance, before pausing to remove their robes and mask. I throw a hand over my mouth so I don't visibly gasp when I see who it is.

Cyrus.

28

CALLAN

It's been two months since school started, and there's still no sign of Jonah. Even worse, we haven't kept our promise to him. I graffitied Olivia's door and have been sending her threatening notes, but nothing is working. She isn't scared enough to leave the school, which means I'm going to have to ramp up my efforts somehow.

One morning, I suggest to Professor Hilda that Tanwen should pair up with Araceli that day. Tanwen went hard on Liv last week, which I'm perfectly fine with, but I want a crack at her now.

"You're with me today," I say. Olivia jumps a mile as she whirls to face me, and I can't help but snicker. She didn't realize I was behind her. Good. I'm glad to have the upper hand. Maybe she'll keep being jumpy, and I can use that against her.

"Did you have a good weekend, half-human?" I drip acid into my tone, but she doesn't react.

"I did, thank you for asking. How was your weekend?" Her polite voice is the opposite of mine and makes me feel like a big jerk. I don't really enjoy bullying her, but I can't let up, though. Jonah would kill us if he knew we still hadn't found a way to get her to leave. He'd been adamant that she had to go for her own safety. And since I can't do a damn thing to bring him back, I have to do this thing for him.

I gesture for her to follow me onto one of the mats. "Today I'm going to attempt to teach you to deflect an attack from behind."

I go through the motions, and she stands there with her hands behind her back, making her breasts push out and look even more noticeable. If I didn't know she hated me, I'd think she's trying to be seductive. Like she needs to try. Even in the shapeless gym clothes, her figure screams at me. I itch to put my hands around her waist. Her curves are what humans sing about. Perfectly proportioned, and a body that would fit mine like a glove.

Frustrated at the direction my mind is going, I attack without warning. Of course, she doesn't have time to dodge me. I've got her pinned to the mat before either of us takes in another breath.

She blinks up at me with big eyes, and I launch off of her. Damn it. Working with her isn't a good idea after all. "Didn't the humans teach you anything?" I growl. "Why don't you go back to them?"

She huffs as she stands up. "I wasn't ready, but I will be this time. Can we try again?"

I grunt, and remind myself I'm supposed to be teaching her. This time I attack slower, giving her the chance to use the move I showed her earlier, and she deflects it easily. We do the move multiple times, until she gets it down. By the time the class is over, I've worked her hard and we're both sweating, but I'm nowhere closer to getting rid of her.

As she walks out of the gym and heads to the lake for Flight class, I rub my palms on my eyes. I keep failing to keep my promise to Jonah, and I can practically hear my dad yelling at me for not living up to my potential. He'd beat the shit out of me if he knew I wasn't keeping my word to someone. As the son of two Archangels, failure is not an option for me.

It's time for some drastic measures. I take no joy in what I need to do, but it's the only way to fulfill my promise to Jonah. I stalk out to the parking lot, where Liv's beat-up old Honda is parked next to my convertible Audi again. I check the area, but no one is around, and even if someone was, what would they do? No one would dare stop me.

I gather light in my palms, and then blast the windshield to pieces with a direct shot. Tiny fragments of glass fly everywhere, covering the car seats and making it impossible for her to drive it until she cleans it out. *Try going on one of your midnight excursions now.*

It's not enough though. She could mistake this for a random act of nature or something. I use my burning light like a laser and write in large letters along the pavement behind her car, "YOU DON'T BELONG HERE." Below it, I add, "LEAVE NOW OR PAY."

I step back and survey the wreckage of her car. There. That should convince her to leave the school. And then my promise to Jonah will be complete.

29

OLIVIA

F light class is over the lake today. If we fall, we get soaked at best, drown at worst. Enough time has gone by that I don't have to pretend to be a terrible flier anymore. I'm an honest but mediocre flier now and using the class to improve. I'm still not the best, but I don't fall in the lake, so I call it a success.

In Demon Studies, we're learning about Lilim now, which amuses me but also makes me a little nervous that someone in class might figure out there's a succubus sitting only a few feet from them. No one does, of course.

"Imagine needing sex to survive," Marcus says with a grin when we walk out of class together. "Doesn't seem so bad to me."

I roll my eyes. "Of course you'd think that. But it also means the Lilim can never settle down with anyone."

"Not unless they had a harem or something, I guess." Marcus wiggles his eyebrows. "Don't tell me that doesn't appeal to you."

I shake my head, but can't help but smile. "But then the trick is finding people who are okay with sharing you with others."

Marcus grins and starts to reply, but then Grace runs over to me. "Liv! Your car!"

My good mood instantly vanishes. "What? What about it?"

"It's been attacked. You need to go look. I'll go report it to the Headmaster."

"I'll come with you," Marcus says, as we rush down the steps and onto the lawn.

I rush to the parking lot with a hollowness in my chest, and when I get there, I freeze. My windshield's been completely destroyed, and tiny bits of glass cover everything. But that's not the worst of it. No, the worst is the message in the pavement.

My eyes water, and it's hard to hold back the tears. For months now I've stayed strong even when people were mean to me, when they left me threatening notes and tagged my dorm room door, but this is too much. I bought that car myself, scraping together enough money to afford it, and even though it's a piece of shit it's *mine*. Now every time I see it, I'll remember this moment.

YOU DON'T BELONG HERE, the message taunts me. And maybe it's right. I don't belong at Seraphim Academy. I'm not an angel, not like these people are. But I don't belong at Hellspawn Academy either. I belong nowhere.

For a second I'm tempted to say fuck it and leave. Give the haters what they want. It would be so much easier to return to my old life and forget about all of this. But I can't. I won't.

Not until I find Jonah, anyway.

Marcus wraps an arm around my shoulders. "I'm so sorry, Liv."

I nod absently. "Who could do this?"

"That's the work of an Erelim. They're the only ones who can burn with light like that."

My hands clench at my sides. Tanwen. It has to be. That bitch is going to pay.

Marcus takes my face in his hands and stares into my eyes. "Don't listen to them," he says. "You do belong here, as much as any of us do."

His kind words are my undoing, and before I know what I'm doing, I press my lips to his. It was either that, or burst into tears, I guess. He kisses me back like he's been dying for this moment as much as I have, wrapping his arms around me and holding me tight. I slide my hands along his strong back, and for a second I feel safe and loved with him, a feeling so rare and nice I never want it to end. But it has to. It's an illusion, because everything between us is a lie, and nothing like this can last.

I pull away from him and run off, leaving him behind, along with my broken car. As I do, I feel the after-effects from the kiss, sending power through my veins. Marcus is the son of an Archangel, and thus stronger than most other angels, and even a kiss is enough to give me a boost and hold off the hunger for a while. Except now that I've had a taste of him, I only want more.

———

I ditch Angelic History, because I can't face Kassiel with lust running through my veins, but I calm down enough to meet Bastien for our special classes. I'm distracted, totally focused on my car being vandalized and the kiss with Marcus, and he can probably tell.

He meets me outside the library today. "Since nothing has worked so far in finding your Choir, we're going to do something different now. Today we'll go to the Ishim class and watch them practice to see if you feel anything. Then next time we'll go observe a different Choir and on until we find the one you belong to."

I nod, but my stomach twists. Why did we have to start with the Choir I should belong to?

The Choir classes are held in a large building on the other side of campus, set back against the forest. I've never been to this building before, but it's divided into four sections. We head down a hallway that leads to both the Ishim classes, and the Malakim training area and school infirmary. On the rare occasions an angel is sick or injured, they come here and the Malakim fix them up.

Bastien takes me inside a room that appears to be empty except for one man, with pale skin, pale eyes, and pale hair. He looks like an angel that's been bleached by the sun.

"This is Professor Nariel, and he teaches the Ishim classes," Bastien says, introducing us. "Olivia here hasn't found her Choir yet, and we wanted to observe some Ishim at work to see if she feels anything."

"Nice to meet you," Nariel says, shaking my hand. "We were just practicing hiding groups of people and objects."

He makes a gesture, and suddenly half a dozen students appear around us, making me jump. They were invisible the entire time, and I had no idea. Bastien doesn't appear surprised, but I bet he saw through their invisibility with his Ofanim sight. Only my necklace prevents him from seeing me when I sneak around.

Grace is one of the students in the class, and she gives me a little wave, her eyes sympathetic. I don't know the other students, but they stare at me with openly curious expressions.

"As Ishim, we bend light around ourselves to turn invisible," Nariel says, telling me nothing I don't already know. "We can also extend this power to other objects and people, with training. The strongest of us can hide entire buildings from view."

"I bet that makes you good spies," I say, sounding impressed. *And assassins*, I silently add.

"Spies and scouts, yes, but we do a lot more than that. We move through the human world more than other angels do, and often act as messengers. Some of us also work as guardian angels, watching over important humans to influence and protect them as needed."

"Oh wow. I had no idea angels were so involved with the humans. How do you pick who to guard?"

"The Archangel Council assigns us the humans," Nariel says.

"Can we show Olivia some Ishim powers in action?" Bastien asks.

"Of course." He gestures at Grace and the other students. "Continue, Grace."

Grace vanishes into thin air, and then the other students do the same. Seconds later, the desks on one side of the room disappear one by one, along with the bags and jackets hanging on them. Soon the classroom appears completely empty, except for the three of us standing there.

"Impressive," I say, my chest tightening. I can make myself invisible, along with anything I'm holding, but that's it so far. I could learn so much more if I was in this class with the others of my kind. But if I reveal my Choir, that would link me to Father and Jonah, and I can't expose my connection to them. For now, I must remain the powerless half-human girl with no Choir.

Grace suddenly appears at my side, though I didn't even hear her move. "Did you feel anything?"

"Nothing." Looking at Bastien, I shrug. "Sorry."

My necklace keeps him from detecting the lie in my words. "Thank you for your help," he tells Nariel. As we walk out of the building, Bastien arches an eyebrow at me. "You truly felt nothing?"

"Nope. Were you expecting me to?"

His cold eyes narrow at me. "I was testing a theory. Don't worry, I have plenty more. Tomorrow we'll watch the Malakim heal people. Don't be late."

As I walk across campus to my dorm, a memory of Jonah comes back to me. It was his second visit after starting Seraphim Academy, and I remember how he flopped on my bed with a big, dreamy sigh.

"What's that about?" I asked.

He came out of his fog with a silly grin on his face. "Hmm?"

"Your goofy smile." I pushed him over, so I could sit beside him. "Let me guess. You met a girl."

"How'd you know?"

"A succubus can tell these things," I said with a wink. "Tell me about her."

"Her name is Grace. We met in Ishim training, and she's just... the best. So smart and kind, and she has the prettiest big brown eyes. Here, let me show you." He scrolled through photos on his phone, and then showed me one. He wore a baseball uniform, except this one had the Seraphim Academy logo on it, and he stood in front of a lake with his arm around a strawberry blond woman with a pretty face. They were both grinning like idiots, and Jonah beamed just looking at the photo.

"We started dating a few weeks ago and everything's been great. I seriously think I might marry this girl one day."

I rolled my eyes and threw a pillow at him. "Let's not get carried away, lover boy. You haven't known her that long."

"Yeah, but sometimes you just know. You just do."

My brother, the romantic. He really loved Grace, and after spending time with her these last few months, I can see why.

I vow again to find him. Not just for me, but for the sadness I still see occasionally in Grace's eyes.

But first...I need to get back at Tanwen for destroying my car. Tonight I'll sneak into her room while she has dinner with the Valkyries at their normal table. Tomorrow, when she goes to get dressed for Combat Training, she'll find every single one of her gym clothes has been cut to shreds. It's the least she deserves. Sure, she can go get more at the student store, but it'll be a hassle for her, and she'll know I'm not going to sit back and take the abuse anymore. I'm done being bullied.

30

OLIVIA

It's been two weeks since my car was vandalized, and tonight's the football game against Hellspawn Academy. Tanwen is one of the cheerleaders, because of course she is. She must suspect that I'm the one who pranked her, but she hasn't said anything to me about it. I keep waiting for some kind of retaliation, but all I get is mocking insults and the regular beatdowns in Combat Training, although I've gotten better at fighting back. On rare occasions I even manage to knock her on her back.

We head out to the field behind the gym, and on the way there we run into Darel, who's wearing his football uniform. Lately he's been spending more time in our dorm than his own. When he's in Araceli's bedroom, the lust coming out of there is more than I can refuse. All I do is sit on the couch and absorb it, even though I feel like a fucking creeper. Like having a light salad, it's great nourishment, but it doesn't fill you up for very long. I need another real meal soon.

I smile at their joined hands. I'm so glad Araceli has found someone that accepts her for who she is.

As soon as we walk behind the gym, we see the huge field there has been transformed. Bleachers line either side and at first glance, it's obvious the visitors are not mingling with the home team. There are easily seven or eight hundred angels crammed into the bleachers. Maybe a thousand. On the demon side, probably half that.

I turn in a circle with my jaw slack. I've never seen so many angels and demons in one spot. "Wow."

"Yeah, I guess it's a lot if you've never been here," Darel says. "My dad took me to a bunch when I was a kid. He's thrilled I made it onto the team this year, even though he had to miss this game. He'll be at the next one though, and then you can meet him."

"That would be great," Araceli says.

"I need to get going. The game's starting soon." Darel gives Araceli a long kiss, and I pointedly look away.

"Good luck!" we call out, as he jogs away to join the rest of the team. Professor Hilda barks some orders at him, and he disappears into the gym.

"Let's find a seat," Araceli says.

We get some beers and find some seats just as the football team comes out onto the field to the major cheers from the crowd. They don't have their helmets on yet, and I catch sight of Callan. I can't help but stare at his ass in those tight little pants as he runs down the field. Even though I can't stand the guy, I have to admit he fills those out nicely. Yum.

I gaze across the crowd and spot Bastien and Marcus in the audience, and a little way behind them sits Kassiel with Nariel and Raziel. I make a mental note to avoid looking that way again, or risk my lust flaring up again. Grace and Cyrus wave at us as they walk by, and grab seats a few rows ahead of us. Ever since finding out Cyrus was a member of the Order, I've been super careful with what I say around him, and Grace too in case she's a member also.

The crowd quiets down as the demons come out. Their bleachers erupt in cheers, but it's nowhere near as loud as the angel side. I guess if we were at a game at Hellspawn Academy, we'd be the lesser represented, too.

"Do they have games at Hellspawn Academy too?" I ask. I can't wait to visit there. In theory, I could've gone to that academy if I could've hidden my angelic side from them. It would've been nice to have been able to learn from both sides of my heritage.

"They do, and normally this game would be held there, but their field was flooded this spring. It should be back in shape for their game against the fae though."

"Why not hold it at the fae school? Ethereal Academy, right?"

"They don't allow us to go to Faerie. I've never even been myself."

"Oh, too bad."

The game starts, and we cheer when Darel makes a touchdown. "He's the best one on the team," Araceli says dreamily. "Even better than Callan."

"It's nice to see Callan isn't the best at something. The Princes think they're so damn good at everything."

"They are. Most things. But football takes more than natural-born skill. It takes practice and learning."

The football game is close, but Callan, big and fast, heads up the angel's defense and blocks many of the demon's attempts to score. Darel is the hero of the night, scoring thirteen touchdowns. When the angels win, I cheer as loud as everyone else.

At the end, the teams shake hands, and even from a distance it's easy to see the tension. There is no happy banter, no real sportsmanship. It's barely-veiled hostility between the two teams.

Darel runs over to Araceli and I smile up at them as he lifts her off her feet in a huge hug. Their fondness for each other is uplifting to see, but it also makes me feel like something of a third wheel. I can't help but be jealous of them for having something I'll never be able to have myself.

"Are you two coming to the party after this?" he asks us.

"Wouldn't miss it," Araceli says.

"Cool, I'll meet you there." He gives her another kiss, and then runs back to celebrate with the rest of his team. My gaze follows him and then lands on Callan. Tanwen stands beside him in her cheerleader uniform, clutching his bicep, but his eyes are on me. I blow him a kiss, just because I know it will annoy him, and I'm rewarded with a sharp scowl.

"I think I'm going to head back to my room," I tell Araceli.

"You're not coming to the party?"

"No, I'm not feeling up to it. I think that hot dog didn't agree with my stomach."

"Oh no! Want me to try healing you?"

I laugh. "I'll be fine. Seriously. Go have fun with Darel."

"Ok, but if you feel better you should come over."

"I will."

I start to head back to the dorms, but I'm stopped by Marcus blocking my path. He's wearing a black shirt that hugs his muscles, his gorgeous hair ruffles in the wind, and his mouth looks deliciously kissable. It hurts to look at him, because I know how good he tastes, and it takes all my power not to take more from him.

"Liv," he says. "You haven't shown up to work on our project. What's the deal?"

I stare at the grass under my feet. "I didn't think we needed to meet anymore. We're pretty much finished with it."

"This is about that kiss, isn't it?" he asks. "You've been avoiding me ever since. Don't deny it."

I sigh. "Fine, I've been avoiding you. That kiss shouldn't have happened."

"Why not?" he steps closer, within dangerous touching distance. "I thought it was pretty amazing, and I'd love to do it again sometime."

My heart squeezes painfully. "Look, Marcus, it was a good kiss, but I'm not looking for anything serious right now. I'm not in the right place for a boyfriend or anything."

"That's fine. I don't want anything serious either. We can keep it casual."

Except my idea of casual would be sleeping with him and a couple other people too. Not because I want to, but because I have to do it to survive. Somehow, even with his joke about a harem, I don't think Marcus would agree to anything like that. Besides, I can't tell him about that anyway, not without revealing my succubus side, and risking everything.

"I'm just not interested," I say, with a nonchalance I don't feel. "Sorry."

His jaw drops, and I bet I'm the first girl who's ever rejected him. He can't even form a reply as I walk away. *Score another point for Liv,* I think, although it doesn't give me any comfort this time, knowing I put another of the Princes in his place.

I make it back to the dorm room and settle down in my pjs with a cup of decaf coffee and my Angelic History textbook. We have a test tomorrow, and even though Kassiel and I meet regularly, I know he's not going to let me off the hook if I don't pass.

Hours later, our dorm room suddenly bursts open. Araceli stands there, obviously distraught. "Have you seen Darel?"

"No, I thought he was with you at the party."

"He never showed up! I waited and waited and he never arrived!"

"That's odd. Maybe he was tired and passed out after the game?"

"No, I checked his dorm and he's not there. No one has seen him. He just...disappeared after the game." She bites her nails, something she does when she's nervous. "Do you think demons took him?"

"I doubt it. Why would they do that?"

"I don't know!"

It tears me apart seeing her so upset, and even though I'm sure there's a simple explanation, I stand up and grab my coat, then toss Araceli's to her. "Come on, let's go look for him."

We spend the rest of the night combing the campus for Darel, but there's no trace of him anywhere. It's like he just vanished after the game...like my brother did.

D arel's body is found the next morning in the forest.
Upon hearing the news, Araceli collapses against me,
screaming and crying. I hold her as her body shakes, and I cry with
her while hating myself a little for being grateful it wasn't Jonah's
body they found.

Rumor gets out that Darel's body was torn apart by what looks
like animal claws, and there were fang marks in his neck. All signs
point to a demon attack after the game, and people are out for blood,
even though all Uriel says is that the investigation is ongoing. Darel
was liked by everyone, not to mention he was the star of the football
team, and his death hits everyone hard. Especially Araceli.

Her normal light has dimmed, and now she hides in her room
most of the time. I can hear her crying through the walls. I give her
some space, because there's not much else I can do, and bring her
her favorite tea and cookies whenever I can.

I find it hard to believe demons would kill Darel, but there
doesn't seem to be any other explanation either.

Two weeks after Darel was found dead, Araceli emerges and sits
beside me on the couch.

"Oliva, I need to tell you something. Something secret."

I put down my favorite mug and sit up straighter. "Anything."

"You asked me one time if there was a secret society on campus,
and I lied to you and said no. But there is one, called the Order of
the Golden Throne, and they're this fanatical pro-angel, anti-demon
group. They invited me to join them, and at first I was so excited
because I've always been such an outcast among the angels, and it
felt good to be wanted and accepted. But then they had us do things
I didn't agree with. Like stealing from a professor."

"You did that?" I ask. Even though I know this was the first task,
I find it hard to picture Araceli stealing anything.

"Yeah, I stole Professor Kassiel's underwear cause I thought it
would be funny, although I felt horrible doing it. I passed that test,
but then they said we had to get a human to confess to something on
camera, and then expose them. I refused and walked away."

Oh shit. She's the one who left that night—and the one they said
they needed.

"Since then, I've been getting notes telling me to come back, and I got one again after Darel died. It's obvious it was a demon attack, but the authorities aren't doing anything so far. The Order says they can help me get revenge against the demons who killed him, but only if I complete the second test and join them. And I do want justice for Darel, I really do, but I don't know if I want to get involved with the Order again." She turns her big, kind eyes on me. "What do you think, Liv?"

I take her hands in mine and give them a squeeze. "I think you were right to walk away from the Order when you did."

She bites her lip. "But should I join now? For Darel?"

"No, I don't think you should. He wouldn't want that."

"He wouldn't?"

"No, he wouldn't. Uriel will make sure that the people who killed him are brought to justice, I'm sure of it. Meanwhile, you can honor Darel by living your life the best you can and staying true to yourself. That's what he would want."

She throws her arms around me. "Thanks, Liv. I knew you would understand. And I'm sorry I lied to you and didn't tell you about the Order. I just wanted to protect you from them."

"It's okay." I feel a pang of guilt, knowing how much I've lied to her about, including this. I'm tempted to tell her I was invited too, but decide against it. That would only open me up to even more questions, and I'm not ready to confess everything to Araceli yet. Besides, it's better for her if she's kept in the dark about all of this. Araceli's heart is so big and pure, and I can't let her get corrupted by the darkness inside the Order. That's my job—and I've already got plenty of darkness inside me anyway.

"I'm going to go make your favorite tea," I tell Araceli. "You just relax here and watch some TV."

She sniffs. "Thanks."

As I head into our mini-kitchen and heat up some water, my mind wanders back to that night I snuck into the cavern below the lake.

"We'll have to convince her to join after all," the leader said.

"Perhaps we'll remind her of the evil of demons, and show her that the Order is the only way to stop them."

"What do you have in mind?" another person asked.

"I have an idea. We'll take action at the football game against the demons."

My hand trembles as I clutch Araceli's mug, and I nearly drop it. Could the Order be responsible for Darel's death? Would they really do something so extreme as to kill one of their own? Thank goodness I steered Araceli away from them. But why do they need her? The only explanation is because she's part fae, and they think that will help them find Jonah somehow. Could he be in Faerie?

I need to pass this next test. The camera arrived a while ago, but I've been putting the task off because I don't want to do it. It's time to suck it up and get it over with, especially because I only have a few more weeks before the deadline. I feel it in my gut, all of this is connected, and I'm getting closer to the truth. The Order is the key to this mystery—and I'll do whatever I have to so I can join them.

31

OLIVIA

As soon as night falls, I double-check the map and take off from my balcony, using my necklace and inborn abilities to leave campus undetected. It's almost summer now, and the air is warmer as it filters through my black feathers. I stretch them wide and savor the feel of flight. I've never traveled this far before, but all that practice in Flight class has been paying off, because it isn't a problem.

The church is empty by the time I get there. I step up to the door and push, finding it unlocked. The large wooden door creaks as I push it open. "Hello?"

Nobody responds, so I walk farther into the sanctuary. Contrary to what you've seen in the movies, demons won't burst into flames in a church. Lucky for me.

"Anybody home?" I look up at the beautiful stained glass as footsteps echo off the stone walls. The church is pretty old, and for a second I feel like I'm in a horror movie or something, walking to my doom. I shake the thought off and steel myself for what I have to do.

A small man in a black suit walks out of the back. "Can I help you?"

"Are you Father Abram?" I ask.

"Yes, I am." His eyes travel up and down my body, and I can feel a hint of his lust. It makes me want to vomit.

"Can I speak with you somewhere privately?" I ask.

"This way."

He leads me into a back office and shuts the door. "What is this about?"

I set the camera down on the desk and turn it on. There's no reason for me to hide it. Abram gives it an odd look, but then he's distracted when I open my trench coat. Inside, I'm wearing a stereotypical schoolgirl uniform, and with my hair in pigtails, it makes me look younger than I am. Closer to the age this monster likes.

Last time I went to feed, I tried to get people in the bar near the academy to confess, but none of them had done anything terrible enough to warrant exposing them for. Then I met a man who was distraught, nearly drinking himself to death, because his daughter claimed a priest had touched her. No one else believed her, and I silently swore to that man that I'd make things right for his little girl.

"I need to ask you a few questions," I say, as I run my hands down my tight white shirt, which clearly shows my pink bra underneath. I let my powers unfurl, and I'm disgusted by the way his lust tastes. It's rotten and vile, and I can't wait to get out of here.

He stares at me, his tongue practically hanging out of his mouth as he ogles my body. I'm sure the camera is getting a great view of my ass under my short plaid skirt.

Abram is evil, every bit of him, from his shaggy brown hair to his sensible brown shoes, but he has the nerve to say to me, "You're a sinner."

If only he knew.

"I am," I say, tugging on my skirt, which barely covers my thighs. "I need you to help me."

Abram steps forward, clasping his waistband now. The evidence of his desire is bulging against his pants, and I have to say, it's not impressive. "I can help you."

"Do you want to hurt me, Abram?" Trailing my hands up my waist, I throw my hair back and moan. "Do you want to make me pay for my sins?"

"I do."

"Except I'm not young enough for you, am I?" I can't bring myself to touch him where he wants me to, but I reach out and touch his hand, and my power latches onto his lust and draws it out.

"You'll do for tonight," he says, as he pulls out his cock.

"You want me, Abram?" I slide a hand under my skirt, pushing it up, revealing more of my bare thighs. "Then tell me the truth. You touch little girls, don't you?"

"They need it," he says, stroking his cock as he stares at me. Ugh, he's disgusting. "Someone has to punish them for their sins."

"And it has to be you, of course."

"I'll punish you too, you little demon."

I laugh, and the sound is evil. "Oh, I'm so much more than that, Abram." My voice lowers. "I'm an angel."

He falls to his knees and reaches for my legs, his desperation to have me so strong he can't help himself. "Please, demon, angel, whatever you are. Let me punish you."

"Tell me the girls' names first."

"Caroline. Melody. Amanda."

I nearly barf with each confession, but this is what I need for the video. When he's done, I reach over and shut it off.

Then I reach over and wrap my hands around this monster's neck. I want to squeeze the life out of him, but instead I throw more of my power into him. He jerks on his cock, unable to stop himself, until his orgasm shoots out of him. I needed him to come, but I was definitely not fucking this guy. Just touching him for a second is horrifying.

"If you want more, you will get up, put your dick back in your pants, and go straight to the police station. Confess everything you told me tonight to them." His eyes are on mine, and my power has done its job. He's glassy-eyed and totally in my thrall. "Do that, and I'll come to you again."

He nods and as soon as I let go of him, he jumps up, running for the door as he stuffs his dick in his pants. I grab my coat and camera and follow, unfurling my wings and going invisible. He's already in his car and pulling out of the parking lot. Damn. I've never unleashed my magic like that before—I usually try to hold it back, so that humans won't be harmed by it. But once I let the magic work, it really did.

I follow Abram to the police station, and when he disappears inside, I creep to the window and turn the camera back on. As it records, I watch the priest speak to a police officer behind a desk. His face goes from bored to pale to furious.

Mission complete.

I need to go home and have a long, hot shower to get the feel of his desire off of me. The Order had better let me in after that—and now there will be one less predator out in the world too.

32

MARCUS

During second period, we head to room 302. Bastien unlocks the door with the key he swiped from the office, and I glance around warily. He shut the cameras in the dorms off, and even if someone was here, they wouldn't stop us or question us. Why would they? We do what we want without any consequences. Olivia's the only one who ever gives us any grief at all.

Maybe that's why I can't stop thinking about her. She's the only woman who's ever rejected me before, and it stings. I know she wants me too, but she's holding back, and it drives me crazy. For once, I don't know what to do about a woman.

I'm pretty sure breaking into her room isn't it, but the guys never listen to me on these things. "This is a really bad idea," I say anyway. "We shouldn't do this."

"Nothing else is working," Callan says. "It's been months and she's still here. We have no other choice."

Bastien pushes open the door, and Callan pushes past him and stomps inside. I pinch the bridge of my nose and follow behind them. It was bad enough when Callan was just sending her notes and being rude to her, but then he went and trashed her car. Now this.

But maybe he's right. Jonah made us promise him we'd keep Olivia away from the school for her own safety, and I trusted my best friend to my core. She was obviously important to him, which makes her important to me. If this is how we keep her safe, I guess we have to do it. I just don't like it. At all.

The living room is neat and unadorned, except for a few cozy pillows they've added, plus some art on the walls with splashes of paint. There are textbooks stacked on the coffee table and a few dirty plates in the sink. Both Olivia and her roommate Araceli have class right now according to Bastien, so we knew they'd be away, but it still makes me feel like a total creeper for being in their room uninvited.

Callan and Bastien don't seem to be bothered by it though. They find Olivia's bedroom and get right to work, first closing her curtains so no one will see. Meanwhile, I keep glancing at the door and wondering if I can sneak out.

Olivia's room is surprisingly boring. There's nothing on the walls, and her bedspread is plain gray and from the student store. Even so, her presence is imbibed into its fabric, and I can practically smell her in the air. Knowing how she affects me, I don't give her unmade bed a second glance, besides thinking how typical it is that she doesn't make her bed.

"She's undisciplined," Callan says, his voice disgusted. "People without proper structure never make their bed in the morning."

I roll my eyes. "I bet you make yours every day."

"Of course I do. It sets the tone for the day. Order and control."

From what Callan's told us, I wouldn't be surprised if Michael drilled that into him. Everyone thinks the former leader of the Archangels was a damn saint, but Callan's hinted at another side to him. A dark side.

Bastien digs around in her desk and looks under her bed, while Callan throws open the closet doors and begins pulling out her clothes and tossing them on the ground. I cringe at this major invasion of privacy, but I don't stop them.

Callan glares at me. "Why'd you come if you're not going to help?"

"This is wrong," I mutter. "Seriously wrong."

Even as I say it, I move to her drawers and begin pulling them open. The top drawer holds her panties and bras. She likes dark lingerie, the color of jewels, and there's not a granny panty in sight. Lace the colors of rubies and sapphires tempts me, but I only look long enough to make sure there's nothing hidden in the drawer.

"Fuck." I slam the drawer shut. "Leave that drawer alone," I warn Callan, but of course, my words make him come straight over and open it.

He sucks in a fast breath. "That's..." Looking at me out of the corner of his eye, he slams it shut, too. "No big deal. Pull the drawer out and sling them around the room."

Nope. Can't do it. If I touch those frilly things, I'm going to run out of this room and find Olivia immediately. Instead, I pull out the next drawer, which holds several pairs of jeans. I can handle that. Taking my time, I pull them out one at a time and shake them to unfold them, then fling them around the room. Meanwhile, Bastien has found Olivia's planner, and is studying it like it might hold the secrets of the universe. From what I've seen of Olivia's room so far, I doubt it contains anything important. She's too careful. Almost like she knew something like this might happen.

By the time I'm done emptying out her jeans and socks, Callan has pulled out the rest of her closet, and Bastien's ripped out all the pages of the planner and scattered them around the room.

"No sign of any white robes," Callan says. "She must not be an initiate."

Well, that's a relief. The last thing we need is for Olivia to be mixed up with the Order too.

Bastien examines her shoes carefully, and then picks up one of her sexy little heels, the ones she wears when she sneaks out at night. He presses something inside of them. "There, now we'll be able to follow her next time."

"What was that?" I ask.

"A tracker."

It keeps getting worse and worse. I feel like the biggest jerk in the world. "Can we leave now?"

"One last thing." Callan picks up a mug, half-full of coffee, from her bedside table. It has a phrase on the side. "I'm a fucking angel," he reads, and then snorts. He pours the coffee out on her bed, then throws the mug against the wall, hard. With a crash, it breaks into a dozen pieces and falls to the floor. He looks at me with hard eyes. "Now we can go."

33

OLIVIA

After Flight, Araceli and I head back to our room to change and heat up some leftovers for lunch while we study before our next classes. It's been over a month since Darel was killed, and she's doing a little better, although I worry she'll never return to her once-perky self.

When we walk into the dorm room, my bedroom door is open. That's odd. I always close it. As I stand in the doorway, my heart freezes and jaw drops. It's totally trashed. There are clothes thrown around everywhere, the pages have been ripped out of my planner and scattered around, and there's coffee all over my bedspread.

"Liv?" Araceli calls out, sounding worried. She peers over my shoulder and gasps. "Oh my gosh. What happened?"

I shake my head as I survey the destruction. I don't even want to walk into the room, but I take a step forward. It was bad enough when my car was attacked, but now this. I'm sure it's retaliation for going into Tanwen's room and messing with her gym clothes, but everything she's done to me has been so much worse than what I did to her.

"Oh, Liv, your planner." She picks pieces of paper off the floor and sighs.

Tears threaten to fill my eyes, but I take in a deep breath and blink them back. These are only things, and I'm not that attached to them. There's only one thing I'm attached to, and I glance around for it. My mug from Jonah was on my bedside table. Where is it?

I pick up clothes around the room and then I spot the mug on the floor.

In pieces.

The tears fall then. Everything else in this room meant nothing to me, but that mug? It was the one connection to Jonah I allowed myself. My most valuable possession. And now it's gone.

Araceli puts her arm around me. "I'm sorry someone did this."

My hands clench at my side. "It has to be Tanwen."

"Probably." She sighs, and then throws my empty planner in the garbage can. "Come on, I'll help you clean this up, and we'll go shopping this weekend."

"Thanks, Araceli." I pick up the tiny pieces of my mug, wiping the tears from my eyes as I drop the shards on top of my destroyed planner.

After she leaves the room, I shut the door, and pull the desk out from the wall. Behind it is a little hole I made where I keep my Order robes and mask, plus a huge wad of cash. Luckily it's all undisturbed.

―――――

I report the break-in of my room to Headmaster Uriel, and he says he'll investigate it, just as he said the same thing about my car. So basically he's no help at all. I'll have to deal with Tanwen on my own.

I'm five minutes late to my meeting with Bastien, and he gives me an icy stare.

"You're late."

"Deal with it," I snap. I'm so tired of getting shit from everyone, I can't even tell you. "Someone trashed my room, and I was busy reporting it to your dad."

"I see." He pauses, and I think he might actually say something nice for once, but then he starts walking. "We're going to watch the Malakim work today."

"Fine, whatever."

We head over to the infirmary, in the same building as the Ishim classes. A blond woman wearing a flower-print flowing dress greets us at the door. "Hello Bastien. What can I do for you?" Her face grows concerned. "Are you injured?"

"Not at all, Professor Lydia. We were hoping to observe the Malakim at work to see if it helps us identify her Choir."

"Of course. You're in luck, actually. We had a mishap during Erelim training today and have a young lady in here needing to be healed."

We step inside and I look around for Araceli, but she must have Malakim training during another period. I spot Marcus immediately, and when our eyes meet, his forehead creases in concern. It must be obvious from my face that I'm both hurt and pissed.

He's sitting beside a bed, and lying on it is a Valkyrie girl a year ahead of me, whose name is Gwen. I've never spoken to her, but she's joined in on Tanwen's taunts, and I glare at her. It's hard to be too mad at her though, because she's holding her arm and wincing, and I can see a painful-looking burn running along it.

"Gwen here was burned during class, and although her body would be able to heal this in a few days, it'll be very painful until then. As such, Marcus here is going to practice his healing and help it along. Go ahead, dear."

Marcus lifts his hands and they begin to glow, almost too bright to look at. He holds them over Gwen's arm and within seconds the burn disappears, soft pink skin knitting over the spot where the blisters were.

"That was amazing," I whisper. I don't have to act. Watching an instant healing is impressive, even if it's not my affinity.

"Did you feel anything?" Marcus asks.

"No, sorry."

Bastien lets out a huff and walks away, no doubt disappointed I've foiled him once again. Gwen thanks Marcus, and then gets up and heads to talk to Professor Lydia, without even giving me a second glance.

"Are you okay?" Marcus asks, lightly touching my arm.

I run a hand through my hair with a sigh. "Yeah, just having a rough day. Thanks."

"I can help you with that."

"If you're offering sex, I'm so not in the mood."

"Not this time, though I'm open to that too." He winks at me. "We Malakim can help soothe the mind and the body in other ways though."

"I don't know..."

"C'mon, let me try. It'll be good practice for me anyway." He tilts his head toward Professor Lydia. "Make me look good in front of the boss."

"Okay, fine."

He rests his hands on my upper arms and closes his eyes. Warm light surrounds me, and the muscles in my back and neck begin to relax. I didn't even realize I was so tense, but Marcus basically gives me a full-body massage with his magic, and I let out a long exhale.

"Wow, that was..."

"Almost as good as sex?" Marcus asks with a grin.

"Almost," I agree. "Thank you, Marcus. I feel a lot better now."

"You're welcome, Liv."

As I walk out of the infirmary, my steps are a lot lighter, and my body feels all loose and warm, like I just stepped out of a hot tub. I'm still upset about my room, but it doesn't bother me as much anymore.

I find Bastien waiting outside with his arms crossed and a sour expression on his face. "What's your problem?" I ask.

"You. You're my problem." He pokes a finger into my chest, in the spot just above my breasts. "My father gave me a task, but you thwart me at every turn. I know you're hiding something. Just tell me what it is already, and we can end this ridiculous game."

"Sorry, but you didn't say please." I take his hand and go to move it off me, but when we touch, lust flares between us. I hate to admit it, but he's sexy when he's angry like this, and I long to melt his cold exterior.

"You're impossible," he says, but then he tightens his hand around mine and pulls me closer. His mouth is near my ear as he whispers. "I'm going to figure out your secrets, little angel. I promise."

"I'll enjoy watching you try," I reply.

And before I know what he's doing, his mouth lands on mine, and he's giving me a thorough kiss that makes my knees weak. If this is his way of finding out my secrets, sign me up.

He pulls back and lets go of me. "Interesting," he says to himself as he walks away, rubbing his chin. "Very interesting."

Okay, then. I guess that was another test. I'm just not sure if I passed or failed it.

34

OLIVIA

S ummer in the mountains of Northern California is like
something out of a movie. Everything is green, the sky is bright
blue and cloudless, and the lake is perfect for swimming after class.
My angelic side loves all the sunshine, and drinks it in hungrily.

On Saturday, Araceli and I take a day trip to go to Redding to
shop for some new clothes. This time, I don't buy new, and Araceli
delights in finding thrift store gems with me. She's never been
secondhand shopping before, but I'm pretty sure I've converted her.

On Sunday, I head out to my morning yoga class, and it's
already so hot I'm sweating by the time I get there. These weekly
yoga classes have been a true blessing, except for the fact that
Tanwen is in them too.

I stretch my mat out as far away from her as possible. As class
begins, I focus instead on the instructor as she moves us through the
complicated positions of advanced yoga. Using the time to meditate
and drink in the light, I think about my brother and what I know
so far.

He disappeared after the championship game against the fae.
The Order knows where he is, and are worried he hasn't returned
yet. They need Araceli for some reason, probably because of her fae

blood. It doesn't seem like a stretch to come to the conclusion that my brother is in Faerie.

I need to know more...and find out if my theory is correct.

I turned in my camera the other week and received a note that I'd passed the second test, and now I'm waiting for the third trial. If I pass it, I'll be invited into the Order and can find out more about what happened to Jonah. Then I can make a plan for finding him.

After class, I roll up my mat and turn toward the dorm, only to run headfirst into Tanwen.

"Get away from me," I snarl. After she destroyed my dorm room, I have no patience for her whatsoever.

"Whoa." She holds her hands up and takes a step back. "Hostility from the half-human."

"Where's your entourage, Tanwen? They can't stand the heat?" She's not so tough without her Valkyrie cronies backing her up.

"They prefer more strenuous exercise, but I've learned that the key to being a good fighter is flexibility."

"Whatever." I don't know why she's trying to explain herself to me. I don't want to hear it. Pushing past her, I take the high road and squash the urge to use my powers on her to make her want me so bad she can't think of anyone else ever again.

I could do it. But I won't. I'm better than that.

"Hey, hang on." Tanwen catches up to me. "What's your deal today?"

I round on her. "You destroyed my car, trashed my room, and you're asking *me* what my deal is? You call me hostile? You've been nothing *but* hostile to me, Tanwen. I'm sorry about the gym clothes, but you've gone way too far. I can't help the circumstances of my birth, and I can't leave. They made that perfectly clear. So, *back the fuck off.*" By the time I finish, I'm shouting and everyone on the lawn stares at us. After shooting them a glare, I stalk off to go have a shower and change.

"Hey, wait!" she calls, as she follows after me. I can see I won't be able to shake her so easily.

"What?" I ask, stopping on the path and crossing my arms.

"I didn't trash your room." She holds up her hands. "Or your car. I swear."

"Yeah, right. And you didn't send me threatening notes either, right?"

"I didn't. Although maybe I should have done all that stuff, if you're the one who tore up my gym clothes. I mean, what the fuck?" She tilts her head and grabs onto her straw-colored ponytail.

I huff. "I only did that in retaliation for what you did. But I'm done with this shit. Seriously over it, and all the insults, and everything else. That stops now."

"Fine, I'll lay off the trash talk. I don't dislike you as a person, Olivia, but you don't belong at Seraphim Academy. I'm obviously not the only one that thinks that if someone trashed your room." She lets out a haughty sniff. "Trust me, I wouldn't want to touch your stuff."

I roll my eyes as she walks away. What a bitch.

Except...I believe her. But if she didn't do all that stuff to me, who did?

———

I head to the lake and breathe in the warm night air. Even at night the campus is beautiful, and I listen to the sound of crickets chirping. Instead of sitting in my normal spot on the bench, I opt to sit in the cool grass instead.

Before I even have time for my thoughts to collect, Kassiel's voice interrupts my quiet meditation. "Fancy meeting you here."

"How are you?" I ask, as he sits beside me on the grass, stretching out his long legs.

"Good. How are you doing? Getting enough to eat?"

His eyes flash in the moonlight, and I can't help but think he wishes he could help provide me some nourishment. "Sure. The cafeteria here is great."

We both know that's not what he means, and he grins. "You did well on your last Angelic History exam. Good work."

"Thanks. I have a pretty good teacher."

He looks at me out of the corner of his eye. "Perhaps. I try to teach history in a way that doesn't paint angels or demons in a negative light. Do you think I've succeeded?"

My time in his class has been difficult at best. Not because of the subject matter, but because watching Kassiel move and talk has been a lesson in suppressing my succubus powers. I answer his question with a question of my own. "Why do you do that? Why do you care?"

He hesitates. "I... I've known demons over the years. They're not so different from angels. Most of them aren't evil or anything, and just want to live their lives peacefully, the same as we do. I've learned it's possible for anyone to be good or evil, even angels. Plus, I was alive for the last several decades of the war."

My eyebrows fly up. "Of course. I should have realized. What was it like?"

"It was horrible. So much death, and for what? Because angels and demons have been enemies for centuries, and no other reason." He shakes his head. "It was the best thing to happen to both races when Michael and Lucifer made the Earth Accords and stopped the war."

I can hear the depth of pain in his voice, and it breaks my heart. "You lost someone, didn't you?"

"My mother."

"I'm sorry."

He nods. "That's why I became a professor here. If I can teach younger angels about what happened, perhaps I can prevent the war from starting again."

"You're doing a good job of it."

"I hope so."

"I'm glad the war is over too. Although I can't help but wish I could have seen Heaven before it was closed. What was it like?"

"Bright."

I laugh. "Obviously."

"During the day, the sky there was the color of dawn, when everything is a soft orange and a golden yellow. It sounds odd, but it was beautiful."

"I can imagine. And Hell? Did you ever go there? What was the sky like there?"

"Yes, I've been there." He stares out at the lake, his face distant, his eyes lost in memories. "You know that moment after the sun sets and the sky is a deep indigo? That's what Hell was like during the day. And at night... it was like living in the space between the stars."

"I can tell it had a strong impact on you."

"It did, yes." He clears his throat. "Maybe one day we'll be able to visit the two other realms and rebuild."

"What about Faerie, have you been there too?"

"No, I can't say I have. Maybe someday, though." Kassiel lays down on the grass and puts his hands behind his head, which pulls his shirt up a bit so I can see his toned stomach and dark happy trail. Urges that have nothing to do with hunger rise in me. Urges that are getting harder and harder to resist the more time I spend with my professor.

I need to feed. Tonight.

35

OLIVIA

I end up back at the bar I've visited many times before. It's not ideal, but it's probably been a month since I last came here. I've been avoiding feeding as much as possible, surviving on sunlight and little lust snacks from people around school, plus the kisses from Bastien and Marcus. But I've gone too long since I've had a real feed, and now I'm desperate.

Naturally, the bar is fucking empty. Nobody but the bartender, and I've been avoiding using her. Employees of places like this are the worst option. If I sleep with her, I can never let her see me again, or she'll want more. I can't give her more.

Damn it.

I sit at the bar and signal her to bring me a beer. I'm so hungry, I may be forced to seduce the bartender after all. I'll give it a few minutes and see if anyone comes in. Maybe I'll get lucky.

Checking my phone, I see it's after two on a Sunday night. I'm not going to get lucky.

As I finish my beer and prepare to lay the lust on the bartender, the door opens and a good-looking guy walks in. He's no movie star, but he looks clean at least, and isn't wearing a wedding ring. I call that a win.

"Hey, Chuck," the bartender says. "How goes it? You still with Louann?"

He sits on the other side of the bar. "No. She took off with that guy from Redding that sold us the Mustang."

"Tough luck."

The phone distracts the bartender, and I take that as my cue. "Hey." I hop up in the seat beside Chuck and trail a finger along his arm. "Want some company?"

Hitting him hard with desire, I make sure he won't say no. His mouth opens into a slow grin. "Definitely."

With one eye on the bartender, I grin at Chuck. "Meet me in the bathroom," I whisper. "Hurry."

The bartender has her back to us as she speaks into the handset, so I hurry past with Chuck right behind me. As soon as we enter the bathroom, I'm on him. I wore a skirt and no underwear just for this. He steps forward, and I grab the waistband of his pants. I'm not interested in kisses or caresses, I just want to get this over with as fast as possible.

I hate that I have to do this with him and not one of the guys I want to be with. After kissing both Marcus and Bastien, I'd much rather be sleeping with one of them tonight. Or Kassiel. But that isn't an option, and I need to feed.

I can't help it. I have to do it to survive.

I didn't choose the Lilim life. The Lilim life chose me.

Before I can get started, the bathroom door bursts open. I shove Chuck back as a tall man walks in. It's the hot guy I spotted the first time I came here, the one who somehow rejected my seduction, and he smiles at me like a cat who just caught a mouse.

"Hello, little succubus. We've been looking for you." He's tall, and seduction rolls off of him. I can feel it, even though it bounces off me. An incubus. A full incubus. Oh shit.

Chuck is caught in a daze of lust, unsure if he should look at me or the new guy. I shove him toward the door and *push* with my magic. "Get out of here!"

He runs out the door, and I enter the fighting pose Callan taught me and prepare to defend myself the best I can. I can't use my Lilim powers against this guy. They won't work. Equally, though, he can't use his against me. Unfortunately, that does me no good when two other men walk in the bathroom, and although I'm pretty sure they're both demons, I'm not sure what they are.

One of them suddenly shifts into a large black bear. A shifter, which Raziel would say represents the Sin of wrath. He definitely looks pretty wrathful as he lets out a terrifying roar, and I can't help but shrink back.

The other one lets out a burst of darkness and multiplies, until I'm staring at three identical versions of him. An imp, like Marcus and I are studying for our project. He's using illusion magic to make copies of himself. I'll have to find the original one to stop him.

Fuck, I am way out of my league here.

"Come with us, and we won't hurt you," the incubus says. He's wielding a big ass knife, which kind of contradicts what he just said.

Father and Mother warned me this would happen one day if I ever revealed myself, and now it's happening. I need to get out of here, fast.

The incubus rushes me, and I try to deflect him the way Callan taught me. It works and I spin away from the knife, but then the bear raises up and knocks me back with his giant paws. I hit the side of the bathroom stalls and stumble, and the three imps grab my arms. The incubus stalks forward, playing with his knife, and he leans close and breathes me in slowly. I have a sudden fear he might kiss me. I have no idea what I taste like, but I don't want to risk him figuring out I taste like an angel.

They can't know what I really am.

I jerk in the imps' arms, and one of the hands moves onto my bare skin. I blast him with a bolt of power, making his emotions flare and dazing him for an instant, giving me a chance to spin around and knee him in the groin. I choose the right one, and he yells and lets me go, while his clones vanish. I dart away, but the bear blocks my path.

The bathroom door bursts open, and I spot three men standing in the doorway with their wings spread, their eyes burning with light, looking every inch like sexy avenging angels.

The Princes have come for me.

I can't believe a strong, capable woman like myself is so relieved to see three Princes riding in on their proverbial white horses, but here I am.

Callan blasts the bear with a bolt of burning light, and Marcus and Bastien rush forward to fight the incubus and his knife. The whole place suddenly goes black, courtesy of the imp's illusion magic, putting my guys at a disadvantage.

Wait. Not my guys. Just guys.

The imp suddenly grabs me and paws at my skirt. The one I'm not wearing underwear under. Damn it, I blasted him too hard and now he wants me. I use my meager skills to fight him off, but then he pulls out long blade. It glows with eerie darkness, like nothing I've ever seen before.

"Get back!" Marcus yells, but then the bear knocks him aside, and he crashes into one of the tables in the bar.

The imp lunges for me with the blade, and I dodge out of the way, but I'm not fast enough. It slices along my side, and I let out a scream of pure agony. Bastien grabs me and drags me out of the bar, and into the cool night air, but it doesn't help. My side is on fire, and all I can do is hang onto him and moan.

"You were hit with a dark-infused blade," Bastien says, sounding way too calm considering I'm squirming with pain. "Don't worry, Marcus can heal you."

Callan and Marcus bust out of the bar an eternity later, and I've never seen them look so angry before.

"We took care of them," Marcus says.

"Fucking demons," Callan growls. "We need to report this."

"No, you can't!" I can't have any questions about what I was doing out here. But then another dose of pain hits me, and I cry out.

"Olivia is injured," Bastien says.

"What happened?" Marcus asks, moving close to inspect the wound.

Callan huffs. "She didn't listen in combat practice, that's what happened."

"I promise to do better next time," I manage to get out, but I'm so weak. Worst of all, my hunger grows so strong I can't contain it. My body is trying to heal itself, but it can't, because I was already so low on power. If I don't get out of here and find someone to feed on, I'm going to do something I regret.

Marcus's hands glow and he heals my side, and the pain fades a little, but it's not enough. I waited too long to feed, hoping that my kiss from Bastien was enough to tide me over, but I was wrong. I squeeze my eyes shut and try to hold my succubus side at bay.

"She's healed," Marcus says.

"There's still something wrong with her." That's Callan. "Try again."

"Whatever it is, it's nothing my magic can fix."

"Please," I find myself begging.

"What do you need?" Bastien asks.

Marcus's tender, masculine hands touch my cheek. "Tell me, Liv. How can I help?"

My eyes suddenly fly open, and I grab Marcus's face and kiss him hard. I can't stop myself, the hunger is too intense, and my succubus side has taken over. I suck the lust from him that springs up when we kiss, and it's oh so delicious, but it isn't enough. The thing I want to do most is spread my legs and let him settle there between them.

"Her eyes are black," Bastien says.

In the back of my mind, I know this is bad. Really fucking bad. But I can't stop myself from rubbing up against Marcus like a damn cat. I reach for his jeans and pop them open, trying to reach inside for his cock.

"Whoa now," he says. "I am all for whatever this is, but maybe we should wait 'til we go somewhere more private."

"Can't wait," I manage to get out. "Need. Now."

Bastien suddenly grabs me and kisses me, and it's enough to calm me down a bit. But I need more, more, more. I paw at his chest, and he pushes me toward Callan, who steps back at the sight of my black eyes.

"Kiss her!" Bastien yells.

"What?" Callan asks, taken aback.

"Just do it!"

I grab Callan's face and pull it to mine. I'm a bit stronger than I was before, but if he fights me at all, I won't be able to feed from him.

Callan resists at first, but then he can't help himself, and he presses a hand to my back and kisses me hard. I suck all the sexual energy I can from Callan through the rough kiss, and he's so powerful his energy fills me up just enough to take the edge off.

When we're done, my head clears a little and I no longer feel so weak. I'm still hungry and will have to feed soon, but I might be able to make it a few more nights before things go bad again.

Bastien glances back at the bar. "We have to get out of here. I'm sure they called the human police."

"She's too weak to fly," Marcus says.

Callan grunts, looking pissed off, but he scoops me into his arms. I cling to him as he takes off, his powerful white and gold wings beating the night air. Curling my face into his neck, I breathe in his spicy scent. I never thought I'd be grateful for the Princes spying on me, but if it weren't for them, I'd be with the demons now...and I have no idea what they would do with me.

"I'm sorry," I whisper against Callan's thick neck. I know he never would have kissed me if Bastien hadn't made him.

He doesn't reply, or if he does, I can't hear it over the sound of the wind whistling past my ears as he flies. He does tighten his grip though.

I doze as we fly, and only wake when Callan lays me down on the couch. They've taken me to their private lounge in the bell tower, and I would feel honored if I wasn't so tired. Callan steps back, and I sit up and press a hand to my side. That blade really messed me up.

As the three men stare at me, I realize what I've done, and my stomach sinks.

Bastien manages to speak first. "You're a succubus."

36

BASTIEN

Olivia's eyes are no longer black, but I can see the truth in them, and I don't even need my Ofanim powers for that. "Yes," she replies to my statement. "Half succubus, anyway."

Callan backs up from her and swears under his breath. "You're a demon. Fuck."

I always knew there was something suspicious about her, but I thought I would feel more satisfaction upon uncovering the truth. "How is this possible?"

She sighs. "My father is an angel, my mother is a succubus."

"But demon-angel relations are forbidden," Marcus says.

"That's why I've been in hiding my entire life. My parents told me if anyone found out what I am, I'd be in danger."

"Why did you come to Seraphim Academy then?" I ask.

She hesitates. "I got tired of hiding. I wanted to learn to use my powers, and it seemed safer here than at Hellspawn Academy."

I get the feeling there's more to it than that, but I'm not done with my interrogation. She's deceived me for months, and it shouldn't have been possible. I need to know more. "How were you able to hide your succubus side from me?"

She touches the aquamarine stone at her neck. "My mother gave me this necklace. It allows me to lie undetected and to hide the truth from anyone. Even an Archangel."

"That looks like a fae relic." I rub my chin. That would explain a lot. What would I see in her aura if the damn thing was removed? Now I want to find out.

"Are you going to expose me?" From her spot curled up on the couch, with her eyes wide and her dark hair mussed up, she looks more vulnerable than I've ever seen her before—and scared. She's terrified that we know the truth about her.

"No, of course not," Marcus quickly says, as he covers Olivia in a blanket.

Callan shakes his head and paces back and forth in front of the window. "We should. We definitely should."

I'm not so sure. I find it hard to believe my father doesn't know, or at least suspect, what Olivia is. "One last question. How do you know Jonah?"

"Jonah..." she says slowly, tilting her head. "The guy that disappeared last year? How would I know him?"

"You're lying." My lips press into a tight line. Another secret of hers to uncover. I have to admit, I'm glad the game isn't over. I like playing with her. Finally, a worthy opponent.

"Sorry, not sure what you're talking about," she says.

"Take off your necklace and tell me that," I snap.

Marcus holds out his hands to separate us. "Okay, that's enough. Liv has been through a lot and she can barely sit up. She needs to rest, not be interrogated by the three of us."

I huff and cross my arms. "If we're going to protect her, we need to know the truth."

"I don't need your protection," she mutters.

Callan snorts. "Obviously you do. Those demons tonight wanted to take you somewhere."

"They somehow knew I was a succubus." She stares off into space. "How did you find me there?"

"Bastien put a tracker in your shoes," Marcus says, his voice guilty.

She sits up at that. "He *what*?"

I shrug. "We knew you were sneaking off and wanted to know why. Be glad I did. It's the only reason you're here and not with the demons."

She narrows her eyes at me and pulls the blanket up to her neck, but doesn't reply.

"We need to report the attack to Uriel," Callan says.

"You can't," Olivia says quickly. "If you do, there will be too many questions, and someone else will find out what I am."

'The Archangels need to know," Callan insists. "First Darel, now this...the demons are growing bolder. We need to prepare for battle."

"Okay, let's not jump straight to war," Marcus says, rolling his eyes.

"I agree, we should keep tonight's events between us for now," I say.

Callan shakes his head. "You're all making a mistake. Olivia's a *demon*. She's one of *them*. And you're just okay with that?"

"She can't change what she is," Marcus says.

"Fuck this, I'm out of here." Callan throws open the balcony door and launches off before his wings are even fully extended. Marcus runs after him, his bronze wings flapping against the night.

I pinch the brow of my forehead. Someone needs to go deal with those two. "I'll be right back."

I fly to the top of the bell tower, where Marcus and Callan are facing off. Callan paces back and forth on the old roof, looking pissed. "She's a demon."

"Half," Marcus reminds him.

"That's a pretty big chunk." Callan's hands are starting to glow. He's gathering an Erelim's burning light and if we're not careful, he'll release that power on something. Or someone.

I don't try to get in front of him or calm him down. He's got to get control of himself, and there's little I can do to help. Marcus though, he's a bigger idiot than I am, and he steps towards Callan. As a Malakim, he can calm Callan down, but it's risky when he's in a state like this. He might explode instead.

"Callan," Marcus says.

"What?" he roars.

"She's half angel, too." Marcus lets that sink in for a second. "Think about what that means. She's supposed to be impossible. Forbidden."

Callan's chest heaves as Marcus's words break through the rage clouding his mind. "She's an abomination."

"She's a woman." Marcus laces light into his words, just enough to have a slightly calming effect on Callan. And me, but I shake it off easily. "She's a person. She has feelings too."

I stand to the side and wait. I'm as useless as Marcus against Callan in combat. Both of us are well-trained and can hold our own in a fight. Against each other, either of us would have a fair shot. But Callan is an Erelim, and he's the son of Michael. He's a warrior, born and bred. It's in his very DNA. Some humans are good at making music. Some are good at math. Callan is very good at fighting. The only thing we can do is work together to restrain him if he loses it.

Callan stares across the dark sky as his chest heaves. Marcus is calming him down, but not enough. Callan has more reason than anyone to hate demons, since they killed his father and his half-brother. Finding out Olivia is part-demon shook him, hard.

"Tell me something you know about Olivia," I say.

"She's a demon."

I roll my eyes. "Something not related to her being a demon."

He sighs, and his glowing hands dim again. He's calming down, and I nod at Marcus. He cuts off the flow of magic to see how Callan does on his own. It's still best for him to come back from this as much as he can on his own. It will help him learn to control it in the future.

Sucking in a deep breath, Callan manages to say, "She's a horrible fighter."

Marcus smiles. "She is. For sure. She's also too stubborn for her own good."

"And secretive," I add. "But I can understand why now."

"We're not asking you to accept her." Marcus steps forward

again, getting within swinging range of Callan's fists. "You don't have to be her friend. Just don't expose her either."

Callan glances at me. "What do you think?"

I rub the back of my neck and scowl. "I think it's likely my father already knows. He probably wanted me to figure it out as a test. Which I failed."

Callan's glow vanishes, and he rests a large hand on my shoulder. "Don't be too hard on yourself. She's spent her life deceiving people."

"Why'd you carry her back?" Marcus asks.

"She needed help," he says, as if that explains everything.

"Jonah must have known the truth about her," I say. "That's why he wanted to keep her away from the school. He worried if she came here someone would find out what she truly was."

"Yeah, he said it was for her safety," Marcus adds. "Now we know why. But how do they know each other?"

"That's what we need to find out, but she's playing innocent. I'll get it out of her in time though."

"Jonah obviously wants her to be safe," Marcus says. "That means we should keep her here and protect her."

"I disagree," Callan says. "Jonah made us promise to get her away from the school. That promise still stands, even more so now that we understand the danger she's in."

Marcus points in the direction of the bar. "She's in danger out there too! You saw those demons tonight."

"Then we'll find her somewhere safe to hide her," Callan says. "We have enough money between the three of us to make sure she lives a life of luxury, at least until Jonah is back."

"I don't think she'll go for that," I say. "The best thing we can do for now is to keep her close and try to figure out what else she's hiding. Then we can decide how to proceed."

"Fine," Callan says. "I trust your judgment. But we can't forget our promise to Jonah either."

"We won't."

"I'm going to take her back to her room," Marcus says, his wings flaring. "Maybe I can heal her a little more too."

I raise an eyebrow at him. "You do know what she needs in order to heal?"

He gives me a cocky grin. "If that's what she wants from me, I'm more than happy to provide."

He's totally missing the gravity of this situation. One quick fuck is not going to cut it. "From what I know about Lilim, she was completely starved tonight. She's probably not getting enough sustenance from the few times she's sneaked out of school. She'll need to feed more often or she'll continue to grow weak."

"Feed?" Callan asks. "Like on sex?"

"Exactly."

"I'll take care of it," Marcus says.

I shake my head. "One person won't be enough. I'll have to sleep with her too."

Marcus's jaw drops. "You?"

I wave my hand dismissively. "Don't worry. I'll only be doing it out of necessity to keep her healthy and safe, as part of our promise to Jonah. I don't have feelings for her or anything preposterous like that."

Marcus relaxes a little and laughs. "Of course you don't. You're as cold as ice. Sex with Olivia will be like a business arrangement for you."

His easy dismissal annoys me, especially as I remember my kiss with Olivia. I definitely felt something then, though I'll never admit it.

"It would be best if three of us provided sustenance for her." I glance at Callan pointedly. "Succubi must feed on multiple people or risk injuring them."

"No fucking way," he snarls. "I am not touching a demon."

"Fine, Marcus and I will handle it. We're much stronger than humans, and we can deal with it later if it becomes a problem."

"Assuming she's on board with this arrangement," Marcus says.

I flash back to the way her lips felt on mine and how her body molded against me. I know she kissed Marcus too—I saw it on camera. Somehow I don't think she'll have a problem with this proposal. "She will be."

37

OLIVIA

While the boys are off somewhere discussing my fate, I drag myself off the couch and pull myself together. I'm still weak and hungry, but I'm not going to sit here and wait for my judgement to come.

I draw out my black, shining wings, and then launch off the bell tower. I'm covered in blood from that demon's blade, and all I want in the world is a hot shower. Then I'll start packing a bag. Just in case I need to make a quick getaway.

When Marcus arrives on my balcony, I'm wearing only a robe and brushing my hair. I cautiously let him in.

"What happened?" I ask.

"We've decided not to tell anyone about you," Marcus says.

My shoulders slump in relief. "Thank you."

"We've also decided we need to help you with your succubus problem. Well, Bastien and I will. Callan isn't a fan of the idea."

I raise my eyebrows. "Is that so?"

"As long as you're okay with it." He reaches out and strokes my cheek. "I understand why you pushed me away after our kiss. But you don't have to do that anymore."

I grab his hand and squeeze it. "Then you know I can't have a real relationship either. We can have sex, but that's all it can be."

"I'll take whatever I can get of you." His hands slide around my waist and he pulls me against his hard chest. His mouth finds mine, and his kiss instantly makes me stronger. I grab his shirt and bring him closer, as his lips and tongue do wicked things to mine.

But then I have a thought, and I pull back to look up at him. "Are you okay sharing me with Bastien?"

His thumb runs along my lip as he gazes down at me. "I don't love the idea, but from what I remember from Demon Studies, you need to feed on multiple people, right?"

"I do. If you were human, I could only feed on you once without killing you, but I can feed multiple times on supernaturals without draining them too much." Or so I'm told. I've never tested the theory.

"That's where we come in. Bastien and I are the sons of Archangels. We're stronger than most supernaturals. Between the two of us, we'll keep you satisfied." He gives me a sinful smile that makes me want to rip his clothes off right this second. "Besides, I'd rather you feed from us than from strangers."

I can't believe the two of them are on board with this plan, but I'm so ravenous and relieved I don't want to say no. Maybe the two of them could actually keep me full without any problems. We won't know unless we try, anyway.

His lips trail down to my neck. "We're going to take care of you. I promise."

In his strong, protective arms, I'm actually willing to believe that fantasy, if only for a few minutes. He grabs the tie of my robe and slowly pulls on it, allowing the terry cloth fabric covering my naked body to fall open. His dark eyes look me up and down with obvious pleasure, and the lust coming off him is so strong it makes my succubus side go into overdrive.

"Damn, you're beautiful." He grabs his shirt and lifts it off him, then tosses it to the side. I lick my lips at the sight of his muscled chest, like some kind of ravenous beast. He grins at my reaction. "Bastien said you've been starving yourself."

"I didn't want to get caught."

"Then tonight you're going to have a five-course meal." He pops open his jeans and slides them down without hesitation. His black briefs go next, and then he's as naked as I am. The size and shape of Marcus's cock is absolute perfection. I've touched so many in my life, and his is one of the best I've seen. Long, thick, and delicious.

I step forward and rest my hands on his chest, unable to stop myself. I press my face into his neck and breathe him in. "Marcus, I need you now, please. I can't hold back the hunger."

"Take whatever you need."

I push him down on the bed and climb onto his lap, wasting no time sinking down onto his cock. I cry out as he fills me up, and he feels like heaven inside me. His sexual energy hits me like a jolt of lightning.

He grunts and grabs my ass to pull me closer, but he lets me lead the show. Swiveling my hips, I ride him hard and fast, positioning us so that his head hits my spot every time I press down on him. It's been so long since I slept with someone I actually liked—since Kassiel actually—and it's amazing how different it feels. You'd think after sleeping with so many people it would get old, but this is like having sex for the first time all over again...except with someone who knows exactly what they're doing.

My orgasm builds fast, and I cry out as it hits me, cascading over me along with Marcus's power. I slump down onto his bare chest as he heaves. He moves to kiss me, but stops just before our lips meet. "Whoa. Your eyes."

I pull back and clap my hands over them. "I'm sorry."

"No, no." He takes my hands away from my face. "Don't be sorry." He kisses my eyelids with the softest touch, brushing his lips against them, feather-light.

I breathe in and open my eyes. "They don't bother you?"

Marcus grips my hips. "On the contrary. They're kind of sexy."

I can't help but laugh. "Oh, so you've got a demon fetish."

"Seems that way." He grins. "Or maybe I just have an Olivia fetish."

"Thank you. I feel a lot better now. Feeding from you is...

intense." Marcus's energy is strong enough I'll be able to go for weeks before feeding again, just like when I slept with Kassiel. Their energy tastes different somehow, though. Maybe because Marcus is a Malakim and Kassiel is... Actually, I'm not sure which Choir Kassiel is a member of, come to think of it, but perhaps that's the reason. Marcus and Kassiel are the only two angels I've fed from, but it sounds like I'll be sampling Bastien soon, and then I can see if that's the difference. I doubt I'll get another shot at Kassiel, unfortunately.

"We're not done yet." Marcus grins and lifts me off him, then spins and plants my back on the bed. He hasn't come yet, and I'm ready for him to enter me again and finish us both off, but he has something else in mind. "Like I said, this is going to be a five-course meal. Time for round two."

"What—" I start, but then he's spreading my legs wide and dipping his head between them. His tongue begins to do sinful things to me, things I've rarely had done before. I usually go straight for sex to get it over with as quickly as possible, and don't have time for foreplay. Plus most of the guys I pick up give zero fucks about making sure I'm satisfied. Marcus, though? He's a real man, and he definitely knows what he's doing and likes to make sure his woman is very pleased. As his mouth and tongue bring me to new heights, I see why he's so popular with the ladies around campus.

I cry out and dig my hands in his glorious hair as he works magic on my clit, and then he slips two fingers inside me and brings me to climax all over again. Two orgasms in one night? I'm a lucky girl.

But he's not done yet.

I'm in a daze of pleasure, when he lifts his head and grins at me. "You taste delicious. I could go down on you all night long."

"I certainly won't stop you," I say with a laugh. "But I think it's time you came too."

"Is it?" he asks, as he slowly stalks up my body.

I nod. "To feed fully, I need you to have an orgasm too."

His eyes gleam with desire as his cock nudges my entrance. "Well, I can't let you go hungry, now can I?"

He's still slick with my juices, and his entry is fast and hard. It takes my breath away when his cock fills me up, and then he sets a relentless pace as he plunges into me. It's exactly what I need from him, and I arch up to meet his every thrust. He captures my mouth as he fucks me hard, and it's somehow both intimate and dirty. I love every second of it.

Another orgasm builds, and we finish together, crying out at the same time as he thrusts his cock into me harder than before. He pushes up on his arms and looks down at me as we both breathe heavily. "Fuck, that was good. But we have another two rounds to go so I make sure you're nice and full."

I laugh. "Should we take a break?"

"No way." He pulls out of me, flips me over, and enters me from behind, already hard again. "Angel stamina, baby. I can go all night."

And he does. We end up having more than five rounds, until I'm so full I feel like I just had Thanksgiving dinner and I need to unbutton my jeans. I finally kick him out just before dawn so we can both get a little sleep, but it's hard. I want him to stay. That's new.

Other than that time with Kassiel, I've never wanted so badly to roll over and cuddle with someone before. But I have to push the urge away, and it unnerves me. This is not a relationship. I can't have one of those. This is just fucking. Really, really good fucking.

Hopefully on a regular basis.

38

OLIVIA

A knock wakes me up.

"You coming down for breakfast, Liv?" Araceli cracks my door open as I sit up. "Hey. You hungry?"

"Yes," I croak. "Starving." And thirsty. Although physically I feel like I could fly from here to New York. Marcus's sexual energy crackles inside me, and I've never felt so...powerful before. I'm even more excited about feeding from Bastien, whenever that happens.

I use the bathroom and run a comb through my hair before throwing on my gym clothes and walking out to meet Araceli. No time for a shower.

The cafeteria is packed. We're having one of those crazy California heat waves, and even at 8am it's crazy hot out already, even for an angel. Everyone wants to sit in the cool air-conditioned cafeteria instead of eating outside. Only one table is open in the entire room, so we grab our food and then hurry over to it, plunking our butts down before someone else can claim it. Seconds later, three trays plop down across from us.

My gut tells me what my eyes haven't seen yet. I look up. Sure enough, I drink in the sight of three gorgeous angels hovering over me. Marcus gives me a knowing grin, his dark hair still messy from last night, while Bastien stares at me with eyes that are slightly less cold, although still inquisitive. And Callan? He glares at me like he wants to wrap his big hands around my neck and squeeze.

"Shit," Araceli breathes. "Sorry, we can eat somewhere else."

She starts to stand, but I shake my head and stare back at the Princes. "I don't remember inviting you to sit with us. Besides, I thought you guys never eat in here."

"These are the last three seats in the entire room, as you can see." Bastien sits down first, on my right. Marcus sits on the other side of me. Callan sits across, next to Araceli, who subtly inches away from him.

"We wanted to see how you're doing this morning," Marcus says, with a naughty gleam in his eye. "Are you feeling well-rested?"

"I'm fine, thank you."

"You do look better," Bastien says.

Araceli is staring at us like she's very confused.

"I ran into the guys yesterday after having a run-in with Tanwen," I explain. "It was nothing."

"Right," she says slowly, but I don't think she buys it.

The rest of breakfast is super uncomfortable. Marcus keeps grinning at me and sneaks in a few light touches on my arm or hand, Bastien stares at me like I'm the most fascinating thing he's ever seen, and Callan throws food in his mouth while glaring at me the entire time.

"Well, as fun as this is, it's time for class." I stand up and grab my tray. Araceli breathes a sigh of relief and follows me. "I guess we'll see you there, Callan."

He grunts as we walk away. I have a feeling he won't be giving me a break in Combat Training today. And Tanwen? I'm not sure where we stand either after our talk.

As soon as we're outside and sweating instantly in the heat, Araceli whirls around on me. "What was that about?"

I shrug. "I don't know. It's weird they sat with us."

"No shit. And Marcus was all over you. Plus last night I definitely heard some sounds coming from your room along with his voice. Are you guys a thing now?"

"No, definitely not."

"But you totally fucked."

I hesitate. She is my roommate, and the walls are not thick. I heard everything she and Darel did together, that's for sure. "Yes, we did."

"So why aren't you dating? Marcus is hot and nice, for a Prince anyway, and he's obviously into you."

"It's...complicated. I'm not looking for something serious right now. He's just a fuck buddy."

Araceli snorts. "Fuck buddy. Right."

"Seriously."

"Okay, Liv. Whatever you want to believe." She slings her bag onto her shoulder and starts down the path. "Let's go."

We head into Combat Training, which has been Araceli's least favorite class since Darel died. For a long time she skipped it entirely, but then Hilda came to our room and talked to her, and she started going again. I think it's actually helped her to be able to take out her grief and anger... Usually on me. I became her regular partner, which at least saved me from more Tanwen beatdowns.

Tanwen and one of the other Valkyries are sparring, and she gives me a little nod as I move to the mat. I guess we're in a truce now.

"Olivia, you're with Callan today." Professor Hilda calls. "We've got to get you up to par."

Callan argues with Hilda in a low voice, but she shakes her head. He scowls, before stomping over to me. "Until you're able to show at least a modicum of an ability to defend yourself, we're going to be working together."

"I didn't do too badly the other night," I say in a low voice.

"You got stabbed. By a dark-infused weapon. How is that 'not too badly'?"

I huff. "What is a dark-infused weapon anyway?"

"It's a weapon made by the fae to hurt angels. There are light-infused ones also, which do extra damage to demons."

"Great," I mutter. I'm probably susceptible to both of them.

Callan looks me up and down slowly, like he's trying to decide what to do with me. No way I'm going to make this easy on him, so I cock one hip and breathe deep so my breasts will push ever-so-slightly against my shirt.

"See something you like?" I place a pinch of husk in my voice, a great touch when seducing someone overtly. The trick is to be seductive without the target realizing you're *trying* to turn them on. It must seem effortless and natural. I could just send some of my succubus magic at him, but where's the fun in that?

"You're not my type," he growls. Liar, liar, pants on fire.

The desire coming off Callan is enough to wake up my succubus side. Even knowing I'm part demon, he still wants me—he just doesn't want to admit it.

"Put your hands here," Callan says, lifting my arms at the elbow. His fingers on my skin cause bolts of fire to shoot down my body, making it really damn hard to hold my arms exactly where he wants them. He's affected too because he lets go of my arms as fast as he can.

"Now, when I move toward you, put your arms here." Showing me how to best deflect his attack, I try to pay attention. Not an easy task.

We walk through the motions several times in slow motion, until Callan says, "This time, I'm coming at you at full speed. You ready?"

"I don't think the bad guys will warn me."

He takes my point and rushes me. Throwing my hands up at the right moment, I'm amazed to see him flip over my shoulder as I twist and curl.

"Nice work," Callan says. Then he realizes he's congratulating me, and his face darkens. "It's about time."

Jumping to his feet faster than I can follow with my eyes, he straightens his clothes and runs at me with no warning this time. I sidestep him, grab his arm and twist around, flipping him again. I wish I'd learned this move before fighting the demons the other night.

A flash of pride crosses his face, just for a second, and then it turns hard again. I hear a smattering of applause from around the gym and look away from Callan to see Professor Hilda and Araceli clapping. Even Tanwen gives me a little nod.

"Great job," Hilda calls across the gym. "Practice the rest of the period."

I turn triumphantly to see Callan giving me a deadpan stare, but the emotions coming off of him betray his thoughts. He's thinking about doing things to me that don't include me flipping him over my shoulders. He runs at me again without warning, and this time I don't move fast enough.

I hit the ground and look up at him without any breath in my lungs. He looms over me, deadly and handsome, and I grin. "You just wanted to get me on my back, didn't you?"

He grunts and gets off of me quickly. "No, I expected you to fight me off. Guess I should have known better."

Whatever. I still managed to flip him twice, even if he got me the third time.

Through the rest of the class, he pins me two more times, but I flip him another three. And even though toward the end I'm growing exhausted, I'm triumphant. If those demons come for me again, I have another way to defend myself, thanks to Callan. Turns out, he's actually a pretty good teacher, when he's not being a dick. Maybe he'll keep it up.

"Thanks for the help."

"It's my job." He gives me a hard stare. "You obviously need a lot of help defending yourself."

I roll my eyes and walk out. Nope, he's still a dick.

39

OLIVIA

Once the Princes take interest in me, the rest of the school notices. The whispers and weird looks stop, and instead everyone starts acting really nice to me and Araceli. Suddenly the outcasts become the cool kids on campus, and all it takes is a couple of overprotective guys following me around all the time. They even invite the two of us up to the bell tower, and I find myself studying up there whenever I can.

As summer turns into fall, the football game against the fae rolls around, but Araceli isn't up for it after what happened to Darel. I skip it to keep her company and watch movies while eating pizza, even though I'm dying to see a full-blooded fae in person. Faerie might be the key to finding my brother, but it's not like I can just walk up to one of the fae and ask them if they've seen him. I highly doubt I'd learn anything at the game, and Araceli is more important.

It's a shame I can't watch Callan run around in those tight pants though.

I keep waiting to hear from the Order of the Golden Throne about the next trial, but so far they've been silent. I'm anxious to confirm my theory about Jonah, or uncover another member or two of the Order, but for now all I can do is wait.

We're watching the newest X-men movie on the couch when Mystique takes the form of a politician, and I grin and nearly turn to Araceli and tell her about my brother. Then I remember she doesn't know he's my brother, and mentioning him now doesn't seem like the best time somehow. Not when she keeps turning the volume on the TV louder and louder to drown out the cheers from the game outside.

But my mind wanders, and I can't help but remember the last time I saw him.

Tap tap tap.

Jonah was flying outside my window, like he did the first time we met, except he was a lot bigger now. I opened the window up and laughed. "What are you doing out here?"

"Coming to see you, obviously."

"You're too big to fit through the window. Come to the front door like a normal person."

"Oh, fine." He went invisible as he floated to the ground. I waited a few minutes, and then he knocked on my apartment door.

I threw my arms around him before I could stop myself. I hadn't seen him in months, not since he told me about Grace. He spent all his time at Seraphim Academy now.

"Hey now," he said, surprised by my rare show of affection. "I missed you too."

"Sorry, it's been a rough day."

"Rough? How come?"

"Oh, the usual stuff. Weirdos at the bar. And all I got was a card from Mother and a note from Father saying he'd be coming by to teach me to use my angelic powers soon."

"Sorry, but I'm here now, so let's get the party started." He was carrying a brown shopping bag, and he pulled out a bottle of champagne. "Happy birthday, Liv!"

I laughed. "Thanks."

"Have you gotten your wings yet?"

"No, not yet."

"I'm sure you will soon. I heard most don't pop out for two weeks. Hey, I got you something." He reached into the bag again and handed

me a pink mug that said, "I'm a fucking angel" on it. "It's not much, but I thought it was appropriate."

I clutched the mug with a grin. "Wow, Father is going to hate this."

"That's exactly why I got it. Along with a large tin of your favorite fancy coffee."

"I love it. Thanks." I gave him another hug.

He popped open the champagne, and we crashed on my bed and toasted to my 21st birthday. Then I asked him about school and he caught me up on things, like how he was still seeing Grace, and how he'd been studying up on the fae.

"There's something I need to show you too," he said, sitting up. "Check out this thing I learned how to do."

As I watched, his skin seemed to shimmer and crawl with light, and then his appearance changed, until he looked exactly like Father. I jerked back in surprise. "What...how? Is that an Ishim power? Father's never mentioned that."

"Nope," when he spoke, he sounded like our dad too. Creepy. "You know how Father has special powers because he's an Archangel? Turns out I have one too—I can change my appearance however I want. It's easiest to copy someone I've seen and heard before, but I'm still experimenting."

"Wow, that's incredible. Do others know?"

"Only Grace and my friends."

"Be careful. With a power like that, everyone will want you to be their spy."

"Don't worry about me." He paused for a second, and then frowned. "Although there is something going on at school."

"What do you mean?"

His face darkened, which was unusual for him. "I'm not sure, but I think it's a good thing you're not going to school there too."

"Why?"

"They're not a fan of demons there, for one thing." He stared off into the distance, and I could tell something was troubling him, but then he turned to me and smiled. "But I'm probably worried over nothing. Let's pour some more champagne."

He must have been talking about the Order then. He knew they were up to no good, and was glad I wasn't there to be involved in it.

It's almost my 22nd birthday now, and all I want is to find him. I'm close though, I can feel it.

———

"Y ou're feeling hungry again, aren't you?" Bastien asks me.

It's been weeks since I had sex with Marcus, and even though he's hinted many times that he wants to do it again, I keep turning him down. Not because I don't want him, but because I'm worried about what might happen to him if we have sex a second time. I've never tested it before, and though I think he'll be okay, I don't want to hurt him.

"How can you tell?" I ask.

We're having one of our afternoon library sessions, although since he found out I'm half demon he's given up on uncovering my Choir and instead questions me about being a succubus. The guy is relentless, and I have to be extra careful with what I say around him, especially since he keeps bringing up Jonah.

"You're more distracted than normal and your eyes are a little wild. Not to mention, you keep looking at my neck like you want to take a bite out of it."

"I'm not that kind of demon." He's right though, and I hate that I'm so obvious. Then again, no other person has ever studied me as closely as Bastien has. It's kind of an honor, having someone so focused on me. He's borderline obsessed.

"No, but vampires and Lilim share many similarities. The hunger, for example." He stands up and begins closing the blinds, even though the library is pretty empty. "You need to feed."

"But Marcus—"

"Not on Marcus." He finishes with the blinds, and moves to sit on the edge of the table in front of me, forcing me to look up at him. "On me."

I swallow. I can't say I'm not tempted, especially after our kiss, and Marcus did say he was okay with it, but I still hesitate. "Are you sure?"

He begins unbuttoning his shirt slowly, and I revel in every inch of skin he reveals. "Yes. But don't take this as anything more than what it is—a business arrangement. I don't have feelings for you. I don't want to date you. This is just sex, and I'm only doing this because it needs to be done. Understand?"

My eyes narrow at him. "Fine with me. I don't have feelings for you either."

"Excellent. Let's begin."

I can't stop myself. Reaching out, I slide my hands up his chest, enjoying the strong muscles underneath. He's not huge like Callan or full of natural sex appeal like Marcus, but his sharp jaw begs to be licked. So, I do. In our private library room, I nibble Bastien's jawline and barely contain my desire as he reaches around and lifts me by my ass. Wrapping my legs around him, I press my mouth to his. He kisses me thoroughly, just like he did the other time, and he's such an expert with his tongue that it makes me wonder what else he could do with it.

He sits me on top of the desk, his fingers digging into my butt cheeks as he stands in front of it. Pressing his groin into mine, he grinds, causing delicious friction. It's not enough and it's too slow. I'm suddenly starving for him, and I'm not sure it's all succubus hunger.

"More. Now." Pushing him away in a show of strength that surprises him, judging by the look on his face, I grab his belt buckle and pop it open. I've had some practice at disrobing a man, and I've got his cock out within seconds. My mouth waters. I want to taste it, but I think that might break the "just sex" part of our arrangement.

But Bastien's not content with letting me take charge, and he pushes me down. My back hits the desk with a thump, and then he's yanking off my flats and tugging my jeans down my legs. My panties slide off next, and then he drags me down the desk until my ass is at the edge of it, and he's spreading me wide. His fingers slide between my legs, and he finds me dripping wet. A wicked smile crosses his lips as he feels how hot I am for him, and I'm so over the arrogant look in his eyes. Or maybe it turns me on more, I'm not sure. Either way, I reach between us and grab his cock, positioning him so my wet slick slides down his length with ease. He fills me completely, large enough to give me a bit of stretch, which is delicious.

I'm lying back on the desk and he's standing over me, looking down at me with his inscrutable gaze. The first time he moves inside me, I gasp. Bastien is excellent at everything he does, and I can already tell he's not going to disappoint in this area either. He pulls out of me almost completely to the hilt, then slides back home so smoothly it makes me moan. He hits me deep inside with expert precision, and I'm tempted to touch him, but I grab onto the desk instead. I've still got my shirt on, his black slacks are still hanging off his ass, and everything about this encounter says this is just a quick fuck, except for how amazing it's making me feel.

He starts moving faster and harder, slamming into me over and over, and I can't help the sounds that erupt from my mouth. I wonder if any librarians or other students will hear us, and decide I don't give a flying fuck at this moment.

I think he's going to make me come without touching me at all, but then his fingers dip between us to find my clit. With a master's touch, he takes me to new heights, even as he fills me with his cock. With his other hand, he slips under my shirt and begins teasing my nipples, almost like he can't stop himself.

I can't help myself either, and I wrap my legs around Bastien as I feed off him. With his fingers and cock stroking me, I scream out my orgasm, and he follows me a second later. His eyes close and his face changes, losing that cold exterior for just a second, as he pulses inside me. Drawing in his orgasm with mine, I suck the last little bit of sexual energy from him as he finishes us both off.

As soon as it's over, he pulls out of me and turns away, tucking his cock back in his slacks. "I trust that will be sufficient to keep you sated for a while."

He's all business again. That was fast. Meanwhile, I'm still panting on the desk, my naked legs hanging off the edge of it, with my shirt pushed up to my breasts. I manage to sit up and smooth my hair at least. "Yes. Thanks."

He buttons his shirt back up, still not looking at me. I wonder why. Is he afraid I'll see a hint of emotion in his cold eyes? Or is he worried he might actually feel something if he looks at me? "You're welcome."

He walks out of the room without another word, and I'm left to pick up my clothes alone. Try as he might to act unaffected, I can tell I'm starting to melt that hard, cold exterior of his.

40

KASSIEL

I've been waiting on the bench for an hour before Olivia shows up. It's been a while since she visited me by the lake, and I was starting to think she wasn't going to come anymore. When she sits beside me, I'm relieved. I see her every weekday in class, but that's different because we don't really interact. I've come to appreciate these quiet chats we have by the lake, and I felt almost hollow when she missed a few of them. If there wasn't this power imbalance between us, I might even call us friends now.

"I haven't seen you here in a while," I say, studying her closely.

"Sorry, I've been kind of busy."

"So I see." For once, she looks like a well-fed succubus. Her hair is extra lustrous, her lips look fuller, her eyes are brighter. Even her breasts seem perkier. Olivia is always beautiful, but now she's down-right stunning...and I'm suddenly awash with envy knowing she's this way because she's been feeding regularly with some of the other students. "You've been spending a lot of time with the Princes."

Her eyebrows dart up. "You know?"

I smirk. "Yes, we Professors do notice these things, and Hilda and Raziel love to gossip." My voice turns serious again. "It's good to see you looking healthier. I was worried you weren't feeding enough before."

I wait for her to deny it, but she lets out a long breath, and I sense she's done with that game. "Thanks. It's been a challenge to feed while I've been here, but it's going better now."

I sigh, knowing she spent months struggling while I did nothing. I feel like a total jerk, but I couldn't risk getting caught. "I wish I could have helped you with that."

Her eyes widen at me. "You do?"

I can't help but reach out and touch her cheek, stroking her soft skin. "I've never stopped wanting you since that night. If it wasn't forbidden, I would take you to bed again. Many times."

She presses her hand against mine, holding it to her face. "I'd like that."

I swallow and yank my hand away before I throw her down on the grass and have my way with her. "Maybe once you're finished with school. It's only another two years. That's nothing for people with our lifespan."

She nods, her face disappointed. "Maybe."

We sit in awkward silence again as we fight off the sexual tension between us, until she asks, "Does that mean I can sleep with an angel multiple times without hurting them?"

"Yes, you definitely can. You're not the first succubus I've been with."

"Really?" Now she looks intrigued.

"I've lived a long time," I say quickly, hoping she doesn't dig further. "Plus the Princes will be extra strong since they have Archangel blood. They won't be as weakened when you take their energy."

"That's good to know."

"Do they know what you are?" I ask.

"Yes, they found out."

"Are you sure you can trust them?"

"No, not really. I'm not sure I can trust you either, though."

"That's probably smart. Just...be careful. If word gets out about what you are, both the angels and demons will want to control you. Or they'll want you dead."

She swallows and nods. "I'll try."

I reach over and squeeze her hand. "I'll do whatever I can to protect you also. I swear it."

She gives me a heart-stopping smile. "Thanks, Kassiel. Being able to talk to you about this has really helped me a lot. I'm glad you walked into my bar a year ago."

"Me too." I stroke her hair softly, just once, and then I stand up. I'm so close to kissing her, I need to get away. Resisting a succubus at her full power is difficult, especially one I like as much as Olivia. "I should go. Good luck on your test tomorrow."

She groans. "Don't remind me."

With a flash of my black-and-silver wings, I'm in the air, and flying back to my room. Like the student dorms, it has a balcony so I can land on it and walk inside, without having to go through the rest of the building. I purposefully left it unlocked, since I knew I'd be coming back here.

But when I step inside, I see I've had a visitor while I was gone, and now an ivory envelope waits on my bed. Inside is an invitation to the third trial to get into the Order of the Golden Throne. It's during the half-time of the championship football game against the demons, which I was planning to skip anyway.

Finally. Father's been waiting for news on my mission to infiltrate the Order of the Golden Throne, and it's been ages since I had anything to report. Now all I have to do is pass this third trial, and I'll be in. Then I can figure out what they're really up to...and see if they're a threat.

41

OLIVIA

I t's hard to believe, but the school year is almost over. It's also November 13, and my birthday. I wasn't planning on making a big deal of it, since it mainly reminds me that it's been a year since I last saw Jonah, but Araceli was relentless. It's the first time she's been excited about anything since Darel died, so I caved in. And once Marcus found out it's my birthday, it turned into a *thing*.

Practically half the school has been invited up to the bell tower tonight. I think people are more excited to check out the Princes' lair than celebrating my birthday, but I don't mind. My birthdays usually consisted of just me and Jonah, so it's a nice change to be surrounded by friends.

"There you are!" Cyrus says, as he and Grace make their way through the crowd to me.

"I haven't seen you in ages. Are you avoiding us, or have the Princes been hogging all your time?" Grace asks.

"Neither," I lie. I totally have been avoiding them ever since I found out Cyrus was in the Order, and I'd bet money that Grace is too. "I've just been busy studying for finals. I started out so clueless compared to everyone else, and I want to make sure I do well."

"You're going to do great," Grace says. "Here, we got you a little something for your next year at Seraphim Academy."

She hands me a small gift bag, and I reach around inside until I find a pretty new daily planner for next year in pink and black, with silver edges. "Thank you, I'll totally use this." Especially since my last one got destroyed with my bedroom. Wait...could they know about that? Was the Order behind that? Maybe another test, or trying to find out if I'm loyal... I don't know. But now I'm even more suspicious of Grace and Cyrus.

"Are we opening presents already?" Araceli asks, bouncing over to us with some of her usual inner light. "Open mine next!"

She hands me a little box wrapped in gold, and I give her a big smile before opening it up. Inside is a silver charm bracelet with angel wings. My throat closes up at the beautiful gift, and once again I feel horrible for deceiving her. I'm going to tell her at the end of the school year. I am.

"I love it." I give her a big hug. "Thanks."

"It's nothing for the best roommate in the world."

"That honor definitely goes to you," I say, as the guilt piles up even higher. "You threw me this party and everything."

"No, I had the idea for the party. The Princes did all this." She nudges me. "You should go dance with Marcus."

I glance over at him, where he's leaning on the wall and drinking a beer, while others come and talk to him, like he's holding court for all his admirers. I hate to admit it, but I've become one of them. Marcus is pretty great, once you get past the arrogant side of him.

The other Princes are another story. Bastien and Callan stand in another corner, glaring at anyone who dares to come close. Callan still hates me, more than ever now, but he's oddly protective of me too and has worked hard to make sure I can defend myself in Combat Training. My situation with Bastien is even more confusing. He doesn't hate me, but he doesn't seem to like me much either, even though he also wants to help me in his own way. The sex is good though, so at least there's that.

I head over to Marcus when he's alone, and he grins at the sight of me and then wraps an arm around my waist.

"Having fun?" he asks, as he draws me close.

"Sure," I say. Big parties aren't really my thing, but it was nice of Marcus to do this for me.

"Uh huh. You want to get out of here, don't you?"

"Maybe," I say with a laugh. Am I so obvious?

"C'mon, let's go to my room. I've got a present for you there."

"Is it in your pants?" I ask, raising my eyebrow.

He gives me a wicked grin. "That's not what I'm talking about, but you can definitely have that too."

We fly off the balcony together, and some of the people at the party cheer. Guess it's no secret I'm sleeping with Marcus now. I bet people would be surprised if they knew I was banging Bastien too though.

Marcus lands on his balcony with a thump, and I set down beside him. We slip inside his dorm room, and I remember when I broke into this place to investigate at the beginning of the school year. I glance at Jonah's door quickly, and then look away.

Marcus hands me a box wrapped in balloon-covered paper, and I rip it open. Inside is a coffee mug with a little cartoon devil on it and the words, "*Coffee fiend.*" I stare at it, wondering if he knew about my angel mug somehow, but he never visited my room until after it was destroyed. Can it be a coincidence he got me such a similar present to Jonah's? Or was he involved in trashing my room?

"I've never met anyone who loves coffee like you do, so I thought it was funny," he says, rubbing the back of his neck. "If it's too on-point I can get you something else."

He sounds so sincere that I set the mug down and then hug him. "It's perfect. Thank you."

The hug turns into a kiss, and Marcus is ravenous as he presses his lips to mine. We haven't kissed like this since that time we had sex, and even though I don't need to feed yet, I can't help but revel in what he's giving me. Marcus puts off a sex appeal that even a nun couldn't refuse, and to a succubus like me, it's like candy.

"I don't need to feed tonight," I tell him, giving him an out.

"Good," Marcus says, as he pulls off his shirt. "Then this will be just for fun."

Sex for fun? A novel concept for me. I did it to live, and sometimes I enjoyed it, but doing it just because...that's new. I'm definitely not complaining though. Plus, I'm more confident that Marcus will be okay after my chat with Kassiel.

I reach out, splaying my hands across Marcus's chiseled chest. He's not as huge as Callan, but he's still more muscular than most guys I've been with, and I want to lick him all over. Damn.

I'm wearing a little flowy dress with spaghetti straps and a cardigan. While Marcus and I kiss, the cardigan hits the floor, and then he pushes my spaghetti straps off my shoulder. His mouth goes there next, planting kisses on the bare skin, as he tugs my dress down and reveals my breasts. The dress falls away, and I open up his jeans at the same time, then push them down.

His hands wrap around me, pulling me close and pressing my bare breasts against his chest as he swoops in for another kiss. He yanks our hips together, and the desire rages through me, potent and compelling. And for once, it's not my succubus side that's hungry for sex.

Marcus walks forward, moving us toward his bed, and I move with him willingly. He drops me back, and shimmies my panties down my legs so I can kick them off.

I slide up the bed, spreading my legs and gliding my hands down my stomach and around my sex. I arch my back and moan. I'm so turned on my touch is enough to make me soaking wet.

The sharp intake of Marcus's breath makes me look at him. He's got his briefs halfway down his legs, but he's frozen, eyes glued to my hands as they circle my mound.

"Spread yourself," he orders.

I grin and do as he says, happy to tease him this way. It's not much of a tease, because he sheds his briefs and falls on me, cramming his face between my legs.

Spreading my lips to give him the best access, I cry out as he sucks my clit into his mouth. My first orgasm crashes into me quickly, turning me into a moaning mess. As I ride it back to reality, Marcus slides two fingers inside me, hitting the perfect spot like he's done it a hundred times just to me. Instead of washing away, the orgasm keeps going, like I'm riding on a surfboard, taking advantage of every inch of the wave.

He uses his teeth to put sharper pressure on my nub as he relentlessly strokes the spot inside me that is driving me wild. Moaning and possibly yelling, the same orgasm builds again, going higher and higher. I'm pretty sure by this point I'm screaming and grunting, but I can't be sure. I've lost all sense of propriety. Not that I had that much to begin with, but still.

Marcus's mouth and fingers leave me in the middle of my sense-less pleasure, but then his cock slams into me with a force that moves me up the bed. He throws my legs back, putting his hands on the backs of my knees to bend my body in half. It means his cock keeps hitting that spot, that amazing, sent-from-heaven spot, every time he enters me.

His relentless pace makes my orgasm continue, and every time he slams home, the noises I make are truncated as my breath leaves me in a rush. I move my hands above my head, grabbing the wooden headboard of the bed. If I don't brace myself, I'm going to slide up the bed until my head is bouncing off of it.

He's not done. His ferocious pace continues to draw out what has got to be the longest orgasm of my life. It's not the most intense, but I'm not sure it'll ever end. He's getting close to finishing because his thrusts grow wilder and more erratic as the headboard bangs against the wall.

He finishes with a grunt and a whisper of my name, before he collapses on me. Careful not to smother me, he props himself up on his elbows and grins. "Happy birthday, Liv."

"That was...wow." I've never complimented a man on his perfor-mance in my life. It's a night of firsts all around. I'm not sure how I feel about it. "Now get off of me."

He chuckles and pops a kiss on my cheek before sitting up. "Want to stay the night?"

"You know I can't."

He strokes my thigh in a teasing way. "I don't see why not."

Shit, he's getting way too attached to me. He's going to think we're actually dating, and then things will get...complicated.

"I have to go," I say, as I get up and pick my panties off the floor.

He sighs, but then nods. "Let me know when you need to do it again."

"We'll see. I don't want to overtax you."

He grins at me. "Angel stamina, remember?"

I pick up my dress and toss it over my head. It's not his stamina I'm worried about, but his heart. How am I supposed to know if he really cares for me, or if it's a side effect of my succubus powers? Can angels resist the allure? There's so much I still don't know. Where's Mother when I need her?

As I walk out onto the balcony, Marcus grabs my hand and tries to stop me. "Stay."

"I can't."

He presses a desperate kiss against my lips, which only confirms that I need to go. "It's weird that you're leaving."

"No. It would be weird if I stayed." I pull away and launch off the balcony, leaving him behind.

42

OLIVIA

The day of the championship football game against the demons rolls around, and I brace myself for what's to come. After my last chat with Kassiel, I returned home to find an invite to the third trial, and I'm nervous about what we'll have to do now. It can't be good. But at the same time, I'm excited too. Jonah disappeared after this game last year, and I'm so close to uncovering the truth. I just have to pass this one final test.

When I get to the field, I see it's twice as packed as it was at the other game I went to. Araceli opted to stay behind again, and I'm glad. Something is going to happen tonight, and the cold air feels taut with tension. I shiver and pull my hoodie up over my head.

Grace lands beside me. "Exciting, isn't it?"

I nod. "I've never seen this many angels."

She smiles as she gazes across the field. "Imagine the power in this one stadium."

I turn my attention to the other side of the bleachers. Demons of all shapes and sizes, looking no different than the angels, fill the stands. "There's three times as many demons as there were before."

"That's normal for the championship game. Cyrus has saved us some seats down in front."

We make our way through the stands, zigging and zagging around bodies. I spot a familiar face in the crowd and my jaw drops. I have to quickly compose myself as my father bumps into me accidentally-on-purpose.

"Excuse me," he says as he puts a steadying hand on my arm.

"No problem." I look at him out of the corner of my eye as he walks the same direction I do, seemingly a coincidence.

"You're well?" he asks under his breath.

"As well as I can be," I mutter.

"Did you say something?" Grace turns to me as she walks ahead of me.

"Just that I could go for a drink."

She chuckles. "I'll get us some. You find Cyrus. He's over there."

I nod, and she takes off, leaving me standing next to my father.

"Looking forward to the game?" He doesn't look at me as he asks, and I don't answer. "My son was on the team last year."

"Oh? But not this year?" I pretend to be interested in the stranger's story.

"Unfortunately, no." His voice is heavy with grief. He looks at me for the first time. "You look good," he says in a low voice. "Healthy."

He gestures for me to follow, and we step behind the port-a-potties that have been set up. A ripple of magic releases from him, and he bends light around us both so we're invisible, along with everything we say.

"Are you eating enough?"

"You're worried about that *now*?" I ask. "Where were you the rest of the year?"

"Looking for Jonah. Don't worry, I had people keeping an eye on you here so I knew you were safe."

They're not doing a very good job, since he doesn't seem to know about the demons attacking me. "Has there been any progress with Jonah?"

He scowls. "No. The Archangel Council has officially closed the case."

The news that nobody official is searching for my brother

anymore infuriates me. How can he let them stop looking? Jonah is his only son and his only legitimate child. "It's a good thing I'm still searching for him then."

"Have you found anything?"

"I don't know yet. I think he might be in Faerie."

Father shakes his head. "I already spoke with the High Court of the fae, and no one there has seen him."

"That doesn't mean he's not there. If there's anyone who can hide from them, it's Jonah."

"Perhaps." He doesn't sound convinced. "You should give up this hunt already, Olivia. It's only going to get you in trouble."

"I'm not giving up until I find Jonah."

He pinches the bridge of his nose. "Why do you continue with this madness? Are you trying to punish me?"

"I'm *trying* to find my brother."

"We both know that's not going to happen, and you're just going to get yourself in trouble in the process. At the end of the school year, it's best if you leave this place and never return."

Wow. I can't even reply to him. He doesn't believe in me at all. What must it be like to have a proud parent?

I'll never know.

"I have to go. Don't follow me."

Turning away, I walk back around the port-a-potties and come into view as I leave his magic behind. He better not fucking follow me. I'll blow the whole operation. I'm that mad.

I sit between Grace and Cyrus. "Sorry, stomach problems," I explain.

"Do you need a Malakim?"

"Nah, I'm okay." I grab the beer Grace got me as the teams run out onto the field. My eyes immediately hone in on Callan and his impressive ass. "Besides, the game's starting now."

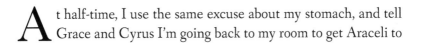

At half-time, I use the same excuse about my stomach, and tell Grace and Cyrus I'm going back to my room to get Araceli to heal me. It's easy to convince them, and I'm sure it's because they need to sneak off too.

I pretend to head back to my dorm, but then go invisible and slip into the woods. I pull my robes and mask out of my bag and throw them on, before going visible again and heading to the meeting spot.

There are only five of us in white robes tonight. I guess two people either failed the last trial or decided not to go through with, like Araceli. I wonder how many will remain after tonight's trial, whatever it is. I swallow hard as we wait.

What did Jonah have to do to become a member himself? I'm almost glad I don't know.

The golden-robed initiates appear, although they seem fewer than last time. I bet some of them are still at the football game.

"Follow us," the crowned leader says, in their garbled voice.

They walk the same way I followed them last time. When they stop near the boulder, one of them turns toward us and hands us each a blindfold. "Put this on over your mask. We will know if you leave a spot to peek out."

One of them must be an Ofanim. Maybe Cyrus. I'm glad I'm wearing the necklace, though I don't need to peek. I know where we're going.

Just to be safe, I put the blindfold on properly, while the other initiates do the same. Then we're told to wait, and I hear the sound of the boulder moving. If I didn't know what it was already, I'd be clueless though.

Someone takes my arm and leads me down the long hallway, and from their nails digging into my skin, I guess the hand is feminine. The initiates are all led down to the main cavern, and then we stop. I wait for them to remove the blindfold, but they don't.

"Congratulations on making it to the third trial," the leader says. "You will each be taken into another room one by one, where you will be given your task. If you fail, you will be escorted out of here. If you succeed, you will be initiated into the Order at the end of the year. Don't let us down."

"You first," someone says to my left. I hear the sound of movement, as the person next to me is taken away. The rest of us have to wait, still blindfolded.

After about five minutes, we hear the muffled screaming.

My stomach twists. I don't know if it's the other initiate screaming, or someone else. What is this third trial? For the first time, I'm questioning whether I'll really be able to do it or not.

One by one the other initiates are led into this other chamber, and then we hear more terrible noises. At one point I think I hear a drilling sound. That's when one of the other initiates turns and tries to flee, then yells, "Let me out!" The person is escorted out of the cave, and then there were four.

I'm the last one to be sent in. When the door slams shut behind me with a heavy *thud*, my blindfold is taken off by a golden-robed initiate. Behind them is a man tied to a chair in the middle of the room. He's covered in blood and his head slumps forward. A few fingers are missing, and I instantly recoil.

"What's going on?" I ask, as I scream a little inside.

"This demon is an abomination," the golden-robed person says.

"Who is he? What has he done?"

"He is no one. A random person watching the games. Does it matter? He is a demon. You will torture him until he gives you any information that can be valuable to the Order. If you come back without this, you will not be initiated into the Order."

The demon is gagged and manages to look at us with furious eyes. Shit. What do I do? I can't torture someone! I am a lover, and getting better at being a fighter, but definitely not a torturer. Besides, the poor guy looks like he's been through enough already.

"We will come get you when your time is up," the golden-robed person says, and then leaves the room, slamming the door shut.

Across the small room is a table with a candelabra and a myriad of instruments of torture. I walk over and examine them, mostly just to give myself time to think, and see all sorts of terrible twisty, pointy objects, many already covered in blood. Including the drill. I cover my hand to stop myself from gagging.

I look around the room, searching for a camera or recording device, but I don't see anything, and I don't think the damp stone walls could camouflage anything. I take out my cell phone and use the flashlight to make sure. It's about the only use it has down here—no reception at all.

I consider using my succubus powers to get this guy to tell me something, but I'm not sure that would work on this demon. I can't tell what he is from looking at him. Like angels, demons all look like humans, until they use their powers.

Making my decision, I kneel in front of the guy and whisper, just in case someone is listening in somehow. "I'm going to get you out of here. I promise. But you have to give me something first."

He tries to talk over his gag, and I remove it carefully. "Bullshit," he says. "You're just trying to trick me."

"I'm not, I promise."

"Why would you help me?"

"Because I'm like you." I was hoping it wouldn't come to this, but this is the only way he will trust me. I remove my mask, then lean in close and touch his arm. As I do, I let my power emerge and draw out his lust for me. It was there, just a tiny bit, and it's enough to activate and feed. As I do, my eyes turn black. He gasps when he sees them.

"A succubus! How is it possible?" he whispers.

"I'm infiltrating the school to find out about what they're doing to demons here. I'll help you however I can, but I'm on a direct assignment from Lucifer, and I can't blow my cover."

"Nope, I've heard that line before tonight. I don't buy it."

"You...what?"

"The whole spying for Lucifer thing." He rolls his eyes. "The guy before you said the same thing."

Whoa. That's...unexpected. Is there another demon infiltrating the school?

I huff. "Fine, don't believe me. I'll just have to torture you, I guess."

He studies me for a long moment, and then nods. "I believe you. Let me free, and I'll tell you what you want to know. Juicy things, things that I didn't even tell your friends who came before you."

I hesitate. It could be a trap, but I also can't let this demon stay down here. I'm 99 percent sure they'll kill him when I'm done with him.

"Okay, but we need to make it look like you overpowered me and escaped."

"I'm a vampire. It won't be a problem."

This is a bad idea, I think, but what other choice do I have? I check out the bindings holding them, and notice they're imbued with light. No wonder he couldn't escape. I find a knife on the torture table that glows when I pick it up, and hope this will work. And if he messes with me, well I can always stab him with it. I know first-hand what these imbued weapons can do.

I saw through the ropes, and then the vampire bursts up and grabs me. I use the move Callan taught me and flip him over my shoulder, knocking him to the ground.

I level the knife at him. "Information. Now."

He grins up at me, and his fangs are out. The fucker was going to bite me. "I'll tell you a good secret. You're the succubus everyone is looking for."

"Why?" And how? I was so careful.

"There have been rumors of an unknown succubus in the area for months. Many of us were told to be on the lookout for you tonight. The Archdemons want us to bring you back alive." He grins wider. "There's a nice bounty on your head, and I'm planning to collect."

Like I have time for this shit. Seriously.

I lower the glowing dagger to his neck. "Sorry, but I really am on a mission here, and I can't have you messing it up. Now give me something useful, and maybe I'll let you go after all."

"That's all I know, sorry. Everything I told the others was a lie." He laughs, and it's a mad laugh, and I feel bad for the guy again. They really did a number on him.

I stand back. "Go. Get out of here. I'm not going with you though."

He rises to his feet and pounces on me. So much for being nice and trying to help him. I dodge him and roll, then get back to my feet and lunge, using more moves from Combat Training. The vampire lets out a blood-curling scream as the dagger cuts him, and he stumbles back, clutching his stomach. He bares his fangs and backhands me across the face, so hard it sends me flying. Damn supernatural strength.

I hit the side of the cave hard, and fall to the ground. I've still got the dagger clutched in my hand though. Everything fucking hurts, but I will cut that fucker again if he comes close to me. But instead, he throws the door open and dashes out, so fast it's hard for my eyes to follow. I have no idea how he'll get out of the cave, but that's not my problem anymore. He's on his own.

Everything hurts, but I manage to crawl forward and grab my mask and shove it back on my face. There's chaos outside the room and lots of yelling as the vampire makes his escape. For a long time I sit there in a daze, and when it quiets down, someone in a gold robes runs in to me. "Are you all right?"

"I've been better," I say, with the weird muffled voice of my mask. "Did he escape?"

The other person nods. "It seems that way. What happened?"

"I was torturing him but then he overpowered me." I touch my head, which is pounding. "He threw me across the room."

"Did you learn anything before that happened?"

Shit. I need something. I decide the truth is the best option.

"I did." I use the wall to help me get to my feet, but everything hurts, and the hunger is rising in response as my body tries to heal itself. "There's a demon on campus, infiltrating the school."

"What?" the other person asks, shocked.

"It's true. I tricked him into thinking I was going to help him escape, and in exchange, he told me that. But then he actually did escape. I managed to cut him with this dagger though."

"Good work. That will slow him down, and we should be able to find him. Do you need a healer to attend to you?"

"No, I'm fine, thanks."

"Then put your blindfold back on, and I'll lead you out of here."

I do as I'm told, and as the arm grabs me again, I feel the same feminine nails. I'm led out of the cave and into the forest, and I wonder if the vampire got away.

He was a dick, but I kind of hope he did. Otherwise, I'm pretty sure he'll be found dead tomorrow.

"You did good tonight," the golden-robed person whispers to me. "You'll receive an invitation to the initiation soon."

The arm releases me, and when I take off the blindfold, she's vanished and I'm alone in the forest.

I did it. I passed their final test. And I did it without losing my soul too.

43

OLIVIA

The demons win the football game, and I keep waiting to hear about a dead or tortured vampire, but it seems both the Order and the demons want to keep that quiet. I'm paranoid that the demons know I'm here now, and look over my shoulder constantly during the last few weeks of school. Then final exams draw near, and I'm so busy studying, I don't have time to worry. At some point during the school year I stopped being here only for Jonah, and started being here for me, and I desperately want to do well on my exams.

The night before our last day of school, I receive my final invitation to the Order of the Golden Throne. At midnight, I'm to head back to the usual meeting spot, where I'll be initiated into the Order. Finally.

When I reach the designated spot, all of the golden-robed members are there. I think it's all of them, anyway. I wonder which one is Cyrus, and if Grace and the Princes are among them too.

"Initiates, step forward," says the leader wearing the crown.

I move two steps forward along with three other people. Who are they? Maybe Tanwen? Other than that, I don't have a clue. All I know is, I'm glad Araceli isn't one of them. I made sure she was asleep in her room before I left.

"Only four of you were strong and loyal enough to pass all three trials, and become full members of the Order. For your initiation, we require one last test of bravery, loyalty, and faith."

Of course. I should have known it wouldn't be just a simple "here's your gold robe, now we'll tell you all our secrets." Nope, they had to make us do one final thing.

We're taken to the lake, near where I met with Kassiel all those nights, and then we stop. One figure steps forward and places a gold-plated medallion around the necks of the other initiates and me. Once we all wear one, they step back. I look down at mine. It's a golden throne with a sun behind it.

"You will wear these around your neck and allow yourselves to sink into the lake," the leader says. "When you emerge, you will be reborn as a member of the Order."

Nope, this does not sound fun at all.

Suddenly someone is picking me up by the arms, and I'm flown over the lake...and then dropped right into the middle of it. The other initiates hit the water a short distance away, and as I fall, I try to spread my wings, but can't. The medallion around our necks must prevent it. I suck in as much air as I can before I plummet into the water. I kick my legs, but my robes make it hard to swim, and the medallion seems to get heavier, dragging me down, down, down, into the pitch-black depths. Thanks to my demon side I can see better than the angels can, but that doesn't help me at all down here.

My feet hit the ground, and I glance around for something to help me, but all I see is darkness. Every time I try to swim up, the medallion drags me back down, and the robes only get in my way. I fight, and I struggle, and I try to do everything I can to get back to the surface, but it's no use. None of my demon or angel abilities can help me with this. I can't see any of the other initiates, and I wonder if they're going through the same thing as I am, or if this is some kind of special trick just for me.

I can't hold my breath much longer. Real panic sets in. I am totally going to die down here, and then Jonah will be lost forever.

This is a test of bravery and faith, I suddenly remember.

Am I brave enough to die? For Jonah, yes. And I have faith that I'll find him, even now.

I let my limbs go limp and blow out my last bit of air. This isn't going to be the end, I'm sure of it.

Just when I think I've made a mistake, my medallion begins to glow with a soft light. I suddenly glide up to the surface, as though propelled by a strong motor, and my head breaks through the surface. I cough and suck in a huge gulp of air, and then arms grab me and fly me back to the shore. I'm dropped on the grass, where I turn on my side and spit out a ton of water, then try to remember how to breathe.

The other initiates lie beside me, coughing as much as I am. We all have our masks on still, somehow. More of the medallions' magic? Other members of the Order come around and take the medallions off our necks, and then the leader stands before us. "You have been reborn, and are now members of the Order of the Golden Throne. Welcome, brothers and sisters."

Golden-robed members help us to our feet and pat us on the back. My head is still foggy from almost drowning, but underneath my mask, a big grin splits across my face.

We're taken around the lake to the boulder and shown how to open it, and then led inside the cave to the great big cavern at the bottom. The four of us who have made it stand in our dripping-wet white robes in the center of the room, while the other members form a semi-circle behind us. I'm given a bundle of gold robes and a matching mask.

"Now that you are members, we shall go over a few things," the leader continues. "First of all, you must always wear your robes and masks to the meetings. You shall not know the identities of other members until you graduate, and they shall not know you either. The only exceptions are a few of us who have been chosen to know your identities."

Except I already know Cyrus is a member, and I have my suspicions about a few others. I plan to keep working to uncover other members next year too—especially if they had something to do with Jonah's disappearance.

"Now that you have proved your loyalty and devotion to our causes, we shall reveal to you the true purpose of the Order, and give you your first mission to accomplish over the winter break. We seek the Staff of Eternity."

The Staff of Eternity? The thing Michael and Lucifer used to close off Heaven and Hell? Why does the Order want that?

The leader answers my question without me even asking. "Once we find the Staff, we plan to use it to return to Heaven so that we may rebuild it, and to lock the demons up in Hell for good."

Oh shit. That doesn't bode well for me. Or Mother. Could they really do it though? Hopefully Michael and Lucifer hid that thing where no one can find it.

The leader continues. "For the last few years we have been searching for the Staff, to no avail. We have reason to believe it is in Faerie, but the people we sent to find it have never returned."

That must be what happened to Jonah! I'm practically bouncing on my heels now. I knew I would find the truth once I was a member...except this doesn't make sense. Jonah must have gone to Faerie looking for the Staff, and he would have been able to sneak into that realm better than anyone with his shapeshifting skills. But why would he want the Staff? The Order is opposed to everything my brother believed in. Like Kassiel, Jonah believed we should have peace with demons, no doubt partly because of me. He would never want to find the Staff of Eternity and use it to kick all the demons off Earth.

And what happened to him once he got to Faerie? Did he find the Staff? Or did something go horribly wrong?

"Your mission is to learn everything you can about the Staff over your winter break, including where it might be hidden. Do this without alerting anyone to your true purposes. Return next term with useful information, and the Order will reward your service. Remember, when you graduate from Seraphim Academy, we will help you find prominent, powerful positions in the community.

Whatever your dream is, we can make sure you achieve it." He spreads his arms. "You are dismissed."

We file out of the cave with golden robes tucked in our arms, and as the cold night air hits my damp hair, I do feel reborn...and more determined than ever to find my brother.

I have no clue how to get to Faerie, but I'm going to find a way.

Guess I'll be taking fae studies next year.

———

F inal exams begin the next morning. My first one is Combat Training, where we have to fight Callan one by one, using all the moves we've learned over the year. It's obvious he's going easy on us, because none of us could actually defeat him in a real fight, not even Tanwen, but he still gives us a challenge.

Araceli does really well, even though she missed a good chunk of Combat Training, and Tanwen of course wipes the floor with all of us. The girl is formidable, I'll give her that.

I'm last.

Callan's eyes narrow as I move onto the mat in front of him. Somehow I don't think he'll go easy on me, but he's also taught me well over the last few months. He rushes me, and I manage to dart out of the way. But then he's back, and there's no use wrestling with him because he's way too strong. I sweep my leg under him, knocking him down, and then land on him with my elbow. He lets out a loud *oof*, before rolling out of the way. Then he's back on his feet almost instantly, and he throws me across the mat. He's on me a second later, pinning me down, and when I look in his eyes I see he's as aroused by this as I am. Luckily he taught me how to get out of this, and I manage to bring my knee up and get him off me. I spin on my back and kick him in his way-too-handsome face, knowing he'll heal fast anyway, and then when he's stunned, I land another one in the chest. He falls back, and I win.

Hilda lets out a little clap. "Nice job, Olivia."

Callan bounces to his feet, and then reaches down to help me up. He doesn't seem to be in pain, even after the entire class beat the crap out of him. Archangel blood is some good stuff, seriously. I wonder what it would be like to feed on him. With two Archangel parents, I bet he's even more powerful than Marcus and Bastien. Yum.

"Good work this year," Hilda says. "You've all improved a lot. See you next year."

We all file out of the gym, and Araceli and I towel off our sweat and then prepare to go take our Flight exam, which is by the lake. It should be easy after all the flying I'm done this year, although we'll be expected to do some fancy maneuvers like spinning and flipping. That stuff scared me before, but not anymore.

"Olivia," Callan says. He gestures for me to follow him.

"I'll catch up," I tell Araceli.

He leads me to the other side of the gym, where we have some privacy from the others. Then he turns on me, and corners me against the wall. "You can't come back next year."

"Why not?"

"It's not safe for you here."

"I'm fine," I try to walk away, but he nudges me back against the wall.

"You're a demon," he growls.

"Half," I remind him.

"You don't belong here."

Not this shit again. "Yes, I do. I'm half angel too, dammit."

"I'll hide you somewhere safe, where no angel or demon can find you. It's the only way to protect you."

"No thanks."

He places his hand on either side of my head, pinning me against the wall. "Why are you so damn stubborn?"

I stare into his eyes, challenging him. "Why do you resist, when you know you want me bad?"

Rage crosses his face. "You don't know what the fuck you're talking about."

"No?" I laugh. "Don't forget, I can sense your lust. I feel it every time we fight. Every time you look at me. And especially now." I wrap my arms around his neck and press myself against him. "Just give in, and this will be easier for both of us."

"Only because you're using your succubus powers on me to make me want you." He yanks my arms off him and pushes me back against the wall. His face is so angry, I think he might explode. "I could never want a demon."

But then he crushes his mouth against mine, funneling all that rage into a kiss so intense, all I can do is let it happen. He presses me back against the wall, kissing me roughly, and it turns me on so much I'm instantly wet and oh so very hungry. Turns out I like it a little rough, from Callan anyway. I can only imagine how domineering he'll be in bed, and if this kiss is any indication, his energy will fill me up for ages.

I didn't feed after the football game, but my body healed anyway, it just left me pretty hungry. Now I take some of his energy through the kiss, my eyes turning black as he devours my mouth like he's just as hungry for sex as I am.

He pulls away and sees my eyes, and that only seems to make him angrier. He stumbles back. "Stay away from me, demon."

He stomps away while I stand there in a daze of his power. His kiss was strong enough to sate my hunger, for now anyway, but I also feel like I only got a few bites of a meal I wanted to really savor.

Stay away from him? He was the one who cornered me and then kissed me! The man has some nerve.

I roll my eyes and pull myself together, then head to Flight for my next exam.

44

CALLAN

With Olivia's taste in my mouth, I head to the bell tower and begin to pace in my usual spot. No matter how much I've tried not to think about her over the last few weeks, Olivia's seductive face keeps popping into my head. Every time we fight, I want to pin her down and spread her legs for my cock. And when I kissed her just now, it took all my power not to fuck her right up against the wall.

Why the fuck do I want that? The son of Michael and Jophiel can't want a half-demon. My father will rise from his grave and hunt me down if I get together with Olivia. And my mother? She would probably disown me if she found out. Especially since her first son, my half-brother Ekariel, was killed by demons when he was a child. It was before I was born, but still. Between his death and my father's, I have plenty of reasons to hate demons.

So why can't I stop wanting her?

Plus, there's the promise I made to Jonah. I know now that he wanted her away from this school for her protection, because it would be too dangerous if anyone finds out what she is. I've failed so far at getting rid of her, but I can make sure she doesn't come back next year.

This is my last chance...and I'm going to have to do something drastic.

I text Bastien to meet me at Uriel's house, and he arrives there fifteen minutes later.

"What's this about?" he asks, as he folds his wings away.

"I need to get a video from one of the security cameras."

He arches an eyebrow. "Why?"

"Because I fucking need it, that's why."

Bastien scowls at me, but I'm the boss, and he doesn't question me. Luckily Uriel is gone, and Bastien lets me into the office and goes right to the security camera footage. "What time?"

"About twenty minutes ago, outside the gym."

He finds the footage of me and Olivia there, and we watch as I kiss her and her eyes turn black. Even on the grainy black-and-white footage, it's obvious what she is.

"You kissed her?"

"Shut up," I tell him. "Can I get this on a thumb drive or something?"

"Sure." He looks at me from the corner of his eye as he transfers the video over. "What do you plan to do with this?"

"What I should have done weeks ago." I grab the thumb drive from him. "It's time the truth came out about Olivia. As an Ofanim, I thought you'd be on board with this."

"This is a bad idea," Bastien says with a deep frown.

I ignore him and leave Uriel's house, the thumb drive tucked in my pocket, along with the picture of Olivia that Jonah gave me a year ago.

I don't want to do this, but I gave Jonah my word—and the word of Michael's son is unbreakable.

That's the reason I'm doing this. Not because I'll lose my fucking mind if I have to spend another year with Olivia on campus. Besides, it's for her protection. I'll make sure she has somewhere safe to go, where no demon or angel can get to her.

But by the end of the day, I'll make sure Olivia can never come back to Seraphim Academy again.

45

OLIVIA

I manage to get through all the rest of my exams, and I think I did pretty well on them, even Angelic History, my hardest class. Kassiel gave me a small smile as I walked out, so hopefully I'm not doing too badly in the class, but I won't know for sure until I get my grades when they're emailed to us in a few weeks.

Once exams are finished, we have one final assembly with Headmaster Uriel, and then the school year will officially be over. It's the end of November, and I haven't even thought about what I'll do during my break, which Seraphim Academy takes during the winter, since most angel families like to go somewhere warm during the colder months. Araceli and her family plan to spend the holidays in the Bahamas. And me...I'm not sure what I'll do yet. Stay here maybe, and keep trying to find Jonah. I'm pretty sure he's in Faerie looking for the Staff, but I can't understand why he would do such a thing, or why he hasn't returned yet.

I head to the auditorium, where everyone is abuzz with end-of-the-year excitement and saying goodbye to all their friends. I see Grace and Cyrus and give them a little wave, then start heading over to them. I'm still suspicious of them, but they're my friends too.

As I'm walking down the aisle toward them, Callan walks out

onto stage, and I pause. He has a determined look on his face, his eyes harder than I've seen before, and I'm suddenly nervous, though I can't say why. What's he doing up there?

He speaks into the microphone. "Students of Seraphim Academy, before you head home, you should know the truth about one of our students here. The half-human named Olivia Monroe is not what she seems."

Oh fuck.

"Olivia, what's going on?" Araceli asks me, appearing at my side, while the entire school whispers and turns to stare at me.

I clutch my necklace and shake my head. "I don't know."

Callan's voice booms through the microphone. "The truth is, she's not half human, but half demon. A succubus, to be precise. She's been lying to us the entire time."

It's happening. Callan's exposing me. My worst fear, now come to life, right when I felt like I was finally fitting in. Why would he do this now?

A gasp goes up through the audience, and I begin to back out slowly, trying to make an escape. Araceli, bless her heart, yells at the stage, "You're the liar!"

"I have proof," Callan says. He turns around, and a video begins playing in black and white. There's no sound, and the angle is weird, cutting off everything but my shoulders and up, but it clearly shows my kiss with Callan outside the gym. Along with my black eyes when he pulls away from me.

This is why he kissed me. He was planning all along to tell everyone about me, even though he promised he wouldn't. I feel sick, and dirty, and used. My stomach twists, and I both want to punch something and burst into tears, but most of all I want to run far away and never see him again.

Were Marcus and Bastien part of this plan? I don't see them anywhere, but they must know about this. The Princes never do anything alone, after all, and that only makes this worse. I trusted those guys, even Callan, and thought they truly cared about me. In the last few weeks, they became my friends. Maybe even something more.

Now they've betrayed me.

Araceli's jaw drops, and she turns to me with shock in her eyes. "What...?"

She doesn't want to believe it, but I can't lie to her anymore. "I'm so sorry," I tell her, and then I dart out of the auditorium as fast as I can, while the rest of the place erupts into chaos.

I fly back to my room and start grabbing my things and throwing them into a bag, including the money in my secret stash. The demons know what I am. The angels know what I am. Everyone fucking knows what I am. I need to get out of here, and go into hiding, fast, except where can I go? There is nowhere safe for me, thanks to Callan. I might need to call my parents for help. Shit. I don't think I can handle telling my father I not only failed to find Jonah, but that he was right all along about me coming here. I'm exactly what he thinks I am—a mistake. And Mother? I'm not even sure how to reach her, or where she is. I'm alone, completely and utterly alone, just like I was before I came to Seraphim Academy.

A knock on the door makes me freeze. Shit. They've come for me already. What will they do to someone whose very existence is forbidden? Kick me out? Lock me up? Execute me?

"Olivia?" Kassiel's voice comes through the door. "Open up."

I let out a relieved sigh and open the door. Kassiel is the one person who might be able to help me. As soon as I throw open the door, he wraps his arms around me and holds me close. I take comfort in his strength and warmth, and nearly start crying, but I manage to hold myself together...barely.

"I'm in trouble," I say against his chest. "I messed up, big time, by trusting the Princes."

"I know, and I'm going to help you however I can...but I'm supposed to take you to see Headmaster Uriel now."

I stiffen and pull away. "How is that helping me?"

"I believe Headmaster Uriel will listen to reason, and I'll help convince him you deserve to be here just like anyone else. Although if you want to run, I can help you do that too, but we need to go now."

I glance back into my bedroom with my half-packed bag and

consider leaving. But then I think about how hard I've worked this year, not just to find Jonah, but to learn everything I could about being an angel, and how I'm so very tired of hiding. I'm tired of being ashamed of what I am and feeling like a big mistake. I didn't ask for this life, or to carry both angel and demon blood, but maybe it's time I owned it already.

I draw in a deep breath and nod. I can do this. "Let's talk to Uriel."

"Good choice."

We jump off my balcony, and I hold my head up and let my wings pull me into the air. Kassiel follows, then flies out in front of me, leading me to my fate.

46

OLIVIA

Once we arrive at Uriel's house, Kassiel walks straight in the front door, through the hallway, and into the office. Inside, Uriel sits behind his desk pinching his nose between his thumb and forefinger.

"Here she is," Kassiel says. I appreciate that he doesn't leave my side.

"Have a seat, Olivia," Uriel says. "You may go, Kassiel."

"With all due respect sir, I'd like to stay."

Uriel glances at me. "If Olivia is all right with that, then fine."

I nod and take a seat. Uriel opens his mouth, but the door opens before he can say anything, and Archangel Jophiel storms in, the angel that recruited me from the hospital to come to the school—and Callan's mother.

"Is it true? Is there a half-demon at your school?" Jophiel asks.

"Yes, it is," Uriel replies.

She stops and looks at me. "You. I questioned you myself. How is this possible?"

"She has a fae relic that allows her to lie," Uriel says.

Jophiel narrows her eyes at him. "You knew all along, didn't you?"

"Of course I did. I know everything that happens at my school."

My eyes widen. Uriel knew all along what I am? I glance at Kassiel and he nods. He isn't surprised by this. He must have suspected all along that Uriel knew. Maybe that's why he didn't feel the need to tell the headmaster about me.

"How could you let a half-demon attend Seraphim Academy?" Jophiel asks, her face enraged.

"She's half-angel as well." Uriel gives a small shrug. "If she wishes to focus on that side of herself in her training, who are we to deny her?"

Jophiel whirls on me, and she's terrifying in her beautiful rage. "What do you have to say for yourself?"

My shoulders slump, but I suck in a breath and prepare to defend myself. "All I want is the chance to learn, like every other young angel out there. I want to attend classes and go to football games and learn how to fly and use my powers. I want to be part of the angel community. I didn't have any of that growing up. Is it so wrong to want that now?"

"You shouldn't have deceived us to get here. You knew you were a succubus from the moment I stepped into your hospital room, and everything you told us has been a lie."

I take a gamble. Callan hates demons, and I'm guessing it partly came from his mother. "I'm sorry, truly I am. But I can't help what I am. What I can do is try to suppress my demon side and overcome it, and that's why I came here instead of going to Hellspawn Academy. I hoped by being here I could bring out my angel half and focus on that."

Kassiel arches an eyebrow at me, and I know he doesn't buy it, but Jophiel softens a little.

"I've taken testimony from her teachers," Uriel says to Jophiel. "They speak highly of her. Even Hilda, and you know how she feels about demons."

"Olivia is an excellent student," Kassiel says. "She has worked hard in all her classes, and done everything that's been asked of her. She deserves to be here."

Jophiel crosses her arms, her nose high in the air. "That may be, but it can't be ignored that she joined our school under false pretenses. Or that you kept her secret this entire time, Uriel. The other Archangels will not be pleased once they find out."

They're not going to let me stay. Where will I go? Soon the whole world will know what I am, and there won't be anywhere I can hide.

Uriel gives her a withering look. "I'm in charge of Seraphim Academy, and how I run it is my decision, not yours, or any of the other Archangels. As far as I'm concerned, Olivia can stay."

I let out a relieved breath, until Jophiel shakes her head.

"Azrael will never allow it," she says. "The girl must leave."

Shit. Azrael leads the Archangels now. If he says I'm out, not even Uriel can stop him.

Footsteps in the hall make Uriel pause. The door flies open, and of all people, my father charges in, looking like he's going into battle. I've never seen his face so determined or his eyes so angry. Holy shit.

"Gabriel!" Jophiel says, dropping her arms. "What are you doing here?"

Gabriel's presence and power fills the room. He was second in command to Michael for thousands of years, and he would be leading the Archangel Council now if he hadn't turned down the job. I can't believe he's here.

"What is the meaning of this?" he demands. He puts a hand on my shoulder and squeezes, letting me know he's with me. "Why is my daughter being questioned like a common criminal?"

"You're her father?" Jophiel asks, so shocked she takes a step back and puts a hand to her chest.

I look up at Father, still in disbelief myself, but he just stares down the other two Archangels.

"Yes, I am."

"I'm sorry, Gabriel," Jophiel says. "We had no idea." Uriel coughs, and Jophiel glances at him. "You knew that also?"

"I had my suspicions," Uriel says.

Damn, is there *anything* Uriel doesn't know?

"Who is her mother?" Jophiel asks.

"That is not pertinent to this discussion, except that she is a succubus," Gabriel says, and his tone leaves no room for argument. He's protecting Mother too now. I've never loved my father more than at this very moment.

"Relations with a demon are forbidden, even for Archangels," Jophiel says, with a hint of a threat in her voice.

"I'll face the consequences for that crime myself, but my daughter is innocent. If she wishes to continue her schooling at Seraphim Academy, she will stay."

"But—" Jophiel starts.

"There is nothing in the guidelines that say demons are not allowed to attend," Uriel adds. "Only that all angels must attend. That includes half-angels."

Gabriel still has his hand on my shoulder as he speaks. "We have been hard at work trying to create more harmony between the angels, demons, and fae. Having a half-demon, half-angel student here could go a long way to ease tensions with the demons."

Jophiel snorts. "I think we all know the truce with the demons isn't going to last. Especially after the recent demon attacks."

"I know no such thing," Gabriel says. "And whether or not the demon truce will last is not the question here. My daughter has a right to continue attending Seraphim Academy, and that's the end of it."

"Azrael will have many words for you about this," Jophiel says, but the fight in her voice is gone. She knows she's lost.

"I'll deal with Azrael later." Gabriel squeezes my shoulder. "Let's go, Olivia."

I jump to my feet, my head spinning, and say a quick thanks to Uriel and Kassiel, ignoring Jophiel completely, before I follow my father out the door.

Gabriel doesn't stop until we're outside the house, and then I throw my arms around him. He hesitates for a second, and then he gives me a firm hug in return. When was the last time we hugged? Or that he showed any affection for me? I can't even remember.

"Thank you," I tell him.

"It's what I should have done years ago," Gabriel says. "You're my daughter, and I should never have tried to hide you away. I love you, and I'm proud of you, and I'm sorry."

My eyes water. I've wanted to hear those words for so long, and now I think my heart might explode. Somehow this horrible day has also turned into one of the best days. How is that even possible?

He notices other students watching us and clears his throat. In fact, there's quite a huge crowd gathered outside Uriel's house, waiting for more gossip. I spot Marcus among them, and turn my back on him quickly.

"Let's get out of here." Gabriel takes my hand. Outside the house, his massive silver wings extend and he lifts into the air, letting go of my hand in the process. I spread my much smaller black wings and follow as he flies off-campus and toward Angel Peak.

I have no idea where he's taking me, but I'm pleasantly surprised when we land on top of a hill, on the front porch of a white cottage with black trim. It's super quaint, with a picket fence, square windows, and a cute red door. "Whose house is this?"

"Mine. Most of the Archangels have a house in Angel Peak." He opens the front door. "Let me give you the grand tour."

Inside, I notice how clean and bright everything is. The living room is huge, with a big fireplace and floor-to-ceiling windows showing off an amazing view of the forest stretching out below us. There's a very modern-looking kitchen with granite countertops and shiny new appliances that we walk past, and then Father leads me down a hallway into the rest of the house. He stops in front of a closed door. "This is where Jonah stays when he's not in school."

His voice is sad, and he doesn't open the door, but continues on to the other two doors. "This is my room. And this room is yours. If you want it, that is."

He opens the third door, and I glance inside a bright room with a soft yellow bedspread and white furniture. It's cute, but looks like a guest room that no one's ever used before.

"I can stay here?" I ask.

"Yes. This is your house now too. I actually got the room ready for you a long time ago in the hopes you'd come live with us, but I was too scared of what would happen if anyone found out about you." He shakes his head. "I was a coward. I should have known that keeping you close would be safer for you. You're the daughter of an Archangel, and should be treated like one."

I don't know what to say. On one hand, I'm finally getting everything I've ever wanted. On the other hand, I'm kind of pissed it took him this long to accept me as his daughter, to be honest. I spent my entire life feeling like a dirty secret, and it's hard to suddenly let that go. But at least he's trying.

He presses a key into my hand. "This is yours. I need to go find Azrael before Jophiel puts her own spin on this. I might not be around too much in the future, as my duties for the Archangel Council require me to travel a lot. But I do hope you'll stay here over the break, and perhaps we can spend some more time together too."

"Thanks, Father." I stare at the room that's now mine. I have a home. With my father and my brother. Once I find my brother, anyway.

I turn back to Gabriel to tell him what I've learned about my brother, but he's already teleported away. Damn Archangels. And seriously, why couldn't I get that power?

I'm tempted to throw myself on that sunny little bed and never get up again, but all my things are back at school. Which means I need to go back and face everyone, even though they all know what I am now.

I head outside and spread my black wings under the sunlight. I'm not hiding what I am anymore—and everyone will just have to deal with it.

47

OLIVIA

As soon as I fly into my room, Araceli runs in, her face streaked with tears. "How could you do this to me?"

"I'm so sorry," I say, emotion making my throat tight. I'm the worst friend in the world, and I deserve whatever she gives me.

More tears spill onto her cheeks. "Why didn't you tell me?"

My heart cracks at the pain in her face. "I wanted to tell you, I really did. But I was scared, I guess."

"Of all people, I would have understood!" She angrily wipes tears off her face. "But you told the Princes and not me. Why, Liv? Why?"

"I'm sorry." I don't know what else to say. Everything else feels like an excuse, but I need to try to explain. "The Princes found out, otherwise I wouldn't have told them either. But you're right, I should have told you. I made a huge mistake, and I understand if you don't want to be friends anymore."

"You lied to me all year long!" She plants her hands on her hips, and she's so upset she's shaking. "And then after demons killed Darel, why didn't you tell me *then*?"

"I should have, but I worried you'd hate me." I swallow hard. I deserve this, but man, it hurts.

Araceli lets out a long sigh. "I could never hate you, Liv. I just wish you trusted me."

"I do!" I sink onto my bed, exhausted after everything that's happened today. "I wanted to tell you so much, but I was scared to trust anyone at first. I've spent my entire life in hiding, worried about what would happen if anyone found out what I am, and I only came here to find my brother, Jonah. Then I wanted to tell you, I really did, but too much time had passed, and I knew if I told you it would feel like a betrayal."

Recognition dawns across her face. "Wait. You're Jonah's sister?"

I nod. "We have the same father, but different mothers. Mine's a succubus, obviously."

Her jaw drops. "That means you're the only true daughter of an Archangel. Wow. Why didn't you tell people who your dad is?"

"He wouldn't let me. My parents were too scared about what would happen if anyone found out about me, so they basically disowned me. I really did grow up in foster care. Almost everything I told you about me is true, other than the succubus bit."

"That's bullshit. You can't help being born to them."

I look down at the key clutched in my hand. "I know. Although that's all changed now. Gabriel came to defend my right to be here, and claimed me as his daughter."

"Good." She sits beside me on the bed. "I'm still upset, but I understand a little better. And I'm sorry about Jonah."

"Thanks. I'm convinced the Order of the Golden Throne has something to do with it." I hesitate, but there's more I've been hiding from her, and it's time she knows the truth about everything. "Jonah was a member, so I joined them too so I could try to find him. I'm sorry I lied about that too, but I wanted you to stay away from them. In fact, I'm pretty sure they killed Darel."

"What?" she practically yells.

"They wanted you in the Order bad, I think because of your fae blood. They thought if they killed Darel and made it look like a demon attack, they could convince you to join them. Luckily you saw through their bullshit and stayed away."

She wraps her arms around herself and trembles, staring off into space as she absorbs my words. "I might have joined, if you hadn't convinced me not to. How do you know they killed him?"

"I don't know for sure, but I followed them after one of the trials and heard them discussing their plans. I stayed hidden using my Ishim powers, and this necklace." I touch the aquamarines. "My succubus mother gave it to me. It's a fae relic that allows me to lie and hide what I am."

"So you do know how to use angel magic after all." She turns to me with wide eyes. "What else have you lied about?"

I hold up my hands in surrender. "That's it. You know everything now. And I've always tried to be as truthful as possible with you about who I am, otherwise. I'm no different than I was before you knew I was part demon, I swear."

"What's going to happen to you now?"

"Uriel says it's okay for me to stay here, so I guess I'm coming back next year. I'd like to be your roommate again, if you'll let me."

"Of course you can be my roommate," she says. "We're still best friends, and next year I'm going to help you find Jonah and take down the Order after what they did to Darel. I just...need some space to come to terms with all this, okay?"

I've held myself together all day, but Araceli saying we're still best friends is what finally makes me fall apart. Tears fall from my eyes, and I'm so grateful to know someone with such a good soul. I truly don't deserve her, and I'll do everything I can to be the friend she needs from now on. I nod quickly through my tears. "I understand."

She wraps her arms around me, and together we cry and rock and hold each other. Then she wipes her face, says goodbye, and leaves the room. As I pull myself together, she gathers her bags and flies off to meet her family. The dorm room feels much darker and emptier after she's gone, but at least I know we're still friends.

There's another knock on my door, and I wonder if it's Kassiel again, but when I open it I see Grace instead.

"Oh, Olivia. How are you?" she asks in a sympathetic voice.

"I'm doing okay," I say, as I let her in.

She gives me a quick hug, and then steps back. "I can't believe Callan did that to you, but at least your father's accepted you now."

"You...don't seem surprised."

"About Gabriel?" She shakes her head. "No, I knew all along. Jonah told me about you. I didn't know about the succubus part though. That was a surprise, but I don't care. You're still Jonah's sister, and that's all that matters to me."

"Thank you, Grace." It's a relief to have another person on my side. I lead her to the sofa, and we sit next to each other, so close our knees bump. "I came here to find him, but I haven't been too successful. I know he was in the Order though—and I'm guessing you are too."

"Yes, I'm the one who nominated you." She gives me a serene smile. "And you're the one who got attacked by the demon at the last trial."

"How did you know?"

"It was me who led you out of the cave, and I had a feeling it was you. Besides, I knew you'd make me proud. You're Gabriel's daughter, after all." She grabs my hands and squeezes them tight. "I'm so glad this is all out in the open now. Next year we can attend Order meetings together, and we can work on rescuing Jonah, plus we'll have Ishim classes. It'll be great."

"You know where Jonah is?"

"Yes, but I only found out recently. He was sent to Faerie to find the Staff of Eternity, but he never returned, and we haven't received any messages from him. I've been so worried about him, and the Order had this plan to send someone back to Faerie, but it didn't work." She sighs and looks down at her hands with sadness in her eyes. "But maybe with your help, we'll be able to bring him back."

"We will. I'll make sure of it."

She nods and stands up. "I need to get going. Did I tell you Nariel is my uncle on my mother's side? Well, we're all going to Orlando for the holidays, and we're heading out tonight. My little brother is going to lose his mind. He's never been to Disney World before."

I laugh at how mundane it all is. Angels like amusement parks too, I guess. "That sounds like fun."

"Do you want to come with us?" she asks.

"No, I'll be okay, but thank you."

She gives me a quick hug and then stands. "Oh, before I go, there's one last thing you should know. The Princes are also in the Order. They know what happened to Jonah too. In fact, they've known from the very beginning. But I guess you already know you can't trust them."

"Yes, I've learned that lesson well today." My anger returns, and my hands clench at my sides.

Grace takes off, and once again I'm alone in my dorm. Soon the entire campus will be empty. It's time to pack my things and leave Seraphim Academy behind for the next few months.

But first, I need to confront the Princes.

48

MARCUS

I fly toward the bell tower, so mad at Callan I can barely see straight, and totally shocked by what I just saw outside Uriel's house. I need to speak to the other Princes, immediately. They had better fucking be there.

When I arrive, Bastien is arguing with Callan, although they both go quiet once they see me. I land and walk straight to Callan, then pull my arm back and punch him in his face as hard as I can. It's like hitting steel, but I don't give a shit. "How could you?"

"I had to!" Callan says, as his head whips back around after my punch. "You wouldn't listen to me, none of you."

"We told Liv we wouldn't expose her, and then you did it anyway. Without even telling us." I turn my angry gaze onto Bastien. "Or did you know?"

Bastien looks away, and I see a rare flash of emotion cross his face. Guilt? Regret? I can't tell. He's so hard to read, even though I've known him my whole life. "I helped him get the recording of their kiss, but I didn't know what he would do with it."

"You knew it wouldn't be anything good!" I yell. I'm actually shaking with rage now. I care about Liv so much, and I can't believe they would do this to her. Don't they care about her at all? "What is going to happen to her now? She's going to be kicked out for sure, but what if the Archangel Council decides she should be killed or locked up or something?"

"They won't do that," Callan says. "All they'll do is make sure she doesn't come back next year."

"How the fuck do you know?" I'm still yelling and I don't plan to stop anytime soon. "And what about the demons? When she gets kicked out, who will protect her then? They're already searching for her!"

"I was planning to hide her somewhere safe." Callan's jaw clenches. "I know this is extreme, but we had to keep our promise to Jonah. He knew she wasn't safe here, and now we can protect her in other ways."

"You idiot," I say. "Olivia is Jonah's sister."

The announcement hits him in the face even harder than I did. "No fucking way."

"How do you know?" Bastien asks. He's probably annoyed I found out before he did, but he can suck it. He should have stopped Callan before any of this happened. "They look nothing alike."

"I saw her and Gabriel outside Uriel's house. He called her daughter, and then they flew off together. Probably to take her somewhere safe." For all I know, that's the last time I'll see her, and my heart clenches tight at the thought. I think I might be in love with her, and I might never be able to tell her that.

"Gabriel's daughter..." Bastien says to himself, as he stares out the window. "This changes everything."

"No, it doesn't," Callan says. "Jonah still told us to keep her away. Now we know why."

"He wanted us to protect her," I argue. "He would never in a million years want you to fuck up her car, trash her room, or expose what she is to the entire school. That's the opposite of keeping her safe."

Callan says nothing, but he looks away, the muscle in his neck twitching. Awkward silence stretches between the three of us as we remember our crimes against Olivia. I feel like a total shithead for being involved with any of that, and then I have another horrible thought. I've been sleeping with Jonah's sister. After I also slept with Grace after he disappeared. Worst. Friend. Ever. I'm no better than Callan or Bastien, it turns out.

The silence is interrupted when Olivia herself bursts through the open window of the bell tower, her black wings spread wide and her entire body glowing slightly. She looks beautiful and fierce, a perfect combination of light and dark, angel and demon.

"You betrayed me," she says, in a cold voice I've never heard her use before. "Why?"

"I made a promise to Jonah," Callan says. He plucks her photo from his wallet and holds it up. "Before he disappeared, he made us swear to keep you away from this school—for your safety. Nothing else I did worked, so I had to expose you. It was the only way."

"Nothing else—" she starts, and then her eyes widen as she puts it all together. "The notes. My car. My room. You did all that?"

"We did," Callan says.

Her eyes sweep across the room, leveling accusations at me and Bastien. "I can't believe I trusted you."

I step forward and hold out my hands in peace. "I had nothing to do with exposing you, I swear. Or the notes, or the car."

"But you helped trash my room! You broke my mug!"

I hang my head. "Callan broke the mug, but yes...I was there. I'm so sorry."

Liv turns to Bastien. "And you?"

He stands a little taller, like he's resigned to his fate, but he still has that guilty look in his eyes. "I am complicit in all of the same things as Marcus, and I also helped Callan retrieve the video of your kiss. I do apologize. I would not have done such things if I'd known you were Jonah's sister."

"So you all know that too." She shakes her head, her hands in fists. "Jonah gave me that mug. It's the only thing I had from him, and you destroyed it."

"I had no idea know he gave it to you," Callan says. It's probably the closest he'll get to saying sorry. Callan does not apologize. "I figured it was just a silly mug."

"I came here to find Jonah. I believe he went to Faerie, and if he told you to keep me away from this school, then he must have suspected he wouldn't return. Do you know what happened to him?"

Wow, she knows a lot. I open my mouth to tell her everything, but Bastien shoots me a look, before saying, "No, we don't."

He must be trying to protect her, even now. We have to keep her safe from the Order. They'll want to use her or hurt her, now that word's out about what she is. Seriously, what the fuck was Callan thinking?

"Sorry, but I don't believe you," she says. "In fact, I'm pretty sure you're lying and you know exactly what happened to him. After everything you've done to me, I can't trust you at all."

"Everything we've done has been to get you to leave and fulfill our promise to Jonah," Bastien says. "And if we're keeping secrets from you now, that's why."

"We're not bullies, not really," I say, but it sounds pathetic, even to my ears.

Olivia snorts. "Even without the way you treated me, you walk around this school like you own the place. If you don't want to be bullies, try treating people like equals instead of the dirt on your shoes."

Okay, she has a point there.

"I stand by what I did," Callan says. "You don't belong here, and Jonah knew it. Plus you showed up here and turned Marcus on his head, and now Bastien is just as bad. I can't stand the sight of you, but I can't help but want you anyway. We can't have a succubus using her powers at this school."

She puts a hand on her hip and cocks it. "Hey, asshole, I've not sent a single ounce of my powers toward you. So, if you can't stop thinking about me, guess what? It's because you want me for who I am, not because of what I am. But I'm happy to tell you that your plan failed. I'm coming back next year. And the three of you? Can stay the hell away from me."

"Liv, wait." I reach for her, but she pulls away, and her glare shuts me up fast.

"No. I thought we were friends, or maybe even more. But we are done."

She flies out of the bell tower, and I'm half tempted to follow her, but sense it would be useless to try to talk to her right now. I spin around and face the other two Princes.

"We're done too. I want nothing to do with either of you. I'm over your bullshit." I shake my head at them in disgust. "Olivia deserves better."

I don't wait for a response before I take off. I need to figure out how to get Olivia back, and I have a feeling it's going to involve a lot of groveling.

49

OLIVIA

I head back to my dorm room and finally let myself fall apart. I cry, and I hit a pillow, and I eat up the last of the ice cream in the fridge, then drown myself in coffee—after throwing the mug from Marcus against the wall. It doesn't break, because even my fucking mug is against me. It's obvious he got it for me as a guilt gift, and I want nothing to do with it.

Or with any of the Princes. I'm certain they're lying to me about Jonah, especially after what Grace said, and I can't forgive them for what they did to me throughout the year. I blamed so many things on Tanwen, and even pranked her in return, when it was the Princes all along. Specifically Callan. He vandalized my door. He sent me horrible notes. He ruined my car. And they *all* trashed my room.

Then they committed the ultimate betrayal by exposing me, after getting me to trust them and promising they wouldn't tell anyone what I am. Marcus might be innocent in that crime, but Bastien is as guilty as Callan is, and I can't forgive any of them. I'm not sure I ever will.

Next year, I'm going to make them pay.

By the time I pull myself together, it's gotten late, and the campus is pitch black and empty. Everyone else has left. But there's one last person I want to talk to before I go, and I have a feeling he's waiting for me too.

I set down by the lake, and Kassiel is already waiting there, still wearing his suit from earlier. He jumps up from the bench and steps toward me with a worried expression.

"Olivia, are you all right?"

"It's been a rough day, but I'm...okay," I say. "Thank you so much for your help today. I appreciate you standing up for me and for just being there."

"Of course. Everything I said was true. You do deserve to be here, and I'll always do whatever I can to help protect you."

All year long I worried he might expose me, but in the end, he proved to be one of the few people I can trust. It's a strange realization that I have only two real friends at Seraphim Academy, and he's one of them.

"Why help me?" I ask softly, stepping close to him. He's so ridiculously handsome, and it's been a while since I really allowed myself to fully take him in. The moonlight enhances the highlights in his dark hair, and his lips look so soft and kissable. I can't stop staring at them.

He reaches up to stroke my hair. "I care about you, Olivia. You know I do."

"I care about you too," I whisper. Originally it was just lust and attraction, but over the last few months it's turned into more. Our little midnight meetings by the lake became one of the highlights of my week, and I wished so many times that he wasn't my professor, even though he was also a damn good one.

He's looking at my lips too, and then our eyes meet again. He looks as conflicted as I feel, and he's still touching me, trailing his hand down my cheek now. We're standing close together, very close, and I'm not sure how that happened.

"Fuck it, I can't wait two more years," he suddenly growls, and then our mouths meet at the same time. His arms pull me against his chest, and I circle his neck with my own, never wanting this moment to end. Our kiss is desperate and hungry, filled with months of longing and the memory of that one night we spent together, and then his energy hits me, hard. He's so incredibly strong, maybe equal to Callan, but he tastes totally different from the Princes, just like I thought. They taste like light, and the finest wine, and hardy potatoes.

He tastes like whiskey and filet mignon.

And darkness.

I pull away from him and stare up at his green eyes. Eyes a lot like mine.

Demon eyes.

"You're a Fallen," I whisper.

He looks down at me in the darkness, seeing me perfectly, and his lips press into a tight line. "How did you know?"

"You taste different from angels. Before I thought maybe I was remembering it wrong, since it had been a while since I fed on you, but now I know for sure—you're a demon. But you have wings too, so you must be a Fallen." My eyes widen as I connect all the dots. "The other demon, the vampire the Order tortured—I told him I was undercover on a mission for Lucifer, and he mentioned another demon at the school said the same thing. That's you, isn't it?"

"It is." He tilts his head and studies me. "You're a member of the Order?"

"I am now, yeah. And so are you."

He nods. "I started teaching here to find out if the Order is a threat. But you're not on a mission from Lucifer."

"No, I just thought it would be something the demon might believe, especially once I showed him I was a succubus."

"You told him that?" he asks, his face concerned. "That means the demons know you're here."

"Yeah, it seems the cat's out of the bag now. Everyone knows about me."

"Things could get very dangerous for you now. Be careful. Why *are* you here anyway?"

"I'm trying to find my brother Jonah, who disappeared last year. The Order sent him to Faerie, and I'm going to bring him back."

He takes my hand. "Then we'll work together. I can't let the

Order get the Staff of Eternity. They'll start another war, and I won't let that happen."

I squeeze his hand. "Me neither. And I promise I won't tell anyone what you are. You can trust me."

He leans down and brushes his lips against mine. "I know."

"Uriel knows you're a Fallen though, doesn't he?" I ask.

"Of course he does. He knows everything, and he thought it would be good to have a demon professor on campus." He hesitates. "I'm not sure we'll be able to hide a relationship from him, and I can't afford to get fired. Now you know why I've had to resist you this year."

"I understand." I take his face in my hands and give him one more quick kiss. "We can't be together. Not yet. But maybe someday."

"Someday," he says, then kisses me again. Harder this time, like he can't stop himself.

I'm the one to pull away. I want him so badly, but I can't get him in trouble either. I need his help. "Until then, we're allies. We'll stop the Order together."

A dark smile crosses his lips. "With the two of us infiltrating them, they have no chance."

"I'll see you next year," I tell him, and then launch myself into the air before I throw him onto the grass and take what I need from him. I have no idea how I'm going to resist him for the next two years, especially when I know he cares about me as much as I care about him, but we'll have to find a way. He's the only one I can count on to help me fight the Order from the inside.

I fly back to my father's cottage and begin to make a plan for my second year at Seraphim Academy. First, I'm going to bring the Princes down, and then I'm going to rescue Jonah. I'll learn everything I can about Faerie and the Staff, and I'll do whatever it takes to find him. He's alive, I know it, and if anyone can bring him back, it's me.

Because I'm not just a succubus. I'm the daughter of an Archangel too.

SINFUL THINGS

SERAPHIM ACADEMY BOOK TWO

1

OLIVIA

S ome days I forget I'm half demon and I live on light like any other angel. Other days I wake with a raging hunger for sex and remember there's no escaping my succubus side.

Today is one of those days.

I held off for as long as I could, and then debated going back to bars to pick up strangers, but in the end, I contacted Bastien for help —again. I've been using him to feed over the last few months, and he's never questioned or commented on my sudden requests. I'm sure he's only here out of some sense of obligation to my brother, but I'll take whatever I can get.

I suck all the lust and desire out of him as I stare at my soft yellow bedroom walls. Allowing myself to get into the feeding isn't an option, so I turn off all my emotions, even the raging anger I feel toward him. It's still a good meal because Bastien is incredibly powerful and damn good in bed, but there's a reason I called him and not Marcus. With Bastien, sex is a quick and easy business transaction between two people, and nothing more. That wouldn't be the case with Marcus—and sex with emotions is an *entirely* different experience.

For a second the emotions manage to creep back in anyway, and my heart pangs as I think about how it could've been if the Princes had been honest with me instead of trying to bully me off campus. Damn it, now I'm mad again.

Bastien must sense the change in me, because he stops pounding into me from behind and flips me over. He takes my chin and turns it to the side, then presses his face against my neck almost tenderly. He breathes me in deeply like he can't resist, but then his cock plunges into me hard, and the moment is over. We're back to business, and it's a relief to lose myself in the feel of him thrusting in and out of me.

He never lets me go unsatisfied, even though it's not part of our deal, and he reaches between us and finds my clit with his very talented fingers. I can't help but groan as he strokes me in the right way to drive me wild. By now, he knows exactly what it takes to get me off, and he doesn't hesitate or delay. I don't want to feel, but for a few seconds all I do is feel, feel, feel, and my legs tighten around his hips to draw him further inside me. The climax ripples through me, and he joins me moments later, hitting me with a rush of power. His face is right beside mine, and I start to turn my head to kiss his perfect lips, before I remember who we are and what we're doing and why I very much do *not* want to kiss Bastien.

When I've soaked up all the energy I can from him, I push him off me and straighten my clothes, avoiding his eyes. Bastien stands and pulls up his slacks, which we only yanked down to his knees in our haste. He buttons them as he walks toward the bedroom door, and I watch his tight ass as he moves away. At least the view is nice.

"I appreciate your assistance," I say in a stiff voice. Nice views don't cancel out what he did to me.

"Are you sufficiently sated?" he asks, his voice equally stiff.

"Yes, thank you."

He nods and then walks down the hall with his nose in the air. *You think you're doing me this huge favor, you ass.* But I don't say it out loud, because technically he is doing me a favor. Of course, he also gets to sleep with a hot succubus as part of the deal, so I think he's doing pretty well for himself.

I open the front door for him, and the beautiful sunset streams through with the still-crisp air. It's the beginning of March, which means school starts in a few weeks. I've been living in my father's house in Angel Peak for the last few months over the break, and although it's been nice to finally have a home, I'm eager to head back to Seraphim Academy.

Bastien pauses in the doorway, while the sun makes his black hair shine like raven feathers. "We'll be in school the next time you need to feed. I'm sure Marcus will be willing to provide that meal."

I cross my arms. "Not going to happen."

Marcus would want to grovel and apologize and tell me how much he cares about me, and I am so not in the mood for that right now. I'm far too pissed to give him an inch, and I doubt he'll be okay with me using his body and sending him on his way, like I'm doing with Bastien now.

Bastien scowls. "We both know feeding on one person alone isn't going to cut it."

"Have a good night," I say in my coldest voice, and begin closing the door on him. He's right, of course, even though I hate to admit it. I'll have to find another solution soon, or risk draining Bastien dry.

He clamps his mouth shut and walks outside. *Finally.* I watch him head down the porch steps, where he spreads his dark silvery wings and launches into the air in the direction of campus. When he's gone, I breathe deeply, trying to calm myself down. My anger is hard to swallow when the Princes are around. Even though Callan was the true instigator of the events last year, Bastien and Marcus were just as complicit. I won't let them off easily, if at all.

Over the break, I've been plotting my revenge. I have several tricks up my sleeve for the coming school year to get payback for what the Princes did to me. All three of them need to be knocked down a peg, not just for my own pleasure, but because they have to realize they don't rule the school anymore. And forgiveness? That's not in the cards. Not unless they convince me they're really sorry. The only one who might succeed is Marcus. Bastien is good for a quick meal, at least. But Callan? He's a lost cause. I picture him on his knees, begging for my forgiveness. Not a chance.

They deserve what I have planned for them.

Other than plotting my revenge, I've spent my winter break trying to figure out how to rescue Jonah. He's been missing over a year now, and my heart aches every time I think of him, but I refuse to believe he's dead. By infiltrating Seraphim Academy's secret society, the Order of the Golden Throne, I learned that Jonah went into Faerie to find the Staff of Eternity, the magical object used by Michael and Lucifer to end the great war, close off Heaven and Hell, and bring all angels and demons to Earth permanently. The Order wants to use the Staff to send all the demons back to Hell and reopen Heaven so they can try to rebuild it. I have no idea why my brother volunteered to get the Staff, but something bad must have happened once he got to Faerie, or he would have returned by now. My guess is the fae found him and have him locked up somewhere— and I won't rest until I bring him back to Earth.

Seraphim Academy has a spectacular library, and over my break I spent much of my time there searching for information on how to get to Faerie or on the Staff of Eternity. Sometimes I ran into Kassiel there, but I tried to avoid him as much as possible. After the kiss we shared at the end of last semester, the sexual tension between us has only grown stronger. The attraction popped and sizzled between us whenever we were in each other's presence, but we've both agreed we can't give in to our lust again, not until I graduate anyway. Teacher-student relationships are forbidden at Seraphim Academy, and I don't want to do anything to put his job in danger. Especially since he's my only true ally at the moment, and I'm going to need his help if I'm going to find Jonah and stop the Order.

I have a huge journal full of notes, but no clear plan yet. I'm hoping that once I take Fae Studies this year I'll be able to fill in all the gaps in my knowledge. It might take me some time, but I won't give up until I find my brother and bring him home. *I'm coming for you, Jonah. Stay alive for me. Please.*

I take a quick shower to wash Bastien off me, and put all the Princes and Kassiel out of my mind. The less I think about them, the better.

2

OLIVIA

I n the morning, I head into the kitchen to fix myself something for breakfast, but groan when I open the fridge. Almost empty. I'll have to head to the store for one last supply run before it's time to return to campus. At least I still have plenty of money left from the allowance Aerie Industries provides students for attending Seraphim Academy. I barely spent any of it last year, so most of it is hidden in my bedroom here under a loose floor board. I keep my new golden robes from the Order in there too.

I grab a slightly stale croissant off the counter and munch on it as I walk into my bedroom, then look around with satisfaction. My room was pretty sparse when I moved in, and I've managed to decorate it on a tight budget with some cute pillows, flowing curtains, and a few little trinkets here and there. The room feels like mine now. For the first time, I belong somewhere. I just wish Jonah could be here too.

I dig my boots out of my closet, where they've been buried under a few days of laundry. With a sigh, I pick up the clothes and drop them in the hamper. No reason to be a total slob just because I'm here on my own without anyone popping in to judge me.

Gabriel comes to visit me every few weeks, but things are always a little awkward between us. We spent Christmas together, but it was a sad affair, between the lack of Jonah and the fact that Gabriel and I have barely had anything to do with each other for the last twenty-two years. He did get me a new winter coat though, which was nice, and I could tell he was trying, at least. He stayed for a week then, and it was almost a relief see him go at the end of it. I appreciate that he's claimed me and is making an effort to be a true parent for once, but we'll need some time to figure out how to be a family.

Especially since Gabriel still doesn't believe me about Jonah being in Faerie. I explained everything about the Order—which he knew about, of course, and said he's been monitoring for years—but he claimed he already spoke with the High King of Faerie, who assured him Jonah wasn't there. Which means the king doesn't know, or he's lying.

Honestly? I think it's easier for Gabriel to believe Jonah has run away, rather than to face the truth that he might be imprisoned...or worse.

I grab the coat he got me, which is bright, lipstick red with white fake fur trim around the neck. It's big and loud and practically screams, *I'm done hiding, deal with it.* I love it, especially because it shows Father does know me, at least a little bit.

Not having to hide who I am has been a welcome change, along with all the snow over the winter. I was in no way prepared for living in the mountains of northern California, but loved it all the same. Every time I wanted to go out, I layered on pretty much all of my wardrobe, but the coat helps with that.

There's no snow now though, and the sun is shining high, filling me with light as I fly into the main part of Angel Peak, the small town near Seraphim Academy that only angels can visit. It's been pretty empty all winter, since angels hate the cold and tend to migrate into warmer climates like birds. But with Seraphim Academy starting in only a few days, people are returning to town, and the quaint little shops are busy again.

I land on the sidewalk and retract my black wings into my back. The entire street seems to pause all at once in order to stop and stare at me, and I can't tell if the looks are angry or fearful. Now that everyone knows I'm both half-demon and the daughter of an Archangel, people treat me differently. No one is outright rude, because no one dares to insult Gabriel's daughter, but some move out of the way quickly to avoid me, and others cast me hateful glares, like I'm tainting their town by being in it. I can't decide which is worse.

I quickly hurry into the local coffee shop, and it's probably my imagination, but I think I hear a collective sigh of relief from the street as the door shuts behind me. It's a relief to be away from their judgmental looks too, except when I move to the counter to order, I see someone who makes me nervous all over again. Araceli.

Things didn't end great between us last semester, and I'm still riddled with guilt over that because I know it was all my fault. Araceli was my roommate and my best friend—sometimes my only real friend—during my first year at Seraphim Academy, but when she found out I lied to her the entire time about who and what I am, she was pretty upset. I tried to mend the relationship as best I could, but she said she needed space, and I respected that.

I debate rushing out of the place, but then she spots me, and it's too late. I have to face her now. She's wearing her lime green combat boots, and has that purple streak in her dark brown hair, and I have to admit, it's really good to see her. I just don't know if she feels the same about seeing me.

I approach her at the counter and we stare at each other awkwardly, before I finally ask, "How was your break?"

Araceli surprises me by throwing her arms around me. I instantly have tears in my eyes as I hug her back. "Oh, Liv," she says. "I missed you."

"I missed you too." My voice only cracks a tiny bit. "Are we...good?"

She pulls back and smiles at me. "We're good. Like I said, you're still my best friend. I just needed some space." She pokes her finger at my chest. "And you better not lie to me ever again."

I let out a long breath as the tension leaves my body. "I won't. I promise."

"Good. I'll get a table so we can catch up."

She grabs her coffee and heads off to a round table in the corner, while I step up to the counter. The barista doesn't meet my eyes, even though I've been coming here once a week for months now. She knows my order by heart though, and hands it to me immediately, then takes my payment quickly before darting off to be anywhere else. I give her a big smile and drop a few coins in the tip jar anyway.

With my giant cup of liquid heaven—yes, the coffee here really is that good—I sit down across from Araceli. "How have you been?" I ask, with more confidence this time.

"Good. I spent the break with my mom, and that was nice, but I came back a little early to get settled in before school starts. I'm staying with my aunt now. She has a five-year-old, and he's cute, but a total monster, so I came here for an escape." She takes a sip of her coffee. "What about you? How was your break?"

I shrug as I warm my hands on the coffee mug. "It was okay. I spent a lot of time researching and learning about the fae. I don't feel like I'm any closer to finding my brother, but I should ace Fae Studies this year at least."

She laughs. "You better, with me as your roommate. I took that last year to see if I could learn anything new about my heritage."

"And did you?"

"A little, yeah. My dad told me some things of course, but he left out a lot. It was good to have an outside perspective on it all too."

Araceli rarely mentions her half-fae dad, and I guess I was too self-absorbed before to notice that. Worst. Friend. Ever. But I'm totally going to do better this year—it's one of my goals, along with getting revenge on the Princes and finding my brother. "You don't talk about him much."

She stares into her coffee mug. "My parents separated a few years ago and things got weird after that. At first he came to visit me every weekend, but then it became more like every month, and now it's like once a year."

"Does he live in Faerie?" I ask. "Have you ever been there?" The

Order wanted to use Araceli to get into Faerie to find Jonah. I won't use her like that, but she did offer to help me however she could.

"No. Dad was a messenger between the fae and the angels, and both sides grudgingly accepted him because he was useful. Then he met mom, they fell in love, and then I was born. The fae excommunicated him after that. I guess having a child with another angel was the final straw for them. He can't go back to Faerie without being killed, and I'm not welcome there either."

"I'm sorry. I had no idea."

She shifts uncomfortably and shrugs. "I don't like to talk about it. I'm only a quarter fae anyway, so I just focus on my angel side and don't worry about the rest."

I take a bite of my burrito and nod, even though I think she might be making a mistake. Try as she might to deny her fae heritage, Araceli will always have some of their blood. There's no escaping it. I know that more than anyone.

"Anyway, Dad lives in Florida now, and we don't talk much. When I do see him, it's pretty awkward."

I snort. "I know all about awkward encounters with dads. Christmas with my father was definitely uncomfortable at times."

"I bet. But hey, at least he's trying."

I nod and take a sip of my coffee. "He is, and I appreciate that. Maybe once Jonah is back it won't be so awkward anymore."

She gives me a pitying look. Like everyone else, she probably believes Jonah is dead. "I'll do whatever I can to help you find him."

"Thanks. I appreciate that."

She sips her drink again before raising her eyebrows at me. "How's the, ah, *eating* situation going?"

I lower my voice, even though there's no one sitting near us. "I've been using Bastien for a quick meal. It's working for now, but I'll need to figure something else out soon."

"What about Marcus?"

"I'm not sure I want to open up that can of worms again." I sigh and sip my coffee. "Marcus would grovel, and try to win me back, and tell me how much he cares, and I'm not interested in any of that.

Bastien is an emotionless bastard, and that's exactly what I need right now."

"And Callan?"

My eyes narrow. "Callan deserves what's coming for him."

"What do you mean?"

"I've been thinking about ways to bring them down a notch or two, and I have a plan."

Araceli grins and leans forward. "I'm in. Whatever it is, I'm in."

3

KASSIEL

I land in front of Gabriel's house in Angel Peak, silently retract my black and silver wings, and adjust my tie. I'm wearing a heavy coat, even though the cold doesn't bother me at all, but I have to keep up the appearance that I'm an angel. Only two people at Seraphim Academy know what I truly am—Uriel and Olivia. Perhaps that's why the Archangel sent me to collect Olivia, and when he asks me to do something, I have little choice but to obey. As a Fallen, I don't need to bow to his authority, but as a professor at Seraphim Academy, I have to respect the headmaster. I'm only allowed to teach at the school because of his good will, and I appreciate that he keeps my secret for me. If the angels found out a demon was teaching their students, they'd have me fired...or worse.

And if anyone finds out about me and Olivia? It would be just as bad.

Not that anything is happening with Olivia at the moment. We slept together before I became her professor, and there's nothing we can do about that. The kissing at the end of last semester is another story, but nothing like that will happen again, not as long as she's a student. We've both agreed to keep things strictly professional between us while we work together to take down the Order of the Golden Throne.

That's the true reason I'm at Seraphim Academy, and I spent the break trying to research them, along with the Staff of Eternity. Of course, that only brought me closer to Olivia, since she was also researching the same things. That's how we ended up at the library together several times this winter. And every time I saw her, it grew harder to deny my feelings for her.

I'm determined not to let my desire for Olivia alter the way I treat her, though. She's my student, and I want her to get the most out of what I can teach her while she's at Seraphim Academy. Even though I have an ulterior motive for being a professor, I take my teaching very seriously, and in Angelic History classes I try to present the past as neutrally as possible. Angels and demons have fought for centuries, but now that the war is over, I hope the new generations can grow up in peace, without the old stereotypes and hatreds. I took this job as a special assignment from Lucifer himself, but I've come to enjoy it, and I care about my students. Especially one in particular.

But I won't take advantage of her, or show favoritism, or anything else that men in authority positions have a tendency to do. Especially human men.

My hand freezes before I strike the door. Coming to Olivia's house feels like a major violation, and an even bigger temptation. I remind myself I'd do this errand of Uriel's for any student, no matter who they were. I raise my fist and knock on her door.

Olivia answers wearing a tight tank top that is trying desperately to hold her large breasts flat and failing, with some matching yoga pants. Her hair is tied back and there's a sheen of sweat on her face that makes me think she was exercising. I can't help but remember when I had that body pressed up against the wall as I pounded into her, and she had that same sheen of sweat as she clenched around my cock.

"Kassiel?" she asks, leaning against the doorway. "What are you doing here?"

I force my gaze upward, away from the allure of her upper

thighs. It takes me a moment to remember why I'm here. "Uriel sent me to fetch you. He wants to speak with you immediately."

Concern floods her features. "Why?"

"I don't know, but he said it was urgent."

"Come in, please."

My eyes can't help but travel the length of her body again. "I'd rather not."

She rolls her eyes. "I won't jump your bones, I promise. I just need a few minutes to change into something else."

"Probably a good idea." I step inside the house. Archangel Gabriel's house. If he knew there was a Fallen standing in his living room, he'd probably teleport here in an instant to eject me from his land. And if he knew I'd slept with his daughter once, he'd probably have my head.

Olivia slips away, and I stand in the living room awkwardly while I wait. The big windows offer a gorgeous view, but I'm more interested in the bookshelves, which are full of human novels. Old classics, written before I was born, and new bestsellers too. The spines on most of them look worn, as if they've been read many times.

"My dad loves to read human books," Olivia says. "Everything from the tawdriest romance novel to the driest of the classics."

I turn as if barely interested and see she's put on a pair of jeans that hug her curves and a black sweater that dips down in a V and accentuates her breasts. I'm not sure she could wear anything unflattering. All succubi are incredibly sexy, and Olivia is the most alluring one I've ever met.

She opens a closet and pulls out a bright red coat with a white fur collar. "Let's go."

I can't help but chuckle. "You can't be that cold, not with demon blood in you."

"I'm not overly sensitive to the cold, like an angel, or the heat, like a demon. I'm more like a human in that way. But I grew up in LA, so I'm still kind of a wimp about the cold." She heads outside and locks the door behind us. "Ready?"

"Are you nervous?"

"A little." She looks up at me with those mysterious eyes. "I'd be more nervous without you at my side."

My chest tightens, and I have to look away before I grab her, kiss her, and tell her everything will be okay, I'll make sure of it. I can't do that, but as much as I can be there for her, I will. She's still my student, I remind myself. The most attractive student I've ever seen in my life, but still. Just a student, for two more years anyway.

I have a feeling they'll be the longest two years of my life.

4

OLIVIA

Flying next to Kassiel is a wonderful kind of torture. He's the only other person I've met with black wings, which are rare but not unheard-of among angels, and common among the Fallen. Most of the angels in last year's Flight class had white, gray, or brown wings, and Araceli has the most beautiful wings of all—white with purple, the same color as the streak in her hair. Along with her pointed ears, they're the only thing marking her as part fae.

As we fly, it's hard not to steal glances of Kassiel in his sexy black suit, with those silver and black wings spreading from his back, especially when I can still feel his lust for me. His reaction to seeing me in my yoga clothes washed over me before either of us had time to utter a word. His desire for me has given me nice snacks in between meals from Bastien. In all the time we spent together over the break, I never felt him crave any other woman in the library, even though there were several very attractive angels shooting him obvious come-hither looks. He never even noticed.

But he's not mine. He can't be mine, not until I graduate from Seraphim Academy in two years. Not unless we want to put his job and everything we're trying to do in jeopardy.

I'm just not sure how we'll be able to resist each other that long.

Now I'm flying toward campus with him right beside me, with his lust hovering between us. I'm starting to think facing Uriel might be easier than being around Kassiel without acting on our feelings for each other. Because it's not just lust we share, but something more. Something I definitely can't think about right now.

The forest below us gives way, and the gleaming white buildings of the campus greet us, along with the sparkling lake. Spring is in the air and the grounds are a verdant green, with flowers beginning to bloom along the walkways. I draw in a deep breath. I came to Seraphim Academy under false pretenses in order to find my brother, but to my surprise I came to love it here over the last year. When the Princes tried to get me expelled, I pleaded my case so I could stay, and it wasn't only because of my hunt for Jonah. I wanted to stay here for me, too.

As we approach the headmaster's house, my stomach twists. Why does Uriel want to see me two days before class starts? Is it to tell me he's changed his mind, and I'm not welcome at the school anymore? What else could it be?

We land in front of Uriel's Victorian house, which looks too quaint to be a part of the campus. I've been in his office a few times before, and it was never a pleasant experience. I hesitate and turn to Kassiel. "Are you coming too?"

"I am," he says, as he leads the way inside.

That's a relief. Going at it all alone has been my MO my entire life, and it's nice to have someone in my corner for once. Someone other than Jonah, anyway. My brother's the only one who ever had my back—and now it's my turn to return the favor by rescuing him.

Kassiel opens the office door and stands to the side so I can enter. As soon as I get a view of the room, my blood runs cold. Uriel isn't alone. Sitting across from his desk in one of the wingback leather chairs is a man so coldly handsome it takes my breath away. With long black hair casually draped around his broad shoulders, piercing blue eyes, and sharp cheekbones, he looks like the kind of man who'd haul you over his shoulder and take you back to his evil lair.

"Please come in," Uriel says, and indicates the chair beside the other man. "This is Baal, the headmaster of Hellspawn Academy."

My eyes widen. Baal is the Archdemon of the vampires. Whatever this is, it can't be good.

"I'm pleased to meet you, Olivia." The vampire stands and holds out his hand. Like Kassiel, he has an English accent, except his sounds more formal. Older. Ancient.

I reach out and shake his hand. I expect it to be cold and clammy, like a dead person's, but then remind myself that just about everything in movies and TV shows about vampires is wrong. They're not dead, they can go out in sunlight, and garlic does nothing to them except give them bad breath. It's only his eyes that are cold as death, even as he gives me a charming smile.

"Please, have a seat. I don't bite." He winks at me with those ice-blue eyes.

Oh, yes you do. I'm reasonably sure he won't do that in front of Uriel though, so I sit at the edge of the leather chair. Kassiel moves to stand directly behind me.

Baal lifts his gaze over my head and narrows his eyes. "Kassiel."

"Baal." Kassiel's voice is flat, and I glance back to see him crossing his arms and staring the Archdemon down. I wonder how they know each other, and if it's safe for Kassiel to be here with me. I appreciate his support, but I don't want him to get in trouble on my behalf.

Baal's gaze returns to my face. "Olivia, I'm here to secure your enrollment at Hellspawn Academy."

I nearly fall out of my seat. "My enrollment?"

"As the first angel-demon hybrid, it's only right you spend half your time at Hellspawn Academy." He smiles at me, but it's the smile of a lord looking down at one of his minions and expecting them to drop into a bow.

"I appreciate the offer..." I swallow. How can I word this delicately? "But I'd prefer to stay here."

"I'm not sure you have a choice." Baal is still the epitome of polite, but he's got a strong undercurrent of darkness too, and it's clear he expects to get his way.

I don't look behind me to see how Kassiel reacts, but he shifts and his hand brushes against my back. I'm pretty sure he's gripped the top of the chair.

Uriel clasps his hands in front of him on his big mahogany desk. "If Olivia wishes to stay here, then she shall. We can assure her safety here."

Thank you, Uriel.

Baal leans forward. "She will be perfectly safe at Hellspawn Academy too. I can promise you that. It's important she learn about her demon side, as much as her angel side. Not only so that she can know our history from our point of view, but so that she can learn to control her powers and not be a threat to others."

"I've been trained," I interject. "My mother spent a considerable amount of time with me when I came of age so I could learn to use my succubus powers safely."

Baal arches an eyebrow. "And your mother is...?"

I shrug casually, and hope my necklace protects me from lying to Archdemons too. "A succubus named Laylah. I don't know much about her."

"Hmm." Baal's face turns thoughtful. "Nevertheless, there are many things we can teach you that the angels can't."

I'm intrigued, I will admit. I do want to learn more about my demon side. But I need to stay here to find Jonah and take down the Order. I can't do that from Hellspawn Academy. "Sorry, but my place is here."

"Would it be an acceptable compromise if a demon taught her about your kind here on campus?" Uriel asks. "I already have one of the Fallen in place who can do that."

Kassiel adds, "It would be my honor to teach her about our ways."

Baal doesn't look happy about this, but he doesn't object either. He shifts in his seat and crosses his long, muscular legs. He really is hot, but his age radiates off of him like a heatwave. He's thousands of years old, as old as my parents. Not for me, thanks.

"Fine," he drawls. "Kassiel can teach her about our history and our laws, but I want a succubus to test her to make sure she is properly trained in that area, as well." I start to protest, and Baal shoots me a hard look that instantly renders me silent. "Even though you say you've been trained, let us be the judge of that. We cannot have an untrained succubus draining humans dry all over California. You'll meet with a succubus of my choosing, or you'll attend Hellspawn Academy. Your choice."

I want to argue that it hasn't been a problem for that last four years, but I guess I understand his need to be cautious. I'm not super excited about more classes with Kassiel either. It's going to be a lesson in restraint for both of us, at least.

"All right," I reluctantly agree. "Anything else?"

"That will be all." Baal stands to his tall height and flashes me a dangerous smile. "It has been an absolute delight, Ms. Monroe. Archangel Uriel." He purses his lips. "Kassiel."

"An honor to see you again, Archdemon Baal," Uriel says.

The vampire gives Uriel a nod, and then walks out of the room. I relax in the leather seat as soon as he's gone, and my eyes wander around Uriel's office. I spot the shadowy black feather floating in a glass case, and wonder again whose wings are missing it. I also eye his private bookshelf and the forbidden book I stole from it last year. I feel a little guilty about that, but I had to do it to get into the Order. At least it got returned at some point.

Uriel steeples his fingers and meets my eyes. "Olivia, as I'm sure you've surmised, Kassiel is a Fallen and not an angel. He's working here as part of an initiative to improve angel-demon relations, but we're not ready to reveal what he is yet to the school. I trust you to keep this secret as part of the condition for remaining at Seraphim Academy."

I nod and pretend this is news to me. "I understand. I won't tell anyone."

"Good. I'll add weekly training sessions with Kassiel to your schedule. I'm not sure when the succubus will arrive, but you'll have to find time for her lessons as well. Do you have any other questions or concerns for me?"

"No," I say. "But I appreciate your support. Thank you for letting me stay here."

"Of course," Uriel says. "You belong here as much as anyone does. I'll see you at orientation tomorrow."

That sounds like a dismissal, so I nod and leave the room, with Kassiel right behind me. Once we're outside, I give him a smile. "Thanks for staying with me."

"You're welcome." Kassiel frowns and stares down the road away from the house, before looking back at me with a warning in his eyes. "This deal with Baal is the best we could have hoped for, although the succubus will obviously be spying on the school for the Archdemons."

"Uriel must realize that," I say. "Otherwise he wouldn't have agreed."

"I'm sure he does, and he probably has a spy of his own at Hellspawn. Just be careful, Olivia."

"I'm always careful. It's how I've stayed alive this long on my own."

"I know, but things are different now. Everyone knows who— and what—you are, and both angels and demons will want to use you." His mouth twists. "Or they'll want you dead."

5

OLIVIA

I t's the first day of school...and time to face the Princes.

Araceli and I moved back into our dorm room yesterday, and then went to Uriel's orientation, where he went over the rules and introduced us to the new teachers. I was relieved to see I'd never slept with any of them this time.

As I head outside into the sunshine and breathe in the crisp air, I glance at the bell tower. It's a habit to look for the Princes' shining metallic wings, even though I dread the idea of seeing them. Luckily, the bell tower appears empty.

Unfortunately, my first class of the day is Combat Training, which means I'll have to face Callan. The one saving grace is that Araceli shares the class with me, so I don't have to walk into the danger zone alone.

I keep my head high and my shoulders square as I walk into the gym with my friend at my side. I spot Tanwen first, who is playing with her straw-colored ponytail, and she gives me a little nod. It's unexpected, and I'm not sure what to do in return. Then my eyes land on Callan.

Somehow over the last few months I forgot just how incredibly handsome he is, and I nearly stumble as it hits me all over again.

Short golden hair. Bright blue eyes. Muscles for miles. He's delicious. And I should know—I've kissed him twice now.

My eyes narrow as I remember how he played the video of our second kiss to the entire school to show I was a succubus. The bastard betrayed my trust and revealed my deepest secret in an attempt to get me expelled. He said it was for my own good, that he was doing it because my brother told him to keep me away from the school, but I don't buy it. He did it because he wanted me, and he couldn't handle wanting a demon. Even one who's half angel.

His eyes are hard as he stares back at me, and he crosses his arms. It feels like a challenge, but he should know by now that I'm not going to back down. I move to stand along the wall, still meeting his eyes, and only look away when Professor Hilda's voice announces the start of class.

"Welcome back, Second Years," Hilda says with a grim smile. She's one of the Valkyries and looks like she could tear a man in half with her bare hands. I pity anyone who would try to mess with her. "This semester, we're learning weapons."

She indicates the far wall, where a myriad of different types of weapons are displayed on several tables. "Callan is going to help me demonstrate the proper use of each of these weapons over the next few classes, and then you're going to try each of them out. Over time, you'll find an affinity for one of them. By the end of the year, I expect you to be able to pick up any weapon and use it without injuring yourself in the process, and to be well-trained in the weapon of your choice."

Callan walks over to one of the tables and picks up the first weapon, a huge two-handed sword. My mouth waters a little as he lifts the heavy blade with ease. Hating him would be a lot easier if he wasn't such a perfect specimen of masculinity.

"Sit," Hilda says. "Get comfortable."

The wrestling mats are on the ground, and Araceli and I settle down behind the Valkyries. Tanwen shoots me a look as I pass by her, and I wonder what her deal is this year. Is she preparing her next verbal attack, now that she knows I'm part demon? I realize she wasn't behind the notes and vandalism last year, like I initially suspected, but it's not like she's ever been nice to me either—and that was back when she thought I was half-human. How much worse will it be this year?

Hilda talks about the proper use of the sword, including stance, grip, and footwork. I try to pay attention to everything she says, but it's hard to keep my eyes off of Callan. Every time that asshole swings his sword, he makes sure to do it while looking directly at me. As if he's imagining thrusting the blade into me with every strike.

Or maybe he's thinking about thrusting something else into me.

I shift a little on the mat at that thought, trying to ignore the growing heat between my thighs. It's hard though, when Callan keeps swinging that sword like some kind of sexy barbarian warrior. I'm a modern woman who doesn't need a man to save her, but sometimes it's pretty hot knowing a guy *could* save you if you were in danger. Even if I hate him.

He glares at me like he knows what I'm thinking about, and I give him a seductive wink in return because I know it will annoy him. He practically seethes, and I only smile wider. I can't wait 'til he sees what I have planned for him.

By the time class is over, I could use a cold shower. The good news is, I'm pretty sure which weapon I'm going to focus on this year—the dagger. It's a weapon of stealth and skill, perfectly suited for me, whereas Callan is more attuned to weapons that require brute strength. Maybe Hilda will be the one training me, instead of him.

As the class heads out of the gym in a big group, someone moves past me and bumps my shoulder hard.

"Sorry," I mutter, the apology coming automatically.

"Why don't you watch where you're going?" The guy that plowed into me jerks away and stares at me as if I've just vomited on him. "Don't touch me again, demon filth."

I blink at the guy as he rushes away, and it takes me a second to remember his name. Jeremy. He was in my Flight class last year, and I never really paid him any attention. He didn't seem interested in being my friend, but he wasn't particularly rude or anything. He never gave me a reason to think badly of him, until now.

"Whoa," Araceli says. "What was that about? He's never acted like that before."

"He obviously has a strong opinion about demons, and I'm sure he's not the only one." I push the door open to go out toward the lake and pretend the encounter didn't hurt my feelings. I'm still the same person I was last year, but not everyone is going to see that. They were already standoffish before when they thought I was half human, and I imagine it will only get worse now.

"Don't sweat it," Araceli says. "Not everyone will be a dick, I promise."

Probably not. But if I expected my second year at Seraphim Academy to be any easier than my first, I'm already being proved wrong.

6

OLIVIA

I'm relieved to see Raziel is teaching Fae Studies this year, and even happier when he gives me a kind smile as I step into his classroom. He looks exactly the same as he did last year, with his friendly face, salt and pepper hair, and quirky bowties. Today's is white with black Scottie dogs on it.

I got an A last year in Demon Studies, naturally, and I'm hoping to do just as well in this class. Thanks to my research over the summer, I know more than the average angel or demon about the fae. I'm hoping this class either reinforces that knowledge or teaches me something I don't know already. I trust that Raziel will keep things fairly unbiased, like he did in Demon Studies, even though the things I most want to know probably won't be covered in the class. Like what the fae do with their prisoners, and how to rescue one.

I take a seat at the front of the classroom and get out my notebook, then groan out loud when Bastien walks in. I should have known I'd share this class with at least one of the Princes.

He doesn't even give me a glance. We might as well be strangers, except he sits at the desk beside me even though most of the classroom is still empty. I arch an eyebrow at him, but he ignores me as he pulls out a black Moleskin journal and a pen. As he slowly flips to a blank page, I glimpse very precise handwriting in black ink, with no doodles or anything else. It's all so very Bastien.

"Welcome to Fae Studies," Raziel says in his cheerful voice once class starts. "I'm so happy to see some familiar faces here. This year we're going to learn all about the reclusive fae, along with the world they live in, Faerie. Though most of you probably won't have any encounters with the fae other than at the school's sports games, it's still important to learn about them, because you never know when things might change."

I lean forward, pen poised, greedy for whatever knowledge Raziel can impart upon me—and not just because I hope it will help me find Jonah. Surprisingly, I'm actually really curious about the fae. The Olivia of a year ago would have laughed at the person I've become. I never cared all that much about school before coming to Seraphim Academy.

"Just like there are different types of angels and demons, there are different types of fae," Raziel continues. "They're divided into four Courts, based on the seasons. Each Court has its own king or queen, but they're all ruled by the High King of Faerie, who united the courts after the Faerie Wars. We'll talk more about those wars in upcoming weeks, but first let's go over some basics. What do you know about the fae already?"

Jeremy raises his hand. Ugh, he's in this class too? "They have pointed ears."

Raziel nods. "Yes, they do, and a few of them even have wings, although that's pretty rare and mostly found in the royal families. What else?"

"They're weak against iron," another student calls out.

"They can't lie," someone else adds.

"All very true," Raziel says. "Although they're very good at misdirection and twisting their words, so that even though they're speaking the truth, they're not actually being honest. You must be very careful to never make any bargains with them, especially since they're famous for being tricksters. They're also known for being cruel and inhuman, mainly because they see themselves as better than all other races, which makes them somewhat callous."

I could say the same thing about some of the angels I've met so far, like the ones in the Order. I wouldn't be surprised if there are demons like that too. Then again, even among humans there are people with superiority complexes and hatred of people who are different. Discrimination and prejudice seem to be universal traits, unfortunately.

Raziel continues giving a basic introduction and overview of the fae, until our time is up and the students begin to file out. I'm starting to think Bastien and I might ignore each other forever, but as we exit the room he gives me a little nod. "See you in class tomorrow."

Before I can reply, he turns on his heel and stalks away. I check out his ass again, because hey, why not. A succubus can look, can't she?

My next class is Ishim Training, taught by Nariel. I met him briefly last year, and he tested my Ishim abilities about a week ago. I debated playing inexperienced again, but decided I didn't want to get stuck in the First Year class with the newbies. Thanks to my father's training, I suspect I could have been placed with the Third Years in skill level, but I'm happy to be in this class with the other Second Years.

When I enter the room, I'm surprised to see Grace there, since she's a year ahead of me. Her normally pale skin has a nice tan, and her strawberry blond hair seems especially bright, like all the Florida sunshine over the holidays made her even more beautiful.

She gives me a kind smile and a light hug. "How have you been?"

"Good. How was your trip to Disney World?"

"So much fun," she says. "My little brother loved it, and it was a nice distraction from everything that happened last year."

Grace was my brother's girlfriend, and she seemed to really care about him and worry about his disappearance. However, she's also a member of the Order of the Golden Throne, so I can't entirely trust her, even though I wish I could. She knew he went to Faerie, and knew I was his half-sister, and didn't tell me anything until I found out on my own. I can't forget that, even though she might have had her reasons.

"What are you doing in this class?" I ask.

"Nariel let me test out of the Third Year class, and now I'm working as his teacher's assistant in the hopes of becoming a professor someday. With the way the school is growing every year, they're going to need a lot more teachers soon."

"That's great. It'll be nice to have a friendly face in the class." The only other student I've heard of testing out of classes is Callan with Combat Training. I bet it helps that Nariel is Grace's uncle. I don't see any resemblance between the two of them though. Nariel almost looks like an albino, with very light hair and very pale skin. He must have lathered on the sunblock while in Florida, because he didn't get even a hint of a tan while they were there.

Ishim class goes by quickly, and after a small lunch in my dorm, I head to my fourth class of the day—Angelic History. Kassiel gives me the subtlest of nods when I walk in, and I raise my eyebrows at him. Last year he only taught the 101 class, but now he must be teaching this one instead. Did he switch to 102 because I'm in it? It feels arrogant to think so, but it feels right too. I'm pretty sure he did it to be close to me, even though it would be a lot easier for us if he wasn't my teacher anymore—no more sexual tension distracting me in class, for one thing. But at the same time, I'm relieved to see him standing at the chalkboard. He's a good teacher, and I like being around him, even if it's torture of the best kind—his classes are always a mixture of barely contained desire and interesting stories.

I sit in the front row and cross my legs, and his green eyes drop down to them. He swallows hard and looks away for a moment, but then he looks back, like he can't help himself.

Oh yeah, he likes the torture just as much as I do.

Light Control is my last class of the day, and it's out by the lake, probably so we can soak up the sunlight. They chose this mountain in northern California for Seraphim Academy because it's one of the sunniest places in America, and today doesn't disappoint. My angel side wants to stretch her wings and soar over the lake, but I settle for taking off my sweater and letting the light sink into my skin.

The teacher, Eileen, is a red-haired angel with freckles on her nose, and her eyes widen with a hint of fear when she sees me. Great, even a professor is scared of me now.

"Angels and demons both use life force to fuel their powers, and they need to recharge that in different ways," she explains. "Angels use light, and demons have different ways of doing this depending on their type. The Fallen use darkness, vampires use blood—"

"And succubi use sex," a Valkyrie I don't know says with a smirk.

Eileen's face turns bright red and she glances at me quickly before looking away. "Um, well, yes. As I was saying, in this class you'll learn how to best recharge yourselves, and how to use your light magic in ways you might not have thought of before."

Like my other classes, this one is mostly an overview of what to expect during the year, and I find my attention wandering. My gaze drifts over the lake, watching the breeze make tiny ripples in the water, and then I spot Marcus standing on the other side. Looking directly at me.

I'm going to have to face him soon—and I'm so not ready.

7

MARCUS

I'm going to be late to my Human Studies class, but I can't keep myself from stopping to watch Liv in her Light Control class. It's outside next to the lake, and her dark brown hair shines under the bright sun as she listens to the professor. She's so beautiful it makes my chest hurt, and I long to go to her and beg her to take me back.

I managed to stay away from her over the winter, even though it was hard. Especially when I found out she continued sleeping with Bastien, even though she's still pissed at him. I understand why she did it, but they both know she needs to feed on more than one person, and dammit, it should be me helping her, not anyone else.

I'm filled with guilt at the thought. Now that I know she's Jonah's sister, I can't look at her the same way without feeling like I've betrayed my best friend somehow. Jonah would kill me if he knew what happened last year, although maybe he'd cut me some slack if he knew I slept with her to keep her safe and healthy. Does that make it okay to sleep with your best friend's sister? Could he ever forgive me?

Of course, that's not the only thing I'm going to have to answer for, if we ever find Jonah. In a moment of weakness, when it was clear Jonah wasn't coming back, I slept with his girlfriend, Grace. It was a monumental mistake and we both regretted it immediately and swore we'd never bring it up again. I've avoided Grace ever since then, but I'll have to own up to that with Jonah, and tell him how sorry I am.

I head to my Human Studies class, but I find it hard to concentrate on anything the professor says. Callan is in it too, but I shoot him a cold look and sit on the other side of the room. I haven't spoken to him or Bastien after they betrayed Liv, and although I miss them, I'm still pissed at them too.

Afterwards, I head back to my dorm to get ready for soccer practice. It's going to be intense, because the fae always kick Seraphim's ass at the sport, but I consider skipping it anyway because I just don't care. Ever since school ended last year, I've been feeling...lost.

I step into the elevator to my dorm, the one I still share with Jonah even though he's been gone more than a year. I hate going back there. It's too empty, and every time I glance at his door, I'm reminded that he's gone and probably never coming back.

Olivia steps into the elevator just before the door closes, and she stiffens when she sees me. For a few seconds we're alone, and I have to say something. I have to try.

"Liv," I say. "I missed you."

She doesn't answer, but just stares at the elevator door. It's going to open any moment now and she's going to leave. Before I know what I'm doing, I hit the STOP button and the elevator jerks to a halt.

"I'm sorry," I continue. "I never meant to hurt you, and everything I did last year was to protect you."

Her unusual green eyes cut to me sharply. "Trashing my room was protecting me?"

I cringe, but at least she's talking to me now. "Yes, in our own way, or at least we thought so at the time. It was stupid though, and I should have stopped Callan and Bastien. We should have been honest with you from the beginning."

"Yes, you should have."

"But you weren't honest with us either. You could have told us Jonah was your brother."

She props her hands on her hips. "I had no reason to trust you. And then I *did* trust you, and Callan betrayed me anyway."

"Callan is a dick, and I haven't spoken to him in months. I'm pissed at him too, but I had nothing to do with him betraying you. You have to know I'd never do anything to hurt you." I draw in a deep breath. "I am sorry for what I did though. I'll say it a hundred times, if necessary, until you believe me. A thousand times. A million."

She glances away, her shoulders dropping. Maybe I'm finally getting through to her. But then she pushes the STOP button again, and the elevator hits the second floor.

"I believe you're sorry," she says, as she walks out. "But I just don't care."

The door shuts with a thud after that, and the hollowness inside me feels like a black hole I can't escape from. I've never felt this way about a woman before. In fact, before Olivia I slept with a new angel every month, and they all knew it was just a bit of fun and nothing serious. Then Liv came into my life, and nothing was ever the same again.

All I can do is keep trying to win her back. I screwed up last year, but I'll make it up to her, somehow. And I think I have an idea how.

8

OLIVIA

My first week of classes is pretty uneventful, other than the constant looks from other students. Most of them avoid me, which is fine by me. At least Araceli still treats me the same. It's good to be living with her again, even if she insists on waking up at the crack of dawn, something I doubt I'll ever get used to.

On Friday, it's time for my first demon lesson with Kassiel, and it's held in his office in the professor's building, with their housing on the floors above. I wonder what his apartment is like. Is it all organized and refined, like he is in class? Or is it super messy, a way of letting himself go in his own private space? I long to find out.

When I step into his office, he's taking off his suit jacket and loosening his tie. I stop in the doorway to admire him as he relaxes a little. When he rolls up his sleeves, I have a hard time not unbuttoning his shirt one pearly white button at a time. I have a feeling these lessons are going to be even more torture than his classes.

Kassiel is off-limits, I remind myself.

"Hello, Olivia. How was your first week of school?" His voice is so formal. I might as well be any other student, not one who's tasted him before.

"Fine," I say, trying to keep my tone even too. I sit in the chair in front of his desk.

He sits across from me. "After what happened the other week, I thought I'd begin our lessons with a little about the Archdemons, starting with Baal."

"Probably a good idea. I know a little about them from Demon Studies already, but I'd like to hear your side of things." Mother also told me about them, but she didn't spend much time talking about demonic history. She focused on how to be a succubus. How I would survive without getting caught and without killing anyone.

"As you probably know, Baal is the leader of the vampires and the headmaster of Hellspawn Academy. What you probably don't know is how well-respected he is among the demons."

"I guess that makes sense, if they trust him to teach their children. Just like Uriel is well-respected among angels."

"Exactly. Plus vampires are a charming bunch at their worst, and Baal is the most powerful vampire there is. He has the power to dominate entire groups of people and bend them to his will, and he's ruthless and determined. I can't be sure he doesn't want to supplant Lucifer as leader of the demons, but if so, he's got another think coming."

"It's 'another thing coming,'" I mutter absently as I remember the darkness in Baal's eyes.

Kassiel opens his mouth to continue talking, but then closes it and stares at me. "No, it's 'another *think.*'"

I roll my eyes. "There's a whole song about it. It's 'thing.'"

"I've been alive for more than a century, and you want to question me?" he asks, with a hint of teasing in his voice.

I tease him back, unable to stop myself. "This has nothing to do with age. I've lived among humans all my life. I know what I'm talking about."

"Let's find out." He opens his laptop, presumably to search online for the answer. It doesn't take him long to find it. "Ha! I was right."

He turns the screen toward me, and I read about the phrase, which has suddenly become the most important thing in the world.

The phrase was originally 'think,' but... "No." I shake my head. "I'm right. Modern slang has changed the phrase to 'thing.' So there." I close his laptop with a click and cross my arms.

"Maybe we're both right, but I was right first because originally it *was* 'think.'" He sits back in his desk chair and grins like he just ate a big canary.

I lean forward and grin even wider. "And I'm right *now*, because we live in this century and not the previous one."

As we stare at each other, something shifts between us, and our fun argument seems more like verbal foreplay. His eyes drop down to my cleavage, which is on display as I lean forward on his desk. I sit up quickly, my cheeks flushed with heat.

He tugs on the collar of his shirt and looks away pointedly. "This is dangerous."

"It doesn't have to be." I fold my hands in my lap like a proper student who is not thinking about banging her professor right here on his desk, nope, definitely not. "We got sidetracked by the argument. Tell me more about the Archdemons. What about the Fallen one?"

Kassiel clears his throat as he gets back into professor-mode. "The Fallen are technically led by Lucifer, but since he's the leader of all demons, Samael acts as his second in command and handles most Fallen issues."

"What's Lucifer like?" I ask. "You must have met him before, since you're here on a mission for him."

"He's...intense. It's hard to say no to him." He stares off into space, and then shakes himself and comes back to reality. "In Demon Studies, did they mention that Las Vegas is a hotbed of demon activity?"

"Yes, and they said that Lucifer controls most of the casinos there."

"He does. In Vegas, demons can feed without drawing too much attention to themselves. What they didn't tell you is that Lucifer set everything up to take over the casinos almost immediately after the Earth Accords were signed. He'd been planning it for a while."

"That's definitely not in the textbooks."

"I'm not surprised. Few know that Lucifer and Michael privately debated for a long time on how to best end the wars. The Earth Accords were in development for many years before they actually happened."

"Really?" I raise my eyebrows at him. "Do you think Lucifer killed Michael?"

Kassiel's eyes narrow. "No. I know he didn't. And why would he? Lucifer and Michael were friends, or as close to friends as they could be, considering the circumstances. What reason would he have for killing Michael now that the war is over, anyway?"

"I don't know." Unlike the angels at the school, I don't have an opinion on the matter. It does seem odd to me that Lucifer would kill Michael now that angels and demons are at peace, but maybe I don't have all the facts either.

Kassiel's face darkens. "The angels want to believe he did it, but they're rarely rational when it comes to demons. It's easy for them to blame Lucifer for everything bad that happens. They've been doing it for centuries, after all. Why stop now?"

He has a point. How many sayings are there about Lucifer? *The devil made me do it.* A convenient excuse, for sure.

Kassiel seems pretty worked up about this topic though, so it might be time to change the subject. "What about Fenrir?" I ask. "The shifter Archdemon?"

"He's angry, as most shifters tend to be, but he's good at controlling it. He's also one of the few Archdemons who doesn't live in Vegas. He prefers to be in the background, usually in the wild, staying out of sight and controlling his kind from the shadows. Lilith is like that, too. A true nomad."

I sit up a little at the mention of the Lilim's Archdemon. "What can you tell me about Lilith?"

Kassiel pauses, like he's considering what exactly to tell me. "She's very old and very powerful. Also, she's smart. Probably one of the most intelligent creatures I've ever met."

"Oh, really?" I've never heard anyone talk about her except with a negative connotation. Her reputation is almost as bad as Lucifer's, but maybe that's more angel propaganda.

"She's very mysterious as well, and is always on the move. I'm told she's impossible to track down, unless she wants to be found. Even though she's technically the Archdemon of the Lilim, she lets Asmodeus handle most matters for her."

"Asmodeus?"

"Her son."

My mouth falls open, although I quickly close it. "She has a son?"

"Yes. I believe she's had a few children over the years. I'm not sure how many are still living though."

"That's unusual, isn't it?" I ask. "For one of our kind to have so many children?"

"It is, although she does get around a lot, if you get my meaning."

I do. I very much do. "Why does she move around so much?"

He shrugs. "Most Lilim are nomadic. They can't take a human lover for more than one night, and they would need multiple demon lovers to survive, so most don't bother with that. Traveling allows them to feed without repercussions." He pauses and his brow furrows. "Speaking of that, are you...? No, never mind, inappropriate question."

I'm very tempted to ask if he wants to give me a snack. The truth is, I'm hungry, and I'm going to need to feed soon, and not on Bastien again—but I can't tell Kassiel that. So all I say is, "I'm surviving."

He nods slowly. "Good." A moment of awkwardness hangs between us before he says, "I think our time is up."

I practically jump to my feet, because now that I've started thinking about feeding on Kassiel, it's hard to stop. "Thanks for this lesson. I wasn't sure if I'd learn anything from these meetings, but I did."

"I'm glad," Kassiel says, as he walks me to the door. My arm brushes against his, and a bolt of lust shoots through me. I'm not sure if it's from me or him. "We'll meet next week at the same time."

As soon as I escape the room, I breathe a sigh of relief—and regret.

I'm starting to think going to Hellspawn Academy would have been easier than this.

9

OLIVIA

I t's becoming increasingly obvious that people are terrified of me. Grace usually has a table full of people sitting with her at dinner, but the minute I sit down, the place becomes a ghost town. Students who would've come to eat with Grace veer off in a different direction. But Grace doesn't seem to mind, and I'm used to people treating me like dirt. At least they aren't actively trying to kill me. Yet.

When I get back to my dorm, there's an invitation to the next meeting of the Order of the Golden Throne sitting on my bed. My first one as a true member.

I still can't believe they kept me in, but I suspect they have ulterior motives. Their main purpose is to rid the world of demons, after all. How can they do that and allow a half-demon in their midst?

Kassiel's words come back to me. *"Be careful. Everyone knows who—and what—you are, and both angels and demons will want to use you...or they'll want you dead."*

Good thing I'm always careful.

The next night, I pull my new golden robes out of my hiding spot behind my desk, along with my mask. Last year I was only an initiate of the Order of the Golden Throne and wore a white robe for these meetings. As I pull the shimmering material over my head, I'm reminded of how far I've come since then. I passed all their tests and proved myself to them, even with my demon blood. I don't agree with the Order's beliefs or their methods, but I infiltrated their ranks in order to find my brother, and now I hope to learn more about their plans and to uncover the identities of their members. I know Kassiel is a member—he was sent by Lucifer himself to infiltrate the Order and see if they're a threat. We've already agreed to work together to stop their grand plan—to retrieve the Staff of Eternity to send demons back to hell.

I need to find out who their leader is, most importantly. He or she is the one who ordered Araceli's boyfriend, Darel, killed. They made it look like a demon murdered him in an attempt to get her to join the Order, but I convinced her to stay far away from them. They want to use her fae blood to get into Faerie, although neither of us is sure how exactly—something else I hope to learn from the Order.

The meeting tonight is earlier than the ones last year, and it's in their secret lair under the lake. I make myself invisible using my Ishim powers, and fly to the large boulder in the forest. As I fly lower, I spot another golden-robed member appear out of the night, as if made of shadow. That must be Kassiel. As a Fallen, he can control darkness, although I've never seen him use his powers before. It eases my nerves to know he's going to be with me at the meeting tonight, that I have an ally among the other masked members.

Of course, I know some of the other people in the Order already. Grace. Cyrus. The Princes. But I'm not sure I can call any of them allies.

Kassiel opens the boulder, and I follow him down into the dark, damp stone tunnels leading under the lake. At the end of the tunnel, far below the surface, is a large cavern with over a dozen people sitting in a circle, all wearing gold robes and matching masks. Kassiel and I take a seat on the last empty stone bench.

The leader of the Order wears a gold crown and stands before us, in front of an ancient gold throne carved with depictions of angels and demons in battle. I've never seen our leader sit on the throne before, but maybe that will happen tonight. Otherwise, who is meant to sit there?

The leader speaks, but the masks are magically enchanted to distort voices, so I can't tell if it's a man or a woman. "Welcome, members of the Order of the Golden Throne. I'm pleased to see you all back with us for another year. We have much work to do."

He or she strides forward, and a shoe peeks out from under the robes. Black loafers, too big to be female, although some of the Valkyries have pretty big feet. It's impossible to tell from the voluminous robes, but I get the sense it's a man.

"As this is the first meeting of the year, let me remind everyone of our three basic tenets. One, angels are superior beings, meant to guide Earth and humanity to a brighter future. Two, demons are evil and must be eradicated from Earth to protect humanity. And three, loyalty to the Order is paramount, along with discretion. Anyone who speaks of the Order outside of these chambers will face dire consequences."

He continues on about the Order's long history, and I glance around at the other members, wondering which is Grace. I look for feminine builds, but the robes are very good at concealing body types, which I'm sure isn't an accident. Everyone else is a mystery. There are three large figures sitting together, who could be the Princes, but it's hard to tell for certain. Cyrus must be here somewhere, probably at Grace's side. I wonder if Jeremy, who hates demons so much, is here too. If so, he'd probably lose his shit if he discovered I was a member. It's probably a good thing my identity remains hidden from most members of the Order at this meeting. Only when people graduate do they learn who else is in the Order.

"Has anyone made any progress in our goal to retrieve the Staff of Eternity from Faerie?" the leader asks, drawing my attention once again. I hold my breath, but no one answers. Good.

Finally one person speaks up, their voice unreadable due to the mask. "Perhaps we should try to get that fae-blooded girl to join us again."

Another person adds, "Or we could kidnap her and force her to help us. She must know how to get into Faerie."

"She doesn't," I speak up, even though it draws attention to me. I don't care though—I can't let them hurt Araceli. "She was raised among angels and knows nothing about her fae side."

"I agree," says one of the people in the cluster that could be the Princes. "She is worthless. We must find another way."

"We could use the fae at one of the upcoming soccer games," a person across the room says. "Perhaps we can kidnap one of them and force them to open a portal."

I have to bite my lip to stop from speaking out against this idea. This is exactly why I'm here—to learn their plans. Even if I disagree with them.

"A valid idea," the leader says. "One that we must ponder. However, getting to Faerie is only the first step. We must find the Staff once we are there, and Faerie is large and dangerous. It won't be easy."

"And we need to find Jonah too," another of the Princes says. My bet is Marcus.

The leader inclines his head slightly. Not really an answer, I notice. "Continue your research," he says instead. "You will also be sent an individual task throughout the year, which you must complete. Do not fail us, or your punishment will be swift and severe."

His chilling words wash over me. What kind of things do they want us to do? Last year they had us manipulate humans and torture demons as tests, so I'm not looking forward to whatever these new tasks are.

"We will meet again soon," the leader continues. "For now, we must welcome the new initiates in the woods. They should be there by now, and we will form a circle around them. Do not speak. I will address them and assign them their first test."

He turns and walks up the pathway to the exit, and the circle follows in single-file silence. Once outside in the cool night air, we move through the forest to surround the initiates in their white robes. I have no idea who they are, but they peer around the clearing and wring their hands. I remember exactly what it felt like to be in their shoes.

Our leader gives the same speech he gave last year, and ends with giving the initiates the task to steal an important object from one of the professors. We're all dismissed, and we disperse silently into the shadows, slipping away like eels into the dark night.

I attempt to follow one of the other members for a short time, hoping to uncover who they are, like I did with Cyrus last year, but they turn invisible and I lose them. And when I get back to my room and remove my mask, only then do I realize that I didn't really learn anything new at the meeting. Dammit.

10

OLIVIA

On Sunday, the school's yoga classes on the lawn start up again, and it feels good to settle into the familiar poses. The combination of yoga and sunlight help keep my hunger to a low simmer, which is easy to ignore as long as I don't let my gaze settle on Kassiel...or one of the Princes.

Tanwen's in my yoga class too, and I cringe a little as I remember our big fight last year. I keep expecting some of her bitchy commentary now that she knows I'm a demon and has even more material to work with. Surely she must hate me—she's a Valkyrie, after all. They're raised from childhood to fight in the Angelic Army against demons, and she probably considers me an abomination, like many others do. My very existence is forbidden, after all.

I wait for the insults or taunts the entire class, but all she does is give me a little nod at the end, when we all grab our things and walk away.

Odd.

I spend the rest of the afternoon doing my homework and reading, which is light since classes just started. Araceli and I order in pizza from Angel Peak and watch old episodes of Friends. Every time I spot the purple streak in her hair—which I know now is not dyed, but part of her fae heritage—I'm reminded of what the Order said and how they want to use her. I'm doubly glad I'm her room-mate again so I can protect her from them. I'm not letting anyone hurt my best friend.

After we say goodnight, I glance out the window toward the bell tower. Are the Princes up there tonight? Do they still gather there to lord over the rest of the school like kings? A pit hardens in my stomach at the memory of being up there with them. When they found out I was a succubus. When they threw me a birthday party. When they betrayed me.

It's time to begin my revenge.

I throw on a hoodie and slip outside, using my Ishim powers to go invisible. The necklace my mother gave me protects me from any Ofanim who might see through my angelic powers, but it hardly matters because there isn't another soul out tonight. Not at this late hour. Angels are definitely not night owls...and I definitely am.

I stroll toward the parking lot with a bag over my shoulder containing the means of my revenge. This is only stage one, my opening shot, and after tonight, they'll know its war between us.

My poor, battered Honda sits on one end of the parking lot. Last year, Callan broke my windshield and left me a note telling me I didn't belong at Seraphim Academy. It wasn't cheap getting it fixed, and now it's time to get even.

Callan's convertible Audi stands out from the rest of the cars, with its ostentatious red color and shiny silver rims. I slowly run my hands along the side of it, knowing no one will see me, not even the video cameras that are trained on this lot. Is Bastien watching them now, wondering if I'll sneak out again for a quick meal? Probably. But he won't see anything tonight.

I remove the canister from my bag and put on a mask over my mouth and nose. Still invisible, I begin my work, and can't help but grin as it comes out even better than I expected.

It takes me hours, but it's worth it. So very worth it.

I can't wait to see Callan's face in the morning.

———

"Y̶ou're up early," Araceli says, when she exits her room in the morning to grab a cup of coffee.

I'm already dressed and getting my bag ready. "I want to get to the cafeteria early. Care to join me?"

"Sure," she says. "Any particular reason why?"

"It might be entertaining," I say with a sly smile.

Araceli raises her eyebrows. "You started, didn't you?"

"Maaaaybe."

She lets out a whoop and runs back into her room to throw on some clothes. Five minutes later, we're heading out of our dorm, and I'm pleased to see there's already a crowd gathering in the parking lot. We join it, along with other students who can't help but be drawn to the spectacle. No one is outright laughing, but I see a lot of grins and hear hushed whispers and giggles, like we're all sharing an amusing secret. And in the center of the crowd is the thing we're all staring at—Callan's convertible Audi, no longer bright red, but now a glittery hot pink that sparkles under the morning light. Across the top of the windshield, pink and white letters spell out PRETTY PRINCESS. It looks like a real-life Barbie car.

"I can't believe you actually did it," Araceli says. "Respect, girl."

A hush comes over the crowd, and even though I don't turn my head, I know the Princes have arrived. Two of them, anyway.

Callan stomps through the parking lot, practically shoving people out of the way. The crowd parts like water, and when he gets that first view of his car, his whole body tightens with fury. His rage is beautiful in its intensity, and the students in the crowd no longer think it's funny. They step back and duck their heads, as if they're afraid to be caught looking at my prank.

"Who did this?" Callan roars, glancing around, sending people scurrying like pigeons.

Bastien leans over and says something quietly in Callan's ear, and then the two of them turn toward me as one. Pure hatred fills Callan's eyes as he glares at me, and an aura of angry white light surrounds him. Bastien rests a hand on his shoulder, and I wonder what would happen if he wasn't there to hold the beast back. Would

Callan shoot me with his burning light? Would he run over and throttle me right here, in front of all these other students?

I stare Callan down, meeting his challenge head on, and give him a sinful smile. His face is absolutely priceless as his fury only grows, but I'm not afraid of him. He's already done his worst to me, and now it's my turn.

I turn on my heels, toss my hair, and walk away. If he wants to retaliate, he'll have to come after me.

Bring it, baby.

———

C allan skips Combat Training that morning. Maybe he's too angry to face me. Maybe he's trying to figure out how to get the pink sparkly paint off his car. Whatever the reason, Hilda isn't pleased by his absence, but shows us how to wield an axe with practiced ease anyway.

"I used this move to cleave through an incubus once," she says with a wicked grin, while she slices the heavy axe through the air. Then she glances at me and her smile drops, like she's worried she's insulted me somehow.

When class ends, I tell Araceli I'll see her later and start to head to Fae Studies. Tanwen passes by me, slinging her bag over her shoulder, and says, "That was dirty. He loves that car more than anything."

I shrug. "He deserved it."

"Probably," she says. "But you better watch your back."

My eyes narrow. Last year she had a thing for Callan, even though he only had eyes for me, and she's probably still pissed about it. "Is that a threat?"

"No, just a warning."

I put my hands on my hips. "If you have something you want to say to me, just spit it out already."

Tanwen tugs on her long straw-colored braid and laughs. "I think I'd rather keep you in suspense for now. Besides, someone else is here to talk to you. Good luck with that."

She walks away, and I turn around to see what she's talking about.

Callan stands behind me, his hands still clenched. Everyone else has vanished. We're alone outside the gym, in the same spot where we kissed.

This is where he betrayed me.

"What the fuck was that?" he growls.

"Payback," I reply. "You messed with my car, and I've messed with yours. Now we're even."

"You think this is a game?" His angry eyes search mine, but he doesn't make a move toward me.

"Isn't it?" I poke a finger at his chest, hitting hard muscle. "A game you started, but one I intend to finish."

"Everything I did was to protect you." He grabs my hand, and I tense, waiting to see what he'll do next. He holds it a second longer than I expect as he stares into my eyes, and then he drops it in disgust. "Just stay away from me, demon."

"Half-demon," I remind him sweetly. "Don't worry, I intend to keep my distance from you. But this game? It's only just begun." I lean close, so close my lips almost brush his. "Make no mistake, this is war."

11

BASTIEN

I sink into the desk beside Olivia and give her a long look. I hoped to get through my final year as a student at Seraphim Academy without any problems, but clearly that isn't going to happen, not with our little half-succubus around. That prank this morning was clever, I'll admit, and a fitting punishment for what Callan did to her, but it was also unwise. Callan is a formidable opponent, and he does not forgive easily. If I hadn't been there, I'm not sure what he would have done.

Olivia ignores me as she pulls out her notebook and pens, while Raziel talks to another student just outside the classroom door. We have a few minutes before our Fae Studies class will begin.

"What do you think you're doing?" I ask Olivia in a low voice.

"I have no idea what you mean," she says with a smile. The picture of innocence.

"Even your necklace can't hide that lie." She goes back to ignoring me, and I pinch my brow before starting again. "Tell me this is a one-time thing. A single prank to get back at Callan, and now it's over."

"I can't do that."

My eyes narrow. "What are you planning next?"

She tilts her head with a taunting smile. "I'm sure you'd love to know."

There has never been a more infuriating woman than Olivia Monroe. Raziel walks in and starts going through some papers on his desk. I pin Olivia with a stern look. "Be careful. Callan is not someone you want to cross. Neither am I."

She drops her smile. "I'm getting really tired of everyone telling me to be careful all the time."

I lean forward and hiss, "Then maybe you should stop being so reckless."

She leans forward too, her face very close to mine. "Or maybe you should treat me like a grown woman who can take care of herself for once."

"I'm only trying to protect you, but you do make it difficult."

She places a hand over her heart. "Aw, Bastien, for a second it almost sounded like you cared."

I scowl at her. "I care about keeping my promise to Jonah. Nothing more."

She bats her long lashes at me, but then Raziel moves to the front of class and clears his throat. He glances at us like he's worried he's interrupting, and I sit back in my chair and gesture for him to begin his lecture.

"Today we're going to start discussing the different Faerie courts, beginning with Summer and Spring," Raziel says. "Together, they're known as the Seelie courts, and in history they've often been depicted as the 'good' fae, although this isn't really correct. They can be just as kind or cruel as any of the Unseelie fae. The Summer court is known for being both brave and volatile, while Spring court members can be both kind and capricious."

He continues on, but I already know everything he's discussing, so I take few notes. Instead, I wonder what else Olivia has planned. Is she going to exact revenge for everything we did to her last year, tit for tat? If so, she'll probably go after our rooms next. Or the bell tower.

As class comes to a close, Raziel says, "Before I forget, I want to pair everyone up for your class project. If you've been in one of my other classes before, this should be familiar to you. You and your partner will write a paper on a topic related to the fae, and this year I've decided to let you choose it."

He begins assigning partners, and when he calls Olivia, he pairs her up with me, exactly as I instructed him. I got the idea from Marcus, who did the same thing last year in Demon Studies. Raziel is a good professor, but he's a weak-willed fool, and like most people, he has no desire to go up against the Princes. Olivia's the only person who has ever tried.

She lets out an audible groan when she hears she's assigned to me, and it sounds just like the one she makes when I'm fucking her. I'm instantly hard, and she glances my way. Can she feel it, my desire for her? I shove it to the back of my mind, along with my other emotions. I feel nothing for her. Nothing at all.

When class ends, she turns toward me in the hallway. "What a coincidence that we're paired together."

"Indeed. What shall we pick for our topic?"

"Magical objects." She touches the gold and aquamarine necklace hanging above her breasts. "I'd like to know more about how they're made."

"Good choice. Let's meet on Mondays in the same time and place as we did last year."

She makes a disgusted face. "Right, when you performed tests on me like a lab rat."

"That was Uriel's decision, and if you'd been honest about your Choir, we wouldn't have had to do that."

"If I'd been honest, they would have kicked me out of school." She shakes her head. "Let's just try to get this paper over with quickly so I can go back to avoiding you as much as possible."

"As you wish." I take her chin as I stare into her green eyes. "But don't forget who provides you with your meals. Unless you want to go back to feeding on strangers?"

She opens her mouth, but can't seem to form a reply, and I gaze down at her perfect red lips. My cock hardens as I imagine what I'd like to do with that mouth. She senses my desire and her breathing hitches, while her eyes glaze over a bit.

"You seem rather hungry," I ask, stroking her soft skin. "Should I come by tonight?"

"Yes, fine," she says with a sigh, before jerking away. "But only for a quickie."

"I'll be there at nine." A satisfied smile crosses my lips as she walks away. She needs me, even if she won't admit it...and I'm more than happy to give her what she wants.

12

OLIVIA

My classes keep me busy, and two weeks pass by in what seems like only minutes. I avoid the Princes, and they stay out of my way too. My hunger grows, since I took as little from Bastien as possible during our last encounter. I ignore it as best I can, and spend extra time soaking up sunlight to give me strength. That won't last forever though, and I know it. But I can't keep feeding on Bastien either. Sooner or later he's going to start to grow weak, and it'll be my fault.

I receive a message from Uriel that my succubus testing will begin on Wednesday after my normal classes, and that I'll meet with her in one of the rooms in his house. I'm excited to meet another succubus other than my mother, although I'm not sure what kind of tests she'll have for me. I hope I pass.

At the appointed time, Bastien opens the door to Uriel's house and instructs me to follow him. He leads me past the office and deep into the house, where I've never been before. We step into some kind of old-fashioned parlor, where Uriel sits in a chair with curled wood arms, sipping tea across from a woman in a red dress. She's the most beautiful woman I've ever seen other than my mother, with dark brown skin, luscious curls, perfectly pouty lips, and amazing curves. All angels and demons are attractive, but the Lilim have something else, something irresistible that makes it hard to take your eyes off them, and this succubus is no exception.

"Ah, there's Olivia now," Uriel says, as I step inside the room. Will Uriel be attending these sessions too? That could get very awkward. Especially if we start talking about my sex life. Or how I'm sleeping with his son for sustenance. I glance at Bastien in a panic, but he discreetly exits the room and closes the door as Uriel begins speaking again. "This is Delilah. She'll be handling your succubus testing, per Baal's request."

"It's a pleasure to meet you," Delilah says, and even her voice is alluring.

Uriel stands. "I'll leave you two to get started. Feel free to enjoy some tea and cakes."

He exits the room, and I hesitate a second before sitting in the chair he vacated. On the table beside me there are tiny little yellow teacups and a steaming tea pot, along with some cute mini cakes with pastel frosting. I pour myself some tea, even though the whole moment feels like something from a dream.

"How strange to be having tea in an Archangel's house," Delilah says, before bringing her cup to her lips for a delicate sip. "I look forward to teaching you here, in Uriel's quaint little parlor. It's so very chaste, and what we'll discuss is definitely not."

"Teach me?" I ask, confused. "I'm not sure how much Baal told you, but I already know how to control my succubus hunger and how to feed without hurting anyone. I don't think there's much more you could teach me."

Delilah's laugh floats through the air like butterflies with gossamer wings. "My dear, you don't know a quarter of what I have to teach you. Besides, that's not why I'm really here, now is it? We both know I've been sent to evaluate you for Baal. Now, what Baal doesn't know is that I'm also here to watch over you, at the behest of your mother."

My eyes widen. "You know who my mother is?"

"I do. I'm one of your cousins. But don't worry, I won't tell anyone who your mother is." She gives me a wink that could bring humans to their knees.

I sit back with a sigh of relief. It's forbidden for angels and demons to have relationships, and Mother's life could be in danger if anyone found out she gave birth to me. Then the other part of her statement registers, and my eyes widen. "We're cousins?"

"Yes, we share closer blood than most."

I want to ask more, but I get the sense she is being purposefully vague, and likely won't tell me anything else. Instead, I ask, "Are you going to test me?"

She picks up one of the little cakes and takes a bite. "No, I already know enough just by looking at you. For one thing, I can tell you're not feeding enough."

"It's not exactly easy on a campus full of angels," I mutter.

She waves a dismissive hand. "There are plenty of places nearby you could go to find prey."

"I tried that last year and it was...challenging. I also got attacked by demons, which didn't make it any easier." I don't mention that I would prefer not to feed on strangers anymore, for fear it will make me seem weak or something.

"You don't need to worry about that anymore. There were rumors of a rogue succubus in the area and a bounty was placed on your head, but that's all over now that you're not in hiding anymore. No demon will attack you, not without facing the wrath of the Archdemons."

That's good to know.

She cocks her head. "If you're not feeing from humans, who are you feeding from?"

"Right now, one of the angels on campus."

"That's it?" She blinks at me. "No wonder you're half-starved. You can't survive on one angel alone—your mother must have taught you that. Not only because it won't sustain you over a long period, but because eventually you will kill this person, just as you would a human."

I stare down into my tea. As much as I dislike Bastien, I don't want to hurt him. "Can we never have a long-term supernatural lover then?"

"No, you can, however you would need many of them. Ideally six to eight, unless they're very powerful, then you might get away with fewer. That way, when you feed regularly from all of them, you take less of their life force and don't put them in any danger." Her lips curl. "Of course, the tricky part is finding multiple supernaturals who agree to share you."

"Have you done it?"

"I have in the past, but it never lasts. In the Lilim world we call it a harem, and many young idealistic succubi and incubi try to create one, but find it challenging to maintain. Lovers get jealous and fickle over time. Personalities clash. People leave." Her eyes go distant, and I sense that she's remembering something in her own past. After a moment, she shakes her head. "It's a lot easier to keep traveling and feeding on human strangers, as you'll soon learn."

I take a sip of my tea and think over her words. She's saying nothing I haven't heard before from Mother, but I foolishly hoped another succubus would have better answers for me. But as Mother said, love isn't for our kind.

"I'll figure something out." I'll have to either start trolling nearby bars again for truckers to bang, or I'll have to take Marcus into my bed again. And probably a few other angels too. But who? Kassiel is off-limits. Callan hates me, and the feeling is mutual. I can't think of anyone else on campus I'd sleep with, unfortunately.

Delilah scrutinizes me. "Have you figured out how to feed off of lust not directed at you?"

"I have." I remember the snacks I used to get from Araceli and Darel, before he was killed anyway. That's not an option now.

"Good. That should help sustain you. One thing you could try is going to a strip club to feed on the lust in the air, but that can only do so much. You could also incite lust in people around you. You do know how to do that, don't you?"

"Yes, but I don't do it often, especially here on campus."

"That's understandable, but I have an idea for how you can do it without getting caught. I assume you sleep in dorms, as they do at

Hellspawn Academy?" she asks, and I nod. "When all the little angels are asleep in their beds, send out a wave of lust through the building. You'll give every student in your dorm a sexy dream that will sustain you for a short time."

I sit up straighter. "That's a good idea. Nobody discusses their sex dreams, right?"

She smiles, pleased at my enthusiasm. "Indeed. You'll have to start small though. A few rooms at a time at first. But that should tide you over until you find more lovers, at least."

"Nothing replaces sex though, does it?" I ask.

"No, but we do what we must to survive." She finishes the last of her tea and sets it down, then rises with the elegance of a queen. "I'll return in a few months to check on your progress. I hope to see signs that you're feeding better by then."

I jump to my feet with a lot less grace. "I'll try."

Delilah reaches out and strokes my cheek tenderly with her red nails for a fleeting moment. I catch a quick glimpse of a gold ring set with rubies, and for some reason it reminds me of the necklace I wear, but then I'm ensnared by her mysterious green eyes, which look just like mine. She's only the fourth member of my family I've ever met, and I almost beg her to stay longer. I have so many questions, but more than that, I just want to spend time with her. But the moment ends as quickly as it began, and she draws herself up and walks out of the room, moving with such confidence you'd think this is her house and not Uriel's.

I stare at the empty doorway with a hollowness in my chest, but then collect myself and set out for the dorms. I have something new to try tonight.

13

OLIVIA

When I get back to my dorm, there's a piece of blue paper taped to the door, announcing something new called Family Day in June. I rip it off and scan it quickly. It says all parents will be invited to explore the campus and attend classes with us that day, plus there will be a big feast out on the lawn. I doubt Father will bother showing up, so I leave the paper on the kitchen counter in case Araceli wants it. Her mom will definitely come, but I'm not sure about her dad.

I head into my bedroom, drop my bag on my bed, peel off my cardigan, and then freeze. There's a gold envelope on my desk, like the ones the Order sends...but it's too soon for another meeting, isn't it? Although last year I was only an initiate, maybe now that I'm a full member, I'll be expected to attend more meetings. But when I rip it open, I see it's not an invitation, but something that sends a chill down my spine.

Find a way to bring your roommate's father to campus before the end of the year. Failure to complete your task will result in the punishment of a loved one.

I ball up the paper in my fist, and then notice my hands are shaking. I should have known the Order would want to manipulate me to achieve their goals. I just didn't expect them to do something like this, or with such an open threat. Then again, they got away with murder last year—what *won't* they do?

I sit on the edge of my bed as I consider my options. I think Araceli wants to reconnect with her dad, and after doing the same with my father, I believe it will be good for her. Convincing her to invite him to Family Day or one of the upcoming soccer games won't be too hard, and I'll be doing it for her benefit, not for the Order. Plus, he must know something about getting to Faerie...which is probably why the Order wants him, of course.

If they want him, it can't be for anything good. What will they do to him if he comes to campus? Kidnap him and force him to open a portal to Faerie? I can't let anything happen to one of Araceli's parents. Then again, it will be easier to stop the Order if we can set up a trap for them, and her father's arrival would be perfect for that. And maybe if he comes to school, he can help us find Jonah too.

My head spins, trying to decide what to do. Manipulate my best friend, and risk her father's life with the best of intentions? Or ignore the Order's task, and put someone I care about—possibly Araceli herself—in danger?

I hear the front door open and Araceli's combat boots stomping through the living room and the kitchen. She pauses, and I imagine she's looking at the Family Day flyer. Probably debating whether or not to invite her father. All I have to do is go out there and convince her it's a good idea. Easy.

No. I've resolved to be a better friend this year, and that means no more lying or deception. The old Liv didn't trust anyone and relied on no one but herself, but I'm trying to change. It's hard for me to accept that I don't have all the answers, and even harder for me to put my trust in someone else, especially after the Princes betrayed me, but Araceli has never done anything to make me question her loyalty.

I touch my mother's necklace. Its purpose is to help me lie and conceal, and I'm very good at both of those things. As an Ishim and a succubus, my nature is to work from the shadows. But maybe truth is the answer sometimes.

I head out into our shared living room, where Araceli is plopping down on the couch and grabbing the TV remote. I pick up the Family Day flyer off the kitchen counter and bring it over to her, questioning my decision with each step.

"Hey, Liv," she says, glancing up at me. She sees the look on my face and sits up a little. "Everything okay?"

"Did you see this flyer?" I hold up the Family Day notice.

"Yep. My mom is going to go nuts when she finds out. I'll never get her to leave." She rolls her eyes. "Are you worried about your dad coming?"

"No, that's not it." I sit beside her on the couch. "You know I joined the Order of the Golden Throne so I could find my brother, and now I'm trying to stop them from the inside."

"Yeah..." Her nose wrinkles in confusion. "After what they did to Darel, I told you I'd help."

"They want all their members to perform tasks this year. I just got mine." I hand her the letter from the Order, which she carefully unfolds.

Her eyes widen as she reads it. "Holy shit."

I let out a long breath. "I told you I was going to be honest and open with you about everything from now on, and I'm trying to do that. I want to know what you think we should do."

She reads the paper again and then looks up at me. "I'm really glad you showed me this, and I know it probably wasn't an easy decision." She chews on her lip a little, and then tugs on her purple strand of hair. "Okay, I'll ask him to come to Family Day."

"Are you sure? It could be dangerous for him."

"I know, but there's no guarantee he'll come anyway, and if he does, then we'll know to watch out for an attack." She hands me the gold letter. "Besides, we have to try. If we don't, they could hurt someone else."

I throw my arms around her. "Thank you, Araceli. I'm so sorry you're mixed up in all this. If I could protect you from it, I would."

She pulls back from my hug and pokes me in the arm. "I'm not the one who needs protecting, girl. You're getting involved with some dangerous people, people who know what you really are now, I might add. Good thing you've got me to watch your back."

I can't help but smile, especially since her words remind me of something Jonah once said. Here I am, trying to protect her from the people who want to use her fae blood, and she's trying to do the same for me. "Yes, good thing."

She rips up the Order's note with her nails, and for a second I think I catch a glimpse of that infamous fae cruelty in her eyes. "Whatever the Order has planned, we'll stop them."

14

OLIVIA

The next month passes in a blur of spring, sunshine, classes, and homework. My classes are harder this year than last, and combined with my extra meetings with Bastien and Kassiel, I barely have time to breathe.

Callan finishes his demonstration of all the different weapons in Combat Training, and now we're starting to try them out ourselves. As expected, I find daggers the easiest to work with, and plan to pick them when the time comes. We still seethe at each other during every class, but otherwise pretend the other doesn't exist, which suits me just fine.

The most curious thing is I don't feel any lust from Tanwen toward him anymore. I wonder what changed? Maybe she found someone else over the break? Or has she finally realized he is the actual worst?

In Fae Studies, we move from learning about the Seelie courts to the Unseelie courts, and on Mondays, Bastien and I do research on famous magical objects throughout history and mythology, like Excalibur. He's not as fun a partner as Marcus was, but he gets the job done at least. Meanwhile, I keep hoping to find clues about how to find Jonah, but always end up disappointed.

In Angelic History, Kassiel has started talking about migrations of angels and demons to Earth in the past, like during the Renaissance. Did you know Leonardo Da Vinci was an angel? No, me neither. Then, during our private sessions, Kassiel gives me the demons' perspective on the same lessons—like how they believe Mona Lisa was Leonardo's secret succubus lover. Kassiel knows all the good gossip, for sure.

In Ishim class, we study how to conceal other people and large objects, which is something I hadn't learned yet, and it takes a lot of energy. As does everything in Light Control, where we started out by creating little hovering lights to guide us in the dark, and are now making big flashes that can temporarily blind our enemies. It's exhausting, and all it does is make me hungrier.

Delilah's trick helps. Every night I set an alarm for 2 AM, and then I practice what we talked about during our meeting. I started with a few rooms on my floor, sending a wave of lust to my sleeping peers, while avoiding Araceli, of course. That topped me off nicely, but it didn't last long. The next few nights, I spread my powers to other floors, being careful to skip around a lot so no one suspects me. I have no idea what the dreams are about, but I can feel their intensity as I feed on the desire they create. I hope the dreamers enjoy it as much as I do. It's not as satisfying as sex, but it does the job. For now.

I'm so busy with schoolwork and trying to stay sated that it's easy to forget about my plan to get revenge on the Princes. Then, on a Friday night, there's a knock on my door while I'm reading my Angelic History textbook. Araceli is out having dinner with her aunt, and I'm careful when I open the door—but it's just Marcus on the other side.

"Hey," he says, leaning on the doorway and looking good enough to eat. "How are you?"

I cross my arms. "What are you doing here, Marcus?"

"I just came to see if you wanted to grab a bite to eat with me. We could even go to Angel Peak. Or maybe order in..."

I raise my eyebrows. "Like on a date?"

"Sure, if you want to call it that."

I'm actually tempted by his offer—we don't have any classes together this year, and I sort of miss him a tiny bit—but I shake my head. "That's not a good idea."

"Are you sure?" He reaches out and brushes a piece of hair back from my face. "You look like you need to eat. I can help you."

His voice dips low, and I know he doesn't mean food. His desire rolls over me like a wave, and it's delicious and irresistible, because it's different from the normal lust I get from people. There's real emotion behind it, which isn't something I feel often. Maybe it's because of that emotion that I grab his shirt and pull him into the room, then shut the door behind him.

We're on each other instantly, lips locked, hands roaming, bodies pressed together. Damn, I really missed kissing Marcus. The boy knows what he's doing with his mouth, that's for sure. And his fingers. And everything else. After surviving on nothing but dreams and light for weeks, I can't get enough of this real desire directed at me. I know I should stop this immediately, and that sex with Marcus can only lead to drama, but I can't do it. I'm so hungry I'm physically unable to tear myself away from the man in my arms, even as he leads me to my bedroom.

Once we're inside, Marcus doesn't hesitate. He pushes me down on the bed and yanks my skirt up, then rips my panties off like they're made of tissue paper. His eyes are determined and a little wild, before he drops to his knees and buries his head between my thighs. His mouth and tongue conduct a little symphony on my clit, and I grab onto his thick, luscious brown hair and moan. It's so good, but I need more. To really feed I need his pleasure too, and I need it now.

"Fuck me," I command him. "Hard and fast. Hurry."

"Someone's feeling a little desperate, isn't she?" he asks, as he slides a finger into me, feeling how wet I am for him. He's teasing me now, but it's so good I don't care, even as it makes me hungrier. I practically drool as he drops his pants and slides his hard cock between my legs. He rubs it against my folds, getting it nice and slick, while he stares into my eyes. "I've got what you need right here."

I grab his cock and slide it into me before I go mad. I hadn't realized how much I needed to feed before Marcus showed up at my door, and nothing will stop this until I'm sated. I'm not sure he could leave now if he tried.

But he doesn't want to leave. He wants to sink his cock into me over and over again, in long deep strokes that make me wonder how I possibly went without sex with Marcus for so long. What was I thinking, when it's this amazing to feel him buried inside me? I grab his ass and pull him even deeper, urging him to move faster, needing us to both get off right now. My nails dig into his skin, and his little grunts in my ear are the best sound I've heard in months. Harder and faster our bodies move together, skin against skin, until we're both right there on the edge. Then Marcus kisses me hard and I'm over it, climaxing around his cock, moaning in his mouth, totally lost in the pleasure. He comes inside me at the same time, and his power fills me to the brim instantly. I don't want it to end, and I know Marcus doesn't either because he keeps kissing me, even as our bodies calm and our hearts slow.

Eventually, I roll away from him and sit up. Shit, I just slept with Marcus in a succubus lust haze. I used him for quick and dirty sex, like I did with Bastien. Except Marcus actually cares about me, unlike Bastien, which makes this much more complicated. I have to make sure he knows this isn't something more than sex for sustenance.

"This doesn't mean I forgive you," I tell him.

"Uh huh," he says with a smirk. He slowly stands and pulls on his pants. It's hard to resist pulling him back into bed with me, so I look away.

"I'm serious."

"It's fine. I know about your deal with Bastien, but you can't survive off of him alone. Make the same deal with me, that's all I ask."

I hesitate, but I can't say no. I'm too desperate, and Marcus is too good in bed. His power rushes through my veins, making me feel like I can light up the entire building with magic. "Okay. But it's just sex. You have to remember that."

He leans over, touches my chin, and then gives me a kiss that's somehow both tender and dirty all at once. "Sure it is."

He's so damn cocky, so sure that all is forgiven between us just because we had sex. It makes me want to lash out at him, but he walks out of my room before I can do anything but seethe.

When he's gone, I pull myself together. This is a dangerous game I'm playing. I have to remind myself that the Princes and I are not friends, not after what they did to me last year. That includes Marcus.

It's time for stage two of my revenge plan.

———

On Saturday, Araceli and I head into Redding, the largest nearby city, to hit up the department stores. We take my car and fill it with stuff that makes us cackle in delight, especially when we imagine the Princes' faces. Then we head back to campus, and we wait.

Araceli lets out a huge groan when I wake her up at 2 AM, but she manages to rouse herself after a few minutes. Thanks to my Ishim classes, I know how to make her invisible now too, as long as I'm touching her. Together we grab some department store bags and fly over to the bell tower, which is dark and empty. The Princes are all in bed, leaving their lair unattended. They claimed this space as their own, another symbol of their authority over the rest of the students, and it's time to mess with it—just like they messed with my room last year.

It takes a few clandestine trips back and forth to bring everything over, and then we begin. Their masculine leather couches are decorated with sparkly pink blankets and pillows. Their dark wood tables get new tablecloths with shiny pink unicorns. Their little mini-kitchen gets pink heart stickers all over it—on the counters, on the microwave, on the fridge—until you can barely see anything underneath them. Sparkly pink streamers hang from the ceiling, while pink shimmering curtains cover the windows. For the final touches, we spray a ton of cheap floral body spray around the room, and cover everything with a heavy dusting of glitter.

"Wait, we almost forgot the best part," Araceli says, as she grabs the last bag. She pulls out tons of little stuffed animals, all super cute and very pink, ranging from unicorns to kittens to bunnies. There's even a pink sparkly llama with a nanny cam in it, which I place in the perfect spot to capture the Princes' reactions when they arrive. We scatter the rest of the stuffed animals liberally around the room, and then stand back to admire our work with a grin.

The Princes' mancave has been completely transformed into a pretty pink princess room, with three sparkly plastic tiaras on the table waiting to be crowned. It's totally over the top and ridiculous, and I love it.

I can't wait to see their faces when they walk in.

15

CALLAN

I fly into the bell tower, with Marcus and Bastien just a few wingspans behind me. The first thing that hits me is the smell as I set down on the alcove. My nose is assaulted by a strong fake floral scent that permeates the space, and I recoil as it hits me hard in the face. Then my eyes catch up to my nose, and my jaw drops as I scan the room, taking in all the pink sparkles, stuffed animals, and glitter. Fuck, there's so much glitter. We'll be finding that stuff in weird cracks for the rest of our lives.

Bastien lands beside me and covers his nose, then scans the room with disgust. When Marcus lands, he bursts out laughing, doubling over both from the smell and his amusement.

"Open all the windows and doors," I command. We can't do anything else until we air this place out. My eyes are watering just from being in here for a few seconds.

We cover our faces with our shirts and open everything up, then use our wings to create a draft that blows some fresh air through the place. But the smell is only the beginning. Our lounge has been twisted into some kind of pink monstrosity.

I stare at the room for a few minutes, and all I can finally manage to say is, "What the fuck?"

"It's so petty," Bastien says, shaking his head.

"We trashed her room, and now she trashed ours," Marcus says with a shrug. "It's nothing more than we deserve." He plops down on the couch, falling into the pile of pink stuffed animals. "Besides, I think it's pretty awesome."

"How long is this revenge bullshit going to continue?" I ask.

Bastien plucks a unicorn off his armchair and tosses it aside. "So far she's gotten back at you for her car, and this is obviously retaliation for what we did to her room. Assuming she ignores the smaller offenses like vandalizing her door and leaving her threatening notes, she should only have one more act of revenge left." He gives me a hard look. "Exposing a secret to the entire school."

"We have to stop her before it gets to that point," I growl.

"Stop her how?" Marcus asks with a snort. "That sort of thing is what got us into this mess."

I scowl at him. "I did what I had to do."

"Did you?" Marcus throws a stuffed dog at my head, which I catch. "Did you really have to threaten her?" He throws a stuffed llama next. "Or fuck up her car? Or betray her?" His words are laced with anger, and he keeps throwing things at me until there's nothing else within reach.

"Are you done?" I ask, knocking the last of the animals aside. "I did what I thought was right at the time. I didn't know she was Jonah's sister, only that I made a promise to him, a promise to keep Olivia away from this school."

"Some of it *was* particularly harsh," Bastien says, rubbing his chin.

I glare at him. I thought he was on my side. Guess I'm alone here. "Maybe it was harsh, but it was a necessary evil."

Marcus stretches his legs out on the couch and puts on a little plastic tiara, like he's totally cool with all this. "We should've been honest with her from the beginning. It would have saved us all a lot of trouble."

"We didn't know if we could trust her," I reply.

"No, but we knew she was connected to Jonah somehow," Bastien says. "We should have made her tell us how from the start."

Marcus nods. "Yes, and once we knew she was his sister, we should have told her that Jonah went to Faerie on a mission for the Order. We could have worked together to find him, instead of trying to get her to leave the school."

I roll my eyes. "And if we'd known Jonah would go missing, we never would have let him go to Faerie in the first place. There's no point wishing the past could be different. We already made the choices we did, and we have to stand by them. Even if we might regret them now."

"The only way to get this to end is to apologize to her," Marcus says. "Convince her to forgive you. That's what I'm doing, and it seems to be working. Very well, if the other night was any indication." A slow grin spreads across his face, and I want to punch it off. He's fucking her again, no doubt. Him and Bastien. She's got them both under her spell.

"Never." I hate all demons, including Olivia, and I hate that every time I look at her, I want her anyway. She must be using her succubus powers on me. There's no other explanation. She doesn't belong here, and even her brother knew it. Her half-demon blood puts her at risk and makes her a threat at the same time. But I'm not going to try to get her kicked out again. I've accepted she's not going anywhere, even though I don't like it. Considering demons destroyed my family, I think that's pretty fucking big of me.

"I'll send someone to clean this place up," I say, as I pick up the llama on the floor. Something in it catches my attention, and I examine it more closely. A hidden camera. She's been recording all this, and now she has the perfect video to show the entire school.

I can't let her do that.

I track Olivia down an hour later, as she's leaving her yoga class. I land right in front of her in a rush, making her jump back.

"Callan," she says, her voice breathy and sexy as hell. "Having a good morning?"

I throw one of the plastic sparkly tiaras at her chest. "Thanks for redecorating our lounge. Pink's not my color though."

She catches it with a wicked smile. "Too bad. I thought it was perfect for such a pretty princess."

I grit my teeth at the reminder of my car. "What are you planning next?"

She starts walking back to the dorm, like she doesn't have time for me. "I'm sure you'd like to know that."

I match her stride easily. "I know you were watching us on that camera. You recorded us, didn't you?"

"I don't have any idea what you mean."

I grab her arm to make her stop and face me. "You need to quit this shit. Now."

Her eyes narrow. "Maybe you should listen to Marcus. This could all end if you just apologize."

"I can't apologize if I'm not sorry."

"Then I guess you deserve everything that's coming to you."

Fury rises up in me as I face her, and I imagine pushing her down on her knees and shoving my cock in that pretty mouth to shut her up. As soon as I have the thought, she smiles, like she knows what I'm thinking. She can feel how much I want her.

I release her arm in disgust and step back. "Quit using your succubus magic on me."

"I'm not doing anything. This is all you." She steps closer and runs a hand down my chest. "It must kill you, how much you want me. I see the way you look at me in class. The same way you're looking at me now." She licks her red lips, and I can't help but stare at them. "Your lust is tinged with hate, but somehow that only makes it more delicious."

She drives me mad, but for a second I'm tempted to kiss her anyway, and it takes everything in me to hold myself back. Maybe because she's forbidden fruit. Maybe because she's the sexiest thing I've ever laid eyes on. Maybe because she's the only woman who's ever challenged me.

Either way, it's not going to happen.

I knock her hand away. "You fucked up my car. You messed with my lounge. I accept your punishment as justice—an eye for an eye. But I'm warning you now...stop this before it goes any further. You don't want to push me."

"You're wrong. That's exactly what I want to do." She steps back with a cruel smile. "I'm going to push you until you break."

16

OLIVIA

When I get back to my room, I sit at my desk and watch the recording again with a wicked grin on my face. I originally planned to show the video of their reactions to the entire school, thinking it would humiliate them, but then they started talking about Jonah and Faerie, giving me concrete evidence they've known all along where he is and that they're part of the Order. A video like this could ruin them. Just like they tried to ruin me. All I have to do is share it, when the time comes.

Even though I acted brave in the face of Callan's anger, I still dread going to Combat Training the next morning. We're still trying out different weapons to see which one we want to focus on, and today we're working with throwing knives.

I ignore Callan as best I can, while Hilda barks instructions at us and has us spread around the room to face targets. But then she sends Callan over to help each student with positioning, starting with me.

"Try not to kill me," I mutter, as he moves beside me.

"I think it's more likely you'll kill me." He grabs my hand and adjusts the knife quickly. "Hold it like this."

"Wow, that's some great teaching there."

"Would you rather I spend a long time with you?"

"No, on second thought, let's get this over quickly."

He crosses his arms. "Show me what you got."

I can feel the steady stream of his hate-lust, and it makes my head spin. Hate is a lot like desire, I've discovered. It makes you all hot and sweaty, and unable to focus on anyone else but that person. You think about them constantly. You imagine all the things you can do to them. You want to do whatever you can to get them out of your system.

Callan's hateful eyes are intense as they stare at me. I wonder if he's thinking about fucking me or strangling me right now. Probably both.

I roll my shoulders and focus on the target in front of me, but then Callan's eyes lower to my ass and his lust flares. I drop the knife instead of throwing it, and he laughs.

It's not a nice laugh.

"Don't mock me," I snap at him.

"Sorry," he says, with a haughty smirk. "Do you need me to show you how to hold the knife again?"

I glare at him as I pick up the knife. "No, I need you to stop thinking about fucking me. Your lust is very distracting."

His smirk falls and his eyes go hard again. "Just throw the damn knives already."

I throw one and it hits the side of the target and then clatters to the ground. I grab another, with even worse results. I bet I could do this if Callan wasn't hate-banging me with his eyes. And every time I fail, his cruel smile gets bigger and bigger.

"This is your fault," I say, after picking up the knives off the floor.

"Your inability to throw the knifes correctly has nothing to do with me."

"I thought you were supposed to be teaching me."

He shrugs callously. "I can only do so much for someone so innately bad at combat."

I'm tempted to bury one of these knives in his arm next, but before I can, he leaves to go work with the next student. Finally.

But even once he's gone, his desire hovers around me like a thick cloud, making it hard for me to breathe, or think about anything else other than how much I hate him. I picture his face on the target and throw, and this time, I don't miss.

———

In Fae Studies, Raziel is discussing time in Faerie, which moves differently than on Earth, and he's wearing a bowtie with stars all over it.

"The early hours of the morning are spring. The temperature warms somewhat, the flowers bloom, the animals wake and frolic. In the middle of the day, it shifts to summer. The air gets hot, the sun beats down, and sometimes there will be summer showers. Late afternoon is autumn. As the sun sets, the trees lose their leaves, the air grows cooler, and the animals get ready to sleep. And finally, full dark is winter. It's very cold, the animals are snug in their burrows, and the trees are bare. However, this does change a bit depending on where you are in Faerie. For example, in the Winter Court, that season will be the longest."

He continues on about the layout of Faerie for some time, and then asks if we have any questions.

I raise my hand to ask the question that's been on my mind for months. "What do the fae do with prisoners caught in Faerie?"

Raziel looks taken aback by my question. "I imagine they either imprison them or execute them, but it's so rare, I'm not sure. No one gets into Faerie these days without their permission."

Not helpful at all.

In the last few weeks I haven't learned anything I didn't already know. The fae are reclusive and rarely leave Faerie. A few of them have wings, and all of them have unusual, colorful hair, unless it's jet black or pure white. They have extraordinary amounts of magic and can glamour people, although that doesn't work on Ofanim. Some powerful fae can make magical objects like my necklace. But nothing is getting me any closer to rescuing Jonah, and I'm starting to get frustrated.

"You should go to Faerie and find out," Jeremy says in a low voice behind me. "Maybe they'll execute you like the abomination you are."

My mouth falls open and I spin in my seat to face him, but I'm shocked into temporary silence by his words. I know many people here hate and fear me, but it's rare for anyone to say something as horrible as that.

Bastien speaks before I can, his voice filled with cold menace. "How dare you speak to her like that."

"She's a demon," Jeremy practically spits out.

"And you think you're so much better? You, whose father abandoned his post during the Great War, letting his entire squad die? Whose mother left her family to marry a human?"

Jeremy's face flushes with murderous rage. I'm impressed Bastien knows so much about him. Then again, he probably knows the dirty secrets of every student at this school.

"Jeremy, please leave this classroom until you can compose yourself," Raziel says with a disapproving tone.

The jerk stands up slowly and gathers his things while glaring at me the entire time. When he leaves the room, I relax and sneak a glance at Bastien, but he's back to ignoring me. Everyone else in class stares at us with wide eyes for the rest of the lecture, and I doubt any of us hears what Raziel's saying at all.

As soon as class ends, I hurry after Bastien to catch him outside. "Thanks for sticking up for me."

"It was nothing." His voice is still cold. He's always cold and emotionless. Or so it seems. But he must have felt something for him to snap at Jeremy that way, and I know from watching the video that he does seem to regret his involvement in what the Princes did last year, at least a little. But he still hasn't apologized either, so he's not off the hook.

17

OLIVIA

A rare thunderstorm sends everyone into the cafeteria for dinner one Thursday night, and it takes me forever to get food from the buffet. I plop my tray down beside Grace's plate and sit across from Araceli, then nearly faceplant into my food because I'm just that exhausted. It's been a month since I got my second revenge on the Princes, and my classes are kicking my ass. I probably need to feed again too, and not just on food. I had to lay off the sex dreams a little when I overheard two people laughing about how they'd both had a bunch of them recently. I don't want anyone to start connecting the dots. On the other hand, people on campus seem to be hooking up left and right, so they should really be thanking me. Love is in the air—or at the very least, a heavy dose of lust.

At least I know why Tanwen is over Callan. After the sex dreams started, she began dating one of the other Valkyries, a broad-shouldered girl named Marila. They sit together on the other side of the cafeteria with their identical blond hair, and I wait for some petty thoughts to come into my head, but they don't. I guess I'm fine with Tanwen these days. How strange.

"Is that a burn on your arm?" Araceli asks me, as I dig in to my burrito.

I glance down, surprised. "Oh yeah. I got it in Light Control today. One of the Valkyries zapped me. I think it was an accident, but who knows."

"Ugh, of course they did." Araceli rolls her eyes and covers the burn with her hand. Within seconds it's healed, thanks to her Malakim blood. "There you go, all fixed up."

"Thanks." It would have healed within a day or two anyway, but it's nice to have a healer on your side.

Cyrus sits at the end of our table, with his new boyfriend Isaiah across from him. Isaiah is like a ginger version of Cyrus, with his nearly identical hipster jeans and robin blue polo shirt. They're even about the same height. They're another of the new couples that spawned after I started turning up the heat in people's dreams, and there's always an invisible cloud of lust swirling around them. I have a feeling it won't last, but they give me a nice snack whenever they're around, at least.

Cyrus immediately jumps into his favorite pastime—gossip. "Did you hear about the attack in Angel Peak?"

"What?" Araceli drops her spoon in surprise. "No?"

He leans forward and lowers his voice. "Two angels were killed right outside the coffee shop. Their heads were severed...along with their wings."

The others gasp. Wings are a big deal among angels, I've learned. Touching someone else's wings without permission is taboo. Mutilation of someone's wings is a truly horrific punishment, only reserved for the most serious of offenders. And cutting them off? It's a rare, ghastly crime, and it makes the others shudder to even consider such a thing.

"Was it demons?" I ask, my stomach sinking. I don't need anyone to have even more reason to hate me for my demon blood.

"That's what they thought at first, but now there's a rumor going around it was humans instead," Cyrus says.

Grace's eyes widen. "Humans? How could they get into Angel Peak?"

"Yeah, I thought the place was warded so humans couldn't even find it," Araceli says.

Cyrus spreads his hands. "No one knows."

Grace pokes at her food with a frown. "That can't be right. How could humans manage to take out two angels? It must be a demon attack. They're the only ones who would be so heartless." She quickly glances at me. "Sorry, Liv. I didn't mean—"

"It's okay," I say, although it does sting a little.

"They're increasing security around the town to make sure nothing like this happens again," Isaiah says. I almost forgot he was here, since he's so quiet. I guess if Cyrus is your boyfriend, you let him do most of the talking.

The next day, the attack in Angel Peak is all anyone can talk about, and the campus is buzzing with fear. No one knows if demons or humans were behind it, and speculations are running wild. I get more dirty looks than usual, like somehow it's my fault.

It's Friday, which means another after-school lesson with Kassiel. Last week he talked a little about what the Great War was like from the demons' perspective. Kassiel lost his mother during it, and he spoke with passion about the horrors he witnessed when he fought. I was hoping to hear more stories about his time as a soldier, but today I have a more pressing question.

"Do you know anything about the attack in Angel Peak?" I ask, after closing the door behind me. "Was it demons who did it?"

One of his eyebrows arches up. "I see the attack has been weighing on your mind. Come. Sit."

I take my usual chair, and he sits behind his desk, a safe distance away from me. Every session with him is a lesson in restraint and self-control. I'm already thinking about banging him right there on his desk, which isn't a good sign.

"As far as I know, it wasn't demons who did it," he says.

"So it's true?" I ask. "Humans killed two angels?"

"It does seem that way."

I lean back. "Wow. I knew there were human hunters, but I didn't think they were a real threat to us."

"Most of the time, they're not. However, I've heard some stirrings about a group of humans that is growing in numbers called the Duskhunters. They're fanatical and cult-like, but worst of all, they're organized and well-funded. They believe all supernaturals should be wiped off of Earth completely, and will do whatever it takes to achieve that goal. It's possible they're behind this attack, although I'm not sure how they could have gotten into Angel Peak."

I knead my hands as I consider his words. "I spent most of my life afraid of angels and demons, worried about what they would do to me if they found me. Then my worry shifted to the fae, and what they might have done to Jonah. I never thought of humans as a threat at all...until now."

"As long as you stay on campus, you'll be fine," Kassiel says. "The Archangels have sent extra guards to Angel Peak, so the town should be safe too. You don't need to worry. Honestly, angels and demons are still a much bigger threat to you. And the fae, if you manage to make it to Faerie."

"Have you ever dealt with human hunters before?"

"I infiltrated a group of them once." He picks up a pen and idly plays with it as he speaks. "When my time as a soldier came to an end, I began working as a spy for Lucifer here on Earth. During the early 2000s, I was sent to deal with a group of humans in London who worshipped demons. They were Satanists with a murderous side, except they weren't very good at tracking down angels and kept killing humans instead. Lucifer didn't want the angels finding out and blaming us for it, since the Earth Accords were still in the early days back then. And frankly, he's tired of all the bad press too. I joined their group pretending to be a human, and discovered it was their leader who was behind the killings...the others were simply too scared to act against him. I convinced them one by one that demons weren't real, and that they should go back to their normal lives."

I could listen to Kassiel talk about his long life forever. He always has the best stories. "What about the leader?"

A sinful grin crosses his lips. "I convinced him I was Lucifer himself, and that I was displeased with his actions. He was so upset, he ended up jumping off a bridge and drowning."

"A fitting punishment."

"I thought so."

We chat a bit longer about his time with the humans, and then our hour is up. It always goes too quickly, and I'm both sad and relieved when it's over.

He gets up and walks me to the door. "It's been a pleasure, Olivia."

I hesitate, and then find myself blurting out, "Do you want to get dinner tonight? I'm free, and we could keep talking about the humans."

His face looks pained. "I wish I could. More than you know. But it's not a good idea."

I shouldn't feel rejected, but I do anyway. "You're right. I'm sorry. It was a dumb idea."

"It wasn't." He reaches for me, but then pulls his hand back with a regretful shake of his head. "Being alone with you during these lessons is hard enough. I can't handle any further temptation."

"I understand." I hover there at the door, knowing I should go, but delaying the moment as long as possible. Finally I step through the doorway and say, "I'll see you in class."

My throat tightens with emotion as I walk out of the professors' building. I'm not sure how long I can keep doing these lessons—because the more time I spend with Kassiel, the more it breaks my heart that I can't be with him.

OLIVIA

Next Wednesday, I'm summoned to another meeting with Delilah in Uriel's house. Bastien lets me in, and there's no sign of his father this time.

"He's at an Archangel meeting," Bastien explains, even though I didn't ask.

"Are you reading my thoughts now?" I ask, raising an eyebrow.

"No, I don't possess that power, but it's obvious you were wondering where he was."

"And you're holding down the fort for him, as usual."

He leads me through the house. "Indeed."

"I guess you already know what you'll do when you graduate this year." I study him closely. It's hard to read anything on his face, but he seems troubled. "Does it bother you, that your path has always been laid out for you? Do you ever wish you could do something else?"

His brow furrows. "No. This is where I belong. Why do you care?"

I shrug, honestly not sure of the answer myself. I'm saved from having to reply when we reach the door to the parlor, which Bastien opens for me. He shuts it immediately after I step inside.

Delilah is already siting in one of the old-fashioned armchairs and sipping her tea, today wearing a deep purple that makes her eyes pop. She gives me a dazzling smile as I sit across from her.

"I don't have long today, but I wanted to check in on you. I'm sorry I couldn't do it sooner, but some other matters called me away."

"It's all right," I say, as I pour myself some tea.

"I can see you're feeding better, at least. There's more color in your cheeks, your eyes are brighter, and your hair is shinier."

"Is it that obvious?" I ask, self-consciously touching my hair.

"To anyone else, probably not, but I know what to look for, after years of training Lilim."

"I've been influencing everyone's dreams, as you told me, and that helped." I hesitate and think of my quick and dirty encounter with Marcus. "I also took another lover."

"Good." She takes a small sip of tea. "You do know that two lovers won't be enough though, don't you? Especially as your powers grow."

"Grow?"

She nods. "You're still young and are just now coming into your powers. As you grow stronger, you'll need to feed more. Your hunger will increase until it's all-consuming. Don't risk the lives of the people around you by getting to that point."

"I understand." I pause, staring into my tea. "What if my lovers are the sons of Archangels? Would that help?"

She arches a perfect eyebrow and smiles at me over her tea. "I did feel the lust from Uriel's son when he led you here. Yes, that would make it easier for you, because their life force is so strong. With Archangel blood you would only need three lovers, perhaps four to be safe. But that is the bare minimum."

"How do you know?"

"I've fed on Archangels before, and Archdemons too. Oh, and a few fae royalty now and then." She waves a hand. "When you've lived as long as I have, you get bored and want to sample a little of everything."

"Can I ask how old you are?" I'm not sure if this is an offensive question to an immortal.

"You've heard of Samson and Delilah?"

My eyes widen. "That was you?"

She gives me a conspiratorial smile as she stands. "I'm sorry for the short meeting this week, but there have been rumors of attacks on angels nearby, and Baal wishes me to find out more. I'll try to visit more often from now on though."

"It was good to see you again," I say.

"No, it was my pleasure." She leans forward and gives me a quick kiss on my forehead, surprising me. I look up at her in wonder, and then she gathers her purse and is out the door.

Once she's gone, I sit and go over her words, from the thought of taking another lover, to the news that the demons are investigating the recent attacks also. They're probably trying to determine if it was one of their people or if it was humans, like some suspect.

Bastien opens the door and finds me still sitting there, wrapped up in my thoughts. "Come," he says.

I obediently follow him out of the room and up the old, rickety stairs with an elaborate wooden handrail. He leads me down a hall and opens a door at the end. We step into a room that seems completely out of place in the old house—everything is black, modern, and very minimalistic, all clean lines and hard angles. It's like someone dropped an Ikea showroom in the middle of this Victorian house. The room is sparse too, except for the large bookshelf along the wall, which is so full of books it's a wonder it doesn't topple over.

It takes me a second to realize this must be Bastien's room. He lives in the dorms with Callan while he's a student, but this is where he grew up, and where he'll likely return after he graduates at the end of the year.

"Why did you bring me here?" I ask, spinning around to take it all in.

"I wanted to speak to you privately."

"About what?" I sit on the edge of his charcoal gray bed.

His brow furrows, and he almost looks...nervous? That can't

be. "I've thought a lot about the events of the previous school year, and I regret my involvement in many of them. I was not truthful with you, and I did things I am not proud of. I should not have spied on you, or put a tracker on you, or helped Callan obtain that video—even though I am pleased with the results of those actions."

I tilt my head at him. "What do you mean, you're pleased with the results?"

"As an Ofanim, it is my nature to seek the truth, and you are especially good at concealing it. Though I regret my methods, I do not regret that your truth was revealed. Once we knew you were part succubus, we were able to help you with your feeding problem and could protect you better. Once we knew you were Jonah's sister, we understood your actions. Once Callan exposed you, it allowed Gabriel to acknowledge you and for you to be your true self. The truth has a way of setting us free."

He isn't wrong, but I'm still confused. "I don't understand why you're telling me all this."

He scowls at me, like it should be obvious. "I'm trying to ask your forgiveness, though such a thing does not come easily to me."

My eyebrows jump. "This is your version of an apology?"

He shifts on his feet. "Something like that, yes. As I said, I regret that I acted in a way that may have caused you emotional or physical harm."

Wow. I did not expect this when I arrived today. Bastien, apologizing? In his own way, at least? I can't believe it.

I try to imagine everything that happened from his perspective. I arrived at Seraphim Academy as a mystery he was ordered by his father to solve, but I thwarted him at every turn. He thought I was a half-human, but discovered that was a lie. He had no reason to trust me or help me, when everything I did went against his own personal code of honor—but he did.

And he kept helping me, even after everything went south. He was there for me, every time I needed him, without question. He always made sure I was satisfied, even though that wasn't required. He never asked me for anything in return. Our "deal" feels a lot more one-sided when I consider it from his standpoint, but he's never complained.

That's when it hits me. Bastien, cold, unfeeling Bastien, actually cares about me.

I stand up and take his hand. "I forgive you."

"Truly?" he asks, searching my eyes.

I reach back and unclasp my necklace, the one thing blocking his powers. He sucks in a breath as it's removed. "Yes, Bastien. I forgive you."

He slides his hand around my waist and pulls me toward him, then kisses me hard. It's been a long time since we kissed. During all our sexual encounters, we avoided kissing as part of an unspoken agreement that it would be too intimate an act. But now his fingers dig into my hip as he kisses me with all the emotion he never shows on his face.

Then he pulls back, and his eyes scan me from head to toe, like he's seeing me for the first time. "Your aura. I've never seen anything like it."

"What does it look like?"

"A perfect mix of light and dark, demon and angel, night and day. With a heavy streak of red, carnal desire." His hands slide down my hips. "You're hungry, aren't you?"

"For you, always," I admit, though it makes me feel vulnerable to say it.

He begins unbuttoning his shirt, drawing my eyes to his smooth chest. "You should have come to me sooner."

"I didn't want to hurt you."

He lowers his head, his eyes gleaming with his own dark hunger. "I'm stronger than you think."

19

BASTIEN

I 've had sex with four women: two angels, one human, and Olivia.

The books say that coitus with a succubus is the most intense sexual experience a person can ever have. My sample size is small, but from my own research, I have to agree.

Then again, it could just be Olivia. She seems to have a strong effect on me, no matter how much I try to resist it. At this point, I've given up trying.

I remove her clothing slowly, savoring the reveal of her smooth, olive skin and feminine curves. Every inch of her seems to be perfectly sculpted to heighten arousal, even in someone as emotionless as me.

Once we're both undressed, we move onto my bed and resume kissing. I rarely sleep here at the moment, since during the school year I share a dorm with Callan. Perhaps it's wrong to do this in my childhood bedroom, but I find I don't much care.

I spread Olivia's legs and move my fingers to her clit. She strokes my cock at the same time, while our tongues dart in and out of each other's mouths. We don't normally do any of this. We always skipped the foreplay before. I never thought I cared about any of that, but it's actually nice to move a little slower this time.

We continue on like this, until neither of us can resist any longer. With both of us on our sides, I hook her leg over my hips and adjust our bodies until we're lined up and my cock can slide into her. We stare into each other's eyes as we move together as one, and it's the most intimate moment of my life.

I take note of every moan, gasp, or sigh she makes, filing it away for future reference, becoming an expert on Olivia and what brings her the most pleasure. I previously thought she preferred things hard and fast, but it seems she also responds well when it's slow and tender. Very interesting.

More experiments are definitely required. Lots more.

She digs her nails into my shoulder and kisses me harder, and I sense she wants me to bring her to completion. That's the best way to feed her as well, I've found. When both of us come almost simultaneously, she seems the most sated. And above all else, I aim for her complete satisfaction.

I reach down to play with her clit in the way I know she likes, while my cock strokes in and out of her. Her eyes close and she breathes heavier, letting out a soft moan. I sense her orgasm approaching, and it makes me more aroused as well. We rock together faster, and I keep up the pressure on her clit, until she climaxes and tightens around my cock, which sets me off too. We keep moving as the waves of pleasure roll through us, until we can only hold each other and try to get our breathing under control.

I stroke her hair when it's over, marveling at the way it shines and curls around my finger. She idly rubs a hand along my arm instead of jumping up and running away. Hmm, I could get used to this.

"What was it like, growing up here?" Olivia asks.

I prop my head under my arm and stare at the ceiling. "I don't know how to compare it to any other childhood, but it was fine, I suppose. I grew up with a big lawn to run around on, a large lake to swim in, and a library with all the books I could want."

"Were there any other kids around? Anyone your age?"

"No."

"That sounds lonely."

"There were plenty of students on campus to interact with, along with professors. Hilda and Raziel were especially kind, and would spend time with me when my father was busy. Which was often."

Olivia runs her nails up and down my chest. "What about your mother?"

"She has never been in the picture."

"No?" Olivia bites her lip. "Can I ask what happened?"

"Nothing happened. My parents had an arrangement, and she fulfilled her part of the deal and moved on." There's a bitter taste in my mouth as I say the words. I dislike talking about such things. It's easier to go about my day without thinking about any of this and keeping it locked away in the back of my mind.

Olivia sits up a little and looks at me with interest. "What was the arrangement?"

"I'm sure they covered this in Angelic History, but as immortal beings, supernaturals do not reproduce easily or often, at least in Heaven, Hell, and Faerie. It could take a hundred years, or even a thousand, for a couple to have a child. But that isn't the case on Earth."

"Yes, Kassiel told us about it in class. He said it's one of the main reasons angels and demons started migrating here."

I sit up too and fix the pillows behind us as I talk. "Indeed. Angels tried to regulate the migration, to keep us from moving too quickly into this world and revealing our kind to humans, but demons shared none of those concerns. Eventually none of that mattered though, once the Earth Accords were signed. Michael and Lucifer used the Staff of Eternity, and all angels and demons were sent to Earth, with Heaven and Hell being abandoned and sealed off. Once all of our people were here on Earth, they began to procreate a lot more frequently. Our population swelled with new angels for the first time, and the Archangels became worried."

"Worried?" she asks.

"Worried they would lose power without any heirs of their own.

Together the Archangels made a pact to all have at least one child. Raphael, of course, had already had multiple children at that point, but was happy to sire another. My father reluctantly agreed, and chose another Ofanim named Dina, who was a prophet. They had me, and then she gave me up to be raised by Uriel as part of the deal. I've only met her a few times."

Olivia touches her neck reflexively, but she's not wearing her necklace still. "How awful. I'm sure she misses you."

"I don't know if she does."

She leans back on the pillows, totally comfortable with her nudity. "I always wondered why you Princes were born around the same time. I guess this explains it."

"Yes. Five male children, all sired from Archangels. Ekariel was the first by a few years. He was Azrael and Jophiel's son."

"And Callan's half-brother," she adds quietly.

"Yes. He was killed when he was a child, presumably by demons, but there's no evidence of that. Or that he's dead, as a matter of fact. Anyway, Marcus and I were born next, followed by Callan and Jonah." I raise an eyebrow at her. "And then you were next."

"Except I was an accident."

"A lucky one," I say, as I pull her into my arms again. Yes, I could definitely get used to this.

20

OLIVIA

When I return to my room, I pull out my laptop and play the video again. As I watch the guys admit they've known all along where Jonah is, I mull over the idea of exposing them. Telling the world they knew my brother was going to sneak into Faerie. Revealing they're all in the Order. It would be the perfect revenge for them exposing me as a succubus.

The problem is...I'm not sure I want to do that anymore.

Callan was the true person behind that betrayal, but this video would incriminate Marcus and Bastien too. More than that, it would reveal my brother was in the Order with them.

Is it worth hurting so many people just to get back at Callan? I'm starting to think the answer is no. I'll have to find some other way to get revenge on him. He must have other secrets, and I'm good at sneaking around. I'll find something.

There's still so much I don't know too. Like why they let Jonah go to Faerie. That part infuriates me. I know the Order wanted him to get the staff, and my brother was uniquely qualified to find it because of his special ability to change the way he looks, but still, it was risky. What did they think was going to happen? The fae would just hand over the Staff and Jonah would walk out of there with a smile on his face? Even I know better than that.

Pausing the video, I study Marcus's expression and body language, then rewind and watch again, smirking as he throws stuffed animals at Callan. He really was pissed at them for getting him so far into this mess, but I've seen them together since then, so he must have forgiven them.

Now that I've forgiven Bastien, who did much worse things than Marcus, I should probably forgive Marcus too. I know he's sorry for what he did, and he's apologized many times, but somehow his betrayal stings more. He and I grew close last year, and he made me think there might be something real to our relationship—and then I learned he was involved in all their bullying. Even though it was mostly Callan's plan, Marcus could've stepped up and been the one to put a stop to it, but he didn't.

A noise outside my room draws my attention to the sliding door that leads to the balcony. I look back at my laptop, trying to ignore it, but then I hear the noise again. It's like a strange gust of wind, and just when I think it's stopped, some music starts. Someone's playing a guitar, and it sounds like it's right outside my room. Probably one of the other students on their balcony. I listen to the words, about walking through fire or some such, and the voice sounds really familiar. My curiosity piqued, I hop off my bed and head to the balcony.

As I open the sliding door, my mouth falls open. Marcus is flying outside, his glorious wings flapping slowly to keep him hovering a short distance from my balcony. There's a guitar in his hand, and he's belting out the lyrics to that song by Harry Styles, "Adore You." It's incredibly corny, especially when he grins and points at me during the chorus, but he has a sexy voice and I find myself captivated anyway.

When the song ends, I hear applause and cheers from some of the other balconies, and realize we have an audience. My face flushes, and I gesture at Marcus to come toward me. "Get in here, you're causing a scene."

Our onlookers hoot, and Marcus gives them all a wave and a charming smile before tucking his wings and shooting toward me.

"I didn't know you played guitar," I say. "Or sang."

He lands gracefully on my balcony and his wings vanish as he sets the guitar down. "I stopped after Jonah disappeared, but you inspire me."

I roll my eyes, but I'm smiling too. "You're so cheesy."

"It's true." He steps forward and holds out his hand. This time, I take it. "No other girl has ever made me feel the way you do. For the first time in years, I want to make music again." He brings my hand to his lips. "I'm so sorry for everything that happened last year, and I want to make it up to you. Let me take you to dinner."

"Okay."

His eyes brighten. "Okay?"

"I think you earned a meal after that performance, if nothing else."

He lets out a whoop, and then picks me up like I weigh nothing and spins me around. He sets me down and steps back with a grin. "Come on. I know a good place that's only a fifteen-minute flight from here."

I throw on a sweater and grab my purse, and then we launch ourselves off the balcony. My wings are jet black and blend into the night sky, while Marcus's are bronze and white, his feathers glinting like metal under the bright moonlight. True to his word, it takes about fifteen minutes of leisurely flying before he starts to veer down, and then we land behind a little diner called Angela's. The logo has a hamburger and milkshake with wings.

I raise my eyebrows at Marcus as we set down. "This seems very on-the-nose."

He winks. "You'll love it. Best food for miles."

I glance around. I've been to this little town once before to feed off a trucker at a bar, but otherwise have never had a reason to come out here.

When we step inside, a short, round woman with curly hair rushes over to us. "Marcus, dear! It's been too long!"

"I've been busy at school," he says, with a sheepish grin.

"Who's your girlfriend?" she asks, smiling at me.

Marcus doesn't bother to correct her. "This is Olivia."

"Is she..." She wiggles her eyebrows. "Like you?"

"Close enough," he says with a wink.

"Come, come." She leads us to a booth in the corner. The place looks like something out of the 1950's, with sparkly laminate tables edged in metal and plastic booth seats in neon blue. There's even a mini jukebox below the window.

We slide into the booth, and Marcus immediately leans over and queues up something. "Elvis," he says with a grin. "My mom's favorite."

I raise my eyebrows, but say nothing.

Angela hands us some menus and tells us to order anything, before heading behind the counter. "On the house, of course."

"What's that all about?" I ask when she's gone.

"I'm a very loveable guy," Marcus says.

"She knows about...our kind."

"Jonah and I used to come here during our first year at Seraphim Academy in the middle of the night to get waffles and chicken. They're the best, you have to order them." He doesn't even glance at the plastic menu in front of him. "Angela was always kind to us. Treated us like a mom. Made us feel a little less homesick, you know? Anyway, one night, she had a heart attack right there behind the counter. A bad one. Jonah called 911, but I knew no one would arrive in time, not out here in the boonies. So I healed her, even though we're not supposed to do things like that. Jonah used his Ishim invisibility to keep anyone else from seeing what was happening, but there was no hiding the healing glow from Angela. She was already a believer in angels and a devout Christian, and she swears she saw my wings. After that, it was impossible to convince her we weren't angels. So I just gave up, and let her feed me."

"A good deed," I admit. "But you could have gotten in a lot of trouble for that."

He spreads his hands. "What's the point in having these powers if not to help people? And not just angels, but everyone here on Earth?"

"That sounds odd coming from someone in the Order."

He looks out the window with a frown. "I was invited to join the

Order, and it seemed like a cool clique that all my friends were join-ing. Once I realized what they were really about, it was too late to back out."

Angela comes and takes our order, and I let Marcus talk me into trying these infamous chicken and waffles.

Once we're alone again, I sigh. "I'm still upset with you."

Marcus shakes his head with a smile. "You said you forgive me. You're not allowed to take that back."

"I forgive you for your part in how the three of you treated me last year. I don't forgive you for letting Jonah go to Faerie."

Marcus's face darkens. "I didn't want him to go."

"Then why did you let him?" I throw my hands up. "All three of you knew where he was going. Even Grace knew. Did not one of you stop and think, hmm, this might be a bad idea?"

"Of course we did. I tried to talk him out of it, but he wouldn't listen."

"What about Callan and Bastien?"

He hesitates. "Callan hates demons, as you know. His half-brother Ekariel was killed by them as a kid, and then there was Michael's murder... Plus Jonah kept talking about duty and honor, and you know Callan is all about that shit."

I nod. "I get why Callan would be on board with getting the Staff, but what about Bastien? I've never gotten the sense that he hates demons."

"No, he doesn't, or no more than he hates people in general, anyway," Marcus says with a snort. "But Bastien is a scholar at heart, and the thought of retrieving the Staff and being able to study it proved irresistible. He warned Jonah of the dangers, but ultimately encouraged him to go."

I shake my head. "This is bullshit. The three of you should have stopped him."

Marcus sighs and slumps his shoulders. "Even if we wanted to, we couldn't have stopped him. The Order found out somehow that Jonah could change his appearance, and then they were determined to use him. And he agreed, all too easily."

Angela brings us some sodas, and then I ask, "So you are all members of the Order?"

"Yeah, we are. Jonah was too."

I already knew all that, but it's good to hear it from Marcus's mouth. "How did they find out about his power?"

Marcus shrugs. "I don't know. He wasn't exactly careful about hiding it. Maybe someone saw him. Maybe he told someone."

I believe it. He was so proud when he showed off his new skill to me, and then he went missing not long after.

"But why would Jonah want to get the Staff anyway? He doesn't want to send the demons back to Hell." Not the Jonah I knew, anyway.

He pokes at his soda with a straw. "At the time, I thought he did. He was dating Grace, who is a true believer in the Order and their purpose, and he kept talking about duty and honor and how it was the right thing to do. He said he had to do this, and that it had to be him."

That doesn't sound like Jonah at all. And then there's Grace... I'll have to talk to her at some point to get her side of the story.

Our food arrives, and it's just as delicious as Marcus said it would be. I can see now why he and Jonah came here all the time. My chest clenches as I think of Jonah, and how he's been gone for so long now.

"Letting Jonah go to Faerie is one of many things I regret when it comes to your brother," Marcus says. "I want to do whatever I can to make things right. With you, and with him. So if you have a plan for rescuing Jonah, I want in on it."

I push around a piece of waffle on my plate. "What makes you think I have a plan?"

He grins at me. "Because I know you, Liv. You always have a plan."

True that.

21

OLIVIA

After my dinner with Marcus, I invited him back to my room, but he gave me a chaste kiss and declined. When he saw my surprised look, he stroked my cheek and said, "I want to show you what we have isn't just about sex."

Naturally, that only made me want him more.

A few days later, we had dinner again, this time in my dorm, and then we slept together. Now we've fallen back into our old groove, and with both him and Bastien giving me regular sex, I have more energy than ever before.

Somehow it's already the beginning of June. This school year is flying by, and I'm no closer to finding my brother. It's frustrating, to say the least. But when Family Day arrives, I jump out of bed with hope for the first time in weeks—hope that Araceli's dad will show up and provide the answers I need about how to get into Faerie and rescue Jonah.

I quickly shower and throw on a cute outfit, one that's not too sexy in case Father comes today, and something I can fight in, in case the Order makes a move against Araceli's dad. I need to be prepared for anything today.

When I head into our little kitchen to grab my coffee, Araceli is already there looking miserable as she eats a banana.

"What's wrong?" I ask, as I pour coffee into my mug, the one Marcus got me after the Princes broke my mug from Jonah. This mug has a little cartoon devil on it with the words, "Coffee fiend," and even though it doesn't replace what I lost, it still makes me smile.

"It's Family Day," Araceli says with a groan. "I'm worried my dad will show up, and I'm worried he won't. I can't decide what's worse."

"Everything is going to be fine," I try to assure her. "If he shows up, then it will give you a chance to reconnect. If he doesn't, then we don't have to worry about him getting kidnapped or anything. Either way, just try to enjoy it, and spend some time with your mom too. I know she's proud of you."

Araceli smiles at me and tugs on her purple streak. "Yeah, she is. It'll be good to see her. But what about you? Are you excited to have Gabriel follow you around all day?"

"Not really." I lean back on the counter and sigh. "I'm afraid it will become a spectacle. I'm one of a kind, and if Gabriel shows up, people will whisper. If he doesn't, they'll whisper even more. Either way, I'll be the center of attention, which isn't my favorite place to be."

She grins. "If it gets to be too much, we can ditch class and hide in our room."

I raise my mug to her in a salute. "Good plan."

There's a knock on our door, and Araceli runs over and opens it. "Mom!" she squeals, and then throws her arms around a woman who looks like a slightly older version of her, but without the purple streak. A pang of jealousy hits me as I watch them hug and smile and catch up. I've never had that kind of relationship with my mother, and in fact, I haven't heard from her in years. Even if I wanted her to come today, she wouldn't be welcome at Seraphim Academy.

I thought that once I was no longer hiding what I was, she would feel comfortable reaching out to me, but I guess that's not the case.

She taught me to be a succubus when I was eighteen, and then she just...vanished. I miss her. A lot.

"Hello, dear." Araceli's mom, Muriel, holds her hand out. "I'm glad to meet you again. Araceli has told me so much about you."

With a nervous grin, I shake her hand, hoping Araceli hasn't told her *too* much. "It's nice to see you again also."

Araceli grabs her bag. "Ready to show off our weapons training?"

"Definitely." I get my things and hold open the door for them. "Araceli is a natural with a sword."

"Is she? I was never very good at fighting, so she must get that from her father's side." Muriel puffs up with pride, and that annoying jealous pang is back. I'm not sure Mother's ever been proud of me.

We chit-chat all the way to the gym, and Muriel tells me about how she's recently opened a wildlife rescue in Arizona, where she heals animals and rehabilitates them before re-releasing them in the wild. It's a great use of her angelic powers, since it doesn't attract too much human attention either.

"That sounds amazing," I tell her.

"I got to help out over the break, and it was really great," Araceli says. "Archangel Ariel came by too at one point. I'd never met her before, but she was sweet, although a little odd."

She quickly glances at me, probably because Ariel is Jonah's mother. I've never met her, but from what I heard from Jonah and Gabriel, she's very quirky and flighty. She's a Malakim, like Araceli and Muriel, but spends most of her time in nature, healing plants and animals. She has always given Jonah tons of love, but tends to flit in and out of his life like a colorful butterfly. Much of his childhood was spent either traveling with her on various wildlife excursions, or living in her little cottage in the middle of a forest. The rest of it was spent with Gabriel living in an angel community, growing up among his peers. Pretty much the opposite of my childhood spent in human foster care, with no real family or friends, but I try not to let that bother me.

"Yes, Archangel Ariel has been a great supporter of my work,"

Muriel says, as we reach the gym. "She actually gave me the funding to get started in the first place. She's a good soul, although she's been miserable ever since her son disappeared." Muriel shoots me a quick frown, as though she's just realized I'm connected to Jonah also. "Oh dear, I'm sorry, that must be tough for you also."

"It's fine," I say quickly as I open the door to the gym, hoping we can drop the subject. And then I freeze.

Gabriel stands against the wall in his perfectly tailored suit, radiating power and authority without even trying. But like Jonah, he also looks approachable, like a friendly neighbor who always waves at you from his front lawn.

His eyes light up when I walk in. "Olivia," he calls out, and my heart leaps a little as I notice how happy he looks to see me. I split off from Muriel and Araceli and go to him.

Father hesitates a moment, before giving me a quick hug. "Surprised to see me?"

It must have shown on my face. "A little. I thought you might be too busy."

He clasps a hand on my shoulder. "No, you're my priority now."

I'm saved from replying by Hilda clapping her hands. "Let's get started, class. Pair up, and show your parents what we've been working on."

"I've decided to choose daggers as my weapon to focus on," I tell Gabriel, as we walk to the table with all the weapons on it. I pick up the knife I like to practice with, a small one with a black hilt that fits nicely in my hand.

"You're focusing on daggers?" He sounds so surprised that I glance over at him, worried I've chosen wrong somehow.

"Yeah, why?"

"It's your mother's favorite weapon, too." He rubs his arm absently with a distant smile. "She got me one time. I teleported behind her in her bedroom once, and she was so startled she reacted by stabbing me in the arm with a dark-infused blade. Hurt like the devil, but what did I expect? I learned after that to never sneak up on her."

I stare at my father with my jaw slack. He's rarely mentioned his time with my mother, and never with any kind of fondness. I always thought I was the lucky—or unlucky—result of a one-night stand or a short affair, but maybe there was more to it than that. "Wow. What was your preferred weapon?"

"I prefer to avoid combat when I can, but in the old days I used a spear. You don't see too many of those around now though." He chuckles softly as he picks up a spear from the table.

As the leader of the Ishim, Father commands a large number of messengers, spies, scouts, and assassins. He also oversees the guardian angel program, which is used to protect important people around the world. He's definitely not a warrior, but more of a hide-in-the-shadows type, only fighting when absolutely necessary. Jonah was—no, *is*—the same.

I'm distracted by Callan sparring with Araceli, both of them wielding swords, although his is much larger. He's putting her through her paces, but she grits her teeth and fights back with every-thing she's got, trying to make her mom proud. She manages to disarm Callan, and ends with her sword at his neck and a big grin on her face. It seems a little too easy, and I wonder if Callan let her win. Araceli is a good fighter, but she's not *that* good. But I have a hard time believing Callan would lose on purpose either—his ego is way too big for that.

When they're done, Muriel claps, and Gabriel and I join in also. "Good show," Father calls out.

Callan pauses, and then walks over to us and bows his head to Gabriel. I've never seen him look so humble before. "Sir."

Father shakes Callan's hand. "It's been far too long. Is your mother here today?"

"No, she couldn't make it," Callan says. "Something came up at Aerie Industries."

Like Jonah, Callan's got the blood of two Archangels flowing through his veins. His father was Michael, the former leader of the Archangels, who was murdered a few years ago. His mother is Jophiel, who took over as the CEO of Aerie Industries when the former CEO, Azrael, stepped up to lead the Archangel Council after Michael's death.

If Callan is upset by being alone on Family Day, I can't tell. For a second I pity him a little, especially as I glance around the room and see all the other students with their family members, but then I remember I hate him and the pity vanishes.

"Callan's the one who exposed me as a succubus to the entire school," I tell Gabriel.

"Is that so?" Father asks, raising his eyebrows. I have a feeling he already knew, judging by his tone. "I get the sense my daughter is not a fan of yours."

Callan lifts his chin. "I stand by my actions. If I hadn't done it, you wouldn't be standing here with her now."

Ouch. He has a point there. Gabriel's only here as a result of Callan's betrayal, and the reminder stings a little.

"I can't deny that," Gabriel says. "What are you doing in the Second Year class?"

I note the quick subject change, but let it go. "Callan's working as Hilda's assistant for these classes."

"Excellent." Gabriel stands back and waves us on. "Let's see what you've learned so far."

I turn to face Callan, who grabs a short sword off the table, before getting into a fighting stance. He lunges for me and I dodge, twist, and thrust. He taught me some of those moves, which means he's expecting them too, and he quickly retaliates. If I thought he might go easy on me like he did with Araceli, I am sorely mistaken. He slashes at me and nearly gets my arm, but I manage to get away in time. He roundhouse kicks me and knocks me down on the mat, but I roll and slice him along the shin. He grunts and steps back, and I jump to my feet. He rushes me again, and I use a move he showed me last year to let his momentum carry him over my shoulder and to the ground. As his back hits the mat, he drops the sword, and I put my foot on his chest with a satisfied smile.

Father claps for me. "Very good."

Callan stands and checks his cut, which is shallow and already healing. "She's improved a lot since she started."

It sounds a lot like a backhanded compliment, so I shoot him a glare, which he ignores. Then I wonder if he meant it as an actual compliment. No. That's impossible.

22

OLIVIA

G abriel sits in on some of my other classes, and then we head
out to the lawn, where the school has prepared a big banquet
in honor of our guests. Picnic tables are spread out across the grass,
and the weather is absolutely perfect—sunny, without a cloud in the
sky, warm, but with a nice breeze. Banners hang between tree
branches, welcoming everyone to Family Day, and there's a cheerful
atmosphere as everyone grabs food, chats with their parents, and
soaks up the sunshine.

I walk onto the lawn beside my father with a bundle of dread in
my stomach, worried all eyes will be on us—and they are. We head
over to the big buffet tables, and people stop and stare at Gabriel in
awe while we grab some corn, barbeque chicken, cole slaw, and
potato salad. I knew he was a big deal, but I've never seen other
angels around him before. The only good news is that no one is
looking at me.

Then everyone forgets about Gabriel completely when Marcus
walks into the area with his dad, Raphael. Marcus is gorgeous, but
he pales next to his father. The guy is practically sex on a stick,
which feels wrong to think about, when he's an ancient Archangel
like my father. Raphael leads the Malakim and is considered to be

the most powerful healer in the world. It's even rumored he can bring back the dead.

But what he's most known for? Being a total player.

I can totally see it too, as he flashes a suave grin at every lady he passes by, while the sun shoots highlights through his dark curly hair and illuminates his bronze skin. He stops at each table, kissing women's cheeks, greeting everyone with warmth and exuberance.

"What a flirt," I say, without really meaning to, just as Araceli and her mom walk over to us.

"Yeah, he's...quite charming," Father says diplomatically.

"He's probably looking for his next baby mama," Araceli says, and then looks at my father and covers her mouth, like she can't believe she just said that in front of him.

"Araceli!" Muriel says, horrified.

But my father just laughs. "No, she's probably right. I can't even remember how many sons Raphael has at this point. Eight, maybe?"

Poor Marcus. He's being dragged along in his father's shadow, and it seems like Raphael is ignoring him completely as he soaks up the attention. I wonder if that's what his childhood was like—and where's his mother?

Uriel and Bastien, meanwhile, stand on the edge of the festivities, speaking to one another in low voices as they watch over the crowd. Uriel didn't bother to join us in Fae Studies, but I suppose he doesn't really need Family Day to see his son. I'm not surprised to see that Bastien's mother is missing either.

We move to an open table, and I wave Araceli and her mom over to join us. They sit down, even though Muriel looks a little starstruck to be eating with Gabriel.

"Aren't you proud of these girls?" Father asks Muriel, as if we're in kindergarten and have just completed a finger painting.

"Bursting," Muriel says with lowered lashes. "Couldn't be happier."

"Any sign of your dad?" I ask Araceli quietly, while Gabriel talks to Muriel about her wildlife center.

"No. I wrote him a long email, and left him a voicemail too, so I really hoped he would show up." She sighs. "At least we don't have to worry about an ambush from the Order. Although I'm sorry you couldn't complete your task. I'll keep trying."

"Don't worry about that. I just want to make sure you're okay."

"I'm fine." She does not sound fine.

"I'm sorry, friend." I take her hand and squeeze it under the picnic table.

Raphael appears at my elbow, with his son behind him. "May we join you?"

"Of course," Gabriel says. Muriel's eyes get even bigger as she takes in the second Archangel at our table.

"This must be Olivia." Raphael holds his hand out and gives me a million-dollar smile. "I can see why Marcus is so taken with you."

I shake his hand and feel a little star-struck myself. He's so charming and attractive, it's hard not to get lost in his warm brown eyes. "Hello."

"Where's your mother, Marcus?" Muriel asks. "I haven't seen her in some time and would love to catch up with her."

"She's at home," Marcus says. "She says she's too pregnant to travel."

Raphael holds up his hands in surrender. "This one's not mine, I swear!"

The table all laughs, and everyone relaxes a little. I had no idea Marcus's mother was pregnant, and I wonder who the father is. Combined with all of Raphael's other sons, Marcus is the only angel I know with a big family.

I glance around at the other tables, and spot Grace eating lunch with a pretty redhead who I assume is her mother, plus a boy with the same fiery hair who must be her little brother. Nariel sits with them too, but there's no sign of Grace's father.

Behind them, I notice Tanwen sitting with a muscular man with very light, shiny blond hair. Like Gabriel and Raphael, he radiates power, although not as strongly. That must be Zadkiel, Tanwen's father, and Michael's replacement on the Archangel council. Beside him is a woman with the same glossy hair tied back in a tight pony-tail. She looks even taller and fiercer than Tanwen, which is saying a lot. Her sister, I guess. I look around for their mother, and then remember Araceli telling me that Tanwen's mom was killed by human hunters.

Seems like most of us have a missing parent. I guess there are not many functional relationships among immortals.

Lunch passes quickly, and both Archangels are especially warm and friendly with Muriel and Araceli. I'm pretty sure they're trying to make an effort to show inclusion, supporting me and Araceli even though other angels consider us outcasts, and I want to hug them both for it. By the time lunch is over, I'm pretty sure Muriel wants to be next in line for making a baby with Raphael.

We get through the rest of my classes, and even though I find it awkward to sit beside my dad while Kassiel lectures us on history, neither of them seems bothered.

When my last class is over, I think Gabriel will probably be more than ready to get out of here, but instead he asks, "May we go somewhere and talk? Privately?"

This is unexpected. "Is my dorm private enough?"

He nods, and I spread my wings and head that way. When we land on the balcony, he chuckles. "I could've teleported us here in half that time."

I roll my eyes. All Archangels have an extra power that's unique to them, and my dad's is teleporting. That's also how Jonah can change his appearance, since he has the blood of an Archangel. I wonder if I'll develop bonus powers too, or if being a half-breed makes that impossible.

We head into the dorm, and I'm relieved to see Araceli isn't back yet. Gabriel sits stiffly on the couch, and I sit beside him and grab a pillow to hug against my chest. I have a feeling something is weighing heavily on him. "What did you want to talk about?"

Father studies me for a long moment, and then he says. "I'm worried about Azrael."

"What do you mean?" Azrael is the leader of the Archangel Council, and I've heard he's pretty scary—he's known as the Angel of Death for a reason.

"As you know, angels and demons are forbidden from having relations, and a hybrid child is unheard of. Your very existence puts you in danger. It's the reason your mother and I kept you hidden for as long as we could."

"I know."

"The secret is out now, and there's nothing we can do about it. In a way, it's a relief. I no longer have to deny your existence and can openly be your father in public. But I am also going to be punished for the crime of siring you."

"Punished?" My eyes widen. "How?"

"I don't know yet. The Archangel Council will vote on my sentence at an upcoming meeting. I doubt they'll do anything too severe, but I wanted you to be aware of it anyway. That's why I wanted to speak with you. They might send me away for a while, possibly to Penumbra Prison, and then I won't be able to look after you. As such, I want you to know about the risks."

"Okay." I clutch the pillow tighter to my chest. I don't want anything bad to happen to Gabriel, especially now that we're getting to know each other. "Will you be all right?"

"I'll be fine. You don't need to worry about that." He reaches across the couch and pats my leg. "But I want to make sure you're especially careful over the next few months. If they send me away, no one will stand between you and Azrael. He hates demons, and if it were up to him, we'd restart the war tomorrow. Now that he's the leader of the Archangel Council, I worry he'll want to use you, or possibly kill you to make an example."

"I'll try to be careful. I think I'm safe here. Uriel won't let anything happen to me."

"I hope so." He sighs and drops his head. I've never seen him look so defeated before. "Things would be a lot easier now if I'd taken the leadership position when it was offered to me. Having Azrael in charge can only lead angels down a dark path."

"Why did you turn it down? You seem like the obvious choice to lead the Archangels."

"I turned it down to protect you." He looks up at me with pain in his bright blue eyes. "I couldn't risk having that level or attention or scrutiny on me at all times, not without it leading people back to you. If I'd taken the job, it would have put you in danger."

He gave up the highest position an angel can have. Turned down the leadership of the Archangels. For me.

"Do you regret that decision?" I ask.

He reaches over and takes my hand. "Never. I know it doesn't seem like it, but everything I've done has always been to protect you and Jonah. I just wish my decision didn't put you in greater danger now."

"Wow. Um, thank you." I stammer through the words, fighting the wave of emotion his confession brings up. He might have been an absent dad, but all along he was doing what he thought was best for me.

He nods and slowly rises to his feet. "Don't worry. I'm going to make sure you're well protected." He bends down and presses a kiss to the top of my hair. "I'll see you again as soon as I can."

I stand up, hating that he has to go, and fearing for his future. "Thanks for coming today. Goodbye, Father."

He gives me one last warm smile, and then disappears in the blink of an eye.

23

CALLAN

G abriel appears in front of me, and I nearly deck the guy. I've seen him teleport many times before, but I doubt I'll ever stop wanting to reach for a sword when it happens.

"Thank you for meeting with me," the Archangel says, as he glances around the lounge in the bell tower. "Interesting décor."

"Courtesy of your daughter." We removed most of the pink sparkly stuff, but Marcus insisted we keep some of the stuffed animals, and we'll never be able to get all the glitter off the floor.

Gabriel laughs. "She's full of surprises."

"Would you like something to drink?" I ask, trying to remember my mother's lessons in politeness. It still hurts that she cancelled on Family Day at the last minute. I get that her new job at Aerie Industries is important, but I never see her anymore. Not that we've ever been super close, but it'd be nice to know she is proud of me, like the other parents were with their kids today.

"No, thank you." Gabriel sits in Bastien's armchair like it's a throne. "I've got a very important task for you."

I sit on the couch, my back stiff and straight. "Yes, sir?"

"Your father and I had our differences, as you know. But the one thing we both agreed was that we wanted peace and unity between demons and angels. Nothing has changed in that regard, even after his death."

I nod. As much as I hate demons, I don't want the war to begin again. That's why I wanted to help the Order get the Staff of Eternity, and why I encouraged Jonah to go to Faerie to get it. If they send the demons back to Hell, another war can be averted. That was my hope, anyway.

Now I'm not so sure I want that anymore. As much as Olivia drives me mad, the thought of sending her to Hell feels wrong. Maybe I'm starting to think she belongs here too, as much as the rest of us.

Damn that woman, I wish she'd get out of my head.

Gabriel leans back in the chair as he continues. "Olivia is a sign that things could change between angels and demons, now that both races are living here on Earth. That also puts her in grave danger at all times. I've tried to watch over her as best I can, but I need your help."

"My help?"

"You are a fearsome warrior, are you not?"

I sit up a little straighter. "I am."

"I would expect no less from Michael's son. And as the son of Jophiel, you must be honorable as well. That's why I've chosen you for the most important thing I could ask of you—the protection of my daughter."

Fuck.

"Are you certain you want to choose me? Olivia and I... We don't get along on the best of days."

"I don't care about that. I only care about her safety, and I know you're the person who can protect her the best."

I glance down at my hands. I've been trying to avoid Olivia as much as possible, and this is going to make that a lot harder. But I can't exactly say no to an Archangel.

"Please, Callan," Gabriel says, with more emotion in his voice than I've ever heard. "I've already lost my son. Please make sure I don't lose my daughter too."

I glance away, my jaw tightening at the reminder of Jonah. I made promises to him too about Olivia. Promises that I couldn't keep. Surely he would want his sister to be safe now that she's staying at Seraphim Academy. If I agree to this, I'm not just doing it for Gabriel, but for Jonah too.

"All right," I say. "On my honor, I'll protect her with my life."

"Thank you." He stands and offers his hand, and I shake it firmly. "I feel better knowing her safety is in your hands."

I swallow hard and nod. What the fuck have I gotten myself into?

He clasps me on the shoulder. "I should've been around more for you after Michael died. And while he was alive too, perhaps."

I stare at him in surprise. It was well-known that Gabriel and Michael didn't get along. As the leader of the angelic spies, Gabriel works in the shadows, trying to get information before making a decision. When he acts, he prefers a knife in the back to an outright confrontation. My father, on the other hand, often acted first, usually with violence, and then thought later. I should know—I often got the brunt of his violence, a secret I'll probably keep to my grave, since there's no way I could tarnish the image of the beloved Archangel Michael. Everyone admired him, and no one knew what a total dick he could be in private. But I think maybe Gabriel knows, from the look on his face now.

"One more thing." His fingers on my shoulder tighten, digging into my skin painfully. "If you ever betray or hurt my daughter again, you'll have to answer to me, and Michael's legacy won't be able to protect you. Do you understand?"

I swallow. "Yes, sir."

"I'm glad we understand each other," the Archangel says.

He vanishes, and I let out a long breath. I better call Bastien and Marcus and get them over here. I'll need their help to protect Olivia, since she won't let me near her. What was Gabriel thinking, putting me in charge of her protection? The woman hates my guts, and the feeling is mutual. Plus she's still plotting some kind of horrible payback for me.

This is going to be a disaster.

24

OLIVIA

Every year the three supernatural schools—Seraphim Academy, Hellspawn Academy, and Ethereal Academy—choose a sport to focus on, and this year it's soccer. It's well-known that the fae always kick everyone's asses at soccer, so our team has been training non-stop, which means I don't see Marcus as often as either of us would like.

Tonight is the first game, and it's against the fae. It's another chance for Araceli's dad to visit her, and another chance for me to complete my task for the Order.

The bleachers are packed as Araceli and I fly over to them. On one side, angels fill the stands, and the other side has a much smaller number of fae. Very few of them like to leave Faerie at all, so these are probably all family members of the players, here to show their support.

As we set down on the angel side, I notice Araceli looks a little paler than usual. "You don't have to be here," I tell her.

Last year, Araceli's boyfriend Darel was killed at one of these games. The Order made it look like it was a demon attack, but we know it was them. She's avoided the games ever since, and as she glances over at the fae side of the field, I think it's not just because of

Darel that she's nervous. Araceli has never tried to hide her fae side, but she hasn't exactly embraced it either. I don't blame her, since they totally rejected her.

She straightens up and tucks her purple streak behind a pointed ear. "I need to do this. For me."

I nod. "Do you think your dad will show?"

"Probably not, but I did leave him another voicemail letting him know about the game." She offers me a weak smile. "I am trying."

She looks so sad while trying to put on a brave face, that I throw my arms around her and give her a big hug. "You're doing great."

She gives me a squeeze and then steps back with resolve in her eyes. "Besides, we need to make sure the Order doesn't try anything tonight. Even if my dad's not here, they might try and kidnap one of the other fae."

"We won't let that happen."

We scan the bleachers, but don't see Araceli's dad anywhere. I think she's probably right that he won't bother coming. It's frustrating, and not because of the Order—after reconnecting with my father, I want Araceli to be able to do the same with hers.

"May we sit with you?" Bastien asks, as he comes up behind me. He rests a light hand on my lower back almost possessively, and it sends a little thrill through me.

Callan's beside him, and he scowls as he notices Bastien's hand, but says nothing. I don't really want him anywhere near me, but I guess he's a package deal with Bastien. Ugh.

"We're not really planning to sit," I tell them slowly, then glance at Araceli. Can we trust the Princes? They're in the Order too, and there's no telling what task they've been given. For all we know, they're supposed to steal one of the fae away.

"You don't plan to cheer for Marcus?" Callan asks, making it sound like an insult.

"Of course we do," I snap back at him.

"We want to check out the fae," Araceli says. "Me, mostly. I'm so curious about them, with my heritage and all."

Bastien narrows his eyes at me. "And no doubt Olivia is interested because of Jonah."

"Fine, but we're going with you," Callan says, his voice leaving no room for argument. For anyone but me, anyway.

I shoot him a glare. "No one's inviting you along."

He stares me down. "Too bad. It's not safe for you over there."

"Since when do you care?"

"Since your father put me in charge of your protection."

"What?" I can't keep the horror off my face. "You?"

He raises his chin and gives me a cocky smirk. "Looks that way. So wherever you go, I'll be there, making sure no one tries anything."

I want to wipe that arrogant look off his face so bad. "That's really not necessary. I'm not the one in danger here."

"You're obviously worried about the fae being kidnapped by the Order," Bastien says in a matter-of-fact tone. "We can help you."

"We don't know if we can trust you," Araceli says, and I'm proud of her for standing up to them. Last year, they scared the crap out of her.

"I swear on the light of truth that I have no intention of harming the fae," Bastien says, and a white glow surrounds him. He makes Callan do the same, and even though he repeats the words with an eyeroll, the light surrounds him too. "There. Now you know we speak the truth."

I glance at Araceli, since I'm not familiar with this, and she nods. "Fine," I say. "Come with us. We're going to patrol the area during the game and look for anything suspicious."

We take a quick walk through the angel side of the bleachers as the game begins. Marcus and the rest of the team run out onto the field to massive cheers. I notice that asshole Jeremy is also on the team, along with Cyrus's boyfriend Isaiah, but don't know the rest of the players.

The fae team runs out next, moving with otherworldly grace across the field. The fae side claps enthusiastically, but don't cheer or yell, like the angels did. Nope, they're way too refined for that. I study them closely, taking my first look at full-blooded fae. Most of the players are men, but there are a few women too. They're all tall and willowy, with pointed ears, sharp, beautiful features, and hair that looks dyed, ranging from sunflower yellow to lime green to snow white.

"How do we know they're not using glamour?" I ask. We learned a little about glamour in the last Fae Studies class, and how the fae can use it to create illusions, change their appearance, or trick people. Only Ofanim like Bastien are completely immune.

"Look up," Bastien says, pointing at hundreds of tiny hovering balls of light scattered above us, which cast a bright glow over the field and the bleachers. "Uriel and I spent hours filling the sky with those. The light of truth prevents fae glamour, along with Ishim invisibility and imp illusions. If anyone plans to make a move today, they will do it without any of those powers."

We stop and grab some hot dogs and beer, while the game continues. I take a minute to watch Marcus run across the field in his sexy little shorts, showing off his sculpted calves, and then cheer with everyone else when he scores. The game is tied so far, which is better than anyone thought we would do, and the crowd is buzzing with excitement.

Then we make our way along the outside of the field to the other side, where the fae are sitting. As we approach, we see two guards at the entrance to the bleachers, who seriously look like extras in the Lord of the Rings. They both hold spears and wear elaborate, shining armor, although the one on the left has bronze leaves on his chest, while the one on the right has copper flowers. They must be from the Autumn and Spring Courts, respectively.

"Halt," the spring fae says, blocking our path with her spear. "What is your business here?"

I hesitate, trying to come up with a quick lie, but Bastien steps forward and offers them the truth, of all things. "I am Bastien, son of Archangel Uriel, and his personal assistant. We come to ensure your people's safety, and to offer our assistance."

The autumn fae looks offended by this very suggestion. "As you can see, we have security well under control."

"Is there anything we can get you?" Araceli asks.

Both fae study her intently for a long pause, before the female guard says, "That won't be necessary."

Their spears continue to block our path, so we turn around and head back. Not much else to do. We're obviously not wanted there, and even though we could fly over them, that seems especially rude, and likely to cause problems between the two schools.

"Whatever happened to fae hospitality?" I mumble, as we make it back to the angel side.

"They're our guests," Bastien says. "If they'd invited us, things would be different."

Araceli asks, "Is there nothing we can do?"

"Not without sneaking over there," Callan says.

"My necklace!" I say, grabbing it. "It should let me go invisible, even with your little light of truth bubbles floating around us. I can fly over the fae side for the rest of the game, just to make sure nothing bad happens to them."

"That could work," Bastien says.

Callan grabs my arm. "I'm coming with you."

I shake him off and step back. "No way."

"I made a promise to your father. Trust me, I don't like this any more than you do, but I must keep you safe. And I know you can make me invisible too."

I pinch my brow, trying to decide if I'm more annoyed with Callan or Father at this moment. "Fine. Callan and I will fly over to the fae side and keep watch. You two make sure everything stays calm over here on the angel side."

Araceli and Bastien nod, and head off to sit with the rest of the crowd. I watch them squeeze next to Grace and Cyrus, and then Callan and I head behind the bathrooms so we're out of sight.

I hold out my hand to him. "We need to be touching for this to work. Don't let go of me."

He nods, but instead of taking my hand, he slides his arm around my waist and pulls me close. He's warm and strong and I get a taste of his hateful desire again as our bodies press together.

"We don't need to be *this* close," I say, although I don't move away.

He looks down at me with inscrutable eyes. "It will make it easier for you. We don't want to accidentally break contact."

I suck in a breath and try to block out my own flaring lust. Then I gather light around us, taking it from the glowing baubles floating above us, the moonlight, and the lamps around the field. I bend it around Callan and me until we're invisible. "It worked. Let's go."

Callan holds me against him and launches into the sky before I can even extract my wings. He carries me like I weigh nothing as we dart over the field, while I make sure to keep us hidden.

"I can fly, you know," I say, digging my nails into his arms. His really strong, masculine arms.

"This is safer."

I huff, but there's little point in arguing with him when we're already there. I'm reminded of the other time he carried me, when I was attacked by demons and hit with a light-infused blade. His wings are pure white and edged in gold, and I have the strongest desire to run my fingers along them.

We do a few passes overhead, but don't see anything unusual, and then we land behind their bleachers in a spot of grass. Callan sets me down and takes my hand, before stepping back, then wipes his other hand on his jeans like he's got to brush my cooties off him. I roll my eyes and sit on the grass to wait, tugging him down with me.

We wait there for the entire game in silence, and though I worry it will be awkward holding his hand the entire time, it's surprisingly not. Turns out, as long as I'm not talking to Callan, or looking at his stupid handsome face, he's somewhat tolerable. Even as he runs his calloused fingers over the back of my hand idly, as though he doesn't realize he's doing it.

The most action we get is when two fae sneak under the bleachers to make out, before being shooed away by one of the guards. They run off with their shirts half-on, and I cover my mouth to suppress a giggle. Out of the corner of my eye I see Callan smile a little too.

The angels lose the game, despite Marcus's best efforts, and then the fae gather outside the field to depart. I stand up, dragging Callan with me, but can't see what they're doing. We move closer as a large portal opens up, shimmering and circling while the fae walk though it and vanish. The guards huddle closely around the portal with their spears raised to prevent anyone else from entering. One by one the fae head back to Faerie, and I think about my brother, and how Jonah must have disguised himself as one of them to join their group, then followed them inside. What I don't know is what happened after that. How long could he pass for one of the fae before being discovered? Did he find the Staff? And most of all, is he still alive?

25

OLIVIA

I have a shadow, and his name is Callan.

He follows me between classes with a glower on his face, like he hates me for existing, and hates himself for having to protect me. At one point I ask him, "What is this, the fifties? Want to carry my books for me too?"

He gives me a scathing look. "I'd rather impale myself on my sword."

I'm so over it.

During Ishim class, we're learning how to conceal larger groups of people by making a chain of hands. We each practice turning the rest of the class invisible, but only Grace and I can do it with ease. Nariel promises everyone will get there eventually, but his eyes linger on the two of us. Not with lust though, but something else. Pride, maybe? I can't tell.

This trick will come in handy when I go to Faerie, because I'm starting to realize I won't be able to go by myself. I'll need other people to help me, and I'll need to conceal them. Plans form in my head. The trick is opening one of those portals somehow.

As class ends, Grace walks out with me. "You did great in there.

You're very powerful, which I guess is no surprise, with Archangel blood in your veins. Jonah was strong too."

"Yeah." I corner her in the hallway and lower my voice. "Is that why you let him go to Faerie?"

Shock registers across her face, and then it twists with sorrow. "Let him? I begged Jonah not to go. I did everything I could to stop him. I even tried to go with him, in the end. But he wouldn't listen to me. He was determined to go, and to go alone." Her eyes water with tears she tries to blink back. "Every day I wish I'd tried harder. It kills me wondering if I could have done something more."

Her grief is so sincere, I feel bad for even questioning her. "I'm sorry. I had to know."

She dabs at her eyes with her knuckles. "I understand. I would want to know too, if it was my brother."

I spot Callan hovering out of the corner of my eye and grab Grace's arm, leading her in the other direction. "Is there anything else you can tell me, like why he went?"

"To get the Staff for the Order, so that we can return to Heaven and begin to rebuild," she says, as though it's obvious.

"And to send demons back to Hell?"

"That too."

"That doesn't sound like my brother."

She gives me a kind smile. "I'm sure he didn't think it would work on you. Your angel blood probably protects you."

"Probably?" Seems like kind of a big risk to take on a *probably*. One I seriously doubt Jonah would take, unless he changed a lot in the year he was at Seraphim Academy. What did the Order do to him?

Grace loops her arm with mine as we walk. "You seem so stressed these days, Liv. Let's ditch our next classes and go to Angel Peak for some shopping therapy."

Getting away from campus does sound good, especially if I can ditch Callan in the process. "Is it safe there?"

"Definitely. The coffee shop attack was weeks ago, and security has been beefed up since then. No human is getting in that town now."

"All right, I'm in, but we have to go invisible before we fly off. I need to ditch my tail."

She follows my gaze to Callan. "Not a problem."

We head outside and agree on a place to meet, since we can't see each other while invisible, and then set off for Angel Peak, leaving Callan behind.

You probably think we're going to get attacked there, but it doesn't happen. We spend the next couple hours buying new clothes for summer, before heading back to campus. It's exactly what I needed to unwind after a stressful couple weeks, and I'm so glad Grace suggested it. I'm still wary about her involvement with the Order, but I know she's a real friend.

I open the door to my dorm, but then a large hand slams into it and closes it in my face. I spin around to face Callan, because who else could it be?

"Don't ever do that again," he growls. His hand is still on the door above me, causing him to lean in close.

I glare up at him. "You can't protect me 24/7."

The hatred in his eyes burns with an inner light. If I'm not careful, he'll set us both on fire. "What if something happened to you? How would I explain that to your father? You know it's not safe out there, not for any of us, but especially not for you."

"Nothing happened. I was fine."

"This time." He grabs my shoulders like he wants to shake some sense into me. "Do I need to put a tracker on you again?"

"No!"

"Then don't be so fucking difficult!"

His mouth crashes down on me, and that pent-up lust and hate and rage all mix into a kiss that scorches me in the best way. I claw at his broad shoulders, his blond hair, his strong jaw, kissing him back hard, until I'm gasping for air.

When we pull back, we both look shocked and dazed by what we just did. Callan steps back, and the menacing glow around him dies down a little.

"I gave my word to your father, and I intend to keep it," he says. "He cares about you and wants to make sure you're safe. Do you know how lucky you are to have that? Instead of throwing it in his face, accept it and try to let him take care of you, however he can."

I jerk back at his unexpected words. I'm not used to people caring about me, especially not my father. For so long I was on my own, with only Jonah looking out for me, and even he wasn't around much. Now I have family who want to keep me safe. And friends. And...Callan. Whatever he is.

Callan's voice sounds tough, but I sense something beneath it, some hidden pain. I remember how he was alone at Family Day, and I swallow my pride. "All right. I'll try to be less difficult about you protecting me, if you agree to be less of a dick about it too. Give me a little space, or I'll lose my mind."

"I'll do whatever I feel is necessary to keep you safe. Trust me, I don't like it either. I'd rather be as far away from you as possible."

"That kiss just now proves otherwise." I can't help but taunt him. "Or were you recording this one too? Was this another trick?"

"You're the one with the recording. What are you planning to do with that?"

"Nothing. I'm not going to use it. I don't want to hurt the other guys." I run my hand slowly down his chest and speak to him like a lover. "I only want to hurt you. I want to hurt you so bad."

"Then do it already." There's hunger in his eyes, and we both know we're not talking about getting payback. "I'm waiting."

"Oh, it's coming." A new plan is forming. One that involves the two of us and that nanny cam. Seducing him won't be too hard. Not with the amount of lust coming off him, and the pent-up desire in that kiss. He wanted the school to believe that he only kissed me because I used my succubus powers on him, but soon everyone will know he wants me, the half-demon, all on his own.

"And it's going to be good," I say, before stepping inside my dorm. "Real good."

I slam the door in his face.

26

OLIVIA

I have a hard time sleeping that night as Callan's words replay in my head. They remind me of a time when I was seven years old and playing on the swing at the park.

I wasn't scared as I flew through the air. Not until I saw the ground rushing at my face, anyway. It all passed in slow motion, like in a movie. The sounds around me faded, the other kids' voices disappeared as I watched the wood chips under the swings get closer and closer.

But at the last second, arms wrapped around my chest and legs, and I was flying up again, in a circle. Silver wings flashed around me, flapping through the air. My fear turned to delight as a male voice said, "It's all right, I've got you. You're safe."

Something about the voice sounded familiar, though I couldn't place it. The man set me on the ground and stepped back. For a second I saw the outline of his silver wings, but then they were gone, and I wondered if I only imagined it. "That was a close one."

"Thank you." I tucked my dark, wild hair behind my ear. The counselors at school said not to talk to strangers, but something about this man made me instantly trust him. He had brown hair that looked soft, and his eyes crinkled as he smiled at me. Sunlight seemed to

shine down on him, highlighting his profile, and I felt a sense of awe when I looked at him.

"You're very welcome, Olivia."

I flinched when I heard my name, and a small stab of fear hit my heart. I looked around the playground, but nobody was paying any attention to us. Almost like they couldn't see us at all. Weird. "Are you a social worker?"

"No, I'm not." He backed up to show me he wouldn't hurt me. "I just didn't want you to fall."

"Who are you?" I asked.

"My name is Gabriel."

"Are you an angel?"

He gave me a warm smile. "I'm someone that cares about you very much, and will always make sure you're safe."

Those weren't words I'd heard very often in my young life. The family I lived with at the time was pretty good. They fed me regularly, and I was never cold or neglected or beaten. But they didn't love me. I didn't know if anyone ever had.

"Like a guardian angel?" I asked.

Another smile lit up his face. "Yes, a lot like that. Please don't jump off of the swings anymore, okay?"

Oh, yeah. I'd been trying to fly. I'd always wanted to fly. I turned to look at the swings so I could explain why I'd jumped out, but when I looked back at my new friend, he was gone. I glanced around the park, but didn't see him anywhere.

"Olivia!" My foster mother ran up to me. "There you are."

Uh-oh. She looked mad. "I've been right here the whole time," I tried to explain.

She grabbed my hand and dragged me out of the park toward our house. "Come on. You can't play at the park if you're going to disappear on me."

I forgot about that moment until tonight. That was the first time Gabriel visited me. Now I realize he was protecting me from the time I was a child, and that maybe he always did care for me after all.

———

The next morning, Uriel cancels all classes and calls an emergency assembly.

"What's this about?" I ask Marcus, as Araceli and I sit beside him in the auditorium.

He shakes his head. "No one knows, but it can't be good."

A nervous buzz moves through the crowd, and the place fills up quickly. I spot Callan moving down the aisles, but he takes a seat a few rows behind me. Bastien stands to the side of the stage, his hands clasped behind his back. Kassiel and the other teachers form lines along the walls, almost like guards.

Cyrus and Isaiah grab the seats next to Araceli. "There's been another attack," Cyrus says, leaning over Araceli to make sure we all hear him. "It has to be."

Uriel comes out onto the auditorium stage, looking every inch the powerful, immortal being he is. His eyes scan the audience, which quickly falls into silence, and then he speaks. "I've called you here today with some grave news. Three of our students, Gwen Svava, Favelyn Kyrja, and Marila Thruth were killed last night in a pattern consistent with the previous attack in Angel Peak."

My jaw drops at the names, and a shocked murmur goes through the crowd. All three of those names belong to Valkyries, and everyone knows they were fierce warriors. I didn't know any of them well, although I watched Marcus heal Gwen once, Favelyn was in a few of my classes, and Marila was dating Tanwen for a short while, although rumor had it they broke up last week.

Cyrus leans over again and whispers, "Told you."

We all shoot him a sharp look, and he shrugs and sits back, taking Isaiah's hand.

Uriel clasps his hand together on the podium and continues. "All of them were on their way back from having dinner in Angel Peak, when they were shot down between the campus and the town."

Oh shit. That wasn't long after Grace and I went to Angel Peak. I feel like the biggest idiot ever for ditching Callan now, especially after all my big words about not needing protection. If I glance over at him, I'm sure his face will convey his grim smugness at being right. Instead, I look over at Tanwen, who sits with the other Valkyries. Her eyes shine with unshed tears, but her jaw is clenched and her face is hard. She and the other Valkyries look like they're ready to go out and avenge their fallen sisters as soon as this announcement is over.

"Rest assured, we are doing everything we can to both investigate these attacks and prevent them from happening again," Uriel says. "However, until we are certain it is safe, we are locking the campus down. No one is allowed in or out without my permission until the threat is over, not even to visit Angel Peak. We also encourage you to wear a weapon on your person at all time. Hilda can assist in providing you one, if needed. Remain vigilant, and we will get through this threat without losing any more lives." He nods to the audience. "You are dismissed."

Panic grips the crowd as everyone stands and rushes out of the auditorium. A few more people shoot me angry or fearful looks, and I realize Uriel never mentioned who they suspected might be behind the attacks. Do some people actually think I could do this, or are they just looking to me because of my demon blood? We don't even know if demons were behind these attacks, but then again, how could humans take down three Valkyries?

I spot Grace talking with her uncle Nariel outside the building, and I'm relieved to see she's safe, even though she came back with me last night. People rush across the lawn, some carrying weapons, while others huddle in groups with heads together as they talk. The worry in the air is infectious, and I have a feeling it's only going to get worse, especially as people go stir-crazy after being cooped up on campus for weeks.

Classes start up again the next morning, but it's hard for anyone to focus when three of our peers were just killed. Combat Training is especially tense, with Hilda reminding us to carry a weapon on us at all times. I have a dagger in my bag, but probably need to come up with a better solution at some point. Tanwen spars with Callan, and the rest of the class stops what they're doing to watch, especially as she grits her teeth and goes at him with everything she's got. They're both so skilled in combat it's like watching a performance, but then Tanwen begins to glow with an angry light and Hilda barks out an order for her to go outside and calm down. Tanwen drops her sword and stomps outside, giving me a glare as she goes.

In Fae Studies, Raziel tries to teach us about the Faerie Wars, which we're also covering in Angelic History from the angel side, but no one is really listening, including me. During Light Control, our professor Eileen bites her nails and keeps glancing at me, like I might attack her at any moment. A fight breaks out in the cafeteria between two Erelim during dinner, while the dorm's common room is packed with people sitting in little groups, gossiping over the latest rumor.

And the week just keeps getting worse and worse. My mug from Marcus goes missing, and I can't find it anywhere in the dorm. Kassiel cancels our lesson with a note that he has to leave campus for the weekend, which shouldn't bother me, but I find such comfort in our extra hour together. I wonder if he is investigating the attacks, or if he has some other demon-related business.

Then I receive an invitation to the next Order meeting, and remember the task they've given me. I'm still no closer to getting Araceli's dad to come visit her. Still no closer to getting to Faerie. And still no closer to rescuing Jonah, dammit.

27

KASSIEL

It's a short airplane flight to Los Angeles, and then I'm in the glass elevator heading up to my father's penthouse condo, staring out over the sprawling city below me. I'm reminded of my last time visiting this city, when I met a gorgeous bartender and took her back to my hotel room, something I'd never done before. I recognized Olivia as a succubus and she ran from me in a panic. Only later, when I met her at Seraphim Academy, did I understand why.

To keep up my disguise, Lucifer and I always meet in Los Angeles, instead of his domain in Las Vegas. This city is a hotly contested zone between angels and demons, although our two kinds battle it out in business instead of war these days. Lucifer has been opening nightclubs across the city as part of a new venture to gain control of it, and he's looking at a blueprint when I enter.

"Kassiel," he says, with his charming smile. He raises a glass in my direction. "Drink?"

"No, thank you."

"Nonsense, you look like you need one." He heads behind the gleaming bar counter and pours me a whiskey on the rocks from his collection of expensive alcohol on the silver shelves. He doesn't ask what I want, and I know he won't let me refuse it.

I sigh, but take the drink. Dealing with Lucifer is always a challenge. "I've been making progress on the assignment you gave me."

"Is that so?" The King of Hell leans against the counter and swirls his drink. "Tell me."

"I've completely infiltrated the Order of the Golden Throne. They trust me and accept me as one of their own. I don't think anyone suspects what I truly am."

"Of course not. There's a reason I chose you." His green eyes shine with pride. "You never fail me."

I bow my head in response to his praise. "As you suspected, they're after the Staff of Eternity. They know it's in Faerie, and they sent a kid to get it last year, but he never came back. Now they're doubling their efforts to get it."

"Those idiots." He takes an angry sip of his drink. "Michael and I worked hard to end the war and stop the extinction of our races, and yet everyone wants to go back to the old ways of hatred and violence. And with Michael gone and Gabriel in disfavor, there's no one to reign the angels in anymore."

I take a sip of my whiskey. It's damn good, and probably as old as I am, knowing Lucifer. Maybe I did need a drink after all. "They still think you killed Michael."

"Obviously." His smile is downright evil. "Who else, but their favorite villain?"

My fingers tighten around my glass. "When I finish this mission, I'm going to clear your name."

He waves a dismissive hand. "I'm not worried about that. Your current task is more important. We can't let the Order get the Staff. Or any of our people either, for that matter. Best it stays in Faerie, but if it does somehow end up on Earth, I want it brought to me for safety."

"I'll do my best." I finish my drink and set it down on the counter. "The Order have given their members tasks this year, and mine is to compile a list of people on Earth with fae blood. I've already included the obvious and well-known ones, but wanted to check with you before adding a few of the more obscure and hidden people, especially on our side."

He strokes his beard as he considers. "Yes, we must make sure you give the Order something they don't already know to prove your value to them as a member. I'll have my assistant get you the information by tomorrow."

"Thank you."

He pours both of us another drink. "What of the half-angel hybrid girl? I understand you've been giving her private lessons."

I hesitate. "Yes, and I've been keeping an eye on her, as you requested."

"And? What is she like?"

I consider my words carefully. "She has a hard time trusting others, which is understandable given her history, but she's level-headed and clever. She doesn't seem biased against demons either."

"Good. She could be a strong ally. The first true hybrid of angels and demons." He stares off into the distance for a beat, perhaps remembering something from his past. "For now, continue your lessons and keep her safe."

"I shall. I assume you heard about the recent attacks in Angel Peak."

"Yes, and I've already sent someone to look into it. The humans are growing bolder every day."

"Have there been any attacks near Hellspawn Academy?"

"So far, no, but Baal has increased the security there as a precaution." He swirls the cubes in his drink. "Do you have anything else to report?"

"Not at this time."

He moves around the bar and faces me, then dusts off the shoulder of my suit. "You look good, Kassiel. Your mother would be proud."

"Thank you."

"Come, now that business is over, we should catch up. There's this amazing Chinese restaurant we could go to nearby. Or we could order in. They have apps for everything now, you know. I do so love this era."

"I should really get back to Seraphim Academy. The campus has been in lockdown after the last attack." Not that it was difficult for me to sneak out. Being able to control darkness in a school of light-users has its perks.

"Already? You've only just arrived." He rests a light hand on my arm. "Stay for a meal at least. I rarely see you anymore."

My resolve falters. "All right. I'll stay for dinner."

It's almost impossible to say no to the devil.

Especially when he's your father.

28

OLIVIA

I don my golden robes and mask, then make myself invisible and fly to the cavern's hidden entrance. It's empty out here and there's a layer of fog throughout the forest, giving the place an eerie vibe. I glance around me, worried someone might attack me, even though I know the campus gates are warded from intruders.

The boulder opens for me, and I head down the dark stone tunnel to the Order's hidden lair. Most of the benches are empty still, and I grab a spot on one of them and wait. The leader walks in and stands in front of the empty throne, and one by one, the room fills up with other members in golden robes.

"Welcome," the leader says. "These are troubling times. We have lost one of our own, and we need to remain vigilant now more than ever."

I glance around the benches and notice an empty spot. One of the murdered Valkyries must have been in the Order.

"With such senseless violence, it only proves how much we need the Staff of Eternity," he continues. "As I mentioned before, you will all be given a special task this year to further our goal of obtaining the Staff. Some of you have already gotten your task, while others will receive it later this year. Has anyone completed their task who hasn't reported it yet?"

"I've compiled a list of all the people I could find on Earth with fae blood," another member says, stepping forward and pulling an envelope out of their robe.

"I've done the same for my task," someone else says.

"Good work." The leader gestures, and another member walks over and collects the two documents. "We shall compare both lists, and see what you have found. Does anyone have anything to report?"

Someone else raises their hand. "I've made small strides toward getting closer to the half-fae here on campus. We might still be able to use her to get to Faerie."

They must mean Araceli. White-hot rage fills my veins, as I wrack my brain trying to figure out who has been hanging around her more lately, but I can't think of anyone.

"Good," the leader says. "Another member is working on getting her father to visit the campus also. Has there been any progress on that?"

Shit, that's me. I step forward hesitantly. "He has been invited to campus twice, but doesn't seem interested."

"Keep trying. Push a little harder. Do whatever it takes to get him here." The leader glances around the room. "Remember, we do not tolerate failure from our members."

I nod and step back, swallowing hard. A few other people talk about the things they've been trying, but no one else has made any real progress, and I'm distracted with thoughts of Araceli being in danger. I'll have to warn her as soon as I get back.

"That concludes our business for the evening. Let's join the initiates in the forest and see who has completed the first trial. It's always one of my favorites."

The leader strides regally out of the underground chamber, and the golden-robed figures follow in single file. We're ordered to join hands, and someone makes us all invisible. Grace maybe? She's definitely strong enough to do it. Nariel could also. Hmm.

We spread out around the clearing where the white-robed initiates wait, nervously shifting their feet in the dirt. Our leader gives his normal spiel, and then he and some other members step forward to collect the items the initiates have stolen from the professors.

The first person has stolen a pair of Kassiel's briefs from his laundry basket, and a member to my left sighs softly, so I assume it's him. The same thing happened last year, and I wonder if this is some new tradition, or if everyone on campus is just a little bit in love with Kassiel. At least I'm not the only one.

The second person claims to have a necklace from Eileen, but when one of our members checks it with the light of truth, they shake their head. Two golden-robed figures grab the initiate by the arms and drag them out of the circle, while the rest of us stand there, doing nothing. I feel dirty for being one of them.

The third initiate holds up a mug proudly. "This is the half-demon's coffee mug."

Wait, what? I nearly jump forward and snatch it from the initiate's hand, but manage to hold myself back. I thought I was losing my mind, looking for it all over the dorm, but someone actually stole it from me. What the fuck!

"The half-demon is not a professor," the leader says.

"No, but she's the most dangerous person on campus," the initiate argues. "That should count for something."

I can't help but snort, and then glance around hoping no one heard me. Then again, if I find out who snuck in my room and stole my mug, I will become very dangerous where they're concerned.

The leader takes it and examines it. "This is acceptable."

The hell it is! I clench my fists inside my robe. I know the mug will be returned, but it still pisses me off, especially since it means a stranger was in my dorm. I'll have to increase our security somehow to make sure it never happens again. Once again, I feel bad for sneaking into Uriel's office and taking his book last year. It's not quite the same, but it was still a violation, even if I had to do it in to get into the Order.

Do good intentions make up for bad crimes? I'm not sure.

Damn the Order. They force people to steal, cheat, and manipulate. They threaten the people we care about if we don't do what they say. They murder their own kind to get what they want.

I've got to stop them.

———

As soon as I get back to the dorm, I wake Araceli. "Hey, it's important."

She rubs the sleep out of her eyes. "What's wrong?"

"I just got back from an Order meeting."

That gets her attention. She sits up in bed. "Any news about Jonah? Or their plans?"

I climb into bed beside her. "They're trying to find more people with fae blood on Earth. They want me to keep trying to reach your dad. And one of them said he or she has been successful in getting closer to you."

Realization dawns across her face. "Cyrus."

I look at her in the moonlight streaming through her balcony windows. "What has he done?"

She shakes her head. "Nothing too bad. He's been extra nice to me in class, hanging out with me a lot during meals in the cafeteria, and he and Isaiah took me shopping two weeks ago, before the last attack. You were at your meeting with Kassiel, or we would have invited you too."

"Damn it. I know he's in the Order, so it must be him." I didn't exactly trust Cyrus before, but now he's definitely on my shit list. "You can't let on like you know, or they'll realize I told you. Just humor him for a few days, then come up with reasons not to be around him."

Her face falls. "I thought he was just being my friend. I hoped it meant people were getting more comfortable with me, and accepting me for who I am. But it was all a lie."

I'm angry all over again. Araceli is the best person I know, but so many people are too close-minded to see that. Now she's going to be convinced that anyone being friendly to her is doing it with an ulterior motive. I should know...it's how I feel too.

She sighs. "Then again, they probably threatened to cut off Isaiah's hand or something if Cyrus didn't agree to do this, so I can't be too mad at him."

"Good point." It's just like her to have sympathy for someone who did her wrong. I pat her on the leg over the blankets. "It just means we have to stick together to take the Order down."

"You should talk to the Princes about it. They're members, right?"

My mouth twists. "Yeah, they are."

"It might be time to get their help. You've forgiven them and given up on your revenge, haven't you?"

"I forgave two of them. I still have plans for Callan. He needs to pay for what he did."

She stares at me with concerned eyes. "Don't become a bully like them in your quest for revenge. You're better than that."

I'm not better though. I'm really not.

29

OLIVIA

The next evening, I spread my wings and fly to the bell tower after dinner. I've finally admitted it's time to confront the Princes.

The three of them are reclining in their private lounge, and I'm sad to see it's no longer pink and sparkly—although there are a few stuffed animals still around. All three of them swing their heads when I land. I'm wearing a little black dress, and they all take a moment to admire how it hugs my curves, giving me a little taste of their lust.

"Olivia," Marcus says with a smile. "What are you doing here?"

Callan raises his eyebrows. "Come to redecorate again?"

I sit in one of the armchairs. "We need to talk."

"About what?" Bastien asks, from where he sits in the other armchair. He sounds tired, and I notice his eyes are bloodshot. Is he not getting enough sleep?

I face each guy in turn. "We need to talk about the Order. I know you're all members. Marcus confirmed it for me."

Callan shoots Marcus a glare, before turning back to me. "And?"

"And I'm a member too. I infiltrated them last year to find out what happened to my brother. Now I'm trying to do everything I can to bring him back from Faerie—but I also want to take down the Order."

"You want to *what?*" Callan's eyebrows are in danger of popping off the top of his head. "Please tell me I heard you wrong and you're not that suicidal."

I scowl at him. "I know it won't be easy. That's why I need your help."

"The Order is thousands of years old," Bastien says. "Its scope extends beyond this school, which is mainly used for recruitment purposes, and stretches to all levels of angel society. They're in every angel community, working in the highest ranks of Aerie Industries, and probably even in the Archangel Council too."

"All the more reason to destroy them," I say. "They're controlling things from the shadows, and most angels probably don't even realize it."

"But why do you want to take the Order down?" Callan asks.

I spread my hands. "Shouldn't it be obvious? They hate demons and they manipulate humans. That alone is enough for me to want to bring them down. But they also killed Darel last year—were any of you involved with that?"

"Of course not," Bastien says.

"Though we did suspect it was the Order," Marcus mutters.

I lean forward. "They sent Jonah to Faerie even though he was just a First Year student. They've asked us to do unethical tasks and have threatened our loved ones if we don't do them. And they want to get the Staff to send all demons back to Hell. What will happen to me if they get it? Will it send me to Hell too? Will it kill me?"

Marcus rests a hand on my knee. "We won't let that happen."

"Good. So you'll help me?"

"Yes," Marcus answers immediately, but Callan and Bastien exchange uneasy glances.

"What?" They can't be uncertain, not after everything they've seen the Order is capable of, firsthand. "You're actually hesitating?"

"How exactly do you plan on defeating the Order?" Bastien asks.

"I haven't gotten that far," I admit. "Right now I'm trying to figure out who their members are and stop them from getting the Staff. Along with rescuing Jonah too."

Callan stands and walks away, rubbing his neck. "You make it sound so easy, but this is more dangerous than you know. They will kill you, without hesitation, if you cross them."

I meet his eyes with a challenge. "I'm not afraid. Are you?"

Marcus clears his throat. "How can we help?"

"Most importantly, we get Jonah back. I'm working on a plan to get to Faerie, and I think I can conceal all of us once we're there—"

"Wait." Bastien holds up a hand to interrupt me. "You plan to go to Faerie?"

"It's the only way to rescue him. I don't trust the Order to rescue him, do you? All they care about is the Staff."

Callan crosses his arms. "If you find a way into Faerie, we'll go with you."

"Thank you." I suck in a breath. "Otherwise, we need to start working together and share what we know. I've uncovered a few other members—Cyrus and Grace, for example—and I can tell you my task is to bring Araceli's father to the school."

"They told me to make sure we win the soccer game against Hellspawn Academy, no matter what," Marcus says, with a shrug. "We're way better than them at soccer, so it shouldn't be a problem."

"I haven't gotten my task yet," Bastien says. "And I know of two of the initiates this year, but that doesn't help us."

We glance at Callan, who frowns, before saying, "Tanwen is a member."

"Okay, that's good to know." I already suspected Tanwen might be a member, and this pretty much confirms it. I debate letting them know about Kassiel, but then decide that's not my secret to share. "Let's all meet here when we can and keep each other updated on anything new we uncover." I stand up and glance between the three of them. "Thank you."

Callan scowls and turns away, while Bastien sits back in his chair and closes his eyes, like he can barely keep them open.

"Are you okay, Bastien?" I ask him.

"Just tired." He waves a hand, but doesn't open his eyes. "It's nothing."

It's definitely not nothing. Delilah's words come back to me. *Eventually you will kill this person, just as you would a human.*

Bastien and I slept together a few days ago. I've had sex with him for months now, using him for my own sustenance, and I must be draining him dry. Adding in Marcus wasn't enough. I was a fool to think I could survive off of two lovers. I need to add another one immediately, or risk losing both Bastien and Marcus.

Marcus puts his arm around me. "Want me to fly back to your dorm with you? Watch a movie?"

I want to. It sounds like a normal thing someone would do with their boyfriend. But it would probably lead to sex, and I don't know if Marcus can take it. What if I hurt him, like I did with Bastien?

"No, I can't tonight. Maybe some other time."

He leans close and kisses me softly. "Okay, some other time."

Bastien and Callan both watch the exchange—Bastien with interest, and Callan with disgust.

I fly back to my dorm, entering the living room through the balcony doors and closing them behind me. I need to visit the library tomorrow and check out that one good book on Lilim and see if there's anything I can do for Bastien. Does he just need time to recover? Or can I—

I'm interrupted from my thoughts by a banging on my balcony doors. I jump like ten feet and spin around, reaching for my dagger, but it's Callan.

I throw open the sliding door. "Are you trying to give me a heart attack?"

He practically pushes me out of the way as he steps inside. "You're hurting Bastien, aren't you? And probably Marcus too."

I tear my eyes away from him, the guilt punching me in the gut. "Yes, I am. Not on purpose though."

"I suppose I can't tell you to stay away from them."

"I would, if I could." I run a hand through my hair as I consider. "I could go back to sleeping with human strangers, but I'd have to leave campus."

"No. Not an option."

"All right, then I'll have to sleep with other people here. I've been trying to feed off of sex dreams and stuff like that, but it wasn't enough. But maybe I can find someone else—"

"How many angels do you need to survive?"

"Three I think. Maybe four. If they're strong."

He nods with a grim set to his mouth. "Then it has to be me."

I take a step back, my mouth open. "You?"

"I don't trust anyone else, and I'm the strongest person on campus, other than maybe Uriel."

"But—I hate you. And you hate me."

"I also swore to protect you. I can't have you running off and fucking some stranger."

"So you'll fuck me instead?" I let out a laugh that sounds a little crazed. How did I get into this mess?

"I'll do what I have to do." He grabs the front of my dress to yank me closer, and then his mouth slants down over mine. It's so forceful and sudden I bring my hands up to circle his neck, as if I might strangle him. I'm tempted, but then his kiss demands my full attention, and somehow my fingers have started caressing his throat instead of choking it.

His large hand slips down and cups my breast through my dress, then pinches my nipple hard, making me gasp. He groans a little at the sound and pushes me back against the edge of the couch.

I spin away from him and move to my bedroom door, knowing he'll follow me. As I reach it, Callan claims me again with his hands and his mouth and his body, and I press myself against him, unable to resist. He reaches behind me and turns the door handle, and we practically fall inside. Someone slams the door shut, and I think it's me, but I barely notice anything except his mouth on mine.

Callan picks me up and slams me back against the door, hard. As hard as his cock, which grinds against me as he lifts me up and wraps my legs around his hips. We're devouring each other, hands and mouth and teeth, and all thoughts are gone as I pop open the buttons on his shirt and tear it off him. My dress is next, yanked up and tossed over my head, and then my bra's gone too. He unzips his jeans, I push my panties aside, and then he's inside me, hard and fast and huge. I can only gasp as I stretch around him, but he gives me no time to adjust.

He plunges into me, and each stroke feels like he's trying to conquer me, possess me, master me. But he's given himself up to me, a half-demon he claims he hates, and even though it looks like he's in control, I'm the one with all the power. Sex is my domain, and after one taste of this succubus, he'll only want more and more. Problem is, I'll want more of him too.

He bounces me up and down on him, pumping into me fast like he can't control himself. I wrap my arms around his neck and throw my head back, and his mouth finds my throat and claims me there too. We're both possessed by some kind of madness, and it has nothing to do with my succubus side. This is all us.

Harder and faster our bodies move, his hips thrusting me back against the door and making it rattle. It's intense and rough and so very good and exactly what I needed. Nothing relieves stress like a good round of hot, dirty sex, even with the guy you hate. Or maybe especially with the guy you hate.

Then he steps back, away from the door, our bodies joined as one in the middle of the room. He reaches down and grabs my ass, shifting me higher so he can get a better angle, and I cry out, but not in pain. Not exactly, anyway. I cling to his muscular body as he keeps pumping, and when the orgasm hits me like a freight train, I sink my teeth into his shoulder. He groans and digs his fingers into my ass as he keeps pounding me, before he fills me with his power. It's so strong I would fall over if he wasn't holding me up. Stronger than Marcus and Bastien. Maybe even stronger than Kassiel. It must be the result of his double Archangel blood.

Damn, a succubus could get used to this.

Of course, that would mean fucking Callan again. Because oh shit, I just fucked Callan. Or more accurately, he fucked me. Oh yeah, he fucked me good and hard.

But damn, it was worth it.

30

OLIVIA

When it's over, Callan drops me on the bed and glares down at me, so I see we're back to our old ways again. He tugs on his shirt, then tosses me my dress, all without saying a word.

Finally I manage to say, "Thanks."

He frowns at me, like he's confused by the word. "How often do we need to do that?"

"Every couple weeks, I think."

"I can do that." Then he wipes his mouth with the back of his hand. "But don't think we're dating or anything. This is just fucking."

I stretch out on the bed, still naked and gleaming with sweat. His eyes can't help but devour me. "Fine with me. I don't want anything more from you. Not now. Not ever."

"One more thing. No one can know about this, or it's over." He grabs my ass hard, kneading the cheeks with his fingers. I wonder if he's an ass guy. Maybe he'd like to put his cock back there sometime. I'm wet again just thinking about it.

I gaze up at him. "What, you don't want anyone to know you're fucking the succubus? Or worse, that you liked it? That even now, you want more and can barely resist?"

He releases me and shakes his head, then stomps to the balcony door. He throws it open so hard the doorframe rattles, and then he launches himself through it with a flash of gold wings. Leaving me there with the door open.

I stand and close the door, then move to my desk, where I've set up the nanny cam that was once in a stuffed llama. After that initiate stole my mug, I made a point to record everything in my room when I'm not in it. Tonight I never turned it off once I got home.

I pull up the recording on my laptop. It got everything from the moment we stepped into the bedroom. Our frenzied fucking. Our conversation afterward. That look of angry desire as he left. It's all there, the perfect video to ruin him. I just have to decide when to strike.

———

A massive crash on my balcony jerks me from my sleep. My heart leaps through my throat as I sit up. Is Callan back? Or am I under attack? I quickly grab for my dagger off the nightstand and jump out of bed, glad Hilda told us to keep a weapon on us at all times.

I slip to the wall and turn on a small light on the balcony, then peer through the curtains. As soon as I can clearly see what's out there, I gasp and drop my dagger. Then I quickly throw open the balcony door.

"Father!" I ask, rushing to his side. He's collapsed on my balcony, completely naked and covered in blood. But the worst part are his wings—they've been butchered, the silver feathers missing and torn, the skin flayed and the bones broken. There's so much blood, I can barely look at the damage without wanting to throw up. "What happened?"

"Help me inside," he gets out through gritted teeth.

I bend down and help him up, and he leans heavily on me as we stumble into my bedroom. He can't retract his wings, and he lets out a small cry as they brush against the doorway. Tears roll down my cheeks at the sound. I may not have a perfect relationship with my father, but seeing him hurt like this is heartbreaking.

I help him onto the bed, not even caring that my sheets will be ruined. He can only lie on his side, with his wings hanging behind him, and every time he moves, fresh agony washes through him and makes his face tighten.

"I'm sorry," he gets out. "I tried to teleport to Angel Peak but I ended up here somehow."

"It's okay. I'm going to get help. Araceli is a Malakim, she can heal you."

"No. Must keep this quiet." He tries to shift a little and groans. "I'll heal...eventually."

"We can trust Araceli." I clasp his big hand and lean close. "I'll be right back."

Rushing out my bedroom door, I yell Araceli's name as I burst into her room. She jumps out of bed with a wild and scared look on her face. She's already got her hand on her sword. "What?"

"My dad. He's in my room and hurt."

It takes her a split second to process, but when she does, she places the sword back in its spot beside her bed, then grabs her robe, running ahead of me out of the room as she throws it on.

She pauses in the doorway of my bedroom and gasps when she sees the bruised and bloody naked angel on my bed. For a second she covers her mouth in horror, and then she gathers her inner strength and composes herself. She rushes into the room and touches Gabriel's arm, closing her eyes as a warm glow emanates from her hands. I've never been so glad to have a healer as my roommate.

As she works, I hover nearby, wringing my hands. "Were you attacked? Was it the human hunters?"

"No," he whispers between groans. "It was Azrael."

"Azrael? Why?"

Father's jaw is clenched tight, but he sucks in a deep breath and opens his mouth. I lean close to hear him. "Punishment. For you."

His words send a shard of ice into my heart. He warned me

something like this would happen, but I never imagined *this*. How could they do this to one of their own?

Gabriel's eyes close, and his wings go slack. I rush forward, fearing the worst, but realize he's just sleeping.

Araceli removes her hands and shakes her head. "This is beyond me. I've put him in a healing sleep, but we'll need someone a lot stronger than me to heal him completely. Raphael might be the only angel who can."

"Raphael isn't an option." If this was punishment for me, then the entire Archangel Council must be in on it. "I'll call Marcus."

The phone rings and rings, but then finally Marcus answers with a groggy voice. "Liv? What is it?"

"I need your help in my apartment. Come quickly."

"Be right there."

He flies up to the balcony doors exactly three minutes later, wearing a worn Beatles t-shirt and loose pajama pants. "Oh shit," he says when I let him in, but he rushes forward immediately to my father's side.

"I put him in a healing sleep, but I wasn't sure what else to do," Araceli says.

"Good thinking." Marcus studies Gabriel's wings and touches them lightly, while his face takes on a look of determination. I've only seen Marcus work once before, but never on something as bad as this. "Dark-infused wounds. Whoever did this made sure it would take a long, painful time to heal. This is going to need intricate healing."

I remember when I was cut with a dark-infused blade last year, and how painful it was. I can't even imagine how much agony my father must have been in when he arrived, and I'm grateful to Araceli for knocking him out, and to Marcus for coming so quickly.

"What can I do?" I ask.

"We'll need some water. Both to drink and to clean his wounds."

I nod. "No problem."

I rush out of the room and gather supplies, including some towels from our bathroom. We'll need new ones after this, but whatever. When I get back, Marcus has begun the painstaking job of moving slowly over Dad's wings with his glowing hands. I stand in the doorway, feeling powerless. Callan left only a few hours ago, and his energy still bursts through me, making me feel invincible, but I'm no healer. All I can do is keep out of their way and hope my father gets through this without too much permanent damage.

31

MARCUS

Healing is a lot like playing the guitar, I've learned. Sure, any Malakim can do it, even without training, just like any idiot can pick up a guitar and strum it to make sounds come out. But to actually be a real healer, you need to study for years. You need to learn all the body parts and how they work together, just like a guitarist needs to learn the notes and chords and how to combine them into a song. You need to practice as often as possible. And to be really good, you need to have innate talent.

My father is the best healer in the world. I've personally seen him bring someone back from the dead. My healing is only a shadow of what he can do, and I'll have to use all of my strength and training to heal Gabriel. Even with Araceli here to assist.

"How can I help?" Araceli asks, at my side.

"The best thing you can do is keep him asleep the entire time. I'm going to try to heal what would take weeks or maybe months for his body to heal on its own." I walk around to the other side of the bed to get a better angle, while Araceli puts her hands on Gabriel's head. Olivia hovers at the edge of the bedroom, and I wish she didn't have to see this, but I know she won't leave either. I can't blame her. If it was my dad, I'd stay too.

Gabriel's wings have been shredded. There's no other word for it. I've never seen anything so horrible before, and when I feel the darkness in the wounds, it's obvious dark-infused weapons were used. Otherwise, Gabriel would be able to heal this himself in a few hours, as powerful as he is.

I use my light to heal his bones first, mending them and making them whole, while drawing out the darkness. As the muscles and tendons stitch back together, I grab some rags and wash away some of the blood. It's not just his wings that need healing, though. His collarbone was broken during the attack, and his shoulders also suffered damage. This is going to take hours to repair.

Some time later, I sit down on the carpeted floor with my back against the side of the bed and take a long sip of water. My hands are covered in blood, and I've done what I can for now, but I need a break or I won't be able to go on. There's still so much to do though.

"Are you all right?" Olivia asks, kneeling beside me.

"Just tired. I'm not sure I have the strength to do it all tonight, but I'll try."

Araceli places a hand on my head and frowns. "You're tapped out, Marcus. You need a break. I can try to heal while you recover."

"It won't be enough. Healing these kinds of wounds takes a lot of energy and life-force. Once the sun comes out it will be easier though. Especially if we bring in more healers to help."

"We can't do that," Liv says. "He didn't even want me to get Araceli involved."

"It's fine. Maybe you can get me something to eat. Or some coffee."

"That won't be enough," Araceli says.

"Can you give Marcus some energy?" Liv asks her.

"No, it doesn't really work like that. I'm sorry."

Liv bites her lip. "Maybe not, but... Hang on, I want to try something."

She sits on the carpet beside me and takes my hands, then leans close and kisses me softly. At first I'm surprised, but it's impossible to resist Liv's soft lips, and maybe we both need a little comforting after the rough night we've had.

A rush of power flows through me, and I realize it's coming from Olivia. From her kiss. Energy crackles in my veins like lightning, and it feels different from my own. Violent. Seductive. Powerful.

It's like chugging ten energy drinks at once. I sit up and look at Liv with awe. "What did you do?"

"I'm not really sure. I felt like I was overflowing with Callan's energy and had the strongest urge to try to pass some of it to you. I didn't know if it would work. Did it?"

"Yes." Then her words register and my jaw falls open. "Callan's energy?"

"Is that who was here earlier?" Araceli asks, her eyebrows shooting up. "Damn, girl. I thought you hated each other."

She grimaces. "We do, but you should have seen Bastien tonight. I'm hurting him by feeding on him so much, and Marcus was next, so Callan stepped in to save them. He's doing it for them more than me, I'm sure."

I don't believe that's true. Callan may pretend he doesn't care about Olivia, but in his own, twisted way, he does. Otherwise he wouldn't go out of his way to torment her, or to make sure she's protected. Even when he bullied and betrayed her, in his mind he was doing it in her best interests.

"Are you upset because I slept with him?" Liv asks.

"No," I say, and wipe the frown off my face. "I was just surprised."

And jealous.

Shit.

Why am I jealous? I can't expect her to only sleep with me. She's a succubus, after all. I knew this would happen when I got involved with her, and she's never tried to hide it. I thought I would be fine with it, and I guess I was, for a while. But I've been struggling with this feeling ever since winter break, when she continued having sex with Bastien and not me. It felt like she chose him over me. Then she forgave him first, which made it hurt even more. Now she's sleeping with Callan, who she claims to hate. Does she care about me at all?

Growing up, I was always one of a dozen of Raphael's sons. He would come by and give me gifts now and then, and shower me with love and attention...but then he would leave again. He would always leave. Even so, I thought he was the greatest guy I'd ever met, and I would do anything to please him. When I got older, I realized he showered his many other sons with the same gifts and love and promises to visit more often. I wasn't special in any way. I was just another one of his many kids.

I'm starting to feel that way with Olivia too.

I offer her a weak smile. "I can't expect you to only have feelings for me."

"The only feeling I have for Callan is loathing. But he is very powerful, so hopefully he can help you." She leans back on the side of the bed and closes her eyes.

"And now you're exhausted and need to feed again," Araceli says with a sigh.

Liv waves her away. "I'm fine. Just heal my dad. Please."

Right. The reason we're here. I stand up again and face my patient, who already looks a lot better, though there's still much work to be done. I rub my hands together, feeling Callan and Olivia's energy bursting out of my skin, plus maybe a little of Bastien's power in there too. I jump back into the healing with renewed vigor, fueled by Liv's gift.

She grabs a pillow and a blanket and dozes on the floor while Araceli and I work through the rest of the night, only taking breaks for snacks and water. Together we manage to heal Gabriel completely by the time sunlight is streaming through the sliding glass doors. I'm tempted to crawl over to a sunny patch of carpet and fall asleep in it, like a dog.

Araceli leans against the headboard with her eyes closed, but I know she's not asleep because her hands still glow against Gabriel's head.

"It's done," I say, and then collapse beside the bed.

A half-asleep Liv crawls to my side and wraps her arms around me. "Thank you for healing him."

I lean my head against hers and close my eyes. "Anything for you."

32

OLIVIA

A loud knock on the dorm room door makes me jerk upright. I blink the sleep from my eyes. The three of us all passed out on the floor after the healing finished, and my dad is still on the bed, though his wings are gone and his naked body has been covered with a blanket. Through the glass doors, the sun is high in the sky, and I check the clock and gasp. We've slept half the day away. No wonder someone has come to look for us.

There's another loud knock on the front door. "Liv, are you in there?" a voice calls out.

"It's Callan," I whisper loudly to Araceli and Marcus, who are also waking up.

Father pushes himself up with a frown. "He can't know about this."

I'm so glad to see him awake that I rush to him and give him a big hug. He holds me close for a second, and then Callan bangs on the door again. I call out, "Be right there."

Father stands, wrapping the blanket around him like a toga, and glances between Marcus and Araceli. "Thank you. I owe you both a great debt."

"Are you okay?" I ask.

"Much better now, thanks to you and your friends. I'm going to the house to rest."

"I'll check on you tomorrow," Marcus says.

"I'd appreciate that," Gabriel replies. Then he vanishes.

"Stay in here and be quiet," I tell Araceli and Marcus. I grab a robe to cover up my blood-stained nightie, before shutting my bedroom door on my way out.

I throw open my door to a red-faced Callan. I think if I waited another few seconds, he would have used his Erelim powers to blast through the door.

"What's going on?" His eyes search behind me like there might be some hidden danger in my living room. "Have you been in here all day? You missed your morning classes."

"I forgot to set my alarm." I shrug and yawn. "I guess you wore me out last night."

His eyes narrow and I'm pretty sure he doesn't buy it. "Get dressed. You don't want to be late to your next classes."

"Yes, sir." I tell him, before placing a kiss on his cheek. "Thanks for checking on me. It's nice to know you care."

He steps back and looks surprised, but then his lip curls in disgust. "Don't get the wrong idea."

"Yeah, yeah." I roll my eyes, but my kiss worked in distracting him. "Now get out of here so I can shower."

I practically close the door on his face, before rushing back to my room. Marcus is gone, no doubt heading back to his room to get some rest, and Araceli is asleep on the floor again. Bless my sweet friend. She didn't hesitate to help my dad, even though he's never done much to warrant her kindness.

She stirs and gives me a weary grin. "Everything okay?"

"Yeah, although we're missing classes."

"It happens," she says with a shrug and a yawn.

I help her up and give her a hug. "Thank you. Now go take a nap."

"I will." She hesitates, her face concerned. She holds onto my hand a little longer than necessary, and I realize she's using her Malakim powers on me. "But what about you? I can feel how weak you are. You gave all your energy to Marcus for the healing. Now you need to feed again."

"I'll figure something out. Don't worry about me. Just get some rest, okay?"

"All right." She shuffles out of my room and back into her own, with another loud yawn.

I want to take a nap too, but I have an impatient angel outside waiting to walk me to my next class. Father doesn't want anyone to know what happened, which means going back to my normal routine. I take a quick shower to wash the blood out of my hair, and a wave of exhaustion and hunger hits me. Shit. I'm definitely going to have to feed soon. But on whom? I can't use Bastien again, not when he's so weak. Marcus is definitely in no shape to feed me either, not when he used all his energy healing my dad. I just slept with Callan last night. I'm going to have to come up with another option, fast.

I raid the kitchen and find a banana, which I devour, along with a bottle of Gatorade. Araceli likes it after a tough healing lesson. Now I know why.

I walk out and give Callan a nod as he falls in step beside me. Once outside, I pause for a minute and soak up the sunshine. It's the end of the summer, the day is scorching, and I instantly feel a little stronger. I should be able to make it through my classes, at least.

———

I get through Ishim class without jumping anyone, barely. The hunger is overwhelming, and I can't decide if I should go back to Callan for round two and hope he can handle it, or sneak off campus to make a quick trip to a human town, despite the danger.

For now, I have to get through my next two classes.

Unfortunately, my next one is Angelic History, and it's a serious lesson in self-control to last the entire hour without ripping Kassiel's clothes off. Not an easy task when I already want to rip pretty much everyone's clothes off and suck their sexual energy from them with a straw. As soon as class is over, I'm going to have to make a quick trip to a nearby trucker bar. I can't wait any longer.

I practically jump out of my seat the minute class is over, but then Kassiel calls out, "Olivia, can you chat for a minute? I'd like to talk to you about your last essay."

No, I really can't, I want to yell, but then the other students would know something is up, so I clench my fists and take a deep breath before heading over to him.

I move beside his desk, and he wipes his whiteboard down with a damp rag while the last of the other students file out. Once the door clicks shut, he whirls around. "You need to feed, don't you?"

"Is it that obvious?"

"Very, at least to someone who has met many Lilim before."

I give him a nervous laugh. "I'll be okay. I'm heading out to find someone to feed on right now."

"Who? A human stranger?" He moves toward me, his green eyes blazing with desire. "You know it's not safe for you to leave campus."

"Stop right there." I hold my hand up to keep him from getting any closer. Damn him and his English accent and sexy scruff and that perfect body in his tailored suit. We both know this can't happen, but it's taking everything in my power to resist him, especially when his lust hovers between both of us.

He takes another step closer. "Let me help you."

Without realizing it, I've backed away from him and pressed myself against the classroom door. The coldness in the wood seeps through my shirt, but it does nothing to calm my need. "You're my teacher. You'll lose your job if we're caught."

"We'll be careful." He offers his hand. All I have to do is reach out and take it, but still I hold myself back. "I'd rather you feed on me than some stranger, so I know you're safe."

"I'm so hungry, I might hurt you." The conviction in my voice is fading. I'm still pressing myself against the door, but my resolve is weakening. And I'm pretty sure Kassiel's resolve disappeared the moment I stepped in the room.

"I can handle it. Trust me."

I remember the power I got from him when we had sex before,

and decide he's probably right. He's over a hundred years old, after all.

I rest my hand in his palm, and he closes his fingers around it. "And the risk?"

"Acceptable." His mouth descends to mine, but stops shy of touching. "Besides, I don't think I can wait until you graduate. Can you?"

I answer by closing the distance between our lips. Waiting is not an option anymore.

Kassiel's lips press against mine, soft and pliant, but neither of us can take it slow. Our tongues meet in a sensual dance as his hands roam my body and his desire flows over me, the sexiest appetizer. He wants me as much as I want him, even though he's not being fueled by my need to feed. Moaning my appreciation for his ardor, I press myself against him, unable to keep my body still. The friction of our bodies together only increases my need.

He buries his fingers in my hair as he explores my mouth. When he pulls my head back with a hand tangled in my locks, I gasp, chest heaving as I wait for him to press his lips to my neck. He takes his time, licking and nipping along my jaw, then the lobe of my ear, before moving to my neck.

I'm not idle while he enjoys himself. My hands roam his body, pushing his jacket off of his shoulders. He shrugs out of it without lifting his lips from my neck.

Kassiel's toned body is one layer closer to my hands now. I lose some of the initial frantic energy as he lavishes my collarbone with attention. He wants to take his time, apparently, but I'm starving here. With frenzied fingers I remove his tie and yank it off his neck. Then I feel for the buttons of his shirt and unbutton them as quickly as I can with my head still held in his grip.

"I wish we didn't have to rush," he says against my neck.

"We'll go slowly next time," I say without thinking. But now it seems obvious there will be a next time. There has to be. This thing between us is too powerful to resist.

He wraps his arms around me and grips my ass, pulling me as close as we can be without being naked. I lift my legs and wrap them around his waist, using his shoulders for leverage. When I'm in his arms, Kassiel walks us across the room without looking. His lips are on mine again, and his tongue is in my mouth, tasting. Teasing.

"Please," I whisper in his mouth. "I need you."

He sets me on the edge of his desk, then sweeps everything off it and onto the floor. Books. Notepads. Pens. All of it.

I'd managed to undo all but one of his buttons. I reach for it. "Off."

His grin is mischievous as he looks down at himself. "What? You want to see my chest when yours is so woefully covered?"

I nod. "I do, *Professor,* if you please."

He steps back and takes care of the last button, then tosses his shirt onto the floor beside his jacket. I'm mesmerized by the sight of his taut abs and hard chest, along with the dark hair trailing into his pants.

I lick my lips. "I want to taste you."

When he hears that, his expression changes and I swear I see the devil in him. He reaches for his belt buckle. "How can I refuse my best student?"

For a succubus, a blow job is like eating dessert before dinner. Every act of sex has a flavor, and blow jobs are sweet, succulent. Rich. Humans can't survive on dessert alone, nor can I survive on blow jobs. But damn if I don't love to indulge.

Kassiel's belt hits the floor with a clank, and his black slacks fall a moment later, along with his boxer briefs. He's hard, as hard as it's possible for a man to be, and I forgot how perfectly sized he is. I suck him into my mouth, and he moans, his lust and attraction feeding my insatiable, gnawing hunger.

I could take my time and try to take him all in my mouth, down my throat. I could savor every lick, teasing, giving him big eyes and fluttering lashes. But I'm fucking hungry. His clenched hands in my hair spur me on to move faster, suck harder, and take him to the edge as fast as I can.

"Olivia, stop," he commands, pulling me off him.

I'm so hungry for more that it's hard not to latch onto him again, but I take a breath and calm down. That was just an appetizer. The real meal is coming soon. It better hurry though.

I open my blouse, revealing my pink lace bra. The weight of Kassiel's gaze feels like hands caressing my skin. I know exactly what he can do with his hands, and I can't wait to experience it again.

"Take off your bra," he says.

I unclasp my bra, and my breasts spill out of it. He grins, the devil in his eyes again, and then buries his face between them. With his hands on my ass again, he pulls me close and sits on the desk, then cups my breasts as he swirls his tongue around one nipple, then the other.

"I can't wait anymore," I said. "Please, Kassiel."

My pants fall around my ankles before I realize he's unbuttoned them. My core ignites, making my previous desire feel like a teenager's crush as Kassiel's fingers move between my legs and find my clit. He knows exactly what to do to make me writhe, moan, and cling to him as an orgasm builds inside me.

But then he pushes me back on the desk and climbs over me, wrapping my legs around him. His cock slips into me easily, filling me to the hilt. We both let out a sigh as we join together again after so long of waiting. With his hands flat on the desk on either side of my head, he begins a slow rhythm that tortures me in the best way, sliding all the way in and out of me so that I truly feel every second of it. I grip his ass and urge him on, craving more of him, feeling an intense desire to take everything he can possibly give me. I want it all.

And he gives it to me. Moving faster. Deeper. Harder.

He grinds me down against the desk as he hovers over me, his green eyes possessive, like a dark lord ravishing his lady. He gives me exactly what I need, and I give into it completely. Tiny explosions ricochet up my body and down my legs as the orgasm hits me. My low moan grows in pitch and volume while my inner muscles clench around his cock. When he comes, he says my name in a hoarse voice, holding me as tightly against him as he can.

"That was so much better than I remembered," he says, before giving me a long kiss. I can't help but agree with him as he stands up and reaches for his trousers.

"I'll get dressed and get out of here before someone comes in," I say, as I get up quickly. I'm not ashamed of what we did, but now that it's over and I'm in my right mind again, I'm worried about him getting caught. I couldn't stand if he left the school. Not now. Not while he's one of the few people I can trust.

"It's fine. I don't have any more classes today." He grabs his shirt and begins slowly buttoning it. "What happened? You didn't seem this hungry yesterday."

I pick up my clothes off the floor. "I had to give my energy to someone else. It's a long story."

"You gave someone your energy?" He arches an eyebrow. "How?"

"I'm not really sure. I figured it was a succubus power I hadn't learned yet."

"No, it's not. Or at least, I've never heard of it. But you're the daughter of an Archangel. Perhaps that's your unique power."

My eyes widen. For some reason, I never considered that. All Archangels—and Archdemons—have a unique power, as does anyone with their blood. That's how my father can teleport, and how Jonah could change his appearance. I just never realized I would have one too. I suppose it's because for the longest time I never felt like an Archangel's daughter. But now I do.

I'll have to ask Delilah about it next time I see her.

33

OLIVIA

That night, I go invisible and sneak off campus. I don't care if it's not allowed, or if it's dangerous, or if Uriel will find out and I'll get in trouble—I have to check on my father.

When I land at the house and step inside, Gabriel's on the couch. It doesn't look like he's moved at all since arriving earlier and collapsing. He's still wearing the same bloody blanket wrapped around him.

"Father?" I ask softly, as I approach.

He opens his eyes and gives me a weak smile. "Hello, daughter."

"How are you?"

"Better than when you last saw me," he says with a grimace, then manages to sit up on the couch. He glances down at himself, as if he's just realized he's butt naked and covered in dried blood.

I keep my eyes averted. "You should take a shower and get dressed. I'll make you something to eat."

"Probably a good idea." He manages to stand and takes a moment to check his balance, then heads off to his bedroom. I hear the sound of running water a minute later, and hope he's okay in there by himself.

After heading into the kitchen, I open the fridge and stare at the shelves in dismay. It's totally empty, except for some moldy cheese and wilted lettuce. Father must not come by much now that I've gone back to school.

I rummage through the drawer and find the menu for the pizza place in Angel Peak, and order a supreme pizza plus a BBQ chicken pizza. I have no idea what Gabriel likes, so I figure that covers all my options.

When Father returns, he looks a hundred times better, although there are bags under his eyes that weren't there before he was punished. Bonus, he's not naked anymore. No one wants to see their dad naked, even if he looks just a few years older than you.

"There was nothing in the fridge, so I ordered some pizza," I tell him, as we sit back down on the couch. "Hope that's all right."

"I'm grateful for anything at this point." He sinks into the cushions with a frown. "I'm sorry I arrived outside your room last night and in such a state. I was trying to come here, but teleporting works by picturing where you want to go, and I guess I couldn't stop thinking of you."

"I'm glad you came to me. If you hadn't, you'd still be injured and in pain." I shudder as I remember the state he was in last night. He really thought he could handle that on his own? Angels truly are the most prideful race out there. "Are you safe here? With the attacks nearby?"

"This property is warded so no one can get in without invitation from one of the three owners—you, me, and Jonah. That's why I came here to recover."

"What happened? How could Azrael hurt you like that?"

"The Archangel Council had a meeting to decide my punishment. I knew it was coming, which is why I warned you and asked Callan to protect you. I hope he's been doing a good job?"

"Yes, he's been annoyingly protective at all times."

"Good." Father closes his eyes and draws in a breath, before speaking again. "At least I know you're safe at that school. Especially now."

"What do you mean?"

"I'm no longer a member of the Archangel Council."

My stomach drops. "Because of me?"

"Because of what I did with your mother, and because I lied about it. They no longer feel I can be in a position of power."

"That's total bullshit. You didn't do anything wrong."

"They believe I did."

I swallow hard and ask the question that's haunted me my entire life. "Do you regret doing it?"

"Not for one second." He rests his hand over mine. "I would take a thousand of those punishments as long as it meant having you as my daughter."

I give his hand a squeeze as emotion makes my throat tight. I'm not used to feeling this way, and I try to shake it off before I start crying or something. Luckily the doorbell rings at that moment and saves me from an embarrassing moment.

I grab some plates and napkins, then head back to the couch. Father looks like he's become part of the cushions, so I'm not sure he has the energy to move to the dining room table. Casual it is.

"Thanks for ordering this," he says, as he fills up his plate with some slices. "How did you know BBQ chicken pizza is my favorite?"

"I didn't—it's my favorite too."

He smiles at me, and I think how nice it is to sit on the couch and eat pizza with my dad, like a somewhat normal family. But the moment's ruined as he continues his story.

"As I was saying, the Archangel Council kicked me off, but they decided that wasn't enough. They want to make an example of me, to show that even an Archangel isn't above the law. Azrael claimed I should be sent to Penumbra Prison for twenty years, which is the normal punishment for my crime."

"Twenty years?" I ask, nearly choking on my pizza. "That's so long!"

"Yes, although Ariel argued I should get a reduced sentence because I'm an Archangel, and some of the others agreed."

"Good." More points for Jonah's mother. "What exactly is Penumbra Prison?"

"It's a prison for all supernaturals here on Earth who commit a crime, whether they are angels, demons, or even fae—although the fae are so rare on Earth that we don't have very many of their prisoners. In Faerie, they handle their own punishments as they see fit."

"Are they sending you to this prison?"

He grabs a glass of water and takes a sip before continuing. "No. Raphael argued that since I was the leader of the Ishim, I was too valuable an asset to imprison. The Council doesn't want a group of angry and rebellious spies and assassins on their hands. Azrael reluctantly agreed because he knows it's true, as an Ishim himself. He tried to take over as Ishim leader before actually, but our kind were loyal to me. When the Archangel Council offered me Michael's position, Azrael thought he would take over as Ishim leader finally. Instead, I refused the position and he became the leader of all angels. And he never forgets to remind me of it."

"He sounds like a real asshole," I mutter, which makes Father laugh. I give him a little smile. "Sorry, but it's true."

"Oh yes, he's definitely an asshole, it's just funny to hear someone say it out loud." He chuckles softly as he grabs another slice of pizza. "Anyway, Uriel suggested that instead of sending me away to prison, they invoke the old punishment of destroying someone's wings with dark-infused weapons. It hasn't been used in many years, since it's considered so barbaric, but the other Archangels agreed to it."

"*Uriel* suggested that?" I thought Bastien's father was a pretty decent guy. Scary, as all Archangels are, but he convinced both Jophiel and Baal to allow me to stay at Seraphim Academy. I can't believe he'd suggest something so horrible.

"It sounds harsh, I know, but if you think about it, he was actually doing me a favor. This punishment was incredibly painful, and they knew it would take me a long time to heal from it, but it's still better than a long prison sentence. At least this way, I can still see you. And Azrael definitely enjoyed giving the punishment to me, the sick bastard."

I've never met the guy, but I already hate him. And it's a different hate than what I feel for Callan. This is deep in my bones, because he hurt someone I love.

"They did strip all my powers as an Archangel though. I'm basically just a regular angel now."

I shake my head, my appetite gone. "I can't believe they did something so horrible to you."

"It was worth it. If they hadn't punished me, they might have gone after you instead. I couldn't let that happen." He lets out a long sigh. "All your life, your mother and I have worried that if anyone found out about you, you'd be put to death. That's why we hid you for so long, and why we will always do whatever it takes to protect you."

That emotion is back, making my eyes water. I cough a little into my napkin. "Have there ever been others like me?"

"No. Plenty of angels and demons have had relations before, of course, but all other pregnancies ended in miscarriage. You're the only one that's survived."

My eyes widen. "But...why?"

He shakes his head. "We have no idea. We always assumed it was because your mother and I are both very powerful, but I suspect it will always be a mystery. Just like some human couples can be infertile for years, and then suddenly become pregnant. Perhaps it's fate. Or luck. Who knows the will of the universe?"

I take a minute to absorb that, and then get mad all over again that my father was punished for having me. "Angels and demons are at peace now. Why keep the old rule that the two races can't be together? It needs to change."

"I agree. But with Azrael in charge, I fear it never will."

"I wish you'd taken the job." It's exasperating to think how much good he could be doing right now instead of hiding in this house.

"Sometimes I do too, but I never would have risked your safety like that."

"But now that I'm in the open, couldn't you challenge him?"

"Probably not. Azrael's powers have increased now that he's the leader of the Council, and he has many people who are loyal to him too, like Jophiel. Even if I was still a member of the Council, it would be extremely difficult to remove him."

Gabriel yawns, and I decide it's time to cut things short, even though it's been nice to talk to my dad so openly for a change. I grab our plates and take them to the kitchen, and make a mental note to do a grocery store run for him tomorrow. He walks into the kitchen behind me, but he's stiff. Is he still hurting?

I rest a hand on his shoulder. "I should get going so you can rest. Marcus will check on you tomorrow, and I'll be back as soon as I can. Please be safe."

Before I know it, I'm enveloped in his arms. Tears well behind my closed eyes. This is the most affectionate hug he's ever given me.

"I love you, Olivia."

My breath catches in my throat. "I love you too...Dad."

I've never called him that before. He was always Father, a formal name for our formal relationship, but maybe we're starting to move past formalities to become a real family. I know I'd like that.

34

OLIVIA

As fall arrives, the trees begin to change, and the campus becomes beautiful in a different way. It's hard to believe the school year will be over in a few more months.

Our soccer team has a game at Hellspawn Academy, and I ask Uriel if I can go, but he denies my request and says it's too dangerous right now with the recent attacks. Our team wins, fulfilling Marcus's Order task, and I'm sad I don't get to see him play or check out the school. Someday I'll make a point to visit it, but not now. I have more important things to worry about anyway.

Father—Dad?—is completely recovered, but he's basically been placed on house arrest, and isn't allowed to leave Angel Peak. I sneak off to visit him when I can, and we have a few more relaxed family dinners. I consider talking to him about the Order and about my plan to rescue Jonah, but he's been through so much lately, I decide it's better to wait until I know something more concrete. Besides, it's not like he believed me last time I mentioned it.

In Fae Studies, Raziel finally starts talking about magical objects and relics, like my necklace. "Some of the fae have the ability to imbue objects with magic, and they're known as enchanters. It's a rare and powerful ability, usually used in conjunction with other magic, including that of angels and demons. For example, Raphael once worked with an enchanter to create a blanket that would heal anyone it was placed upon. Unfortunately such a relic was lost during the Great War."

He goes on to talk about some of the objects the Fae have made, and I twirl my pen as my mind wanders. I have my meeting with Delilah at the end of the day, and I want to ask her about what happened to me on the night my dad was injured.

"This is also how angels, demons, and fae moved between the worlds," Raziel says, drawing my attention again. "Fae enchanters created special keys that can open portals to the other worlds. Most open portals to two worlds, i.e. between Earth and Heaven. A few rare keys can open portals between any world. The most famous of these is the Staff of Eternity, of course."

He has my full attention now. It's been over a month since the guys promised to help me defeat the Order and find Jonah, and not one damn thing has happened, other than they asked me to start spending more time in the bell tower with them. The request came from Callan, oddly enough. He was a total jerk about it, but explained that he takes his promise to my father seriously, and he'd appreciate it if I helped him by staying close when I could.

"The Staff is one of the most powerful relics in existence." Raziel rubs his hands together in excitement. He clearly loves talking about it. I wonder if he's in the Order. "It was created by an enchanter named Culann with the help of Michael and Lucifer, and it can work as a key between any world. But it also used their power as leaders to send both our races to Earth, and to close off Heaven and Hell from anyone who might try to open a portal to it."

"Can it work in reverse to send all the demons back to Hell?" Jeremy asks. He narrows his eyes at me as he says it. Prick.

"Yes, and it could also send all of us back to Heaven too. Not that anyone would want to go there. Both worlds were pretty much decimated by the time Michael and Lucifer signed the Earth Accords. Our only hope of long-term survival was moving to this world."

A girl I don't know raises her hand. "Couldn't we try to rebuild Heaven?"

Raziel gives her a sad smile. "Perhaps eventually we will. For now, we're focusing on replenishing our population while on Earth and finding a way to live in harmony with both demons and humans."

"Where is the Staff now?" someone else asks.

"No one knows. Michael and Lucifer hid it after the Earth Accords so that it wouldn't fall into the wrong hands. Of course, it requires both an Archangel and an Archdemon—or one of their children, perhaps—to unlock its full power, and it's unlikely anyone could find two of them to agree to such a thing."

He continues telling us about different Fae relics, but Bastien and I have already finished our paper on this topic and he's covering things I already know. I shift in my seat, impatient to meet with Delilah, and my pen rolls off the desk. When I bend over to get it, I realize it's rolled all the way under me and into the row to my right. I stretch my body and reach for the pen, and see something gold in Jeremy's bag. I snatch my pen and knock the bag at the same time, just enough to get a better look at the gold mask inside.

I quickly sit up straight, bumping my elbow in the process. Bastien gives me a quizzical look, but I just shake my head. I should've known Jeremy was in the Order. He's definitely a believer in their cause.

When class is over, Jeremy grabs his bag and purposefully kicks my chair on his way out. I can't wait to take the Order—and that asshole—down.

———

"I s your dad out of town again?" I ask Bastien with a wink, as he leads me to the parlor.

He smirks. "Alas, he is not. But I can come to your dorm tonight."

"I'd like that." We pause outside the doorway and I reach up to touch his sharp jaw. I gave him a few weeks off to recover, but he's back to his normal strength now, and I can't wait to spend some time alone with him tonight.

He takes my hand and kisses my fingers in a move that's surprisingly tender for him. Then he drops my hand and walks away, like it meant nothing to him. *Oh, Bastien, you'll never change.*

I step into the parlor and smile at Delilah, who's wearing a sleeveless black sheath dress that accentuates her shapely arms and legs. As always, I'm momentarily dazzled by her beauty for a split second, and then I recover and take my seat across from her.

"You look much better," Delilah says.

I pour myself some tea. "Thanks. At your advice, I took additional lovers and I'm feeding more regularly now."

"Good. You should be feeding once a week, at least. Remember that the more often you feed, the less you'll need to take at each meal."

"Just like if you skip a few meals, you'll be starving and stuff yourself until you can barely move?"

"Exactly. It's much better to have a steady diet, both for you and for your lovers." A naughty smile crosses her dark red lips. "And if you can convince two of your lovers to join you for one meal, it will be even better."

Two at once? That does sound amazing, but I'm not sure any of my guys would agree. I take a sip of my tea and stare off into space.

"Is there something on your mind?" Delilah asks. "You seem troubled."

"A few weeks ago I transferred some of my energy into one of my lovers. Is that a succubus power we haven't covered yet?"

She pauses while holding her tea mid-sip. "No, it isn't. In fact, that shouldn't even be possible. It must be your unique power due to your...special parentage."

"I thought that might be it."

She leans back with a proud smile. "Now that you're feeding more often your powers are growing, although I would guess something probably triggered this one's emergence."

"Someone I cared about was hurt, and this was the only way to help them."

"Yes, that explains it. Just be careful with such a power. Don't give too much of yourself, or you'll risk growing weak."

"I understand."

"Is there anything else you wish to discuss?" she asks.

I hesitate. "Have you ever been to Faerie?"

Her face changes, her lashes lowering as she stares into her tea cup. "Yes, though it's been many years. I used to have a lover there named Culann."

"The one who made the Staff of Eternity?"

"The very same. Alas, we had a falling out some time ago, and I haven't seen him in many years since it's so difficult to get to Faerie now."

I lean forward in my seat. "Do you know how to get to Faerie?"

"I do. You need a special relic called a key to open a portal to Faerie, but those keys have mostly been destroyed over the years, or are being held by the fae themselves. Some keys can only be used by fae too. Getting one now would be near impossible." She taps her fingers on her tea cup. "I used to have one, but it's long gone now. Probably for the best, since I have no interest in facing the High King again, and he would definitely notice if I stepped into his lands."

Sounds like we're not getting a fae key anytime soon, dammit. I remember Raziel telling us about the High King in class, and wonder how Delilah knows him. "Is it true the High King killed his wife?"

"Oh yes. Titania was a powerful fae queen, but could not bear him any children. Oberon desperately wanted a son and had many affairs in the hopes of having one, and because he has a hard time keeping his dick in his pants. In retaliation, Titania cursed him to sire only daughters. When he discovered what she'd done, he killed her. Yet the curse remains."

"He sounds horrible." And speaking of horrible men... "What about Azrael? Do you know him?"

"You're full of interesting questions today." She sets her empty tea cup down. "Yes, I've met him, though you'd be wise to stay far away. Before he became the Archangel leader, he was their assassin.

They call him the Angel of Death for good reason, and he has a personal vendetta against demons since he believes we killed his son. Not that there's any proof of that, mind you."

"He seems to have a vendetta against my father too," I mutter.

"They've always had something of a rivalry, or so I'm told." She rises to her feet, and reaches down to rest her hand upon the top of my head, lightly stroking my hair. "Be cautious. There are people on both sides watching you at all times."

"Including you?"

That makes her smile. "Especially me."

35

KASSIEL

E very time I sleep with Olivia, I put everything at risk. My job.
My mission. My heart.

But I can't stop myself from going back for more.

I tell myself I do it because she needs me. Or because Lucifer
wants me to keep her safe, and making sure she's well-fed is part of
that. I tell myself all sorts of excuses, anything to make it easier on
my conscience when I meet her alone. In my classroom. In my
office. In my room.

She sits up in my bed after our latest round, and I run my hand
up and down her back. Even her back is beautiful, with soft, smooth
olive skin. I roll on my side and press a kiss to the curve of her hip.

She smiles at me over her shoulder. "I should get going. We both
have classes tomorrow."

"Don't remind me." I lean back and prop my head up on my
pillow. "You could stay though. If you wanted."

She shakes her head. "I don't do that, and I don't allow anyone
to stay over either. It's one of my rules."

Probably smart. I know she's sleeping with other men too, but it
doesn't bother me since I grew up around Lilim. Her angel lovers,

on the other hand, might get jealous to find another man in bed with her.

It wasn't hard to figure out who her other lovers are either. The Princes hang around her like they're her personal bodyguards, even after what they did to her last year. But three angels aren't enough, even ones with Archangel blood. Olivia needs me too.

Besides, I have to be up way too early. Damn these angels and their love of mornings. I let out a yawn, and Olivia pauses while putting on her dress, then stares at me with a worried expression.

"Are you feeling all right? No weakness or exhaustion?"

I laugh softly and sit up. "You don't need to worry about me. I'm just struggling with this angelic schedule. I have a hard time sleeping at night still."

She searches my eyes. "Are you sure?"

"Liv, I'm not a young demon. I can handle feeding you."

"I know, but the others have Archangel blood, and they were still weakened by me. You don't."

"Ah, I see." I pause as I consider my next words. I haven't revealed this secret to anyone in a long time, but I trust Olivia and care about her more than any other woman in many years. "As I said, you don't need to worry. I have the demon equivalent of Archangel blood."

"Your father is an Archdemon?" she asks, but then frowns as she remembers our discussion. There is no Fallen Archdemon, not really.

"My father is Lucifer."

Her mouth opens and closes, opens and closes, before finally she asks, "Lucifer?" She stares at me. "Like, *the* Lucifer?"

"The very one." I scan her face, trying to read her. Is she going to panic? Run away? Scream? People tend to have pretty strong reactions to me being the son of the devil. "How does that make you feel?"

"Wow. I suppose I really don't need to worry about you then." She lets out a soft laugh. "No wonder you're so powerful and know so much inside information about him. I hope you can tell me more sometime."

My eyebrow arches up. "That's it? You learn my father is the most powerful demon in the world and the greatest villain of all time, and you just want to learn more about him?"

"How else would I feel? Your father could be Azrael, who I hate much more than Lucifer." She tilts her head as she considers. "I mean, I don't hate Lucifer at all. I don't have any feelings about him one way or another."

"Maybe I can change your mind about that." I take her hand and caress it softly. "Perhaps someday you can meet him."

"I'd like that." She pauses. "Maybe. The real question is, how does he feel about me?"

"He thinks you could be an ally, and has asked me to protect you."

"Does he want to punish my mother?"

"I don't believe so."

She blows out a breath. "That's a relief. After what they did to my father, I've been extra worried."

"Demons are much less strict about that stuff. We're all about personal freedom, after all."

She nods. "It's angels who are fixed on the old traditions. We need to find a way to change things, so demons and angels can be together if they want."

"It's hard to overturn ancient laws and thousands of years of hatred. We've only been at peace for a little over thirty years. We'll get there eventually."

"I hope so." She bends down and gives me a kiss, before moving toward my balcony. "I'll see you in class tomorrow."

She goes invisible before flying back to her own dorm. I lean back in the bed and stare at the night sky through the open sliding door, soaking in the darkness that creeps inside. When I was born in Hell, angels and demons were at war, both intent on wiping the other race out. Now I'm teaching at an angel school, and sleeping with the first angel-demon hybrid. Change is coming, whether the angels or demons are ready for it—and I have a feeling Olivia will be leading the charge.

36

OLIVIA

A week later, Araceli and I are heading to the cafeteria for dinner, when there's a loud boom and a tremble in the earth. We freeze, whirling around to find the source of the sound. It's not close, but it's definitely on campus.

"Was that an explosion?" Araceli asks.

I zip up my hoodie. "I think so. It came from the direction of the lake."

We both sprint toward the sound, heedless of the danger, and spot Hilda outside the gym.

"Gather to me, students!" she calls out to anyone nearby, and some other students run to her. She gestures for them to enter the gym, while she stands guard outside.

Another boom fills the air, closer this time, and I hear a few nervous screams. Wow am I glad that Hilda had us all start carrying weapons. My dagger's already in my hand, while Araceli's unsheathing her sword.

There's a flash of gold and white feathers, and then Callan sets down beside me, wielding his huge barbarian sword. "You should be in the dorm," he snaps at me.

"If the school is under attack, we want to help."

"You want to get yourself killed, as far as I can tell," he grumbles, as he falls in step with us.

"Do you think it's the humans?" Araceli asks.

"Possibly," Callan says, before eyeing me. He's probably thinking it could be demons too.

Marcus and Bastien land beside us, and I'm relieved to see they're all right.

"I've done a quick sweep of the area, and it seems like they've moved away for now," Marcus says. "But it appears they can throw whatever is causing the explosions."

"That could explain how they're getting them past the gates," Bastien says. "They're warded against both humans and demons right now."

"We should take cover somewhere until it's over," Callan says.

"No way," I say. "Don't you want to defend the school?"

"Of course I do, but your protection is more important."

"And I'm going to fight," I say, stomping off toward the gates. "So you'll just have to stick with me."

"I wouldn't be anywhere but by your side," Marcus says and grabs my hand to give it a quick kiss. Callan grumbles, but he and the others move with me toward the forest.

A group of angels fly overhead, and I spot Kassiel's black and silver wings. The professors must be going to investigate. I wonder if Uriel's already there. What will we find when we reach the gates?

We creep through the woods, weapons ready, but it's pitch black and I'm the only one who can see much of anything, so it's slow going. There's no moon tonight either. A perfectly timed attack against angels.

"If they can't get onto the campus, why are we moving like they can?" Araceli whispers.

"Because what if they could?" Callan asks. "What if we're wrong? We must be prepared for anything."

We hear a rustling in the woods and ready our weapons, but then Tanwen emerges from behind a bush, her eyes bright and determined. She clutches a mace tightly in her hand, and her straw-colored ponytail whips behind her as she moves with purpose. She shoots us a quick glance, sizing us up, and then continues forward.

A black shape comes toward us in a hurry, just above the tree line. It's so dark, I'm probably the only one who can see it, with my demon vision. I squint, watching it fly, but it's too small to be an angel, and it moves in a way that seems almost familiar.

"Look out!" I scream, my heart clenching as I realize it's a drone —and it must be behind the explosions. I grab Tanwen's arm and yank her to the side, just as the drone drops an object. A bomb.

As everyone takes cover, Callan raises a hand and shoots a beam of burning light at the bomb. It explodes with a horrible sound and a bright flash, making dirt and leaves fly all around us. We all slowly stand up again, while Callan brushes dirt off his shirt. That brave idiot.

"They're using drones," Bastien says with a voice full of appreciation. "It's genius."

Callan gives him a chastising look. "You sound like you're on their side."

"Don't be ridiculous. But you have to admit it's smart. They can't get through the gates, so they're using drones. With cameras on them, almost certainly."

"Not too smart," Marcus says, as his wings snap out. "Or they'd know the sky is our domain."

I search the night sky but the drone is gone. "There must be more of them. Araceli, you should fly back and make sure everyone knows to take cover."

She hesitates, but then nods. "On it."

The rest of us take off and fly toward the gates. Up ahead, we see other angels flying with balls of light by them, helping them see in the dark. And also making them targets.

A burst of automatic gunfire pierces the night, and one of the angels goes down. My chest clenches, and I pray it's not Kassiel who's been hit. Marcus dives down after the angel, presumably to heal them. One of the angels up ahead blasts the drone with Erelim light, but more approach and begin firing at us. With a roar, Callan flares out his wings and faces the oncoming drones, his arms wide.

There's a flash of white light that spreads all around him, both above and below, and the gunfire bounces off it. He's created a giant shield to protect us all.

His Archangel power, it must be. I've never heard of any other angel doing that.

The angels fly forward to attacks the drones, since there's no telling how long Callan can hold his shield. It quickly becomes total chaos, with wings flashing in the night, swords slashing into machinery, and bursts of light that make me blink back white spots. I've never fought in anything like this before—year three of Combat Training is where we learn things like aerial combat—and it's chaotic. I lunge for the nearest drone with my dagger, but then someone shoves me hard, and I miss. I glance back and spot Jeremy, who hovers there with an evil grin.

"Two birds, one stone," he says, before darting away.

The drone unleashes a volley of gunfire as I spin to the side, and I scream as something hot and sharp hits me, sending excruciating pain through my arm. Then there's a blast of light and I'm yanked aside, before the drone explodes. Another drone appears at my side, but the person who saved me swings her mace and knocks it to the ground. Tanwen.

"That was close," she says, her white wings slowly flapping to hover at my side. All around us the battle is ending, with the drones either defeated or flying away. "Are you all right?"

I check my arm, which is bleeding quite a bit but doesn't seem to have a bullet stuck in it, at least. Marcus or Araceli can heal it when they get a chance. "I got hit, but I'm okay. Thanks for saving me."

"What kind of warrior would I be if I didn't protect the weakest of us?" Tanwen says with a haughty sniff. "Besides, I saw what that asshole Jeremy did. Not cool."

No. I'll have to deal with him at some point. Like I need more shit added to my To Do List.

Bastien flies over to us. "They're gone, but we've confirmed it was the Duskhunters. Their symbol is on the drones."

Tanwen grips her mace tight, her eyes glowing with angry light. "We need to go after them. They have to pay for what they did."

Bastien shakes his head. "The headmaster has ordered all students back to their dorms, while the professors finish up here."

"I'm not going back while they're still out there!"

"I know you want justice for your friends, but this isn't the time," I tell her.

"Not just my friends. Those bastards killed my mother too." With a great flap of her shining white wings, she takes off.

I sigh as I watch her go, then turn back to Bastien. "What were the Duskhunters trying to do?"

"They were testing our defenses, I believe." His brow furrows as he gazes across the forest. "I fear this is only the beginning."

37

OLIVIA

I n the aftermath of the Duskhunter attack, defenses are increased around the school, with regular patrols along the gates at night. My father personally takes over Angel Peak's security, and I feel a little better knowing he's got it handled.

Three angels were seriously injured in the attack, including Hilda, but thanks to Marcus and the other healers, they recovered quickly. Otherwise, there was no real damage done, luckily. Still, it seems like the wrong time to throw a birthday party, so I decide to just have a small gathering in the bell tower, with absolutely no gifts allowed. Instead, I set up a little jar to collect money for the families of people who were killed by the Duskhunters.

"What's she doing here?" Araceli whispers to me, as Tanwen steps inside the lounge.

"She helped me during the attack, so I invited her here," I say, with a shrug.

Tanwen stuffs a wad of bills into the donation jar, then heads over to me. "Happy birthday, Liv."

"I'm going to get a beer," Araceli says, and I get the impression she just wants to bolt. "Want one?"

"Sure," Tanwen replies.

I decide to just come out and ask. "You're being a lot nicer to me this year, and you protected me from Jeremy. What gives? I thought you hated me."

"No, I hate humans." Her nose wrinkles, and it's annoying how cute it is. "But I guess I realized I was a total bitch to you last year, and that wasn't cool. You got back at me too. So hopefully we're even now."

My jaw practically hits the floor as I process her words. "Yeah, we're cool. But if you don't hate demons, why are you in the Order?"

She glances around us quickly, her face worried. "Don't say that so loud! And how do you know?"

I drag her off to a corner where no one can hear us. "I'm in the Order too."

She blinks at me. "You? They let you stay in even after they found out you're part demon?"

"I was surprised also. Maybe they kept me because Gabriel's my dad?" I shrug. "Either way, I'm in it, but only to find my brother. What about you?"

She bites her lip, and for the first time ever, she actually looks a little worried. "I'm working against them."

"Why?"

She pauses, but then she must decide to trust me. "My sister is in love with a demon."

"Oh." Was not expecting that. "Wow."

"She's set to be the next leader of the Valkyries, but since her relationship with the shifter is forbidden, she keeps delaying taking on the job." Tanwen tugs on her ponytail. "At first I joined the Order because all the other Valkyries were doing it. Now I stay to try and thwart their plans against demons, for my sister. And because her boyfriend is a pretty good guy. His family is nice too. They've opened my eyes a lot to the fact that demons and angels are not all that different. Most of us want the same things."

"I know what you mean. My dad was punished for being with my mother. It was horrible."

"That's why I'm worried for my sister. Angels are strict about this, much more so than demons. The law needs to change if we ever want true peace between the two races."

I nod. "Totally agree."

"I'm guessing you don't believe in the Order's crap then either?" she asks.

"No." I hesitate, but decide to trust her, since she trusted me. "I joined at first to find my brother, which I'm still working on. Now I want to stop them from getting the Staff, and eventually find a way to take them down."

"Whatever you're planning, count me in." She offers her hand, and I take it. Tanwen, my ally? Maybe even...a friend? It's hard to believe, but she gives me a fierce smile, before heading off to talk to Callan.

My dad shows up with a bunch of pizzas like he's a delivery boy, and everyone laughs and cheers. He gives me a big hug and then goes to start serving, and I look around the room at the people I care most about, and smile. The only person missing is Kassiel, but he gave me a birthday orgasm earlier to make up for it. I couldn't exactly invite him to the party, after all. Not without a lot of questions.

As the party is winding down, Callan corners me outside the bathroom. "I got my Order task," he says quietly.

"What is it?"

He looks behind us, where Grace, Cyrus, and Isaiah are sitting on the couch, laughing about something. "They want me to beat up Isaiah to punish Cyrus for failing his mission."

My hand flies to my mouth to cover my gasp. Cyrus's mission was to get close to Araceli, but ever since I found out about it, she's been avoiding him. The Order must have noticed. "That's horrible. Are you going to do it?"

His face darkens. "Of course not. Do you really think I'm the kind of man who would?"

I consider this. He rules over the school and intimidates everyone. He bullied me, although he did it thinking it was in my best interests. He never actually hurt me or anything else though. "No, I know you're not like that." Then I have another thought, and it makes me grip his shirt. "But if you don't do it, they'll punish you next. Someone you love. Maybe your mom."

"They can try, but I won't be intimidated by them," he growls. "Besides, we're going to take them down anyway, right?"

He always seemed like he was on the fence before about going up against the Order, but not anymore. He's willing to do what's right, even if it's dangerous. The last little ice in my heart melts, and I give him a hug, resting my head on his chest. "Yes, we are."

He stiffens and awkwardly pats my back, probably worried about people seeing us. I don't care. I can finally admit that I don't hate Callan, not anymore. I don't think he hates me either. If he did, he wouldn't protect me so fiercely, and he wouldn't kiss me so hard. He cares about me, even if he won't admit it.

When I get home, I'm destroying that video of us having sex. I'm done with revenge.

Araceli's right—I'm better than that. Or at least, I want to be.

38

OLIVIA

W hen I get to my bedroom, I find someone waiting for me. I grip my dagger tight as I hit the light switch.

"Lilith?" I ask, so shocked I drop my weapon.

She's been lounging on my bed like it's her own while playing on her phone in the dark. She looks up at me with a smile. "Hello, daughter."

How does one describe the Archdemon of the Lilim? She's so beautiful it nearly hurts to look at her, yet so alluring you can't do anything but stare. We share the same olive skin, dark brown curls, green eyes, and seductive curves. If someone were to look at us side by side, they'd probably think we were sisters, except she has this magnanimous power that is unique to her. And much like the Archangels, when you look into her eyes you can somehow sense the thousands of years she's lived.

"What are you doing here?" I awkwardly bend down and pick up the dagger, then close the door behind me.

"It's your birthday. I came to give you a gift."

"I haven't seen you in years!" My shock is starting to give way to anger. "Where have you been all this time?"

Lilith rises from the bed like a queen, and I'm reminded of the first time I met her, when I was six years old.

"Are you a princess?" I asked with awe in my voice.

She laughed. "More like a queen."

"An evil queen?"

A wicked smile touched her red lips. "Some would say so. But you have nothing to fear from me."

"I'm sorry for my absence, but it was unavoidable," she says now.

"I haven't seen you since I was eighteen." She vanished right after she finished my succubus training, and all I got after that were a few birthday cards and postcards from various places around the world. Even when I was revealed as a half-succubus to the world, she didn't come for me. Only Gabriel did.

"I didn't mean to stay away so long, but someone I care about dearly went missing. I've been searching for her ever since." Lilith moves to stand in front of me and brushes the back of her hand against my cheek. "But this past year I've come to visit you, many times. You simply didn't know it."

She takes something from her pocket and puts it on. A gold ring with rubies on it. As she does, her appearance melts into something else. Her hair and skin turn darker. Her nose and mouth shift slightly. The only thing that remains are her eyes. Even her presence and power are lessened a little. A perfect disguise.

"Delilah?" I step back, my stomach twisting. "You were her all along?"

"Yes, thanks to a fae relic from Culann." She gestures at my neck. "Much like your necklace, it allows me to hide myself. He made that for me too, you know."

I can barely process what she's saying, because I have so many other questions. "Why would you hide? Is Delilah real?"

"I hid because I couldn't exactly show up on your campus as Lilith. Delilah is one of my disguises, like Laylah. She doesn't exist, but everything I said to you during our meetings was true otherwise."

Laylah's the name I was said to use whenever anyone asked about my mom. I was told demons might have heard the name, but wouldn't know exactly who she was—unlike the name Lilith, which everyone knows.

"But why hide from *me?*"

She looks down, her lashes lowered. "I worried you'd be mad, since I've been away so long. I wanted to get to know you as a friend or peer, not as your absent mother. I am sorry for that."

I sigh, but it's hard to stay mad with her. I think it's probably part of her magic. Or maybe I'm just so happy to see my mom again and to know she's been there for me over the past few months after all.

I open my arms to her. "I'm happy to see you, Mother."

She moves close and embraces me tightly, and I breathe in her rose-scented hair. Yes, she even smells amazing.

I pull back with a frown. "Why didn't you tell me about my brother?"

She waves a light hand. "Asmodeus is thousands of years old. He's your brother by blood, but his concerns are very different from yours. He used to rule for me in Hell, and he's had a hard time adjusting to Earth. I thought I would introduce you someday, when you were both ready. For now, he doesn't know you're related. I never told him about you for your own protection."

"Are there others?"

"Yes. Some living. Some not." Sadness crosses her face. "Some lost."

"Lost?"

She takes my face in her hands and kisses my forehead. "I'll reveal all in time, I promise. For now, I must continue my travels. After you open your present, of course." She picks up something off the bed that's wrapped in a dark silk shawl, then places it in my hands carefully. I remove the fabric and find two daggers, one glowing with pure white light, the other pulsing with inky black darkness.

"These daggers have served me well for many years, but I wish for you to have them now."

I hold one in each hand, feeling the weight of them, and how perfect they fit. Like they were made just for me. "I understand the dark-infused blade, but why do you have a light-infused blade too?"

"Sometimes the greatest threat to us comes from one of our own."

I nod, thinking of my father and Azrael. The daggers have a belt sheath, and Lilith helps me attach it, so the daggers rest on either side of my hips.

"Perfect." She claps her hands together. "I feel a lot better now, knowing you have those."

"Thank you."

"I'll try to visit more often. I promise." Her phone makes a noise and she checks it, then lets out a short laugh. "Sorry, I'm totally addicted to this Star Wars game and my energy is full."

"You...what? You like Star Wars?"

"Oh yeah. Saw the first movie in the theater, and I've loved it ever since." She winks at me. "I'm an original fangirl."

Wow. That is something I never knew about my mother...and totally unexpected.

We embrace again and she kisses me on the cheek, before she walks out my door and slips away into the night. Without wings, she has to find some other way off campus, but I have no doubt she'll manage.

That's my mom—ancient demon, leader of all Lilim, queen of lust...and a Star Wars geek. Who would have thought?

39

BASTIEN

School is almost over, and it's time for our penultimate Order meeting. We go as a group this time—me, Callan, Marcus, and Olivia. After we put on the golden robes and masks in the bell tower, we link our hands in a chain, allowing Olivia to turn us all invisible. Flying is difficult and feels rather foolish, like we're holding hands and about to sing songs or something. Good thing no one can see us.

The woods are quiet and dark at this early hour of the morning, as we set down in the soft dirt. Olivia leads us forward, her hand tightly grasping mine. It feels small in my own, and I rub my thumb reassuringly along the back of it as we wait for the boulder to open. As I do, I realize this is not normal behavior for someone who cares nothing for her.

I can't deny it any longer. I've developed feelings for her.

How peculiar.

As I ponder this new development, we release each other's hands and lose our invisibility, then move down the corridor to the cavern at the bottom. We split up and join the other Order members, sitting beside them on the bench. Others continue to file in, until we're all present, and our leader steps from the shadows, wearing his crown.

He clasps his hands together. "You should all have been given tasks by now. Some of you have completed them. Some have not." His gaze scans the crowd, and even though we can't see his face or hear his voice, his displeasure is obvious from the tilt of his head. "Remember there will be consequences should you fail."

"I completed my task this week," I speak up.

"Excellent. Come forward."

I move closer and open a small, clear container. Inside is an inky black feather that emanates darkness, which once lived in my father's office. My task was to steal it, though I'm not sure what it does. Uriel told me it was one of Lucifer's feathers, and I can't imagine why the Order would want it.

I hold it out to the leader, who takes it carefully at the end and holds it up to the light. Shadows cling to it like mist, and the room seems a little darker.

"You have done well," he tells me with a nod. "This, my friends, is a feather from Lucifer's wings, stolen from Headmaster Uriel's office." A few people gasp, while some cringe backward, and others lean forward like they want to get a better look. "The feather has many interesting properties, but we're only interested in one of them. It can lead us to the Staff of Eternity."

Soft murmurs go around the room at this. "How does it work?" someone asks. I think it's Olivia.

"The feather will try to seek out its master. Here on Earth, it would fly to Lucifer. In Faerie, it will seek out the Staff, which contains a touch of Lucifer's essence."

"What about Jonah?" That's Marcus, I'm sure of it. "Can it find him too?"

"It is my hope he is with the Staff, but if not, we will do what we can to find him. However, we must stay focused on our purpose."

Another member nods. "Jonah knew the risks when he volunteered. He would want us to make finding the Staff the priority."

Callous, but practical. I would say the same thing, if I believed in this foolish mission. I still have a hard time understanding why

Jonah went to get the Staff in the first place, especially after meeting Olivia. Why would he put his sister at risk?

"But how will we get to Faerie?" someone else asks. Callan maybe.

"Do we have a key?" the person I think is Olivia asks.

"We do not, but the fae coming to the championship game will have at least one, possibly more. There are also ways of getting to Faerie without keys, using fae blood."

I've heard rumors along those lines, and it explains why they want Araceli so badly, but it must be a highly guarded secret among the fae if it's true.

The Order's leader continues. "We will kidnap a few fae from the game tomorrow. The initiates will be tasked with torturing them into opening a portal to Faerie for us. If they don't succeed, I'm sure one of us can be very convincing. You'll receive your instructions after this meeting." He stops and looks around the circle, his gaze landing on each of us for a second. "If all goes well, we will have the Staff within a few days' time. It's taken us many years to get to this point, and soon our hard will work all pay off—and the demons will be returned to Hell."

A few of the Order members begin to clap, and more join in a moment later, so I add my applause so I don't stand out. Then we're all dismissed, and we exit the cavern and disperse into the woods. The four of us split up, and then meet back in the bell tower.

"How could you give them that feather?" Olivia asks, as soon as I land.

"I didn't know what it did." I scowl, angrier with myself than her. I should have made more of an effort to find out why they wanted it first.

She slumps down on the couch and rests her head in her hands. "Now they can find the Staff, and we're no closer to finding Jonah or getting to Faerie."

"We'll need to stop the kidnapping and then convince the fae to let us go with them to Faerie, in the hopes that Jonah is with the Staff," Marcus says. "Oh, and steal the feather from the Order."

Callan rolls his eyes. "You make it sound so easy."

"At the very least, we need to stop the kidnapping attempt," Olivia says. "We can try to get the feather too."

Suddenly there's a rush of wind and Tanwen lands on the balcony. "If you guys are planning something, I want in."

Marcus glances at us and then back at her awkwardly. "Uhh... I'm not sure..."

Olivia stands up. "It's okay. Tanwen is on our side. She's agreed to help us take down the Order."

Callan's jaw drops. "What?"

Tanwen tosses her blond hair. "It's true. I want to take the bastards down, and I have inside information that can help you—if you agree to help me fight the Duskhunters in return."

I nod as the rightness of her words makes my Ofanim senses tingle. "She's speaking the truth."

"Then we agree to that deal," Callan says, crossing his arms.

Tanwen gives a short nod in response. "When I got back to my room there were instructions waiting for me. I'm supposed to pack a light bag with supplies and food for a few days of travel, and then I'm supposed to join them in the Order's cavern during halftime. Someone else must be handling the kidnapping. Probably an Ishim."

"Maybe Grace or Nariel," I speculate. We know Grace is a member, and it makes logical sense that her uncle would be one as well. Plus the Order tends to favor using invisibility to hide its members, a trick only a few powerful Ishim can handle.

Callan rubs his chin. "Do everything they said, and keep us updated if anything changes. They obviously trust you more than us, since we weren't invited to go on this mission, so you'll be our inside woman."

"Got it," Tanwen says.

"Marcus can keep an eye on Jeremy, since they're both on the soccer team." Callan's eyes scan the group. "The rest of us will split up and follow the other members we know are in the Order, or have suspicions about. Grace. Cyrus. Nariel."

"And Professor Kassiel," Tanwen adds. "He's a member."

"How do you know?" I ask.

"During the final test last year, when the demon escaped, there was chaos and fighting, and his mask got dislodged slightly. I recognized him."

"Kassiel is working to take down the Order also," Olivia says. "We can trust him."

"How do you know?" Marcus asks.

She hesitates, considering her words. "He and I made a pact at the end of last year to stop the Order. He has his own reasons for doing so, which aren't mine to share. I was going to ask him to help us tomorrow."

"I don't like it," Callan says.

Marcus shrugs. "If Olivia says we can trust him, then we can."

I cross my arms. "You realize that if we do this we'll be going up against the Order, and they'll know it. There won't be any turning back."

"That's why we have to succeed," Olivia says, her eyes burning with determination. "This is our one chance to stop the Order from getting the Staff, and to rescue my brother at the same time. Failure is not an option."

It's the day of the final tournament game against the fae, and I step back and check myself in the mirror. I'm wearing a new pair of black jeans that happen to make my butt look amazing, with my mom's infused daggers on my hips. A long, flowy red shirt covers them up and hides my butt too, which is probably for the best. I don't need anyone's lust distracting me. Then I double-check my necklace and make sure it's secure. We're going to need it today.

There's a knock on our door and I head to answer it, thinking it must be one of the Princes, or maybe Tanwen. When I open it, there's a man with sharp features who is wearing a hood over his head, even though we're indoors.

"Oh, hello. Is Araceli here?"

Araceli walks out of her bedroom at that moment, and her face goes from confusion to disbelief to delight. "Dad?"

He gives her a hesitant smile. "I got your messages. I'm sorry I couldn't make it to Family Day, but I was halfway around the world at the time. I hope it's okay that I'm here now."

"It's great." She walks over and I see her eyes are wet. "Thank you for coming."

"I'm so happy to see you, my little plum." The two of them

embrace, and as they do, his hood falls back and I see pointed ears and shiny purple hair, slightly darker than Araceli's.

"I'll give you two a few minutes to catch up," I tell them, before retreating to my room. I'm happy they're reconnecting, but also worried. I've now completed my Order task, of all the irony, but it puts Araceli's dad at risk.

As I shut the door, I hear Araceli's dad apologizing. Even with it closed, I can hear them talking through the walls, although it's muffled.

"I'm so sorry I haven't been around as much," he says. "I've been traveling a lot, working for the angels, but that's no excuse. I guess the real answer is that every time I saw you, it made me feel guilty."

"Guilty...why?" Araceli asks.

"Your mother never told you why we split up?"

I don't hear Araceli's answer, but I'm guessing the answer is no, because then her father continues talking.

"Muriel wanted to have another child, and I said no. After what my people did to me, and how hard it's been for you, I didn't think it was fair to put another child through that. I left your mom in the hopes she would find another man who could give her a pure angel child. One who wouldn't suffer for having fae blood, like you have."

"That's why you two split up?" Araceli asks loudly.

"Yes, and I've been wracked with guilt ever since. I love your mother, and I wanted her to be happy, even if it meant being with someone other than me. I hoped you might get a sibling out of it too."

"That's not going to happen. She doesn't want anyone else. And you don't need to worry about me. Sure, the other angels treated me like an outcast when I was a kid, but it just made me stronger." She pauses for a second. "A sibling would be cool though. Would you ever reconsider?"

"I don't know. It depends if Muriel would ever take me back."

"She would. You should talk to her."

"Maybe."

I feel like a jerk for invading their privacy, so I walk out onto the balcony to watch as the field is set up for the soccer game. A short while later, Araceli enters my room. "Liv? Can you come chat?"

"Sure."

As we head into the living room, she says, "Dad's given me some information that will help us get to Faerie."

"I'm Fintan," he says politely, offering his hand.

My heart races as I shake his hand. This is it. He's going to tell me how to find Jonah. "Do you have a key to Faerie, by any chance?"

"I do not, I'm sorry to say. I used to, but it was taken from me when I was excommunicated from Faerie. Most keys have been lost or destroyed, and the others are well-protected or hidden. But there are other ways to get there." He studies me with kind, intelligent eyes. "Araceli tells me you have a fae relic."

I lightly touch my gold necklace. "I do."

"May I see it?"

I hesitate, but then lean forward so he can look at it closer. I refuse to take it off, even for my friend's dad.

"Yes, this will work. It's very old and very powerful. Since it's not made for opening portals, it will require some blood from a fae to activate."

I stare at him open-mouthed. "That's all we need—Araceli's blood and my necklace?"

"Yes. Araceli will have to activate it with her fae magic, while picturing where she wants to visit. Since she's never been to Faerie before, it's best if I take her now for a few minutes. Then she'll have somewhere to envision."

"We're going to Faerie?" Araceli asks, her eyes dancing with excitement.

"If you'd like," he says with a smile. "Is there anywhere in particular you want to visit? The Summer Court, perhaps, to see your own kind?"

"Do you know where the Staff of Eternity is being kept?" I ask.

Fintan shakes his head. "No, I don't know anything about that."

I sigh. "Then I guess it doesn't matter. We won't know where to find the Staff or Jonah until we get that feather from the Order."

"Just take us somewhere safe," Araceli says.

"I shall." He clears his throat. "Trust me, I don't want to get caught. If they find out I took you to Faerie, they will kill me."

We clear some space in the middle of our living room and then Araceli grabs a knife and hands it to her dad. He cuts his hand, and then presses his bloody palm against my necklace. As he does, he mutters a few words in a language I've never heard before and holds out his other hand. After a few seconds, a portal opens up, a lot like the one we saw the fae make, but smaller.

Fintan drops his hand and wipes it off with a dishtowel. The wound is already closing up by the time he's done. "Let's go."

Fintan walks through the portal first, and Araceli gives me an excited, goofy thumbs up before following him. I take a deep breath and move through the portal, which makes my skin tingle, sort of like when your foot falls asleep. The world goes hazy, and then I'm standing in the middle of an overgrown forest. Everything is verdant green, and we're surrounded by the sounds of birds calling out and the wind rustling through the trees.

"Where are we?" Araceli asks.

"A forest in the Summer Court near my family's holdings. I figured if they caught us, they would probably be more merciful than other fae, though I could be wrong about that." He takes a few steps and touches the side of a thick, gnarled tree. "I carved my initials here when I was seven. It's an easy place for me to envision when I need to travel here, and few people venture into this forest anymore."

Araceli stares at the initials on the tree and nods. "I think I can envision it."

"Good. Now open a portal back to your dorm."

He instructs her in the phrase she should say, and then she cuts her hand, gives me an apologetic look, and touches my necklace. A portal opens up, and we return through it back into the dorm.

"I did it!" she says with a laugh.

"You've done well, little plum." Pride shines in his eyes. "Your fae magic is stronger than you know."

She shakes her head. "I don't have any fae magic."

"Of course you do." He smiles at her, but then it turns to a frown. "Speaking of magic, be careful using any angel magic in Faerie. Someone nearby might feel it." He turns to me. "Your necklace should protect you from being detected though, as long as you're wearing it."

I nod. "Thank you for helping us."

"It's the least I can do. Now, shall we head to the championship game? I haven't been to one of those in years, and I'd love to watch it with my daughter at my side."

I glance at Araceli. "Actually, it's not safe here for you. It's probably best if you leave."

"Leave?" he asks, blinking at us both.

Araceli nods sadly. "I'm sorry, dad. I would love to watch the game with you too. Maybe when school ends we can have a longer visit?"

"I'd like that." He kisses her on the cheek. "Be careful if you go to Faerie. I'd go with you, but I fear I'd only put you in more danger. Remember, the fae are powerful allies, but terrible enemies. Most importantly, don't get caught. I worry about what they would do to you."

"We'll be careful," she says.

She walks him out and I clutch my necklace tightly. We're so close. All we need to do now is get the feather. Oh, and stop the Order's nefarious plan along the way. Piece of cake.

41

OLIVIA

The crowd cheers as the Seraphim Academy soccer team runs onto the field, and I take a second to give Marcus an appreciative glance, before going back to scanning the crowd. Araceli and I are sitting with Grace and Cyrus in the bleachers, keeping an eye on them in case they run off. So far, they mostly seem excited to cheer for Isaiah, who stands next to Marcus on the field. Jeremy is on the team too, although I don't see him run out with the other players. Hmm.

"I'm going to get a soda, anyone need anything?" I ask, while giving Araceli a pointed look. She nods at me in response.

"No thanks," Grace says.

I head off to the closest food stand, and spot Callan leaning against a nearby wall. He meets up with me as I buy a soda.

"Jeremy's missing," I tell him quietly.

He gives a short nod as his eyes scan the field. "I'll have Bastien look into it. Have you seen anything else?"

"No, not yet."

"What about Nariel?" he asks.

I gesture to one side of the bleachers. "Kassiel is sitting with him and some of the other professors."

"I hope we can trust him."

"We can." We all met up briefly before the game started and went over the plan, then shared our new information on how we can get to Faerie. We're all ready for multiple scenarios. Now we just have to wait.

I grab my soda and head back toward my friends. The fae team is on the field now, and the game's about to start. We believe nothing will happen until half-time, but we want to be prepared when it does. Our plan is to try and prevent the kidnapping from happening at all, but if we fail, then we'll head to the forest with Tanwen and stop the Order there.

We watch the game, cheering for the angel team, who manage to hold their own against the fae. Still no sign of Jeremy though. Cyrus spends the entire time either cheering for Isaiah, talking about how hot he is, or sharing the latest rumors and gossip about the Duskhunter attack. Grace cheers along with him and nods at his newest story. They give no indication they're up to something.

As halftime approaches, Cyrus stands up. "I'm hitting the bathroom. Be right back."

Araceli gives me a quick look and then jumps up. "I need to pee too. I'll walk with you."

They head over to the bathrooms together, while I wait with Grace and watch the game. But Araceli and Cyrus take longer than I expect, and I can't help but glance back to look for them.

"Are you okay?" Grace asks.

"Yeah, fine." I shrug casually. "That bathroom line must be long, eh?"

Just as I'm about to go look for them, there's a huge boom behind us and a drone flies overhead. People scream and duck and someone yells, "The drones are back!"

Professors and other angels assigned to security launch into the air immediately, while others run to take cover. Everyone in the bleachers stands up and tries to shuffle away, while the players on the field are whisked into safety, including the fae. It's total chaos.

Shit, a Duskhunter attack is the absolute last thing we need right now. Although it might stop the Order from kidnapping any of the fae, so there's that at least. I extend my wings and fly up into the air to do whatever I can to help. As I do, I see Hilda blast the drone with burning light, and it explodes in a flash. Other angels continue to fly around, searching for more, but after the initial panic, it seems there was only one drone.

As Kassiel flies past me, I grab his arm, my eyes wide. "It was a diversion!"

"I think you're right." He glances around. "I don't see Nariel anymore. I was following him, but he must have slipped off and gone invisible."

"Grace too. I lost her in the chaos as everyone panicked. Dammit!"

I scan the crowd, which is dispersing quickly, but still don't see Araceli or Cyrus. This has all gone to shit.

"Time for plan B," I tell Kassiel, who nods. We know where the Order is meeting thanks to Tanwen. We'll have to try to stop them there. I just hope everyone else realizes it, since I have no way of finding them in this chaos.

I go invisible, and when I look back for Kassiel, he's gone too. He probably slipped into a shadow or something. I head toward the forest, and land near the boulder to throw on my golden robes and mask.

When I get to the cavern, there's a group already gathered there, some in gold, and some in white. Someone is already screaming from behind a closed door. It's just like when they wanted us to torture a demon last year. I messed that up for them, and now it's time to do the same this year.

As I walk in, the prison door opens and someone drags a shaking initiate out of the room. Behind them, three people are tied to chairs. Araceli. Her dad. And the female fae guard from the Spring Court that I met at the previous game.

My blood boils as I see my best friend's forehead covered in blood. Those fuckers are going to pay for this.

"Stop," I yell, but it sounds odd since the mask distorts my voice. I remove my dark-infused dagger, leaving the light one at my hip. It won't help here. "Let the prisoners go!"

"We can't do that," the leader says, standing near the prison door. He waves a hand, and some of the other golden masked people rush toward me to grab my arms. I slash at them and they dart back, but another one manages to knock off my mask—revealing my face.

Everyone stares at me, but I'm officially done with this cat and mouse game. I stand up to my full height and adjust the grip on my dagger. "Don't make me use my succubus powers."

A few people gasp, mostly the initiates. I figured focusing on my demon side would get a response.

"Put down your weapon," the leader says, as other members draw their weapons and surround me. "You're going to get hurt. You must realize this is the only way to get to Faerie...and to find your brother."

How dare that asshole use my brother to justify torture. I'm done playing nice. I haven't used my succubus powers like this in a long time, since I stopped seducing strangers, but now I reach out and incite lust in the leader. I used to need to touch someone to do it, but not anymore. I'm so angry that my power radiates out of me like a bomb, slamming into some of the other members too.

The ones holding weapons immediately drop them and step toward me. I can feel their desire, and how much they want me. How much they'll do anything to have me.

"You want me, don't you?" I ask in my most seductive voice. "I'll be yours...you just need to let the prisoners go."

"Do it," the leader stammers. "Anything."

That was too easy. He must already have wanted me a little.

"Don't listen to her!" someone calls out from the back. My power must not have extended that far. "She's using her dirty demon magic on you!"

I have a pretty good idea who that is. I slam some of my dirty demon magic into Jeremy in response, and he falls to his knees while reaching for me at the same time. "Be quiet, asshole."

The leader shakes his head and tries to resist my power, and others break free and rush toward me with their weapons. But then three people move in front of me, protecting me with their own swords. With everyone in masks, it's hard to tell who is who, but I'm guessing these are my friends. One of them is definitely Callan, judging by the size. Two others rush into the prison room and begin working to free the fae, starting with Araceli. The person who freed her hands her a sword, and she guards them as they free her dad and the fae woman.

"Remove your masks," I tell everyone under my power.

The kneeling scumbag removes his mask, and to no one's surprise, it's Jeremy. Cyrus removes his too, he's one of the ones who dropped his weapons. Which meant he was going to stab me, if he had to. That hurts. I knew he wasn't trustworthy, but I thought we were friends. A few others remove their masks too, but I don't see Grace among them, thankfully.

The leader rips his off last, and his crown hits the floor. Nariel stares up at me with a mixture of lust and hatred. "I should've killed you."

"I'd like to see you try," I snarl. "Give me the feather."

He snorts, and I raise my chin, then release more lust into him. He tries so hard to fight it, but in the end he crawls to me on his hands and knees, then removes a clear plastic container from his robe, which holds the feather. He offers it up to me with love-struck eyes, and I kick him in the chest to push him back.

Araceli and her dad stumble out of the other room, with the fae woman held between them. She's in the worst shape, and I cringe at the realization one of her ears was torn off. "We need to get this woman back to her people," Araceli says.

"Let's go." I hold my dagger out to the members and initiates who are either under my spell, or held back by my friends. "Don't even think of following us."

I lead the way out of the cavern, and draw in a deep breath of fresh air when we get outside. Araceli and the other fae are right behind me, followed by my golden-robed allies. They all rip off their masks, and my chest swells with pride to see Callan, Bastien, Marcus, Kassiel, and even Tanwen all on my side. Unlikely allies? Definitely. But it worked.

42

OLIVIA

We move some distance away and hide in the forest, so Marcus can heal the fae woman with Araceli's help. Our group spreads out around them, keeping an eye out for anyone following.

"Have they taught you how to create a bubble of invisibility yet?" Fintan asks me.

"No, not yet."

"Let me show you."

He bends light around our group, bouncing it off the trees and the ground, creating a little dome around us. No one from the outside can see us, but we can see everything inside our little shell. It's definitely an advanced Ishim move, and one only someone very powerful could accomplish. No wonder Fintan was such a good messenger.

"I think I got it," I tell him. "Thanks, that will come in handy in Faerie."

"Will she be all right?" Callan asks, kneeling beside the fae woman.

"Yes, she's already recovering," Marcus says. "Araceli managed to grab the ear on the way out, so we re-attached it. She should heal completely within a few hours."

Araceli stands up and wipes blood on her pants, like it's no biggie. "We need to take her back to the fae before they realize she's missing and attack the school."

"I can take her," Fintan says.

"Are you sure?" I ask. The fae don't seem to like him much, from what I've heard.

"Yes. It has to be either me or Araceli, and you need her to get to Faerie." He gives Araceli a warm smile. "Don't worry about me."

"I'm sorry your visit turned into this," Araceli says, as she hugs her dad.

"It was worth it to spend time with you."

The fae woman stirs and looks up at us, then focuses on me. "Thank you. Your rescue will not be forgotten."

Fintan takes the fae guard's hand to help her stand, and then they go invisible as they walk into the woods.

As they leave, I turn to the others and hold up the container with the feather. "Now that we have this, we can go to Faerie. I vote we leave immediately, before the Order can regroup and come after us. Go back to your rooms and gather whatever supplies you need for a couple days in Faerie. Food, water, weapons, extra clothes, whatever. Then we'll meet in the bell tower in thirty minutes."

"Remember that the weather in Faerie fluctuates from very hot to very cold every day," Bastien says. "Dress accordingly. We won't want to have to use our magic unless absolutely necessary."

"Why not?" Callan asks.

"It might alert them to our presence," Araceli says.

"I'm going to stay behind and do what I can here," Tanwen says. "Things are crazy after the drone attack, and someone needs to keep an eye on the Order from this side. But I wish you the best of luck."

"Thanks for your help, Tanwen," I say. "This wouldn't have been possible without you."

"Just remember our deal." She gives me a little nod, before flying off with a beat of her bright white wings.

The rest of us split up and head back to our dorms. Araceli and I are already packed, so all we do is grab our bags, run around doing one final check to make sure we have everything, and go. We don't want to spend a second longer in our dorm, in case Nariel or Jeremy or even Cyrus comes after us there.

Back in the field, it looks like they're trying to get the championship game underway again, but it might be tough with two of their players missing, and half the audience hiding in fear of the Duskhunters.

"What happened at the game?" I ask Araceli, after we land at the bell tower.

"When I came out of the bathroom, Cyrus knocked me out and kidnapped me. He apologized and said he had to do it to fulfill his Order task. That snake." Her eyes harden. "When we got to the cavern, Jeremy was already there with my dad, and someone else brought the fae guard in after that."

My hands clench into fists. "They must have been watching our dorm or something, and grabbed your dad on his way out."

"Probably." She shudders a little. "Then they had the first two initiates torture us for info on getting to Faerie. They barely roughed me and my dad up, but you saw what they did to that poor woman."

I give her a warm hug. "I'm so sorry you had to go through all that."

"I'm going to make them pay for what they did," Araceli says, and I've never seen her look so bloodthirsty before. Not that I can blame her. First they killed her boyfriend, now they kidnapped and tortured her and her dad. I'd be out for blood too.

"We will," I say, as the Princes arrive carrying backpacks and weapons. They begin moving furniture to give Araceli space for the portal, and I move to help them, but then I'm distracted by a knock on the door.

I open it and find Grace outside. "What are you doing here?"

"You're going to Faerie, aren't you?" she asks. "That's why you took the feather. I'm coming with you."

"No way," Araceli says. "We can't trust her."

I shake my head at Grace. "Sorry, but she's right. Your uncle is the leader of the Order."

"Bastien will know I'm telling the truth," she says, looking at him for confirmation. "I want to help you find Jonah."

"True," he says.

"Were you involved in kidnapping or torturing Araceli, her dad, or the other fae?" I ask.

"No!" Grace looks horrified by the very idea. "I was there because Nariel made me go, but I had no part in any of that, I swear."

"Also true."

I stare at her for a long moment. I know Bastien can sense truth, but that doesn't mean I trust her.

She takes my hands and looks at me with pitiful eyes. "Please, Liv. I care about your brother, and I have to know what happened to him. Whether he's alive or dead. Whether he found the Staff or not. I need to know, or I'll never be able to find peace."

I glance at Bastien, who nods.

"All right." She does seem to really care about my brother, and I guess she can't help it if her uncle is the leader of the Order. "You can come, but we'll be watching you closely."

"Thank you," she says, with a relieved sigh.

Kassiel lands on the bell tower then, and everyone stares at him. I sense an awkward moment approaching.

"Kassiel is coming too," I tell them.

"Can we trust you?" Bastien asks.

"Yes," Kassiel says. "I want to stop the Order as much as you do, if not even more. They can't ever get ahold of the Staff."

Bastien crosses his arms and nods. "He's telling the truth."

"Let's hurry," Araceli says, as she cuts her hand. "Everyone stand back."

She presses her palm to my necklace and mutters the fae words, and I hold my breath in anticipation. We're actually going to Faerie to rescue my brother.

It's about damn time.

43

MARCUS

I n Faerie, everything is a little...*more*. It's like someone turned up the volume to max on the entire world. The plants are greener. The sky is brighter. The flowers smell sweeter. Even the birds sound better somehow.

Our group made it through Araceli's portal, and now we're just standing in the middle of a forest, taking it all in. It's different from the forest around Seraphim Academy. This one looks more like a rainforest, and the air is humid and hot.

"Where are we exactly?" Bastien asks.

"We're in the Summer Court," Araceli says. "This is where my dad's family lives."

"Does that mean you have Summer Court magic?" I ask her.

She spreads her hands. "I guess so? I don't really know. Once we get back, I should probably find out."

"Okay, I took Fae Studies two years ago, so I might be a little rusty, but time moves differently here right?" I ask.

"Yes, the season changes depending on what time of day it is," Kassiel says. He's still acting like our professor, even here in Faerie. "Right now it's probably summer, which means it's mid-day. Since we're in the Summer Court, that season will last the longest. At night it will be winter."

"I knew Faerie experienced all four seasons over the course of a day, but not so drastically," Grace says with awe in her voice. "I figured the temperature changed a little."

"We need to hurry," Callan says. "We need to find shelter before it gets dark and becomes too cold."

Liv pulls out the black feather, which pulses with darkness, even here in Faerie. "Our best bet is to find the Staff, and hope Jonah is being held prisoner somewhere nearby. If not, maybe someone there will know where he is."

I notice she doesn't mention the possibility that Jonah's been killed. It must be too hard for her to consider when we've come this far, although it will probably be a relief when she knows his fate, one way or the other.

Liv holds the shadowy feather up in the air. "Return to your master."

She lets the feather go and it flitters and floats and twirls, like feathers do in the wind, before blowing on the breeze toward Kassiel. At first I think it's not working and we're screwed, but then it seems to hover around him for a second. He takes a step back with a frown, and the feather continues onward, flying higher into the sky with clear purpose.

Grace claps her hands together. "It's working!"

Liv creates an invisibility bubble around all of us and the feather, and then we take off after it. First we travel by foot through the forest, moving past clueless rabbits and deer, plus some weird glowing flowers I wish we had time to investigate, and some huge green insects I'm glad we don't. Then the feather gets too high, and we have to fly after it, careful not to move too far from Liv. As the day grows hotter, we soar over the dense canopy of trees, which stretch for miles, only to be broken up by a castle sitting on a hill in the distance.

"What is that?" Grace asks.

"No clue. I only know a few random things about Faerie." Araceli gives us an apologetic look. "Sorry."

"Don't apologize," Liv says. "It's your dad's fault."

"We should probably steer clear of it," Callan says.

We take a break in the forest, after plucking the feather from the air and putting it back in its case. The sun beats down on us as we eat some granola bars, but none of us mind the heat. When it gets cold, we'll have to bundle up because we can't use our magic to stay warm. I just hope we can find somewhere indoors to hide for the night.

We set off again down a dirt road, with no hint of concrete or asphalt. I feel like we've stepped a thousand years into the past. The sun heads lower in the sky and the air begins to cool, while the leaves begin to change color, turning red, yellow, and orange. It's hard not to stop and stare at the beauty all around us, but we put on some jackets and keep moving.

Then Araceli whispers, "Someone's coming!"

Callan grabs the feather, and Liv keeps her little invisibility bubble around us as we move off the road and onto the grass. We hide in the trees as a fae male comes down the road on a beautiful white horse. He has hair the color of lemons, and he looks like he's stepped out of a Tolkien novel in a floor-length silver tunic and a gold jacket. His shoes look like they're made of cloth.

We crane our necks as he walks by, and I breathe as quietly as possible without moving too much. When he's past us, we wait a while for him to go out of sight. Finally we can move back onto the road.

Liv starts to get the feather, but then more people appear on the road, probably a half-dozen of them, wearing similar clothes to the other fae we saw. After they pass, Callan says, "We don't have time to hide every time more people appear. We need to keep flying."

Liv nods, but her face is paler than normal and she moves a little slower. "I guess it's the only way."

"Are you all right?" I ask her. I press a hand to her forehead, and can feel how weak she is with my powers. She's going to need to feed soon. Sunlight alone isn't going to be enough to keep her going.

She waves off my hand. "I'm fine. It just takes a lot of energy to keep this bubble around us. Let's keep moving."

"We'll have to find somewhere to stop soon," Kassiel says, his brow pinched with concern.

"Keep an eye out as we fly," Callan says. "Otherwise we'll have to sleep outside, and I don't think any of us brought our camping gear."

We continue on as the sun sets, the air grows colder, and the leaves turn brown and begin to fall. A frigid rain soaks our clothes and sends a chill through my wings. We pass a town, but decide it's too risky to stop there. I don't see anything else for miles, while it gets darker and colder, and Liv grows weaker.

"There," Kassiel calls out, pointing down below. "A ruin of some kind."

I don't see anything in the darkness, but we all follow him anyway, just as snow begins to fall. He leads us to a group of old stone buildings that are clearly abandoned, with some missing walls or with holes in their roof, and vines growing up the side. There's one building that still looks mostly intact, and we land in front of it.

Callan tries to use a flashlight, but it doesn't work. Something about Faerie blocks technology, if I remember correctly. Bastien uses some matches with some shrubbery to create a makeshift torch. We head into the building, which looks like it was abandoned long ago. At least it's a little warmer inside.

Liv staggers as she steps inside, and I know I need to help her somehow. She needs all her strength for what's to come tomorrow.

Once everyone is settled in, I pull Bastien aside. "Liv needs us."

His eyebrows dart up. "Us?"

I swallow and push my lingering jealousy aside. "I read once that a succubus can feed off two men at once for an extra boost. Liv needs that tonight."

He nods slowly. "Yes, you're probably right. Do you think she'll be open to such a thing?"

"Definitely."

44

OLIVIA

"I'll take first watch," Kassiel says. Probably a good idea, since he doesn't feel the cold like the angels do, and can see much better in the dark. It's how he found this place.

As everyone spreads out and tries to get comfortable while shivering, Araceli gathers some sticks and stones, building a little fire pit in the center of the room.

"What are you doing?" I ask.

"I'm not sure." She sits back on her heels and holds out her hands, then squints in concentration. A few seconds later, the little bundle of twigs catches fire, instantly bringing heat and light to the room.

I blink at the flames. "How did you do that?"

She grins as she warms her hands over the fire. "Ever since we arrived it's like my fae side has started waking up. Summer Court fae have fire magic, so I thought I would try it. I wasn't sure it would work though."

"That's incredible."

"When I get back, I think I'm going to learn more about my Summer magic. I've been trying to forget my fae side all my life, but I don't want to do that anymore. I'm not ashamed of my fae blood, and it's time to own it."

"I think that's a really good idea." I'm so proud of Araceli. She's grown so much this year, and it's a real honor to be her best friend.

"Nice fire," Callan says. "We should get more sticks to keep it going all night."

He heads outside with Grace and Araceli, and I'm about to follow, when Marcus grabs my hand and pulls me back. "Come with me," he says.

He leads me through the ruined building, down a long hallway, to another intact stone room. It's much colder in here without Araceli's fire, but Bastien is waiting next to a makeshift bed of blankets surrounded by candlelight.

"Sorry it's not more romantic," Marcus says. "But we did the best we could under the circumstances."

"It's really sweet," I say, smiling at him.

"You need to feed," Bastien says, getting straight to the point as usual. "On both of us."

Sex with two guys at once? It's like a Thanksgiving feast. I'm going to need to wear my stretchy leggings afterward. Too bad I left them at home.

I wonder where they got the blankets, but the whole thing is so sweet—and sexy—that I don't care. Plus, I'm starving and weak. I didn't realize how bad I felt until they mentioned feeding, but now I can't stop thinking about it.

Marcus puts his hand on my back and nudges me toward Bastien and the blankets. I taste their desire. They want to do this, together. It turns them on, the thought of sharing me.

It turns me on too.

"What are your intentions with me?" I ask with a coy smile.

Bastien looks at me with confusion on his face. "We thought you'd enjoy both of us together. Is that not the case?"

I shake my head quickly. "No, I do want it. Very much."

"Good." Bastien takes my hand and pulls on it, inviting me to join him on the makeshift bed. I step out of my shoes and drop to my knees, surprised to find the blankets rather comfortable.

"We found some furs," Marcus explains. "They're surprisingly plush and clean, once we shook out the dust."

He sits beside me and presses his lips to mine. His desire overwhelms my nerves and my body ignites. In all my time using men for food, I've never had a threesome, and my heart beats faster in anticipation.

The two of them take off my shirt, then make quick work of my bra. Marcus bends over me, pushing my back against Bastien's chest. Bastien slides his hands around my front and cups my breasts as he buries his face in my neck. I throw my head back, as Marcus moves my hair to the side so he can also press his lips on the nape of my neck. They kiss along my skin, both of them sending little sparks through my body with each soft touch.

From behind me, Bastien lifts one breast up, holding it for Marcus to lean down and wrap his lips around my nipple. He runs his tongue across the tip before sucking hard, then going soft again. I moan as he drives me mad with wanting.

My hands find their way up and into Bastien's hair as Marcus moves his lips to my other nipple, while his hands drift down my stomach to the curve of my hips. I push back on Bastien and lift my hips up so Marcus can pull off the rest of my clothes.

While Marcus gets undressed, Bastien slips his hand down between my legs and begins stroking me there, preparing me for his friend. Then Bastien digs his fingers into my thighs and spreads my legs wide. Marcus moves in, and the hunger in his eyes matches my own. His cock pushes inside me, and I cry out in pleasure as I lean back against Bastien. Marcus starts off slow, rocking me back and forth between the two of them, and I've never felt more adored in my life than at this moment. Having both of their bodies pressed against me, with their mouths on my skin and their hands roaming my curves, it's the best feeling in the world. It hits me then how much I care about these two, so much more than I did even a year ago.

Lilim aren't supposed to love, but I'm starting to wonder if maybe I can. If I do already.

Marcus's pace increases and all thoughts flee my mind as he fills me over and over again with his amazing cock. I suck up all the sexual energy he has to offer, immediately feeling a lot better, while also wanting more. I turn my head and find Bastien's lips, as he reaches down to rub my clit. The combination of sensations sweeps an orgasm through me, and I tighten up around Marcus, but he's nowhere near done.

He pulls out and grabs my hips, rolling me over on the blankets. "Bastien could use some attention too, don't you think?"

"Definitely," I agree.

Bastien unbuckles his pants, and I reach in and pull his hard cock out. After giving him a few strokes, I lick him slowly, then take him into my mouth. He groans and his lust spikes, while his fingers tangle in my hair.

Marcus presses kisses to my back and shoulders, then slides inside me again from behind. With each stroke, he pushes me onto Bastien's cock, making me take him further in my mouth. I have two of my lovers inside me, giving me their sexual energy, and it's amazing.

Opening my mouth wider, I use Marcus's rhythm to push me up and down on Bastien's cock. The erotic feeling of his head sliding deeper and deeper down my throat combined with the stimulation of Marcus slamming into me helps me get close to another orgasm. I sense Marcus is close too, as he moves faster and harder, slamming into me from behind. He rubs my clit too at the same time, knowing exactly what to do to make me climax.

Moaning through it, I tense up and ride it, my voice getting louder and louder around Bastien. The jolts of pure pleasure keep me moving back against Marcus until he comes inside me too with a loud groan.

When we're both sated, Marcus pulls out of me and drags me onto the blankets, holding me close. We stare into each other's eyes, and I see how much he cares for me too. But I can't ignore Bastien. I pull away and turn back to my other lover.

"I hope you're not full," he says. "I've got plenty more to give you."

"I can take it."

He hums deep in his throat. "Come here."

He stretches out on the blankets beside Marcus, and holds his long, hard cock up in invitation. I straddle him and sink down onto it, with a delirious sigh. This is so much better than sex with strangers.

I begin to rock up and down on Bastien, getting into a good rhythm. Marcus moves behind me, his hands roaming my body and caressing me, while Bastien's fingers dig into my hips. Each time Bastien fills me, tiny waves of pleasure shoot through me. He fits inside like he was molded just for me.

My third orgasm grows, making me move faster and faster. Bastien is growing close as well, and his sexual energy rolls into me in waves of delicious intensity.

"Yes," I cry. I can't say much more. I'm moving too fast and the pleasure is too high. "Harder."

Bastien thrusts up into me harder in response, while Marcus cups my breasts and begins working my nipples. They work together, focusing on my pleasure, and it's incredible.

I cry out and throw my head back as the orgasm crests. Bastien pulls me forward against his chest, almost into an embrace, then finds my lips. Flexing his hips, he rides out his orgasm inside me as we kiss. As he finishes, I soak up his pleasure, his lust, his passion. It feeds me, sates me, sustains me. I'm filled to the brim, possibly fuller than I've ever been before. And more than that, I'm happier than I've been before too.

With a sigh, I move to Bastien's side, cuddling up between him and Marcus, who pulls a thin, fresh-smelling quilt over the top of us. "I had this one rolled up in my backpack," he whispers.

None of us have any desire to get up and dress, and even though it's cold, we don't feel it at all. They wrap their arms and legs around me and we fall asleep, safe and comfortable in each other's embrace. Or as safe as we can be in an abandoned ruin in the middle of Faerie, anyway.

45

OLIVIA

I n the morning we continue on, and the temperature is absolutely perfect as we set off, with bright blue skies and vibrant flowers blooming everywhere. Faerie is beautiful, but there's something about it that feels unusual too. It's like a deal that's too good to be true, and you're just waiting for the catch.

Thanks to the boost I got from Bastien and Marcus, I'm able to maintain the bubble of invisibility around us as we fly, which saves us a lot of time over walking. After a few hours, the feather starts moving faster and faster, and I think we must be getting close. It leads us toward a dark, imposing stone building with a wall around it, with armored guards perched in regular intervals and at the gates. Our only bit of luck is that they're not looking for an attack from the air, which gives us a chance to sneak inside.

"It's heavily guarded," Callan says. "The Staff must be in there."

And hopefully Jonah too. It definitely looks like a prison, with small windows and heavy defenses.

"Everyone stay close," I tell them as we approach.

We slowly fly over the gate and hover above the building, looking for a good place to land. I spot a small empty alley and gesture for everyone to follow me. The feather practically quivers with excitement, so we know we're close now.

We land next to some trash bins, and everyone takes a moment to collect themselves and look around for a way inside. Around the corner, two fae women stand on a small porch outside a closed door, one with rosy pink hair, and the other's snow white. They seem to be arguing, and they're both wearing plain green dresses with aprons, so I'm guessing they're servants or cooks or something.

"Fine. I'll do it," the one with white hair says. It's pulled back into a dozen or more intricate braids that fall way down her back. "But you owe me."

The pink-haired fae rolls her eyes. "I don't owe you anything. Now go."

The first one pushes the door open with a huff, and they both slip inside. Callan launches forward in a half-jump half-flight and manages to get his hand on the door just before it swings shut.

He waits, listening for the sound of the women to recede, and then opens the door and lets us inside. We enter the building in some sort of mudroom. There are benches, shelves, and hooks along the wall with a few coats hanging from them. The coats seem to be well-made, but not as nice as some of the clothes we saw other fae wearing. This is likely a servant's entrance.

It's crowded with all of us in here, and I glance among the faces of my friends. We all look exhausted from the lack of sleep and the non-stop flying or walking. Not to mention, the time difference. But we're so close now, I can feel it. Soon we'll have the Staff and my brother too.

Bastien holds the feather by the end, and it twitches for us to go further into the building. We walk into a long, empty hallway made of whitewashed wood planks. Most of the doors leading off the hall are closed, but the feather keeps telling us to go forward.

Bastien stops at a closed door, and glances back at us. Callan moves to the front, back in over-protective mode, and turns the door-knob slowly. It's locked.

Luckily, I knew something like this might happen, and I brought my trusty lock picks. It takes me a few minutes because the lock is a harder one to crack, but then the door swings open.

One the other side is a stairwell with broken steps that disappear into darkness. If this was a movie, this is when people would yell, "Don't go down there, you idiots!" So naturally, we start going down.

It's narrow and twists into a tight spiral, and if we meet anyone going up it, we're in trouble. We try to make as little noise as possible while both staying close together and moving quickly, and I just hope no one is right there at the bottom of these stairs.

The stairs seem to go on forever. We pass some doors, but the feather wants us to keep going down. We've got to be several stories underground now.

"We're getting close," Bastien whispers, as he holds the feather back so it doesn't dash away.

We reach the bottom of the stairs, and discover a new problem. Ahead of us is a large stone door that's clearly bolted shut. Two guards in bronze armor stand beside it wielding spears.

How are we supposed to sneak past that?

We never get a chance to formulate a plan, because the second my feet hit the ground, the invisibility bubble vanishes. I quickly reach for light to bend it and hit something like a magical wall, but it's too late anyway.

The two guards start when they see a group of us suddenly appear, but they're obviously well-trained, because they lower their spears at us. "Halt!"

"Shit," Marcus mutters.

So much for not getting caught by the fae.

There's an open door to the right, and I wonder if we can dart through it and escape, but no, someone would get stabbed by one of those spears. The fae are as quick as we are, if not more so. We could try to overpower these guards, ideally without really hurting them, but there's no telling if there are more nearby. And we can't seem to use our magic here.

"State your business," one of the guards says.

The others glance at me, like I'm supposed to get us out of this mess. Crap.

I step forward and hold up my hands in surrender. "We're looking for the Staff of Eternity...and for an angel named Jonah."

The two guards glance at each other, and I have a feeling they're about to arrest us, when I hear a familiar voice ask, "Liv?"

I turn toward the open doorway and gape at the man standing there.

Jonah.

46

OLIVIA

My brother is alive. He's *alive!*

I thought he would be a prisoner. I worried he might be dead. I spent two years trying to find him—and he's standing there, with a book tucked under one arm.

"Jonah!" I rush toward him, and he drops the book to embrace me. I hold him tightly with tears in my eyes, then pull back to look at him in disbelief. Is it really him? Is he really okay? He has a new beard, he's wearing fancy fae clothes, and there's a sword on his hip, but he looks good otherwise. Healthy. Unharmed. *Alive.*

I've envisioned this moment for so long. I pictured him lifting me off the ground and spinning me around, ecstatic to see his baby sister. But instead he frowns at me. "What are you doing here?"

This is definitely not the reunion I was expecting.

"I'm here to rescue you," I say. It sounds silly, since he obviously doesn't need rescuing.

"You shouldn't be here," Jonah says. The guards eye us warily, but he raises a hand to them. "It's fine. I know them."

I step back, wounded by his words, as the others rush forward.

Grace throws her arms around Jonah and gives him a kiss. "It's been two years," she says. "I could have moved on, but I didn't. I never gave up hope you were still alive."

"I'm sorry," Jonah says, as he holds her close. "I'll explain everything."

Marcus moves forward to give Jonah one of those quick man-hugs. "You better."

"We've been worried," Callan grumbles.

Bastien clasps Jonah's hand. "Well, some of us assumed you were dead."

Jonah lets out a short laugh at that. "It's really good to see all of you. But how are you all here together?"

"That's a long story," I say. "The short version is that I started attending Seraphim Academy in an attempt to find you. All of us worked together, including Araceli, my roommate, and Kassiel, one of our professors, and it led us here. To you, and to the Staff." I glance at the heavily guarded door. "Is it in there?"

"It is," Jonah says, but then he turns to Callan with hard eyes. "I thought I told you to keep Liv away from Seraphim Academy."

"I tried," Callan says. "Believe me, I did everything short of actually harming her, but none of it worked. She's very...stubborn."

"More like determined," I mutter.

"It's not safe for her at Seraphim Academy. Or here." Jonah shakes his head. "You should go back."

"We're not leaving without you," Callan says. I was about to say the same thing.

"Why did you even come here?" I ask. I'm feeling at my wit's end at this point. "Were you really trying to get the Staff for the Order?"

His eyebrows dart up. "I see you know a lot. No, I wasn't. I came here to protect you from the Staff—and that's why I stayed." He sighed. "C'mon, let's go inside, and I'll show you."

He gestures to the guards, who move aside, and then Jonah touches an unremarkable spot on the wall behind them. The bolts unlock, and the heavy stone door slowly opens. Inside is a large stone dais, and floating above it is a staff that glows with both dark-ness and light. It's made of twisted silver and gold metal, and at the top is an orb that shifts and swirls with a rainbow of colors, surrounded by two wings, one black and one white.

I step forward slowly. "Is this it? *The* Staff?"

Jonah walks beside me. "Yes. I've been guarding it all this time."

Our friends walk in behind us, and I hear Araceli gasp. The Staff radiates power and beauty, and it's hard not to stare at it in awe.

There's another guard inside, a beautiful fae woman with hunter green hair and matching eyes. She's wearing Autumn Court armor, and draws her sword as we approach. "Jonah? Who are these people?"

"Eveanna, this is my sister, Olivia," he says. "She came to rescue me."

"It's a pleasure to meet you," she says, with a slight bow. "Jonah has spoken of you many times."

"Eveanna is the current guardian of the staff," Jonah explains. "Michael and Lucifer entrusted it with the fae, and it moves to a new Court every year to keep its location hidden."

She sheathes her sword. "It is my great honor to protect the Staff."

I turn to Jonah to demand some answers, when suddenly there's a loud bang and a flash of light on the floor near us, and then the air fills with white smoke. It smells horrible and burns the eyes, and we're all instantly coughing and trying to wave it away.

"What was that?" I ask, spinning around and trying to see in the darkness.

"We're under attack!" Eveanna yells. "Protect the Staff!"

I move toward it, and as the smoke clears, I see a portal like the one we came through. Grace is holding something long and using it to open the portal. The Staff of Eternity.

"Grace?" I ask. "What are you doing?"

It's a dumb question. She's obviously stealing the Staff. I'm just so shocked by what I'm seeing that I can't say what I really want to ask, which is *what the fuck, Grace?*

"Getting a present for my father," she says, with a devious grin I've never seen before. Her father? Who is he?

I'm gaping at her, trying to wrap my head around what she's doing, when Nariel, Cyrus, Jeremy, and five other Order members appear through the portal.

"Grace," Jonah whispers. "How could you?"

She glares at him. "It's our duty to retrieve the Staff. You failed in that task. I will not."

As she says it, she shoves the Staff into Jonah's chest, and there's a burst of light as he goes flying backward. Fury overtakes me and I grab my succubus magic, but nothing happens. It's still trapped inside, along with my angelic powers too. This room must block magic somehow. But I'm not defenseless, thanks to my mother. I draw my dark-infused dagger, and my friends grab their weapons too.

"Cover her," Nariel calls out, and all the Order members raise their weapons as they make a barrier between Grace and the portal.

The place interrupts into chaos as the Princes—including my brother—clash with the Order members. Kassiel and Araceli fight too, along with Eveanna. I dodge through the mayhem and try to get to Grace and the Staff, but she runs into the portal with it before I can reach her. Dammit!

Cyrus follows her, right at her heels. I try to go after them, but Nariel grabs my arm and yanks me back, hard.

"Die, demon spawn," he growls, as he raises a light-infused sword over me. There's no time for me to get away.

Before he can strike, Callan's huge sword slams through Nariel's chest from behind. My Ishim teacher lets out a gurgling gasp, before his body goes slack. He hits the floor, and I stare at the blood covering him in horror. How did it come to this? My own professor trying to kill me. Callan saving my life. Dead bodies on the floor. All because of the Staff.

"Are you okay?" Callan asks, touching my arm and shaking me from my thoughts.

"Yes. Thank you."

He gives me a brief nod, then spins around to stop another attack coming my way. As I do, I see Jeremy running toward the portal. No way, fucker. I grip my dark-infused blade and go after him, blocking his path to the portal.

He swings his short sword, his eyes wild, and I have the sense to duck and roll. Good thing I paid attention in combat classes. Jeremy turns, ready to attack again, but I raise my dark-infused dagger and block him, even though the blow is so strong it sends waves of pain through my wrist. But then I spin away and slash, cutting his arm with my dark-infused blade. The arm holding the sword, which hits the ground. Jeremy screams and stumbles back, as the darkness sinks into him. I remember how painful it was and can only smile.

"How does it feel?" I ask. "You're in a room devoid of magic, and you were taken down by a half-demon."

He sneers at me as he backs away, holding his arm against his chest. "It doesn't matter, because soon you'll be back in Hell...or you'll be dead."

He leaps into the portal, and I lunge after him, but it closes the split second he's inside.

"No!" I yell, as I stumble through the empty space that once had the portal. They got the Staff. *They got the Staff!*

All around me, the fighting has ended. Nariel lies dead, along with three other Order members whose names I don't know. All of my friends are alive, thank goodness, but they're staring at the spot where the portal was, and every single one of them looks defeated.

We failed.

47

CALLAN

"Arrest them," a voice commands behind us, and before I know what's happening, dozens of armored fae are swarming into the room and clamping us in chains. None of us fight back. We're too shocked by what just happened.

Jonah tries to explain things to a fae captain, who doesn't look impressed, as the rest of us are dragged out of the room. I glance back and spot Olivia just behind me, physically unhurt, though I've never seen her look so broken before. Grace's betrayal must have hit her hard.

My magic comes back the second my feet touch the stairs and we're no longer on this floor. We go up and up the swirling stairs, until a door in unlocked on a random floor, and we're brought into a prison cell. They shove us all in one and slam the metal door shut.

Jonah's not with us. He must be trying to explain to the fae what happened. I don't see his fae friend either.

I stare at the guards perched outside the prison cell, and then turn around to look at my friends. Araceli wraps an arm around Olivia, and they lean against each other, both exhausted. In one corner of the cell, Bastien is bleeding from one arm, but Marcus is taking care of it. Kassiel stands alone, staring at nothing, his gaze haunted.

We wait there for at least an hour. None of us says much. What is there to say? We lost, and the Order won. Now Olivia's at risk. Fuck.

Food and drink are brought to us, and we all eat like we're starving. I guess it's been a long time since we ate, actually. I have no idea. Time is so odd in Faerie, and it's impossible to tell anything in this damp, dark cell.

I lean my head against the bars and close my eyes, trying to get a little rest so I'm alert in case we need to fight again. Olivia soft voice wakes me up, and I see she's speaking quietly with Kassiel in the corner of a cell. Everyone else seems to be asleep, except for the two of them. As I watch, Olivia's head drops, and Kassiel reaches up to touch her face. The moment looks so intimate, I glance away, feeling like I'm intruding.

Then it hits me—is Olivia sleeping with our Angelic History professor? Is that why he's really here? I'm not sure how I feel about that.

Before I can figure it out, guards arrive, and everyone in the cell stands up. "Come with us," one of the guards says.

They lead us up the stairs and onto the main floor, and then we're taken down a long hall with a dark green carpet decorated with red and orange leaves. All the guards wear bronze armor decorated in leaves as well. At some point we must have entered the Autumn Court lands, though none of us realized it.

Tall double doors open up, leading us into a grand room. A long red and gold carpet leads us to a throne, upon which sits a man with long black hair and cruel eyes. He wears a large crown covered in gems and taps his long, sharp fingernails on the arm of the throne as he waits for us to be brought down to him.

"Kneel before High King Oberon," one of the guards orders.

I grit my teeth, but go along with it, dropping down to my knees. A son of Michael should never kneel, but I've also heard of the power and brutality of Oberon, and since this is his realm, it's best to play it safe.

Jonah is led in next, with Eveanna at his side. He gives us a worried glance, before facing the king and kneeling.

"Such interesting specimens we have found lurking in our basement," Oberon says, as his eyes move down the line. "A child with diluted fae blood who should never have come to this world."

Araceli's head lifts and she meets his look with hard eyes. She's grown a spine somewhere in the last two years. Good for her.

"A son of Uriel and a son of Raphael," the king continues, and then smirks. "Who shared the same bed last night."

My eyebrows lift at that. How does he know? Jonah's gaze jerks to Bastien and Marcus, clearly very confused.

He pauses on me and a chill runs down my spine. There's something very unnerving about him, and I'm not scared of anything. Then his gaze continues to Kassiel and Olivia.

"And finally, a son of Lucifer and a son of Michael, both consorting with the daughter of Lilith and Gabriel." He throws back his head and cackles. "How wickedly delightful."

My jaw practically hits the floor. Everyone's head turns to Kassiel, whose brow is furrowed. Did Oberon just call him the son of Lucifer?

Things quickly snap into place from the last twenty-four hours. His desire to come on this mission. His excellent night vision. His resistance to the cold. He's not an angel, he's a Fallen who's tricked us all.

My hands tighten into fists. That asshole kneeling next to me is the son of my father's murderer. And he's sleeping with Olivia.

Olivia, who is the daughter of Lilith. The *Archdemon* Lilith.

I knew she was half demon, but I had no idea she was the daughter of the most powerful succubus in the world.

All of that goes through my mind while High King Oberon taps his fingers on the arm of his throne. He watches me like he senses my turmoil and delights in it. I want to burn this whole fucking room down.

"We've guarded the Staff of Eternity for over thirty years, as part of a deal struck with Michael and Lucifer," he says, finally ending the long silence. "Today the Staff was stolen, and shame has been brought upon our people. Needless to say, if any of you had different parentage, you'd be dead by now."

"Your majesty, I can explain—" Jonah starts.

Oberon holds up a hand. "Silence. I already know what happened. Your half-sister and her friends came to find you, but one of their own betrayed them and stole the Staff."

I heard Oberon is wise, and that his power comes from the land itself, but he seems to know everything. Way too much.

"All of you are responsible for this disturbance, and all of you must return to Earth and correct it. That includes you, Eveanna of the Autumn Court. You are henceforth banished from Faerie until the Staff is returned or destroyed."

The green-haired fae's eyes are saucer-wide, but she lowers her head. "Yes, your majesty."

"Now go, I tire of looking at your faces," he says, waving his hand in dismissal. "I'd forgotten how much I loathe angels and demons and their drama."

We're escorted out of the throne room and into another room, where a fae in a bronze robe opens a portal. One by one we head through it, including the new member of our group, Eveanna.

We emerge in the bell tower, and it's pitch black. The sun is down. I wonder how long we've been gone.

I switch on the nearest light, and look around for Kassiel, but he's gone. Fine. Right now we have more pressing matters.

I'll deal with him later.

48

OLIVIA

We're all shell-shocked and exhausted, but we're back and Jonah is with us. It's not a total win, but it's something.

I throw my arms around him again, now that we're on Earth and the danger has passed. He hugs me back hard, and then I'm crying into his shirt. Crying because I'm so relieved he's alive. Crying for the two years we lost. Crying because Grace betrayed us.

"I missed you so much," I tell him, while wiping my eyes. "I never stopped looking for you."

"I should have known you'd find me, even in another world," Jonah says, with that crooked grin I've dreamed about seeing for so long. His eyes are wet too.

"Stubbornness runs in our family." I release him and step back, then take a deep breath to steady myself. "We have a lot to talk about."

"No shit," Callan says. "Where's Kassiel?"

He's gone. Probably gathered darkness around himself to escape as soon as we returned. I don't blame him. The others are going to have a lot of issues with the news about who and what he is.

"Are you actually banging him?" Araceli asks, then sees the

truth of it on my face. "Daaaamn, girl. I mean, I get it, he is crazy hot, but he's also a teacher."

"He's also the *son of Lucifer*," Callan practically yells.

Marcus yanks the couch back into the center of the room, since we pushed it aside for the portal. Then he plops down and grabs one of the pink unicorn stuffed animals I left for them. "Forget Kassiel, I want to know what the hell Jonah's been doing in Faerie for two years."

"Yes, tell us everything," Bastien says, pulling up his armchair.

We all sit close together, and find some cheese, crackers, and wine, which we spread out between us. Eveanna sits stiffly to the side of us, glancing around in wonder.

"Let me start from the beginning," Jonah says, as he pours himself some wine. "I was recruited into the Order, along with Grace and the other Princes. We were just initiates, but Grace had inside knowledge because her uncle Nariel was the leader."

Was being the key term. We left him for dead in Faerie. Even though he led the Order, my gut still tightens at the thought of him being gone. He'd been my teacher for months now. He taught me a lot about my powers. And then he called me demon spawn and tried to kill me. It's a lot to wrap my head around.

Jonah continues, interrupting my thoughts. "A few years ago the Order found out that the Staff was being kept in Faerie, but everyone they sent to retrieve it ended up dead. Once my Archangel power emerged, Grace wanted me to volunteer to get the Staff." He stares into his wine glass. "Grace was a true believer in the Order's tenets. I should have seen her betrayal coming."

"We all thought she was our friend," Araceli says. "It's not your fault. She even passed Bastien's lying test."

"Yes, using careful words," Bastien says, his eyes narrowing. "I suspect she planned everything from the beginning. She knew Olivia would try to stop the fae being tortured, so Grace made sure she had no part in it, and then she knew we would go to Faerie and use the feather to find the Staff. All she had to do was come with us."

I close my eyes as I remember things she said, both this year and last. "She's been manipulating us this entire time."

"Yes, I see it all clearly now," Jonah says, with a sigh. He really loved her, so it must be killing him to know their relationship was all a lie.

"Who is her father?" I ask.

"Her father?" Jonah frowns. "An Ishim named Malcolm. He dated her mom for a short while, but otherwise hasn't been in her life much. Why?"

Curious. I'll have to find out more about this guy, and why he might want the Staff. "Just something she said. Sorry, go on."

Jonah nods. "I knew if the Order ever got hold of the Staff, Liv would be in danger. They were going to keep sending people to get it, which is why I volunteered...with the intention of making sure they never got it."

"How did you manage to stay alive in Faerie?" Araceli asks. Then she offers her hand with a smile. "I'm Araceli, by the way. Liv's roommate."

"It's nice to meet you," he says with a warm grin. "I managed to fool the fae for a few days. Longer than I expected." Eveanna rolls her eyes at this, but doesn't respond. "But eventually they caught me and threw me in prison. I explained who I was, and why I was there, and they weren't sure what to do with me. As the son of two Archangels, they didn't want to kill me. They also didn't feel they could send me back. Eventually I won over the High King and he let me stay in Faerie as long as I helped guard the Staff."

"You're lucky the High King was amused by you," Eveanna says.

Jonah winks. "Everyone is amused by me. Even you."

I glance between the two of them. "Are you..."

Eveanna wrinkles her nose. "Definitely not. I have no interest in men."

I hold up my hands. "Sorry, had to ask."

"No, I've been faithful to Grace, much good that did," Jonah mutters.

"Why didn't you send word to us?" Bastien asks.

"I was too afraid the Order would find out and know I was still alive. Or worse, be able to track me down somehow."

Tears fill my eyes again. "You have no idea how hard it was for all of us, not knowing what happened to you. If you were alive or dead. Your parents have both been distraught."

"I'm sorry," Jonah says. "I never wanted to hurt everyone. I was just trying to protect you." He glances at the other Princes and his eyes harden. "I even made my best friends promise to keep you away from this school, but that didn't work. And now you're sleeping with Callan?"

"All three of us actually," Bastien says, like it's an obvious fact.

Jonah's jaw drops. "What the fuck?"

"Sorry." Marcus looks down with shame in his eyes. "It wasn't something we planned, developing feelings for your sister."

"Feelings?" Jonah half yells. "What do you mean, *feelings?*"

"Speak for yourself," Callan snaps. "I only slept with her to protect her."

"You were supposed to protect her by keeping her far away from this school and from the Order!" Jonah says, shaking his head. "Now that they know what she is and have the Staff, Liv is in more danger than ever."

"What do you mean?" Araceli asks.

Jonah runs a hand through his hair, but he looks anything but calm. "The Staff requires both an Archangel and an Archdemon to activate it's full powers, but they have to work together. If they wanted to send the demons back to Hell, for example, they'd both have to agree to do that."

"That's good," Marcus says. "That means Grace doesn't stand a chance of using it. Unless she has both an Archangel and Archdemon in her pocket, anyway."

"And no Archdemon is going to agree to send everyone back to Hell," Callan says.

Bastien rubs his chin. "No, but it also works for anyone with Archangel or Archdemon blood."

"Exactly." Jonah leans forward and meets my eyes. "Olivia, you have both."

I have both. The idea sinks in slowly, leaving me reeling.

I have both.

"You understand now?" Jonah asks. "You're the only person alive that can use the Staff by yourself. That's why I never wanted it to leave Faerie, and why I asked these idiots to keep you far away from this life. If nobody knew you existed, they couldn't try to force you to use the Staff."

"Shit, Olivia is in more danger than we realized," Callan says.

"Yeah, especially since you exposed her as a half-demon," Marcus mutters.

"You did *what?*" Jonah asks.

"We have many things to catch up on," Bastien says. "But the most pressing matter is to figure out how to get the Staff back."

"Agreed," Araceli says.

I nod, trying to focus. "We need to look for Grace, Cyrus, Jeremy, and anyone else who came back. They could still be on campus, although I doubt it."

"If they are, I'll find them," Bastien says. "I need to speak with my father about all this too."

"We have a lot to do." I stand up slowly. "But first, Jonah needs to see our dad."

The group splits up with a loose plan to look for Grace and the Staff. Marcus, Callan, and Eveanna are going to scour the campus for Order members, while Bastien consults with Uriel, and Araceli finds out what happened while we were gone from Tanwen. I have no idea what Kassiel is doing—probably reporting to Lucifer what happened.

I want to join the hunt too, but family comes first. I take Jonah to the house in Angel Peak, where our father opens the door and drops the cup of tea he's holding. As it shatters, Gabriel rushes forward to embrace his son.

"You're alive," he says into Jonah's hair. He looks up at me with proud eyes. "You brought him back."

Dad gestures for me to come closer, and I join their group hug, all of us holding each other tightly. Our little family, reunited at last. I may have failed in every way regarding the Staff, but at least I did something right.

49

OLIVIA

J onah sits beside me as we stare at the stage where all the
graduates line up. Callan, Marcus, and Bastien stand tall in the
front, wearing all white caps and gowns. I didn't go to the ceremony last year, and I'm surprised to find it's almost exactly like a
human graduation. Uriel is in the middle of a speech, but he lost me
about three minutes into it. My mind keeps drifting to the events of
the past few weeks.

We were in Faerie for two days in Earth time, but luckily it was
a weekend, so no one was too worried about us. Tanwen managed to
cover for us as needed, though she couldn't stop the Order from
coming after us. I think she feels guilty about it, because she's
announced she's staying in Angel Peak during break to help protect
the town and the school from the Order or the Duskhunters. Some
of the other Valkyries are staying too. They've offered to train some
of the students who stay behind too, like me. Tanwen seems way too
excited about that. She's going to kick my ass, but I suppose it'll be
good for me.

The Order should have had its final meeting and initiation for
its new members a few days ago, but we never saw any hints of it by
the lake, in the forest clearing, or in the cavern. With Nariel dead

and Grace missing, I have no idea what the state of the Order is—
and Jeremy and Cyrus aren't talking. Cyrus is up there now, graduating and accepting Grace's diploma on her behalf. My one consolation is that he and Isaiah broke up in the last week, as I predicted.

"Does it bother you that you're not up there?" I ask Jonah. He's
not graduating since he missed an entire year of school. He talked
Uriel into letting him test out of a few classes and double up on
others. If he manages to keep up, he'll graduate next year with me.

"Not really," he replies. "Sure, it sucks that I'm not graduating
with my friends, but I learned a lot in Faerie, things I never would
have learned here." He nudges me with his shoulder. "Besides, now
I get to go to school with you for the first time."

"Lucky me," I say sarcastically, shoving him back. "Who doesn't
want their overprotective brother following them around?"

He gives me a pointed look. "It's not being overprotective if
you're actually in danger."

I sigh and tug my jacket tighter around myself. My plan was to
spend winter break searching for Grace and the Staff, but the
Princes overruled me. For my safety, they want me to stay in Angel
Peak with my dad while they investigate. Jonah gave me his puppy
dog eyes and I couldn't refuse, but we'll see how long I manage to
keep that promise before I go stir crazy.

Eveanna will be going with them on the hunt. She's staying with
my dad at the moment, using glamour to make herself blend in. She
leans over and whispers, "When do they prove themselves?"

"I'm sorry?" I ask, not following.

"At Ethereal Academy, all students must prove themselves by
showing off their skills, whether they be talented at combat,
enchanting, cooking, or sewing. If they impress the headmistress,
they may graduate and move into their chosen profession. If not,
they must return to school for another year."

That sounds harsh. "We're a lot more relaxed here," I tell her.

She sniffs and sits back with a disapproving look. She's an interesting one, no doubt.

Uriel finishes his speech, pulling me back to the present. He
calls the names of the graduating class one by one, and they walk

across the stage to receive their diplomas. I clap when Callan, Marcus, and Bastien walk across the stage. Next year it's going to be me up there.

After the ceremony, we file out to the field where the sporting events are held each year. It's been transformed under a huge tent into a big dinner for the graduates and their families. As we all head inside, I catch sight of Kassiel standing in the shadows of the forest nearby. I haven't seen him in a few days, and I tell Jonah I'll be right back, and then head over to him.

"Is everything okay?" I ask him. He cancelled all of our private sessions, and I've only seen him during the last few Angelic History classes. I've started to think he's been avoiding me ever since we got back from Faerie.

He looks down at me with his green eyes. "Yes. I just wanted to say goodbye."

"Goodbye?" I blink up at him, my throat suddenly tight. "What do you mean?"

"I won't be teaching here next year." He glances behind me, and I turn to see the Princes entering the tent. Callan stops and shoots a hateful glare at Kassiel, before slipping inside. "Now that the Order has the Staff, my mission has changed. My priority is recovering the Staff before they can use it." His mouth twists. "Besides, word got out that I'm the son of Lucifer, and some of the Archangels are very upset that Uriel's allowed me to teach here. He claims he didn't know who my father was, but I think he's simply covering his ass."

"What do you mean, word got out?"

His eyes narrow. "I'm sure Callan told them."

"No..." I shake my head. "He couldn't."

"He hates demons, and believes my father killed his father. It's fine." Kassiel tucks a piece of hair behind my ear. "This was a temporary assignment anyway. I always knew it could never last beyond my mission. I did enjoy teaching though. I will miss it. And you, Olivia. But at least we don't have to hide our relationship anymore."

"That is a relief, but will I ever see you?" I move close and slide my arms around him, making us invisible at the same time to avoid any onlookers. "I need you, after all."

He gives me a sad smile. "I'll try to visit you as often as I can. I don't want you to starve again."

"It's more than that." I can't help but speak the words I've been wanting to say to all of them for so long. Well, maybe not Callan. That asshole. "I care about you. A lot."

"I care for you too. More than you know. More than any woman in all my long years." He lowers his head and presses his lips to mine, giving me a long kiss that feels a lot like a final one. "Which is another reason I must find the Staff and destroy it."

He launches into the air with his sparkling black and silver wings, and my heart aches as he flies away. The thought of not having him as my teacher next year is terrible, but even worse is the idea of not seeing him as often. Or ever again.

How could Callan betray him? I realize he didn't know Kassiel as anything but our teacher, but we fought together in Faerie on the same side. Didn't that count for anything? The stupidest part is that Kassiel and the Princes all have the same goals. They should be working together to find Grace and the Staff.

I throw off my invisibility and stomp inside, then catch Callan in line at the buffet. I grab his arm and drag him out of the tent. "What have you done?"

He looks down at me with his arrogant eyes. "You'll have to be more specific."

"You told everyone about Kassiel," I hiss.

He crosses his arms and his face turns hard. "Of course I did. We can't have the son of Lucifer teaching at our school."

"Why does that matter?"

He drops his arms. "His father killed my dad."

"You don't know that for sure."

"No one else is even a suspect."

I pinch the bridge of my nose. "Even if Lucifer did kill Michael, that doesn't mean Kassiel had anything to do with it. Do you want people to judge you based on your father's actions?" He frowns at that, but I'm not done. I poke my finger into his chest. "I thought you had changed. That you were better than the others who saw demons as the villains. That you cared about me."

He grabs my hand and pulls me against him, his mouth so close I think he might kiss me. "I do care," he growls. "I hate it, but I do. That's why I had to get rid of him. I can't have you fucking the son of Lucifer. Just be glad I didn't mention *that* to Uriel."

I push him away and take a step back. "Wow. I get it now. You did all of this because you're jealous that I'm sleeping with Kassiel."

His eyes narrow. "I'm not jealous. I'll share you with Marcus and Bastien. But not him. Never him."

"Luckily you won't have to share me at all. We are done."

I turn on my heel and walk away, silently fuming. Why did I think Callan could change? He hates demons, and can't see beyond that. Well, too bad, buddy, because I'm half demon, and that is never going to change.

For the past two years, I've allied myself with the angels, but maybe it's time to embrace my demon side even more. I might have to, if I'm going to find Grace, stop the Order, and get the Staff back. If anyone can do it, it's me.

Because I'm not just the daughter of an Archangel.

I'm the daughter of an Archdemon too.

FALLEN KINGS

SERAPHIM ACADEMY BOOK THREE

1

OLIVIA

C ool night air sifts through my black feathers as I fly over the dark forest. No angel likes being caged, not even a half-angel like myself, and I've been cooped up all winter. It's about time I got to stretch my wings.

Callan flies in front of me, the bright moonlight making the gold trim on his white wings gleam like metal. There's a huge sword strapped to his back as he leads the way to our destination—a house where we might find the Staff of Eternity.

We've been looking for it ever since my second year at Seraphim Academy ended. Grace and Cyrus, our former friends, betrayed us and stole the Staff from Faerie for the Order of the Golden Throne, a secret society of angels. They plan to use it to send all demons back to Hell, permanently. Including me. Or maybe it will kill me. It's not clear. All we know is that we have to stop them before they start another war between angels and demons.

The one good thing is that they need an Archdemon and an Archangel—or someone with their blood—to activate the Staff. The Order might be able to pull off the Archangel side, but no Archdemon would ever help them.

That's why I'm in danger, at least according to my annoyingly overprotective brother, Jonah. With the blood of both an Archangel and an Archdemon, I'm the only one who can use the Staff alone. The Order would love to have me under their control—which is no doubt why they let me join their ranks during my first year at Seraphim Academy, and why they kept me around during my second year. That all ended when we opposed them and killed their leader, Nariel.

Jonah flies beside me now, and the two of us use our Ishim powers to keep the rest of the group invisible. He's carrying Eveanna, a green-haired fae warrior from the Autumn Court who acted as the guardian of the Staff in Faerie. She and Jonah became friends during his two years there, and when we lost the Staff she was banished to Earth by the High King of the fae. Only once she rescues or destroys the Staff can she return home. The two of them share such a close bond I thought perhaps Jonah and Eveanna had a thing, but Eveanna is only interested in women. Jonah was loyal to his girlfriend Grace during his entire time in Faerie, until she betrayed us, that is. Now he glowers anytime her name is even mentioned.

Marcus and Bastien fly behind us, guarding me from behind like my own sexy angel entourage. And damn are they sexy. Marcus is pure temptation with olive skin, a sensual mouth, and beautiful brown hair that curls a little at the ends, not to mention his muscular body and bronze-and-white wings. Bastien is just as mouth-water-ingly delicious, but in a different way. While Marcus looks like an underwear model, Bastien looks more like a sexy movie villain, with shiny black hair, intelligent eyes, and strong cheekbones, plus dark gray wings streaked with silver. I feel like a lucky girl to call them both my lovers.

Along with Callan, Marcus and Bastien graduated from Seraphim Academy last year, and have spent the last few months searching for the Staff. Jonah and Eveanna often go with them to track down leads. But me? They always make me stay behind.

Until tonight.

I begged and cajoled and threatened until they finally agreed to let me go on a mission with them. My father, Gabriel, would never have let me go—he wants me to stay away from anything involving the Order and the Staff. If it were up to him, I'd never leave the house at all. Luckily tonight he's busy at a meeting in Angel Peak. After getting kicked off the Archangel Council, he took over the little town's defenses after the Duskhunter attacks last year, and he's really settled into the new role. Which makes tonight the perfect opportunity to go on a mission without him trying to stop me.

Callan leads us toward the ground, and I know we're close. For two hours we've been heading north from Seraphim Academy and Angel Peak, which are both located at the top of a mountain in northern California, and we just crossed over the border into Oregon. A thick, dense forest of dark trees stretches below us, and we glide down to a small clearing.

Callan lands first, and he looks like a damn superhero as he sets down on the ground with his broad, muscular body, shining gold hair, and strong jaw. Add in his arrogant blue eyes and commanding attitude, and everything about him screams alpha male. He scans the area and then gestures for the rest of us to land.

With silent steps, the rest of us set down in front of a derelict old house in the middle of nowhere. It looks like it's been abandoned for a very long time, but it also looks like the perfect place to hide.

I retract my shiny black wings and rest my hands on my twin daggers, one infused with light and one with darkness, both presents from my mother, Lilith. The others ready their weapons too. If the Order is inside, we'll be ready for them.

While Jonah and I keep our team invisible, we circle the house as one group. Several windows are broken, and the paint, once white, is gray and peeling. I'm not sure we can even get to the front door because vines have grown up so thickly on the porch. We move as quietly as we can, but it's difficult with everything so overgrown. As we continue around the house, it's clear the sides and back are in as bad shape as the front, and there's no sign anyone is inside.

Once in the backyard, Bastien points upward at an open window on the second story. It's a stark difference to the rest of the closed windows, though most have broken and cracked panes.

Someone could have used that window to go in and out of the house. Someone that could fly up there. Like an angel.

My heart beats faster at the thought we might finally catch Grace and get the Staff. I step forward and unfurl my wings, but a hand on my right wing pulls me back. I whirl in shock, and Callan yanks his hand back as if scalded. Narrowing my eyes, I give him a look cold enough to make sure he knows I don't appreciate him touching my wings. It's an intimate act reserved for lovers and family, and we are neither of those right now. Not after what he did.

He scowls at me and points to the window, then whispers, "I'm going in first."

Using all my energy not to snarl at him, I step aside and sweep out my arm. *After you, asshole.* Of course he wants to be the first inside. One of these days he's going to realize I don't need his brute strength to save me all the damn time. I can take care of myself.

He flies to the window and slips inside, tucking his wings at the last second to go through the narrow opening. Jonah pushes in front of me with Eveanna in his arms, then hovers in front of the window while she enters first. With a sigh, I grit my teeth and enter the same way, slamming my wings together to slide in the window. I land on my tiptoes to stay quiet and straighten up. Bastien and Marcus arrive only seconds behind me.

We stop and listen, but all I hear is the soft creaking of the trees outside in the breeze. The house is pitch black, with a damp, moldy smell that makes me wrinkle my nose. The air carries the chill of an Oregon that hasn't yet felt the touch of spring, but luckily cold doesn't bother me the way it does angels. Thanks to my demon blood, I can also see better in the dark than they can.

Dust covers every inch of the bedroom we've landed inside, including on the rusted metal frame of a twin bed and on a wooden rocking chair in the corner. The rest of the room is empty, with a small bathroom that Eveanna scopes out, and a closet door standing open. I stick my head in the closet and nearly jump out of my damn skin when I see what's inside—a creepy doll with glass eyes. I shudder and close the door quickly before the doll steals my soul or some shit. I've seen plenty of horror movies, thank you very much.

Callan makes his way into the hall, followed by the rest of the crew. I'm mildly miffed at being last, but at least I'm here and not waiting at home for them to get back, worried sick yet full of hope they'll find the Staff. The only other times I've been off my father's property in Angel Peak all winter was to go visit Bastien at Seraphim Academy, to see Marcus at the house he shares with Callan, or when I sneaked out to meet Kassiel.

The thought of Kassiel sends a quick pang through my chest. After quitting his job as professor at Seraphim Academy—partly because Callan told everyone he's the son of Lucifer—Kassiel has been following his own leads on the Staff. I only see him once a month when he makes time to visit me. I hate the idea of him searching alone, but he refuses to work with the Princes, and I know Callan would never agree to it either. Stubborn, prideful, idiotic men. Don't they know we're all on the same side here?

The hallway is empty except for a ratty dust-covered rug that I think used to be blue. There are two other doors, and Callan gestures for Bastien and Marcus to take one, while Jonah and Eveanna take the other. That means Callan and I are going downstairs.

This time I go first, and I make it to the bottom step before Callan catches up. He grabs my wrist to make me stop and gives me a hard look. I roll my eyes at him. He can try to intimidate me all he wants, but that's never worked on me before, and it's definitely not going to start now.

He releases my wrist and turns away, shaking his head. We quickly do a sweep of the first floor, my hands hovering over my sheathed daggers the entire time, ready in case someone jumps out at us with a weapon. But all we find are empty rooms.

In the kitchen, Callan pulls out a trash can and opens it up, finding frozen food containers and empty water bottles inside. He holds up a Valentine's Day themed candy wrapper and raises his eyebrows. Valentine's Day was a few weeks ago. The stores have all moved on to Easter candy now. Dammit. Another dead end.

"House is clear," Jonah says, and I nearly jump out of my skin. "Find anything?"

"Some food and candy wrappers," Callan says, as he continues to riffle through the trash. "It looks like they stayed here for a few days last month."

Bastien enters the room with Marcus. "We found some blankets and pillows in the cleanest bedroom upstairs, but I sensed they hadn't been used in some time."

"How can you tell?" Eveanna asks.

Bastien tilts his head. "Sometimes I simply know."

"Ofanim are like that," Jonah explains to Eveanna. "They detect truth and stuff. Some of them even have visions."

Callan rises and brushes a cobweb out of his golden hair but doesn't get it all. Before I realize what I'm doing, I reach up and pluck the rest of it out. He stares at me as I jerk my hand back, before turning to the others. "Another false lead, as expected."

"As expected?" I bristle and glance at the others. "What are you talking about?"

"I knew this house was empty as soon as my feet touched the ground," Eveanna says, as though it's obvious. As an Autumn fae she has earth magic, but I didn't know she could do things like that.

Jonah rubs the back of his neck and won't meet my eyes. "Uh, yeah, we were pretty sure this was a cold lead. The tip we got said no one had been seen here in a while."

My jaw falls open and anger surges through me. "On the way here, I got my hopes up thinking we might actually find the Staff. Then I was crushed when I realized it was a dead end and we'd have to keep looking. But you knew all along we weren't going to find it here? Why even come?"

"You've been begging us to take you on a mission for weeks, and this seemed like the perfect opportunity," Marcus says with a shrug.

Bastien nods. "A low risk mission with very little danger."

I'm so pissed my hands are clenched at my side, my nails biting into my skin. "So you brought me along tonight just to placate me? Like I'm some little kid who needs to be coddled and lied to for her own protection?"

Callan crosses his arms. "You can't actually think we'd bring you if there was any real danger."

"I thought you would treat me like an adult who can protect herself!" I want to punch him in his perfect face. I want to punch all of them, in fact. Instead I turn on my heel and walk out of the house before I do something stupid like unleash my succubus powers on them. Especially Callan. I'd love to see him grovel before me.

I have to really struggle to get the back door open, which ruins my dramatic exit somewhat, but then it slams loudly behind me and that makes me feel a little better. Once I've stomped away from the house, I hear the door open and shut again, and whirl around to see Marcus trailing after me.

"What?" I snap.

He rests his hands on my upper arms and his touch immediately calms me a little. "I'm sorry, Liv. We know how upset you've been, and we wanted to get you out of the house for a bit. This seemed like a good opportunity, and we really did need to investigate this lead. We just have to make sure you're safe too. None of us could bear it if anything happened to you."

"Fine, I get it." I sigh and my shoulders slump. "I'm just so tired of this. I really hoped we would find the Staff tonight."

"I know," he says, as he draws me in to his warm, muscular arms.

I relax against him for a second, but then push back. "Wait, are you using your Malakim calming on me?"

He holds up his hands. "Nope. I promise."

"Good." I can't handle any more of their coddling tonight.

His lips brush mine, and the angers slowly leaves me as I kiss him back. Most of it. I'm still pissed at Callan, but that's normal for me.

It's hard to stay too mad at the others. I did enjoy getting out tonight, and I can't blame them for wanting to protect me. Even if it's annoying, I know they do it because they care about me, and I try to appreciate that—especially since I lived most of my life without having anyone to care for me like that.

"Are we done here?" Callan snaps, breaking me from Marcus's amazing kiss.

I linger in Marcus's arms, hoping it annoys Callan to see something he can't have. "I guess so."

It takes us another two hours to fly back to Angel Peak, and once we're there everyone splits up. Marcus and Callan head back to the house they're sharing just outside town, while Bastien takes Eveanna to Seraphim Academy, where they're both living. Jonah flies home with me, and it's late enough I hope Dad will be asleep and will have somehow missed our absence.

My heart sinks as the house's back porch comes into view. Dad's sitting on it and boy, does he look pissed.

2

OLIVIA

"In the house." Gabriel stands as Jonah and I land on the porch. "Now."

He sounds like he's about to ground me, and the ancient power that emanates from him is enough to make anyone cower, even me. I follow his orders, but I scowl the entire time. I've just about had enough of people treating me like an errant child tonight. I'm a grown woman and a powerful angel-demon hybrid in my own right, not some rebellious human teenager.

Gabriel slams the door behind us. "What were you thinking?"

I give him a defiant glare. "I've been trapped in this house all winter. I needed to get out and do something useful for once."

"You're not trapped. You've been training on campus with that Valkyrie girl. You head into town with Jonah sometimes. I even allow you to visit your men to feed on them."

Jonah makes a slight gagging sound in his throat. He still hasn't come to terms with the fact that I'm sleeping with his three best friends. If he knew what kind of torture they put me through while he was in Faerie he'd be doubly pissed, but I kept it from him on purpose. I didn't want Jonah to know, especially since Callan did all that bullying because of the promise he'd made to my brother. That would only make Jonah feel guilty and strain his relationship with the guys. I don't want that, especially since I already forgave them for what they did. Besides, I don't need my brother to handle my problems. I dealt with the Princes myself, just like I can deal with the Order too.

I prop my hands on my hips as I face my father. "I've been on my own since I was eighteen years old. Longer than that, really. Most of my foster parents didn't do squat to help me, growing up. It's not easy for me to bend to your rules, but all winter, I've done it." Gabriel opens his mouth, but enough is enough, and I hold up my hand to stop him. "No. You're my father, and I respect that. I respect why you left me as a kid. You believed you were doing what was right." Pain and regret flashes across his face, and I soften my voice. "I forgave you for that. But being on my own made me into a strong, independent woman. I'm not a child. I'm not even a teenager. You can't stop me if I choose to go help with a lead."

"I know you're an adult." Even though he looks only a decade or so older than me and Jonah, suddenly I see every year of his age on Gabriel's handsome face. "You're my only daughter, and your life is at risk, now more than ever. All I ask is that you stay out of the action when it comes to the Order."

"I can't promise that."

Gabriel raises his eyes to the ceiling and sighs, then turns to my brother. "You were supposed to be keeping her safe."

"She looks okay to me," Jonah says, with a shrug. With light brown hair, bright blue eyes, and a friendly smile, he looks so much like Gabriel you might think they were brothers instead of father and son.

Dad presses a hand to his forehead, but whatever he's about to say is interrupted by a sharp knock at the front door. Jonah gives me a blank look when I turn to him with eyebrows raised. With every-thing that's gone on, an unexpected visitor isn't exactly welcome here.

Before any of us can move, the front door flies open and an angel swoops inside the living room. His long, white hair is like nothing I've ever seen, as pale and shining as fresh snow under the sunlight.

His wings are the same color but covered in long black gashes, as if someone took an angry paintbrush to them. They remind me uncomfortably of when Gabriel had his wings slashed by a dark-infused blade. But the worst part are his eyes. They're pitch black, as black as my wings, as black as Lucifer's feather, which I have tucked away in my bedroom.

"Azrael," Dad says under his breath.

My eyes widen, but of course this is Azrael. Who else could it be? He's even wearing a long black robe and carrying a freaking scythe. No wonder they call him the Angel of Death.

My hands immediately rest on the daggers on my hips and I take a step back. Azrael hates my father and destroyed his wings as punishment for siring me. He hates demons even more and likely wants me dead. Worst of all, he's the leader of the Archangels. His presence here can't be good.

Azrael's nightmare eyes land on me and send a shiver down my spine. "So this is the hybrid child everyone is talking about."

"I'm very popular at the moment," I manage to say, before I can think better of it.

He studies me with a cold expression and his fingers tighten around his scythe. Oh shit, I should not have said that. Jonah moves to stand in front of me protectively, and Dad looks like he's ready to jump into action too, should Azrael make a move. But then Azrael throws his head back and laughs.

It's not a nice laugh. It's the laugh of a villain about to tell you their diabolical plan. I swallow hard.

"What brings you here?" Gabriel asks.

Azrael's eyes snap to my father. "I need a word with you in private."

Dad lets out a long breath. I know what he's thinking—Azrael isn't here for me after all. It's obvious from the relief on his face. "Of course. Let's go into my office."

He leads Azrael into the other room and shuts the door. My shoulders slump as soon as Azrael is out of sight. The man is terrifying, and powerful too. As soon as he's gone it's like a weight has been lifted off my shoulders. I'm used to being around Dad and his power, but Azrael's is even stronger and more oppressive—like trying to walk through tar.

Jonah gestures for me to follow him into the kitchen, where our voices won't carry as much, but we can still see the front door. As soon as we're in there, he asks, "What do you think that's about?"

I lean on the island and wrap my arms around myself. "I don't know, but whatever it is, it can't be good. I'm just glad I don't have to look at those creepy eyes anymore."

"Seriously." Jonah runs a hand through his short hair. "When he flew in, I thought he was here for you. Scared the shit out of me."

"Me too." I shudder a little and Jonah wraps his arm around my shoulder.

"Don't worry. Dad and I won't let anything happen to you."

I roll my eyes and punch him in the arm with a smile. "My heroes."

While we wait for Dad and Azrael to come out, I empty the dishwasher and Jonah wipes down the already-clean counters and table, and as the minutes tick by we exchange several long, worried looks. What could they be talking about? Is Dad in trouble again?

After an eternity they come out of the office, and Gabriel leads Azrael back into the living room toward the front door. The black-eyed angel shoots me one last soul-chilling gaze before turning to Dad with a pointed look. Gabriel meets his eyes without backing down, and the leader of the Archangels finally steps outside.

As soon as Gabriel shuts the door behind Azrael, he turns back to us with a creased brow. We stare at him and wait for him to tell us what that was about. Instead he says, "It's late. We should all head to bed."

"What the hell?" Jonah asks. "What did Azrael want to talk about?"

Even though Dad looks distinctly frazzled, he waves off Jonah's question. "He was just making sure I understand I'm not to leave Angel Peak."

"That's it?" I ask. There must be more to it than that.

"That's it." But then Gabriel walks over and gives me a hug, and waves Jonah over too. My brother and I share a wtf-is-happening look over Dad's shoulder as we all have a family group hug. Our second one ever. The first one was on the night I brought Jonah back from Faerie.

"Um, Dad? Everything okay?" I ask.

"I'm just glad you're both home safely." Gabriel straightens up and pats my hair, then smiles at Jonah. "Good night."

Jonah and I exchange another long look as our father heads off to his bedroom and shuts the door behind him.

"Well, that was bullshit," Jonah mutters.

"Agreed." There's no way I'm going to be able to sleep now. Not after that.

Maybe some fresh air will help clear my head.

3

CALLAN

I slip behind a tree and narrowly escape being seen by Azrael when he leaves Gabriel's house. I've met Azrael many times and he's one scary bastard. I have no idea how my mom had a kid with him, but Jophiel has always been his most loyal ally, even after my half-brother Ekariel was killed. Azrael even put her in charge of Aerie Industries when he took my father's place as leader of the Archangels.

I relax a little once he's gone. Or at least, I assume he's gone. Damn Ishim and their invisibility. I better stick around a while longer, just to be sure. Azrael's hatred of demons is well-known, and I was worried he might have come here for Liv. If he'd tried to hurt her, I'd have been in that door in an instant ready to defend her. Even though she hates my guts.

I do a quick patrol of the outside of Gabriel's house, and the door opens again while I'm in the front yard. I consider hiding, but I'm no Ishim and it's too late anyway. The second the door shuts, Liv sees me standing there among the trees. The porch light above her illuminates her dark wavy hair, seductive red lips, and amazing curves, along with the twin daggers on her hips. At least she always wears those now.

She narrows her green eyes at me. "What are you doing out here?"

Shit. I'm too damn honorable to lie. "I'm patrolling the grounds to make sure you're safe."

She rolls her eyes so hard it looks uncomfortable. "You really don't need to do that."

I cross my arms. "You're in more danger now than ever before. Especially if Azrael is showing up in the middle of the night."

She frowns a little at that, but then glares at me even harder. "First of all, I can take care of myself. I've had years of combat training now, and thanks to you, Hilda, and Tanwen, I've gotten damn good. Not to mention, I have both angel and demon tricks up my sleeve. Second, I'm living with a former Archangel and an over-protective brother, so I'm more than safe here. And third, your promises to Gabriel and Jonah to protect me don't apply anymore. So I ask again, why are you really here?"

"It's my duty. If the Order came for you, all your training, your powers, and your family wouldn't be enough."

"But you would be?"

I lift my chin. "Maybe."

"Your arrogance is truly astounding." She shakes her head and sits on the porch step. I'm surprised she hasn't left yet. Something must be bothering her more than my presence here. "What are you going to do when I go back to school? Follow me to every class? Sleep in the hallway outside my dorm room?"

I lean against the nearest tree since it seems like she wants to chat a while. "You should be fairly safe there. Uriel has the school locked down. Bastien will be teaching this year. And I'll be around too."

Her eyebrows dart up. "You will?"

"Yeah, I'm still working as Hilda's assistant in Combat Training classes."

"Really? I thought you were done with that and off to some big job in the angelic army. What does your mom think about this?"

I can't hide a scowl. "She's not thrilled."

This is an understatement. Jophiel practically demanded I leave

Angel Peak and follow in my father's footsteps as a warrior. And it's not like I don't want that, but I have other things to do first. Like make sure Olivia is safe, find the Staff, and stop the Order. Mother doesn't understand any of that. But then again, she hates demons as much as Azrael does.

"I bet." Liv lets out a dramatic sigh. "And here I thought I'd finally be free of you."

"Someone has to make sure you learn to defend yourself."

"Tanwen's been helping me a lot this winter."

"Tanwen is good, sure. Hilda is better. I'm the best."

"Angels and their damn pride," Liv mutters, shaking her head.

"What are you doing out here anyway? You should be asleep."

"You're one to talk." She shrugs and gazes up at the moon. "I needed some fresh air."

I don't blame her. "What did Azrael want?"

"I don't know. He spoke to Gabriel alone. Dad wouldn't tell us anything, but he seemed shaken by the meeting." She blows out a long breath. "Go home, Callan."

I grit my teeth, annoyed she won't take this threat seriously. "I will when I'm sure you're safe. For all I know, you're sneaking out to see Kassiel tonight."

Her face pales. "Have you been following me?"

"No, but it's not hard to figure out," I snarl. Just the thought of her sleeping with that Fallen makes my blood boil.

"I wouldn't have to sneak around if you hadn't betrayed him!"

"I didn't betray him. I did what I thought was best for you and for the school. We can't have the son of Lucifer teaching Angelic History, for fuck's sake! And have you forgotten that Lucifer killed my father?" I let out a long breath and try to compose myself. "I know exposing the *truth* about Kassiel brought you pain. But it had to be done."

She jumps to her feet and points at the road. "Leave. Now. And don't come back."

"I can't. Hate me as much as you want, but I'm still going to protect you."

"Go home!" With a huff, Olivia heads back into the house, slamming the door behind her.

"Not a chance," I mutter. I'll sit out here until I'm sure Azrael isn't coming back. Maybe longer.

It's the right thing to do.

4

OLIVIA

After months of living with Jonah and Dad, it's a relief to move back into my dorm at Seraphim Academy, and not just because it means I'll see Araceli again—although that's a big plus.

"Hey!" she calls as I open our dorm's front door. "You're finally here!"

I drop my bag and rush over to give her a hug. "I'm here!"

"Our final year, can you believe it?" she laughs and flips back her dark brown hair streaked with purple, a sign of her fae blood.

"Nope. The last two years have gone by so quickly, but also feel like an eternity. How's that possible?"

Araceli crashes on the couch with a grin. "That's just life, I guess. Whatever, we're seniors now. We get to rule the school. Especially now that the Princes are gone."

I sink into the couch beside her and prop my feet up on the coffee table. "Well, most of the Princes. My brother's going to be here this year."

Her voice softens. "How's he doing after everything that happened?"

"I think he's okay, but it's hard to tell. He gets upset whenever we mention Grace, and he spends a lot of time by himself." I shrug. "School will be a good distraction for him."

Since Jonah missed two years of school, he couldn't graduate with the other Princes. Uriel allowed him to test out of some of the second year classes and to double up on the other classes so that he can graduate with me this year. Jonah's going to be extra busy with all those classes, but maybe it'll keep him out of my hair a bit.

She nudges me. "And how are you doing? Glad to get out of that house?"

"You have no idea. At first it was great to spend so much time with Dad and Jonah, but I need my space too. My succubus side really likes her privacy."

"I bet." She gives me a knowing grin. "How's it going with all your guys?"

"Things with Bastien and Marcus are good, and I see them multiple times a week. Jonah is grumpy about it, but he's just going to have to get over it. I see Kassiel a lot less, maybe once a month, which sucks. He's out there searching for the Staff and I worry about him. If only Callan hadn't exposed his secret..."

"Callan's such a dick."

"He is." I smirk and can't resist adding, "He also has a very nice one."

Araceli cackles and throws a pillow at me. "I'm sure you miss that about him."

"Sometimes, yeah. But that's *all* I miss." I clutch the pillow to my chest and try to pretend I don't care at all. "Besides, three guys is plenty."

"I can't believe you have three boyfriends. Lucky girl."

"Ugh, 'boyfriend' sounds so juvenile."

"Yeah, but lovers sound ridiculous too. Even Taylor Swift can't make that one cool."

"True. I'll just call them my men." I throw the pillow back at her. "What about you? It's about time we got you a guy."

She frowns and looks down at her lap. "Yeah, maybe."

Uh oh. I probably shouldn't have said that. It's been almost two years since her boyfriend's death at the hands of the Order, and maybe she's still not ready. I just know how amazing she is and wish some great guy would see that too.

Time for a quick subject change. "Tell me all about your break. How are your parents?"

Araceli's face cheers instantly. "They're back together and seem happier, but it's been slow progress. Dad still isn't sure about having another kid with fae blood, and Mom isn't sure she can forgive him for leaving. I've been trying to get them to make up all winter. It's so obvious they love each other and won't be happy with anyone else."

"They'll get there. They just need time."

"Good thing angels have a lot of that," Araceli says. "And fae too. Speaking of, Dad's been teaching me some new tricks. Check this out."

She holds up her hand and traces letters in the air. Flame bursts from her fingertips and spells out her name in fire. It hovers there for a second, and then she waves it away, making the flames vanish.

I clap my hands. "Impressive. You've improved so much."

"Thanks. I'm hoping Eveanna can help me too. Even though I'm Summer Court and she's Autumn, I think she can teach me some new tricks."

"No doubt." I glance at the clock and sit up quickly. "Shit, it's almost time for Uriel's annual orientation. We better get going."

Araceli groans but stands up, and we head out the door a few minutes later. When we step into the elevator, we run into my brother and squeeze in beside him.

"Hey." He shoves his hands in his jeans and grins at us. "All moved in?"

"Yep," I say. "How about you?"

"Yeah, although it's weird being back there. They kept my dorm room the same the last two years, so some of my stuff was already there. Now Marcus has graduated, and they didn't want to give me a first year roommate, so I have the place to myself."

"That sounds lonely," Araceli says, her eyes sympathetic. "You can come to our dorm anytime you want to hang out."

"Thanks," he says, and the two of them smile at each other.

We head across the lawn toward the auditorium, and Tanwen catches up with us. "Hey. Any new leads on the Staff?"

"Nothing," Jonah says.

"Damn." She tugs on her straw-colored ponytail. "Don't worry. Grace won't be able to hide forever. We'll find her soon, and the Staff too."

"I hope so," I say. It's weird having Tanwen walk with us and not with her usual group of Valkyries, but we've grown close over the break during the endless hours we spent sparring together. Plus she helped us stop the Order last year. She's one of us now.

As we walk across campus, I soak up the sunlight and marvel at how things have changed over the last two years, while trying to imagine what things will be like when this year is over. I came here on a mission to find my brother, but now it feels like my second home. I'll be a sad to leave when we graduate.

As we enter the auditorium, I spot Jeremy in the crowd, and remember it's not all good here. He's been a prick ever since he learned I was half demon, and then he fought with the Order against us. He even tried to get me killed by a drone once. We questioned the asshole after we got back from Faerie, but he told us nothing and we had to let him go. What else could we do with him? We couldn't hold him prisoner. We couldn't turn him over to the authorities. As far as we know, the Order reaches far wider than the school. We can't even trust the Princes' parents or the other Archangels.

Once we're seated, Uriel walks out onto the stage and the entire room quiets immediately. Even from a distance, Uriel's Archangel presence radiates power, and when he gazes across the crowd it's like he can see into your soul and uncover all your darkest secrets. I hate it every time those eyes fall on me.

"Welcome to another year at Seraphim Academy," Uriel begins. He then launches into his usual speech about the history of the school, how it was founded in 1921 with only fourteen students, and after the Earth Accords it expanded a lot. I tune him out and think back to the end of last year.

After graduation, Uriel summoned us all to his office and asked us what happened. We couldn't lie. Well, technically I could thanks to my necklace, a fae relic from my mother that allows me to conceal the truth. But the others? No way. Uriel's the most powerful Ofanim around. Not to mention, his Archangel power allows him to see glimpses of people's past when he looks them in the eye, according to Bastien. We had no hope of lying or hiding the truth, so we told him everything. How we fought the Order during the soccer game against the fae. How we found the Staff and Jonah in Faerie. How Grace betrayed us when she took the Staff. Nariel's death. Eveanna's banishment to Earth. *Everything.*

We had no choice.

Uriel already knew about the Order, of course. How could he not? But he claimed he thought they were a harmless secret society on campus acting as an elite fraternity, and nothing more. He didn't realize they were killing people or going after the Staff, and he thanked us for bringing it to his attention. He said he'd be diligent this year in working to remove them from campus and asked us to report anything else we found out about the Order's activities at Seraphim Academy. He also covered for our absence while we were in Faerie, along with Nariel's death, and made Eveanna an official fae representative to the school in order to explain her presence here. He even let her stay in one of the professor's dorms.

"Although there have been no Duskhunter attacks in months, we must be vigilant in case they return," Uriel says, bringing my focus back to the present. "Until we are sure the area is safe, you are not allowed to leave campus without permission. We will plan two days a month for each student to visit Angel Peak, and these will be staggered for safety. In addition, we recommend all second and third years carry their weapons on them at all times."

I glance at Araceli in surprise. I didn't expect that one. The attacks have stopped, and Gabriel and Uriel have worked hard to make sure both Angel Peak and Seraphim Academy are safe. Do they expect another attack soon?

"Now I would like to introduce the new members of our staff," Uriel says.

Three people emerge from the side of the stage, and the first one is Bastien. He's wearing a black button-up shirt with slacks and his sharp, handsome face is serious and cold as he faces the auditorium. Last year he sat in this audience, and now he'll be teaching his peers, including some people he shared classes with. Is he nervous about that? It's impossible to tell with him. I doubt anyone would question him as a professor though—he's much too scary for that.

"Professor Bastien will be teaching Angelic Studies this year," Uriel says. He doesn't mention Kassiel at all, which makes me scowl. Technically Kassiel quit his job to find the Staff, but he would have been forced out anyway once people realized who he was.

I nearly laugh at the realization that once again I'll be sleeping with my hot professor. Uriel knows, of course, but he asked us to keep our relationship on the down low this year until I graduate. I'm just glad he didn't forbid us from seeing each other, but maybe he knew that wasn't going to happen.

"Professor Rosangela is the new teacher of Ishim Studies," Uriel continues, gesturing at a woman beside him. Again, no mention of what happened to Nariel. It's probably better this way. If people knew he was dead there would be too many questions, and possibly an inquiry into his death at Callan's hand. He did it to protect me, but other angels might not see it that way, or they might feel that my life wasn't worth protecting over Nariel's. Especially if they're secretly in the Order. Until we stop them, our little group is on our own.

We can't trust anyone except ourselves.

5

OLIVIA

C lass starts the next morning, and while I'm excited to be back
at Seraphim Academy, it's hard to focus knowing the Staff is
out there somewhere. We don't have any new leads at the moment,
and we have no idea how close the Order is to using it. My blood
boils just thinking about Grace, imagining when she used the Staff
to shoot a bolt of light at my brother. I'm going to find her and make
her pay.

Until then, all we can do is wait.

At least Jonah is in school with me. My first class of the day is
Ishim Training, and I can't help but grin when I see him already in
the class when I arrive. I searched for Jonah for two years, and I
found him when no one else could. Granted, he wasn't locked up in
Faerie like I presumed, or dead like everyone else thought. He
stayed in Faerie of his own choice to protect the Staff, mainly to
keep me safe.

Turns out, we've both been trying to save the other one for the
last two years. Jonah and I might not have grown up together, but we
would do anything for each other. Including going to Hell—or in our
case, Faerie—and back. That's family for you, I guess.

Professor Rosangela looks like someone's favorite aunt, with soft curves, super curly brown hair, and laugh lines around her eyes. "Welcome to Ishim Training. I'm Rosie. Please don't feel like you have to call me professor, and for the love of apple pie, don't call me Rosangela. That's what my grandmother calls me before she starts yelling."

The class chuckles along with her, and I find myself smiling too. She's so damn likeable, it's impossible to resist.

"You may be wondering why I'm qualified to teach this course. I've worked for Gabriel for six hundred years. I've been a spy, a scout, and a guardian angel to kings, presidents, and even a few celebrities." She gives us a kind smile, and I bet her appearance makes her perfect for any of those roles. I already want to invite her over to bake cookies in my kitchen while I spill all my secrets to her. "Now that I have grandkids I'm taking a break from that life, and this seemed like the perfect position for me."

I wonder if Gabriel recommended her for the job. I wonder what she thinks of Azrael, who tried to take over as leader of the Ishim for years, until he got a better job as leader of all angels. I wonder who will take my father's place now that he's been kicked off the Archangel council.

Yeah, I'm wondering a lot of things these days.

"By now, you've probably learned most of the advanced Ishim moves, so this year we're going to focus on preparing you for life after graduation," Rosie continues. "As an Ishim, you'll be expected to serve the angelic community as a spy, scout, messenger, guardian, or even assassin. There are plenty of skills you'll need for any of those roles, and that's what I'll be teaching you. How to observe your surroundings and take in all the details. How to move silently. How to sneak into places. How to protect from the shadows...or kill."

I share a wide-eyed glance with Jonah. I'm starting to rethink inviting Rosie over for cookies. It's hard to imagine her sneaking around or killing anyone, but maybe that's why she was so good at her job.

It's also hard for me to imagine what I'll be doing after graduation. None of those jobs sounds right to me. I'm already good at sneaking around, and a master at breaking and entering, but I'm not sure I want to be a spy. Definitely not an assassin either. Guardian angel? No thanks. I have enough on my plate already.

"Once we see what you're good at, we can help you decide your career path, and whether you'd like to work for the Archangels, for Aerie Industries, or do something else entirely." Rosie smiles at the class. "Think of me as your career counselor."

She lets us leave class ten minutes early, and says we'll be starting our training tomorrow. Jonah and I head out of class together, but neither of us are in a hurry, so we sit in the grass and soak up some sunlight.

Jonah stretches out his long legs and looks up at the bright sky. "It's so weird being back here," he says as he glances at the students walking by. "I don't know any of the other students. All my classmates graduated last year, and I was gone before any of these people came here."

"Well, you've got me," I point out. "And Araceli."

"True." He gives me one of his easy-going smiles that make him look just like Dad. "Being in school with you for the first time is the only thing making this tolerable."

"Do you miss Faerie?" I worked so hard to rescue him, but over the break I caught him staring off into the distance or poring through some of my books on the fae, and sometimes I wonder if he wished I hadn't brought him back.

He idly rips up pieces of grass. "Sometimes. It's so different there."

I bite my lip and look away. "Maybe you can go back sometime. Do you have any idea what you'll do when you graduate?"

He shakes his head. "Not a clue. You?"

"Nope."

Time's up. We get to our feet, and he slings an arm around me. "We'll figure it out together. With Rosie's help, I guess. Can you believe our new professor?"

I lean against him as we head to our next classes. "She's very different from Nariel, that's for sure."

"No kidding. I bet she's a mean assassin."

"Seriously. No one would ever suspect her. You and Dad have the same thing though."

"What thing?" he asks.

"That thing that makes people immediately trust you. You're like the quintessential boy next door, and Dad is like that friendly neighbor who throws BBQs for the entire block." I shrug. "Whatever it is, I don't have it."

Jonah shoves me a little. "No, you look like trouble."

I grin at him. "Damn right I do."

Yeah, it's good to have my brother back.

6

OLIVIA

Next up, Combat Training. I've been working with Tanwen all winter to improve my skills and I was looking forward to showing them off, until I learned Callan is going to be there. When is he going to get it through his thick skull that I don't need or want his constant protection?

Araceli catches up with me and Jonah halfway to the gym, and we all head in together. Tanwen is already inside standing with her Valkyrie friends, but she gives us a little wave, which surprises me. I wasn't sure if she'd still be cool once her friends were around.

"Everyone gather close," Hilda calls out. She stands in the center of the gym with her hands on her hips and a huge sword strapped to her back, looking every inch the formidable Valkyrie. "This year we're going to continue to work with your chosen weapon until you're an expert. We're also going to learn some more advanced maneuvers, such as aerial combat. It's my hope you won't ever have to fight in the sky, but it's a skill all angels need to learn. It certainly helped in the fight against the drones last year. If they come back, I want you to be ready for them."

I remember those attacks, and how chaotic and difficult it was trying to fight and fly at the same time. The only reason I'm still alive is because Tanwen saved me at one point.

"I guess this is why this gym has such a tall ceiling," Jonah mutters, and Araceli grins.

"Callan and I will demonstrate some of the things we'll be practicing this year," Hilda says, before turning to the man I've been trying very hard to ignore. It's impossible, of course. Callan dominates any room he's in, even when he's just standing to the side with his hands behind his back. That plain blue t-shirt shows off every muscle in his hard chest, and those sweatpants cling to his tapered waist. I tear my eyes away.

Callan grabs a sword, and then his gold-tipped white wings spread wide to launch him into the air. Hilda leaps up with her own pearly white wings and raises her large sword, and the clash of their weapons makes the class gasp. I can't help but watch with rapt attention as they pivot, slash, and fly around each other with a speed and beauty I could never achieve. They're both Erelim, bred to be warriors, with the thrill of combat running through their veins. When the dance comes to an end, the entire class applauds. Even me.

After that, we're given some time to pair up and spar using our preferred weapons. Lilith's daggers are too dangerous to use in class —one touch of the dark-infused blade would be enough to make an angel scream—so I grab some practice knives instead. I try to get paired with Araceli or Jonah or even Tanwen, but of course Hilda puts me with Callan. Who else?

"How does it feel, slumming it with us students?" I ask, as I grip the hilts of the practice daggers.

Callan grits his teeth and raises his sword. "Show me these new moves Tanwen taught you."

He comes after me and I use both daggers to fend him off, spinning and slashing the way I practiced for hours with Tanwen.

Hilda comes to watch and nods her approval. "I can tell you've been practicing, Olivia. Nice work."

Her praise makes my chest swell, and I wipe the sweat off my brow and smile at her. She heads over to watch Jonah and Araceli next. Jonah picked up some fae moves while in Faerie—I've seen him practicing with Eveanna sometimes—and he's showing one of them to Araceli now. She nods with determination in her eyes and tries it herself, while Hilda adds her own notes.

Class is over before I know it, and then it's time for lunch. I grab a quick bite to eat in the cafeteria with Araceli—Jonah has another class, unfortunately—and then we head to our third year angelic class, Immortal Ethics. Except on the way there, Araceli realizes she forgot her bag in the cafeteria and has to run back. I promise to save her a seat in class.

This class is in the main building, the one with the Princes' bell tower on top, and I make my way up to the second floor. When I get to the room I'm a little early, but the professor waves me inside. He's wearing jeans and has close-cropped dark hair and warm eyes. I've never seen a professor wear jeans in class before.

"Please, come in," he says. "I'm Professor Simiel."

"Hello. I'm Olivia." I step into the room and finger the strap on my bag. I've never met this guy and have no idea how he feels about me being half demon. Last year my Light Control teacher was downright terrified of me.

He gives me a wide smile, showing perfect teeth. "I've been eager to meet you. Please, have a seat." He maneuvers me to sit right at the front of the room. "So, you're the hybrid."

"That's me," I say, as I take a seat. I'm still not sure where he's going with this.

He leans on the edge of his desk, crosses his arms, and stares at me intently. "Have you found being a hybrid to be more difficult than if you'd been born a pure angel or demon?"

Wow, he's just jumping right in with the questions, isn't he? "Sometimes."

"I'm sorry, I won't pry. I'm simply fascinated by your parentage. Do you know your mother?" He cocks his head and doesn't seem to realize his second question pries even more than his first.

"I do..." I shift in my seat, really wishing someone else would show up. Where are the other students?

"The fact that she's the only one to become pregnant out of all the demons and angels that have consorted over the years..." He gives me a grin that makes the hair on my arms stand up. "She must be something special."

I'm saved from having to answer when other students begin to pour into class and Simiel's attention is diverted. When Araceli drops into the seat beside me, I want to hug her in relief.

"Welcome, third year students, to Immortal Ethics," Simiel says, once class begins. "This is a required course to graduate, and while many write it off as boring, I suggest you take good notes because we'll be discussing things that will affect you for hundreds of years to come. Possibly thousands."

He drones on and on about what we'll be learning, from angelic laws about marriage and property to the proper way to behave around humans so they never learn about our presence. I'm sure it's all very important, but it also sounds really dull. It doesn't help that he keeps giving me a creepy smile as he talks either.

The bell doesn't ring soon enough, and I make a beeline for the door, vowing to never, ever come to this class early again.

My next class is Human Studies with Raziel, and to my delight he's wearing a green plaid bowtie today. Since I grew up among humans this class should be a breeze, at least. Jonah is in this one too —he took Fae Studies his first year, so now he has to double up and take both Human and Demon Studies in order to graduate on time. I already told him I'd be happy to help out with either of those areas if he needs. Plus my brother can be my partner on whatever group assignment we'll no doubt be given.

That asshole Jeremy slides into class just before Raziel closes the door and I nearly groan out loud. He takes a seat on the opposite side of the room, just before Raziel launches into his usual jovial welcome speech. I glare at Jeremy as he sits down, and he sneers at me. He may not know where Grace or the Staff is, but he's still a member of the Order, and I'm going to keep an eye on him. He's our one link to the Order's activities on campus, and soon he'll lead us right to them. I'll make sure of it.

7

BASTIEN

F or the last few years I've been the headmaster's assistant while also being a student, but this is my first year as professor.

I didn't plan to become a professor right away. I was supposed to continue as Uriel's assistant for a few more years. However, Kassiel's sudden departure left a gap in the roster that needed to be filled, and Father thought I would be a suitable replacement. I hope he's right.

I teach six classes a day, two per school year. I'm going off of Kassiel's lesson plans, which he kept in very neat order. I admire his organization and the way he covered the material with seamless transitions, and I only made a few modifications to the curriculum.

Olivia walks into my last class of the day. I've been waiting for this moment. A true test of my skills as a professor. Can I be unbiased when it comes to her? Can I give her a fair grade and not treat her better than any other student? I'm not sure. I'm even more impressed by Kassiel, knowing he was able to do it for two years.

At first I was worried that some of my former peers might have a hard time adjusting to me as their professor, but so far that hasn't been a problem. Being one of the Princes probably helped. No one questioned my authority then, and no one questions it now.

Olivia gives me a little smile and a thumbs up as she sits down. I keep my face free of emotion and don't respond in any way, instead letting my eyes wander to the other students. That ignorant fool Jeremy is in this class too. He'll also be a test of my ability to be unbiased. Every time I see him, I remember the way he spoke to Olivia in Fae Studies last year and I want to grab him by the throat. I'm not a violent man, but he brings it out in me.

The minute the clock hits the hour, I clear my throat. "Welcome to Angelic Studies. I'm Professor Bastien, and this year we'll be covering the last one hundred years, including the founding of Seraphim Academy, the destruction of Heaven, and the signing of the Earth Accords. First I shall give a brief overview of what you should have learned in the previous two years."

The class goes by quickly, and I find it easy to tune out the audience and lose myself in the subject matter. Last year Olivia asked me if I ever wanted a different fate, but I've always felt my place was here at Seraphim Academy. I was a student, now I am a professor, and someday I will be headmaster. Uriel has been grooming me for the role my entire life. I've never wanted anything else.

Until Olivia, anyway.

At the end of class all the students file out of the room, but Olivia hangs back until everyone is gone. Now that I'm her professor, we must keep our relationship discreet. I prefer it that way, truthfully.

"That was great!" She throws her arms around me and I stiffen, but then relax and return the embrace. I'm not used to people hugging me. "How was your first day as professor?"

"It went well, thank you." I touch the gold and aquamarine necklace hanging above her breasts. It blocks me from seeing her magnificent aura and I'd rather she took it off, but I understand why she wears it. "How was your day?"

"Pretty good, although Professor Simiel was weird and asked me about my mother."

My brow creases. "He's always been rather odd, but he's been here many years. No one has reported any issues with him before."

Olivia waves it away. "He was probably just being nosy."

I hope so, but I can't help but worry about her. I feel this overwhelming desire to protect her, and that includes from nosy professors. "I'll look into it."

"Thanks." She slides her arms around my neck and draws me in for a kiss. As our lips meet, I forget about being a professor and lose myself in my feelings for her. At first, Olivia was a mystery I wanted to solve. Then she was a unique specimen I wanted to study. Now she's become so much more.

I've never felt like this before. My mind has always shied away from emotional connections, except with the Princes, whom I've known most of my life. Uriel and I have never had a particularly loving relationship, and my mother Dina only had me as part of a business arrangement with my father. I've only met her a few times, and I haven't seen her in at least ten years.

I don't know anything about love or relationships. I never wanted or expected a partner. Yet I crave Olivia with every fiber of my being.

"I have to admit, it's going to be hard to sit in your class and not want to jump you the entire time," she says, as she runs her hands down my chest. "I seem to have a thing for sleeping with professors."

I arch an eyebrow. "Just don't add Raziel to your harem next."

"Raziel? You can't actually think—oh, you made a joke!" She playfully swats me on the arm. "Nice one."

"I try." I pull her into my arms and kiss her again, harder this time. Until we're both breathing heavier, and I'm sure she's feeding off my lust for her. But it's not just lust I'm feeling...and perhaps it's time to accept that.

8

OLIVIA

The door to the bell tower is unlocked, and I throw it open and charge inside, flipping on lights as I go.

Araceli trails behind me at a much slower pace. "Are you sure this is a good idea?"

"I'm sure this is an *excellent* idea."

Our first week of classes is over, and we're no closer to finding the Staff or uncovering the Order. I need to do something to get my mind off of things, and this is it.

I stand in the middle of the room with my hands on my hips and quickly scan the area. The large open space looks like it hasn't been touched since the end of last semester, but all the furniture is still there. The big couch. Bastien's armchair. The kitchen area. All abandoned...and ready for us to claim.

Footsteps in the hallway catch our attention, and I turn to see Eveanna standing there with a frown. "You summoned me?"

"Yes, you're right on time!" I gesture for her to come inside. Even though she's living on campus, since she doesn't go to classes we hardly ever see her. I want that to change, especially since she's good friends with my brother. "You remember Araceli?"

"Indeed. The angel with Summer Court blood." Eveanna dips

her head in acknowledgment. The overhead light shows some of the highlights in her hunter green hair, and it's hard not to stare at it in awe.

"It's good to see you again," Araceli says, her eyes wide. Maybe she's nervous to be around a full-blooded fae, but Eveanna doesn't seem to mind Araceli's heritage.

Eveanna glances around the bell tower, eyeing the huge floor-to-ceiling windows and sliding doors that lead out to a balcony. "Why did you request my presence?"

"You'll see," I say with a grin. "We have one more person coming. Let's rearrange the furniture a bit while we wait, and maybe wipe some of the dust off of things."

"I shall take care of it," Eveanna says. She cocks her head and the dust lifts off all the nearby surfaces and flies toward her. She swirls her hands, and the particles gather into a small ball of moving dust hovering in front of her. She then walks outside onto the balcony and spreads her arms far apart. The ball of dust disburses on the wind, disappearing from our sight instantly in the waning daylight.

"That was so cool," Araceli says.

Eveanna walks back inside and gives us a nod. "In Faerie that would be the job of a lowly servant. Any Earth Court fae can dust their home without a thought. But I am pleased I can be of assistance."

"Araceli has been learning fire magic over the break," I say, smiling at them both. I'd really like the two of them to connect, which is one of the reasons I came up with tonight's plan.

"My father's been teaching me a little." Araceli shrugs. "I still have a lot to learn though."

"I would be happy to teach you what I can," Eveanna says. "Though we are of different Courts, there are many things I can help you with."

"That would be great," Araceli says, her face brightening. "There's so much more I want to learn about my heritage and my powers. Thank you."

Tanwen lands on the balcony, her bright white wings spread

wide and glinting in the fading sunlight. They disappear behind her back as she walks inside. "What's going on? You told me to meet you here?"

"Yes, and now that we're all here we can begin." I grin and gesture at the space around us. "For years, this has been the domain of the Princes, but they're gone and we're taking it over. This is our space now. From tonight on, this is officially the Princess Lounge."

Eveanna looks confused. "I didn't think angel society had royalty."

"We don't, not exactly," Tanwen explains. "The children of the Archangels are often called Princes though."

Araceli nudges her with a grin. "Which makes you and Olivia Princesses."

Tanwen scowls. "I guess."

"Araceli and I are not royalty though, not even in Faerie," Eveanna says with a frown. "Are we welcome in this Princess Lounge?"

I wave her concerns away. "Forget the princess thing. We all need a place where we can hang out and plan our next moves against the Order. Or just relax and have fun. This is it."

"Ah, I understand." Eveanna nods. "A place for social enrichment among females."

Araceli giggles. "I think what she means is a girls' club."

"Close enough." I glance around the room. "First up, we should try to make the place ours. Feel free to bring your favorite blankets, pillows, or whatever else you want. For now, let's see what the Princes have left behind."

Araceli and Eveanna take the kitchen area, while Tanwen and I check the living room cabinets. Many of them are empty, but then I find one stuffed full of the pink princess decor Araceli and I used last year to redecorate the guys' space. It was part of my revenge against Callan, and I grin remembering how angry it made him. Even more reason to reuse this stuff now.

"Look what I found!" I pull out pink stuffed animals, ranging from llamas to unicorns, plus pink sparkly streamers, tablecloths, and pillows. Tanwen gives me a skeptical look, but then she finds some pink feather boas and wraps them around the lamps. We perch the stuffed animals on the bookshelves and put the pink table-cloth back on the dining table.

When we're done, we look around at our handiwork and Tanwen snorts. "I feel like I'm in a five year old's room."

My grin is huge. "I admit, it's a bit much. We can bring things from our dorms to add some other colors to the room."

Eveanna shakes her head, obviously perplexed by us. "The cold box was empty of any food. However, Araceli found something in the pantry we can eat."

Araceli walks over with a bowl of popcorn and plops down on the couch. "Microwave popcorn, the perfect food for a girls' night. If only we had some drinks to go with it."

"If only we had some *alcohol* to go with it," Tanwen corrects, as she grabs a piece of popcorn and throws it in her mouth.

I sit in Bastien's armchair, which I've decided is mine now. "We'll have to bring some food and drinks over when we can."

"Oh, don't forget these." Araceli grabs the tiaras off the table and hands them out. We bought a six-pack of them at the party store the year before, and I'm surprised the guys kept them—or any of this stuff.

"Perfect." I don one of the tiaras on my head, while everyone else hesitates. I raise an eyebrow expectantly at Tanwen and she scowls and grumbles, but puts the tiara over her blond hair. Araceli grins and follows suit, and eventually Eveanna does too, although she obviously finds us all very strange.

"Thanks for inviting me," Tanwen says, adjusting her tiara. Out of all of us, she's the only one who looks like it belongs on her. "I know we haven't always gotten along before."

"That's in the past, and we both did things we regret." I grab a handful of popcorn. "After helping us fight the Order last year, you're one of us now."

She glances down at her hands and nods. "I appreciate that. After everything that happened, it's weird hanging out with the other Valkyries now. I can't really tell them what went down because I'm not sure who we can trust anymore. Plus, they don't know about..." She trails off and looks at Araceli and Eveanna.

"About what?" Araceli asks, munching on popcorn and obviously excited to hear some juicy gossip.

"Its okay," I tell Tanwen. "You're among friends here, and none of us will reveal your secret."

Eveanna turns to Tanwen. "We have only met once before, so you have no reason to trust me. However, fae cannot lie, and I promise that I shall keep any secret revealed in confidence behind these walls."

Araceli nods too. I know for a fact she can lie—maybe because she's only a quarter fae. But I trust her more than just about anyone else.

Tanwen sucks in a deep breath. "My sister Rhiannon is secretly in love with a demon. A shifter. She's supposed to be the next leader of the Valkyries, but keeps turning down the job, because she knows if this gets out it will be bad. Really bad."

"That's got to be so hard for her," Araceli says. "Don't worry, your secret is safe with us. After all, we know some demons are cool."

"You have my sympathies," Eveanna. "Your sister will face many difficulties."

"Thank you," Tanwen says. "As long as both angels and demons forbid relationships between the two groups, I must keep this a secret even from my friends. It's nice to be able to talk about it with all of you."

I'm about to respond when I spot Jonah landing on the balcony outside. He opens the sliding door and sticks his head in, as his silvery white wings vanish. "Can I join the party?"

I glance at the others, who shrug and nod. "Sure. As long as you like pink."

"Love it. My favorite color." He grins as he checks out our decorations. "I saw the lights on up here but didn't expect this. I love what you've done with the place."

"We've claimed it as our Princess Lounge, but I guess you can hang out in it too," I tell him.

Eveanna nods as if this, finally, makes sense to her. "Yes, he is a Prince, is he not?"

"He is," Tanwen says, although she crosses her arms. Maybe she preferred it being a girls' club.

Araceli scoots over on one of the couches to give Jonah space, and he grins and plops down beside her. She grabs another tiara and sets it on his head. "There. Now you're one of us."

Jonah adjusts the tiara with a smile. "I'm honored."

I suddenly feel a trickle of lust, and realizes it's coming from my roommate as she gazes at my brother.

Oh shit. Araceli has a crush on my brother, and he is so not over Grace.

This can't be good.

9

OLIVIA

The second week of classes goes by as quickly as the first. It's nice seeing Bastien every day in Angelic History, even though I have to wait until after class to talk to him. Simiel regularly gives me creepy looks during Immortal Ethics, but I make sure I'm never alone with him again. Callan continues to annoy me during every Combat Training class. Hilda has begun the difficult process of teaching us to use our wings in combat, and Callan comes over to help me far too often. I've taken to sticking close to Tanwen, who is a natural at it, of course. Her Valkyrie crowd gives me weird looks because they're confused by our sudden friendship, but they're not rude to me anymore, which is a bonus. Meanwhile, Araceli and Jonah keep ending up as sparring partners, and it's like a repeat of her relationship with Derel all over again. Except, from what I can tell, Jonah only sees her as a friend. Ouch.

When I return to my room on Friday afternoon, I find a note on my bed. It's from Kassiel, just a quick message telling me he's staying at a nearby motel tonight. For a second I thought it was a letter from the Order and my heart started racing. They used to leave them in the exact same spot. I snort as I fold the note up. The Order won't be inviting me to their meetings this year, but that's okay because I'd much rather visit Kassiel.

Pulling out my phone, I shoot a message to the newly formed group chat between our girls' club. We're supposed to watch a movie tonight in the Princess Lounge. We've been hanging out there just about every night, sometimes watching TV and sharing dinner, or doing homework while Eveanna reads books she's checked out from the library, usually about humans.

Can't meet tonight, sorry. I have something to do.

The replies pour in, Araceli first. **Is that what you call Bastien now? "Something?"**

Tanwen replies, **Maybe it's Marcus.**

Eveanna sends a bunch of eggplant emojis and I burst out laughing. Jonah managed to get her a phone over break, although she's still figuring out how to use it. I am one hundred percent sure he taught her that emoji and ninety-nine percent sure she has no idea what it means. Either that, or she is way dirtier than I thought. It's hard to tell with fae.

With a wide grin, I slip my phone in my bag and ignore the pings that keep coming after that. The topic of my love life is a source of constant amusement for my friends, and I can't say I mind their teasing. It's nice to have a group of women to share things with.

Even though the school is still on lockdown, I have no problem flying off campus after night falls. My Ishim powers keep me invisible, and my necklace stops me from being detected. Kassiel has stayed at this same hotel before, so he must feel somewhat safe there, and it only takes me about twenty minutes to fly over. When I get there, I knock four times on his door, as instructed, while my heartbeat quickens in anticipation.

It's been weeks since we last saw each other, and my heart aches every time I think of his absence. I'm able to push it out of mind when I'm in class or hanging out with the girls and Jonah, but when I'm alone at night I often think of Kassiel. I worry about his safety or wonder what he's doing, and it often keeps me up late. Sometimes I even sit by the lake where we used to meet, and I think back on those days when he was my professor. I saw him just about every day for two years and took it for granted. Now I'd do just about anything to see him that often again.

Kassiel throws the door open and grabs my hand, pulling me inside in a flash. We don't say a word, just cling to each other, and I realize he missed me as much as I did him. Then our lips find each other like two magnets unable to resist the attraction, and I lose myself in his touch, taste, and scent. His lust rolls over me, making me crave him even more, especially since I've been on an angel-only diet for weeks now. I've missed the dark decadence of his Fallen energy.

"You're okay?" he asks huskily when he lifts his lips from mine.

"I'm fine. It's you I worry about. Where have you been?" I press my hands to his cheeks and look deep into his green eyes. He's absolutely gorgeous with hair just a shade short of black, perfectly trimmed stubble along his sharp jaw, and a mouth made for kissing. "Are you staying safe?"

"Safe enough." Did I mention his English accent? Yeah, even his voice is sexy.

We kiss again, and my hands slide between us so I can unbutton his shirt. He almost always wears a dark suit, which only makes him more handsome somehow. When he realizes I fully intend to start our reunion with sex he growls against my mouth and grabs the tie of my red coat. The coat falls mid-thigh, just long enough to keep me covered.

His growl turns to a moan when he sees I'm only wearing a red lace teddy under it. "Damn it, you're so sexy."

I run my hands down my sides. "I bought this just for you. No one else has seen it."

He grips my waist possessively. "Even better."

Kassiel leans down and clasps my nipple in his mouth through the lace. My hands can't stay still, and I run them through his thick hair, gripping it when he sucks harder. He runs his fingers along my hips, then pulls the teddy down. The lace scrapes my nipple, separating it from his mouth. He watches as his fingers pull the lace farther and farther down until my breast pops out, the nipple pebbled and aching for his mouth again. He devours it like he can't get enough of my taste, making me moan with pleasure, and then he does the same to the other breast.

Kassiel moves his hands down to my ass, and grunts in masculine approval when he finds it bare. He falls to his knees and grabs both cheeks, caressing and kneading, while peppering my skin with kisses.

One hand reaches up and pushes on my stomach so that I fall back onto the bed, and then his mouth is on me. I cry out and spread my legs to give him the most access. He sucks my clit into his mouth immediately, then strokes my sensitive skin with his tongue. Sucking and stroking, teasing and tasting, he works his magic until I'm gripping the sheets and writhing in pleasure. But he demands more. He slides two fingers into me and pumps them in and out, quickly leading me into an intense orgasm.

I ride it out, moving my hips rhythmically against his mouth and his fingers, unable to help myself. Before I have a chance to catch my breath, he kneels on the bed and plunges his thick cock into me, causing me to arch my back and cry out again.

Kassiel wraps an arm under my back and lifts me up, pulling my chest against his, and our eyes meet. His shirt has been pulled open and his trousers are shoved down. In our haste, we didn't bother to undress him properly. Seeing him so undone only makes him look even hotter.

"Did you miss me?" he asks, as he begins thrusting into me.

My words come out low and husky. "Yes."

"Did you miss my cock?" He punctuates his words by slamming into me.

"Yes!" I cry out.

His hand moves down to grip my ass and he uses my body as leverage, moving me on and off his cock. I moan with each thrust, thoroughly enjoying not being the one to take the lead. He knows I love it when he takes control in the bedroom, and his tight grip on my body proves he likes it just as much.

Letting go of my ass, he presses me back onto the bed and grabs my ankles, forcing my legs onto his shoulders. I'm totally under his control, my body moving in time to his hard length pumping into me, while his fingers reach down to tease my clit again.

"Come with me," Kassiel commands. "Now."

I cry out again, looking up into his intense green eyes as I do exactly what he ordered. My entire body shudders as the pleasure spreads through me, and I tighten up around his cock as his potent sexual energy fills me. He keeps pumping into me until I've soaked up every last drop, and then he finally slows.

He lowers himself onto the bed beside me and pulls me into his arms. "I love it when your eyes turn black. It means I've done my job."

My cheeks flush with pleasure as he kisses me again, this time a leisurely kiss without the pent-up need from before. I feel a lot better too with my hunger sated. I'm still sleeping with Marcus and Bastien on a regular basis, but without Callan or Kassiel in the mix, it's been a lot harder. I make sure not to take too much from either guy so I don't hurt them, but it often leaves me a bit hungry. Especially since I got used to being nice and full all the time when I was sleeping with all four men. A night with Kassiel always makes my inner succubus purr with delight and keeps the hunger away much longer.

"How have you been? How's school?" He idly runs his fingers through my hair. "Tell me everything."

I laugh and spill the details on my first two weeks of school, although there's not that much to tell. It's nice to snuggle up against him and talk though, especially since he's a really good listener.

"I'm glad Bastien is doing a good job teaching Angelic History in my absence," he says, once I'm done.

"Do you miss teaching?"

"I do. More than I expected." He sighs and keeps playing with my hair. "But the work I'm doing now is more important."

I run my hands along his hard chest. "Have you found anything?"

"That's actually one of the reasons I came to see you tonight." He sits up a little in bed and faces me. "I have a promising lead on the Staff. The best one I've had yet. I'm going in the morning, but I wanted to stop by first."

I sit up too. "I'm going with you."

He shakes his head with a sad smile. "There are a dozen reasons why that's a bad idea."

"Then let me call Marcus and Bastien. They can be your back-up." I don't understand why he insists on doing this stuff alone.

His eyes harden. "I'd rather handle this by myself. I don't feel comfortable working with them."

I grip his arm, like somehow I can stop him from going. "Then take someone with you. Don't do this alone. Please."

He leans close and kisses my nose. "I have an army of demons at my disposal. I won't go alone, I promise."

I sigh. "Tell me where you're going at least."

"Utah."

"*Where* in Utah?" I insist.

"I'm not sure yet. When I have some more information, I'll let you know."

"Fine. Just be careful. Please." I wrap my arms around him and press my face against his shoulder. It's been hard enough only seeing Kassiel once every few weeks. I couldn't bear it if something bad happened to him.

He holds me against him too, his touch tender yet strong. "Stay with me tonight."

I stiffen in his arms. I've never stayed overnight with any of my men, and I never let them stay with me. It's one of my rules. We have sex, and then we go our separate ways. I do it to prevent jealousy between them, and, if I'm being honest, to protect my heart. It's a way of keeping everyone distant and making sure our sexual relationships never turn into something more.

But maybe I'm ready for something more. Maybe it's time to open my heart a little.

"Okay," I tell him. "I'll stay. Until you leave in the morning."

The look of happiness on his face makes my decision worth it. I've longed to sleep beside Kassiel since the very first night we met, long before we knew anything about each other, when we couldn't resist the attraction between us. Things have changed a lot since then, and my feelings for him have only grown stronger.

He pulls me harder against him and kisses me deeply, and I know he understands the significance of my choice. I'm taking this thing between us to another level, and there's no turning back now. And if I'm going this far with him, I should do the same with Bastien and Marcus. It's only fair, after all.

But first, I need more of Kassiel. I push him back and move down his body, then yank his trousers down to take his hardening cock into my mouth. I'll never get enough of him, and I only have a few hours with him before he ventures out into danger. I'm going to make every one of them count.

10

OLIVIA

It's the next night, and I'm perched on my balcony while invisible. From here, I have a clear view of Jeremy's balcony a level below mine on the corner of the building. I spy on him every night, and if he flies out of there, I'll know it.

I yawn a little. It's getting late, but I know how the Order works, and they always have a meeting on one of the first weekends at school. If a meeting is going to happen, it'll probably be tonight. Besides, I doubt I'll be able to sleep anyway. All I can think about is Kassiel. Waking up beside him this morning was one of the best things I've experienced, but now he's run off to chase down this lead on the Staff, and I'm back to worrying about him.

I'm just about to give up and try to get some sleep, when I hear the sound of a sliding door opening. It's faint and I almost miss it, but then Jeremy quietly steps onto his balcony, already wearing his golden Order robes and his mask. I instantly jump up, fully awake now. I knew he would lead us to them eventually.

He spreads his dull brown wings and takes off into the night. He's not an Ishim, and although he tries to be discreet, I manage to follow him easily. Except he doesn't go to either of the places I expect—the spot in the forest where the Order met new initiates, or the tunnel leading under the lake where they have their lair. Instead, he flies to the large library on campus, although he doesn't go in the front door, but to the slanted gray roof where a skylight window is open.

He dives inside the window and disappears. I hesitate, then land on the roof silently, still invisible. My necklace keeps me safe from any Ofanim who might see through my invisibility, but it won't protect me from bumping into someone or the sound of my footsteps. I have to be careful.

I kneel on the roof and peer through the window, where I see a large attic space filled with members in gold robes. This must be their new meeting spot in a place I didn't even know existed. The golden throne sits empty on one end of the room, and in front of it stands someone wearing the crown. The one Nariel used to wear, when he was alive.

How do they have a new leader already? Who could it be? It's impossible to tell when the faces, bodies, and voices are all disguised by the robes and masks, and my heart sinks at this revelation. Killing Nariel was never part of our plan, but I hoped it had set the Order back a bit. That doesn't seem to be the case. I'm starting to think the Order is like a hydra—as soon as you cut off one head, another two appear.

I was in the Order for two years, but I only knew the identity of a few of its members. The Order keeps that information a secret, although if things had been different, the Princes would have learned a lot more about the members upon graduation. That obviously didn't happen.

One more person in a mask approaches the window, and I have to quickly move out of the way so they don't brush against me as they drop inside. As soon as they land, the person in the crown nods and the meeting begins.

"We have much reason to rejoice." The crown-wearer raises their arms into the air. "We have the Staff!"

The group cheers, each voice sounding exactly like the last, but their numbers are noticeably smaller this year without me, Tanwen, and Kassiel. Not to mention the Order members we killed in Faerie during the battle for the Staff, including Nariel. I would've loved to have been a fly on the wall when the Order figured out that Kassiel was one of their members *and* the son of Lucifer.

"We're making great progress toward using it," the leader continues. "It should only be a matter of days before we can begin our noble work. As soon as certain things fall into place, we will notify each of you with further instructions."

They cheer again, and a chill runs down my spine. A matter of days? How is that possible? Unless they've got an Archdemon under their control, there's no way they can use the Staff. What do they know that we don't?

"We have a large batch of initiates this year, with the hopes of bolstering our numbers," the leader continues. "Please note we must remain diligent with the half-demon on campus. It is the duty of each member of this group to make sure she doesn't interfere with our glorious mission. You will receive instructions if it comes time to intercede and subdue her. Remember, she is *not* to be harmed."

Intercede and subdue me? I do not like the sound of that. Maybe the guys have a reason to be so overprotective of me. Then again, I bet I could handle most of the people here. My succubus powers are pretty good at bringing both men and women to their knees, I just prefer not to use them unless I absolutely have to.

The masked faces murmur amongst themselves, but I can't make out individual conversations. Then a door opens, and I lean forward through the window to get a better view as the white robed initiates walk into the attic. The leader wasn't lying—there are a ton of them. It makes me sick seeing how many people have been invited to join their ranks, although I wonder how many of them will make it past all three trials. Do they all hate demons? Or are they just here because they're curious? Or because their family members told them to do it?

I sit through the rest of the meeting while the leader gives his normal speech and the same task to the initiates of stealing something from a professor. I wonder if any of them would dare steal from Bastien, or if everyone is too intimidated by him.

As the meeting ends, I launch into the air and fly away before anyone discovers me. In the morning I'll have to tell the others what I learned. Not just about their new location and leader, but how they believe they're almost ready to use the Staff.

Which means we're running out of time to find it.

11

MARCUS

As I move around the kitchen, putting the finishing touches on dinner, a knock on the door makes my heart soar. Today is one of the two days a month Olivia gets to escape Seraphim Academy under Uriel's new rules, and I invited her over tonight to the house I share with Callan here in Angel Peak. I knew Callan would likely be here too, but it can't be helped. Besides, the two of them need to get over their issues already. If Callan apologized and quit being such an idiot, everyone could relax.

I hear Callan let Olivia in the door and her icy voice as she asks, "What are *you* doing here?"

"I live here too, you know," he replies.

"I hoped you'd be gone tonight. I see enough of you at Combat Training, after all."

I quickly hurry over before they start fighting again and slide an arm around Liv's waist to pull her against me. "Hey, gorgeous. Is that a new dress? You should warn a man before you show up wearing something like that."

She flushes and smiles at me, and for a second she's forgotten how much she hates Callan. Mission accomplished. "Yes, I went shopping with the girls earlier today and got a few new things. I'm glad you like it."

"I love it." I bring her in close and nibble on her ear. "I'll love it even more when I'm yanking it off you later tonight."

Callan rolls his eyes and crosses his arms, but he doesn't leave. It's his house too, but the dude could give us some privacy at least. Why torture himself by watching us together when he can't have her?

"Come on." I take Liv's hand and lead her into the kitchen. "Dinner is ready."

"You cooked?" She looks so shocked I don't know if I should laugh or be offended.

I wink at her. "Don't sound so surprised. I'm a man of many talents."

She follows me into the large, modern kitchen with gleaming white cabinets, brand new appliances, and smooth quartz counters. Only the best for Callan, of course. Not that I'm complaining.

When Callan follows us, Olivia turns and gives him a hard look. "I thought we were eating alone."

"It's fine," I say quickly. "I made enough for all three of us."

"Next time we should go somewhere else," Liv mutters.

I sigh, starting to get frustrated with both of them. "I wanted to cook for you tonight. I made chicken enchiladas from an old family recipe."

She gives me an apologetic smile. "I'm sure it will be delicious. I just wish we had some privacy."

"Fine, I can take a hint," Callan snaps. "I'll leave you two to your little date. But you might as well accept that I'm not going anywhere, Liv. You're sleeping with two of my best friends, and my other best friend is your brother. We're all searching for the same thing. *And* you're in my house."

"I accept that I can't seem to get rid of you, no matter how much I try," she snarls back.

"And have you accepted that three guys isn't going to cut it?" He steps toward her so they're right in each other's faces. I don't need to be an incubus to see the hate-lust coming off them. "You need me, or you need to find someone else. Otherwise you're going to hurt Marcus and Bastien again. I won't let that happen."

She pokes a finger at his chest. "Who I sleep with is no longer your concern. You gave up that right, and news flash, I will definitely not be sleeping with you again. Not after what you did. Besides, you refuse to share me with Kassiel, and I'm not giving him up. Unlike you, he actually treats me well."

"Okay, that's enough." I step between them and push them both back. "All I wanted was a nice quiet dinner at home with the woman I care about. Callan, you're welcome to have dinner with us if you're going to be civil."

"Hard pass," he says, before walking out of the room. A moment later I hear the front door slam.

Liv blows out a long breath. "I'm sorry. I shouldn't have antagonized him like that. He just drives me crazy."

I kiss her on the cheek. "He's easy to antagonize. Don't sweat it. He'll get over it."

The worst part is that Callan's right. Olivia does need to take another lover, or we'll all grow weak. I remember how bad Bastien got last year when she was only feeding on two of us. Three is better, but she's not seeing Kassiel very often, and it will start to tax us over time. It probably already is.

"Let's eat and you can tell me all about school." I gesture for her to sit down and then begin serving up the food on plates. "I miss it, you know. Being an adult is so boring."

She laughs and the tension from before slips away. "How's the new job?"

"Like I said, boring. Angels don't need much healing, after all. I have nothing to do all day." I'm a part-time assistant at the one and only clinic in Angel Peak. Another Malakim named Sienna runs the place, and I fill in for her and help out as needed, but in a town of angels, there's really not much for us to do. As the son of Raphael and a powerful healer myself, I was offered many prestigious jobs all around the world, but I turned them down so I could stay close to

Liv, and so I would have enough free time and flexibility to keep looking for the Staff. Plus, this gives me plenty of time to visit my mom, who had a baby a few months ago—my little half-brother Griffin. They live out in the big angel town near Yuma, Arizona, with my mom's current guy, an Ofanim named Ervin.

I sit beside Olivia at the table. "The highlight of my week was when a pregnant woman came in for a routine check-up. Reminded me of my mom."

"How's she doing? And little Griffin?" Liv asks. "He's so cute in his photos."

I smile, thinking of his happy smile and chubby cheeks. "They're good. Really good. I hope you can meet them sometime."

"Me too. It's so exciting that you have a little baby brother. I'd love to meet your mom finally." She takes a bite and makes happy sounds. "Also, this is amazing. You need to cook for me more often."

I can't help but grin. "I'd love to. Maybe when this is all over we can get a big house and live together. I'll cook for you every night."

She laughs, but it sounds a little nervous, and I worry I've crossed a line. I got too serious too fast or something. Olivia can be skittish about that stuff. But surely she knows how much I care about her. And not just me, but Bastien too. That guy has never loved anyone, but I'm pretty sure he loves her. Kassiel must also, if he risked so much to be with her while he was her professor.

And then there's Callan. I hope the two of them can get over their issues and make up, but it won't happen unless he apologizes and does some serious groveling. I think Liv needs him, even if she doesn't want to admit it.

When we're done eating, I take Olivia's hand to pull her out of her seat and into my lap. I instantly see the change my touch brings, as her breath quickens and her eyes darken. Not because she's using her powers on me, but because neither of us can touch the other without a spark of desire. Her hands rest on my chest and for a few seconds we just stare into each other's eyes. Then we start kissing, and I taste the red wine on her lips while my cock hardens at the feel of her body against mine. The dress she's wearing is a little black number with tiny straps and a slit up the thigh, which I'm sure is just taunting me. I slide a hand along her leg and up that slit, savoring the feel of her smooth skin and the way she kisses me harder at my touch. My fingers find some little lace panties under her dress and I easily shove them aside to discover her already wet and slick with desire for me. She moans her approval as I tease her clit, while my tongue slides into her mouth.

With my other hand I tug the tiny straps of her dress down, and then I drag my lips away from her sensual mouth so I can taste her neck. Her shoulder. The swell of her breast. She shoves my shirt up at the same time, her fingers trailing across my chest, finding my own nipples and pinching a little. We're both driving each other wild, and although I was planning to take this to the bedroom, I sense we both can't wait that long. I know I promised to take this dress off, but I kind of want to fuck her in it, and those sexy little heels too. I yank her panties down her legs, then adjust her so she's straddling me, her core pressed right against my hard cock. Her fingers work quickly to unbutton my jeans and yank them open between kisses, until she frees my length and grips it in her hand. I groan at the way she pumps me once, and then she adjusts her hips so my cock slides right into her.

We both gasp as our bodies connect, like it's been way too long, even though it's only been days. I wrap my arms around her and hold her against me as I slowly move in and out of her. Her thighs straddle me, her hips rotating as she rides me, and all I can think is that I want more of her. I'll never get enough. Together we move faster, and I lift up just as she sinks down on me, our bodies in perfect rhythm, while the pleasure builds.

Olivia whispers in my ear. "I'm close."

I already knew she was by the way her voice changed. Her moans grow higher pitched as her orgasm builds.

"Me too." Without breaking my pace, I grunt in her ear and grip her hips harder. Her eyes turn black, and I know she's feeding on me. It only turns me on more. I thrust up into her faster, pushing us both over the edge at the same time. She cries out my name and I press deep, stopping my movements and pressing a kiss to the soft place under her ear. I cling to her as my orgasm wanes, thankful beyond belief that this woman came into my life.

She relaxes against me and I hold her close while we catch our breath and float back to ourselves. She runs her hands along my shoulders and rests her forehead against mine with a contented sigh.

I pick her up, our bodies still joined together, and carry her into the bedroom so we can relax. Once we're both on the bed we can properly snuggle up against each other. My feelings for her swell and I press my hand to her cheek, marveling at how beautiful she is, and not just on the outside. I can't wait another minute to tell her how I feel.

"Olivia, I love you."

Her eyes widen and I see something in them like panic before she looks away. My heart squeezes painfully. I didn't expect her to say it back, but I hoped for something better than that look on her face. Shit, maybe I should have waited.

She sits up, her gaze conflicted. "Marcus..."

This is horrible. I want to rewind time and take the words back. "It's fine. I shouldn't have said anything. You don't need to respond."

"No, I want to say something." She wrings her hands as she finds the words she's looking for. "I have strong feelings for you too. Of course I do. You were the first to accept me, even after you saw me for who I truly am. That means a lot to me."

"But..." I already know it's coming.

"But I'm a Lilim. I'm not sure I'm capable of love. We're taught not to form attachments to our lovers, because they can't last. Mother always told me relationships weren't possible for us. Not real ones, anyway."

"I don't believe that." I touch her chin and redirect her gaze back to me. "I know you're capable of love. I see it in your eyes when you look at me, or at Bastien. Besides, you're half angel too, and that has to count for something."

"Maybe. I hope you're right." She grabs my hand and holds it tightly. "Can I stay the night?"

I blink at her, my mouth open. She's never stayed with me before, and never let me stay overnight with her either. It's always been one of her rules with her men. But something's changed. Maybe she can't say the words out loud, but at least she's making an effort. I pull her back into my arms and press a kiss to her forehead. "I would love that."

12

OLIVIA

Another week passes, and still no word from Kassiel. I'm starting to get worried, especially since he won't respond to my texts, although he often goes dark for a while when he's chasing a lead. I try to tell myself he's fine, but the worry nags at me constantly.

Uriel's given all students two days a month to leave Seraphim Academy. I used my first to go shopping with the girls and visit Marcus, and I used my second one today to hang out with Jonah and our dad at his house. With the weather warming up, Dad decided to do a BBQ outside and got enough food to feed a dozen people. Way too much for the three of us, but at least he'll have leftovers now.

When I get back to my room, I jump at the sight of someone sitting on my bed. Then I relax when I see it's my mother. She loves to show up in my room out of the blue. I have no idea how she gets on and off campus undetected, but I guess when you're an ancient Archdemon you've picked up some tricks.

She's playing on her phone and wearing jeans and a t-shirt, but she still looks like a goddess come to life. Every inch of her is beautiful and flawless, making it hard to take your eyes off her. I look like a lesser version of her, with the same olive skin, green eyes, and wavy dark hair, but I'm missing that extra something that comes with being the queen of lust.

"Mother, what are you doing here?" I ask, as I close the door behind me.

"Hello, daughter." She smiles at me and stands, holding open her arms for a hug. I hesitate, not used to this sort of affection from her, but then I step into her embrace and breathe in her familiar rose scent. She's trying to be a better mom, and I appreciate that. Reconnecting with my parents has been one of the major perks of going to Seraphim Academy.

"I wanted to check in on you," she says as she steps back. "See how you're doing."

"It's good to see you." I sit at my desk chair and smile at her. "In fact, I could use some motherly advice right now."

Her eyebrows dart up as she settles back on my bed. "Is that so?"

"I'm wondering about relationships. During our training you told me I shouldn't form any attachments. You said relationships were impossible for us because we need so many lovers to survive. But I have multiple men I have feelings for, and they're powerful enough that they've been able to sustain me. Isn't it possible we could make it work?"

"Possible...yes. Probable...no." She sighs. "I've tried to have relationships with multiple men at once and it's always been difficult, especially as the years pass. Other Lilim have also tried and failed. But you are half angel. Perhaps you can make it work where we failed. Although angels don't have the greatest success rate with long-term relationships either."

My hope deflates. She and I have discussed this before several times but for some reason I keep hoping for a different answer. Maybe because I have a hard time accepting this one. "But you've been in love before, haven't you?"

"Oh yes, many times. With multiple men at once, even. It's possible, for sure." She looks away and a hint of pain crosses her face. "Yet in the end I always end up alone with my heart broken. I only wish to protect you from such pain. Learn from my mistakes and guard your heart as best you can."

"I understand." I lean back in my chair and sigh. "But I'm worried I'm too far gone already."

"I'm sorry, darling. I've cared for many powerful men in my years. Culann, Baal, Gabriel...even Lucifer, for a short time. I know how hard it can be to let go of them."

My breath catches in my throat. "Wait. Lucifer? When was this?"

She laughs and pats my leg. "It was ages ago. Literally ages. We were both young then and foolish. Lucifer is a tasty meal, no doubt, but he is so not the type to share. We're much better as friends, anyway. After thousands of years, we're more like brother and sister than anything."

"Okay, good." For a split second I worried Kassiel and I were related, and I did not need to deal with that mess. "And Baal?"

"Yes, he's been one of my lovers, from time to time, for centuries." Her face darkens and I sense there's more there, something that brings her pain. Their relationship must have ended badly. But then she smiles again. "Speaking of past lovers, how's your father doing?"

"He's okay. He's stuck in Angel Peak, but he's taking his demotion from the Archangel council pretty well, I think. He's taken over the town's security, and he's been a lot more cheerful since Jonah returned." I shrug. "How did the two of you meet, anyway?"

Lilith tucks her legs underneath her on my bed, getting comfortable. "I suppose we've never really told you that story, have we? Well, you might have heard that Gabriel and Ariel had an on-again, off-again relationship for over a thousand years."

I nod. Archangel Ariel is Jonah's mom, and although I've never met her, I've heard stories from my brother about her. She's a Malakim who loves nature and is known for being kind but also rather flighty.

"Gabriel had strong feelings for Ariel, but she was never interested in a commitment," Lilith says. "From what I heard, Gabriel wanted more from their relationship after Jonah was born. He hoped the three of them could be a real family, but she ended things with him instead. Supposedly to spare his feelings, but he was still heartbroken." Her lips curl up with amusement. "I was his rebound."

"Really?"

"Back then, the truce between our people was fairly new and there were regular meetings in Los Angeles between the Archangels and Archdemons to discuss territory disputes, anyone breaking the Earth Accords, and any other issues that came up. That ended when Michael was killed, unfortunately. Anyway, after a particularly boring meeting I could tell Gabriel needed some distraction from his heartbreak, so I started flirting with him. One thing led to another and we found ourselves in bed together. We had a short, passionate affair, but we both knew it could never last. Relationships between our kind were forbidden, so we decided to end it before things went too far. Besides, he still wasn't over Ariel yet, and I just wanted to cheer him up a bit. I never intended for it to be anything more than that." She looks down at her hands. "Then we discovered I was pregnant."

I hold my breath, waiting for the next part. I've wanted to know this story my entire life, and I'm desperate for her to continue.

"As you know, it's very rare for a succubus to get pregnant. Even more rare than it is for other angels and demons. You also probably know that pregnancies between angels and demons always result in miscarriage. We assumed that would happen to me also, but it didn't. We were both shocked and thrilled when you were born as healthy as can be." She closes her eyes and smiles. "My goodness, you were the cutest baby."

"Has there ever been any explanation as to why I survived?"

"Not really. Maybe it's because Gabriel and I are both so old and powerful. Maybe our Archdemon and Archangel blood made you strong enough to survive. Or maybe it has nothing to do with that, and it's a mystery we'll never solve. Sometimes life persists, against all odds." She leans over to take my hand with a warm smile. "Maybe it was destiny."

It's a nice notion, that I was destined to be born as the first angel-demon hybrid for some greater purpose. I guess that's the best explanation I'll ever get for my existence. "What did you do after I was born?"

Her smile fades and her eyes turn sad. "We both knew from the beginning we would have to keep you a secret. Your existence was forbidden and supposedly impossible. Some would want to study you. Others would want to control you. Most would want you dead. Gabriel and I both agreed we would do anything to protect you from that fate. At first, we tried to hide you when you were a baby. I raised you for the first year, with Gabriel visiting me in secret to spend as much time with you as possible. Sometimes he would bring Jonah too, and the two of you would play. That year was one of the best ones in all my long life. But people started to ask questions of both of us, and then a demon tried to kidnap you. Gabriel and I stopped them, of course, but we realized It was only a matter of time before others discovered what you are. So we made the hardest decision a parent could ever make—we gave you up to protect you." She breaks off and wipes a tear from her eye. "It broke my heart. I sobbed for weeks straight. I wasn't sure I would ever recover from the despair of losing you, and I know Gabriel was miserable too. But we thought it would keep you safe, so we did it."

Tears fill my eyes too at the emotion in her voice. For years I thought my parents had abandoned me. That they didn't care. But hearing Lilith talk about it makes me realize how hard it must have been for her to let me be raised by other families. "I understand."

"No, you don't. There's more." Another tear rolls down her cheek and this time she doesn't stop it. I get the sense she needs to get this confession out. "We gave you to a perfect family in the suburbs, where you would have two other siblings near your age, but an angel found out about you. The family was killed by an assassin, and you were almost taken, but Gabriel got there in time. He couldn't save that family, and their blood is on our hands forever. But he saved you. After that, we decided foster care was the only way. We made up a new identity for you and hoped you would get lost in the system. It worked. You were overlooked by both angels and demons. But I do know you suffered for it, and I'm sorry. I often worry we made the wrong choice, but at the time we did what we thought was right."

Her voice breaks, and some wall within me crumbles. I climb onto the bed and wrap my arms around her, pressing my face against her shoulder while the tears flow freely. She lets out a surprised sound, and then hugs me tight, stroking my hair. We cling to each other and then I manage to say, "I know you did your best...Mom."

She lets out a little sob at the word Mom, which I've never used before, and then hugs me tighter. "I love you, Olivia. More than you know."

"I love you too."

We sit back and wipe our eyes, but anything we might say next is interrupted by someone appearing out of nowhere on my balcony. To my great surprise, it's Gabriel. He must have teleported here.

Dad looks through the glass at us in shock, as we hastily pat our faces and try not to look like we were just crying. I wave him inside, and he opens the balcony door but hesitates, his eyes on Lilith.

"Sorry, um..." He seems flustered at seeing her, and she's staring intently at him too. This could get awkward fast.

"Hey Dad, what's up?" I stand and move between them. "Is something wrong?"

"No, you just forgot this." He holds out my black cardigan, which I must have left at the house during our BBQ.

"Oh, thanks." I put it on my dresser and look back and forth between the two of them. They haven't taken their eyes off each other.

"Are you all right?" Gabriel asks. I'm not sure if he's talking to me or her.

"We've been having a little heart-to-heart," Lilith says with a smile. "One that's been long overdue."

Gabriel nods. "Well, don't let me interrupt. I just came by to drop off Liv's sweater, and now I'll be on my way."

"It's probably time I left as well." Lilith rises to her feet, oozing grace and sex appeal. No wonder my father couldn't resist her.

"Do you need help getting off campus?" Gabriel asks.

She cocks her head with a sultry smile. "No, but I wouldn't turn down a quick flight. For old time's sake."

My mouth just hangs open as I glance back and forth between the two of them. I'm pretty sure they've completely forgotten I'm in the room at this point. Do they still have feelings for each other? Mom said it was a quick affair, but Dad spoke fondly of her before and I'm starting to sense there's something still there.

Gabriel offers Lilith his arm like a gentleman and unfurls his silvery wings. "I'd be happy to give you a lift."

She tosses me a smile as she takes his arm. "It was so wonderful to see you, Olivia. I'll try to come back to visit again soon."

"Thanks, Mom. And Dad. See you both soon." I give them a little wave as Gabriel sweeps Lilith into his arms like they're in a movie, and then flies off the balcony with her.

I step outside into the cool night air and watch them go, until they're only a tiny speck in the distance. For the first time ever, I think I might understand them a little.

13

OLIVIA

I t's the start of May, and spring has arrived in full force. It's a
good thing angels don't suffer from seasonal allergies the way
humans do because there is pollen everywhere. If an angel with
white wings stands still for too long near the trees, their feathers
turn yellow. That doesn't stop everyone from being outside all the
time though, soaking up the sunshine and warmth. Angels sure do
love their sunlight.

If it weren't for my worry over Kassiel, I'd be having a great time
too. Senior year is zooming by and my classes are going well. In
Combat Training, we've started working on aerial attacks and
defense over the lake, which makes for some awkward moments
when someone gets hit and falls into the water. Luckily, I've
managed to avoid that so far, even when I spar with Callan,
although I've had a few close calls. Araceli wasn't so lucky though.
During one class, Jonah managed to stun her for a second and she
took a dive. He immediately swooped down and rescued her, apologizing profusely while holding her in his arms, and I could practically see little hearts floating out of her eyes. The girl's got it bad. I'm
worried about her, but I'm not sure there's anything I can do to stop
it. That train has left the station, and honestly, she could do a lot

worse than my brother. I'm just not sure when he'll be ready to date again after his heart was crushed so badly by Grace.

Bastien continues being a sexy professor in Angelic History and makes it hard for me to focus without undressing him with my eyes, while Simiel keeps giving me those creepy, toothy smiles during his very boring class. At least Raziel's Human Studies class is a breeze, and he keeps me entertained with his bowties (the other day he had one with rubber ducks on them—seriously!).

In Ishim class we head outside to practice moving silently and sneaking through the forest. I've already learned a lot of this from my parents, who drilled these things into me most of my life. Just like they taught me to take care of myself, and to be ready to bolt at a moment's notice. Now I know why, of course, and I appreciate it. Although it's nice I no longer have to hide anymore.

Of course, I'm always aware in the back of my mind that the Order is watching me all the time. I watch them too though. I keep an eye on Jeremy whenever I can, but there haven't been any new meetings. I keep my eyes and ears open for any new rumors about their activities, but it's been quiet. Marcus and Callan sometimes take off for a day or two to investigate something, and I keep hoping they'll come back with news of Kassiel, but so far everything is a dead end.

Every day that goes by makes me more and more worried about him. He's long past the normal amount of time for him to be gone, and he never responds to any of my messages. Plus, without him stopping by regularly, I've had to feed off Marcus and Bastien more than I like, which isn't good for them. I've started giving people in the dorms sex dreams again, which helps a bit, but I can't do that forever. I might have to suck it up and have another round of hate sex with Callan soon. For Marcus and Bastien, of course. Not for me. Nope. Definitely not.

Eventually, I've had enough waiting. I can't sit by and do nothing anymore. I text everyone to meet me in the Princess Lounge, aka the bell tower. I've been hanging out there almost every day with Araceli, Tanwen, and Eveanna, and on Fridays we have movie night, which Jonah always crashes. Eveanna had never seen a movie before coming to Earth, so we quickly introduced her to the movies we decided were must-see. We started with the original Star Wars trilogy (Tanwen's pick), then moved to The Princess Bride (Araceli's), then Jurassic Park (my choice). Tonight we're supposed to watch Titanic, but that will have to wait.

As soon as everyone's arrived—including Callan, who I grudgingly invited too—I explain everything to them. How Kassiel came to me weeks ago and said he had a promising lead somewhere in Utah, and how I hadn't heard from him since. "We need to do something," I conclude. "He has to be in danger. Otherwise I would have heard from him by now."

Marcus and Bastien exchange wary looks, while Callan shakes his head with a stern expression. Araceli and Tanwen look sympathetic, and Eveanna's face is as hard to read as ever.

Jonah spreads his hands. "I'm really sorry, Liv, but what do you want us to do?"

"Mount a search party. Track him down. I don't know. Something!" I pace back and forth in front of them. "I can't sit here any longer knowing the Order might have him!"

"That is troubling," Bastien says. "As the son of Lucifer, he could use the Staff."

"He would never do that," I quickly say.

"Do you have any more specifics on where he went?" Tanwen asks. "Utah is a big place."

"Or is there anything we could use to find him?" Araceli asks.

"Unfortunately, no." I pull out Lucifer's feather, which I've kept all this time. It quivers as soon as I take it out of the case it's in. "I was wondering if we could use this somehow."

"Doubtful," Bastien says. "It went to Kassiel before when we were in Faerie, but the pull is much stronger toward Lucifer."

"Then maybe some of you can go looking for him. Please." Desperation tinges my voice, but I'm past caring. When no one volunteers or jumps to my aid, I let out a sound of frustration. "Fine, then I'll do it myself. I'll find him on my own."

"No," Callan says, his voice firm. "What are you going to do, fly all around Utah hoping you'll find him? Even if we knew where he was, it's too dangerous. Especially for you."

I want to throttle him more than I ever have, and my fists clench of their own accord. "I'm getting really tired of hearing that. If it wasn't for you, Kassiel wouldn't be out there alone, risking his neck. I'm not sure at this point why you're even here. Why do you care about the Staff, anyway? Wouldn't you be happy if all demons went back to Hell?"

He doesn't answer. He just glares at me, and I glare right back at his stupid, handsome face.

"Of course he doesn't think that," Jonah says, breaking the awkward silence.

"The two of you need to quit bickering," Marcus says. "You've got some stuff to work through, but constantly being at each other's throats helps nothing."

"Yeah, why don't you two fuck again and get it out of your system?" Tanwen asks.

"Not going to happen," I growl.

Callan looks like he's about to answer, when suddenly we hear a rush of wind outside the balcony door. Everyone turns their heads just as huge black wings fill the windows. They're so dark the feathers seem made of the essence of night itself, and they're attached to the most gorgeous man I've ever seen in my life. A man who looks a lot like Kassiel, with thick, dark hair, sculpted cheekbones, and a black suit that probably cost more than my car. He swoops inside and lands in front of us in a cloud of darkness, and when it dissipates, the feather in my hand quivers.

He glances between all of us and the shadowy power emanating from him is stronger than anything I've ever felt before. Even from my parents.

There's only one man this could be.

"Where the hell is my son?" Lucifer demands.

14

OLIVIA

H oly shit.
Lucifer is here. In our Princess Lounge.
The King of Hell. Prince of darkness. Father of lies.
The devil himself.
Lucifer.
And he looks absolutely furious.
Everyone is stunned into silence, their faces as shocked as mine must be. I quickly decide I better do something before Callan opens his dumb mouth or lunges at Lucifer with his sword. Besides, I'm the only one here with demon blood, so I guess I should probably take the lead.
I swallow my nerves and step forward. "We were just discussing Kassiel's absence, actually."
"Were you?" Lucifer arches one perfect eyebrow at me. When he speaks, he has a sensual English accent, just like Kassiel. I notice he hasn't put his wings away, and darkness rolls off them like fog. It's beautiful and chilling all at once.
I nod. "He left several weeks ago looking for the Staff. He said it was his most promising lead yet and mentioned he was going to

Utah. I haven't heard from him since, and I'm worried. We were just debating what to do about it."

Lucifer's eyes look me up and down. They're green, just like Kassiel's, and the thought makes my heart clench. His study of me seems to take an eternity, before he says, "I see why he likes you, although I hoped you would have more information for me on my son's whereabouts. He was supposed to check in last week, and he's never failed to report in before."

"I wish I knew something more." My heart breaks at the thought of what the Order might do to Kassiel to try to get him to use the Staff. "I'm so sorry. If there's a way to find him, we will do it. I promise."

"No way." Callan's defiant voice behind me makes me flinch. I narrow my eyes as I slowly turn to glare at him, but he ignores me as he faces down Lucifer. "After you killed my father, why would I ever help you?"

Lucifer's penetrating gaze falls on Callan. "I did not kill your father."

Callan's defiance never wavers, and I have to admire his courage, even if he's being a total idiot. "Then you ordered someone to do it."

If Lucifer is offended by this accusation, he doesn't show it. "I swear I had nothing to do with Michael's death."

"Callan, he's telling the truth," Bastien says.

Callan shakes his head. "You can't know that for sure! He's the father of lies, after all."

"And I'm the son of Uriel." Bastien sounds offended that Callan didn't believe him. "No one can lie to me."

"Unless they have a fae relic like Olivia's," Eveanna says in her calm, even tone.

Lucifer lets out a laugh, as if this is the most amusing thing he's heard all day. He spreads his arms wide. "Would you like me to strip naked in front of you so you can check?"

It's impossible not to stare at him. He's crazy handsome and ridiculously charming, not to mention insanely powerful. He could flash from friendly to deadly in a second, I have no doubt about that. But as curious as I am about what the King of Hell looks like under that fine black suit, I shake my head. "That's really not necessary. We believe you."

"No, the son of Michael still has his doubts," Lucifer says. "Even though I had no reason to kill his father. Michael and I worked tirelessly for years to bring peace to our people. We were allies fighting for a common goal, not enemies. Why would I want him dead?"

"Perhaps if I examine you privately, I can confirm you have no fae relics and are telling the truth," Bastien says. "If you would permit such a thing."

"If it gets us back to discussing my son's disappearance, then I will allow it." Lucifer's wings vanish, and he gestures for Bastien to lead on.

They enter the bathroom together, while the rest of us just stand there with our mouths open. How is this happening? It's kind of like having a celebrity in our lounge, except one who's also a dangerous criminal who could kill us all with barely a thought. None of us are quite sure how to react.

They're in the bathroom for several lifetimes, I'm sure of it. When the door opens, we all freeze as Lucifer saunters out, buttoning up his shirt. He's followed by Bastien, who says, "He's telling the truth."

I glance at Callan, who clenches his jaw and crosses his arms but remains silent. I'm sure he refuses to believe it, but he needs to get over his issues for the moment. We have more pressing problems.

"Now that we've settled that, let's discuss how we're going to find my son," Lucifer says. "Tell me, how did you find the Staff of Eternity in the first place?"

"We used this," I say, holding up the quivering feather. "We stole it from Uriel and took it to Faerie, where it led us to the Staff."

I let go of the feather to show him how it works, and it flies straight for Lucifer. He spreads his black wings in a flash, and the feather disappears amongst them with a small burst of shadows.

"The Archangels did always like to keep tabs on me," he muses, as he rolls his shoulders and his wings disappear again. "Unfortunately, that trick will not help us now. You said Kassiel is in Utah?"

I bow my head. "Yes, but that's all I know. I wish he'd told me more."

"I'll send some of my people there to search for him. If you learn anything else, you are to inform me immediately." He straightens up and looks each of us in the eye one by one, as if taking our measure, before handing me a business card. "Should you need any assistance, you only have to contact me. The entire power of the King of Demons is at your disposal. We must find my son and retrieve the Staff from the Order."

He gives me a quick nod, and then strolls out onto the balcony and disappears into the night. Literally disappears, his body turning to darkness in front of us. He doesn't even need his wings.

We all stare at the spot where he vanished for a long time, and then I glance down at the business card. It's for a Lucas Ifer, CEO of Abaddon Inc. I tuck it in my pocket and shake my head, still wondering if that just happened.

15

KASSIEL

A prod to my ribs sends pain shooting through my body and jerks me from a restless sleep. If you could call it sleep, that is. It's more like finally passing out after severe exhaustion and endless hours of torture.

Now it begins again.

I've been tied up in the basement of an abandoned farmhouse for more days than I can count, my wrists bound in light-imbued chains. At first the chains rubbed my skin raw and made them sting and ache constantly, but they went numb a few days ago. A small blessing.

Another prod to my ribs makes me groan. I crack open an eyelid crusted with blood to see Grace hovering over me, holding the Staff of Eternity beside her. The Staff is made from twisted silver and gold metal from Faerie and ends with two wings at the top, one black and one white. Held between the wings is a glowing orb swirling with colors, radiating both darkness and light.

"Time to wake up, devil-spawn," Grace says. She looks even paler than usual, and her strawberry blond hair is held back in a tight bun.

"Nice to see you again too," I manage to get out between

chapped lips. "Though I do find your hospitality rather lacking these days."

"Agree to use the Staff, and we'll be a lot more hospitable." She's holding the Staff like she owns it, and that only makes me more defiant. She wants me to use the Staff to send all the demons back to Hell, but I'll die first.

I use what little energy I have left to sit up against the wall I'm chained to and squint up at her. Artificial light makes the room almost blindingly bright—another trick to weaken me and prevent me from using my powers. "That will never happen. Besides, you need someone with Archangel blood to use it too."

"We have someone. Me."

"You?" I let out a mad, rasping laugh. A few months ago, I graded her final paper, and now she's holding me prisoner and having delusions of grandeur.

She grips the Staff harder and an aura of light surrounds it, feeding off of Grace's power. "My mother had an affair with an Archangel. Now that I have the Staff my father will finally acknowledge me."

I lean my head back against the stone wall. "Ah, daddy issues. I know all about that."

"You know nothing!" She prods me with the glowing Staff again, and I cry out, playing up the pain. It's horrible, but my father's power inside the Staff helps soften the blow. Otherwise, it probably would've killed me by now.

Cyrus walks into my dungeon and frowns at the sight of us. Every time he sees my injuries, he cringes a little. I'm pretty sure he's my best shot at getting out of here.

"Is that really necessary?" he asks Grace.

"Yes, it is." She shoots a bolt of light at me from the Staff, and this time my screams are real. "Use the Staff, and all this goes away."

"Even if I wanted to use the Staff, I'm too weak," I mutter, then begin to cough, my lungs burning in pain. "You've kept me in light all this time. I need to feed on darkness, or I won't last much longer."

"He's speaking the truth," Cyrus confirms. I've never been so grateful to have an Ofanim around. "And he does look like he's in pretty bad shape."

Grace purses her lips. "Fine. I'll turn off the lights for fifteen minutes. Keep an eye on him."

She exits the room and the lights flip off, except for a small one over Cyrus. Blissful darkness surrounds me for the first time in an eternity, and I bask in the feel of it soaking into my skin and giving me strength. As my body heals itself, I think back on how I got into this mess.

It started with a few covert messages from Olivia's father. As the leader of the Ishim he has an army of spies all over the world, and although I was surprised he wanted to work with me, Lucifer told me Gabriel had always been a decent sort. I blindly went to check each lead, and knew I was getting close. The Staff had been in those locations mere days before I arrived. I felt my father's residual power like a calling card.

It was too fucking easy.

The fourth location was a trap. I took a few trusted demons with me to be safe, only because I promised Liv, but when we reached the farmhouse we were ambushed. My companions were killed, and I was placed in light-imbued chains in this brightly lit basement. All because I was cocky. I should have known the messages weren't really from Gabriel. Now I might never see Olivia again because of my mistake.

When I've gathered enough energy, I tell Cyrus, "Thank you."

He nods and doesn't meet my eyes. For a while I've sensed he's uncomfortable with the lengths Grace is willing to go to, and now that I've soaked up some darkness, I can use that against him.

"You know this isn't right, don't you?" I ask, putting some power behind my words. As the son of Lucifer, I've inherited some extra tricks. This is one I don't like to use very often, except in dire circumstances. "They're going to kill me."

He runs a nervous hand through his curly hair. "You're the son of Lucifer."

Why does everyone always gets hung up on that fact?

"I taught you for two years. Isn't that worth something?" When he doesn't respond I throw more power into my voice. "What about your friends back at school? Olivia? Araceli? They trusted you, and you betrayed them. You must realize that if we use the Staff, it will hurt Olivia too."

"I..." His voice quivers and I know I've gotten hold of him.

"You can't let this go on. Free me, and I'll put a stop to it."

"I can't," he says forcefully, throwing off my coercion. "They'll kill me and my entire family."

That isn't going to work. I try a new angle. "Then please get word to Olivia. Or the Princes. Tell them where I am. They can stop the Order, and then your family will be safe."

There's a long moment of silence, before I hear a sharp intake of breath. "Do you think they can really stop them?"

"I know they can, but they need your help." I throw the last of my power into my voice. "Cyrus, you're a good man. You want to do what is right. Find the others. Tell them where I am. It's the only way out of this mess, for both of us."

He stares at me with his mouth open and I think my suggestive power's done its trick, but then the door flies open and Grace walks back in with the Staff.

"Time's up." She levels the Staff at my chest and blasts me with light until I scream. Any leftover power I got from the darkness burns away as it works to keep me alive. She grabs my hair to haul my head up, so I'm forced to look at her. "I'll ask you again. Will you use the Staff?"

I spit in her face. "Never."

With a sigh, she releases my head, and I don't have the strength to hold it up. "We're going to have to try something else," she says.

I see the Staff swing at my face, before everything goes black.

16

OLIVIA

"**E**arth to Olivia," Jonah says, waving a hand in front of my face.

I blink and refocus on him. "What?"

"We're supposed to practice sneaking up on someone. You're my partner. Remember?"

"Oh. Right." We're in the middle of Ishim Training, but it's hard for me to focus on any of my classes knowing Kassiel is still missing and now Callan, Marcus, and Eveanna have gone to Utah to search for him. Lucifer found out from his people that Kassiel asked a few demon warriors to meet him near Salt Lake City, and he sent us the location. Marcus and Eveanna went to investigate two days ago, along with a somewhat reluctant Callan. We haven't heard anything from them since.

"I should be out there looking for Kassiel too," I hiss to Jonah as we move through the forest. "It's wrong that I'm the only one still here."

"I'm here," Jonah murmurs. "Bastien is too. You're not the only one."

I sigh. I know he's right. As third year students, we can't just up and leave whenever we feel like it to chase down a lead—but I care a lot more about finding Kassiel and retrieving the Staff than my classes at the moment. I just wish I could do something more.

I feel Callan's absence strongly during Combat Training, but I also have some success ambushing Tanwen from the air without being distracted by his stupid face, so at least there's that.

In Immortal Ethics, Simiel lectures us on how we should treat humans, especially since we won't age, while our human contacts will grow older and eventually die. He cautions us against developing strong relationships with any of them and to avoid human-angel romances entirely. A few people in class look annoyed, and I wonder if they have humans they're close with, but otherwise I tune everything out as I worry about Kassiel some more. At the end of class, Simiel pulls me aside and asks me if I'm okay. Luckily Araceli is there, so he can't be too creepy, and I wave off his concerns easily. As we walk out, I can't help but wonder if he's the new leader of the Order on campus. It would explain his weird fascination with me for sure.

In Human Studies, Raziel is telling us about a hunter group in the 90s who wiped out a lot of demons, and Jeremy makes a comment under his breath about how they missed one. I turn and glare at him, clutching my pen tightly, and then get an idea. I quickly text the others and they all agree to my plan.

We wait until midnight when most angels are sleeping, and then we land on Jeremy's balcony, my Ishim powers keeping us invisible. It's locked, but Bastien was able to get the key, and he eases the door open as quietly as possible.

Jeremy's room is a total mess. Dirty clothes everywhere. Empty food containers. Full glasses of soda. It even smells like a boy's locker room. Tanwen pinches her nose and makes a face as we enter, while Araceli covers a yawn. Jonah frowns at me—he thinks this is a bad idea—but then he takes Araceli's hand, keeping her invisible, and leads her out of the room. They return a minute later and Araceli nods, signaling she was successful in putting the roommate in a Malakim sleep trance. He shouldn't wake up, even if Jeremy screams.

Then I remove the invisibility and flip on the light. Jeremy opens his eyes and then lets out a little pathetic scream when he sees the five of us hovering over his bed. I sit down on the edge of it, with Bastien and Tanwen to my left, and Araceli and Jonah to my right.

"Wh-what the fuck are you doing here?" Jeremy asks, trying to sound tough as he scrambles to sit up.

"Tell us where Kassiel is being held," I demand.

Jeremy laughs. "Yeah, right. Like I would help you demon lovers."

Jonah grabs one of Jeremy's arms and Tanwen grabs the other, holding him in place. He struggles, but he's no match for them and his eyes bulge out as I draw closer. I grip his chin, digging my red nails into his skin.

"Tell me," I demand, sending desire into him. "Where is Kassiel?"

Jeremy's eyes change from panicked to adoring as he gazes at me and the magic takes hold. "I want you," he sputters. "I want you so bad."

"You can have me as soon as you answer the question."

"It's why I hate you so much." He struggles against Jonah and Tanwen, but now it's because he feels a desperate need to touch me. There's a tent in his trousers for sure. "You're so fucking sexy I can't stand it. I stare at you in all our classes."

Ugh. His lust tastes oily and disgusting, but I grip his chin tighter and smile sweetly at him anyway. "I know. Now answer the question. Where is Kassiel?"

"I don't know." Jeremy's face is consumed by primal lust and his hips thrust to get close to me.

I stroke the side of his face and try not to gag, while I send even more seduction power into him. "Tell me where the Staff of Eternity is."

"I don't know anything!" he cries out, practically sobbing in his desperation to please me.

"Truth," Bastien says, crossing his arms.

Dammit. I figured Jeremy was just another of the Order's grunts, tasked with carrying out their missions while not being told anything important, but I had to try.

"What do you know about the Order?" Araceli asks him.

Jeremy looks at me, as if asking my permission, and I nod. "The Order controls Aerie industries. If I graduate as a member, I'll get a job with them and make my parents proud." Jeremy's hips thrust at me again. "That's all I know."

If the Order controls Aerie, they're far bigger than we ever knew. And it's a good thing we kept the Princes' families out of this —Callan's mother Jophiel is the CEO of Aerie Industries. Further proof we can't trust anyone else.

"Who is the new leader of the Order?" I bend over and press my arms against my breasts, so my cleavage spills out of my half-unbuttoned shirt.

"I have no idea," Jeremy says.

"He doesn't know anything," Tanwen says with disgust. "Let's get out of here. The smell is killing me."

"Agreed," Jonah says.

Jeremy suddenly lunges forward, and I jump back as Jonah and Tanwen get a better grip on him. He goes slack and throw his head back, then lets out a truly mad laugh that sends chills down my spine. "The Order controls everything. The whole fucking world. You'll never win."

"I think you pushed him too hard," Bastien says.

He's right, and what did we learn? Nothing. I press a hand to Jeremy's chest and tell him, "In the morning, you'll think this was a dream."

Araceli touches his forehead, and Jeremy slumps down into a deep sleep. I stand up and pull out some hand sanitizer from my pocket, then thoroughly coat myself in the stuff. Everyone else wants to use it too, and then we fly away.

We head back to the bell tower, but there's nothing really to say. We don't know anything new. We're no closer to finding Kassiel or the Staff. And we're in way over our heads.

17

OLIVIA

The next night I get a text from Marcus telling us to meet in the bell tower, and I rush over as quickly as I can with Araceli in tow. Within minutes, the entire group converges in the Princess Lounge, and I hurry inside to find Marcus, Callan, and Eveanna there. I immediately throw my arms around Marcus, and he squeezes me tightly and buries his face in my neck.

"I'm so glad you're okay," I say. "I was worried."

"It's good to be back," he whispers, before placing a soft kiss on my lips.

I pull back and glance at Callan, and for a second I have the urge to go to him too, to throw myself against his hard chest and feel his muscular arms surround me, but then I quickly look away.

Araceli is hugging Eveanna, and then Tanwen does the same. Our fae friend looks distinctly uncomfortable with all the attention, and Jonah laughs and pats her on the back. I give her a warm smile, while Bastien gives Callan and Marcus a nod. But as happy as I am to see them, I can't help but notice they didn't bring Kassiel or the Staff.

"Did you find anything?" Bastien asks.

"We found someone," Marcus says, and nods to something

behind me. I turn slowly and spot Cyrus cowering in the corner, wringing his hands together, like he's afraid of us.

He should be.

"What's he doing here?" I ask, unable to hide the venom in my voice. We thought Cyrus was our friend, but he manipulated, used, and betrayed us just like Grace did.

"He found us," Marcus says. "He said he was turning himself in, but he would only speak to you."

"Time to start talking," Callan commands, glaring at Cyrus.

"I'm in over my head," Cyrus says, his eyes wide as we gather around him. "I never meant for anything like this to happen, I swear."

"Maybe you should have thought of that before you turned on us," Araceli says. "We thought you were our friend, but you were just hanging out with us to get close to me!"

Cyrus drops his head. "You don't understand. Grace was my best friend as a kid, and she convinced me to join the Order. She said it would help me get a good job after I graduated, and her uncle Nariel could pull some strings for me. I thought it was just an elite club, but when I found out what they were really doing, I realized I was in way over my head. I did not sign up for murder, blackmail, or torture." He sucks in a long, ragged breath. "I only stayed so long because I was scared. Last year they threatened to hurt Isaiah if I didn't do what they wanted. But I *was* your friend. I swear it."

Araceli crosses her arms with a harrumph. I know Cyrus's betrayal hurt her a lot since he was one of the few people who accepted her early on even though she was part fae. Then we found out he was ordered to get close to her because the Order wanted to use her fae blood. It was hard to trust him after that.

I glance at Bastien with raised eyebrows and he nods. Cyrus is telling the truth so far. "Have you been with Grace and the Staff all this time?" I ask. "Does she have Kassiel?"

"Yes," Cyrus admits in a pathetic tone. "I've always gone along with whatever Grace told me to do, but she's gone too far now. She's obsessed with the Staff and is torturing Kassiel to get him to use it, but he refuses. Soon she's going to get fed up and kill him, I know it.

That's why I decided to escape." He glances down at his hands, which won't keep still. "I liked Kassiel when he was our professor. I know he's the son of Lucifer and all, but I don't want him dead."

My heart clenches painfully at the confirmation that Kassiel is being held captive and being tortured. I stalk forward and back Cyrus further into the corner. "Tell us where Kassiel is being held."

"I'll tell you, but only if you promise you'll protect me and my family. If the Order finds out I helped you, they won't just kill me, they'll kill everyone in my family. I have a little sister. She's only seven." His eyes water at this, and I actually believe him. He's terrified of the Order. For good reason.

"We'll protect you," Callan says, with his authoritative voice. "Just give us the location."

"Gabriel can hide your family," Jonah says. "I promise you this."

Cyrus nods slowly and then gives us a location, which Bastien writes down. Callan grills him for more details about the security of the place, how many people are there, and so forth, and Cyrus tells us everything he can. When he's done, Araceli puts Cyrus in a magical sleep, so we can discuss what to do next.

"Even though he was telling the truth, can we really trust him?" Araceli asks. "It could be a trap."

"Of course it's a trap," Tanwen says. "But we still have to check it out."

Eveanna nods. "If we are cautious, it should not be a problem."

"I'm going this time," Jonah declares.

"We're all going," I say. "No one is getting left behind this time. We need everyone's help to rescue Kassiel and get the Staff." I glare at Callan. "And do not tell me it's too dangerous. I'm going, end of story."

Callan grits his teeth, but he says nothing, and everyone else nods at me. They're all in.

"Should we notify Lucifer?" Bastien asks.

"No," Callan says. "We don't know if we can trust him. He could take the Staff from us."

"We could ask our dad for help," I suggest.

"Or Uriel?" Tanwen asks.

Jonah shakes his head. "No. The Staff is too powerful for any Archangel or Archdemon to possess, and we don't know if we can trust any of them. Even our dad."

"Jonah is correct," Eveanna says. "The Staff should be returned to Faerie, where the fae can protect it. We are neutral in this battle, which is why Michael and Lucifer entrusted it to us to safeguard."

"The fae couldn't keep it safe forever though," Marcus says. "Eventually the Order found it."

Everyone starts arguing about what to do with the Staff and it's clear no one is going to agree on a plan. Meanwhile, Kassiel is out there being tortured and there's a ticking clock counting down to his death. We do not have time for this shit.

I hold up my hands and yell, "Enough!" Everyone quiets down immediately and stares at me. "This is not the time to argue about this. If we manage to get the Staff, we can figure out what to do with it then. Right now we need to rescue Kassiel. That's our number one priority. Trap or no trap, we need to leave immediately."

With a sense of impending doom, the others agree, and we make our plans.

18

OLIVIA

F lying long distance as an angel is possible, but exhausting. We did it in Faerie, of course, but we want to save our energy while getting to Kassiel as quickly as possible. As such, we decide to book a flight to Salt Lake City and go from there. The plane leaves early the next day, and since it's Saturday we don't have to skip classes at least. I've only been on an airplane twice before and it's a bit odd to be trapped inside a flying machine when we have wings ourselves, but I'm so focused on rescuing Kassiel I barely notice.

We land around noon, get our things, and head outside the airport, where Jonah and I make our group invisible so we can spread our wings and take off. It takes another hour to get to the location Cyrus told us, an abandoned farmhouse in the middle of nowhere.

As we land just outside it, I'm reminded of the other abandoned house we investigated a few months ago. I pray this place isn't also a dead end.

Jonah sets Eveanna down and we all ready our weapons. Callan directs us with hand gestures, sending Marcus, Bastien, Araceli, and Tanwen to approach from the air around back, while Callan, Jonah, and Eveanna are with me on the ground in the front. I draw out

Lilith's daggers, one glowing brightly, the other writhing with shadows, as I nod at Callan.

I'm ready. I'm so fucking ready.

It's mid-afternoon now and the sun is bright and hot, bolstering the angels' powers. We approach through the overgrown field slowly, carefully stepping over rusted metal fences. I lose sight of the other group in the air, but I can see the farmhouse clearly up ahead. Peeling white paint. A quaint little porch with a swing creaking in the breeze. Dusty windows. No sign of life anywhere.

The second I step on the porch a loud alarm blares. Callan shoves me back, blocking me with his large body and his huge sword. Angels pour out of the house wielding weapons, and our group stands back to back in the front lawn, ready for their ambush.

As the fighters reach us, Callan shows everyone why he really should be at the head of the angelic armies. With one hand he shoots bursts of Erelim burning light, and with the other he slices through the crowd with his sword. Jonah shows off the moves he learned in Faerie with his own sword, and rocks fly at our opponents thanks to Eveanna's powers.

None of them let anyone get close to me. I wield my daggers, prepared to fight, but I'm well-protected. I can do something else though. As more angels surge forward, I unleash my succubus powers on them, inciting their desire. A few men and women drop their weapons and gaze at me with feral lust, and I give them a seductive smile. "Kneel to me."

They drop to their knees and the others knock them out. No need to kill them if we don't have to—especially if they're trapped in the Order like Cyrus was. He's with my Dad now, who's promised to get Cyrus's entire family into some sort of protective custody.

As we approach the porch again, more angels swarm us and it's way too many for me to control when I've only been feeding on Bastien and Marcus for a while. Callan's face is a mask of rage as one angel after another tries to get at me. They must have orders to capture me because they are relentless. One of them shoots an Erelim beam of light toward me, but a shield of shimmering gold goes up to protect me just in time. Callan's Archangel power. I've seen it once before when we were fighting the Duskhunters.

There's fighting in the air above us too. Marcus and Bastien fly overhead, fighting together to hold off the attackers on the roof. Tanwen swoops over us, blasting angels with light and wielding her Valkyrie sword. Araceli flies right behind her and lands beside Jonah, engulfing one of the angels he's fighting in flames.

"Whoa," he shouts as he jumps back.

"Sorry! I'm still learning." A few more bolts of fae flame shoot out of her hands and hit two of the angels running toward me with their swords raised.

Still no sign of Grace though. Or Kassiel. They must be inside.

With everyone distracted, I weave my way through the fighting, slicing down anyone in my path with my daggers. I make it inside the farmhouse and it's quiet in here. Way too quiet. I hear a footstep behind me and spin around to find Eveanna's followed me.

"I sense people in the basement," she says. "This way."

I hurry after her as she busts through a locked door with her shoulder and takes us down a staircase. The lights in the basement are blindingly bright, but I immediately focus in on two things— Kassiel, beaten and chained to a wall, and Grace, holding the Staff of Eternity as it glows white. She grins in triumph as she points it at me and a beam of light shoots at my chest, sending burning pain through my body and knocking me back against the stone wall.

"Get her!" Grace commands, as I gasp through the pain and struggle to stand.

Two angels rush after me, but Eveanna makes the wall crumble and collapse on them, keeping them at bay. It gives me just enough time to get up, and my eyes land on Kassiel's unconscious body. When I see his condition, my fury chokes me. I send out a wave of succubus power and it forces the other angels to submit to me, but Grace isn't weakened by it at all. She narrows her eyes and shoots another beam of light at me from the Staff, but this time I manage to dodge it just before it sears a hole into the wall.

Callan flies down the stairs, with Jonah and Tanwen only a few steps behind him, and even with the Staff, Grace can't fight all of us at once. I hope.

"Grace!" Jonah calls out, and I hear the pain in his voice.

She barely gives him a second glance as she shoots the Staff's light at us. Callan and Tanwen both rush her at once, knocking the Staff aside, and Jonah quickly rushes forward to retrieve it. The second they grab her arms though, she seems to fade out of view, and they're left holding nothing. Somehow, she slipped free. No...she became intangible. What the...?

Jonah spins and shoots Grace with the Staff, and she's knocked back. It's over for her. We've beaten her. Especially when Araceli, Bastien, and Marcus run down the stairs to join us.

Suddenly the entire ceiling is ripped open like it's tinfoil, and someone flies over us with white and black wings, long white hair, and menacing black eyes. Azrael.

He swoops down and picks up an unconscious Grace, then goes invisible as he flies away, holding her in his arms. We all gape after them, wondering what the fuck just happened. Why did Azrael save her? Is he in the Order?

I don't have time to work that out right now. I rush forward to Kassiel's limp body, but his head lolls and he's barely alive. I send some of my power into him, using my Archdemon gift in the hope it will help, but what he really needs is darkness and some Malakim healing. Will that work on a Fallen? Guess we'll find out.

I can't get the light-imbued chains off him and I let out a futile cry as they burn my fingers. Eveanna is at my side seconds later, and she uses her magic to break them—the light doing nothing to hurt her. Good thing they're not iron or we'd be in real trouble. I let out a sob as Kassiel falls forward into my arms and I stroke his blood-soaked hair, willing more energy into him. I'll give him whatever I can as long as he lives.

"Let us help," Araceli says, with Marcus at her side. They pry Kassiel away from me, and I sit back against the stone wall to catch my breath while they work on healing him.

"Uh, Liv?" Jonah asks and points at my chest.

I glance down and let out a soft whimper. My mother's necklace, the one her fae lover made for her that kept me safe and hidden for so many years, is no more. The aquamarine in the center is gone, replaced by a scorch mark. It must have been destroyed by the Staff's beam of light.

"We need to get out of here before they come back with reinforcements," Tanwen says.

Marcus has his hands on Kassiel's head. "This is going to take time. He's got several broken bones throughout his body and a bad concussion, along with the light-imbued wounds."

"I'll carry him to safety," Callan says.

I look at him in surprise. "Thank you."

He gives me a quick nod as he scoops Kassiel into his arms. We fly straight up and out of the house, since Azrael basically tore the entire thing apart. Jonah carries the Staff, while Tanwen carries Eveanna.

We did it. We rescued Kassiel and got the Staff. But Grace escaped...with Azrael.

19

CALLAN

K assiel's in bad shape. There's no way we can get him on a plane like this, so we find a motel in the middle of nowhere about five hours away from the farmhouse. The entire way there, Jonah and the other guys kept offering to take Kassiel off my hands, but I refused. I had to do it on my own.

I don't owe Kassiel anything. He's still the son of Lucifer. But he didn't break under torture, and he was a good teacher once, even if he was deceiving us the entire time.

More importantly, Liv cares for him.

Bastien manages to get us four rooms with two beds each, and the others sort it out while I stand in the shadows with Kassiel in my arms. He hasn't stirred at all. I'm not sure if he's just that far gone, or if the Malakim did one of those healing trances, but I'll feel a lot better once they have a chance to work on him some more. For Liv's sake, obviously. She's been a worried wreck this entire time, hovering near me and casting concerned glances at the Fallen. He better not die on her.

"This way," Marcus says, once the rooms are ready. "Araceli and I will be taking turns between healing him and sleeping during the night."

I grunt as I carry Kassiel inside the dimly lit room. The motel seems to be decorated in what can only be described as 70's puke yellow, green, and brown, but it looks clean enough. I set Kassiel down on one of the two beds in the room, and then back away so the healers can do their thing. My job is done, and I'll only get in the way now.

As Araceli and Marcus discuss who should sleep first, Olivia rushes in and sits on the edge of Kassiel's bed. He manages to open his eyes and gives her a weak smile, and she lets out a soft cry and kisses his forehead. Pure adoration shines from her eyes as she whispers something to him, and the expression on her face makes my chest ache.

She loves him.

I pull the door closed and stand outside the motel room as a great hollowness fills me. She looks at Marcus and Bastien the same way sometimes.

But not me. Me, she hates.

"You're with me tonight," Jonah says, from the doorway of the next room over. "We're guarding the Staff."

"Fine." I gaze across the courtyard and spot Tanwen and Eveanna heading into a room together, while Bastien slips into the one next to it. "Where is Liv staying tonight?"

Jonah grimaces. "With Bastien."

Of course. She'll need sex after using her powers today. Kassiel is injured, Marcus is busy, and I'm off the menu, so Bastien it is.

I try not to feel bitter and jealous about it, but it's hard.

Jonah heads inside, but I need to be alone with my thoughts or some shit, so I wait outside, leaning against the wall while inspecting a wound on my side that's slowly healing up. A few minutes later, Olivia emerges from the motel room and looks at me with exhausted eyes and dried tears on her cheeks. The sight makes me want to wrap my arms around her and hold her tight, but she'd probably punch me in the face if I tried.

As she heads across the courtyard, I call out, "Olivia, wait. We need to talk."

She gives me a suspicious look and crosses her arms. "About what?"

I suck in a breath. "I never apologize."

She snorts. "Tell me something I don't know."

"It's not in my nature," I continue, ignoring her snark. "But I was wrong about Kassiel. And Lucifer. I was wrong about a lot of things."

Her arms fall to her side. "Callan—"

I cut her off before I get frustrated or say the wrong thing. "I care about you, Olivia. I know I've made mistakes. Lots of mistakes."

"No kidding."

"I hurt you with some of my actions, but I did what I thought was right at the time. I always do."

"Yes, but—"

"Let me finish." I grit my teeth and force the words out. "For years, I've been taught that demons are the enemy. That they killed my brother Ekariel. That Lucifer murdered my father. That it was my destiny to avenge my family and lead the next war against Hell." I take a step forward. "I don't want that anymore. I'm not sure I'll ever be able to trust Lucifer, but I've accepted that demons are not evil. I don't want a war. I just want you."

Olivia's jaw drops and she stares at me for an eternity. I keep hoping she'll accept my apology, rush into my arms, and tell me she cares about me too, but instead she just sighs. "I can't do this right now." She shakes her head, her eyes weary. "Good night, Callan."

She heads into the room with Bastien and I turn away, my jaw clenched. All I want is to make peace with her. I know I've fucked up in the past, but I'm doing the best I can to change. It isn't easy, but the thought of Olivia hating me for the rest of our immortal lives is gut-wrenching. I can't live without her. I realize that now.

And I vow to do whatever it takes to win her back.

20

OLIVIA

I n the morning, I throw my arms around Kassiel and practically sob into his chest, seeing how he's recovered. Thanks to some sleep, some darkness, and some major healing from Marcus and Araceli, he's almost as good as new, although he's thinner and paler than before, and there's an exhaustion in his eyes I've never seen before.

I hope that a good meal will cheer him up, so I drag us all to a local waffle house where we can chat. Jonah brings the Staff with us —it's not like we can leave it at the motel—but Eveanna glamours it to look like a golf club bag. No one gives it a second glance as we walk inside and set it beside us.

The waitress seats us at a huge booth in the corner, and we all scoot in. I'm wedged between Callan and Kassiel, which might have been awkward before, but I'm so over it all I can't find the energy to care anymore. I can't even wrap my head around Callan's speech last night, or how he carried Kassiel for hours to the motel yesterday.

After we've all squeezed inside and given our drink orders, Kassiel glances around the table at the faces of all my friends. "Thank you," he says sincerely. "I would have died there if you hadn't come for me. I owe each of you a great debt."

"Of course we came" Araceli says. "You're one of the group."

"Yeah, we couldn't let them kill our favorite professor," Marcus adds.

Jonah offers his hand. "Liv cares about you a lot, which makes you important to me too. Welcome to the family."

Kassiel shakes it with a weak smile. "I appreciate that."

I take Kassiel's other hand and squeeze it, but then my eyes dart to Callan, who's been sitting there with a face like stone this entire time.

"It was our duty," he simply says, as if that explains anything. Classic Callan.

"Indeed," Bastien says. "Besides, it was imperative that we retrieve the Staff."

"Yes, and now that we have it, what are we going to do with it?" Tanwen asks.

"I still maintain that it should return to Faerie," Eveanna says.

"Of course you do," Tanwen replies, sounding almost bitter. "You just want to end your banishment and return home."

Eveanna's nostrils flare a little at that. She's glamoured herself to look like a brunette without pointed ears while we're in public, but she still has something otherworldly about her that sets her apart. Getting rid of her hunter green hair isn't enough to make her look human.

The waitress sets down a huge steaming cup of coffee in front of me and I wrap both hands around it and take a long sip. I'm going to need a lot of it to deal with this group so early in the morning.

"That is not true," Eveanna finally says to Tanwen, after the waitress leaves again. "I have come to appreciate many things about Earth, such as your coffee and your movies and your internet. However, Faerie is the safest place for the Staff."

"Obviously not, since we were able to track it down without a problem, and then the Order was able to steal it," Bastien says. "Faerie may have been safe before, but no longer."

"I'm sorry, but he's right," I tell Eveanna. "We can't send the Staff back to Faerie. It's what the Order will expect. But if we can do anything to convince the High King to allow you to return home, we'll do it, I promise."

"We can take it to my father," Kassiel says, his voice still weak but firm. "He created it with Michael, and together they sent it to Faerie. He can keep it hidden again now. Or destroy it."

"No way," Callan says. "I'm willing to give you a pass, but we don't know if we can trust your father. Things might have changed since he sent the Staff to Faerie."

"Who do you suggest instead?" Kassiel asks. "One of the Archangels? We can't trust them either."

"He's right," Jonah says. "While you were searching for Kassiel, we learned from Jeremy that Aerie Industries is controlled by the Order. That could include Jophiel."

Callan sits back with a frown. His mother became the CEO of Aerie Industries after Azrael stepped down from the position to become the Archangel leader. We definitely can't trust her. I haven't totally forgiven him, but I hate the pain that blooms on his face. After losing his father, the thought that his mother could be corrupt and working against everything his father stood for must be torture.

"What about our other parents?" Marcus asks. "Raphael? Uriel? Gabriel?"

Bastien shakes his head. "No. We can't trust anyone except ourselves."

"Jonah was right when he said it's too powerful for any Archangel or Archdemon to possess," Araceli says. "Especially now that we know Azrael is working with the Order too."

"He's Grace's father," Kassiel says. "She's able to use the Staff because she has his blood, and she was doing all this to prove herself to him, so he would publicly acknowledge her as his child."

I nearly spit out my coffee at this revelation. "That explains a lot, and if Azrael is working with the Order, there is nowhere that is safe for the Staff. We have to destroy it."

"Are you sure that's what you wish to do?" Eveanna asks.

I nod, my mouth set in a grim line. "It's the only way things will ever be truly safe for both demons and angels. If one side has it, the other side will always be at risk. Lucifer and Michael tried to leave it with the fae, but that only lasted so long. The Staff must be destroyed."

"But...how?" Jonah asks. "Fae relics are nearly impossible to destroy."

I touch the remains of the necklace on my chest. I'm still wearing it, even though its power is gone. "There must be a way."

"Oh, Liv, what happened?" Araceli asks, leaning forward to look at the damage. "Your mother's necklace is ruined."

"Grace shot me with a bolt of light right in the chest, and I think the necklace absorbed the blow."

"I'm sorry," Marcus says, reaching across the table to take my hand. "I know that necklace meant a lot to you."

"What's done is done," I say with a sigh. "But it shows that fae relics can be destroyed. Including the Staff."

Once we're done eating, we continue flying back to Angel Peak, but we stop in the middle of the hot, dry Nevada desert to perform our tests on the Staff. There's no one around us for hundreds of miles, and nothing but empty, flat land and a couple tumbleweeds.

We prop the Staff up between some rocks and then stand back. Way back.

"I'll try light," Callan says, rubbing his hands together. He throws up one of his golden Archangel shields, and it shimmers in the air in front of us. "Everyone stay behind the shield."

Callan steps forward and spreads his hands, which begin to glow so brightly I have to look away. With a mighty yell, he claps his hands together, and an enormous bolt of burning light flies at the Staff. I watch while holding my breath, ready to spread my wings and fly away, poised for the impact.

The Staff glows bright white as the blast hits it, but then it seems to absorb the power. The Staff's orb continues swirling and shifting colors between the white and black wings, as if nothing happened.

Walking closer, Callan studies the Staff, which looks no different than it did a second ago. "Let me try again. I think I can get it a little stronger."

"Don't burn yourself out," Marcus cautions.

"Yeah, right." Callan snorts in reply.

Cocky bastard.

He does the same thing as before, but this time he clenches his hands into fists. This time I notice how the large muscles in his arms bulge. As irritating as he can be, he has nice arms. Very nice.

His yell is more guttural this time as he claps and sends an even bigger beam of light at the Staff. Again, I prepare for impact.

Nothing.

"Let me try," Kassiel says. "I don't have my full strength, but I have enough to tell if it's going to absorb my power."

He holds his hands in front of him, palm to palm, with about two inches distance between them. Inky black smoke appears and grows into a thick tar-like ball, and he shoves it toward the Staff.

The Staff flares with darkness this time, and again absorbs the power.

"Maybe we should stop," Tanwen says. "For all we know, you two just made it stronger."

I let out a long sigh. "You're right, this is getting us nowhere."

"This is one of the most powerful relics in all history," Eveanna says. "Created by the great Culann himself and imbued with the essence of the strongest of demons and angels. It can't be destroyed with simple magic or violence."

"So what do we do with it?" Jonah asks.

"We'll have to hide it," I say.

"Where?" Kassiel asks.

There's only one place. "The bell tower. No one goes up there but us. We'll shove it in a closet and Eveanna can glamour it to look like a broom or something. Hide it in plain sight."

"Azrael or Grace might come looking for it," Bastien says.

"We can create a diversion," Marcus says. "Make it seem like Eveanna took the Staff to Faerie or something."

"I can spread some rumors among the Valkyries along those lines," Tanwen says. "I'd bet a million bucks at least one of them is in the Order."

"We can make sure Jeremy overhears us talking about it too," Araceli adds.

"It's decided then," I say. "We'll each take turns hanging out in the bell tower to make sure the Staff is never unguarded for long, while we research how to destroy it. There must be something in Seraphim's library that can help us."

Or so I hope.

21

OLIVIA

The next morning, Eveanna packs all her things, informs Uriel she is returning to Faerie, and disappears from campus. In truth, she's moved into a guest room in Marcus and Callan's house while glamouring herself to look like an angel, but the trick works. Tanwen helps spread the rumor that Eveanna's returned to Faerie, and Jonah and I chat about how we miss her loudly during Human Studies to make sure Jeremy overhears. No one ambushes me and interrogates me on where the Staff is, so I assume the Order believes the ruse.

But we know the con won't last forever. Eventually the Order will realize the Staff is still on Earth. We need to destroy it before they come looking for it.

Weeks pass, and none of us find anything, and every day I get more frustrated. I've spent much of my free time in the library, pouring through books on fae relics, but there's little information on the Staff. The others aren't having any luck either. Kassiel's returned to Lucifer to give him a report and to see if he could learn anything that would help us, but hasn't returned yet. Bastien's scoured Uriel's private library, to no avail. Callan went to visit his mother for a weekend under the guise of speaking to her about his career prospects, while trying to get information from her on the Order or the Staff. When he returned, he refused to talk about it, so I assume it didn't go well.

After another unproductive session in the library, I return to my dorm to work on an essay for Immortal Ethics, but as soon as I open the door I freeze. There are two women inside I don't recognize, just sitting on my couch. They both glance over and smile when I enter, and I quickly yank out my daggers. Has the Order come for me?

"Who are you? What do you want?" I ask.

Both girls laugh. "It's us," one of them says, and then her form shimmers and fades away, until all I see is Araceli. "Eveanna's been teaching me how to glamour myself."

Eveanna's glamour fades away too, and soon I'm looking at her pointed ears and green hair again. "Araceli is a fast learner. Though all fae can do a few paltry glamours, very few can change their appearance so quickly and thoroughly."

"I have a good teacher," Araceli says.

"That's really great," I tell them. I'm so glad Araceli can embrace her fae side and learn these things from Eveanna. She's been a lot happier this year, and I think this is a big reason why.

The other reason seems to be my brother, but I try to ignore that.

They try changing themselves to look like men next, and I head into my room to work on my paper. Simiel insists on making us write these ten-page essays on ethics every couple weeks and they're such a drag, especially when I have more important things to worry about at the moment.

I throw my bag into my desk chair and turn toward my closet to change into some comfier clothes, but then I spot a brown paper bag on my bed. Instantly apprehensive, I approach slowly and knock the bag over. When nothing comes shooting out of it, I grab it between my fingers and carefully open it.

Inside is a bag of my favorite coffee from Angel Peak, along with a note. From Callan.

Hope you enjoy the coffee.

I crumple the note up into a ball and hurl it into the trash. How dare he sneak into my room again! My blood boils at the thought of him in here, poking around like he did when he trashed the place two years ago. He should know better than to come in here without my permission. After his speech about how he was trying to change and be better, he's still doing shit like this, and just thinks it's okay?

Hell no.

I toss the bag of coffee on the bed, throw open my sliding doors, and launch off my balcony while going invisible. A few minutes later I land on the porch of Callan's house, then bang on the door as hard as I can. I already know Marcus is gone—he's in Arizona visiting his mom and brother—so I'm sure Callan will be the one to answer. When he does, I'll have a lot of words for him.

Callan jerks the door open with a murderous look on his face, wearing nothing but a towel. Water drips down his chest. His very large, sculpted chest. Oh, damn it.

When he sees it's me, his expression softens a little. "Hey. Is everything okay?"

I tear my gaze away from his amazing, muscular body, and shoot daggers at him with my eyes. "Who do you think you are? Leaving something like that in my dorm room?"

"Come inside." He holds open the door so I can step into the house. As soon as it's closed, he faces me down with annoyance in his voice. "Excuse me for trying to get you a gift. I thought you would like the coffee."

"Yes, I like it! But I don't like you going in my room without my permission!"

He gives a casual shrug, making the hard muscles roll in a way that is very difficult to ignore. "I figured you wouldn't want to see me, so I dropped it off. I know you love the coffee at that shop in Angel Peak, so I got you some to show I was thinking of you. Remind me never to do something nice for you again."

I blow out a long breath and try to keep my voice even as I explain. "I appreciate the gift, but if you were truly thinking of me, you would've considered how it would feel to have you invade my space again, after you destroyed it last time."

"I did think about that," he snaps. "But I thought you were over it. You got me back for that. You forgave me. We were past all that."

"Obviously not!"

He walks into the kitchen as he shakes his head. "What do you want me to do? I admitted to making mistakes in the past. I told you I'm trying to do better. I gave you a gift to show I care. Tell me what else I can do!"

"I don't know!" I yell back as I follow him. "I get that you're trying, but your gifts and apologies are meaningless. You're still never going to say the word 'sorry.' I'm not sure you'll ever be able to share me with Kassiel. Has anything between us really changed?"

He lets out a frustrated growl and yanks me toward him, then slants his mouth over mine. I dig my fingers into his massive shoulders as I kiss him back, unable to help myself. We haven't touched in months, and now that we've started, we can't seem to stop. My hands roam his strong chest, his hard back, his perfect hips, while his fingers tangle in my hair, moving my head so he can get a better angle to devour my mouth. And hot damn, does he devour it.

His mouth leaves mine as he presses his towel-covered hips against me. "Admit it. You want me as much as I want you."

I push against his chest, but his hands tighten in my hair, which only turns me on even more. I glare up at him. "I hate you."

"You know what they say about that thin line." He pulls my head back and presses his lips to my neck. I practically melt against him. My body explodes with desire, but my brain is offended that I'm so turned on. Blame it on my succubus hormones. Not because I need Callan so badly I can't think straight. Or because I might actually care about him. No way.

I tell myself hate-sex with Callan is probably a good thing, anyway. I slept with Kassiel after he was healed up, but otherwise I've been relying too much on Bastien and Marcus. I don't want to hurt them. I need to bang someone else, fast.

Yes. This is my excuse.

"We both know you just wanted a reason to come over here," Callan says, against my neck. It's like he can't help but try to piss me off.

"You wish."

He takes my chin in his strong grip and looks me in the eyes, challenging me as always. "Tell me to stop and I will."

I grab the towel and yank it off his hips. "Don't you dare fucking stop."

He lets out a throaty, arrogant laugh and steps back so I can get a good, long look at his naked body. That muscular chest. Those defined hips. That hard cock.

Then, when I've practically drooled all over myself, he grabs my waist and yanks me against him, pressing that irresistible body against me. He claims me with a burning hot kiss and I reach down to grab his cock, squeezing it tight.

"Put this inside me already," I demand.

"So fucking bossy." He spins me around and bends me face-down over the island, then yanks my skirt up. "Don't you know I'm in charge around here?"

"Never." Except I secretly love how he takes control in the bedroom.

His large fingers rip my panties off, and then he's reaching between my legs, feeling how soaked I am for him. He lets out a low, masculine sound of approval, and then he forces my legs wider and moves behind me. With one hard thrust, he fills me up, hips flush against my ass, his body caging me against the countertop.

"That what you want?" he asks, as he pulls out and then slams back into me.

I lift up a little and turn to glare at him. "Shut up and fuck me."

"Maybe I want to take my time." He kneads my butt cheeks, the tip of his dick still inside me. "Damn, I could look at this perfect ass all day."

Impatient, I push my hips back, making him fill me up again. He gets the hint, and with his hands on my ass he begins a steady glide, in and out, back and forth, give and take. Our bodies move together in perfect harmony, in a way that only happens when we're having sex.

Then I feel his large finger tracing my back entrance, sending all new feelings through me. He bends over my back, his lips on my ear, as he probes me from behind. "One day, I'm going to put my cock in here. You want that, don't you?"

I can't speak, not with him pumping into me so hard I'm moving back and forth along the countertop, but my moans must be enough for him. He slides his finger into my ass, thrusting into me in time with his cock. The sensations that shoot through me are almost overwhelming.

I always knew he was an ass man.

His other hand reaches between us and finds my clit, taking the pleasure to another level. He controls my body like it belongs to him, and maybe it does, at least at this moment. Another finger enters me from behind. His pressure on my clit increases. His thrusts grow harder and faster. He's pushing me to the edge, but I'm not falling without him.

An orgasm explodes like fireworks through my body. I moan even louder and throw my head back, my hips moving in time with Callan's cock and fingers, taking everything he can give me. I feel his energy slam into me like a freight train as he climaxes too. Fuck, I forgot how strong he is. His powerful light fills me up until it's practically spilling out of me. Damn, I missed this.

I missed *him*.

Callan gives my ass a tender squeeze as he pulls out of me. I regret the loss of connection immediately. I could do this all night long and never get enough of him. I spin around and face him with challenge in my eyes, but then he kisses me, softer this time. Almost...tenderly.

The front door slams shut, and we freeze. Marcus walks into the kitchen and raises his eyebrows, a bemused expression on his face. "Well, it's about time you two made up."

I realize what this must look like. "We did *not* make up."

Callan, still naked and glistening with sweat and sex, bends over and grabs his towel. "Isn't that what we just did?"

I yank my skirt down and pick up my ruined panties. "You've got a lot to learn."

Without another word, I stalk out of the kitchen.

22

OLIVIA

Two days later, I arrive back at my dorm and find a bouquet of red roses with a note that says, *Better?* I sigh and throw the note away but set the roses on prominent display on the dining table. At least Callan got the hint.

We're no closer to finding out how to destroy the Staff and I'm starting to get antsy, but I have a new plan. If Seraphim Academy's library doesn't have anything, maybe Hellspawn Academy's will. Baal invited me there over a year ago and I turned him down, but I assume the offer still stands. Besides, I'd like to embrace my demon side even more.

The opportunity comes at the first sporting event this year, which is being held at Hellspawn Academy. The sport this year is basketball, and since I'm not friends with anyone on the team I couldn't care less about the game, but a free ride to Hellspawn Academy is exactly what I need right now.

The guys are against it, of course, but do they control me? No, they do not.

It isn't too hard to convince Uriel to let me go, since there have been no Duskhunter attacks all year, but he did give me one condition: I had to take someone with me for protection. I grumbled and asked my brother, who wanted to go anyway since he loves sports.

So here we are, joining the basketball team and their guests as we head out into the forest. I have no idea where we're going, but excitement makes my blood race. I've always been curious about Hellspawn Academy and now I finally get to visit it.

Hilda and Raziel chaperone the students, and they stop in front of two trees whose branches have fused together, forming an arch. Raziel touches a certain spot on it and says a few words in Latin, and then the arch shimmers and a door forms between it, made from golden light. This school continues to surprise me with its secrets, even after all this time.

"This doorway was built between Seraphim Academy and Hellspawn Academy about thirty years ago, after the Earth Accords were signed and the yearly sports games were established," Raziel says, loving this opportunity to lecture us on some angel-demon history. He adjusts his basketball-covered bowtie and opens the door, through which we see another forest that doesn't line up with this one. "It's a symbol of the peace between our two schools and—"

"Yeah, yeah, enough history," Hilda says, as she waves us forward. "Let's get in there and kick some demon ass!"

The basketball team cheers and begins heading through the magical doorway. I give Jonah an excited smile before following them. There's a slight tickle against my skin as I walk through the glowing door, and then I'm in a different forest. The trees are shorter, skinnier, and closer together, with lighter colored leaves. The crisp, mountain air has been replaced by a warm, earthy scent. We've gone from northern California to upstate New York in the blink of an eye.

A small contingent of demons awaits us on the other side, led by Baal, the vampire Archdemon and the headmaster of Hellspawn Academy—and one of my mother's former lovers, apparently. The others are probably professors here, and they range from a somber woman wearing a black dress that looks like it was from the Victorian era, complete with a veil over her face, to a scruffy guy in jeans and a well-worn t-shirt with a raven sitting on his shoulder. I'm super curious about them, but I hang back with Jonah while Hilda and Raziel speak with Baal about the game. After a few minutes they wave for the team and the guests to follow them. They take off with the Hellspawn professors, but Baal holds up a hand for me to wait.

He looks like an old-school vampire with long black hair and an all-black suit, and he's mouth-wateringly handsome and oozing power, money, and age. I can see why Lilith would go for him. "Welcome to Hellspawn Academy, Olivia. It's about time you visited us."

"Thanks. I tried to come last year, but Uriel said it was a bad idea with the Duskhunter attacks." I gesture to Jonah, who keeps glancing past Baal at the basketball team as they walk away. "This is my brother, Jonah."

"A pleasure." Baal begins heading in the same direction through the trees. "I'd like to give you a tour of our school, and I'd be happy to answer any questions you have about it, or about demons in general. Unless you'd like to watch the game, of course."

"No, I'd love a tour," I say. "If possible, I'd like to visit the library. I'm trying to research some of the darker, more dangerous fae relics for a paper I'm writing, and the Seraphim library isn't cutting it."

Baal lifts his chin. "I'm sure their library is extensive, but heavily curated to protect the students from many dark truths. Here, we embrace such darkness. I'm sure you'll find what you're looking for among our shelves."

"Thank you." I knew appealing to his ego would work.

We emerge through the trees to a massive, emerald green lawn with a perfectly trimmed hedge and purple flowers leading to a courtyard with a large fountain. It's dwarfed by an imposing, gothic building in dark grey stone with pointed arches, tall paned windows, and a black roof with a few stone gargoyles on the corners. Beyond it, I spot other smaller buildings in the same style, and a dark stone path leading to them.

"Our grounds once belonged to a human university, but we took it over when they shut down during the Great Depression," Baal explains, as he leads us past the main building along the winding path. "This is the main building, Archfiend Hall, which houses my office, the library, and some of the classrooms. You may notice this campus is somewhat larger than Seraphim Academy, and we have about double the students. Our other main differences from your school are that we start at eighteen instead of twenty-one, we hold classes year-round but give more frequent breaks, and our school is entirely optional."

"Demons don't need to attend?" I ask, surprised. I was told Seraphim Academy was mandatory, and I assumed that was true of Hellspawn also.

"No. In fact, many demon families prefer to train their young themselves, in particular the vampire houses and shifter clans."

"If that's true, why do you have so many more students than Seraphim does?" Jonah asks.

Baal lets out a haughty laugh. "Do they not teach you these things? Interesting. Demons outnumber angels on Earth by about four to one. We came here in much larger numbers throughout history and have been breeding here ever since. Vampires and shifters are the largest in number, while dragons are the rarest. We also teach many Cambion here—those who are half human."

I'm learning a lot of things they never mentioned at Seraphim, and it makes me wonder what it would be like to be a student here. I was treated poorly when people thought I was half-human—are Cambion treated any better at Hellspawn?

Baal leads us on a quick tour around the massive school grounds, revealing a myriad of outdoor activities, including tennis courts and swimming pools. Behind the tennis courts, we enter a large indoor stadium that puts our gym to shame. We stand on the sidelines and watch a few minutes of the game, before heading outside again. Jonah keeps glancing back inside, dragging his heels as Baal continues the tour.

"Go. Watch the game," I tell him. "I'll be fine."

My brother flashes a look at Baal with a frown. "I'm not sure..."

"Olivia will be perfectly safe here on campus," Baal says. "She's under Lucifer's protection, as well as my own. And unlike Seraphim Academy, we haven't had an attack during any of our games in a decade."

Jonah still hesitates, but then a huge cheer goes up in the stadium, and he relents. "All right. As long as you're okay with it."

"Very okay with it. We both know you'd be bored to tears in the library." I'm actually excited to do this alone, without anyone watching over me. I can almost pretend I'm just another student here.

Jonah heads back into the gym, and Baal continues our tour. He shows me the food court, which has a bunch of different restaurants, and the student housing, before adding, "We also have many class-rooms and tunnels underground, in the dark depths below the school. We are demons, of course."

Of course.

"As I mentioned before, our library is housed under Archfiend Hall," Baal says, as he leads me back to the large gothic building we first saw. He opens a thick black door for me, and I step into a grand entrance with rich, dark wood and a sweeping staircase that twists around after splitting in the middle. The windows dim the bright afternoon sunlight from outside, and a huge black chandelier hangs above us with tiny crystals dangling from it.

"This way." Baal takes me around the back of the staircase to another one that leads deep underground. He stops in front of black double doors carved with intricate designs and opens both with a flourish.

We enter a large circular space with tables in the center and bookshelves that stretch all the way up to the top of the very tall ceil-ing, complete with those skinny ladders that roll along the shelves. A few hallways lead off into other similar rooms with more massive bookshelves. It's a shame Bastien isn't here—he would love this place.

Baal speaks to a redhaired woman behind a counter, and she nods and points to one of the hallways. Baal gestures for me to follow, and we pass some students who openly stare at me with a mixture of awe, fear, and hatred like I'm used to getting at Seraphim Academy. Will I ever fit in anywhere? Probably not. Not 'til angels and demons have better relations, anyway. I want to make that happen, somehow.

Baal takes me into an adjoining room and gestures to a large section of books. "These shelves house everything we have on fae relics. You're welcome to stay as long as you would like to do your research."

"Thank you." My eyes scan the massive bookshelves. "Would it be possible to return here again? To continue my studies if I can't finish up today?"

Baal's eyes gleam in triumph. "You are always welcome at Hellspawn. In fact, there's still a spot for you here, if you'd like. We'd love to have you attend the school. Even for only a few days a week."

"Unfortunately, I don't have time for that right now, but I'd love to come visit sometimes."

He nods. "Of course. You may use the doorway in the forest anytime you desire. Before you leave, I will show you how to open it from our side."

"That would be great, thanks."

"If you are satisfied, I will leave you to your research. Simply let the librarian know when you wish to depart." He starts to leave and then pauses in the arched doorway. "Actually, there is one more matter to discuss. I'd like to invite you to Lucifer's Ball."

"What is that?" I ask.

"It's the social event of the school year, similar to a high school prom, I suppose. The graduating class is presented to Lucifer by their parents and he gives them his blessing before they go out into the world. It's a tradition going back oh, hundreds of years. There's also food, wine, and dancing, of course. We'd love for you to come. If you don't wish to be presented by your mother, I'd be happy to do it myself."

"That sounds nice," I say, although it sounds terrifying too. A fancy ball surrounded by demons I don't know, who will all be staring at me and wondering who my mother is? Hmm. "I'll think about it."

"Please do. Lucifer himself has requested your presence there."

Well, shit. Now I can't say no, can I? Not when I'm seeing his son.

Baal gives me another nod and then departs, and I start pulling out some books. I probably won't find anything today, but at least I have a new place to look, and it sounds like I can come back anytime I want. I'm not a student of Hellspawn Academy and never will be, but I have to admit, I like the idea of coming to visit sometimes.

23

KASSIEL

I slowly run my hands through Olivia's dark curls, careful not to wake her. It's a rare, wonderful thing to have her asleep beside me, and for once I'm grateful for my night owl tendencies.

I haven't seen Olivia in weeks, and it's good to be back again, even if we have to meet in a motel room. After I was rescued, I wanted nothing more than to stay with Liv, but that wasn't possible. For one thing, I'm no longer welcome at Seraphim Academy or in Angel Peak now that everyone knows who I am. More importantly, I had to report back to my father, especially since he dared to enter angel territory to find me. I was shocked when Liv gave me the run-down of Lucifer's visit, but pleased that he seemed to like her. I hope to properly introduce them again someday. Maybe at the ball, if Liv agrees to go. I understand why she's hesitant, but I think it's important for her to start moving in the demon world too, and this would be a good start.

Thinking about my father makes my stomach twist. He was relieved to see me alive, and although I gave him a complete report about what happened, I lied to him about the Staff. I told him Eveanna took it back to Faerie, going along with the story the others concocted, but even now I feel conflicted about it. I've never lied to my father before.

At some point, my loyalty shifted from Lucifer to Olivia. I know why, of course. There's no denying my feelings when I'm around her. But as a succubus, Olivia is never going to be satisfied with only one lover. I'll always have to share her with the angels too. It's not the sharing I have a problem with though, but the men themselves. I'm not sure they'll ever accept me as one of them.

A soft knock at the motel room door interrupts my turbulent thoughts. I slip out of bed, trying not to disturb Liv, and grab my sword. When I look through the peephole, I'm surprised to see Callan illuminated in the light in front of the door.

I stand back with a frown, debating what to do, and decide to keep the sword handy. Unless there's an emergency, there's no reason for him to be here unless he wants to pick a fight with me for sleeping with Olivia.

I unlock the door and slip outside, trying not to disturb Olivia. "What are you doing here?"

"We need to talk," Callan says, his eyes hard.

I gesture at him with the sword. "Talk away."

"I know Lucifer didn't kill my father."

His blunt declaration leaves me somewhat speechless. "Is that so?"

"I was wrong about you." He looks like the words leave a sour taste in his mouth, but he continues. "I was wrong to judge you based on what I thought your father did, anyway."

"I appreciate you saying that...." I'm not sure where he's going with this, and I keep expecting a 'but' to show up somewhere, followed by a speech about how I'm evil and should stay away from Olivia. Although I'm told he went out of his way to help me after I was tortured, which never made sense to me. "And I appreciate your help rescuing me."

Callan nods. "You never broke. You didn't give us up. I respect that."

"I would never do that." I glance back at the closed motel room door. "I care about her too much."

His jaw clenches. "That's why I'm here. I care about her too, and if we're both going to be in her life, we need to come to terms with the arrangement."

I cross my arms. "I never had a problem with it, until you did."

"Well, I don't anymore. Not exactly." He gives me a challenging stare. "We want the same things—to keep Olivia safe and happy, and to destroy the Staff. And I think we'd both like to find out who really killed Michael."

One of my eyebrows arches up. "Yes, I hope to clear my father's name someday."

"Our fathers wanted peace between angels and demons. Together they ended the war between Heaven and Hell." Callan thrusts his hand toward me. "This isn't easy for me, but I'd like for us to work together too."

I'm too shocked to move at first, but then I accept his peace offering. "I'd like that very much."

After we shake hands, Callan nods toward the door. "I'll leave you to it then."

He walks away and gets into his red sportscar, while all I can do is stand there replaying the last few minutes in my head and wondering if they really happened.

The door opens behind me, and a sleepy Olivia joins me outside while Callan's car speeds away. "Was that Callan?"

I wrap my arms around her and lead her back inside. "Yeah. He apologized...in his own way. He wants us to work together."

Her jaw drops. "Wow. I never thought I'd see the day. Maybe he really is trying to change."

I stroke her cheek softly. "I'm sure you're the reason for it. He seems to truly care about you. In fact, he told me so."

"Did he?" She shakes her head, still in shock.

"We all do." I pick her up and carry her back to bed. "More than you know."

"Hmm, maybe you should show me," she says with a naughty little smile.

So I do. All night long. And when we're both thoroughly worn out and satisfied, I curl up around her and whisper into her hair that I love her.

24

OLIVIA

What am I supposed to wear to dinner with Bastien *and* Uriel? I settle for my nicest pair of jeans and a silk blouse with the buttons done up all the way to my neck. After putting on a minimal layer of makeup and clipping my hair in a low bun, I'm ready.

Ugh, I look like a librarian. I let my hair down and shake it out, then pop the top two buttons of my shirt and stick out my chest. Great, now I look like a sexy librarian. Oh well. It's not like Uriel hasn't seen me while I'm out and about on campus. I can't help being a succubus. Being sexy is like breathing for me.

I fly straight to Uriel's Victorian house on the far side of campus, worried I took too long and might be late. Landing on the porch, I smooth my shirt and tuck a flyaway piece of hair back. As I raise my hand to knock, the door opens.

Uriel inclines his head at me. "Welcome, Olivia. Please come in."

"Thank you." Now what do I say? Uriel has always treated me well, but our interactions were in a more official capacity before. "Hope you're well."

He pauses after closing the door and the corners of his mouth tilt up. "Indeed."

Bastien walks down the hallway, saving us from further awkward small talk. Giving him a genuine smile, I step toward him, about to hold out my arms for a kiss, then stop myself. I can't greet him like that in front of Uriel. "Hello, Bastien."

Bastien stands in front of me with his hands at his side. His gaze flits from me to his dad and back, then he kisses me lightly on the cheek. "Thank you for coming tonight."

Their dining room is gigantic, with an enormous cherry wood table with hand-carved decorations along the side of birds in flight. Bastien holds out a chair to the left of the head of the table, and I nearly laugh at how formal and awkward this is, except I wouldn't dare do such a thing in front of Uriel.

Bastien scoots the chair under me and then he and his father sit at the exact same time, like some sort of planned synchronization. Uriel's seated at the head of the table, with the two of us on either side of him. The plates have gilded edges and the silverware looks just as fancy, and I'm pretty sure I'm in way over my head here. I swallow hard as we sit through the longest moment of silence ever.

An angel I've never seen before walks out of a door in the back of the room carrying a large silver tray. She sets it in front of Uriel and removes the domed lid. An entire roast duck rests on the platter, and we watch as the angel carves the bird and serves us each a portion.

I can't think of a single thing to say, so I sit there with them and wait for a duck breast to be put on my plate. The woman returns three more times with potatoes, vegetables, and rolls. Finally, we begin to eat.

"I'm pleased you could join us tonight," Uriel says, startling me. I'd started to assume we were just going to eat in silence.

"Thank you for inviting me." I take a bite of the duck, which is delicious.

Uriel nods. "I thought it was time we grew more acquainted, since you seem to be an important part of my son's life now."

Bastien clears his throat at that, and I wonder if this was a point of contention between the two of them. Does Uriel have a problem with me seeing his son?

Uriel changes the subject before I can wonder about it too long. "How do you find living with Gabriel?"

I take a sip of water to wash down a bite of potatoes. "It was a little awkward at first," I say, while thinking *nowhere near as awkward as this dinner.* "But it's become more natural as time has gone by."

"And your brother?"

"It's been great having him back. Jonah is a wonderful brother."

"He's fortunate you were able to locate him." He gives Bastien a sharp look at that, and I remember that Bastien's the one who stole Lucifer's feather from Uriel's office. Which we never returned. Oops.

Uriel doesn't speak for several moments as he takes bites of his food, so I pick up my fork and continue. Just as I slice off a piece of duck and wrap my lips around it, he speaks again. "Tell me, what are your plans after graduation?"

I nearly choke on the duck. I have no clue what I'm going to do. I look across the table at Bastien for help, but he's staring at me with rapt attention, as if waiting on the answer himself.

After another sip of water, I say, "I'm not sure yet."

Uriel's lip twitches. I think that means he's not pleased with my answer. "That's unfortunate. There are only a few months left in the school year. Make sure you speak with Professor Rosangela to discuss your options."

"I'll do that, thanks."

"I hope you're finding it possible to keep your other appetites sated even with the ban on leaving campus," Uriel says casually, as if we're talking about the weather or the color of his shirt.

"Father!" Bastien says. "That's hardly proper dinner conversation."

Uriel looks at Bastien as if he's the one being inappropriate. "I was only asking after her welfare."

I school my features into a calm expression instead of the shocked horror his question evoked. "I'm managing, thank you."

"Do you have plans for how you will carry on once school has finished?" Uriel shoots Bastien a quelling look. "You can't expect to settle down with Bastien, given your succubus nature, of course."

This time, I'm pretty sure I can't hide the shock and horror on my face, and I can't even begin to know how to answer that.

Bastien holds up one hand. "What Olivia and I do with our lives after graduation is between us. If I decide it is your business, *I* will let you know."

Bastien and Uriel stare at one another for several painfully long seconds, until Uriel inclines his head. "Very well. I apologize for the personal nature of my questions. We shall move on to a less sensitive topic. Tell me, have you ever been to the symphony?"

Of course I haven't. And things don't get any less awkward after that.

The dinner ages me by about ten years. I'm pretty sure I'll have a gray hair when I wake up tomorrow. But eventually Uriel shows me to the front door and thanks me for coming, and I'm allowed to escape.

"That went better than I expected," Bastien says, as he offers me his arm so he can walk me to my dorm.

"It did?" I laugh at that. "Now I'm wondering what you thought would happen."

He shrugs as we leave the house behind. "I wasn't sure. I've never brought a woman home to meet my father before."

My heart melts a little at that, and I stop in the middle of the lawn and turn toward him. "No one's ever brought me home to meet their parents before either. I don't think Lucifer showing up and scaring the crap out of us counts."

"No, I'd say it doesn't." Bastien's hands rest on my waist. We're not being as discreet as we probably should be, but I don't see anyone nearby either. "I apologize if he offended you with his questions."

"I'm used to everyone being weird about me being a succubus. And he's right, I probably should figure out what I want to do after graduation."

"You've had more pressing things on your mind lately. Perhaps you need to relieve some stress."

I raise an eyebrow. "What do you have in mind?"

"Let's go somewhere a little more private," he says, as his wings spread out behind him.

He takes my hand and we fly above the roof of the gym, which is tall enough that it affords us some privacy.

"Have you ever had sex while in flight?" Bastien asks, his silvery gray wings slowly flapping behind him.

"No. Have you?"

"Not yet, but I've read it's quite the experience."

I've never even considered such a thing, but maybe I should have. After all, if you can fight while flying, you can fuck while flying.

I'm already unbuttoning my jeans. "Let's try it."

Desire flashes in his eyes and he flies toward me as I yank my jeans down, wiggling out of them as fast as I can. He pops open the buttons on my shirt and eases it off me, then quickly removes my bra and panties. It's a warm night, and the moonlight against my bare skin feels wonderful. I wrap some light around us to make us invisible, just in case someone's up late, and hope no one notices the pile of discarded clothes on the gym roof.

Once we're both naked, we come together, kissing, stroking, melting into one. Slow wingbeats keep us flying in place, and then he wraps my legs around his hips and glides his thick cock into me. He takes my hand and puts it on top of his dark wings.

"Touch them," he says.

I hesitate, never having touched another angel's feathers before. It's an intimate act only done with people you're close to. People you love. Then he grabs my ass and rocks my body with his, his cock sinking deeper into me, and I have no choice but to obey him.

I lightly rest my fingers on his wings, feeling how smooth they are, and then stroke them gently along their length. Bastien closes his eyes, his throat clenching. His feathers are longer than mine, but I think mine are softer. The silver parts are particularly rough, as if they're brushed with metal. That needs exploring further.

He groans and lowers his head to kiss me. While I continue touching his wings, he moves in and out of me in lazy, decadent strokes. His eyes gaze into mine the entire time, and everything about this moment is intimate. It's not just sex, but so much more.

Bastien takes it to the next level as he suddenly runs a finger along the top of my wings, making me shudder. "Your wings are the most beautiful I've ever seen."

I've never felt anything like this before, with our bodies joined as one, our wings beating to keep us in the air, and our fingers stroking each other's feathers. It's both arousing and soothing, all at once.

Bastien begins to pick up the pace, his wings moving to push him deeper inside me. He hits me at the exact right spot to make me moan, and I clutch his wings reflexively. They flex under my hands, the soft feathers shifting against my grip.

"Olivia!" he cries out.

Oh, he likes that. He thrusts into me harder as I hold onto his feathers, and he grips mine too. With each flap of his wings he drives me higher and higher, pushing me up so gravity brings me back down hard on his cock. An orgasm breaks over me unexpectedly, and I moan through the intense pleasure, clutching Bastien for dear life as my body squeezes around him. He lets out a low groan as he loses himself inside me, and I stroke his wings until he's finished.

"Put your wings away," he says.

Without arguing, I do it, and he wraps his arms around me. Carrying me like a bride, he flies us across the campus and I distantly think about how we'll have to fetch our clothes later. At this moment, I really don't care if I never see them again.

We enter my dorm through the balcony, and he gently sets me on the bed, before settling in beside me. Neither of us speaks, until he presses a soft kiss to my lips. "Olivia," he whispers. "Do you know how I feel about you?"

I shake my head, although I'm pretty sure I have an idea. I just want to hear him say it.

"It's been quite a surprise to me." His hands glide up and down my stomach absently. "I didn't expect to develop real feelings for you."

I lift a hand to his jaw. "Bastien..."

He takes my hand and kisses it. "It's a curious thing. I've examined the situation thoroughly, and I'm certain I've fallen in love with you."

His words shock me to my core. I didn't expect him to just flat out admit it like that.

"I never believed I was capable of such a thing, until I met you," he says.

I let out a sigh. "I'm not sure I am either."

"If I can, then there's hope for anyone."

He presses his lips to mine, and emotions surge inside me. They feel a lot like love, but what does a succubus know of love?

25

OLIVIA

The night of Lucifer's Ball comes before I know it. Kassiel convinced me to go with him, even though my mother won't be there. Last weekend the girls took me shopping, and I spent way too much money on a new dress and accessories. It amuses me to no end that I've been saving my monthly stipend from Aerie Industries all this time, and now I'm blowing a huge chunk of it so I can go to a demon ball. I'm sure their Order members would just love that.

Besides, this dress is worth it. It's the sexiest thing I've ever had on my body. Including lingerie. It's made of the softest red silk and is backless, scooping all the way down so it almost shows the curve of my ass. The front would be demure, with a high neckline and long sleeves, except the dress hugs my curves in a way that makes it clear I'm wearing nothing underneath. The hem brushes the ground and hides the black pumps I chose to wear with it.

I spin in the mirror, checking myself out one last time, admiring the expensive lipstick that perfectly matches the dress, the bare expanse of my back, and the way the fabric clasps at my shoulder with a delicate silver flower. If nothing else I'll be turning heads tonight, as a proper succubus should.

I can't find my matching black purse so I fly over to the Princess

Lounge, where the regular crew is watching Lord of the Rings. Jonah and Araceli sit together on one couch, with Tanwen and Eveanna on the other, and they all look very cozy sharing popcorn and beer. It makes my chest swell with pride and happiness to see them all hanging out like best friends, even if I can't join them tonight.

"I'm telling you," Jonah's saying, as I step inside. "Tolkien knew some fae. He had to."

"I suppose there are some similarities," Eveanna reluctantly admits.

Araceli squeals as soon as she sees me. "Girl, you look sexy as hell! Err, no pun intended."

"Thanks." I grab my purse. "I'll be back in a few hours."

"Have fun, but not too much fun," Jonah says, and then Araceli shoves him playfully. Yep, she's still got it bad. Jonah grins and shoves her back though, which gives me hope.

I fly slowly to the forest so I don't mess up my hair, and then open the doorway just like Baal taught me. As soon as it shimmers into view and opens up to Hellspawn Academy, I spot Kassiel on the other side, looking good enough to eat in a black tuxedo. And I thought he looked good in a suit. Damn.

A smile spreads across his lips. "Wow," he whispers. "You're..."

I walk through the doorway and give him a slow twirl. "You like?"

His lust slams into me like a bullet. "You know I do."

His hands are all over me, touching my waist, my arms, then he leans in for a kiss. He doesn't even hesitate with the threat of red lipstick all over him. The brand promised it wouldn't smear, and it was right. When he pulls back from the searing kiss, his lips are lipstick-free, so it was money well spent.

The doorway closes behind us. On this side, it's made of shadowy darkness instead of light, and only those with demon blood can activate it, just like only angels can activate it from the Seraphim side. Lucky for me, I can do both.

Kassiel takes my arm, and together we walk out of the forest. The campus is pitch black, except for some magical twinkling lights hovering at eye-level that look like tiny stars, leading us to another building just past Archfiend Hall. This one is called Morningstar Hall, and I hear the soft sound of classical music coming from its closed doors.

"All of the graduating seniors attend this event," Kassiel says, as he leads me around the back of the building, instead of through the open doors. "They walk down the stairs one by one and meet their parents, who present them to Lucifer. You will be going last, as a guest of honor."

I nod and try to ignore how nervous I am. "Did you have to go through this too? Or is that not required when you're the son of the guy you're being presented to?"

He laughs softly. "No, I was raised and schooled in Hell, not here on Earth. The school didn't exist when I was a child."

Oh. Right. Sometimes I forget he's over a century older than me.

He leads me into the back of the hall and up some stairs, where a man in a suit is waiting for us. He speaks with Kassiel quietly and nods, before stepping back. After another minute, the door opens and Kassiel puts his hand on my elbow to lead me inside.

We step into the upper level of an enormous ballroom with tall windows and doors that open onto balconies under the night sky. It's stunningly beautiful, but black crystal chandeliers and gold filigree trim can't distract me from the horde of demons below. I've never been around so many demons before, not even at the sports games or when I visit the library here. And these aren't all students. Their parents are here too. Their old, powerful parents.

The man who let us inside raises his voice. "Presenting Kassiel, son of Lucifer, and Olivia Monroe."

My legs don't want to move, but Kassiel nudges me forward to a sweeping staircase with a red carpet leading down it. The crowd murmurs as we slowly descend, and I pray I don't trip on these heels or drop my purse. I'm not especially clumsy, but it would be just my luck to ruin this moment in front of everyone. If I were a normal student, my mother would meet me at the bottom and take me to meet Lucifer. But I'm not normal. At least Kassiel is by my side.

I gaze across the great hall, trying not to look down, and spot

Baal in the crowd. He's met me in the library a couple of times when I came to research and I've gotten to know him a bit better. While he's still severe and a little scary, he's become sort of endearing too.

Then my eyes move to the bottom of the staircase and I freeze. Standing there in the crowd is a gorgeous woman wearing a long black dress that looks as if it's covered with tiny diamonds, giving the impression of stars in the night.

My mother.

As my foot hits the bottom of the stairs, Lilith steps forward and holds out her hand. Several people gasp. I blink back tears, trying to keep my face composed, as I realize what she's doing. I always secretly hoped she would show up tonight, but I never thought it would happen.

She's officially claiming me as her daughter.

I take her hand, and she gives me a dazzling smile that could bring kings and queens to their knees. The crowd parts without a word, though I hear shocked whispers tittering throughout the group. Kassiel follows a step behind us as we slowly walk down the red carpet. As people move aside, I get a good view of Lucifer sitting on a massive black throne up ahead. His shadowy wings are spread behind him and a silver crown sits on his forehead.

Lilith stops a few feet in front of him and bows. "My lord, I wish to present my daughter, Olivia."

I quickly copy her and rise when she does. Even though I've met Lucifer before, it's hard not to be intimidated by him. The power and majesty radiating off him is undeniable.

Lucifer looks me in the eye with the hint of a smile upon his sensual lips. "Nice to see you again, Olivia."

"My lord," I murmur softly, unsure what I'm supposed to say in this situation.

He makes a twirling gesture and the small orchestra starts playing again. He then rises from his throne, and his wings vanish. "May I have this dance?'

It takes me a second to realize he means me. Before I can respond, he takes my hand and sweeps me off to the side. In case enough people weren't staring at me already.

Lucifer puts one hand on the small of my back while the other holds my hand. I put my other hand, the one holding my tiny clutch, on his shoulder, as the music begins. Is this the time to mention to the King of Demons that I don't know how to dance? Probably not.

Then we're off. The crowd moves to the edges of the room, revealing a big dance floor. Before I know what's happening, Lucifer takes the lead, his dancing so skillful that even when I stumble nobody can tell. I catch sight of Kassiel and Lilith dancing gracefully on the other side of the floor. Soon other people join us, kicking off the night in style.

"Thank you," I say, sure nobody can hear me as we move swiftly across the floor.

"No, thank you for rescuing my son. It saved me from having to get involved directly and possibly starting another war."

When the music ends, Lucifer presses a kiss to the back of my hand, and then offers me to his son. I melt all over again at the sight of Kassiel looking incredibly handsome in his black tuxedo, and desire races along my spine as he touches the small of my back.

The night passes by in a whirlwind of introductions and dances. I even dance with Baal and a few other demons my mother introduces me to, and everyone is gracious and seems to be accepting of me. On the surface, anyway. When Lilith turns away, I see the jealous looks and hear the suspicion in their voices. But at this point in my life, I'm used to those.

After a few hours, Lilith drags me outside into one of the alcoves, which is covered in night-blooming jasmine, and we sit on one of the stone benches together. It feels nice to take a break and get off my feet.

"Are you having a good time?" Lilith asks, swirling her wine.

"I am, yes." I turn toward her, noticing how the moonlight only makes her more stunning. "Thank you for coming tonight. It means a lot to me."

She entwines her arm with mine. "It was time. There's no need to hide who you are anymore. Although I do have to ask, what happened to the necklace I gave you?"

I touch my chest reflexively, but of course it's gone. I stopped wearing it because it only made me sad. "The stone in it broke when I was hit with a blast from the Staff of Eternity. I'm sorry."

"How did that happen?"

I sigh and quickly explain everything to her, ending with how we have the Staff hidden away. It's been a while since we saw each other, and we have a lot to catch up on. "Do you know how to the destroy the Staff, by any chance?"

"I don't, but I know the man who would. My former lover Culann is the enchanter who made it, along with your necklace. I could ask him. If I had a way to get to Faerie."

"Damn. I have some fae friends, but no fae relic anymore."

"A fae relic won't be a problem. I still have the ring I use to change my appearance, which was also made by Culann." She downs the last of her wine and stands. "If you take me to your fae friends, one of them can open a portal for me."

I hastily get to my feet. "Right now?"

"Why wait?" She winks at me as we return to the ballroom. "Besides, this party is growing dull. Better to leave now so we make an exit everyone will remember. We need to give them something to gossip about, after all."

I've never been so proud to be her daughter before.

26

OLIVIA

W e pay our respects to Lucifer, and then I give Kassiel a goodnight kiss, both of us sad that we can't spend the rest of the evening together, especially when we're dressed as we are. I promise him I'll wear the dress again sometime, and then I lead Lilith into the shadowy doorway to Seraphim Academy's side. We both bend down and take off our heels with a short laugh, and then I make us invisible as we continue toward the school.

"I'm looking forward to meeting the rest of your men," Lilith says, as we walk through the forest. "Although I suppose I've already met Bastien, even though he didn't know it." Last year, Lilith came to train me as a succubus under the disguise of a woman named Delilah. I'm not even sure Uriel knew her real identity.

"They might all be asleep," I say, realizing it must be the middle of the night by now. "It's late."

"Ah yes, I didn't think of that." She lifts her diamond-covered dress to step over a rock. "Sunlovers, we used to call them during the war."

I love getting this glimpse of the past. "And what did they call demons?"

"Nightwalkers."

We make it back to the bell tower, and to my surprise, everyone is there and awake. Mostly. Marcus is passed out on the couch, but Callan jumps up as soon as I walk into the Princess Lounge. "Are you okay?"

"I'm fine," I ask, while mother hangs back in the hall, probably trying not to startle them with her presence. "What are you all doing awake at this hour?"

Marcus sits up and rubs sleep from his eyes "Callan's been like a little old lady, worried the whole time you've been gone. He wouldn't leave, so we thought we'd keep him company."

Bastien stands as well, but that's his nature. "Welcome back, Olivia."

Jonah, Araceli, Tanwen, and Eveanna look at us from the table. They're playing some sort of card game. "Did you have fun?" Araceli asks.

"I did. And there's someone I'd like you all to meet." I turn toward the door as Lilith saunters inside, her jeweled dress sparkling like stars under the light. Every head swings around to her as she crosses the room. "This is my mother. Lilith."

"It's a pleasure to meet you all," she purrs, and the look of shock on all their faces is priceless. I wish I had a camera to capture it.

Marcus steps forward first and gives her an unexpected hug. "It's so nice to finally meet you. I'm Marcus."

"I see Raphael's charm in you," she says, patting his cheeks. When his eyes widen, she laughs. "Don't worry, he's never been my type."

Bastien offers his hand. "It's nice to meet you properly."

"Forgive me for the ruse, but sometimes a little deception is required." Lilith gives him a mischievous smile as she shakes his hand. Her gaze then swings to Callan, who has been standing back this whole time.

"This is Callan," I say, hoping he doesn't say something stupid when faced with an Archdemon.

He steps forward, his movements stiff. Is he...nervous? "It's an honor."

She takes both his hands and looks him in the eyes. "The honor is mine. I can see you have the courage of Michael, the integrity of Jophiel, and a heart that puts both of theirs to shame. How lucky for my daughter that you've given it to her."

She winks at him as he coughs and steps back, his face turning red. All I can do is shake my head. She knows way too much about each of them, but I shouldn't be surprised—she's always been watching over me from the shadows.

I gesture to the others sitting at the table. "This is my brother Jonah, my roommate Araceli, and my friends Tanwen and Eveanna."

Lilith gives each of them a smile and squeezes Jonah on the shoulder. "Thank you for being there for my daughter."

I clear my throat. "Lilith is here because she thinks she can help us with the Staff."

"Yes, I was once intimate with the man who made it. If one of you lovely fae ladies can open me a portal with my relic, I can find him and ask him how to destroy it."

Eveanna slowly rises to her feet and speaks with awe in her voice. "You speak of Culann, master enchanter of the High Court. No one has seen him for many years."

"He's very reclusive, but I know where he lives." Lilith tilts her head with a sly smile. "He might not be happy to see me, but he was never able to resist me for very long. I'll get the information from him." She turns to me. "I can ask him to fix your necklace too."

I consider it, but then shake my head. "Thanks, but I don't need it anymore."

She gives me a proud smile. "No, you don't have to hide now."

"I can take you to Faerie," Araceli says. "I'd love to meet Culann."

Lilith shakes her head. "That is a kind offer, but you're needed here at school, and it will take me a while to find Culann and convince him to give up his secrets. If you open the portal for me, I can go alone."

"I will accompany you on this journey," Eveanna says, in a matter-of-fact tone. "It is unsafe for a demon to travel alone in Faerie."

"But you've been banished from Faerie," Jonah says.

"We shall be careful." She lifts a graceful shoulder in a shrug. "Most believe I am there already. If anyone sees me, it will only reinforce our fabrication. Whereas if I stay here much longer, someone will see through my glamour. It is only a matter of time."

Tanwen rises. "Don't get caught."

The two of them exchange a long look, before Eveanna says, "I was chosen to be the guardian of the Staff of Eternity for a reason. We will not get caught."

"We'll be fine," Lilith says, waving her hand. "I've had centuries to practice hiding from the fae. I can do this on my own without a problem, although I wouldn't mind having someone by my side for the journey."

Lilith removes her ring and hands it to Eveanna. Tanwen gives her a small knife from a sheath on her thigh, and the green-haired fae responds with a nod. Eveanna slices open her hand and clutches the ring in her bloody fist, then says a few words in the fae language while holding out her other hand. A shimmering, swirling portal opens in front of her, just tall enough for the two of them to enter.

Lilith pulls me into a hug. "I'll be back soon with the answer. I promise."

"Thanks, Mom." The word slips out without any thought now. Lilith freezes and her breath catches. She pulls back and looks at me with tears in her eyes, and warmth spreads through my chest. She's moved because I called her mom again. She touches my cheek lovingly before stepping through the portal. Only then do I realize she went in her sparkling dress with no supplies...but she's Lilith. She'll figure it out.

Meanwhile, Araceli and Jonah are shoving the entire contents of our little pantry into a bag for Eveanna to take. Eveanna thanks them, and then turns to Tanwen to give her back her knife. They stare at each other for a heartbeat, and then Tanwen places her hands on Eveanna's shoulders and kisses her. It's a shock to all of us, although I immediately feel the lust stirring between them. It must have been there all along, but they were both hiding it or trying to deny it. Eveanna slides her hand around Tanwen's neck and kisses her back, before breaking away. The rest of us avert our gazes and try to pick our jaws up off the floor. I knew the two of them had become close friends, but I never saw this coming. As a succubus, I should have, but I guess I've been busy lately.

"Come back safely," Tanwen tells her.

"I swear it," Eveanna replies. She steps into the portal, and it immediately vanishes.

Tanwen stares at the spot where it was, and then turns toward us with a scowl. When she sees our expressions, she snaps, "What?"

Araceli lets out a squeal. "Tanwen! Why didn't you tell us? Jonah, did you know?"

He shakes his head with a laugh. "I had no idea."

Tanwen glares at both of them. "Oh, shut up. Like you two are fooling anyone."

Araceli turns bright red and ducks her head. Jonah rubs the back of his neck and avoids looking at anyone. Things are getting awkward fast.

I grab my little purse and my shoes with a yawn. "I appreciate all of you staying up and waiting for me, but it's late. Go to bed. Hopefully we'll have some good news soon."

"I'll fly back with you," Marcus says.

I'm too tired to argue that I don't need a chaperone, and besides, I think he just wants to kiss me goodnight.

We land on my balcony, and I ask Marcus, "Do you want to come in?"

He flashes me a naughty smile. "No, I should really get some sleep, and that won't happen if I go in there. We both know that."

I yawn again. "True."

"I wanted to invite you to meet my mom and my little brother next weekend. It's his first birthday and they're coming to visit me."

I can't help the giant smile on my face. "I would love that."

I guess it's time to bond with all the parents. It's a big step, but it also feels right.

27

MARCUS

I'm waiting for Liv on the porch when I see her black wings come into view. As soon as she lands, I pull her close. "I missed you."

She melts into my arms with a laugh. "It's only been a few days."

"True, but I always miss you when you're not around." We kiss for a few moments, then I take her hand. "Ready?"

She nods and I notice she's tightly clutching a small present with dinosaur wrapping paper. She didn't have to get Griffin a gift, but it's nice that she did. Mom will love it.

I open the door to the house I share with Callan, and Griffin immediately crawls over to me with a squawk, then reaches up with the universal baby symbol for "pick me up." I laugh and bend down to haul the little guy up into my arms. He looks at Olivia with big brown eyes.

"Hello Griffin," she says. "I'm Olivia."

He just stares at her, as little kids do, and she glances at me like she's worried she's done something wrong. Then he says, "Mama mama," and reaches back in the direction of the other room. I chuckle and lead Olivia further inside, where my mom is sitting on the couch with her partner, Ervin. They both stand when we enter and wear smiles, although I notice my mom wringing her hands.

I've been trying to get her to meet Olivia for months now, but she's been hesitant because of the half-demon thing. Although most people at Seraphim Academy and in Angel Peak have come to accept Olivia, out in the other angel communities no one knows her personally and they find her existence to be rather shocking. I learned that when I went to visit my mom in Arizona and the angels were horrified when they heard I was friends with the half-demon. It's going to take some time to change centuries of prejudice, but the fact that my mom agreed to meet Olivia is a good start.

"Hello, I'm Charmeine," Mom says with a kind smile. "And this is my partner, Ervin. Marcus has told us so much about you."

"It's so good to meet you." Olivia holds out the present. "I got Griffin a little something for his birthday."

"You're too kind. Thank you." She takes Griffin from me and sits down, then hands him the present. Together they unwrap it and find a baby bongo drum inside. "Oh, he'll love this. He adores music, just like Marcus. Are you still playing the guitar?"

I guide Liv to the other couch, and we sit down. "Sometimes, yeah. I haven't had much time lately."

"I hope he serenades you with it sometimes," Mom says to Olivia.

"Last year he played guitar for me while flying outside my balcony," Liv says with a fond smile. "I think the entire school saw him."

"That does sound like my boy. Always a charmer." She pinches my cheeks and I roll my eyes. "He gets that from his dad, of course."

"Yes, I met Raphael last year. He was definitely...charming."

"There's a good reason he has so many kids, and he was definitely fun for a fling." Mom turns and takes Ervin's hand. "Although I'm happy to have settled down with Ervin here."

"Mom and Ervin met at Aerie Industries, where they both work," I tell Olivia. Her eyes widen a little, and I sense she gets my meaning. I love my mom, but she *is* hesitant about demons, and I don't know about Ervin's loyalties at all. I don't think they're involved with the Order, but it can't hurt to be careful either.

"How do you like Seraphim Academy?" Ervin asks. "I went myself about fifty years ago. I remember it well."

"My first year was difficult," Liv admits. "I grew up among humans and had a lot to learn. The second year was a little easier, and this year I finally feel like I'm fitting in there."

"That's good to hear," Mom says. "I was worried someone might have treated you unkindly due to your special...background."

"Many did. Some still do. But it's getting better."

We're interrupted by Griffin banging on his new drum from Olivia, which lights up and plays a noise when he hits it. He squeals in delight and does it again, making everyone laugh.

"I'm going to grab us some food and drinks," I say, standing up.

"I'll help you," Olivia says, jumping up quickly. As soon as we're in the kitchen she asks, "Where's Callan?"

"He left to give us some privacy. I think he's playing video games with Jonah, actually."

"That's good." She leans on the counter and blows out a breath. "Do you think it's going okay?"

"Definitely." I wrap my arms around her and bring her in close, touched that she's worried about impressing my mom. "You're doing great."

Griffin suddenly crawls into the kitchen wielding his new drum, and we break apart with a laugh. I start plating some easy appetizers, which I prepared earlier, but Griffin keeps tugging on my leg. I pick him up and pinch his cute chubby cheeks, but then hand him to Liv. "Here, can you take him?"

She gets a complete deer-in-the-headlights look, but then accepts the squirming one year old, who immediately starts crying. That only makes Liv look more panicked, but I hand Griffin a tiny piece of strawberry and he calms right down. Like me, he loves to eat.

"Can I help?" Liv asks, shifting Griffin to the other arm.

"Nope. Just hold him and feed him some fruit. He'll be happy." I chuckle as she nearly loses a finger when he chomps on the strawberry slice she offers. "I'm guessing you've never been around babies."

"No, my foster homes never had babies, and I've never been close to anyone who's had a kid." She stares at Griffin as he gives her a big smile, showing off his new front teeth. "You seem pretty comfortable though."

"Part of the third year Malakim training is in pediatrics. But I've always been around kids and babies. Comes with having a big extended family. You know about my father's reputation and his many sons. Well, some of them have kids too. Or even grandkids."

Liv sets Griffin down on the floor and he crawls off to find his mom again. "It must be nice to have such a big family."

"Sometimes." I empty a bag of tortilla chips into a bowl, then pull out the guacamole I made earlier.

"I always felt so alone growing up," Liv says. "I had Jonah, but he only visited me occasionally, and that was it. Things are a lot better now that we get to see each other all the time."

"It's good that you two are so close. I'm not close to any of my brothers. We're all far apart in age and have different mothers." I shrug as if this doesn't matter, even though this is something I've never told anyone before, and I turn toward the counter to cut up some celery. "Growing up, I always felt like just another one of Raphael's many kids. I'm glad Griffin won't have that problem. He'll be special."

Liv throws her arms around me from behind. "Oh, Marcus, you're special too."

"Am I?" My throat tightens, but I've been keeping this inside too long and need to get it out. "I have to admit, sometimes I have a hard time being just one of your many lovers too. I know it's your nature and you can't help it, and most of the time I'm fine with it, but sometimes it's hard not having any kind of commitment from you. Raphael used to drop in, give me gifts and take me on fun outings, then vanish again for months while he was off visiting his other kids. I worry you're going to leave too when you graduate, only stopping in now and then for sex. I can't handle that kind of relationship. I'm sorry."

Liv turns me around and touches my face with compassion in her eyes. "That is not going to happen. You're special to me. I know I can't say the words you want to hear or make the kind of commitment you want, but I care about you a lot, and I'm not going anywhere, even after graduation. I promise."

I press a kiss to her lips, feeling better now that I got my worries out in the open. "Thanks. I love you, Olivia. I know you can't say it back and that's fine, but I want to say it anyway."

She nods, but ducks her head, and I get the feeling it bothers her. She's been told for so long she isn't capable of having a real relationship, but I know that's not true. And I think I can make her change her mind.

28

OLIVIA

Another week passes in a blur of school and research, and there's no sign my mom and Eveanna are returning anytime soon. I'm starting to think we'll never learn anything about destroying the Staff or the Order's movements, when I spot Jeremy leaving for another meeting in his golden robes and mask.

I quickly swing by Jonah's dorm and pound on his sliding glass door. He made me promise to take him with me after the last time, and I agreed because I wouldn't mind the company. He rubs the sleep out of his eyes, yanks on a t-shirt over his pajama pants, and we take off.

The night is still warm now that summer has finally arrived in the mountains, and it feels good to stretch my wings alongside my brother. Not that we have to go very far to get to the library. Without my necklace there's a chance an Ofanim could see through our invisibility, so we hang back until we're sure everyone is inside the attic and the meeting has started. Then we perch outside the open window like crows, straining to listen and get a peek of what's happening inside without blowing our cover.

"We've had a minor setback with the Staff," the leader is saying. "However, the fae accomplice has been spotted in the Winter Court of Faerie, and we're told she has the Staff with her. We have sent members to retrieve it, and we're certain it will be in our grasp again soon."

Jonah and I share worried looks. Eveanna must have purposefully been spotted to lead them away from us, but the news that they're in Faerie looking for her is troubling. I have to trust that my mom will keep them both safe. She is an Archdemon, after all.

"You should have received your tasks by now," the leader continues. "Many of you have been assigned to watch the half-demon and her associates. We know she is leaving campus regularly, but don't know where she goes. We must uncover this information."

He suddenly glances back at the empty throne behind him, and then nods. Almost like he's communicating with someone sitting there. Is it possible? Is there someone invisible on that throne? Is that why it's always been empty?

But who?

They discuss the comings and goings of Marcus, Bastien, and Callan and report nobody has seen Kassiel in some time. Jonah is mentioned, along with everyone else who went with us on the rescue mission. They're watching all of us and we don't even know who most of them are. Lovely.

Then they allow the white-robed initiates inside to accept their stolen offerings, and Jonah and I sit back so we can keep an eye on them but still talk.

"Who do you think the new leader is?" Jonah whispers.

"I bet it's Simiel." I shudder a little. "He's always giving me these creepy looks."

"Possibly. Either way, it sounds like we need to be extra careful from now on."

I scowl. I hate that the Order is spying on us and tracking our movements, but it's nothing we didn't expect. "We're always careful."

"It can't hurt to warn the other's we're being watched."

I nod, and then we watch the initiates for a few minutes. "What did you steal? For your first test."

He chuckles. "I stole a piece of Hilda's Valkyrie armor."

"No way." I don't know if I should be impressed or should smack him for being an idiot. Hilda's Valkyrie armor is thousands of years old and has been coated in much demon blood. She told us all about it in class. "If she found out, she would've murdered you."

"I took a piece from the gauntlet that wasn't super obvious. Either she's a part of the Order and never found out or they got it back in time." He shrugs and stretches out his legs. "What about you?"

"I stole a forbidden book from Uriel's private library."

Jonah coughs. "That's even more dangerous than what I took!"

"Probably, but it worked. It got me in the Order after all."

"Grace stole something from Uriel too," Jonah says, with a sigh.

It's a shock hearing her name from his lips. Jonah's avoided talking about her this entire time. "I'm sorry about what happened with her."

Jonah picks at a small hole in his pajama pants. "I thought we were in love. I stayed loyal to her during my entire two years in Faerie. Now I see it was never real. She manipulated me the entire time. And not just me." He turns toward me, his face pained. "Did you know she slept with Marcus after I left?"

"What?" I ask a little too loudly, then cover my mouth with my hand. The meeting continues below us without interruption and after a minute I lower my hand. "Are you sure?"

"Yeah, Marcus told me after we got back from Faerie. Grace came to him one night, crying over how worried she was about me, and she started kissing him, and one thing led to another..." Jonah shakes his head. "Marcus was seriously torn up with guilt over it, but I forgave him immediately. It's obvious to me that she manipulated him too. She wanted to see if I'd contacted the Princes at all, and to learn how much they knew about my disappearance. She never cared about either of us. She just wanted to get the Staff."

I hate her even more now than I did before. "She lied to me too. So many times. We all thought she was our friend, but everything she did had an ulterior motive behind it."

"That's the worst part of all this. I feel like such a fool. How could I not have seen it?"

I lean against him. "None of us did. Don't beat yourself up over it."

"I didn't even know her real father was Azrael." His mouth twists. "Sometimes I stay up all night questioning everything she ever told me. Was anything she said true?"

"We might never know." I take Jonah's hand and give it a squeeze. "What I do know is that none of this is your fault. Grace tricked and used us all. Even her best friend, Cyrus."

He sighs and looks down at our joined hands. "At least it brought you here. That's the one silver lining to all this."

My eyes tear up a little at the sincerity in his voice. One of the best parts of this school year is being able to spend so much time with my brother openly for the first time in my life. But even when we were little kids, when our relationship had to be kept secret for my safety, he was there for me. He even spent two years in Faerie to keep me safe. I'd die to protect Jonah, and I know he would do the same for me.

I rest my head on his shoulder. "I love you, big brother."

"I love you too, little sis." He puts his head against mine for a second, but then we hear the Order members approach the window out of the attic. Our sibling bonding moment ends abruptly as we jump into the air and fly away, then giggle like little kids at how we almost got caught.

I sober up again as we hover outside the dorms. "Hey, Jonah. We'll make Grace pay for what she did somehow. I promise."

"A long stay in Penumbra prison would do her some good. Even Azrael couldn't get her out of there." He runs a hand through his messy hair. "Either way, I'm over it. I'm ready to move on."

For Araceli's sake, I hope that's true.

29

OLIVIA

The next morning is Sunday and I sleep in a bit. When I finally roll out of bed, nobody is around. After a shower, I head to the cafeteria and take my breakfast to the Princess Lounge.

To my surprise, Callan is there. He freezes with his hand reaching out toward the table in the small kitchen area. "Oh. Hey."

"What are you doing here on the weekend?" I set my breakfast, a bagel and packet of cream cheese, on the table.

"I was dropping this off for you." He holds up a tiny blue jewelry box. "I didn't mean to get caught, honestly."

I eye the box with curiosity. "What is it?"

"Just something I saw in a shop window." He hands me the box and then steps back and shoves his hands in his pockets. "I don't know. I thought you might like it."

I pop open the jewelry box and find a necklace inside with a silver crescent moon inlaid over a gold sun, almost like an eclipse. I pick it up and thread the chain through my fingers to examine the charm. It doesn't look like something cheap he just happened to pick up in a shop. It looks expensive, and I know he got it because it symbolizes my two halves.

"It's nothing big," Callan mumbles. "I thought it suited you."

"It's perfect." Emotion makes my voice tremble a little. I walk around the table and rest my hands on his strong chest, then look up into his stormy blue eyes. "I love it. Thank you."

"You do?"

I nod and hold out the necklace. "Put it on me?"

He takes it and I turn around, then feel the light touch of his fingers as he moves my hair to the side so he can put the gift around my neck. Somehow this small act feels more intimate than anything we've done before. When he finishes, he rests his hands on my shoulders and buries his face in my hair from behind.

"I lied," he says, as he presses a soft kiss to my neck. "I had it custom designed."

"I figured." I lean back against him and close my eyes. For once we're not fighting, and it feels good.

"I wanted to show you that I accept both sides of you. Angel and demon. Day and night. Light and dark." He turns me around to face him. "I love it all."

The word love makes my heart stutter, and to save myself from answering, I slide my hands around his neck and pull him down to me for a kiss. His arms enclose me in a tight embrace as he kisses me back, his mouth tender as it moves against mine. This is our first kiss that isn't fueled by anger, lust, or hatred, I realize. This one feels like it means something.

"Do you forgive me?" he asks as his mouth moves across my jaw to my neck.

I close my eyes and tilt my head, giving him better access. "I suppose."

A loud blaring noise makes us both jump, abruptly ending our tender moment. We stare at each other for a second, and then Callan shoves me behind him. "It's the school's alarm. We're under attack!"

"Do you think it's the Order?" I ask, and we both glance at the closet where the Staff is hidden, still glamoured to look like a broom. With Eveanna gone, Araceli makes sure the glamour gets renewed and never fades. But we always knew that was only a temporary solution.

"Probably." He storms across the space to the cabinet under the TV, touches something on the side, and the whole thing slides open to reveal a secret compartment full of weapons. Whoa. Did not know that was there. He grabs two large swords. "I'll defend the Staff. You fly to your father's house."

I reach for my daggers, then frown. The one time I happen to leave them in my room, and this happens. "What? I'm not leaving you or the Staff here!"

He tests each of the swords in his hands. "This is the protocol we developed in case of an attack. Half of us guard the Staff, while the other half guard you at Gabriel's house."

"And was anyone going to tell me about this plan?" I ask, annoyed again. I should have known my tender feelings for Callan wouldn't last long.

"No. We knew you wouldn't like it."

I let out an annoyed huff, then move to the closet and grab the Staff. It shimmers the second I touch it as the glamour fades, and I feel a wave of power as I wrap my hand around it. This is the first time I've held it, and wow. What a rush. "Your plan sucks. We should both go to Gabriel's and take the Staff with us."

Callan considers for a moment. "Fine. I don't want you going anywhere on your own."

Araceli suddenly lands on the balcony, drawing our attention. "The humans have breached the gates!"

I breathe a little sigh of relief hearing it's not the Order, but the relief is short-lived as a drone follows Araceli to the bell tower. Callan blasts it with a beam of burning light, and it explodes on our balcony in a flash. We all duck and cover our heads, until the smoke clears.

"Let's go," I say, as I rise up again.

"Uh, Liv, you probably want to leave the Staff here," Araceli says. "I'll glamour it again. You guys go help the others. They're fighting at the gates and the humans have guns. Be careful."

I hold the Staff out to her, but then I'm reluctant to let go of it. It's so powerful, and I could use it in this battle. Why should I give it up?

"Liv?" Araceli asks.

I shake my head to clear my thoughts and hand her the Staff. Shit. I should probably stay away from that thing.

"I don't like the idea of you fighting out there," Callan says, as we walk onto the balcony.

"Too bad, because you can't keep me in a bubble all the time. Besides, the Duskhunters aren't after me."

"That's the only reason I'm letting you go." He grabs my arm and pulls me in for a scorchingly hot, possessive kiss. "Besides, I know you had the best combat teacher."

"Yeah, Hilda is great," I reply with a wink. He rolls his eyes as we take off.

As we launch into the air, we immediately see more drones up ahead, and Callan zooms toward them. He's faster than me, but I'm right behind him, ready to end this battle quickly before the humans hurt anyone. The Duskhunters haven't attacked in about a year, but we're ready for them this time.

Before I reach the gates, someone grabs me around the waist from behind and tugs me back. At first I think it's Callan, but no, he's in front of me. And it's not one of the other guys either. This isn't a protective grip, but a dangerous one—I'm being dragged away against my will. I open my mouth to scream as I fight back, but then a hood goes over my head and everything goes dark and silent.

"Callan!" I scream. "Help me!"

The person holding me is flying away, and no one stops them. We must be concealed somehow, whether through darkness, like a Fallen, or light bending, like an Ishim, I can't tell. All I know is that I'm being kidnapped, and no one is coming to help me.

I scream and fight, using every move I can pull from the training sessions with Callan and Tanwen, but nothing works. It's like I'm fighting an invisible enemy. No matter how hard I fight, I can't get my arms free or even hit the person holding me. I can feel the steel grip on my arms and my back pressed against them, but when I try to hit them, I pass through thin air. How is this possible?

Grace. It has to be. She did something like this to Callan when we fought her at the farmhouse. Intangibility must be her Archangel power.

Panic and rage war for control inside me as I try to do something, anything, to escape. I create a burst of light, but it's not much and wouldn't do much to Grace anyway. I do have another trick though. I let loose my seductive powers, silently willing Grace to desire me and bow to my will.

It works, but only barely. Her grip loosens for a second, and I'm able to wiggle the hood free enough that I can see the trees under us. Grace tries to yank the hood back down, but I struggle and twist in her arms. That's when I realize it's not Grace holding me, but a man.

A man with black and white wings.

I manage to scream and flail harder, directing more of my power at him. For a split second, my fingers grasp skin and feathers, before he goes intangible again. I try to wiggle away, but it's like struggling against a boulder. He's not going to let me go, no matter what I do. Damn it, I wish I could teleport like my dad!

Below us, I spot the arched trees with the secret doorway to Hellspawn and know that if I can just get to them, I'll be safe. Once on the other side, I can find Baal or someone else to help me. *Please let me make it there somehow.*

And then, without any reasonable explanation, I'm free.

I'm standing in front of the archway, with a fistful of black and white feathers. Up above me by about twenty feet is the angel who kidnapped me. He's ridiculously handsome with shortly cropped hair the color of spun gold and those striking wings that remind me a lot of Azrael's. In fact, other than the hair he looks a lot like Azrael, minus the scary black eyes.

He spots me below and starts to lunge toward me, but then Callan yells, "Liv!"

"I'm here!" I call out, just as Callan flies overhead.

When I look back at the other angel, he's gone. He either disappeared into thin air, or he went invisible.

Callan lands beside me, still wielding his twin swords. "What happened? I looked back and you were gone. Are you okay?"

I throw my arms around him. "I'm fine. Someone kidnapped me, but I got away."

"What?" he roars. "Who?"

"An Ishim, I think." I glance down at the feathers in my hands. Who was that man? Was he working with the Duskhunters? Or for the Order?

30

OLIVIA

As soon as it's safe, we all meet in the bell tower. Jonah and Tanwen are sitting on the couch bleeding from gunshot wounds, while Araceli and Marcus heal them. Bastien gets everyone something to snack on and to drink from the kitchen, while they give me a rundown of what I missed.

"The Duskhunters used some kind of fae relic to blast the gates, destroying the magical wards," Jonah says, wincing as Araceli moves his arm into a different position. "They sent their drones in to attack us first, but they had fighters on the ground too. Most had guns. Some had dark-infused weapons."

"How did they get those things?" Callan asks.

"Good question," Tanwen growls. "We fought them off, but many of them were able to retreat."

"Yeah, all at once they turned tail and ran," Marcus says. "Guess they realized they'd made a big mistake attacking us."

"Or maybe it was something else," I mutter, still clutching the feathers.

Kassiel suddenly lands on the balcony with blood tricking down his forehead. "Everyone okay?"

I run over and hug him tightly. "What are you doing here?"

"I was on my way to see you when I got wind of the attack."

"Kassiel fought alongside us during the battle," Bastien says, with respect in his voice.

Kassiel ducks his head. "This is still my school, even if I no longer teach here."

"Come over here so we can heal you," Araceli says.

"Where were you during the fight, Callan?" Jonah asks with a wry grin. "I thought you'd be out there on the frontlines, slicing through any human who dared breach the gates."

Callan's jaw clenches. "That was the plan, but then Liv got kidnapped."

Half a dozen shocked responses all happen at once. I quickly explain to them what happened and assure them I'm fine.

"He had wings similar to Azrael's and sort of looked like him too. But hair..." I pause and stare at Callan. "Hair like Callan's."

"Are you sure?" Bastien asks.

"Pretty sure. He also went intangible, like we saw Grace do in the farmhouse. At least, that's what I think happened."

"It can't be." Callan suddenly stumbles over to the armchair and sits in it. "How? After all these years?"

A heavy silence falls over the group as everyone stares at Callan. I feel like I'm missing something. Something big.

"Do you know who that was?" I ask.

Callan covers his face with his hand but can't seem to answer. Bastien moves to his side and rests a hand on his shoulder, a rare display of affection and sympathy. Then again, Bastien has opened up a lot in the past few years.

"Ekariel," Bastien says quietly. "It's the only explanation."

It takes me a moment to remember where I've heard the name. Callan's half-brother. Son of Jophiel...and Azrael.

"He was killed by demons twenty-five years ago. Only a few months before I was born." Callan lowers his hand and looks up with haunted eyes. "Or so we thought."

"Are you sure it's him?" Marcus asks.

"It's the only explanation," Bastien says. "He has Azrael's wings and Jophiel's hair, and the same Archangel power as his half-sister, Grace."

"Could the two of them be working together?" Jonah asks.

Callan shakes his head. "I doubt it. Ekariel was killed—or something—when he was four years old. Azrael and my mother were both distraught. Jophiel was pregnant with me at the time."

I can see how something like that would have shaped Callan's life, even though it happened before he was born. He would have heard all sorts of horrible things about demons. It also explains why he's had so much pressure on him to be the best, not just because he's Michael's son—but because he's Jophiel's surviving one.

"Grace's mom would have been pregnant with her around the same time," Jonah says. "Your birthdays are only a month apart."

"Maybe that's why Azrael never acknowledged her," Tanwen says. "If Grace's mom had an affair with Azrael and then his son died, he might have been too consumed with grief to want anything to do with her. Especially if she was unplanned, unlike the other Archangel children."

"That's horrible," Araceli says. "I never understood them getting together for the sole purpose of having powerful children anyway. But not acknowledging one of them? That's harsh."

"Could Ekariel be working with the Duskhunters?" Kassiel asks. "Perhaps they kidnapped him as a child?"

"Have they been around that long?" Jonah asks.

"It's possible," Kassiel says, stroking his chin. "They could have been working in the shadows all this time. Hiding. Growing. Planning."

"Well, that's terrifying," Araceli mutters.

"They'll be stopped," Tanwen says, slamming her fist into her palm. "They killed my mother and I won't rest until they pay."

"I'm not sure what's worse," Callan says, his voice rough. "The thought of Ekariel dead, or the thought of him working with the Duskhunters."

I sit on the edge of the armchair and wrap my arms around him. "I'm sorry."

He leans against me, his eyes staring off into space. "I need to tell my mother."

"Of course." I gently stroke his hair, wishing I could do more. He must be in shock.

"If he has that intangibility, how did you get away from him?" Tanwen asks me.

"I'm not sure. One second I was in his arms, and the next I was somewhere else."

Marcus's eye widen. "It must be your Archangel power!"

Jonah sits up a little. "Ooh, maybe you teleported like Dad! Try to do it again."

"I'm not really sure how I did it, but I'll try." I close my eyes and picture my bedroom in Angel Peak, then will myself to be there. Nothing happens. I open one eye and look at my friends. "This isn't working."

"Maybe it's not the same as your father's power," Bastien suggests. "Try to recreate the moment as it happened before."

I go over everything that happened and remember staring intensely at the arch to Hellspawn, wishing I could be there. I stare at the kitchen pantry and in an instant, I'm beside it. The others look around confused, and then spot me in my new location.

"That was so cool," Araceli says.

I try to do it again, this time teleporting out into the hallway. Or onto the roof. Nope.

After a few minutes of practicing and a little trial and error, we discover I can only blink to locations I can see. That keeps it pretty limited to short distances, but I think it could come in handy in a fight.

Just as Callan walks back inside with a long face, a fae portal appears in the middle of the room. We all move out of the way before Lilith steps through, followed by Eveanna. I jump forward and hug my mom, so relieved she's back, and then move to hug Eveanna, except Tanwen's gotten to her first. I grin at the sight.

"You all look a bit glum," Lilith says. In contrast, she looks like she just came back from Lucifer's Ball. Her gown is spotless, her hair and makeup impeccable. How could she travel through Faerie and come back looking like that?

"It's been a rough day," I reply. "How did it go in Faerie?"

"It was lovely." Lilith drapes herself across one of the armchairs like it's a throne. "I forgot how much I love the place."

"We found Culann and convinced him to give us the answer," Eveanna says dryly. "It was not easy."

Lilith waves her hand. "Yes, he needed a little persuasion, but he could never refuse me anything. I knew he would give us what we came for eventually."

"And?" I ask.

"Only Lucifer and Michael can destroy the Staff, since it's made from their essence," Lilith says. My heart sinks until she adds, "Their sons might be able to do it too."

"We tried to do that," Callan says, his voice bitter. "It didn't work."

Kassiel meets Callan's eyes. "We tried separately before, not together."

"Yes, you'll need to both be touching the Staff," Lilith says.

"Let's get it over with then." Callan stomps over to the broom closet and throws it open. But then he just stands there.

"What is it?" I ask.

"The Staff is gone."

"What do you mean it's gone?" Jonah asks.

"That's impossible," Araceli says, jumping to her feet. "I glamoured it myself and put it back after Callan and Olivia left."

"What happened after that?" Tanwen asks.

Araceli shrugs. "I flew to the gates, saw Marcus healing people, and dropped down to help him."

"The Duskhunters took the Staff," Bastien says.

Lilith suddenly sits up. "The Duskhunters were here?"

"The attack on the gates must have been a diversion," Marcus says. "But how did they know it was here?"

"The drones." Callan slams the broom closet shut so hard the door nearly falls off. "One of them followed Araceli here while Olivia was holding the Staff. The cameras must have seen it."

"For all we know, Ekariel has been spying on us for a while," I add.

"Ekariel?" Lilith asks. "Son of Jophiel and Azrael?"

"Yes, we think he's alive and possibly working with the Duskhunters," I explain.

Lilith sits up, her voice anxious. "Was there a girl with them? Around sixteen? Dark brown hair, green eyes?"

"I didn't see anyone like that," Araceli says, and the others confirm the same thing.

"Is she the one you've been searching for all these years?" I ask, vaguely recalling Lilith mentioning that last year.

Lilith's eyes fill with tears. "Yes. Her name is Lena. She went missing five years ago and I've been trying to find her ever since. I believe the Duskhunters kidnapped her."

"Like they must have done with Ekariel," Kassiel says.

"If they have Ekariel, Lena, and the Staff, then we are doomed."

"Why?" I ask, my stomach twisting in knots. "What are you talking about?"

She meets my eyes. "Lena is your sister."

I step back, feeling like someone punched me in the chest. "I have a sister?"

"Half-sister, yes." Lilith's voice trembles. "The daughter of two Archdemons. Much like Ekariel is the son of two Archangels. Together they would be powerful enough to use the Staff and rid all demons *and* angels from Earth."

"That must be why the Duskhunters took the Staff," Marcus says. "They want us all gone."

I know this is bad. Really bad. But I'm still in shock over the fact that I have a sister. I stare at my mother. "Why didn't you tell me? First Asmodeus, and now this?"

She holds out a hand that is trembling a little, and I reluctantly take it. "I'm so sorry. After Gabriel and I agreed to keep your identity a secret, we decided that applied to your siblings as well."

"Yeah, that didn't work for us," Jonah says dryly.

"In retrospect, we were probably wrong to do that, especially now that we've seen how important the two of you are to each other." Lilith says. "But Asmodeus is so much older and things with him are...complicated. Lena was born when you were seven, Olivia, and already in foster care. I planned to introduce you two when she was older and I could trust her to keep your existence secret, but she was taken when she was only eleven. After that...I couldn't speak of her. After sending you away and then losing her, it was just too painful to bear."

I draw my mom in for a hug. "I wish you'd told me, but I understand."

She embraces me tightly. "I've spent the last five years chasing down every lead, trying to find her. I believe the Duskhunters have her, but I'm not certain. If they do, we have to stop them before they can use the Staff."

"How can we find them?" Araceli asks.

"I still have Ekariel's feathers." At some point I put them in my pocket, but now I pull them out again. "Can we use these somehow? Like we used Lucifer's feather?"

"I'm afraid not. That feather was enchanted somehow." Bastien tilts his head and holds out his hand. "May I examine them?"

31

BASTIEN

For a cold, emotionless bastard, I'm feeling a lot today. With the news of Ekariel and Lena, along with Liv's near-kidnapping and the threat of the Duskhunters using the Staff, I'm suddenly overwhelmed with turbulence inside me.

The people I care about most are in danger. I must do something.

Drifting forward by some force I can't explain, I reach out and take the black and white feathers from Olivia's hand. The second I touch them my eyes slam shut, and yet I can still see. My gaze stretches across a forest, as if I'm flying over it. My head turns slightly, and I see wings with black-and-white feathers like the ones in my hand.

I'm somehow in Ekariel's head, seeing through his eyes. A vision, of some sort.

My brain catalogs the passing scenery, which changes as he continues flying over houses and shops, plus some larger stores, heading toward the coast. The ocean comes into view in the distance, along with a larger town, and Ekariel begins to fly lower. Just outside the town, he drops down onto the pavement in front of a large warehouse.

Ekariel opens a steel door and steps inside a huge high-ceilinged building with dim lighting. Bunkbeds line the walls in the front, with people sleeping in some of them. I try to count them, but then Ekariel swivels his head and gives me a view of the entire warehouse. To the left, some people are sparring with weapons, and I spot guns mounted to a wall. Others are fixing drones, with a few hovering in the air beside them. In the back metal stairs lead up to two other floors, with some free-standing modular offices, some with windows, and some without.

Before I can get a better look, a man walks up to Ekariel. He's older, maybe fifties, with gray-streaked brown hair and a beard. He has the confidence of someone who think he's the boss. "Any news?"

"The abomination is going to a ball at Hellspawn Academy tonight," Ekariel says, confirming this vision is from the past. "It's the perfect time for an attack."

The other man strokes his beard, but then shakes his head. "No, we want to capture the abomination if we can, in case Lena is too young to use the Staff. For now, we will wait and keep watching."

"I understand."

The man pats him on the arm. "You're doing good work, Ekariel. Never forget that."

I have the sensation of nodding. "Thank you."

Ekariel walks past the bunks, up the stairs, and into one of the modular offices. Inside is a cage. An actual human-sized cage. A teenage girl with wavy brown hair sits on the floor inside, and when she looks over at Ekariel, her ice-blue eyes light up with something like hope. She looks like Lilith and Olivia, only younger.

"You're back." The girl who must be Lena stands and moves to the side of the cage. "Did you see my sister?"

"I did." Ekariel reaches inside the cage and takes Lena's hand. "This will be over soon. I promise."

The vision ends abruptly and I'm back in the bell tower, where everyone is staring at me.

"Bastien?" Liv asks, waving a hand in front of my face.

I take a long breath to regain my bearings and process what just happened. "I had a vision."

"What kind of vision?" Jonah asks.

"The second I touched the feathers, I experienced what I believe is a form of psychometry, allowing me to see a past event through Ekariel's eyes." I turn to Callan. "His name was said during the vision. I'm sure it's him." Then I swing my eyes to Lilith. "I also saw Lena there."

"Are you sure?" Lilith jumps up and grabs my shirt. "Is she safe? Is she hurt?"

"She's trapped in a large cage but isn't hurt. Ekariel isn't caged though. He's able to move freely, and he's been spying on us for some time. The vision I had was the day of Lucifer's Ball." I quickly give them a run-down of everything else I saw, including a description of the warehouse. I leave out the part where they called Olivia an abomination.

"It must be your Archangel power," Marcus says. "It's finally emerged."

Yes, that would make sense. Uriel is able to see glimpses of the past in someone's eyes, so it would follow that my own power would be related in some way.

"Did you see anything else that might help us?" Callan asks, his voice insistent.

"No. I can try again though." I close my eyes and clutch the feathers tighter, reaching for that burst of power again. Nothing happens. I shake my head and offer the feathers to Callan. "I'm sorry."

"Bastien's vision confirms they're planning to use the Staff, and now that they have it, they can do it any time," Eveanna says.

"She's right," Lilith says. "We must stop them immediately—and rescue Lena."

"And Ekariel," Callan adds.

I almost reply that it didn't look as though he wanted to be rescued, but decide it's better to keep my mouth shut. "I believe I can trace his flight back to the location of the warehouse."

"Then we leave immediately," Olivia says.

Tanwen holds up a hand. "Hang on. We killed a lot of them at the gates, but they had guns and drones. Even with fewer numbers, they'll be dangerous. We can't do this alone."

"My mother is already on her way," Callan says.

"Did she tell Azrael?" Liv asks, biting her lip.

"No, I used the excuse that she shouldn't tell him yet in case we're wrong."

"Good. We can't let him get the Staff." Liv gives Callan an apologetic look. "Or Jophiel."

"If Ekariel really is there, she'll be too worried about rescuing him to care about the Staff," Lilith says. "I know I will be."

"Who else can we trust?" Araceli asks. "Uriel? Raphael? Gabriel?"

"Gabriel we can trust," Lilith says. "But not the others, with my apologies to Bastien and Marcus."

"No apologies required," I tell her. I don't trust my father either.

"So we can't trust anyone except the people in this room, but we need a larger force to attack the Duskhunters," Marcus says. "How are we supposed to get that?"

"Maybe we're looking at this all wrong," Liv says. "If we sneak inside, we don't need large numbers. We have powers they don't have. We can use them to get in and out quickly."

"Good idea," Callan says with a firm nod. "Covert. Quick. And deadly."

It's decided then. A stealth mission to rescue two missing people, retrieve the Staff...and save every angel and demon on Earth.

32

OLIVIA

We land on top of the warehouse from Bastien's vision, already invisible thanks to me, Jonah, and Gabriel. I admire the small force we've assembled as the July afternoon sun burns bright in the sky. We have a few hours of daylight left, and we're not going to waste them.

Dad sets Lilith down on the metal roof, and I can't help but notice his hand lingers on her back. Tanwen carried Eveanna over, and they share a quiet moment before we begin. I've only ever seen Jophiel in a business suit before, but now she wears bronze armor and wields a spear. Remind me not to pick a fight with the CEO of Aerie Industries. Lilith's changed too, no longer wearing her ballgown, but some jeans and a t-shirt borrowed from my closet.

"Good luck." I turn toward Callan and give him a hug. Our siblings are in there, and we must get them out alive. He clutches me tightly, while his mother eyes us with a frown but doesn't say a word. She has bigger things on her mind.

I give Kassiel, Marcus, and Bastien a quick kiss too, partly to take a tiny bit of their energy, and partly because we have no idea how this is going to go down. Then Araceli and I hug, and she whispers, "Don't worry, we got this."

Eveanna bends metal to open the skylight, which is large enough for us to each slip inside. The third floor of the warehouse is below us, and we drop down onto the top of a large modular office. Once we're all inside, we split into three teams, each with an Ishim for invisibility. Gabriel leads Lilith, Tanwen, and Eveanna around the back, toward the room Bastien saw in his vision. Their job is to rescue Lena from that cage. Jonah takes Araceli, Marcus, and Kassiel, who can help conceal them with shadows if light fails us. They're tasked with getting the Staff and flying it to safety. Then there's my team: Callan, Jophiel, and Bastien. We're getting Ekariel. Somehow.

Except when we move to the front of the third floor and glance down, we see splitting up wasn't necessary. All the Duskhunters are gathered in one spot, standing in a circle, wearing gray hoods. A man with a beard stands in the center holding the Staff, while Ekariel and a chained Lena face him on either side.

Oh fuck. They're about to use the Staff. I turn to Callan with panic written across my face.

"Time for plan B," he says.

Callan's gold-tipped wings flare out as he drops down silently behind the group of humans, and he immediately snaps one of their necks. His huge sword is out a second later, cutting through two more nearby. Shit, he is not messing around.

There's no way I can keep him invisible like that, but he doesn't seem to care, and neither does Jophiel. At the sight of her lost son she lets out a cry, then raises her spear and charges into battle.

So much for stealth.

It turns to pure chaos after that. Callan throws up a golden light shield when the humans fire guns at our group in quick succession. Other Duskhunters pull out weapons imbued with light and darkness and charge us. Tanwen immediately gets in the fight, cutting through the Duskhunters with her sword and blasting them with burning light. Araceli and Eveanna use their fae magic, while us Ishim try to remain invisible and focus on the reason we're here. I slip through the battle using my invisibility and my new blinking power while heading for the group in the middle.

I nearly stumble when I see my sister. Bastien was right. She looks like a younger version of me. I feel an immediate wave of protectiveness toward her and continue forward with renewed determination.

"Do it! Now!" The man with the beard thrusts the Staff into Ekariel's hands, and the angel moves closer to Lena. She hesitates, then lifts a hand to wrap it around the Staff with Ekariel, looking at him with devotion.

That's when my mother lets loose her succubus powers. It washes over the entire room of Duskhunters, making them pause. No one can resist her. Or disobey her when she commands, "Kneel!"

The leader drops down to his knees, and Tanwen grabs him around the neck, lifts him up into the air, and sets him on fire with her burning Erelim light. "That's for my mother, asshole."

Note to self: do not piss Tanwen off.

The Staff begins to emit pulses of light and darkness. My mother's power does nothing to stop Lena, who is immune since she's part succubus, or Ekariel, who must be either ridiculously powerful...or in love. I had the same problem when he was holding me.

I don't know what to do, but I have to stop this. I run full tilt toward Lena and grab her around the waist, knocking her to the ground with me. She's chained to the floor so we don't go very far, and she lets out a yell and then shoves me off her. At least she's away from the Staff.

Callan's fighting Ekariel for the Staff, but he's careful because he doesn't want to hurt his brother. Ekariel doesn't have the same problem. He glares at Callan with pure hatred as he picks up a dark-infused blade off the ground.

"Ekariel!" Jophiel's voice fills the air, and the other angel freezes with the Staff raised. He turns toward his mother and something like recognition crosses his face, before Marcus grabs him from behind and makes him fall asleep. The Staff hits the ground, and Jonah rushes forward to grab it, while Jophiel runs to her son.

"Mom?" Lena asks, and I turn toward the sound.

Lilith's holding the girl in her arms, stroking her wild hair, while they both sob. "I've got you, baby. Mama's here."

I can't help but stare at the two of them. Lena looks just like me, but her eyes are haunted and I can tell she's been through a lot. My heart breaks for her, and I hope I can help her recover from this somehow. If nothing else, I'll be there for her however I can.

Eveanna comes over and breaks Lena's light-infused chains, and I realize most of the fighting has stopped. The Duskhunters have all fled or are lying dead around us. Tanwen and Bastien finish off the last brave fools who try to take us down.

As soon as she's free, Lena throws Lilith back and crawls toward Ekariel, screaming his name like she's in pain. It's so shocking most of us don't react fast enough, but then Araceli steps in and puts the poor girl to sleep.

Lilith kneels beside Lena's unconscious body, and Gabriel moves in to speak softly with her. His hand slowly rubs circles on her back, and then she stands and presses her face to his chest while he holds her close. Oh yeah, there's something going on between them. Try as she might to deny it, I feel that surge of love between them, and know there's hope for my parents yet.

Kassiel pulls me into his arms for a fast hug. "I'm going to go with Lilith and Lena. They'll need help, but I'll return tomorrow to destroy the Staff. I promise."

"Thank you." I appreciate him so much. He stayed close to my mom through the entire battle, and now he's doing so much more. He gives me a quick kiss, and then moves to Lilith and shares a few words with her. She nods, and then he bends down to pick up Lena.

"Thank you," Lilith says to the group, with tears still in her eyes. She turns to Jophiel, and the two mothers share a shell-shocked look of understanding. They both have a long road ahead of them. I hope they can get past whatever issues they might have with each other to work through this together.

Gabriel wraps his arms around Lilith, and then the four of them take off. Callan starts to pick up Ekariel, but Jophiel yells, "Don't touch him!"

Callan steps back with his hands raised, while Jophiel takes

Ekariel in her arms. Her copper wings flare out and she flies away, carrying him with her angelic strength.

"We should quickly search the premises," Bastien says. "We know they had fae relics and infused blades."

I nod, although I'm feeling so emotionally and physically drained my hunger is rising up in full force. Good thing it doesn't take too long to search the warehouse and confiscate everything important we find. Then Araceli sets the entire place on fire, while Eveanna causes a localized earthquake to make the building crumble. No wonder the fae are so feared.

Jonah's still holding the Staff, and even through the exhaustion and my complicated feelings about Lena, I breathe a tiny sigh of relief. We've got it back, and now we can destroy it—once and for all.

33

OLIVIA

"I can't believe he's alive," Callan mutters. He looks utterly defeated, even though we won.

It's late now, and everyone's gone home to recover from the day's events. Tanwen and Eveanna are protecting the Staff tonight, while Bastien and Marcus are hiding the relics and infused weapons in the house in Angel Peak, with plans to go through them after the Staff is destroyed. I should head to bed myself, but Callan seemed like he needed to talk, so we decided to have a drink together in the bell tower.

He takes a long swig of his beer. "I knew Ekariel wouldn't recognize me, since we've never met or anything, but I didn't expect him to try to kill me either."

I'm sitting next to Callan on the couch, and I lean against him. "He's been living with the Duskhunters since he was four. It's all he knows. But he'll come around in time, I'm sure of it, especially with your help."

"I'll try to help, but I'm not sure what I can do." He wraps a muscular arm tightly around me. "At least Lena recognized Lilith. She wasn't all gone."

"It's going to be a long road to recovery for both of them. And

Ekariel seemed to recognize Jophiel too, at least on some instinctual level."

"It's got to be hard for him. He grew up without either of his parents around."

"True, although look how Grace turned out. Maybe it's better he didn't grow up with Azrael as his father."

"Maybe." His jaw suddenly clenches. "Maybe that's why I'm so fucked up too."

I sit up and turn around to face him, shocked by his words. He's usually so arrogant. "What do you mean?"

Callan stares into his empty beer bottle. "Michael wasn't the greatest father either."

I blink at him. "I thought Michael was the golden boy, the perfect leader who could do no wrong, loved and respected by all."

"Yeah, in public." He lets out a bitter laugh, then covers his face with his hand. "Shit, I've never told anyone this."

I rub his arm and keep my voice soft. "You can tell me, Callan."

He leans forward and sets the empty bottle down on the coffee table. "Everyone knew Michael had a temper. It's common among Erelim. But in public he controlled it or directed it at our enemies. In private, he would get...angry. He had high expectations of me as his son, and when I didn't live up to them it got ugly."

"Ugly how?" I whisper. "Did he hurt you?"

Callan won't meet my eyes. "Sometimes."

My heart breaks at the pain in his voice. "I'm so sorry. Did you mother know?"

"I think she suspected, but she was in denial or something. She could never see Michael as anything but our glorious leader. And it's not like she was winning any mother-of-the-year awards either. I barely saw her or my dad when I was growing up, unless they wanted to train me, show me off, or scold me for doing something wrong, which happened a lot. Failure was not an option, not for the son of two Archangels."

I think of how relaxed Gabriel and Ariel have always been with Jonah and bite my lip. "It shouldn't have been that way."

"No, but that's my legacy." His eyes finally meet mine. "It feels wrong to speak of him like this when he's dead. And even though he could be harsh with me, I still cared for him and wanted to please him. I still mourned his death and wanted revenge. Even now I hope he's proud of me."

I take his hand and grip it tightly. "Michael wanted peace with demons. He made the Staff of Eternity and the Earth Accords. I'm certain he would be proud."

"Thanks," he says, but he still sounds distant.

"Callan, no matter what happened with your parents or what they did or said, you're not them. You've risen above your past and changed for the better. I've seen it myself these last three years." I touch the sun-and-moon necklace he gave me, which I always wear now. "You've become a much better man. One I care about a lot."

Callan gazes into my eyes and then slides a hand to the back of my neck to pull me close. His mouth slants over mine and kisses me softly, but the second his lips touch mine, my suppressed hunger surges. I grip his arms, digging my nails into them, as I devour his mouth while pressing my body against his. He tastes so good, so masculine and powerful, and I can't get enough. I need more.

He pulls back with an amused grin. "Whoa, someone is hungry."

"You have no idea. I could gobble you up and then have seconds with Marcus. Maybe Bastien for thirds."

Lust flashes in his eyes. "We might be able to arrange that."

He grabs his phone and sends off a text, while I slide my hands up his thighs, heading for the erection I see growing in his jeans. He tosses his phone to the side as I unbutton his pants and drop down to kneel in front of the couch. I wrap my lips around his bulging cock and suck him into my mouth fast.

Fuck, he tastes amazing.

His fingers thread through my hair as he groans. I swirl my tongue along the head of his cock, but then I hear something that makes me pause. The sound of wings.

Bastien and Marcus fly into the bell tower, and I realize Callan was serious. He told the other Princes to head over here so I could have sex with all of them. Oh yeah, he really deserves this blow job. I give it to him good, while the other two men approach. Their lust hits me hard, and it's obvious they like the show.

"Enough," Callan orders, pushing me back.

I'm pulled to my feet by the other two men, and then their hands are all over me. Undressing me. Kissing me. Turning me between them so they can suck and pinch and caress. I reach for their clothes too, yanking them off. Callan joins us in our circle of lust, and soon he's naked too. We all are.

"Are you hungry enough for all three of us?" Marcus asks, as he squeezes my breasts.

Callan's hands reach between my thighs and he shoves a finger inside me. Then he pulls it out and holds his finger up. "See how wet she is? She wants us. All three of us."

"Yes," I practically purr. My succubus side is going wild with all of them touching me. "I've never wanted anything more."

"She's going to need to feed a lot after today's events," Bastien says in his coldly logical tone, as he grips my ass. "But I'm certain we can sate her if we work together."

Callan sits on the couch and grabs my hips, dragging me down onto his lap, with my back to him. His intentions are clear. He's the leader, and he goes first. But facing out like this, I'm free to give Bastien and Marcus some attention too. I pull Bastien toward me and slide his cock into my mouth, while I work Marcus with my hands. At the same time I flex my hips, which slides Callan through my folds. He grabs my breasts as his cock moves inside me, and I cry out at the sudden fullness. Just having him there gives me a rush of pleasure as I feel him deep inside, as deep as he can go.

Callan bucks his hips, thrusting up into me, making me ride him. Someone's hands find my clit, and others pinch my nipples, and I'm so lost in the feel of it all I can barely concentrate on pleasing my men. Not that they seem to mind.

Callan wraps his hand around my neck and pulls me back, kissing me on the throat while exposing my body for the other two. They both move in, Bastien sucking my breasts, while Marcus flicks my clit with his tongue, and then the orgasm floods me with pleasure. Callan pumps into me the entire time, and then he stops, just as I'm coming down from my climactic high.

The guys get me back on my feet and change position, working together like they have this all planned. Bastien lies down on the couch and pulls me onto him, and I immediately straddle him and sink onto his cock. The need to be filled is intense, and oh so good once I scratch that itch, especially with someone as big as Bastien.

Just as I begin riding Bastien, Callan moves behind me, and he grips my ass hard. I freeze as his finger begins probing my back entrance.

He leans close and whispers in my ear, "I said I was going to fuck you here. Tonight's the night. My cock in your ass, with Bastien's in your pussy and Marcus's in your mouth. Think you can handle it?"

"Yes," I whimper, as a second finger joins his first and he begins to stretch me. Preparing me for what's to come.

Marcus hands him some lube, and Callan smears it all over his cock, and slides some into me too. I bury my face in Bastien's neck as Callan moves into position behind me, then I moan deep in my throat as something bigger than a finger presses at my tight hole.

His cock feels impossibly big as it pushes inside. "That's it," Callan says, as he fills me slowly. "You can take it all."

I've had anal before with some of the men I've been with, and I enjoyed it a lot. I'm a succubus, after all. I enjoy everything. But I've never had this—two men inside me at once. The pleasure is so intense I can only tremble as they both fill me up. With both of them inside me, I have to let them do all the moving.

When they do, I shudder as overwhelming sensations wash over me. Callan and Bastien find a rhythm so that when one pulls out, the other pushes in. Their hands roam my skin and massage my breasts, plucking and kneading at my nipples.

"Open your mouth," Marcus says, and I realize I've neglected him. I need my third Prince too.

His hard length slips between my lips and slides deep inside, just as Callan thrusts hard from behind. It sends Bastien deeper in me too, and all I can do is hold onto his shoulders as they work me into a frenzy of pleasure.

Moaning, I lose myself in the moment. All I can do is ride out the intense orgasm while Marcus holds my head and flexes his hips, moving in and out of my lips. I can't help the moans and cries, and he seems to like them. He throws his head back and pumps into my mouth, in time with the other two men who work me in tandem. I give up trying to move with them and just let them use me. Except it's really me who's using them, draining their sexual energy and life force to make myself stronger. I take it all and still want more, and then I'm coming again. The pleasure only gets more intense, almost painful, as it makes my body tighten up around my men. They're close too. I can feel it.

Marcus pulls out of my mouth, allowing me to focus on the other two guys. Bastien grips my hips and thrusts up into me harder, while Callan slows his own movements. I capture Bastien's mouth with my own as his orgasm fills me.

As soon as Bastien finishes, Callan grabs my hips and pulls me back against him, spreading my legs wide. Bastien moves off the couch, and Marcus takes his place. His cock enters me easily and his mouth devours mine while Callan pumps into my ass hard and kneads my breasts roughly. Marcus's fingers slip down and find my clit, teasing it in the way he knows always drives me wild.

"I want to feel you come around my cock," he says, as he thrusts into me faster.

I'm squeezed between Callan and Marcus, their muscular bodies pressing tight against me, and it's too good. I let out a loud cry as my third orgasm bursts out of me. Callan rocks into me with abandon from behind, and his cock surges as he spills himself inside me. Marcus joins us a second later, kissing me hard as he rides out the intense pleasure.

We collapse against each other on the couch in a naked, sweaty heap, while Bastien drops to the floor and rests against my legs, his head on my lap. I stroke and kiss all of them, feeling such warmth and affection for my three Princes. Once my enemies, now my saviors.

"Thank you," I say, once I can finally speak. "That was incredible. I've never felt anything like it. And I'm not sure I'll ever be able to move again."

Marcus grins. "Good work, guys. We managed to out-fuck the succubus."

"Don't tell Callan," Bastien says. "His ego is big enough as it is."

Callan folds his muscular arms behind his head. "Egos are like cocks. Girls like 'em big."

I grab a pink sparkly pillow and hit Callan with it, and we all laugh. We start getting dressed, as we continue to tease each other, and I feel a strong bond between the four of us. I had no idea how much we needed a moment like this. All of us together, united...like a family.

It feels right.

And tomorrow we'll destroy the Staff. We'll go after the Order next. Everything is going to work out.

Just as I've finished donning my clothes, bright lights flash on the balcony. Half a dozen angels land on it, all wielding weapons and wearing armor. Uriel lands in front of them and stalks toward us, a look of grim determination on his face. Another angel lands beside him with light blond hair, and it takes me a second to place him. Zadkiel. Tanwen's father, and the newest member of the Archangel Council.

"The four of you are under arrest for the theft and concealment of the Staff of Eternity," Uriel's voice booms out, as the other angels rush us. His eyes focus on Bastien and he shakes his head. "My own son."

"Father?" Bastien asks, sounding as confused as I feel.

None of us get to say anything else as the angels grab us. I start to fight them off, but my body freezes up. There's some power holding me in place, and I can't move my limbs. The angels slap a silver cuff around my wrist and I try to throw out seduction at them, but nothing happens. On either side of me, Callan, Bastien, and

Marcus are taken captive too, while Zadkiel and Uriel watch with solemn expressions.

I scream and try to look back at my men as I'm hauled away, before everything goes black.

34

OLIVIA

M y eyes fly open and I jump up, prepared to fight off the guards arresting us. When my brain catches up with my eyes, I realize I'm in a small, stone room. Whirling in a circle, anxiety floods me and makes my heart race. There's no door in the room. No window either. Just four stone walls, a stone floor, and a stone ceiling that's not much taller than I am. The only things inside the room are a toilet on one wall and a bed that's more of a wooden shelf with a thin mattress over it.

Where the hell am I?

"Hello?" I call out.

No one answers.

My wrists are encased in those silvery cuffs the guards slapped on me. They look perfectly seamless, except for a spot where chains can be added. I'm wearing different clothes too. Not that I was wearing much when Uriel arrived—that asshole—but I was definitely not wearing this scratchy, uncomfortable shirt and pants that are somewhere between a dark blue and purple. Indigo maybe? Whatever. The shirt is too tight in the boobs and too big everywhere else, and the pants are way too long yet narrow around my hips.

The worst part is that someone put these on me while I was

unconscious. They took off my other clothes. Touched me while I was naked. And then dressed me in this drab uniform.

I've never felt so violated.

To add insult to injury, they took my necklace from Callan too. I have nothing at all connecting me to my previous life.

I sit on the edge of the bed as the intense silence presses around me. I'm not claustrophobic, but this small, soundless room is almost unbearable. So is the despair at the realization that I'm being held prisoner. Are the Princes here also? They must be. Unless they're dead, but I refuse to consider that possibility. I can't believe Uriel would let that happen, but then again, I never thought he would betray us either.

I pull my legs up and bury my face in my knees. If I keep my eyes shut, I can pretend I'm somewhere else. Anywhere else.

Eventually I roll onto my side on the uncomfortable mattress and curl in a ball, willing myself to sleep. It doesn't work. My brain just replays everything that happened as I try to piece together Uriel's actions. We didn't tell him about the Staff, but he knew we were trying to stop the Order and get the Staff. How could he do this to us?

After several lifetimes pass, I hear something. I open my eyes in time to see a door appear in the opposite wall like a shimmering illusion. It opens, and a woman in a black guard uniform snaps, "Lunch time." She stands beside the open doorway and stares at me while I try to process what's happening. "Move!" she shouts.

I quickly stand up, but my legs wobble a little. As my head stops spinning, I try to access my powers to go invisible, blink out the door, or slam lust into her.

Nothing. This place is a total dead zone.

"Trying to use your powers on me?" the guard asks with a cruel laugh. She has mean little brown eyes and blond hair cropped close to her head. "Everyone does that when they get to Penumbra Prison. The cuffs block your magic, and there's no way to get them off. Don't even bother trying."

Penumbra Prison. The supernatural prison that houses fae, demons, and angels alike. During this year's Angelic History course,

Bastien explained how it's ruled over by an independent council with members of the three races, and none of them are Archangels, Archdemons, or members of the High Court of Faerie. They have utmost control over the prison, superseding Azrael, Lucifer, and even High King Oberon.

Which means no one is coming for us.

The guard leads me out into the hall, where two more female guards wait. None of them have weapons of any sort. I guess if they did, I'd try to take them. As it is, I don't think I can fight three of them without a weapon and no magic. Damn.

A door appears at the end of the hall out of nowhere. "How?" I ask. I can't seem to form coherent sentences. I'm still in shock, I guess.

"We're going to the cafeteria, so a door to the cafeteria appears," one of the other guards says with a shrug. It must be some kind of fae magic, because I've never heard of such a thing.

Before we enter the room, she holds a hand out in front of me. "Any signs of collusion or rebellion between you and the other prisoners, and you'll be taking your meals in your room. Understand?"

I nod as I drag my feet forward through the magic door. I can't tell if I'm hungry or not, but I know I should eat so I can keep my strength up.

I step into a large drab space with long tables with empty plates on them. As I step forward, trying to figure out what to do, more doors open, and dozens of women walk through, all wearing the same indigo uniform. They look haggard and desperate as they make a beeline for the tables and sit in front of the trays.

I spot a familiar purple streak in the crowd and my heart leaps. Araceli's moving toward someone with hunter green hair and another with straw-colored hair in a braid. I rush forward and they all spot me at the same moment, their faces as relieved as mine must be. Araceli hugs me tight, while Eveanna and Tanwen move in for a kiss, when a guard yells, "No touching!"

We quickly break apart. We'll have to be quiet and selective with what we say, but at least we're together for a little while. We sit at the end of an empty table, and a few women sit at the other end, leaving several seats between us.

As soon as we sit down, food begins appearing on the plates. It's the same meal on every one—chicken, green beans, mashed potatoes —but it doesn't look too bad. I grab the plastic cup first, gulping down the water. When I set the cup down, it refills. It's a small cup, so I let it refill three times before I slow down.

"Looks like they don't mean to starve us to death," Araceli says.

"We must assume they're not intending to poison us," Eveanna says as she picks at her food.

I grab my fork and stare at the food. Starving myself won't do us any good. And who knows? This may be our only meal today. I shove a green bean in my mouth.

"What are you guys doing here?" I finally ask.

"Uriel and my dad came and arrested us," Tanwen says with a scowl. "I assume the same thing happened to you?"

"Yeah." I sigh and take another long sip of water. "I'm happy to see you and to know I'm not alone in this awful place, although I was hoping you were out there coming up with a plan to rescue me."

"Do you think the guys are locked up on the men's side?" Araceli asks.

I nod. "Callan, Bastien, and Marcus were arrested with me. I don't know about Jonah or Kassiel. Maybe they escaped."

"Jonah was with me," Araceli says, her cheeks turning red. "Nothing happened though. I was hoping it would, but then we were interrupted by the guards."

"Tanwen and I were together as well," Eveanna says in her matter-of-fact way. "Uriel and Zadkiel took the Staff."

I'd been holding onto some hope that the Staff remained hidden, but now cold dread grips my stomach. "We have to assume they're working for the Order."

Tanwen slams her fist on the table. "I can't believe my dad would do something like this. Uriel maybe. He's a cold bastard, but my dad? No."

Eveanna reaches over and lightly rests her hand over Tanwen's in a show of sympathy. A mean-looking female guard walks by us and glares, and they jerk apart. I stuff some potatoes into my mouth. The others do the same. No colluding here, nope, no way. The guard carries on and we all relax again.

"I'm sorry," I tell Tanwen, once the guard is out of range. "None of this makes any sense. Uriel turned on his own son too. He betrayed all of us."

A woman at the table behind us starts cackling loudly. Our heads swivel to look at her, and we see she's staring right at us. "You made a big mistake, trusting that one."

I have no idea who this woman is, and she looks a bit mad, with long, wild brown hair, but I get the sense she knows something. "What do you mean?"

"Lunch time is over," a guard calls out. "Everyone back to your cells."

The food in front of us vanishes and the other women stand up and shuffle away. I barely touched my food and now it's gone. We'll have to eat faster next time.

The guards circle us and hustle us back to the open doors, and I let them take me away, after telling my friends, "I'll see you again soon. We will get through this."

Then I'm shoved into the door by the guard and taken back to my cell. As I sink down on my mattress, I think of that woman at the end. I only got a quick look at her, but something about her seemed familiar. She obviously knows something about Uriel.

I have to find her again.

35

MARCUS

After a few hours pacing my prison cell, I can't take the silence anymore, and begin to hum. It's bad enough being in here by myself, but I can't stop thinking about Liv and how she screamed as the guards dragged her away. Is she in prison too? Or have the Order taken her and the Staff? Are they now torturing her like they did Kassiel to make her use it?

When my throat is dry and ears pounding, I stretch out on the cot with my eyes closed. I have to stop humming, so I tap the wall beside the bed to create noise in the space. Anything to distract me from my thoughts.

Then I begin to count. One, one hundred, two, one hundred, three, one hundred.

By the time I hear something and scramble into a sitting position on the hard bed, I'm up to a million and something. A magical door opens up and a burly guard comes inside and grabs my arms, then drags me through it.

He lets me go and shoves me forward, past another group of scowling guards, and I walk through another doorway that leads outside, into a yard with grass and a few benches surrounded by a very tall chain-link fence. There are three other yards around us, forming a square, each divided by the same fence with about twenty prisoners in each one. All men.

I immediately spot Callan and Bastien standing together in the yard next to mine, and I rush to the fence. I reach out to grab it so I can talk to them through it, and I'm hit with a large bolt of electricity that would probably have killed a human. I fall on my ass and can't move for a minute, then a hand reaches down to help me up. Jonah's hand.

I shake off the buzz, my hair sizzling a little. "Jonah! They got you too?"

"Yeah, me and Araceli." He glances at the other Princes. "Was Liv with you guys?"

"She was, yeah." My chest hurts at the reminder of Liv. "I don't know if she's here or what."

"If she is, she would be on the women's side," Bastien says, his voice way too calm considering the situation we're in.

"Where are we exactly?" Jonah asks him.

"Penumbra Prison."

"Shit," Callan says under his breath.

I know what he means. Not even our parents can get us out of here, and no one has escaped before. We're fucking doomed.

"Hey, things could be worse," I try to find the upside in this situation because that's what I do, even though things seem hopeless. "We're not dead, and things don't seem too bad here. Sure, it's not like we're at a five-star hotel, but at least we're not being starved or beaten."

"Speak for yourself," Callan grumbles and rolls his shoulders.

I furrow my brow at him. "What do you mean? Did they beat you?"

He ducks his head. "I might've decided to test them when they brought me here. They got a few good hits in."

"That's not smart," Bastien advises. "Don't bring violence into play unless you think you can win."

He shoots him a look. "I think I can win."

"He always thinks he can win," Jonah adds.

"Marcus!" A familiar voice calls out. "Jonah!"

We turn to see Kassiel walking toward the fence in the next yard over. We move to the corners of our squares, where it forms a cross in the center, allowing all of us to talk.

"What are you doing here?" Callan asks, but it doesn't sound hostile.

Kassiel looks so different with his hair mussed up and his ever-present suit replaced by a prison uniform. "After I made sure Lilith and Lena were safe, I flew back to Seraphim Academy to help you destroy the Staff. Uriel and Zadkiel got me the second I crossed the school grounds."

"Shit," Jonah says. "We have to assume they got all of us then. Including Tanwen and Eveanna."

"And the Staff," I mutter. "The Order must have it now."

"Are we sure Uriel is working for the Order?" Kassiel asks.

"He must be," Bastien says, his voice cold.

"That fucker betrayed us and locked us up," Callan snaps. "It seems pretty damn clear to me he's not on our side."

Jonah gives him a sharp look. "Hey, that's still Bastien's dad."

"Which is why he should be the angriest one of all of us."

"I'm angry," Bastien says in a level tone. "But I'd rather focus on a solution, not the problem."

Callan's hands tighten into fists. "I'd rather pound your dad's face in."

"If we ever get out of here, I might let you."

I kick at the grass in front of me. "Do you think Olivia is in here too?"

"Hard to say," Kassiel says. "They might have taken her somewhere else if their plan is to use her."

I sigh. "That's my fear."

Jonah starts to reach for the fence, then thinks better of it. "We have to find a way out of here. There's no fence above us. Can we fly out?"

"I tried, but the cuffs block us from accessing our wings too," Kassiel says.

Bastien shakes his head. "There's no escaping Penumbra Prison."

Callan puffs up his chest. "Maybe not for regular people, but they've never locked up anyone like us before."

"He has a point." I rub my chin and glance at the guards, who are watching us closely with hard expressions. "Four sons of Archangels plus the son of Lucifer, all working together. We're a force to be reckoned with."

"Yes, we are," Kassiel says. "If we stick together and are smart about this, we'll figure something out."

The five of us share determined looks, and I feel an unbreakable bond forming between us. It was already there between me and the other Princes, but now it's grown stronger and Kassiel is part of it too. Angel or demon, it doesn't matter. We're brothers now.

And we're in this together until the end.

36

OLIVIA

"Time to go outside." My surly guard points to the other side of my cell, where another door opens.

I head through the opening and shield my eyes at the drastic change from dim room to bright sunlight. After hours being in that dark, drab cell, it feels like the greatest thing in the world to be outside again, soaking up the light and breathing in the fresh air.

I turn and look around the yard, noting the grass and the benches and nothing else. The space is not very large and is separated from other similar yards with a tall fence. I'm surrounded by women in prison garb, but don't see anyone I recognize.

"Olivia!" Tanwen says, behind me.

I spin around and smile, relieved to see my friend. "Where are the others?"

"I haven't seen them. They must rotate the prisoners out here." She starts walking around the perimeter of the yard. "This is probably our only time to get exercise and soak up the sun. We've got to make it count."

I feel so lethargic I can barely move my legs, but I manage to scramble after her. "Let me guess, you're in your cell doing sit-ups and shit."

"You know it." She pumps her arms, making her power walk even faster. "Aren't you doing the same?"

"Yeah, right," I say with a laugh, but then we near one of the other yards and I spot the woman from the cafeteria earlier. She's sitting on a bench with her hair draped over her face, her head down as she stares at the grass. I break off from Tanwen and rush over to the fence to try and get the woman's attention. "Hey!"

She looks up at me through her long, stringy hair and then says, "Don't touch it."

I jerk back, realizing I was about to grab the fence, grateful for her warning. "How do you know Uriel?"

She reaches down and picks a weed out of the grass, then studies it intently. "I gave him a son."

I gasp and nearly grab the fence again. "You're Bastien's mother?"

She cocks her head. "You know my son?"

"Yes, he's my..." How do I describe our relationship?

"Boyfriend," Tanwen supplies. Close enough.

"I'm Olivia and this is Tanwen. Uriel arrested us and threw us in here."

"My name is Dina." She stands and moves closer to the fence, studying me intently. "You truly know Bastien? Has he ever spoken of me?"

I study her in turn, as I think back on everything Bastien told me about his mother. "He said you had him as part of an arrangement with Uriel, and then you gave him up and moved on. He told me he'd only met you a few times."

"Is that what he believes? My poor son." Dina pulls at her hair, her eyes cast downward. "Uriel and I did have an arrangement, yes. It's often how angels, especially Archangels, sire children. However, I always intended to be part of Bastien's life. I'm his mother, after all. But Uriel betrayed me and locked me up here. Like you, I made the mistake of trusting him."

"Why would he do that?" Tanwen asks.

"I saw too much."

"You're a prophet, right?" I ask. Bastien mentioned something like that. It's a rare gift among Ofanim and highly prized, which is probably why Dina was selected to be Bastien's mother in the first place.

"I was. Until Uriel sent me here." She holds up her wrists. "These cuffs block my visions."

"What did you see that landed you in here?" Tanwen asks.

"I saw Uriel donning the crown of the Order of the Golden Throne. Have you heard of it?"

"The crown?" I ask, my stomach dropping. "Are you sure?"

She huffs. "Of course I'm sure. I also saw my own son being arrested by Uriel. Has that occurred?"

"Unfortunately, yes. I assume he's on the men's side somewhere."

"He's *here*?" Her face falls. "Oh, Bastien. He must be heartbroken by his father's actions."

Tanwen snorts. "I don't think anything gets through to Bastien's heart."

I elbow her, but then jerk back, worried a guard will appear and yell at me for touching her.

"My biggest regret in life is not finding a way to be with my boy. I've missed him so much. And now to learn he thinks I abandoned him..." Dina's face crumples. "If only I could speak to him."

Bastien would lose his mind if he learned his mother's been in prison for all this time. I must get her out of here. The rest of us too, of course, but it's suddenly become very important to me that I reunite them. Maybe because I know how hard it was growing up without my own parents, and how better my life is with them back in it now. I want that for Bastien too. Especially since his dad has turned out to be a total asshole.

I step forward, nearly touching the fence, and lower my voice. "Listen, Dina. I'm going to get you out of here, okay? And Bastien too. Then we'll make Uriel pay for what he's done."

Dina laughs, the sound bordering on maniacal again, like in the cafeteria. "Many have tried to break out of Penumbra. None have succeeded."

"Have hope. They've never imprisoned someone like me before."

"Someone like you?"

"I'm the daughter of Lilith and Gabriel." I stand a little taller, totally owning my ancestry. About time, right? "The first child of an Archdemon and an Archangel."

"The hybrid child. Yes, I saw you in a vision too." She frowns. "I saw you wielding the Staff of Eternity, controlling both light and darkness, while standing over a dead angel."

Well, that sounds ominous. "Can you tell me more?"

"No."

"This is why no one likes prophets," Tanwen mutters.

As our time is up and we're forced back inside, I resolve that I'm going to figure out a way to escape somehow. I'm not spending my entire immortal life stuck in this prison, and neither are my friends.

37

OLIVIA

I'm not sure how long I've been trapped in this prison, but it feels like a lifetime already.

The other day I asked the mean-eyed guard, whose name is Nisha, if I was allowed to have any water in my cell, and she let me keep a cup from the cafeteria. She said it gave her something to take away from me if I decided to act up.

How gracious of her.

My days are filled with routine. We're taken to the cafeteria for breakfast, lunch, and dinner, and we're given exactly ten minutes to eat. There's no time to talk if we want to eat, not that any of us has anything to talk about. Two times a day we're let out into the yards, but they rotate the prisoners, probably so we can't get too close to anyone. I've only seen Bastien's mom once more, but she wouldn't speak to me. I still haven't seen Eveanna, and Tanwen hasn't reappeared since the first day. Araceli was put in my yard yesterday, but as soon as we hugged, Nisha threatened to take my cup away.

And damn her, but it worked. I didn't touch my best friend again. I don't want to lose my cup.

I've been taken for a shower twice now. Both times I was woken from my sleep—if you can call it that. Since the lighting in the cell never changes, I try to go to sleep after dinner, but a true eight-hour deep sleep never happens.

Other than the time I hugged Araceli, I've been a model prisoner. I might ask for a real pillow soon. I've been able to question other prisoners enough to discover the cup thing is pretty common, at least throughout the women's side. Supposedly the men's side is stricter. They try to riot and escape more often. Figures.

All in all, it's boring, but not torturous. Nobody beats us. We eat, we shower, we walk. The worst thing is that we're stuck in here while the Staff is being held by the Order, who must be trying to find a way to use it. If they get an Archdemon to help them, I'm royally fucked. We all are.

It's after dinner, so I should be trying to sleep, but that's all there is to do in here. Sleep. I stand and start doing my yoga routine from my classes on campus. That's the other way I've been passing the time. Random bouts of exercise. I got the idea from Tanwen, naturally.

As I move into downward dog, I wonder how the guys are doing. I picture Callan starting fights every day, Marcus slumping in his cell, Bastien giving lectures on the prison, and Jonah trying to keep everyone calm. Is Kassiel free and working on a plan to get us out of here? Or have they gotten him too?

The thought of my men stirs the succubus hunger inside of me. Thank goodness I feasted on the Princes' energy right before I got thrown in here, or I'd be a lot worse off. I've been doing my best to ignore the hunger and keep it pushed to the back of my mind, and it's a lot easier than it used to be. For the last few years, I've been training in succubus fasting without realizing it, and I can go for a long time as long I get sunlight and don't overuse my powers. But at some point, the prison will have to feed me, and I wonder how they'll handle it.

I'm moving into warrior pose when my door opens, and Nisha walks inside. She looks even nastier than she normally does. "Let's go."

I freeze and lower my arms, trying to figure out where we're going. Time has lost all meaning while in here. She points to the door, and I step through into the small hall, where two more guards stand a few feet away, prepared to take me down if I try anything.

"Where are we going?" I ask. "Shower?"

"Just walk."

I walk to the end of the hall and a door appears, but this time, it leads to a long, stone hallway with low ceilings, dim lighting, and no doors whatsoever. Nisha grips my arm and directs me to a spot on the wall, where a doorway appears in the stone.

"Feed," Nisha says. "Don't kill him. We'll be watching."

She shoves me inside, and the door immediately disappears behind me. The room is empty except for a bed that's a lot bigger and more comfortable-looking than the one in my cell, and a man wearing inmate's indigo. Another prisoner.

The first man I've seen in what feels like forever.

He pulls off his shirt, as his eyes rake over my body. "Hello there."

I hold up a hand. "Wait. Who are you?"

"Inmate 1-8-7-5. Fox shifter." He shoves down his pants, where his erection is growing. "You new here? They don't give us much time. Get those clothes off fast."

I gape at him. "You want me to feed on you?"

"Fuck yeah. I volunteered. If we're on our best behavior for a month, we're allowed a conjugal visit with a succubus. Or an incubus, for the gay dudes." He's naked now and stalking toward me with lust in his gaze. I can't feel it, thanks to the cuffs, but I don't need my powers to know it's there.

I step back and hold up my hands. "No, I'm not doing this. I can't."

"What's the problem?" he asks with obvious annoyance. "You need to feed, and I'm horny. Let's fuck already."

As I look at this naked guy in front of me, my hunger surges and I'm tempted. The old Liv would have done it. Then I met the Princes and Kassiel and discovered there was something better than meaningless sex with strangers. It's the thought of them that allows me to turn away from this naked shifter in front of me and bang on the walls.

"Let me out!" I yell. "I'm not doing this!"

The door opens and Nisha drags me out of the room, her grip painful on my arm and her laugh cruel. She lets go as soon as the door closes. "You're one of those types, eh?"

I glare at her as I straighten my clothes, feeling dirty even though nothing happened. I hate this place, and everyone in it. Especially Nisha.

Her cruel eyes mock me. "You'll cave soon enough. They all do."

I clench my fists, but she's right. The hunger will only get stronger. Soon I won't be able to resist anyone they throw at me.

I have to get out of here.

38

OLIVIA

Nisha nudges me forward, toward my cell, and I stumble along. One of the guards in the hallway asks, "Back already?"

The other one snickers. "Must have been a quickie."

"She refused her feeding," Nisha says. "I'm going to have a little chat with her, so she sees the error of her ways."

She shoves me roughly back into my cell, so hard I fall to my knees. I look up at her, feeling too listless to do anything but stare at her. What's her problem? Nisha's a bitch, sure, but she's never been like this before.

She towers over me as the door traps us inside together. "Succubus cunt. You think you're so much better than us?"

Okay, now she's gone too far. Getting pissed off, I start to struggle to my feet, and she grabs my wrists and hauls them forward. Something clicks, and she...winks.

What the fuck?

She throws me down to the floor again and then bends over me, grabbing my hair to yank my head back, her mouth close to my ear. "Lucifer sends his regards."

Now I'm really confused.

"That's right, stay down, you hybrid slut," she yells. Way louder than she needs to, considering how small the room is. Something small and light hits the floor with the quietest tinkling sound. Then she leaves me there on the floor, face down.

As soon as she's gone, I sit up slowly, trying to process what just happened. She never actually hurt me, I realize. She just made a show of acting like she did. And what was that wink and that comment about Lucifer?

I reached around on the floor for whatever she left, and my fingers tighten around the metal of my necklace, the one from Callan with the sun and moon. I'm so relieved to have it back I clutch it tightly to my chest. Nisha left this here on purpose so I would know she's helping me.

I check my wrists, wondering what that clicking sound was, and the cuffs slide off into my hands. Magic blooms inside me, and I'm hit with the overwhelming sensation of being fully myself again. Sucking in a deep breath, I nearly cry in relief. I didn't realize how empty it felt to be cut off from my Lilim and Ishim powers until they returned.

I'm back, bitches.

I'm temped to rise to my feet like an avenging warrior and blow through this place, but I have to be smart. I'm outnumbered and outgunned. I put the cuffs back on loosely, curl up in my bed, and wait.

By the time Nisha comes for breakfast, I'm ready.

She acts like nothing happened, and I do the same. Her eyes are still cruel. I walk steadily to the cafeteria with my head down, trying to look defeated. The other guards barely spare me a glance. Which is good, cause if they look closely they might notice the chain around my neck and the pendant tucked under my shirt.

When I sit at our usual table, Araceli asks, "Are you okay?"

"I will be soon," I whisper. "We all will. Follow my lead."

Tanwen and Eveanna sit across from us, and Dina is alone at the table next to ours. I eat quickly, knowing I'll need the energy from the food. The others copy me. In my head, I count the minutes.

After exactly five minutes, I whisper to my friends, "We're getting out of here. Make sure Dina comes with us."

"On it," Tanwen says. Eveanna gives the subtlest of nods. Araceli bites her lip.

It's now or never. I throw off the cuffs and send out a wave of seductive power through the room, directing it at the guards. A few of them resist, because maybe they're succubi themselves or in love, but most heads swivel toward me. I swallow, hoping this plan works.

"If you want me, you'll protect me," I order the guards under my thrall, using my most seductive voice.

Nisha is the closest to me, but I purposefully left her free of my control. She understands what to do though, especially when I point at her.

"Free us," I order.

She rushes forward and removes the cuffs on Eveanna, who straightens up as soon as she's freed. Tanwen and Araceli are next, and then I direct Nisha to remove Dina's cuffs also. The older angel starts crying the second they're off.

We're free of the cuffs now, but still have to get out of here somehow. The guards who aren't under my control begin closing in fast. The other prisoners are standing up too, looking at me with hope or expectation. I considering removing their shackles too, but I don't know what any of them did to get them locked away in here. They could be serial killers for all I know. I can't let them go free.

A few of the guards, both my thralls and the free ones, make weapons out of light and darkness, and some of them turn into bears or wolves. Both sides face each other, and I know this could get ugly soon.

"Stop this now, and no one will get hurt," one of the guards calls out.

Araceli calls fire into her hands, and Tanwen creates a blade made of burning light. I wish I had my daggers, but they must be back in my bedroom, unless Uriel confiscated those too. I grit my teeth and expand my seductive powers to the prisoners, grabbing onto most of them, who join in the protective circle around us. Some of the other prisoners join in too, even without my control—my succubi sisters. Now we outnumber the guards, but I've never held so many people before, and it's been so long since I fed. I need to hurry this up, especially because some of the guards are already shaking off my seduction.

"Move everyone to that side of the room," I order, lacing more power into my words.

The guards and prisoners under my control start herding the few others, and Araceli and Tanwen make sure no one gets any ideas about attacking us. At one point, Araceli has to throw up a ring of fire around a charging bear shifter, and that makes everyone hesitate before trying anything else.

Once everyone is on one side of the room, Eveanna raises up walls around the guards and prisoners alike, blocking them in with her earth powers. The only one we've kept free is Nisha.

"Let's go," I tell her. I try to make it seem as though she's under my control too, so no one suspects she helped us.

Nisha opens a door in the other wall. Before we go through it, I use my Ishim powers to cloak our group, while Tanwen yanks Dina close. If we run across any Ofanim guards they might be able to see through my invisibility, but hopefully I'm stronger than they are.

"Take us to the men's side," I command Nisha, and she nods.

We head through the door one by one. It's time to rescue the guys.

39

CALLAN

It's another fucked up day in Penumbra Prison. I'm outside in one of the yards with Kassiel this time. Bastien and Jonah are in the yard to my right, and I don't see Marcus at all.

"I'm worried about Liv," Kassiel says. We're sitting together on one of the stone benches, because there isn't much else to do.

"Me too." We have no idea if she's even in here, or if the Order dragged her off somewhere to be tortured. Kassiel's still here, along with plenty of other demons, so we know they haven't used the Staff yet. Time's running out though, and I'm getting antsy. The son of Michael and Jophiel isn't meant to be caged, and I'm going to bust free soon.

Every day I test the guards a little more, while Bastien studies how the prison works. Marcus, Jonah, and Kassiel try to chat up their guards for info. During mealtimes, we exchange what we've learned while shoving food in our mouths.

So far, we know that Araceli, Tanwen, and Eveanna are on the women's side of the prison, but that's it. If Liv *is* there, the guards have been ordered not to talk about her.

We've tested the fences a few times, and there's no way to touch them without getting shocked. The first time isn't too bad, but the longer you mess with them, the worse it gets. And I can't do anything with these fucking cuffs on.

Kassiel stares off into the distance. "If they use the Staff, another war will begin between angels and demons. There will be no way around it. My father will have to retaliate."

"We won't let that happen." I clench my fists. "Our fathers didn't work for years to bring peace to our people just for it to end now."

Kassiel's demon-green eyes meet mine. "And if it does, and I'm sent back to Hell?"

"Then we'll find a way to drag your ass back here to Earth."

The slightest smile touches his mouth. "I appreciate that. If it comes to war, I'll do whatever I can to hold back my father and the Archdemons."

"It won't come to war. Even if Liv..." Fuck, I can barely get the words out. "Even if she's gone, we won't let our people turn against each other. We owe that to her, at least."

Kassiel nods, and we fall into companionable silence. A year ago, I'd never believe I'd be sitting here with Lucifer's son as my ally, or that we'd both love the same woman and be fine with it. But here we are.

A guard suddenly bumps into both of us from behind, hard. We spin around, and the guard stares intently at Kassiel. "Your father says it's time to go."

Kassiel's eyebrows dart up, but before he can reply, an inmate near the fence picks a fight with another guy. They throw some blows while the guards rush forward, and then the first guy picks up the other one with both hands, turns him sideways like they're wrestling, and throws him against the fence. Nothing happens.

This is our chance.

The other guards try to break up the fight, and the guard who spoke to us removes our cuffs in the chaos. My light floods into me like a long-lost friend. Finally, I can breathe again. At my side, Kassiel rubs his hands together, and then our eyes meet. It's time to get the fuck out of here.

More prisoners join the fight, and while the guards are busy, I grab the fence and yank as hard as I can. Kassiel gets the idea, and together we pull the metal away from the frame. As soon as it comes down, we're joined by Bastien and Jonah.

"What's going on?" Jonah asks.

"We're getting out of here." I glance around. "Where's Marcus?"

"I'll find him," Kassiel says, before slipping away into the shadows and vanishing.

Other prisoners have the same idea and start pulling down the fences until our carefully separated enclosures become one massive yard. More guards run out of the magical doors with weapons. They normally don't carry them, but it's turning into a full-fledged riot out here.

One of them makes the mistake of coming after me. He must have no idea who I am. I punch him in the face, and he drops like a rock. It's all too easy to take his sword.

Turning from his unconscious body, I raise my weapon and yell, "The prison is ours!"

All around me, prisoners overpower the guards and grab their weapons. Bodies drop around us. I don't like unnecessary death, but I'm trying to stop a bigger war here. Some casualties are expected. I fight other guards and prisoners alike, knocking them unconscious instead of killing them. Kassiel returns with Marcus, and our friends all get their cuffs removed at some point. Jonah makes our group invisible and we move away from the fighting as best we can, then spread our wings.

"How do we get to the women's side?" I ask Bastien, since she has encyclopedic knowledge of this place stored in his brain.

"It's over there in that building." He points across the prison grounds toward a stone building that looks just like the one we've been locked up in for who knows how long.

We fly up and over the battle that's spreading through the yard, and head in the direction he pointed. I can't see a way inside—it's like one big gray stone cube, just like the men's prison.

"Everybody back up!" Sucking in all the light I can, I channel my powers and send a burning hot bolt of pure light at the nearest wall. It hits with a booming explosion, the stone flying all over the place as a gaping hole appears. I peer through the rubble and spot a hallway, then gesture for everyone to follow me inside.

We're coming for you, Liv.

40

OLIVIA

We ask Nisha to take us to a room with weapons, and she manifests the door there. We're loading up with every weapon we can carry when we hear a massive explosion, like a wrecking ball hit the building. The ground under us shakes.

"What was that?" Araceli asks.

"My partner on the men's side must have done his job and freed your allies," Nisha says. "Hurry. More guards will be here soon."

Hope blooms in my chest at the mention of the men. When this is all over, we're going to have to send Lucifer a big thank you present. Maybe one of those edible flower arrangements or something. "Take us to that explosion."

She opens another magical door—I'm not sure how, but I suspect the guards have a fae relic on them somewhere—and we rush through, nearly stabbing the guys with our newly-stolen weapons. There's a huge gaping hole behind them in the side of the building. Subtle, they are not.

"We were just coming to rescue you!" I cry out, as I rush toward them.

"No, *we* were coming to rescue *you!*" Callan says, as he wraps me in a big bear hug.

"As you can see, we don't need rescuing," Tanwen says, wielding her sword.

Marcus grabs me from Callan. "We were so worried about you. We had no idea if you were in here or if the Order took you."

"I'm okay." I move to hug Bastien, Kassiel, and Jonah. I'm so relieved to see them that my eyes well up with tears, especially as the girls all hug them too.

Then the group hug clears up and Dina steps forward. "Bastien?" she asks softly.

He does a double take as he looks at her. His mouth falls open, but no words come out at first. Finally, he says, "Mother? Is that you?"

Now I'm really going to cry.

"We need to get moving if we're going to reach the helicopter before more guards arrive," Nisha says, interrupting their tender reunion.

"Helicopter?" Eveanna asks. I'm honestly not sure if she's asking what Nisha is talking about or asking what a helicopter is.

"It's the only way off the island," Bastien says. "We're too far out to fly back to land. We'd end up stranded in the middle of the Pacific."

Crap. I didn't know this place was an island. I can blink us a short way, but at best, I could go maybe the length of a football field. And I need to see where I'm going, too. No wonder this place is impossible to escape from, even for people who can fly.

"Let's blast our way out then," Callan says, and I swear half the room rolls their eyes at him.

"Is that always your solution?" Kassiel asks, but it's in a good-natured way. Something's changed between them. The animosity is gone.

"It usually works, doesn't it?" He shrugs. "We have our powers back, we can overpower everyone and steal the helicopter."

"Can anyone even fly a helicopter?" Araceli asks.

"I can." Kassiel strokes his chin. "Granted, that was during World War Two, but it probably hasn't changed much since then, right?"

"We're doomed," Jonah mutters.

"We'll figure things out as we go," I say, as I start forward. All I know is that if we stand around here much longer, we'll be surrounded.

We head back outside, and it feels amazing to spread my wings again. I glance back, and spot Dina hesitating at the edge of the building, before spreading her dove gray wings. They look pale, as if some of the color has washed out of them. She takes off, but struggles, and Bastien goes after her to help. I wonder how long it's been since she used her wings.

Tanwen grabs Eveanna, and Nisha surprises us all with her black and brown wings. A Fallen. She leads us across the compound, and I spot palm trees surrounding the perimeter and other signs of life we weren't allowed in the prison yards. At one end is a square landing pad, with three helicopters sitting there.

Before we can arrive, a group of flying guards, both men and women, head our way. A wave of darkness flies out from one of them and obliterates our Ishim invisibility, which requires us to bend light. Kassiel counters it by wrapping some of the darkness around himself and sending it away, but it's too late—they've seen us now.

We clash in the air with weapons and magic, and I'm so very grateful for Hilda's aerial combat class. A Fallen wraps me in tight, tar-like darkness and I start to panic, but then I look at Marcus and blink toward him. An instant later I'm free and by his side. This new power is already coming in handy.

Callan plows through the group, probably delighted he gets to blast his way out after all. Tanwen shoots burning light while holding Eveanna, who rips chunks of earth out of the ground to throw at the guards. Araceli launches fireballs, while Kassiel wields a sword made of shadows. I blink between guards, disarming them and confusing them, so then Marcus can knock them out with his sleep magic. We kill as few as possible. They're just doing their jobs, after all.

Another wave of flying guards comes toward us, and in this group I see a fae with shimmering, translucent butterfly wings. I've never seen anything as beautiful before and it nearly stops me in my tracks, but then we hear the sound of a helicopter approaching. At first I think it must be more reinforcements arriving and feel an impending sense of doom, until the helicopter gets close enough for me to read the logo on the sign of it: Abaddon Inc. Lucifer's company.

The pilot spots us and heads straight for us, instead of toward the landing pad. The helicopter is larger than I expected up close, big enough for all of us to get on it.

Kassiel suddenly takes off, flying carefully under the dangerous blades before landing inside the hulking machine. Callan throws a shield around the rest of us, blocking us from any incoming attacks, as we all follow Kassiel and climb onboard.

Once we're all safely inside, the helicopter ascends and picks up speed, getting us out of there. Soon we're flying over an endless expanse of dark blue sea while we stare at each other, shell-shocked but mostly unharmed and free. Nisha is with us—I guess there was no way she could keep working at that prison after this, but I'm sure Lucifer will take care of her.

"Where are we headed?" Jonah asks, yelling over the loud sound of the blades.

"Las Vegas," Nisha yells. "You'll be safe there with Lucifer."

Bastien shakes his head, his eyes narrowing. "No. I need to speak to my father."

I'm dreading going back to the school, but I know we have to do it. Going to Las Vegas to hide under Lucifer's protection would be the easy option, but not the right one. Besides, nowhere is safe while the Order has the Staff.

If we want to destroy it, we'll have to confront them.

41

OLIVIA

We can't exactly show up in Angel Peak on Lucifer's helicopter, so we have Nisha drop us off about an hour away, and then we fly the rest of the way to Marcus and Callan's house. We plan to confront Uriel, but first we need time to recover after everything we've been through.

A quick glance at Marcus's phone, which we find on the kitchen counter, shows we've been in Penumbra Prison for three weeks. It felt like longer, and we all damn near lost our minds. How did Dina manage it for all these years?

We each grab something to drink and a bite to eat, but we're too exhausted for much more than that. Jonah winces as he pours himself a glass of water, and Araceli goes over to fuss on him. Jonah laughs and pulls up his shirt, revealing a massive bruise.

"Why are you always getting injured, dude?" Marcus asks, shaking his head.

"I don't know," Jonah says with a grin. "It's a good thing I know such fine healers, isn't it?"

Araceli reaches over and places a light hand on Jonah's muscular stomach. "Let's go in one of the guest rooms. I'll take care of it."

As they leave the kitchen, I feel their lust—and something more

—swirling around them. If they haven't done something to kickstart this relationship yet, they will soon.

Callan pops open a beer. "I think we all know why he keeps getting injured."

"I'm not injured, but I'd really like to be alone with my girl-friend," Tanwen says.

"Let me show you to my room here," Eveanna says. I forgot she'd been staying here, pretending to be an angel, before we were captured. It's a good thing Callan bought the biggest, most ostenta-tious house he could find in Angel Peak, because we need a lot of extra bedrooms tonight.

Before they head leave, I hug them both tight. "Thank you. For everything."

"This is my fight, too," Tanwen says. "I've got your back."

Eveanna faces me with solemn eyes. "It's my duty to find the Staff. However, I do value our friendship as well."

Tanwen grins. "Let us know when it's time to kick some ass again."

They walk away, just as Bastien leads his mom toward Marcus's room, which I assume he gave up for the night, because that's the kind of guy he is. Dina looks truly exhausted and a little over-whelmed, as Bastien helps her inside and shuts the door. I can't imagine how hard this must be for both of them, but at least we got her out of there.

"She's already asleep," Bastien says, when he walks out. "She's so weak. So...different."

"Give her time," Marcus says. "She's been through a lot. I'll check her out tomorrow too."

"I appreciate that."

I collapse on the couch beside Marcus. "We can't stay here long. I'm not sure it was a good idea to come here at all."

Kassiel sits on the other side of me. "We'll reevaluate in the morning. Right now, we need to regain our strength. Especially you, Liv."

Now that I've sat down, it hits me how tired I am. I used more magic today than I realized, and my succubus hunger claws at me.

And I'm sitting in a room with all four of my lovers, none of whom I've touched in weeks.

"Yes, she needs to feed," Bastien says. "It's been too long."

"I'm in," Marcus says. "Whatever you need, however you need it."

"Are you sure?" I ask, glancing between them. "I know you're all exhausted too. Maybe we should talk about this after we've all had a good night's sleep."

"I think we'll all rest better tonight knowing you're sated." Kassiel puts his hand on my thigh and squeezes, sending jolts of desire straight to my core. Yep. That's what I want. Him. And the others. All of them.

Callan's gaze is on my leg where Kassiel's hand sits, but he's not angry. He meets my eyes and I let the question show on my face. I don't want him to do something he's not comfortable with. He was fine when it was just the Princes, but he and Kassiel haven't always gotten along in the past.

Without saying a word, he stands and holds out his hand. "I think we could all use a shower. Luckily, I have a big one in my room."

I rise and take his hand, my pulse already racing with anticipation. He leads me up the stairs and into his room, while the other men follow behind us. We step inside a large, very tidy bedroom with a huge four-poster bed, which is perfectly made. I would expect nothing less from Callan.

As soon as we're inside, Callan shuts the door, and then the four men look at me with their own hunger in their eyes. I feel lust coming off them in waves, and something else too.

Love.

I've felt it enough times now that I've come to recognize it, and it gives me a stronger burst of energy than any desire could. They love me, and I can't deny my feelings for them any longer either.

With a mischievous grin, I remove my prison inmate shirt. It's not the sexiest thing in the world, but I'm not wearing a bra underneath it, so I immediately have their attention. "I have a great need to be sated."

"Oh, really?" Marcus asks, as he pulls off his own prison shirt. I think we're all eager to get out of these clothes for many reasons.

"We can assist you with that problem," Bastien says.

Callan heads into his totally ridiculous bathroom and turns on the shower, which is large enough to fit all of us if we squeeze in a little. Somehow, I don't think that will be a problem.

I slide my ill-fitting pants and underwear to the floor and stand naked in front of them. "Strip."

The men follow my orders, revealing hard muscle and harder cocks. I feel like I'm at a buffet, and I can't wait to sample all of them.

"Touch yourself," I whisper. I don't know what's come over me tonight, but I want to watch them.

Marcus's eyebrows fly up as his hand grasps his dick at the base. "Like this?"

I nod. "Stroke it."

I barely notice his grin. My gaze is stuck to his hand as it moves up and down his shaft. He squeezes the head every time he passes over it.

"Now you," I tell the other guys.

Kassiel and Bastien follow my orders, sliding their large hands along their hard lengths, and I'm growing more wet by the second watching them touch themselves.

But Callan refuses to take orders from me, and instead picks me up in his strong arms. "I think it's time to get you clean, dirty girl."

He carries me against his own naked, dirty body, and then sets me down in the shower under the hot water. I sputter and glare at him as the spray hits me, but then I close my eyes and revel in the feeling of getting clean again. It's been way too long since I had a good shower.

As the other men enter the shower, I have a feeling this is going to be my best one yet. Callan grabs some shower gel and squirts it into his hands, then slathers it on my chest, taking extra time to squeeze my breasts. I take the gel from him and rub it all over his body next, and then we're kissing. Someone else starts massaging me from behind, stroking my back and kneading my ass while I let my hands explore Callan's hard body, from his shoulders to his stomach, until I finally have my hands around his hard cock.

Another set of hands begins working shampoo into my hair, while someone else slides a finger between my legs and strokes my clit, and I tilt my head back and revel in how good it feels to be pampered like this. Someone's mouth is on my neck, someone else is kissing my shoulders, and I have no idea which man is where, and I don't care. They're all mine, anyway.

I rinse off the soap, while they each lavish attention on me. Soon I'm clean enough, and the real fun can begin. Callan washes off his own soap, and then bends me over so my hands fall flat on the tile, and with one quick move he pushes his cock inside me from behind.

"Yes!" I cry out, my succubus side purring at finally getting what she's been craving for so long.

While he grips my hips and pumps into me, the other men watch with eager eyes, while rubbing soap all over their bodies. It's hot watching them get clean, and there's so much raw lust in this shower, I'm surprised the place doesn't combust.

Callan slips a finger inside my ass, making me moan, as he pounds into me harder. He's not wasting any time tonight. But then he pulls out of me and hauls me back up, sharing me with the other freshly washed men. Kassiel is closest, and it's been the longest since I've been with him, so I pull him toward me for a desperate kiss, pressing our slick, wet bodies together. But then he turns me toward the other guys, letting them go first, like the gentleman he is.

Marcus grabs me around the waist and lifts me up, sliding my legs around him as his cock moves into me. I grip onto his shoulders and kiss him hard while he bounces me up and down on him, sending a wave of pleasure into me as the friction hits my clit in the exact right way. Then Bastien's behind me, his hands on my breasts while he kisses my neck. With the two of them worshipping my body, it doesn't take long before Marcus wrings my first orgasm out of me. My first of many, I'm sure. As I tighten up around him, he thrusts into me faster, then hits me with his sexual energy as he climaxes.

We kiss for a long time, and when he breaks it off, he looks in my eyes and I feel his strong love for me. Then he passes me to Bastien, who sits down on the bench in the corner and has me straddle him. I glide down onto his cock and he fills me to the hilt, while the other men watch from around us. Kassiel is beside me, and I direct him closer, then wrap my lips around his cock. I ride Bastien, suck Kassiel, and spot Callan stroking himself out of the corner of my eye, while Marcus rinses himself off. It's all so erotic, and so intimate too. I never thought I would find four men who not only cared for me but would be willing to share me like this too.

Bastien brings me to another orgasm just in time for him to come inside me, bucking his hips up in time to my own movements. Then he takes my chin in his hand and gives me a possessive, scorching hot kiss, before lifting me off him.

"We're clean enough," Callan says, as he turns off the shower.

Marcus is already out and has a towel around his waist, and he wraps me up in a big fluffy towel and begins drying me off. The other guys get out too, but Kassiel and Callan can't be bothered to towel off. Instead, Kassiel grabs my hand and leads me to the bed. He pushes me down onto it, spreads my legs, and dives between them, using his tongue to make me moan.

"Kassiel!" I cry out. "I need you now."

He slowly climbs up the bed, sliding his slick body along mine, the water making his hair black and messy. His hard length nudges against my entrance, and then slowly he slides home. Both of us take a moment to relish the feeling of him deep inside me before he begins to move. It feels amazing. I bury my face in his neck and moan as he fucks me deliberately, so I feel every single stroke.

But then he rolls us over, so I'm on top of him. I get a better grip with my knees and move faster. Bouncing up and down, I moan as he goes deeper, the angle perfect.

"Join us," Kassiel says, looking to the side. I follow his gaze to see Callan watching us intently while stroking his cock.

I can only watch in awe as Callan grabs the lube and moves behind me. Are we really doing this? The two of them and me?

Callan's fingers already prepared me earlier, and honestly, I'm so wet I'm ready for anything. He lubes us both up and then pushes me down, so my breasts are pressed against Kassiel's chest. My Fallen lover captures my mouth in a seductive kiss, while Callan grabs my butt, pulls the cheeks wide, and slides his cock between them. I gasp as his large length fills me up from behind and I bury my face against Kassiel's neck. With Kassiel already inside me, it seems impossible Callan can fit too, but he keeps pushing until he's in to the hilt, and I'm squeezed tight between their bodies.

The three of us, joined as one. Angel and demon. Light and dark. Day and night. I never thought it would happen, but everything about this moment feels right. Like destiny.

The two of them look each other in the eye, and something passes between them. Kassiel begins to move under me, throwing his hips upward, bucking Callan along with us. For once, Callan lets someone else lead the show for a while, our bodies rolling together like a wave. I suck up all the potent sexual energy flowing off them, which gets stronger with every thrust.

Then they suddenly switch so Callan is controlling us, and he grips my hips and picks up the pace, pounding into me from behind. It rocks me forward onto Kassiel's cock, and I can only gasp as they work together to bring me to the most earth-shattering orgasm of my life. I'm pretty sure I scream loud enough to wake everyone in the house. Maybe the entire block. I can't help it. Both men come at the same time, and I'm hit with so much energy it makes my body tremble. I throw my head back and just ride it out, sucking everything from the two most powerful men I've ever slept with.

With a sigh, I rest my head on Kassiel's shoulder, so full of their energy I think it's probably bursting out of my skin. Callan squeezes me tight, and then drops down beside us on the bed. I roll off Kassiel and wedge myself between the two men. Bastien and Marcus move onto the bed and somehow curl up against me too, and I stroke their hair lovingly.

"That was incredible," I tell them when I can finally speak again. "I never imagined I could have something like this." I sit up a little as emotions threaten to overwhelm me. "I want you all to know that I care for each of you a lot. I've been told my whole life that a Lilim can never have love, or have a long-term relationship, but I refuse to accept that. I do feel love, and I want to be with all of you for as long as you'll have me."

Marcus presses a kiss to my lips. "We're here for you, Liv, always. And you already know I love you."

"I do as well," Bastien adds. "Though I'm sure you know that too."

I laugh softly. "I have some idea."

Kassiel runs a hand along my stomach. "I've lived a long time, and I've never loved anyone like I love you."

My heart soars, but then I turn to Callan. He reaches over and touches the sun and moon pendant hanging above my naked breasts. "I know it hasn't always been easy between us, but I'm yours, if you'll have me."

It's not a full declaration of love, but it's a big step for Callan. I lean over and press a kiss to his lips. "Yes, I think I'll keep you." I snuggle up between all of them. "I think I'll keep all of you."

42

OLIVIA

We fall into a deep sleep, all nestled together on Callan's big bed. Even Kassiel. No insomnia plagues him tonight.

In the morning, the angels wake with the dawn, while Kassiel and I yawn and beg them to let us sleep a little longer. They oblige us and let us stay in bed, curled up together. Neither one of us can sleep though, and soon Kassiel's giving me a sleepy fuck from behind while his fingers dance across my clit. Then the other guys come back with my coffee and see what we're doing, and next thing I know it they're all taking me in turns until every one of us gets off again. Me, multiple times. I'm starting to wonder if this is my new life now. If it is, I'm certainly not going to complain about it.

Eventually, we get dressed and make our way downstairs. I'm surprised to find the kitchen and living room empty. Everyone else must be sleeping in too...or not sleeping like we were. Marcus and Kassiel start cooking up some pancakes and bacon, while Bastien stares off into space, and Callan does a quick perimeter check to make sure we're safe. I sip my coffee and relax, wondering if this is how our life could be every day if we manage to stop the Order.

A noise in the hallway makes us all turn our heads. "Bastien?" a soft voice calls out.

Bastien heads out of the kitchen as we all exchange sympathetic looks and remember that our little bubble of happiness can't last. I hear quiet murmurs from the other room, and after a few minutes, I go peek my head in to make sure they're okay.

"I thought you didn't care," Bastien is saying. "Or that you didn't want to be my mother."

"Oh, my son. I hate that you believed that." Tears flow slowly down Dina's face. "I thought about you every single day I was in that prison. Remembering your little chubby cheeks and way too intelligent eyes was the only thing that kept me sane all these years. Of course, now you're a man. I wish I could have seen you grow up."

My heart breaks for the two of them and I start to leave, but then Bastien waves me over. "Stay."

I sit on the couch and hold his hand as Dina gives me a shaky smile. I feel awkward sitting here, but maybe they both need someone to be part of their reunion.

Dina reaches over and takes my other hand. "I have this young lady to thank for getting me out of there."

"It was the least I could do. Tell Bastien everything you told me about Uriel."

She gives a solemn nod and explains to her son how Uriel locked her up after her visions. I notice she leaves out the part about seeing me standing over a dead angel.

"I will never forgive Uriel for taking me away from you and making me miss out on your life," Dina says, with more venom than I expect from her frail body. Then she softens again. "But at least we're together now. For however long it lasts."

Bastien leans over and draws her into his arms. I bet he wouldn't have done that before I came into his life. "I'll take care of everything, and then we'll have the rest of our lives to catch up on what we missed. You are not going back to Penumbra. I swear it."

More tears fall down her cheeks as she strokes his face lovingly. "My dear boy. I always knew you were destined for great things."

Marcus pokes his head in the room. "Breakfast is ready. Can I bring you something, Dina?"

She nods. "That would be wonderful. Just a little something, please."

"I'll help." I jump up and run into the kitchen to get her food, giving her a little more alone time with Bastien.

A few minutes later, I take a bottle of water and the plate of pancakes and bacon to Dina. Bastien has moved her back into the bedroom and is fussing over her, putting another blanket on the bed even though it's not even cold. He sets up a tray on the bed, and I set the plate on it, like room service.

"Thank you, this is wonderful," Dina says. "I haven't been able to relax and eat in so very long."

"If there's anything I can do for you, please let me know," I tell her.

Dina suddenly grabs my arm and looks deeper into my eyes. "You're very special."

My heart beats faster. Can she tell me something about my future? Something about her other vision?

She lets go, grabs a piece of bacon, and takes a big bite. "Mmm. I haven't had bacon in so long."

Okay, guess not.

"I'll leave you to it." I head outside, leaving Bastien to give his mom a kiss on the forehead. Dina obviously needs more time to rest and recover, and we have things we need to do too.

The mood's changed as we sit down for breakfast together. The light, fun, romantic feeling has vanished, and now we're remembering everything Uriel has done to us. I make sure to quickly get the other guys up to speed on Uriel's full betrayal, and Dina's accusation that Uriel leads the Order. Bastien's eyes are blazing with barely controlled fury the entire time he eats. I've never seen him like this before.

"Are we safe here?" I ask, thinking more of Dina than myself.

"For the moment," Callan says. "We might want to find somewhere else for Dina to stay though, for her protection."

Bastien suddenly slams his fork down and rises to his feet. "I have to confront my father."

"Now?" Kassiel asks.

Bastien's eyes narrow. "Now."

I exchange a look with Marcus, who says, "Maybe we should discuss this first. Come up with a plan."

"I'm with Bastien." Callan grabs his last piece bacon and stands up. "Let's get this over with. Our headmaster has a lot to answer for."

Bastien's already heading out the door, but I grab his arm. "Wait! You're acting rash for the first time in your life. Give us a second at least to tell the others to protect your mom while we're gone."

"On it," Marcus says. He rushes off, while the rest of us gather our weapons, and I cloak us in invisibility. Bastien paces impatiently the entire time. I'm seriously worried about him.

When we're ready, Bastien leads the charge, launching into flight with his silver-streaked dark gray wings.

It's time to face the leader of the Order.

43

BASTIEN

I don't think I've ever been this furious before. I'm cold. I'm calculated. I don't fly off the handle or act rashly. But I can't stop the white-hot rage coursing through my veins as I fly toward Seraphim Academy. I'm certain I could single-handedly break us through Penumbra Prison's walls with this much anger inside of me.

He betrayed me. My friends. My mother. There is nothing he can say that will explain how he locked her up for *years*.

He stole the Staff. He runs the Order. He lied to me my entire life.

I am *livid*.

As soon as we fly over the gates, we head directly for my father's Victorian house. The others keep up with me, and Olivia keeps casting worried glances at me, but I ignore them. This is something I must do.

I'm ready to bust through the house, throw my father against the wall, and demand answers, but the front door opens before we even touch down.

"I've been expecting you." Uriel holds the door open and steps back. "Come in."

I stand in the doorway and try not to snarl as my breath comes out in heaving gasps. "How could you?"

He looks at me with a certain heaviness in his gaze. "I have my reasons. Come in. I'll explain everything."

As much as I want to hear his explanations, I'm so angry I don't know if I can sit through them.

Olivia walks forward and puts her hand in mine. My anger cools considerably as soon as she touches me. Suddenly, I can think again. I can be rational. I can be calm.

Somewhat calm.

Once we're in the foyer, my father leads us into the small, formal sitting room that we never used unless we had company over. Last year, Olivia met Lilith in here for her succubus training. I suppose I've been demoted to guest now. I certainly don't plan to live here ever again.

Uriel drapes himself in one of the armchairs, like this is a casual chat. "Sit."

None of us move. I cross my arms. "Explain."

Uriel faces our group with a solemn expression. "I sent you to Penumbra Prison for your protection."

"Bullshit," Callan says. "Try again."

"It's true. If I didn't, Azrael would have gotten to you. Once he learned you had the Staff, it was inevitable."

"How did he find out?" Kassiel asks.

"Jophiel told him when she informed him of Ekariel's rescue."

Callan glares at my father. "Is Jophiel working for him?"

Uriel looks at him as if he's an idiot. "Of course she is. He put her in charge of his company. She's always been loyal to him."

"Why send us to prison?" Marcus asks.

"Azrael can't get to you there. Not easily, anyway. The prison is run by a neutral council of angels, fae, and demons, and they have complete oversight over it. Azrael has no influence there. I figured it would buy us some time."

"And my mother?" I ask, the fury rising again.

A dark shadow passes over his emotionless face. "I sent her there for the same reason. To protect her from Azrael."

"You're the one she needs protecting from!" My fists clench at my sides. "She saw you leading the Order, and you locked her up for it! I thought she abandoned me!"

Uriel sighs. "Yes, that's what she saw, but she is incorrect. I lead the Order on campus, but Azrael is the true leader."

"The golden throne at the meetings," Olivia suddenly says. "Neither you nor Nariel sat on it. Azrael was there the entire time, invisible and watching, wasn't he?"

"That's correct. Nariel was always a puppet, acting at my command. But we all bow to Azrael." Uriel's eyes meet mine again. "When Azrael found out Dina was having visions about the Order, he wanted to control her. He planned to use her to his advantage. Just like he wants to do with Olivia now."

"What do you mean?" Callan asks.

He fixes Olivia with a level stare. "Azrael wants to make an example of you. Now that he has the Staff, all he must do is convince you to use it. And he can be very convincing."

"He only has the Staff because you gave it to him," I snap.

"Zadkiel did that, not I." Father waves a dismissive hand. "Azrael would have gotten it either way. I saved your lives by doing it my way."

"My mother was locked up for years!" I yell. "You could have told me at least. I could have visited her!"

Uriel sighs, like he's tired of this conversation. "Penumbra Prison was the only safe place for Dina because it stopped her visions. I convinced Azrael she was worthless, and he soon forgot about her. I did not want her speaking to you about visions. I worried every day you would develop that gift, and Azrael would come for you too. Perhaps it was an error on my part."

"I'd say so," Kassiel mutters.

"None of that matters now," Uriel says, rising to his feet. "Azrael will soon find out you've escaped, if he doesn't already know, and he'll be coming for you. This time, I won't be able to protect you. He'll have the entire Archangel Council and the might of the angelic army under his command. There will be no escape."

"The entire Archangel Council?" Marcus asks, his face paling. "Even my father?"

"Yes." Uriel meets his eyes. "All of them."

"What are you saying?" Olivia asks. "Are you telling us they're *all* in the Order?"

"Correct. Including Gabriel."

She drops my hand and steps back, shaking her head. "No. No. No. It's not possible."

My mind whirls. I can't grasp what he's just said. *Every Archangel?*

"When Michael was alive, he kept Azrael in check," Uriel continues, while we stare at him in shock. "After his death, things got a lot worse. We tried to put Gabriel in charge, but Azrael made sure that didn't happen. For years Azrael has blackmailed, threatened, and manipulated the other Archangels into doing his bidding. He controls all of us."

"Why didn't you stand up to him?"

"As the leader of the Archangel Council, Azrael can draw upon the power of every angel. He cannot be stopped. Even if we tried, he has too many allies and followers. The Order. Aerie Industries. Even this school. We all bow to his will."

Olivia sucks in a sharp breath. "I can't believe this."

I put my hand on her shoulder. I know exactly how she feels. Betrayed. Angry. Like her life is a lie. I feel it too.

"I know you won't believe me, but I do care for you, my son," Uriel says. "I will not let Azrael harm you. When he comes for you this time, I will fight, even if it means my doom. Unless you wish to hide."

"We could go to Lucifer," Kassiel suggests.

"No," Callan says. "Azrael will never stop. We need to confront him and get the Staff, then destroy it. It's the only way we'll ever be safe."

Uriel nods, his mouth set in a grim lime. "In that case I suggest you stay here on campus, where it'll be easier to defend."

I suppose that's the best option. Running away will only buy us some time, but we'll have to fight Azrael at some point. Doing it here with all of Seraphim Academy's defenses at our disposal is our best chance of success.

"Fine," Olivia says, still sounding shaken. "We'll stay here and fight. After I speak with Gabriel."

"Then I shall prepare the school for an attack," Uriel says. "I won't let him take either of you. I promise."

I wrap my arm around Olivia's shoulders and lead her toward the door, while the others follow. We have a lot of work ahead of us. But before we go, I turn back and meet my father's gaze. "I won't forgive you for this."

A rare flicker of emotion crosses his face for the briefest instant, and then it's gone. "I know."

44

OLIVIA

With shaking hands, I text my brother to meet us at Gabriel's house, and then our group takes off. With this hurricane raging inside me I can barely keep the light bent around us to hide our flight out of Seraphim Academy.

Could my father really be in the Order?

I don't want to believe anything Uriel said, but it would explain a lot. Like why Gabriel dismissed my concerns when I said Jonah was in Faerie. Or why it seemed like he was never looking very hard for my brother. Or why he never did anything about the Order and told me to stay out of it.

All the lies. All the secrets. It's too much.

Especially since I just started to bond with him again after growing up feeling like he abandoned me. I finally trusted him, and now this. I don't know how to process it all. I can't.

My heart is in my throat during the flight to Gabriel's house, and my four men stick close to me the entire time. I know they're worried about me, but I can barely look at them. I can only think about what Uriel said. It's not just my father. It's all the Archangels. Every single one of them. All controlled by Azrael.

How can we ever win against them?

Jonah beats us to the house but waits in the yard like I asked. We land beside him, and he looks a little rumpled. From the lingering lust hovering around him, I know it's not from sleep, and if this were any other time, I would pester him with questions about what happened. Instead I look at him with sadness, knowing what we're about to tell him will hurt him as much as I did me.

"Are you feeling any better?" I ask, unsure how to start this conversation.

He ducks his head. "Yeah, Araceli works wonders."

"I bet," Marcus mutters.

"What's going on?" Jonah asks.

I open my mouth but can't get the words out. I send Bastien a desperate plea with my eyes, asking for his help.

"According to Uriel, he sent us to Penumbra Prison to protect us from Azrael," Bastien explains in a level tone. His anger from before is still there in the background, but it's been reduced to a low simmer he can easily control. "Azrael is the true leader of the Order, and every member of the Archangel Council is in it."

"Including Gabriel," I whisper.

"What?" Jonah looks back and forth between Bastien and me. "There's no way."

"I hope you're right," I manage to say.

"Hang on." Jonah's brow furrows. "Let's give him a chance to explain, okay?"

I nod, and then we hesitate at the door. Do we knock? Or do we use our key and walk in, like it's still our house?

We decide to knock.

Gabriel opens the door and gazes across our group. "What are you doing here? You're supposed to be in Penumbra Prison."

"You knew we were there?" Jonah asks.

Gabriel's eyes fall on Jonah, but instead of answering he asks, "How did you escape?"

"Lucifer," I say, my voice flat.

"Of course." Gabriel sighs. "All of your parents agreed Penumbra Prison was the safest place for you, but we didn't inform

Lucifer of our plans. We're not used to consulting on him on these things."

"Get used to it," I snap. "Kassiel is with me now."

"He's with all of us," Callan says. I look at him in surprise. He's the last one I expected to say that, but something between them has definitely shifted. Kassiel gives him a warm nod in response.

"I know," Gabriel says. "Come, sit down. I'll pour us some coffee so we can chat."

I want to argue, but I never turn down coffee. We all shuffle into the kitchen, where the coffee has already brewed. Marcus, Kassiel, and Bastien all sit at the dining table, but Jonah and I are too antsy, and Callan leans against the walls with his arms crossed, his eyes on my father like he's ready in case he tries something.

Gabriel begins pouring coffee into a bunch of different mugs. "You know, you've all made things infinitely more complicated by not staying put."

"Sorry for not wanting to stay locked up in prison," Marcus says dryly.

"We did it to protect you from Azrael," Gabriel says, as he hands me a steaming hot mug of coffee. The smell instantly hits my nose and makes me feel a hundred times better. Which is probably Gabriel's plan. I can't let my guard down.

"Uriel told us everything," Bastien says.

I grip my mug tighter. "He told us you're in the Order."

Gabriel finishes setting down coffee mugs in front of everyone, along with sugar and milk. Callan shakes his head when offered a mug, glaring at my father. I'm starting to think Gabriel isn't going to answer when he picks up his own coffee and takes a sip. Then he sets it down and says, "Yes. I'm in the Order. All the Archangels are."

I close my eyes as the cold truth washes over me. Up until this point I still held some hope that Uriel was lying or there was some explanation for all this. But hearing my father say it out loud confirms it.

Gabriel's blue eyes get a distant look as he begins speaking. "The Archangels started the Order when we first started visiting

Earth, and we placed Azrael in charge of it. He was one of the angels that regularly traveled between Earth and Heaven in those early days. Back then we were at war with the demons and they were coming to Earth in large numbers. Many of them were influencing humans in ways that were...detrimental. The Order of the Golden Throne was created to balance their power and guide humanity into a better tomorrow." He takes a sip of his coffee. "But like many things, what was started with good intentions became twisted over time."

"What happened?" Jonah asks.

"During the industrial revolution, Azrael started Aerie Industries as a front for the Order, with Jophiel as his second in command. She wasn't an Archangel back then, but he made sure she became one when a spot opened. As CEO, he helped Aerie Industries grow into one of the most powerful corporations in the world. Michael kept him in line as best he could, but Azrael is incredibly sneaky, and he has many loyal followers. Over the years, he amassed lots of secrets about all the other Archangels. Secrets he used to blackmail us." He sighs and stares into his cup. "After Michael's death, Azrael became the Archangel leader, and he made Jophiel CEO of Aerie Industries in his place."

"What did he have on you?" Bastien asks.

I can guess. "He knew about me, didn't he?"

"Yes." Gabriel looks at me with sad eyes. "Somehow Azrael knew about my relationship with your mother from the beginning, and as soon as you were born, he used it against me. He threatened to expose you to the angel community. He made it seem like if anyone found out, you would be killed. I believe he's the one who murdered your adopted family. He tried to make it look like demons, but I'm certain he did it to prove his point—your life was in danger."

"He blackmailed you to make sure you didn't become the new Archangel leader," I say.

"Yes. And now that he's taken Michael's place and controls both the Archangel Council and Aerie Industries, his power and reach are almost limitless. I've tried to subtly work against him over the years, but the fear of him hurting my kids has prevented me from outright acting against him." He glances between me and Jonah. "I tried to keep you both out of this mess, but I should have known that wouldn't work."

"Did you know Jonah was in Faerie all that time?" I ask.

"I did. I hated it, but I figured it was safest for everyone if he stayed there, guarding the Staff."

"You *knew?*" Jonah asks.

Gabriel meets his eyes. "Of course I knew. I do run the angelic spy network, after all."

"We thought you were just really bad at it," Marcus says, making Callan snort.

Gabriel smiles a little at that. "Azrael thinks that as well. I've used it to my advantage many times to undermine him and the Order over the years. I could never oppose him openly though— Azrael made it clear if I did anything to interfere with the Order getting the Staff and using it, he would kill Olivia." His eyes meet mine. "That's what he came to talk to me about at the beginning of the school year. He reminded me to stay out of the Order's business with the Staff, and to keep you away as well."

"What about our parents?" Marcus asks. "Are they working with Azrael, or are they under his control like you were?"

"Zadkiel works for Uriel and is very loyal. Azrael made sure he got the empty spot on the Archangel Council after Michael's death. Jophiel has been loyal for years as well but is more concerned with Aerie Industries than the Order and the Staff. Raphael, Ariel, and Uriel are all held under Azrael's thrall. He holds something over all of them, and they're too scared of him hurting their children." He draws in a sharp breath. "But it's time we finally stood up to him. No more living in fear. I will contact the others and convince them to fight alongside me. We will defend all of you and stop him from using the Staff."

"Are we sure he will come for Olivia?" Kassiel asks. "He could try to find another Archdemon."

"He could," Gabriel agrees. "And while you were in Penumbra Prison, I heard some rumors he would go after Lena, if he couldn't get Olivia. However, Lucifer has the Archdemons and their children locked down tight. It would start another war if Azrael tried to kidnap one of them."

"It's going to be war here too, if he comes for Olivia," Callan growls.

"Yes, and he knows that, but he thinks it's worth it. Azrael plans to force Olivia to use the Staff to make an example out of her. The only child with both angel and demon blood, sending the demons back to Hell? It's exactly the kind of thing he eats up." Gabriel dons a wry smile. "Plus, he just really wants to punish me. We've been rivals for thousands of years. I can't wait to stand up to him finally."

"What is Azrael's Archangel power?" I ask.

Dad's brow furrows. "I... I don't know. That's odd. It's like...a memory that's slipped away."

Marcus exchanges a look with Callan. "That's Jophiel's Archangel power."

Callan nods. "My mother can remove or cloud memories."

Bastien strokes his chin. "That seems to confirm she's working for him. Or has in the past."

"Whatever his power is, Azrael doesn't want anyone to know about it," Kassiel says.

"Uriel thinks Azrael will come for Olivia soon," Jonah says. "We're planning to stand our ground at Seraphim Academy."

Gabriel downs the last of his coffee. "I'll contact Raphael and Ariel and let them know."

Callan straightens up. "We should all begin our preparations."

The others finish off their drinks and set them down, then begin to file out, leaving me and Jonah alone with our father. Gabriel stands and crosses over to us, his arms slightly extended as if wanting to hug us or something, but Jonah and I recoil. I'm not there, not yet, and it seems my brother isn't either.

"I'm sorry," Gabriel says.

Jonah steps back, shaking his head. "You should have told us about all this before. We might have been able to avoid all this mess."

"You might be right. I was simply trying to protect you." Gabriel looks at me with weary eyes. "Both of you."

I let out a long sigh, as I think of all the secrets and lies I've both uncovered and perpetuated myself over the last few years. "Our family has never been good at honesty. Going forward, we need to do better."

"Agreed," Gabriel says. "I'll do whatever I can to regain your trust. But first we need to face Azrael."

45

OLIVIA

W e return to the house and catch everyone up on what Uriel
and Gabriel told us. Tanwen is really pissed about her
father and has to go outside and blast some trees before she can calm
down. Marcus finds some frozen pizzas in the kitchen and heats
them up for all of us to share. Jonah and Araceli sit awfully close
together on the couch, and even with everything that's going on, it
makes me happy to see them together.

"Is this finally happening then?" I ask, waving my slice of pizza
at the two of them.

"I don't know what you mean." Jonah glances at Araceli with a
slight smile, and she flushes under his gaze. Whatever he sees in her
eyes makes him change his mind, and he sits up a little and wraps an
arm around her shoulders. "Actually, yeah. It is."

She rests against him and looks more content than I've seen her
in years. I can't think of a better match than my kind-hearted best
friend and my loyal and true brother.

"We need a girl talk session as soon as possible after this is over,"
I tell Araceli. "But I love what I'm picking up so far."

She rolls her eyes with a smile. "Oh, hush."

I'm about to tease them some more, mainly to get my mind off what my dad said, when Dina emerges from her room, as pale as a sheet. She stumbles forward and Bastien catches her.

"Mother?" he asks.

She looks up at him with horror in her eyes. "Azrael is coming, with many angels in masks. At dawn."

"You saw it?" Marcus asks. "In a vision?"

"It came as a shock. It's been so long since I had one. But I'm sure." Dina suddenly grips Bastien's shoulders with a mad look in her eyes. "You must get Michael's sword. It's the only thing that can stop Azrael."

"Michael's sword?" Bastien's brow creases and he glances at Callan.

"My father's sword has been missing since he was killed. We assumed Lucifer had it, but now we know that isn't the case."

"Can you tell us where the sword is?" I ask.

Dina shakes her head. "No, I can only see snippets of the future at the moment. I need more time before my full sight returns. I'm sorry."

"It's all right, mother," Bastien says.

We offer her some pizza and then she heads outside to soak up some sunlight while she eats. It's going to take some time for her to adjust to life outside of the prison.

Callan wipes his hands with a napkin. "Azrael is coming at dawn, which doesn't give us much time. We need to start preparing for war immediately."

"We'll need allies," Kassiel says. "I will contact my father."

"I can ask the High King for help," Eveanna says.

"He banished you from Faerie," Jonah says. "I know you managed to sneak through with Lilith, but this is different. You'll be facing the High King himself. That's way too dangerous."

"Perhaps. The High King tasked me with returning or destroying the Staff. I could argue that to do so I require his help."

"No, if you go, you might never be allowed to come back," Araceli says. "Jonah and I will go instead. The High King likes him, and I can get us in and out of Faerie. Assuming we can find a fae relic."

Marcus rises to his feet. "After the Duskhunter ambush, we confiscated all their fae relics and infused weapons. They're still hidden in the house. I can take you to them."

"Perfect," Callan says. "We can use those infused weapons too."

"I'm going to Hellspawn Academy to ask Baal for help," I decide out loud. "This is the demons' fight too. If Azrael succeeds, they'll be the ones who suffer the most."

Callan nods. "Good thinking. The rest of you, I'll need your help getting the defenses ready."

When it's all decided, we go our separate ways to tackle our tasks. Most of us fly over to Seraphim Academy together in one big group. It's a Saturday so there are no classes, but I see some of the Professors herding everyone out and sending them away for their safety. The others split off toward Uriel's house, while I keep going into the forest until I reach the arched trees. I speak the words and a shimmering door appears, and I hurry through it.

It's three hours later in the day here, putting the sun in a totally different spot, and I don't think I'll ever get used to that. I rush across campus and a few students give me odd looks, but no one stops me. I manage to run into a familiar librarian on my way into Archfiend Hall, and she directs me to Baal's office on the second floor.

I knock on the door, and Baal opens it quickly. He looks almost... frazzled. If an ancient vampire Archdemon can be called such a thing.

"Olivia, hello. To what do I owe the pleasure?" He turns away from me as soon as I step inside and goes back to a box he's packing. He grabs books off the shelf and drops them inside.

I blink at the state of his office. It's all packed up. "Going somewhere?"

"I'm taking a leave of absence as headmaster. Archdemon Mammon will be taking my place for the time being."

"Why?"

He pauses to look me in the eye. "I need to help Lilith with our daughter, Lena."

"Lena is your daughter?" I gasp. "Lilith never told me."

"She is." He rests a hand on my shoulder. "I owe you and your companions a great debt in return for rescuing her. I'd long given up on ever finding her alive. Now I must be there for her, however I can."

I suddenly have a lot more respect for Baal. "With both you and Lilith taking care of her, I know she'll be in very good hands."

"That is kind of you to say. I do hope you can come visit us and spend some time with her. I'm sure it would help Lena to get to know you."

"I would love that, more than you know," I say truthfully. All I ever wanted in life was a family, and the urge to get to know my sister is strong. "But I might need to call in that debt sooner than later. Or more specifically, right now."

He pauses while packing away another book and turns to face me. "What is it?"

"Azrael has the Staff of Eternity. He's going to arrive at Seraphim Academy at dawn and try to force me to use it. I have no plans to do that, but..."

"But it's Azrael," Baal finishes for me.

"Exactly." I swallow hard. "And if we don't stop him, he'll go after Lena next."

Baal sets the book down and slowly turns to me with darkness in his eyes. The concerned father and headmaster is gone, replaced by the terrifying ancient vampire always lurking underneath the surface of his aloof demeanor. "We will not let that happen."

"That's the plan. We're going to fight back and destroy the Staff, but we could use whatever help you can spare. I know it breaks the Earth Accords for angels and demons to fight, but we could argue Azrael's the one who is breaking them in the first place by trying to use the Staff."

"A sound argument." Baal grabs a huge, medieval-looking sword off the wall. "I must protect Lena, but I will send what warriors I can to fight by your side. I swear it."

I let out a relieved sigh. "Thank you."

———

On my way back, I stop by my dorm briefly to pick up my knives and some clothes that I can fight in tomorrow. Then I look around the place that's been my home for most of the last three years with a hollowness in my chest. I've missed so much school, and things have changed so much for me in the last few weeks. Do I even belong here anymore? If I survive the battle tomorrow, should I return?

I don't know the answer.

It's a relief to head back to the guys' house in Angel Peak, which is starting to feel more like home than anywhere else.

Those of us at the house have a quick regroup over dinner. Callan's been coordinating things with Uriel, and they've sent the students to safety, along with some of the professors. Araceli and Jonah haven't returned yet from Faerie, and I worry about them the entire time we're eating. Kassiel reached out to his father, who agreed to send any warriors who can make it by dawn, but said he couldn't intervene himself due to the Earth Accords. With luck, we'll have a large group of demons and fae to supplement our small angelic numbers.

Araceli and Jonah return just as we're heading up to bed, but we can immediately tell from their faces that they don't have good news. Jonah meets my eyes and shakes his head.

"No help from the fae?" I ask, my hope quickly vanishing.

"Unfortunately, no," Araceli says. "The High King said he could not assist us."

Eveanna turns away, muttering something in the fae language. Tanwen goes to comfort her, leading her back to their room. Araceli and Jonah vanish as well. Dina's already asleep in Marcus's room. I'm not sure what will happen tonight, until Callan stands, eyes me and my other lovers, and says, "Let's head to bed."

At first, I'm tempted to have a repeat of last night, but decide against it. I'm still feeling very sated, and I need the men to be at their full strength tomorrow. Instead, we all climb into Callan's big bed together. I get lots of kisses and cuddles, and then we fall asleep in one big heap.

As I drift off, my last thought is *yes, this is where I belong.*

———

W e wake a few hours before dawn to suit up for battle. My stomach is tight with anticipation and dread as we prepare and wait for Azrael to make his appearance.

Callan's made the bell tower his command center, and we all fly over there just before sunrise, except for Dina, who stays back at the house. Out on the big lawn there are dozens of people lined up and waiting, but I don't recognize any of them. When one of them turns into a large raven, I realize they're demons. In the group, I spot shifters, vampires, Fallen, and more. Baal and Lucifer came through for us.

As we enter the Princess Lounge, I have a fleeting moment of amusement seeing Uriel and Gabriel sitting stiffly among our sparkly pink cushions, before we get down to business. Raphael and Ariel are there too, and Marcus and Jonah take a few moments to speak with them privately. The gym has been set up for the healers, and Araceli heads off to make sure it's all ready. Tanwen lets out a little squeal at the sight of her sister, Rhiannon, who wears full Valkyrie armor. There's a handsome man beside her with black hair, who I assume is her demon lover. They all hug, and then Tanwen introduces Eveanna to them. Hilda's there too, wearing her Valkyrie armor, and I'm touched she's decided to fight for us. I was told Raziel and Rosie are on our side too, but they're with the students in hiding, protecting them in case things go badly.

Callan barks out orders, and then spots me standing there, gazing at the people all around me while they prepare for battle. I'm so impressed by everyone who came to fight. Not just to protect me, or to stop Azrael, but to defend this peace that Michael and Lucifer forged between angels and demons. It feels like the start of something bigger.

Assuming we survive the next few hours.

Callan moves to my side. "Just stick close to me, all right? We'll get through this."

I offer him a smile, but then I spot Kassiel moving through the crowd with another man by his side. He's absurdly handsome, with wavy dark hair that curls up over his mysterious green eyes, plus smooth olive skin and the body of a god. More importantly, he's got that certain come-hither appeal that makes many heads in the room turn, the tell-tale mark of a Lilim.

Kassiel brings the man over to me with a smile. "Olivia, I'd like you to meet Asmodeus, son of Lilith. Lucifer sent him to help lead the demonic forces."

My mouth falls open. Asmodeus, my brother. No wonder he's turning heads. He's old, really old, and even though his incubus allure doesn't work on me, I can feel his power crawling under the surface. I know so little about him, only that he used to live in Hell and had a hard time adjusting to life on Earth, but now runs a chain of strip clubs in Las Vegas, where he acts as Lilith's second in command, reporting directly to Lucifer himself.

"It's really nice to meet you," I manage to say.

"It's about time, wouldn't you agree?" Asmodeus asks with a wry grin, resting his hands on my shoulders. It's not quite a hug, but it's more familiar than a handshake, and it really hits me then that I have another brother. "Mother sends her regrets, but she could not leave young Lena unprotected. Baal is with them, as well."

"I understand. I'm just glad they're safe." I offer him a hesitant smile. "When this is over, I hope we can all get to know each other better."

He nods, and then turns to Callan. "Lucifer apologizes for his absence, but he cannot get involved directly due to the Earth Accords. I hope my presence here as Lilith's second-in-command suffices."

Callan holds his hand out. "Thank you for coming."

Asmodeus's eyebrows raise ever so slightly. "The son of Michael, shaking my hand? If they manage to send us back to Hell, I'm sure I'll find it frozen over."

Callan actually laughs at that. I like Asmodeus already.

"What is the plan, if I may ask?" my demon brother asks.

"The plan is to get the Staff from Azrael, and then Kassiel and I will destroy it together," Callan says. "Everyone else will buy us time so we can accomplish that."

Easier said than done.

As the sun crests the horizon, Araceli lands on the balcony, her face pale. "Azrael is here." She sucks in a breath. "And he's brought a lot of friends."

46

OLIVIA

On the other side of the campus, dozens of angels fly over the trees in gold robes and masks. From the balcony we survey their numbers and I wonder how many of them once sat beside me in class or stood in line behind me in the cafeteria. Grace must be among them, along with Jeremy. There's no sign of Azrael yet, but I know he's coming for me.

But the thing that turns my blood cold is the sight of people walking out of the trees. Tall, thin warriors emerge wearing shining bronze and silver armor with elaborate designs on them, along with pointed helmets that gleam under the sun. I don't need to see their pointed ears or colorful hair to know they're fae.

"What are they doing here?" I ask.

"I guess that's why the High King said no," Jonah mutters. "That dick."

"Why would he help Azrael?" Tanwen asks.

"He must have decided Azrael was more likely to win this battle," Eveanna says. "Mark my words, High King Oberon will turn on the angels next. He is no one's ally but his own."

A burst of light slams into the gates of the academy. They'll be inside soon.

"Get into position," Callan shouts. "You all know your orders. And remember what we're fighting for—peace between angels and demons, like my father and Lucifer wanted!"

A rousing cheer goes up, as everyone disperses. Asmodeus gives my arm a quick squeeze, and then he heads down the stairs to join the demons on the lawn. Eveanna goes with him. The rest of the angels launch off the balcony and into the air, filling the air with shining wings as the sun rises and turns the sky pink.

I give Jonah and Araceli quick hugs, telling them both I love them, before they set off with Tanwen beside them. I hope they can protect each other.

Soon the bell tower is empty except for me and my four men. I stand on the balcony, my hands resting on the metal railing, and face the dawn and what's to come. On my right stand Callan and Marcus, and on my left, Kassiel and Bastien.

"Are you sure about this plan?" Marcus asks.

Callan nods, while surveying the battlefield. "We have to draw Azrael out. This is the best way."

I swallow hard and rest my hand on the hilt of the dark-infused dagger on my hip. I agree with him, but I'm also nervous about what's to come.

Because I'm the bait.

The angels and fae get our gates and wards down in no time. Our people barely have time to get into position. The fae warriors march forward into the school, while the angels in gold masks fly toward our own forces. Soon the fae army hits the covered trenches Eveanna dug yesterday, using her Autumn Court magic. I wasn't sure what good they would do when Azrael's forces can fly, but Callan said we should prepare for anything. Guess he was right.

The trenches slow some of the fae down, but the rest advance on us. We're outnumbered, even with the help of the demons. The first angels reach us and their Erelim send out burning light across the sky, while our angels dodge and retaliate, and our Fallen block them with darkness. Ishim on both sides fight while invisible, while Ofanim use waves of truth to blink the fighters back into view.

Down below, the fae throw out fire and ice, while the demons create illusions, shift into raging animals, or dominate the fae into fighting each other. Malakim grab anyone who falls to the ground injured or dead, to drag them away and heal them if possible.

It's total chaos, and I hate that all we can do is stand here and watch. I can tell my men are frustrated and antsy too. Callan grips the railing of the balcony so hard I'm worried he might break it, while his eyes scan the battle going on in front of us. Kassiel has his arms crossed as he stands beside me, his jaw clenched tight. Marcus wrings his hands and sighs anytime one of our people fall, probably wishing he could get out there to heal them. Bastien is like a statue beside me, his face cold and expressionless, but I see the turmoil in his eyes—he's worried too.

Our efforts aren't enough. The Order and their allies are advancing on us, and as fast as we take one down, three more appear. If we don't get the Staff soon, this battle will go down as a spectacular defeat. But where is Azrael?

Then I see a huge bolt of light fanning out like a wave, knocking down demons in its wake, and I know he's arrived. Azrael wields the Staff instead of his normal scythe, and with his white hair flying back, his black eyes gleaming, and his black-slashed white wings spread wide against the sun, he's truly terrifying. He lets loose another huge blast of light from the Staff, but then someone blocks it. Someone wearing gleaming Valkyrie armor. Hilda.

She and Tanwen, plus Rhiannon and some of the other Valkyries, hold back the light with their own Erelim powers, protecting the demons and other angels behind them. Hilda barks orders, and the few Valkyries fighting for us fan out in a group. It seems like they might actually be able to ward off the Staff's power, but then Zadkiel and Grace move into position beside Azrael. Grace wields a huge sword pulsing with light so bright it's impossible to look at.

Callan leans forward with fury in his eyes. "That's my father's sword!"

"How does Grace have it?" Marcus asks.

"We need to get it from her, according to my mother's vision," Bastien says.

Before we can discuss it further, Azrael launches another huge bolt from the Staff—directly at the cafeteria. Where Araceli is healing our injured, with Jonah protecting her.

I scream, but I'm too far away to do anything. The entire battle melts away as I watch Hilda throw herself in front of the light. She blocks it with her Valkyrie armor, spreading her arms out wide to make sure she sucks up the entire blast. Oh, Hilda, no.

The cafeteria is safe, but our beloved Combat Training professor falls to the ground, her armor singed and her wings charred. She doesn't move again. Callan lets out a guttural roar and unleashes his own blast of burning light at Azrael, hitting him in the right wing. It knocks Azrael back a tiny bit, but he shakes it off fast—but it got his attention. Just like we wanted.

The other Valkyries yell and rush forward with their swords, fury and retribution written on their faces, spurred by the death of one of their own. They clash with Grace and Zadkiel, but Azrael goes invisible.

"Get ready," Kassiel says. "He's seen us."

We move inside the bell tower and I use my Ishim powers to make everyone but me and Callan invisible. Then we wait, while my heart races.

Suddenly an eerie voice sounds just behind me. "Did you think you could hide from me?"

I spin around just as Azrael turns visible. Callan throws up a light shield around us, just in time to block a blast from the Staff. Kassiel and the others move forward while invisible, wielding dark-infused blades.

But then Azrael raises his other hand and somehow sends us all flying back, and everyone becomes visible again. I try to reach for my succubus powers, but there's something blocking them. Callan lifts his hand to shoot Azrael with light, but nothing happens. We can't use any of our powers.

"There's no use in fighting me." Azrael stalks toward me with those horrible black eyes, and I'm completely powerless against him. I see now why none of the Archangels could stand up to him. He's like a black hole, an empty void, sucking away all our powers and only making himself stronger.

Kassiel gets up and launches himself at Azrael with his dark-infused sword. Our powers may be blocked, but we can still move. Azrael dodges and hits Kassiel with a bolt of light, knocking him back into the TV, while Marcus and Bastien move in with their own infused weapons. Callan and I jump to our feet too, and I pull out my daggers. We're not going down without a fight.

But Azrael's too strong, and he's had thousands of years of experience. My paltry three years of combat training are nothing against him, and he knocks my blades away. Within seconds, we're all on the floor, injured and moaning. The only one with any chance is Callan, who wields his sword against the Staff while he tries to protect us all, but then Azrael knocks him down too.

It's impossible. How can we ever defeat the leader of the Archangels?

A burst of darkness fills the room, and a man forms in the middle of it. A ridiculously handsome man with wings made of shadows.

Lucifer is here.

My heart pounds faster as he wraps inky darkness around Azrael's wrists and pins him in place. Somehow, he isn't affected by Azrael's nullification powers. He must be stronger than Azrael, which is terrifying in its own way.

"Get the Staff!" Lucifer says. "I'll take care of Azrael."

"You've broken the Earth Accords," Azrael hisses at Lucifer, while struggling to get free. "This will be war."

"Isn't it already?" the King of Hell growls back.

Kassiel manages to wrestle the Staff away from Azrael's hands, and then steps back with wide eyes. "Father."

Lucifer waves a hand at us, while struggling to hold Azrael with his shadows. "Go! Destroy it! Do what Michael and I should have done years ago!"

I sense Kassiel's hesitation, so I grab his hand and tug him out onto the balcony, only stopping to grab my daggers. Callan, Marcus, and Bastien follow right behind us. I wrap a bubble of invisibility around us as five sets of wings flare out and launch us into the air.

It's time to destroy the Staff of Eternity once and for all.

47

KASSIEL

With the Staff clutched in one hand, I enter the auditorium with Liv and the others at my side. Our plan completely went to shit when we discovered Azrael could block all our powers, but we're back on track now, thanks to my father's arrival. I'm still shocked he showed up here at all. I never expected him to outright defy the Earth Accords like that. On the other hand, Azrael's really the one breaking them by trying to use the Staff, so Lucifer probably felt it was justified. Still, I worry for him, and wish we didn't have to leave him alone with Azrael.

"Let's do this up on the stage in case there's a blast of energy when it's destroyed," I suggest.

Callan nods. "Good thinking. The three of you should guard the entrances."

"I need to heal Bastien," Marcus says. "He took a bad hit from Azrael, but it should only take a minute."

"I'm fine," Bastien snaps, but he limps over to a chair so Marcus can heal him.

"I'll cover the door." Olivia grabs my face in a tight grip and presses a kiss to my lips. "Don't die," she says, then follows with a whisper. "I love you."

I hold her close and have the strongest urge not to let go. "I love you, too."

After releasing me, she wraps her arms around Callan's waist. "Please be careful."

He hugs her tight and kisses the top of her head. "You don't need to worry about us. We've got this."

She looks up at him with love and fear in her eyes. Then she runs to the double doors at the back of the auditorium, while pulling out her daggers, her dark hair flowing behind her. She's sexy and dangerous and I love every inch of that woman.

I see in Callan's eyes that he feels the same, but then we turn away and climb the stairs to the auditorium stage. I have a brief flashback to the last time I stood on this stage a few years ago, when Uriel introduced me as the new Angelic History professor. My chest tightens a little at the memory. I miss teaching here. I worry about my former students out there, now fighting for or against us. I wish things could be different.

Perhaps they can be once the Staff is destroyed. Angels and demons alike are out there fighting together so that we can have peace between our people. That must count for something.

Callan and I wait until Olivia's in position, then we face each other. The sons of the two most powerful men in history. All animosity between us is gone. Once enemies, now allies, united in our purpose and our love for Olivia.

I hold out the Staff to Callan. "It's time to end what our fathers started."

He clasps the Staff just below my hand with a firm nod. "Let's do this. Brother."

As soon as we both touch the Staff, the dark and light energy at the top of it seems to grow stronger. Power rushes through me, and from the way Callan grits his teeth, I'm sure he feels the same thing. It's overwhelming, this much power, and it's hard to even consider destroying such a thing. Couldn't we use it for good? Maybe we should—No.

Callan's eyes meet mine and we both snap back to our purpose. We rest our other hands on the Staff and focus on willpower on destroying it. Eveanna told us fae relics work on intent, and this one is no different.

I gather my power, all my darkness and shadow, and push it into the Staff with the intent of destruction. Callan does the same with his own light and heat. The Staff vibrates, and I can feel how unstable it's becoming as the mix of light and darkness creates chaos inside the orb, where it's nestled between the white and black wings. White and black beams shoot out of the top, blasting into the ceiling.

It's working. We're destroying the Staff.

Without warning, a flaming sword appears over Callan's head, about to slam down onto his neck. I yell and yank both of us backward as hard as I can. I slam into someone behind me, and all three of us the floor. Our attackers appear out of thin air. Grace, wielding Michael's sword, and Zadkiel stand over us, along with some of their gold-masked angel warriors.

Callan tucks and rolls, getting to his feet in half a second, and then he launches himself at Grace with a ferocity I haven't seen before. The person I fell on holds a knife to my throat, and says, "Don't move, devil spawn."

I recognize that voice. I turn a bit and get a glimpse of Jeremy behind me. My former student, now holding a light-infused knife at my throat.

"You don't need to do this," I tell him, lacing power into my words.

He grunts. "Yes. I do."

I throw a blast of shadow energy at him, but all that does is make him jump and scrape the knife against my throat. I clamp my mouth shut to fight back against the pain from such a little cut as the light hits me. Bastien and Marcus run up to fight the other golden-robed angels, and I notice the Staff is missing. Callan and I must have dropped it. Fuck.

Zadkiel raises his arms and we all freeze, suddenly unable to move. It's the same way he and Uriel captured us and took us to Penumbra Prison. He caught me by surprise then, but not now. Even without moving, I can control the darkness. I make it reach for him, long tentacles stretching out from the shadows to attack him.

But then I hear a whimper toward the back of the auditorium. I can turn my head just enough to see Olivia being dragged up the stairs to the stage by Azrael, who holds the Staff in his other hand. Cold dread floods me.

Azrael has the Staff. He has Olivia. And where is my father?

48

OLIVIA

While guarding the door something hit me hard in the head, knocking me out for a few seconds. I come to when I'm dumped on the auditorium stage. I try to shake my head to fight off the daze, but I can't actually move. I'm frozen in place in a lump on the floor, clutching one of my daggers uselessly. Around me, my lovers kneel in a semi-circle with their hands behind their backs. Not tied, just held there by Zadkiel's Archangel power. Between him stopping us from moving and Azrael blocking our powers, things look pretty hopeless.

"You're all trying so hard to use your powers, but haven't you learned by now?" Azrael stalks toward me with a menacing smile, while gripping the Staff. "Even Lucifer couldn't stop me."

"What did you do to him?" Kassiel asks, and I see from the strain in his eyes that he's trying so hard to break free of their control...and failing.

Azrael just laughs, a sound that gives me chills. Grace stands beside him with Michael's burning sword trained on Callan, who glares at her with so much hatred I'm surprised she doesn't shrivel up and die from it. Jeremy's beside her, waving a light-infused blade at Kassiel. Zadkiel paces back and forth in front of Bastien and Marcus with his brow pinched, I'm guessing from the effort it takes to hold us all in place. He's an Archangel, but a new one, and he's probably never held so many powerful people in place before.

Azrael grabs my hair and yanks me up, making me cry out. "It's time for you to use the Staff of Eternity to send the demons back where they belong."

"I won't do it." I try to struggle, but Zadkiel's hold is too strong. I reach for my powers again, angel or demon, but it's impossible to resist Azrael's control.

He lets out another spine-chilling laugh. "See the men under your thrall, all lined up for execution? We'll go down the line, one by one, until you use the Staff of Eternity."

Grace moves to the end of the line to raise the burning sword over Marcus. My eyes widen and I panic at the sight, fighting with everything I have. "No!"

"I think we'll kill Lucifer's son last," Azrael says. "If you won't use the Staff, perhaps he will, to save you."

I squeeze my eyes shut. This can't be happening. I can't use the Staff. But I can't let them kill the men I love either.

"We have another one to add to the lineup," Simiel says, emerging from the back of the stage. That creepy asshole, I knew he was in the Order! My stomach drops when I see who he's dragging along with him—my brother.

Azrael's smile widens. "Even better. Gabriel's son can be our first sacrifice."

Jonah's dropped into position beside Marcus, and Grace moves the sword to his throat. Their eyes meet and she looks away quickly, like she can't watch what she's about to do.

"Stop!" I yell. "I'll do it. I'll use the Staff." I have no intention of doing it, but I can't let them hurt Jonah.

Azrael throws me down on the stage, hard. "I don't believe you. I think you need to see how serious we are about this." He turns to Grace. "Kill him."

Her face pales as she slowly raises Michael's sword, but then she hesitates. The sword hovers in the air, but she can't bring the sword down on my brother's neck. A part of her must actually care about him. She looks at Azrael with imploring eyes. "Father..."

He lets out a disgusted sound and grabs the sword from her, shoving her aside like she's nothing. As he hands Simiel the Staff, he says, "It seems I must do everything myself."

The sword goes up again and in an instant it's going to come down on my brother and end his life. I scream and break into a million pieces as the sheer horror of what's about to happen hits me. Time seems to stop, and then I'm there, in front of Jonah, blocking Azrael with the dagger I'm still holding. Luckily, it's the dark-infused one.

Azrael gapes at me, completely shocked I managed to break free, and I use that split second of hesitation to stab him with the dark-infused dagger. Then I grab Jonah and blink us away to where Zadkiel is standing across the stage. Before anyone can react, Jonah takes the dagger from my hand and thrusts it at Zadkiel's chest. The Archangel staggers back, clutching his chest, then sinks down to the ground, while I silently pray that Tanwen can forgive us.

The second Zadkiel is down, my men jump to my feet, his control over them broken. The battle starts up again, but our side is hindered by Azrael blocking our magic. I hone in on the Staff, still in Simiel's hands, and go after it. I forget about Jeremy, though, and he blocks me with his light-infused blade. How many times is this asshole going to thwart me?

I still have my magic though. Somehow, Azrael can't control me anymore. I blink around Jeremy, through the battle, until I reach Simiel, who levels the Staff at my chest. I grab his arm and throw a huge dose of succubus lust at him, making his jaw drop and his eyes widen.

"Give me the Staff," I tell him. "You know you want to."

"Anything for you," he says, handing it to me. "I always knew you were special."

Barf. I grab the Staff, while Marcus knocks him out with a sharp blow to the head.

Power surges through me from the Staff, but then Jeremy is back, and he slashes at me with the light-infused blade. I manage to jump back, using my wings to lift me up a little, but the knife slices through my thigh, sending red hot pain through me. He comes for me again and I grab the light-infused blade from Jeremy's hand in a disarming move that Callan taught me, then slide it into the fucker's throat. His eyes go wide as the dagger hits home, and I let him fall.

I fly up higher, trying to see how I can help the others, but Azrael appears in front of me, his black and white wings blocking my vision. His shoulder is bleeding from where I stabbed him, but it doesn't seem to slow him down as he raises Michael's sword.

"If you won't use the Staff, then you will die," he growls, as he shoots toward me.

I try to blink away, but nothing happens. I'm weakened by the light-infused injury, and he's got me in his grip again. As the burning sword fills my vision, I see my own death clearly.

"Liv!" Callan yells.

Suddenly I'm shoved aside, while Callan takes the blow that was meant for me. His father's sword sinks into his chest. The blow would have killed me instantly, but Callan manages to grab the hilt of the sword as the light overwhelms his body. He wrestles it away from Azrael, just as his body burns up in light so bright it hurts my eyes. Then the light blinks out.

As Callan falls, my heart shatters. I scream at the sight, then drop down to him. His body is physically unharmed, but there's no life left in his eyes. He still holds Michael's sword, but the burning light has been extinguished. I choke back a sob as I clutch him close to my chest.

He's gone.

49

OLIVIA

I rise to my feet as the agony and grief become a raging storm inside me. Shock pounds through me like one of those headaches you feel throughout your entire body. I stand over Callan's body and clutch the Staff tighter in my hand while I face Azrael with hatred and sorrow giving me strength. I'm Dina's vision come to life.

As the people around me reel from the shock of seeing the son of Michael murdered by Azrael—something even Azrael didn't *actually* want to happen, judging by the look on his face—I flood the Staff with my power.

I have to gasp as the Staff takes what I give it and increases it tenfold, filling me with strength. Azrael wants to use the Staff to send the demons back to Hell, but it can do so much more. With it, I can reshape the entire world and bend both angels and demons to my will. It feels like it was made for me, and me alone. And maybe it was. After all, I'm the only one with both light and darkness inside me.

I'm the only one who can access its true potential.

I unleash my succubus powers on the members of the Order, and with the Staff, I'm so strong they all immediately fall under my spell. They all turn to me and wait, now my loyal thralls. Even Grace. Only Azrael resists.

Marcus rushes forward to kneel beside Callan, while Bastien grabs Michael's sword from Callan's limp hand. Jonah puts Grace into a choke hold, while Kassiel overpowers Simiel.

Azrael lets out a roar and flies toward me with a scythe made of light, his wings spread wide. I level the Staff at him and hit him with a mix of light and darkness, so strong it knocks him back into the auditorium seats. He jumps up immediately, shaking off a blow that would have killed a normal angel, and comes at me again, his eyes seething with rage. Even with the Staff, I'm not sure I can defeat him.

Suddenly light fills the auditorium as more angels stream inside. Not just angels. Archangels.

Gabriel, Uriel, Ariel, and Raphael all surround Azrael, wings spread wide, hair flying back as they glow with bright light. Uriel's voice booms across the auditorium. "Azrael, by a majority vote of the Archangel Council you have been removed as leader of the angels."

"How?" Azrael asks, glaring at them. "I only count three Archangels who oppose me here."

"Oh, didn't you hear?" Raphael asks with a smirk. "We reinstated Gabriel earlier this morning."

"You can't do that," Azrael snaps, and then he spreads his arms and unleashes a huge wave of his void power. The glow around the Archangels dims, but the energy seems to bounce off me while I hold the Staff. I direct another blast of light and darkness at him, which makes him grunt and stagger back, but he fights through it.

There's a burst of shadows behind him, and then Lucifer wraps Azrael in chains made of darkness. I let out a relieved sigh, knowing Kassiel's father is all right.

"You," Azrael practically spits. "I got rid of you."

Lucifer lets out a laugh that's somehow both charming and terrifying. "Sorry, I'm not that easy to kill."

Uriel clears his throat. "For the crime of stealing the Staff of Eternity and trying to use it against demons, thus breaking the Earth

Accords, you and your followers are hereby sentenced to life in Penumbra Prison."

"I'm the leader of all angels," Azrael snaps, as he tries to break free of Lucifer's shadow chains. "If I decide we must act against the demons, then my word is law."

"You also killed Callan, son of Michael and Jophiel," I yell, my body trembling at the words, and all the Archangels look over with horror at Callan's prone body.

"That was an accident," Azrael says. "I would never harm the son of Jophiel intentionally. I was trying to kill the filthy hybrid. She's the one who stole the Staff of Eternity in the first place."

"Can you save him?" I beg Raphael, whose Archangel gift allows him to bring people back from the dead.

Raphael bows his head. "No, I can't. It takes a great deal of energy, almost enough to kill me, and I used that power on a young student caught in the crossfire just now. I won't be able to do it again for some time, and by then it will be too late. I am truly sorry."

I nod my understanding, while biting my lip and wiping away tears. It was a desperate plea, and I knew it probably wouldn't work, but I had to try.

"Azrael killed Michael too," Bastien says, stepping forward with Michael's sword raised. It no longer burns with light, but it's still huge, shiny, and impressive.

"How do you know?" Lucifer asks.

"Bastien's Archangel power," Jonah says. "He can see the past when he touches objects."

"Is this true?" Uriel asks, his chest swelling with pride.

Bastien nods. "The second I touched the sword, I saw it. Azrael arrived at Michael's home and asked to speak with him. Zadkiel was already there."

I vaguely remember hearing that Zadkiel had been Michael's right-hand man before his death. It's one of the reasons it made sense for him to take over the vacant spot on the Archangel Council after Michael's death. But now it sounds like he was secretly working for Azrael all that time.

"Azrael pleaded with Michael to do more about the demons and to accept that peace was impossible," Bastien continues. "Ekariel was killed by demons, in Azrael's mind, and Michael wasn't retaliating against them. Zadkiel agreed with Azrael, but Michael wouldn't budge. He said there was no evidence demons had killed Ekariel, and for the most part, the Earth Accords were working. That's when Azrael said new leadership was required."

"This is nonsense," Azrael says. "You can't truly believe this child over me."

"Silence," Uriel says. "I can read the past in his eyes and the truth in his voice."

"Yes, let him continue," Ariel says.

Bastien glares at Azrael and lowers Michael's sword. "Azrael took this sword off the wall and ran Michael through with it, catching him off guard. With the element of surprise, combined with Zadkiel holding him immobile and Azrael rending him powerless, they managed to defeat him. As they watched him die, they agreed to make it look like Lucifer had done it, and Azrael took the sword as they flew away."

A hushed silence fills the auditorium as the truth of Bastien's words settle over us, along with the enormity of Azrael's betrayal. It's nothing compared to the grief I feel over losing Callan though.

"Even if we excuse the crimes you committed against Callan or with the Staff, the death of Michael is something we cannot overlook," Ariel says, in a clear, feminine voice. "We remove your Archangel status and sentence you to eternity in Penumbra Prison."

The Archangels surge forward and slap those silver cuffs on Azrael, blocking his powers. He struggles and fights and claims he is innocent, then threatens to use what he knows against them, to send his followers after their families, until he is dragged out of the auditorium by Uriel and Gabriel, who look triumphant. Lucifer follows a step behind them, while Raphael slaps cuffs on Simiel and Grace is hauled away by Ariel, who has her in a vice-like grip. She must know that Grace broke her son's heart.

Just before they reach the door, Grace shouts, "Jonah, Liv... This isn't me! He made me do it. I swear!"

"I don't believe you," Jonah says, his voice cold, before Ariel drags Grace away.

Outside it sounds like the battle has ended, but in here, all I see is death. Zadkiel and Jeremy are dead, along with a few other golden-masked people in the room.

And Callan. I swallow hard as I stare at his body.

Marcus is kneeling over Callan and has been trying to heal him. I can tell by the frantic movements and panic on his face that it isn't working. "You can't be dead. There must be something in you that's still alive."

We gather around them, and I hand Jonah the Staff, eager to get it out of my hands. It's too powerful, especially for a hybrid like me. Then I sink to the floor and press my face against Callan's chest, sobbing hard. I can't believe he's gone. I never even got to tell him how much I loved him.

"Can you resurrect him?" Jonah asks. "Like your dad?"

"I've never tried..." Marcus says with a frown.

Bastien tilts his head as he considers. "Your Archangel power hasn't emerged yet. It's possible this is the reason."

"We won't know unless you try," Kassiel says.

I sit back and wipe my tears, giving Marcus space to work. His eyes take on a look of concentration as his hands begin to glow with healing light. I've seen him heal many times before, but this time Marcus's face twists and the light glows bright white with touches of gold woven through it. He gasps as the light surrounds Callan's body, but then it seems to get absorbed, and the glow fades.

Marcus sits back on his heels and wipes his forehead, which is now covered in sweat. "I'm close, but I think if I do this, it might kill me in the process. I can see now why my father doesn't do this very often."

I put my hands on Marcus's bare arms and use my Archdemon power to push some of my own energy into him. Energy I took from him, Callan, and the others. "Take it all," I tell him. "Everything I have. Whatever it takes to bring Callan back."

Marcus looks at me with sad eyes. "That might kill you too."

"Not if we help." Kassiel kneels beside me and grabs my chin, then kisses me hard, filling me with his potent energy. Other than Callan, he's the strongest man I've ever been with, and I send all that power directly into Marcus.

He gasps. "That's it, yes!"

Bastien gets the idea and kneels down too, then wraps his arms around me from behind and begins kissing my neck. I turn my head toward him to find his lips to share a desperate, mournful kiss. His energy fills me too, and I give it all to Marcus.

With the four of us sharing power, the glow around Callan increases until the energy swirls and twists all around him. Marcus lets out a laugh filled with surprised relief. "It's working!"

Suddenly the light vanishes inside Callan, and Marcus sits back, looking exhausted. Callan sucks in a deep, ragged breath, like he's been deprived of oxygen for too long. I break into tears again, relief washing over me like a tsunami.

I let go of Marcus to grab Callan's hand. "I'm here. We're all here. Come back to us."

Callan's bright blue eyes pop open, and his hand squeezes mine tightly. He blinks a few times and I hold my breath, too scared to believe this is real, and then he sits up and faces me. I throw myself against his chest and wrap my arms around him, letting out another happy sob.

"You're alive," I whisper.

"I'm okay." He hugs me tight and his deep voice rumbles through me. I didn't think I'd ever hear it again. "Thanks to all of you."

Then I push against Callan's chest and glare at him through my tears, remembering how he took the blow meant for me. "Why did you do that, you idiot?"

He wipes a tear off my cheek as he gazes into my eyes. "Because I love you."

"I love you too, you brave, noble, arrogant fool." I shove him again and then pull him back to kiss him hard.

"Is that supposed to be a compliment or an insult?" he asks with a laugh, before kissing me again.

I look up at the other men, who surround us with grins on their faces. "I love all of you. Thank you for bringing him back."

"Marcus did most of the work," Kassiel says, clasping him on the back.

"I couldn't have done it without all of you." Marcus lets out a little laugh. "Maybe I'll be able to someday, when I'm older, but for my first resurrection I definitely needed the help."

We all help Callan to his feet, and he hugs every single one of the guys, including Kassiel.

"Here," Bastien says, holding out Michael's sword. "This belongs to you."

Callan hesitates, probably for the first time in his life. "Did your mother's prophecy come true? Did it stop Azrael?"

"Yes, but not in the way we expected," Bastien says.

"When Bastien got the sword, he saw a vision of how Michael died," Jonah says. "It was Azrael."

Callan swears under his breath, while Bastien tells him everything he saw. As the tale ends, Callan says, "I should have known it was him."

"This belongs to you," Bastien says, offering Michael's sword again.

"I saw my father briefly, just before you pulled me back." Callan's brow furrows. "He apologized for some of the things he did, and he said he was proud of me."

"We all knew he would be," Marcus says.

Callan's jaw clenches and he takes Michael's sword. The second his hand clasps around the pommel the burning light ignites, brighter than it was before. It's clear it was meant for Callan to wield, and no one else.

"But you stopped him?" Callan asks. "Azrael is defeated?"

"The Archangels took him to Penumbra Prison, along with Grace and Simiel," Kassiel says. "Zadkiel and Jeremy are dead. The battle is over."

"There's just one more thing left to do," Jonah says, holding out the Staff.

The entire group stares at it as the enormity of this moment sets in. Kassiel reaches for it, and Callan gives him a firm nod. They move close together and grasp the Staff together, facing each other with determined eyes. The rest of us gather around them, for protection and for strength. Whatever happens, we're in this together.

A swirling mixture of light and darkness surrounds the top of the Staff, and it grows stronger as Kassiel and Callan continue to stare at each other. Then the light and darkness burst out of the Staff in every direction, washing through me. It makes the others stagger back, but not me. The Staff fills me with power and energy, replacing everything I gave up to help Callan.

With a huge blast of energy, the Staff breaks apart into a million tiny pieces of black and white crystal, which then disintegrate in front of us, until the entire thing vanishes as if it never existed at all.

"It's done," Callan says.

"We did it," Kassiel says. "It's over."

I let out a relieved laugh and rush toward them, wrapping them both in my arms. Marcus, Bastien, and even Jonah join in our group hug, and we all cling to each other as we laugh and cry and smile. It's over. It's really over.

The auditorium door opens, and three more people rush inside, and I let out another relieved sob at the sight of them. My three best friends are alive, and jumping up onto the stage, and asking a million questions.

Tanwen's forehead is bleeding and her armor is dented and blackened in a few spots. "Was that blast the Staff?"

"Has it been destroyed?" Eveanna asks, looking as good as she did a few hours ago. No marks on her armor, no hair out of place, no signs she was in battle at all. That's the fae for you.

Jonah sweeps Araceli up in his arms and they share a long kiss, and then she laughs and looks over at me with hope in her eyes. "Did we win?"

I pull them all into our group hug, and when we're all holding onto each other, my heart grows a thousand times bigger. "We won."

50

OLIVIA

U riel moves to the podium and gazes across the rows of people sitting in plastic chairs on the lawn, underneath dark clouds that threaten rain at any moment. "Thank you for joining us today, as we celebrate another year at Seraphim Academy coming to a close and honor our graduating students. We've had quite a year, full of hardship and turmoil, but I'm confident it only made us stronger in the end."

Quite a year? That's an understatement.

It's been three months since the battle for the Staff of Eternity. After everything calmed down, Uriel closed the school for two weeks for repairs and to take care of Archangel business. When school resumed, Callan temporarily stepped in as Combat Training professor, Bastien went back to teaching Angelic History, and Kassiel, of all people, returned to finish up Immortal Ethics with us. Having the three of them there made the last few months fly by, especially since I moved back into the dorms with Araceli. At first, we weren't even sure if we'd return to Seraphim Academy after what Uriel did to us, but then we decided we all wanted to finish up the school year anyway—for us.

Jonah and I sit onstage, along with Araceli, Tanwen, and the rest of our graduating class. Our parents and friends are in the crowd, and I smile at the sight of them. Kassiel's wearing one of his sexy suits, looking every inch like Lucifer's son, and very few people give him a second glance at his presence in the crowd. Callan sits beside him and they occasionally lean close to share a word, like they're old friends. It still shocks me to see that. Marcus nudges Callan, like he wants in on the joke, and they grin at him. He's been going back and forth a lot to visit his mom and his brother lately, and I come with him whenever I can.

My eyes land on Bastien next. Dina was invited to the graduation, but she declined, saying she had no wish to lay eyes on Uriel ever again. I can't blame her. Bastien found her a small cottage in Angel Peak and made Uriel pay for the rent. It's the least he could do. She's still adjusting to life outside of prison, but she and Bastien are making good progress in their relationship.

Eveanna is on the other side of him, sitting very straight but wearing a small, proud smile. Tanwen's sister Rhiannon is at her side, along with her shifter boyfriend. Neither sister harbored any ill will toward us for Zadkiel's death—I think finding out he was not only working for Azrael but involved in Michael's murder really soured their memories of their father. But he's still their dad, and now he's gone. I'm glad they have people who love them to help them get through this time.

Beside them sit Araceli's parents, Muriel and Fintan, and I'm pleased to see they're holding hands. It looks like Araceli managed to reunite them after all.

And then there are my parents, seated in the row behind my friends and their families. Dad has the biggest, proudest smile on his face and keeps waving at me and Jonah in a most embarrassing way. Mom just shakes her head with an amused smile every time he does that. To my surprise, both Asmodeus and Lena came too. My whole family, all in one spot for the second time ever.

The first time was on my birthday a few weeks ago. Dad threw a small family dinner at his house, partly so I could get to know my succubus siblings better. It was...awkward. Asmodeus was charming and funny, but Lena sulked and wouldn't speak to anyone, much like she's doing now. Lilith told me for the first few weeks all Lena would do was scream for Ekariel and try to escape. Lilith and Jophiel finally worked out an arrangement so the two can see each other now and then, which has helped them both calm down. Ekariel still has a long way to go though, from what I've heard. He sees all angels and demons as the enemy, with the exception of Lena. Every time he sees Callan, he tries to kill him. I'm not sure he'll ever fully recover. Callan's worried Jophiel might resort to erasing Ekariel's memories, but so far she hasn't done that yet.

Despite working for Azrael in the past, Jophiel claimed to have no involvement in his search for the Staff, and since she was with Ekariel during the battle, they couldn't arrest her. She's still on the Archangel Council and CEO of Aerie Industries, but for now she seems more concerned for her sons—both of them—than anything. She was especially upset when she learned Michael was murdered by Azrael and then killed her son, so even if she was loyal to Azrael before, she's probably not now. We're going to watch her closely though, just in case.

And Azrael? He's locked up in Penumbra Prison, where he belongs, along with Grace, Simiel, and everyone else we caught who was working for the Order. A few people they let off the hook, due to them being coerced or scared for their lives, but the rest were imprisoned with Azrael.

Gabriel gives us a thumbs up and I'm starting to wonder if he's a sitcom dad instead of an Archangel. Actually, not just an Archangel. The new leader of the Archangel Council. Like he should have been all along.

Mom yanks his hand down with a laugh, and I sense lust and more between them. They're not together yet, but I have a feeling it won't be long. I just don't know if he can handle her succubus life-style. I'm so lucky I found four men who can.

Uriel drones on about unity and togetherness and how hard they all fought to overcome tyranny and ensure peace. It's tough not to roll my eyes. The Archangels spent hundreds of years dealing with Azrael. I came onto the scene and took care of it all within three years.

Bitches get shit done.

"It is with regret that I announce I'll be stepping down as headmaster from this point forward," Uriel says, making many in the crowd gasp. Most of the students and parents are in the dark about the battle and the real stakes of what happened here. They know Azrael tried to use the Staff, that he murdered Michael and tried to kill Callan and me, and that the school was half-destroyed. What they don't know is how the entire Archangel Council was complacent in Azrael's actions for years. They let the Order torture, blackmail, and even murder people—including students at this very school—to further their cause. There's no way Uriel can continue as headmaster now that those things are starting to come to light. Besides, I think the guilt of it all finally got to him.

"In my place, the newly appointed Archangel Raziel will be headmaster of Seraphim Academy," Uriel continues. "We look forward to many years of prosperity under his tutelage."

Professor Raziel waves at the crowd, then looks surprised by the raucous applause. I don't think he has any clue how much he's loved by the students, both current and former. He flushes a cute pink and adjusts his bowtie, which has dinosaurs on it. I hope he never stops wearing those.

"Now we request a moment of silence as we honor those we lost this year in our battle for peace." Uriel steps aside, and the screen behind him comes to life. Faces flash on the screen, with names and other information below. The first is a Valkyrie I recognize from Combat Training and my throat clenches up. The next two I don't know, but the fourth one is Jeremy and I have to look away.

I did that. I killed him. In self-defense, but still. Maybe he deserved it for all the things he said and did, and maybe he didn't. Either way, I'm going to have to live with his blood on my hands for the rest of my life. I've come to terms with that.

The video continues, showing more students and professors

who fought on either side of the battle. Then Hilda's face fills the screen, while harp music plays, and a tear rolls down my cheek. Her death still hits me hard every time I think about it. She taught me so much and never once treated me unkindly because of what I am, even though she once cut down demons on the battlefield with glee. She's proof that even though we were enemies in the past, we don't have to continue that way now.

Callan rises to his feet and climbs up to the podium. "Hilda of the Valkyries was an inspiration to us all. She was a former member of the angelic army, known for her fearlessness in battle, but she retired when Uriel opened the school to become a Professor here. She taught many of the people sitting here now not just to fight and defend, but to have confidence in oneself." He bows his head, the grief getting to him for a moment before he continues. "Many of you have been touched by her legacy and now mourn her passing, as I do. The one consolation is that Hilda died in battle, as all Valkyries should, protecting the people she cared about most—her students. Thanks to her brave sacrifice, countless lives were saved that day."

Professor Rosie, who stands off to the side of the stage, waves a hand, removing invisibility from around a glass box with Hilda's Valkyrie armor inside. It hasn't been cleaned. The huge scorch mark from the blow that killed her is still on the front. From my angle, I can see it goes right through the amazing armor.

Callan looks at the armor with a grave face, before turning back to the mic. "The gym was heavily damaged in the battle, and the Valkyrie families have generously donated the repair funds. This armor will stand at the entrance, and the building will be renamed the Hilda Memorial Gymnasium."

Many people jump to their feet and applaud as Callan steps back. On my left, Tanwen subtly dabs at her eyes, and I wrap an arm around her. "Hilda would be honored," I whisper. She nods and leans against me as the graduation ceremony continues.

Finally, Uriel starts the proceedings of handshakes and name announcements. When it's my turn, black and white confetti suddenly falls onto the stage all around me, like it's pouring from the dark clouds above us. I shoot a look at the guys, who laugh and cheer. I don't know how they did it, but I know it was them.

And then, just like that, I'm a graduate of the Seraphim Academy.

———

I t's our last night in the bell tower, aka the Princess Lounge, and it's packed. For our graduation party we invited all our friends, family, and the remaining members of the Archangel council, plus any students and professors who fought on our side. Lilith and Gabriel insisted on organizing the event, trying to outdo each other the entire time, which is why we have angels in gleaming armor and Lilim in skimpy outfits handing out hors d'oeuvres and champagne. It's like the perfect mishmash of my two sides and I love it.

Angels and demons alike move across the small dancefloor or mingle on the sides with each other, and I feel like I'm seeing a vision of the future. That's my hope anyway.

I find Jonah and Araceli sitting practically on top of each other on a couch in the corner, and I squeeze my way between them like the super annoying best friend and sister I am.

"What are you two doing over here, hmm?" I ask, as if I didn't already know.

Araceli laughs. "Nothing."

"Only because our parents are here," Jonah says with a smirk.

I love seeing the two of them together and how their relationship has blossomed over the last few months. But it's bittersweet too, because of what they've decided to do after graduation.

I drape my arms across both of their shoulders. "I'm going to miss you both so much."

Araceli rests her head against mine. "We'll come back as often as we can, I promise."

Araceli and Jonah have decided to go to Faerie, both so she can learn more about her heritage, and so they can try to improve relations with the fae. It's dangerous, but they're determined to try.

I think Jonah just misses it there.

Jonah nudges me. "Besides, you'll be too busy to hang out with us while hunting down the Order, right?"

"That's the plan." Dad offered me a job in his spy network, but I turned it down. I love him, but his deception hit me hard, and it'll take a while before that relationship is repaired. Uriel also wanted me to stay on at Seraphim Academy in some way, but I declined that too. I need some space from the school for a while.

When Callan pitched the idea of a taskforce to unmask the remaining members of the Order, I jumped on the idea. Marcus did too, claiming someone needs to make sure Callan doesn't get himself killed again. We know there are still members of the Order out there, lurking in the shadows, probably plotting a way to break Azrael out of prison. The three of us will track them down and dismantle the secret society, freeing those people still being black-mailed and living in fear of them.

As we chat about Jonah and Araceli's plans in Faerie, Tanwen and Eveanna squeeze onto the couch with us. "Nice party," Tanwen says. "I'm going to miss this place though."

"You sure you don't want to come with us?" Jonah asks. "We could use your expertise."

Eveanna shakes her head. "I've decided not to return to Faerie, even though my banishment has ended. The High King has brought dishonor to our people, and I can no longer work for him." She turns and tilts her head at Tanwen. "Besides, I'd like to watch more movies and eat more popcorn."

"I think we can manage that," Tanwen says, before giving her a quick kiss. Then she turns back to Jonah. "We may be traveling a lot here on Earth anyway. We've both been asked to be on the new Duskhunter initiative Gabriel is putting together. I want to take them down after what they did to my mother, and to Ekariel and Lena."

"The task force is lucky to have you both," I say.

As a slow song starts to play, Kassiel makes his way through the crowd and offers me his hand. "Can I steal you away for a dance?"

I slip my hand into his. "Yes, although I'm not very good at it."

"Not yet," Kassiel says, as he lifts me to my feet and pulls me into his arms. "But we have an eternity for me to teach you. Assuming you don't get bored of us before then."

"Never." I kiss him as he sweeps me onto the dance floor. My succubus grace keeps me from making too big a fool of myself as we move, but I honestly don't care anyway. I'm having too much fun just being in his arms.

"What class have you decided to teach next year?" I ask him, as we sway together.

"Raziel thought I should take over Demon Studies."

"That makes sense. Either way, you're a great teacher. Those students are lucky to have you."

He raises a shoulder in a casual shrug. "Perhaps. Some students will be upset about me being there, along with their parents, but if we want change, we have to create it."

"It will help angel-demon relations to have you teaching there openly. I heard they're adding an angel teacher at Hellspawn Academy too."

"Now all we need is to get the fae onboard," he says with a grin.

I shake my head. "It might be some time before that happens."

When the song is over, Kassiel leads me over to Bastien, who's been watching us from the sidelines while sipping some whiskey.

"Care to dance?" I ask him.

Bastien gives me a cold look. "You know I don't dance."

"Well, I had to try." I wrap my arms around him anyway, and he squeezes me close. "Are you okay?"

"Yes. Why?"

"You've lived your entire life at Seraphim Academy. Uriel groomed you to be the next headmaster. Now Raziel's taking that job."

"I don't mind. I'm not ready for that position. I need a few more decades of experience first. Centuries, perhaps." He picks up a strand of my hair and wraps it around his finger. "Right now, I want to focus on my mother's recovery. Besides, I like teaching. I'm happy to continue as the Angelic Histories teacher for some time."

I run my hand along his chest. "It suits you."

Marcus comes up behind me and nuzzles at my neck. "I miss you. When are you moving back into the house?"

"Tomorrow, along with Kassiel."

"Good," Bastien says. He's been living there ever since we returned from the prison. After the battle, he got all his things from Uriel's house, and never returned.

I turn to face Marcus and move into his arms. "Are you sure there's enough room in the house for all of us?"

"I'm sure. If not, we'll find a bigger house." He grins at me. "None of us want to be apart from you."

"It does please me when you're all close," I say, as I play with the collar of his shirt.

He pulls me hard against his body and nibbles on my ear, whispering, "And we'd be very happy to please you later tonight."

We snuggle against each other, while Bastien looks on with amusement, and then I spot my mom moving through the crowd with Lena and Asmodeus in tow. I give Marcus and Bastien each a kiss and then head over to them.

"Ah, there you are," Lilith says, wrapping me in a warm embrace. "Congratulations on your graduation, my dear daughter. I'm so proud of you."

"Thanks, Mom."

Asmodeus clasps me on the shoulder with a wry grin. "Yes, you've done well, even if you mistakenly chose to attend the stuffy angel college instead of the fun demon one."

"I had my reasons. I'm going to spend some time at Hellspawn Academy though, checking out their classes and doing more research in the library. I really liked it there."

"It will be good for you to spend some more time among demons," Lilith says with a smile. "We're trying to introduce Lena to our society now, but we're taking it slow."

"I really hope we can get to know each other better," I tell Lena.

She crosses her arms and looks away. "Whatever."

Lilith's smile grows pinched. "We're going home. I think this is a bit much for her. I love you, dear."

I give her a hug. "Love you too, Mom."

The three of them head out, and I marvel at how much my family has grown and expanded over the last few months—and not just because of my siblings. I spin and take in the room, watching the people I care about most mingle with each other.

Callan wraps his arm around me. "Lena will be okay."

I reach up to grab his hand, pulling his arm closer. "Ekariel will be too."

He sighs. "I sure hope so."

"All we can do is be there for them."

He nods. "My mother wants to invite you for dinner."

I spin around to face him. "Are you sure? Jophiel actually said that?"

The woman hates demons, and I'm pretty sure she hates me the most. First, because I tricked her into thinking I was half-human, and then because I was sleeping with her son and keeping him from fulfilling his destiny in the angelic army.

"With Ekariel back, and then my near-death experience, she's trying to change. Trying to be a better mom, I guess." He touches my chin and gazes into my eyes. "I think she realized you're going to be a big part of my life, and if she wants to be in it, then she better get over her issues with you."

"What does she think of your taskforce against the Order?" I ask.

"She doesn't love it, but she finds it slightly more tolerable than when I was an assistant professor for a year."

I laugh, but it's cut short when huge shadowy wings fill the night sky. Lucifer lands on the balcony, his wings snap back, and he strolls forward wearing an impeccable black suit, looking like a model on a runway. He adjusts his tie as the crowd parts, both angels and demons alike staring at him with awe and fear. He gives them each a charming smile and a little nod, as he makes his way over to us.

"Callan," he says, offering his hand.

Callan shakes it without hesitation. "Lucifer."

"I'm pleased the matter with your father has been resolved." He inclines his head slightly at Callan, before turning to me. "Olivia, I apologize for not making it to the ceremony."

"That's okay." I never expected him to show up, honestly. Allowing a few demons to attend Seraphim Academy's graduation was fine. Adding the leader of all demons might be pushing it.

"I'd like to speak with you and your father alone, if that's possible," Lucifer says.

"Um. Sure." I lead him across the room toward where my Dad is talking to Professor Rosie. "Is something wrong?"

"No, not at all."

He and Gabriel step aside to speak in hushed tones, and I see Dad nod a few times. Then they return and ask me to follow them. We head down the stairs and find an empty classroom, and Gabriel perches on the edge of the desk in the front like he's a professor.

"There's something Lucifer and I would like to ask you," Gabriel says.

Lucifer adjusts his coat, even though it's impeccable. "Yes, we've been discussing it for some time, and we've decided we need an official liaison between angels and demons. Someone who understands both sides and doesn't show any favor or bias. Someone who can dedicate their life to fostering peace between our people."

"We'd like you to be this person," Gabriel says.

My mouth hangs open as I look between the two of them. "You do?"

Lucifer nods. "We think you're uniquely qualified for the job."

"Thank you." I press my hands to my chest, overwhelmed as a sense of rightness settles over me. This job is exactly what I wanted to do after graduation. I just didn't know such a thing could be possible. "I would be honored. Truly."

"It's settled then." Lucifer heads to the door, but then pauses. "Oh, one more thing. I thought you'd like to know that we're changing the law. Effective immediately, angels and demons are no longer forbidden from having relationships with one another."

Tears prick my eyes, but my voice fails me and all I can do is nod my thanks. This means my existence is no longer forbidden either. It also means Rhiannon can take her rightful place as the leader of the

Valkyries and stop hiding her demon lover. I can't wait to tell Tanwen.

"Oh, and welcome to the family," Lucifer adds. He steps through the door, leaving me alone with my dad.

"I had a feeling you'd want the job," Gabriel says with a warm smile.

"It's perfect. Thank you." I lean on the desk next to him. "How does it feel to finally be leader of the Archangels, as you should have been all along?"

"Good. Stressful. Overwhelming. But mostly good." He hesitates, then wraps an arm around me. I let him. "I can finally make some real changes...for the better, I hope."

"You're already off to a good start."

We chat for a little while longer, and then I head back up to the party. It's later than I expected, and the place has cleared out. Lucifer has that effect on a party, I guess. All that's left are some silver and gold decorations from the party, plus our pink pillows and a few stuffed animals from our redecoration months ago. I pick up a sparkly plastic tiara from the shelf and set it on my head, then slowly turn around the space, taking it all in for the last time. I wonder who will take over the bell tower next year in our absence.

Out on the balcony, my four men wait for me. Kassiel, who stood by me from the beginning. Marcus, the first one to teach me it was possible for a succubus to love. Bastien, who grew from cold and emotionless to a secret softie. And Callan, who taught me it was possible for hate to turn to love, and for someone to change.

Kassiel laughs at something Marcus said, while Bastien crosses his arms and Callan shakes his head. From here, they look like brothers giving each other a hard time. Then they turn toward me, sensing my presence, and I walk into their open arms with a smile.

All my life, I was always taught that Lilim weren't meant for love. That we couldn't have real relationships. That we could never have anything that lasts. For a long time, I believed it.

Now I'm certain all of that is false.

I have the proof right here in front of me, as they wrap me in their arms, adjust my tiara with a laugh, and press soft kisses to my face. I've found love four times, with four different men, and I'm never letting them go.

Maybe I'm different because I'm part angel. Or maybe I'm the start of something big, something that will spread to others of my kind, something that will change us all.

I'm the daughter of an Archangel and an Archdemon...and I'm just the beginning.

ABOUT THE AUTHOR

Elizabeth Briggs is the *New York Times* bestselling author of paranormal and fantasy romance. She graduated from UCLA with a degree in Sociology and has worked for an international law firm, mentored teens in writing, and volunteered with dog rescue groups. Now she's a full-time geek who lives in Los Angeles with her family and a pack of fluffy dogs.

Visit Elizabeth's website: www.elizabethbriggs.com

Join Elizabeth's Facebook group for fun book chat and early sneak peeks!

Made in the USA
Las Vegas, NV
25 November 2022

60283096R00426